Presumed Guilty
Whistleblower
Never Say Die

TESS GERRITSEN

PRESUMED GUILTY
WHISTLEBLOWER
NEVER SAY DIE

Three Complete Novels

Years ago, when I was still in medical training, I would sometimes ease the tension of late-night hospital duty by curling up in my on-call room with a book. Romantic suspense novels by my favorite authors, Daphne Du-Maurier, Helen MacInnes, and Victoria Holt, comforted me through the most stressful nights of my medical career. These were stories about love and peril, about desperate heroes and heroines fighting for their lives even as they stuggled against the irresistible pull of sexual desire. Whether the plots involved spies or cops or English noblemen, the theme of these books remained the same: that passionate men and women will risk everything, even their lives, for love.

To this day, I am still enchanted by the genre. It's no surprise that when I began a new career as an author, the first nine novels I wrote were romantic thrillers.

I'm delighted that my early romance novels are now being re-released. I hope readers who know me only as a medical suspense author will also enjoy a slightly different Tess Gerritsen thriller—one in which love and danger are deliciously intertwined.

Contents

PRESUMED GUILTY

1

He called at ten o'clock, the same time he always did.

Even before Miranda answered it, she knew it was him. She also knew that if she ignored it the phone would keep on ringing and ringing, until the sound would drive her crazy. Miranda paced the bedroom, thinking, *I don't have to answer it. I don't have to talk to him. I don't owe him a thing, not a damn thing.*

The ringing stopped. In the sudden silence she held her breath, hoping that this time he would relent, this time he would understand she'd meant what she told him.

The renewed jangling made her start. Every ring was like sandpaper scraping across her raw nerves.

Miranda couldn't stand it any longer. Even as she picked up the receiver she knew it was a mistake. "Hello?"

"I miss you," he said. It was the same whisper, resonant with the undertones of old intimacies shared, enjoyed.

"I don't want you to call me anymore," she said.

"I couldn't help it. All day I've wanted to call you. Miranda, it's been hell without you."

Tears stung her eyes. She took a breath, forcing them back.

"Can't we try again?" he pleaded.

"No, Richard."

"Please. This time it'll be different."

"It'll never be different."

"Yes! It will—"

"It was a mistake. From the very beginning."

"You still love me. I know you do. God, Miranda, all these weeks, seeing you every day. Not being able to touch you. Or even be alone with you—"

"You won't have to deal with that any longer, Richard. You have my letter of resignation. I meant it."

There was a long silence, as though the impact of her words had pummeled him like some physical blow. She felt euphoric and guilty all at once. Guilty for having broken free, for being, at last, her own woman.

Softly he said, "I told her."

Miranda didn't respond.

"Did you hear me?" he asked. "I told her. Everything about us. And I've been to see my lawyer. I've changed the terms of my—"

"Richard," she said slowly. "It doesn't make a difference. Whether you're married or divorced, I don't want to see you."

"Just one more time."

"No."

"I'm coming over. Right now—"

"No."

"You have to see me, Miranda!"

"I don't have to do anything!" she cried.

"I'll be there in fifteen minutes."

Miranda stared in disbelief at the receiver. He'd hung up. Damn him, he'd hung up, and fifteen minutes from now he'd be knocking on her door. She'd managed to carry on so bravely these past three weeks, working side by side with him, keeping her smile polite, her voice neutral. But now he was coming and he'd rip away her mask of control and there they'd be again, spiraling into the same old trap she'd just managed to crawl out of.

She ran to the closet and yanked out a sweatshirt. She had to get away. Somewhere he wouldn't find her, somewhere she could be alone.

She fled out the front door and down the porch steps and began to walk, swiftly, fiercely, down Willow Street. At ten-thirty, the neighborhood was already tucked in for the night. Through the windows she passed she saw the glow of lamplight, the silhouettes of families in various domestic poses, the occasional flicker of a fire in a hearth. She felt that old envy stir inside her again, the longing to be part of the same loving whole, to be stirring the embers of her own hearth. Foolish dreams.

Shivering, she hugged her arms to her chest. There was a chill in the air, not unseasonable for August in Maine. She was angry now, angry about being cold, about being driven from her own home. Angry at *him*. But she didn't stop; she kept walking.

At Bayview Street she turned right, toward the sea.

The mist was rolling in. It blotted out the stars, crept along the road in a sullen vapor. She headed through it, the fog swirling in her wake. From the road she turned onto a footpath, followed it to a series of granite steps, now slick with mist. At the bottom was a wood bench— she thought of it as her bench—set on the beach of stones. There she sat, drew her legs up against her chest and stared out toward the sea. Somewhere, drifting on the bay, a buoy was clanging. She could dimly make out the green channel light, bobbing in the fog.

By now he would be at her house. She wondered how long he'd knock at the door. Whether he'd keep knocking until her neighbor Mr. Lanzo complained. Whether he'd give up and just go home, to his wife, to his son and daughter.

She lowered her face against her knees, trying to blot out the image of the happy little Tremain family. *Happy* was not the picture Richard had painted. *At the breaking point* was the way he'd described his marriage. It was love for Phillip and Cassie, his children, that had kept him from divorcing Evelyn years ago. Now the twins were nineteen, old enough to accept the truth about their parents' marriage. What stopped him from divorce now was his concern for Evelyn, his wife. She needed time to adjust, and if Miranda would just be patient, would just love him enough, the way he loved her, it would all work out. . . .

Oh, yes. Hasn't it worked out just fine?

Miranda gave a little laugh. She raised her head, looked out to sea and laughed again, not a hysterical laugh but one of relief. She felt as if she'd just awakened from a long fever, to find that her mind was sharp again, clear again. The mist felt good against her face, its chill touch sweeping her soul clean. How she needed such a cleansing! The months of guilt had piled up like layers of dirt, until she thought she could scarcely see herself, her real self, beneath the filth.

Now it was over. This time it was really, truly over.

She smiled at the sea. *My soul is mine again,* she thought. A calmness, a serenity she had not felt in months, settled over her. She rose to her feet and started for home.

Two blocks from her house she spotted the blue Peugeot, parked near the intersection of Willow and Spring Streets. So he was still waiting for her. She paused by the car, gazing in at the black leather upholstery, the sheepskin seat covers, all of it too familiar. *The scene of the crime,* she thought. *The first kiss. I've paid for it, in pain. Now it's his turn.*

She left the car and headed purposefully to her house. She climbed the porch steps; the front door was unlocked, as she'd left it. Inside, the lights were still on. He wasn't in the living room.

"Richard?" she said.

No answer.

The smell of coffee brewing drew her to the kitchen. She saw a fresh pot on the burner, a half-filled mug on the countertop. One of the kitchen drawers had been left wide open. She slammed it shut. *Well. You came right in and made yourself at home, didn't you?* She grabbed the mug and tossed the contents into the sink. The coffee splashed her hand; it was barely lukewarm.

She moved along the hall, past the bathroom. The light was on, and water trickled from the faucet. She shut it off.

"You have no right to come in here!" she yelled. "It's my house. I could call the police and have you arrested for trespassing."

She turned toward the bedroom. Even before she reached the doorway she knew what to expect, knew what she'd have to contend with. He'd be sprawled on her bed, naked, a grin on his face. That was the way he'd greeted her the last time. This time she'd toss him out, clothes or no clothes. This time he'd be in for a surprise.

The bedroom was dark. She switched on the lights.

He was sprawled on the bed, as she'd predicted. His arms were flung out, his legs tangled in the sheets. And he was naked. But it wasn't a grin she saw on his face. It was a frozen look of terror, the mouth thrown open in a silent scream, the eyes staring at some fearful image of eternity. A corner of the bed sheet, saturated with blood, sagged over the side. Except for the quiet tap, tap of the crimson liquid slowly dripping onto the floor, the room was silent.

Miranda managed to take two steps into the room before nausea assailed her. She dropped to her knees, gasping, retching. Only when she managed to raise her head again did she see the chef's knife lying nearby on the floor. She didn't have to look twice at it. She recognized the handle, the twelve-inch steel blade, and she knew exactly where it had come from: the kitchen drawer.

It was her knife; it would have her fingerprints on it.

And now it was steeped in blood.

Chase Tremain drove straight through the night and into the dawn. The rhythm of the road under his wheels, the glow of the dashboard lights, the radio softly scratching out some Muzak melody all receded to little more than the fuzzy background of a dream—a very bad dream. The only reality was what he kept telling himself as he drove, what he repeated over and over in his head as he pushed onward down that dark highway.

Richard is dead. Richard is dead.

He was startled to hear himself say the words aloud. Briefly it shook him from his trancelike state, the sound of those words uttered in the darkness of his car. He glanced at the clock. It was four in the morning. He had been driving for four hours now. The New Hampshire-Maine border lay ahead. How many hours to go? How many miles? He wondered if it was cold outside, if the air smelled of the sea. The car had become a sensory deprivation box, a self-contained purgatory of glowing green lights and elevator music. He switched off the radio.

Richard is dead.

He heard those words again, mentally replayed them from the hazy memory of that phone call. Evelyn hadn't bothered to soften the blow. He had scarcely registered the fact it was his sister-in-law's voice calling when she hit him with the news. No preambles, no are-you-sitting-down warnings. Just the bare facts, delivered in the familiar Evelyn half whisper. *Richard is dead,* she'd told him. *Murdered. By a woman. . . .*

And then, in the next breath, *I need you, Chase.*

He hadn't expected that part. Chase was the outsider, the Tremain no one ever bothered to call, the one who'd picked up and left the state, left the family, for good. The brother with the embarrassing past. Chase, the outcast. Chase, the black sheep.

Chase, the weary, he thought, shaking off the cobwebs of sleep that threatened to ensnare him. He opened the window, inhaled the rush of cold air, the scent of pines and sea. The smell of Maine. It brought back, like nothing else could, all those boyhood memories. Scrabbling across the beach rocks, ankle deep in seaweed. The freshly gathered mussels clattering together in his bucket. The foghorn, moaning through the mist. All of it came back to him in that one whiff of air, that perfume of childhood, of good times, the early days when he had thought Richard was the boldest, the cleverest, the very best brother anyone could have. The days before he had understood Richard's true nature.

Murdered. By a woman.

That part Chase found entirely unsurprising.

He wondered who she was, what could have ignited an anger so white-hot it had driven her to plunge a knife into his brother's chest. Oh, he could make an educated guess. An affair turned sour. Jealousy over some new mistress. The inevitable abandonment. And then rage, at being used, at being lied to, a rage that would have overwhelmed all sense of logic or self-preservation. Chase could sketch in the whole scenario. He could even picture the woman, a woman like all the others who'd drifted through Richard's life. She'd be attractive, of course. Richard would insist on that much. But there'd be something a little desperate about her. Perhaps her laugh would be too loud or her smile too automatic, or the lines around her eyes would reveal a woman on the downhill slide. Yes, he could see the woman clearly, and the image stirred both pity and repulsion.

And rage. Whatever resentment he still bore Richard, nothing could change the fact they were brothers. They'd shared the same pool of memories, the same lazy afternoons drifting on the lake, the strolls on the breakwater, the quiet snickerings in the darkness. Their last falling-out had been a serious one, but in the back of his mind Chase had always assumed they'd smooth it over. There was always time to make things right again, to be friends again.

That's what he had thought until that phone call from Evelyn.

His anger swelled, washed through him like a full-moon tide. Opportunities lost. No more chances to say, *I care about you.* No more chances to say, *Remember when?* The road blurred before him. He blinked and gripped the steering wheel tighter.

He drove on, into the morning.

By ten o'clock he had reached Bass Harbor. By eleven he was aboard the *Jenny B,* his face to the wind, his hands clutching the ferry rail. In the distance, Shepherd's Island rose in a low green hump in the mist. *Jenny B*'s bow heaved across the swells and Chase felt that familiar nausea roil his stomach, sour his throat. *Always the seasick one,* he thought. In a family of sailors, Chase was the landlubber, the son who preferred solid ground beneath his feet. The racing trophies had all gone to Richard. Catboats, sloops, you name the class, Richard had the trophy. And these were the waters where he'd honed his skills, tacking, jibbing, shouting out orders. Spinnaker up, spinnaker down. To Chase it had all seemed a bunch of frantic nonsense. And then, there'd been that miserable nausea. . . .

Chase inhaled a deep breath of salt air, felt his stomach settle as the *Jenny B* pulled up to the dock. He returned to the car and waited his turn to drive up the ramp. There were eight cars before him, out-of-state license plates on every one. Half of Massachusetts seemed to come north every summer. You could almost hear the state of Maine groan under the weight of all those damn cars.

The ferryman waved him forward. Chase put the car in gear and drove up the ramp, onto Shepherd's Island.

It amazed him how little the place seemed to change over the years.

The same old buildings faced Sea Street: the Island Bakery, the bank, FitzGerald's Café, the five-and-dime, Lappin's General Store. A few new names had sprung up in old places. The Vogue Beauty Shop was now Gorham's Books, and Village Hardware had been replaced by Country Antiques and a realty office. Lord, what changes the tourists wrought.

He drove around the corner, up Limerock Street. On his left, housed in the same brick building, was the *Island Herald.* He wondered if any of it had changed inside. He remembered it well, the decorative tin ceiling, the battered desks, the wall hung with portraits of the publishers, every one a Tremain. He could picture it all, right down to the Remington typewriter on his father's old desk. Of course, the Remingtons would be long gone. There'd be computers now, sleek and impersonal. That's how Richard would run the newspaper, anyway. Out with the old, in with the new.

Bring on the next Tremain.

Chase drove on and turned onto Chestnut Hill. Half a mile up, near the highest point on the island, sat the Tremain mansion. A monstrous yellow wedding cake was what it used to remind him of, with its Victorian turrets and gingerbread trim. The house had since been repainted a distinguished gray and white. It seemed tamer now, subdued, a faded beauty. Chase almost preferred the old wedding-cake yellow.

He parked the car, grabbed his suitcase from the trunk and headed up the walkway. Even before he'd reached the porch steps the door opened and Evelyn was standing there, waiting for him.

"Chase!" she cried. "Oh, Chase, you're here. Thank God you're here."

At once she fell into his arms. Automatically he held her against him, felt the shuddering of her body, the warmth of her breath against his neck. He let her cling to him as long as she needed to.

At last she pulled away and gazed up at him. Those brilliant green eyes were as startling as ever. Her hair, shoulder length and honey blond, had been swept back into a French braid. Her face was puffy, her nose red and pinched. She'd tried to cover it with makeup. Some sort of pink powder caked her nostril and a streak of mascara had left a dirty shadow on her cheek. He could scarcely believe this was his beautiful sister-in-law. Could it be she truly was in mourning?

"I knew you'd come," she whispered.

"I left right after you called."

"Thank you, Chase. I didn't know who else to turn to. . . ." She stood back, looked at him. "Poor thing, you must be exhausted. Come in, I'll get you some coffee."

They stepped into the foyer. It was like stepping back into childhood, so little had changed. The same oak floors, the same light, the same smells. He almost thought that if he turned around and looked through the doorway into the parlor, he'd see his mother sitting there at her desk, madly scribbling away. The old girl never did take to the typewriter; she'd believed, and rightly so, that if a gossip column was juicy enough, an editor would accept it in Swahili. As it turned out, not only had the editor acquired her column, he'd acquired *her* as well. All in all, a practical marriage.

His mother never did learn to type.

"Hello, Uncle Chase."

Chase looked up to see a young man and woman standing at the top of the stairs. Those couldn't be the twins! He watched in astonishment as the pair came down the steps, Phillip in the lead. The last time he'd seen his niece and nephew they'd been gawky adolescents, not quite grown into their big feet. Both of them were tall and blond and lean, but there the resemblance ended. Phillip moved with the graceful assurance of a dancer, an elegant Fred Astaire partnered with—well, certainly not Ginger Rogers. The young woman who ambled down after him bore a closer resemblance to a horse.

"I can't believe this is Cassie and Phillip," said Chase.

"You've stayed away too long," Evelyn replied.

Phillip came forward and shook Chase's hand. It was the greeting of a stranger, not a nephew. His hand was slender, refined, the hand of a gentleman. He had his mother's stamp of aristocracy—straight nose, chiseled cheeks, green eyes. "Uncle Chase," he said somberly. "It's a terrible reason to come home, but I'm glad you're here."

Chase shifted his gaze to Cassie. When he'd last seen his niece she was a lively little monkey with a never-ending supply of questions. He could scarcely believe she'd grown into this sullen young woman. Could grief have wrought such changes? Her limp hair was pulled back so tightly it seemed to turn her face into a collection of jutting angles: large nose, rabbity overbite, a square forehead unsoftened by even a trace of bangs. Only her eyes held any trace of that distant ten-year-old. They were direct, sharply intelligent.

"Hello, Uncle Chase," she said. A strikingly business-like tone for a girl who'd just lost her father.

"Cassie," said Evelyn. "Can't you give your uncle a kiss? He's come all this way to be with us."

Cassie moved forward and planted a wooden peck on Chase's cheek. Just as quickly she stepped back, as though embarrassed by this false ceremony of affection.

"You've certainly grown up," said Chase, the most charitable assessment he could offer.

"Yes. It happens."

"How old are you now?"

"Almost twenty."

"So you both must be in college."

Cassie nodded, the first trace of a smile touching her lips. "I'm at the University of Southern Maine. Studying journalism. I figured, one of these days the *Herald*'s going to need a—"

"Phillip's at Harvard," Evelyn cut in. "Just like his father."

Cassie's smile died before it was fully born. She shot a look of irritation at her mother, then turned and headed up the stairs.

"Cassie, where are you going?"

"I have to do my laundry."

"But your uncle just got here. Come back and sit with us."

"Why, Mother?" she shot back over her shoulder. "You can entertain him perfectly well on your own."

"Cassie!"

The girl turned and glared down at Evelyn. "What?"

"You are embarrassing me."

"Well, that's nothing new."

Evelyn, close to tears, turned to Chase. "You see how things are? I can't even count on my own children. Chase, I can't deal with this all alone. I just can't." Stifling a sob, she turned and walked into the parlor.

The twins looked at each other.

"You've done it again," said Phillip. "It's a lousy time to fight, Cassie. Can't you feel sorry for her? Can't you try and get along? Just for the next few days."

"It's not as if I *don't* try. But she drives me up a wall."

"Okay, then at least be civil." He paused, then added, "You know it's what Dad would want."

Cassie sighed. Then, resignedly, she came down the steps and headed into the parlor, after her mother. "I guess I owe him that much. . . ."

Shaking his head, Phillip looked at Chase. "Just another episode of the delightful Tremain family."

"Has it been like this for a while?"

"Years, at least. You're just seeing them at their worst. You'd think, after last night, after losing Dad, we could pull together. Instead it seems to be driving us all apart."

They went into the parlor and found mother and daughter sitting at opposite ends of the room. Both had regained their composure. Phillip took a seat between them, reinforcing his role as perpetual human buffer. Chase settled into a corner armchair—his idea of neutral territory.

Sunshine washed in through the bay windows, onto the gleaming wood floor. The silence was filled by the ticking of the clock on the mantelpiece. It all looked the same, thought Chase. The same Hepplewhite tables, the same Queen Anne chairs. It was exactly the way he remembered it from childhood. Evelyn had not altered a single detail. For that he felt grateful.

Chase launched a foray into that dangerous silence. "I drove by the newspaper building, coming through town," he said. "Hasn't changed a bit."

"Neither has the town," said Phillip.

"Just as thrilling as ever," his sister deadpanned.

"What's the plan for the *Herald?*" asked Chase.

"Phillip will be taking over," said Evelyn. "It's about time, anyway. I need him home, now that Richard . . ." She swallowed, looked down. "He's ready for the job."

"I'm not sure I am, Mom," said Phillip. "I'm only in my second year at college. And there are other things I'd like to—"

"Your father was twenty when Grandpa Tremain made him an editor. Isn't that right, Chase?"

Chase nodded.

"So there's no reason you couldn't slip right onto the masthead."

Phillip shrugged. "Jill Vickery's managing things just fine."

"She's just a hired hand, Phillip. The *Herald* needs a real captain."

Cassie leaned forward, her eyes suddenly sharp. "There are others who could do it," she said. "Why does it have to be Phil?"

"Your father wanted Phillip. And Richard always knew what was best for the *Herald.*"

There was a silence, punctuated by the steady ticking of the clock on the mantelpiece.

Evelyn let out a shaky breath and dropped her head in her hands. "Oh, God, it all seems so cold-blooded. I can't believe we're talking about this. About who's going to take his place. . . ."

"Sooner or later," said Cassie, "we have to talk about it. About a lot of things."

Evelyn nodded and looked away.

In another room, the phone was ringing.

"I'll get it," said Phillip, and left to answer it.

"I just can't *think,*" said Evelyn, pressing her hands to her head. "If I could just get my mind working again. . . ."

"It was only last night," said Chase gently. "It takes time to get over the shock."

"And there's the funeral to think of. They won't even tell me when they'll release the—" She winced. "I don't see why it takes so long. Why the state examiner has to go over and over it. I mean, can't they *see* what happened? Isn't it obvious?"

"The obvious isn't always the truth," said Cassie.

Evelyn looked at her daughter. "What's that supposed to mean?"

Phillip came back into the room. "Mom? That was Lorne Tibbetts on the phone."

"Oh, Lord." Evelyn rose unsteadily to her feet. "I'm coming."

"He wants to see you in person."

She frowned. "Right this minute? Can't it wait?"

"You might as well get it over with, Mom. He'll have to talk to you sooner or later."

Evelyn turned and looked at Chase. "I can't do this alone. Come with me, won't you?"

Chase didn't have the faintest idea where they were going or who Lorne Tibbetts was. At that moment what he really wanted was a hot shower and a bed to collapse onto. But that would have to wait.

"Of course, Evelyn," he said. Reluctantly he stood, shaking the stiffness from his legs, which felt permanently flexed by the long drive from Greenwich.

Evelyn was already reaching for her purse. She pulled out the car keys and handed them to Chase. "I—I'm too upset to drive. Could you?"

He took the keys. "Where are we going?"

With shaking hands Evelyn slipped on her sunglasses. The swollen eyes vanished behind twin dark lenses. "The police," she said.

2

The Shepherd's Island police station was housed in a converted general store that had, over the years, been chopped up into a series of hobbit-size rooms and offices. In Chase's memory, it had been a much more imposing structure, but it had been years since he'd been inside. He'd been only a boy then, and a rambunctious one at that, the sort of rascal to whom a police station represented a distinct threat. The day he'd been dragged in here for trampling Mrs. Gordimer's rose bed—entirely unintentional on his part—these ceilings had seemed taller, the rooms vaster, every door a gateway to some unknown terror.

Now he saw it for what it was—a tired old building in need of paint.

Lorne Tibbetts, the new chief of police, was built just right to inhabit this claustrophobic warren. If there was a height minimum for police work, Tibbetts had somehow slipped right under the requirement. He was just a chunk of a man, neatly decked out in official summer khaki, complete with height-enhancing cap to hide what Chase suspected was a bald spot. He reminded Chase of a little Napoleon in full dress uniform.

Though short on height, Chief Tibbetts was long on the social graces. He maneuvered through the clutter of desks and filing cabinets and greeted Evelyn with the overweening solicitousness due a woman of her local status.

"Evelyn! I'm so sorry to have to ask you down here like this." He reached for her arm and gave it a squeeze, an intended gesture of comfort that made Evelyn shrink away. "And it's been a terrible night for you, hasn't it? Just a terrible night."

Evelyn shrugged, partly in answer to his question, partly to free herself from his grasp.

"I know it's hard, dealing with this. And I didn't want to bother you, not today. But you know how it is. All those reports to be filed." He looked at Chase, a deceptively casual glance. The little Napoleon, Chase noted, had sharp eyes that saw everything.

"This is Chase," said Evelyn, brushing the sleeve of her blouse, as though to wipe away Chief Tibbetts's paw print. "Richard's brother. He drove in this morning from Connecticut."

"Oh, yeah," said Tibbetts, his eyes registering instant recognition of the name. "I've seen a picture of you hanging in the high school gym." He offered his hand. His grasp was crushing, the handshake of a man trying to compensate for his size. "You know, the one of you in the basketball uniform."

Chase blinked in surprise. "They still have that thing hanging up?"

"It's the local hall of fame. Let's see, you were class of '71. Star center, varsity basketball. Right?"

"I'm surprised you know all that."

"I was a basketball player myself. Madison High School, Wisconsin. Record holder in free throws. And points scored."

Yes, Chase saw it clearly. Lorne Tibbetts, rampaging midget of the basketball court. It would fit right in with that bone-crushing handshake.

The station door suddenly swung open. A woman called out, "Hey, Lorne?"

Tibbetts turned and wearily confronted the visitor, who looked as if she'd just blown in from the street. "You back again, Annie?"

"Like the proverbial bad penny." The woman shifted her battered shoulder bag to her other side. "So when am I gonna get a statement, huh?"

"When I have one to make. Now scram."

The woman, undaunted, turned to Evelyn. The pair of them could have posed for a magazine feature on fashion make-overs. Annie, blowsy haired and dressed in a lumpy sweatshirt and jeans, would have earned the label Before. "Mrs. Tremain?" she said politely. "I know this is a bad time, but I'm under deadline and I just need a short quote—"

"Oh, for Chrissakes, Annie!" snapped Tibbetts. He turned to the cop manning the front desk. "Ellis, get her out of here!"

Ellis popped up from his chair like a spindly jack-in-the-box. "C'mon, Annie. Get a move on, 'less you wanna write your story from the inside lookin' out."

"I'm going. I'm going." Annie yanked open the door. As she walked out they heard her mutter, "Geez, they won't let a gal do her job around here. . . ."

Evelyn looked at Chase. "That's Annie Berenger. One of Richard's star reporters. Now a star pest."

"Can't exactly blame her," said Tibbetts. "That's what you pay her for, isn't it?" He took Evelyn's arm. "Come on, we'll get started. I'll take you into my office. It's the only private place in this whole fishbowl."

Lorne's office was at the far end of the hallway, past a series of closet-size rooms. Almost every square inch was crammed with furniture: a desk, two chairs, a bookcase, filing cabinets. A fern wilted, unnoticed, in a corner. Despite the cramped space, everything was tidy, the shelves dusted, all the papers stacked in the Out box. On the wall, prominently displayed, hung a plaque: *The smaller the dog, the bigger the fight.*

Tibbetts and Evelyn sat in the two chairs. A third chair was brought in for the secretary to take accessory notes. Chase stood off to the side. It felt good to stand, good to straighten those cramped legs.

At least, it felt good for about ten minutes. Then he found himself sagging, scarcely able to pay attention to what was being said. He felt like that wretched fern in the corner, wilting away.

Tibbetts asked the questions and Evelyn answered in her usual whispery voice, a voice that could induce hibernation. She gave a detailed summary of the night's events. A typical evening, she said. Supper at six o'clock, the whole family. Leg of lamb and asparagus, lemon soufflé for dessert. Richard had had a glass of wine; he always did. The conversation was routine, the latest gossip from the paper. Circulation down, cost of newsprint up. Worries about a possible libel suit. Tony Graffam upset about that last article. And then talk about Phillip's exams, Cassie's grades. The lilacs were lovely this year, the driveway needed resurfacing. Typical dialogue from a family dinner.

At nine o'clock Richard had left the house to do some work at the office—or so he'd said. And Evelyn?

"I went upstairs to bed," she said.

"What about Cassie and Phillip?"

"They went out. To a movie, I think."

"So everyone went their separate ways."

"Yes." Evelyn looked down at her lap. "And that's it. Until twelve-thirty, when I got the call. . . ."

"Let's go back to that dinner conversation."

The account went into replay. A few extra details here and there, but essentially the same story. Chase, his last reserves of alertness wearing thin, began to drift into a state of semiconsciousness. Already his legs were going numb, sinking into a sleep that his brain longed to join. The floor began to look pretty good. At least it was horizontal. He felt himself sliding. . . .

Suddenly he jerked awake and saw that everyone was looking at him.

"Are you all right, Chase?" asked Evelyn.

"Sorry," he muttered. "I guess I'm just more tired than I thought." He gave his head a shake. "Could I, uh, get a cup of coffee somewhere?"

"Down the hall," said Tibbetts. "There's a full pot on, plus a couch if you need it. Why don't you wait there?"

"Go ahead," said Evelyn. "I'll be done soon."

With a sense of relief Chase fled the office and went in search of the blessed coffeepot. Moving back down the hall, he poked his head into the first doorway and discovered a washroom. The next door was locked. He moved on and glanced into the third room. It was unlit. Through the shadows he saw a couch, a few chairs, a jumble of furniture off in a corner. In the sidewall there was a window. It was that window that drew his attention because, unlike a normal window, it didn't face the outside; it faced an adjoining room. Through the pane of glass he spied a woman, sitting alone at a small table.

She was oblivious to him. Her gaze was focused downward, on the table before her. Something drew him closer, something about her utter silence, her stillness. He felt like a hunter who has quite unexpectedly come upon a doe poised in the forest.

Quietly Chase slipped into the darkness and let the door close behind him. He moved to the window. A one-way mirror—that's what it was, of course. He was on the observing side, she on the blind side. She had no idea he was standing here, separated from her by only a half inch of glass. It made him feel somehow contemptible to be standing there, spying on her, but he couldn't help himself. He was drawn in by that old fantasy of invisibility, of being the fly on the wall, the unseen observer.

And it was the woman.

She was not particularly beautiful, and neither her clothes nor her hairstyle enhanced the assets she did have. She was wearing faded blue jeans and a Boston Red Sox T-shirt a few sizes too big. Her hair, a chestnut brown, was gathered into a careless braid. A few strands had escaped and drooped rebelliously about her temples. She wore little or no makeup, but she had the sort of face that needed none, the sort of face you saw on those Patagonia catalog models, the ones raking leaves or hugging lambs. Wholesome, with just a hint of sunburn. Her eyes, a light color, gray or blue, didn't quite fit the rest of the picture. He could see by the puffiness around the lids that she'd been crying. Even now, she reached up and swiped a tear from her cheek. She glanced around the table in search of something. Then, with a look of frustration, she tugged at the edge of her T-shirt and wiped her face with it. It seemed a helpless gesture, the sort of thing a child would do. It made her look all the more vulnerable. He wondered why she was in that room, sitting all alone, looking for all the world like an abandoned soul. A witness? A victim?

She looked straight ahead, right at him. He instinctively drew away from the window, but he knew she couldn't see him. All she saw was a reflection of herself staring back. She seemed to take in her own image with passive weariness. Indifference. As though she was thinking, *There I am, looking like hell. And I couldn't care less.*

A key grated in the lock. Suddenly the woman sat up straight, her whole body snapping to alertness. She wiped her face once more, raised her chin to a pugnacious angle. Her eyes might be swollen, her T-shirt damp with tears, but she had determinedly thrown off that cloak of vulnerability. She reminded Chase of a soldier girded for battle, but scared out of her wits.

The door opened. A man walked in—gray suit, no tie, all business. He took a chair. Chase was startled by the loud sound of the chair legs scraping the floor. He realized there must be a microphone in the next room, and that the sound was coming through a small speaker by the window.

"Ms. Wood?" asked the man. "Sorry to keep you waiting. I'm Lieutenant Merrifield, state police." He held out his hand and smiled. It said a lot, that smile. It said *I'm your buddy. Your best friend. I'm here to make everything right.*

The woman hesitated, then shook the offered hand.

Lieutenant Merrifield settled into the chair and gave the woman a long, sympathetic look. "You must be exhausted," he said, maintaining that best-friend voice. "Are you comfortable? Feel ready to proceed?"

She nodded.

"They've read you your rights?"

Again, a nod.

"I understand you've waived the right to have an attorney present."

"I don't have an attorney," she said.

Her voice was not what Chase expected. It was soft, husky. A bedroom voice with a heartbreaking quaver of grief.

"We can arrange for one, if you want," said Merrifield. "It may take some time, which means you'll have to be patient."

"Please. I just want to tell you what happened. . . ."

A smile touched Lieutenant Merrifield's lips. It had the curve of triumph. "All right, then," he said. "Let's begin." He placed a cassette recorder on the table and pressed the button. "Tell me your name, your address, your occupation."

The woman sighed deeply, a breath for courage. "My name is Miranda Wood. I live at 18 Willow Street. I work as a copy editor for the *Island Herald.*"

"That's Mr. Tremain's newspaper?"

"Yes."

"Let's go straight to last night. Tell me what happened. All the events leading up to the death of Mr. Richard Tremain."

Chase felt his whole body suddenly go numb. *The death of Mr. Richard Tremain.* He found himself pressing forward, against that cold glass, his gaze fixed on the face of Miranda Wood. Innocence. Softness. That's what he saw when he looked at her. What a lovely mask she wore, what a pure and perfect disguise.

My brother's mistress, he thought with sudden comprehension.

My brother's murderer.

In terrible fascination he listened to her confession.

"Let's go back a few months, Ms. Wood. To when you first met Mr. Tremain. Tell me about your relationship."

Miranda stared down at her hands, knotted together on the table. The table itself was a typically ugly piece of institutional furniture. She noticed that someone had carved the initials JMK onto the surface. She wondered who JMK was, if he or she had sat there under similar circumstances, if he or she had been similarly innocent. She felt a sudden bond with this unknown predecessor, the one who had sat in the same hot seat, fighting for dear life.

"Ms. Wood? Please answer my question."

She looked up at Lieutenant Merrifield. The smiling destroyer. "I'm sorry," she said. "I wasn't listening."

"About Mr. Tremain. How did you meet him?"

"At the *Herald.* I was hired about a year ago. We got to know each other in the course of business."

"And?"

"And . . ." She took a deep breath. "We got involved."

"Who initiated it?"

"He did. He started asking me out to lunch. Purely business, he said. To talk about the *Herald*. About changes in the format."

"Isn't it unusual for a publisher to deal so closely with the copy editor?"

"Maybe on a big city paper it is. But the *Herald*'s a small-town paper. Everyone on the staff does a little of everything."

"So, in the course of business, you got to know Mr. Tremain."

"Yes."

"When did you start sleeping with him?"

The question was like a slap in the face. She sat up straight. "It wasn't like that!"

"You didn't sleep with him?"

"I didn't—I mean, yes, I did, but it happened over the course of months. It wasn't as if we—we went out to lunch and then fell into bed together!"

"I see. So it was a more, uh, *romantic* thing. Is that what you're trying to say?"

She swallowed. In silence she nodded. It all sounded so stupid, the way he'd phrased it. A more romantic thing. Now, hearing those words said aloud in that cold, bare room, it struck her how foolish it all had been. The whole disastrous affair.

"I thought I loved him," Miranda whispered.

"What was that, Ms. Wood?"

She said, louder, "I thought I loved him. I wouldn't have slept with him if I didn't. I don't *do* one-night stands. I don't even do affairs."

"You did this one."

"Richard was different."

"Different than what?"

"Than other men! He wasn't just—just cars and football. He cared about the same things I cared about. This island, for instance. Look at the articles he wrote—you could see how much he loved this place. We used to talk for hours about it! And it just seemed the most natural thing in the world to . . ." She gave a little shudder of grief and looked down. Softly she said, "I thought he was different. At least, he seemed to be. . . ."

"He was also married. But you knew that."

She felt her shoulders droop. "Yes."

"And did you know he had two children?"

She nodded.

"Yet you had an affair with him. Did it mean so little to you, Ms. Wood, that three innocent people—"

"Don't you think I thought about that, every waking moment?" Her chin shot up in rage. "Don't you think I hated myself? I never *stopped* thinking about his family! About Evelyn and the twins. I felt evil, dirty. I felt—I don't know." She gave a sigh of helplessness. "Trapped."

"By what?"

"By my love for him. Or what I thought was love." She hesitated. "But maybe—maybe I never really *did* love him. At least, not the real Richard."

"And what led to this amazing revelation?"

"Things I learned about him."

"What things?"

"The way he used people. His employees, for instance. The way he treated them."

"So you saw the real Richard Tremain and you fell out of love."

"Yes. And I broke it off." She let out a deep breath, as though relieved that the most painful part of her confession was finished. "That was a month ago."

"Were you angry at him?"

"I felt more . . . betrayed. By all those false images."

"So you must have been angry."

"I guess I was."

"So for a month you walked around mad at Mr. Tremain."

"Sometimes. Mostly I felt stupid. And then he wouldn't leave me alone. He kept calling, wanting to get back together."

"And that made you angry, as well."

"Yes, of course."

"Angry enough to kill him?"

She looked up sharply. "No."

"Angry enough to grab a knife from your kitchen drawer?"

"No!"

"Angry enough to go into the bedroom—your bedroom, where he was lying naked—and stab him in the chest?"

"No! No, no, no." She was sobbing now, screaming out her denials. The sound of her own voice echoed like some alien cry in that stark box of a room. She dropped her head into her hands and leaned forward on the table. "No," she whispered. She had to get away from this terrible man with his terrible questions. She started to rise from the chair.

"Sit down, Ms. Wood. We're not finished."

Obediently she sank back into the chair. "I didn't kill him," she cried. "I told you, I found him on my bed. I came home and he was lying there. . . ."

"Ms. Wood—"

"I was on the beach when it happened. Sitting on the beach. That's what I keep telling all of you! But no one listens. No one believes me. . . ."

"Ms. Wood, I have more questions."

She was crying, not answering, not able to answer. The sound of her sobs was all that could be heard.

At last Merrifield flicked off the recorder. "All right, then. We'll take a break. One hour, then we'll resume."

Miranda didn't move. She heard the man's chair scrape back, heard Merrifield leave the room, then the door shut. A few moments later the door opened again.

"Ms. Wood? I'll take you back to your cell."

Slowly Miranda rose to her feet and turned to the door. A young cop stood waiting, nice face, friendly smile. His name tag said Officer Snipe. Vaguely she remembered him from some other time, from her life before jail. Oh, yes. Once, on a Christmas Eve, he'd torn up her parking ticket. It had been a kind gesture, gallantry offered to a lady. She wondered what he thought of the lady now, whether he saw *murderer* stamped on her face.

She let him lead her into the hall. At one end she saw Lieutenant Merrifield, huddled in conference with Chief Tibbetts. The polite Officer Snipe guided her in the opposite direction, away from the pair. Miranda had gone only a short distance when her footsteps faltered, stopped.

A man was standing at the far end of the hall, watching her. She had never seen him before. If she had, she certainly would have remembered him. He stood like some unbreachable barrier, his hands jammed in his pockets, his shoulders looming before her in the cramped corridor. He didn't look like a cop. Cops had standards of appearance, and this man was on the far edge of rumpled—unshaven, dark hair uncombed, his shirt a map of wrinkles. What disturbed her the most was the way he looked at her. That wasn't the passive curiosity of a bystander. No, it was something far more hostile. Those dark eyes were like judge and jury, weighing the facts, pronouncing her guilty.

"Keep moving, Ms. Wood," said Officer Snipe. "It's right around the corner."

Miranda forced herself to move forward, toward that forbidding human barrier. The man moved aside to let her pass. As she did, she felt his gaze burning into her and heard his sharp intake of breath, as though he was trying not to breathe the same air she did, as if her very presence had somehow turned the atmosphere to poison.

For the past twelve hours she'd been treated like a criminal, handcuffed, fingerprinted, intimately searched. She'd had questions fired at her, humiliations heaped upon her. But never, until this man had looked at her, had she felt like a creature worthy of such disgust, such loathing. Rage suddenly flared inside her, a rage so fierce it threatened to consume her in its flames.

She halted and stared up at him. Their gazes locked. *There, damn you!* she thought. *Whoever you are, take a look at me! Take a good, long look at the murderess. Satisfied?*

The eyes staring down at her were dark as night, stony with condemnation. But as they took each other in, Miranda saw something else flicker in those depths, a hint of uncertainty, almost confusion. As if the picture he saw was all wrong, as if image and caption were terribly mismatched.

Just down the hall, a door swung open. Footsteps clicked out and stopped dead.

"Dear God," whispered a voice.

Miranda turned.

Evelyn Tremain stood frozen in the washroom doorway. "Chase," she whispered. "It's her. . . ."

At once the man went to Evelyn and offered her his steadying arm. Evelyn gripped it with both hands, as if holding on to her only lifeline. "Oh, please," she murmured helplessly. "I can't stand to look at her."

Miranda didn't move. She felt paralyzed by guilt, by what she'd done to this woman, to the whole family. Though her crime might not be murder, still she had committed a sin against Evelyn Tremain and for that she would always be tormented.

"Mrs. Tremain," she said quietly. "I'm sorry. . . ."

Evelyn buried her face against the man's shoulder. "Chase, please. Get her out of here."

"He loved you," said Miranda. "I want you to know that. I want you to know that he never stopped loving—"

"Get her out of here!" cried Evelyn.

"Officer," said Chase quietly. "Please. Take her away."

Officer Snipe reached for Miranda's arm. "Let's go."

As she was led away Miranda called over her shoulder, "I didn't kill him, Mrs. Tremain! You have to believe that—"

"You tramp!" shouted Evelyn. "You filthy whore! You ruined my life."

Miranda glanced back and saw the other woman had pulled away from Chase and was now facing her like some avenging angel. Strands of blond hair had fallen free and her face, always pale, was now a stark white.

"You ruined my life!" Evelyn screamed.

That accusing shriek echoed in Miranda's ears all the way down that long walk to the jail.

Drained of resistance, she quietly entered the cell. She stood there, frozen, as the door clanged shut. Officer Snipe's footsteps faded away. She was alone, trapped in this cage.

Suddenly she felt as if she were suffocating, as if she would smother without fresh air. She scrambled over to the one small window and tried to pull herself up by the bars, but it was too high. She ran to the cot, dragged it across the cell and climbed on top. Even then she was barely tall enough to peek over the sill, to gulp in a tantalizing taste of freedom. Outside the sun was shining. She could see maple trees beyond the fenced yard, a few rooftops, a sea gull soaring in the sky. If she breathed in deeply, she could almost smell the sea. Oh, Lord, how sweet it all seemed! How unattainable! She gripped the window bars so tightly they dug into her palms. Pressing her face against the sill, she closed her eyes and willed herself to stay in control, to keep panic at bay.

I am innocent. They have to believe me, she thought.

And then, *What if they don't?*

No, damn it. Don't think about that.

She forced herself to concentrate on something else, anything else. She thought of the man in the hallway, the man with Evelyn Tremain. What had Evelyn called him? Chase. The name stirred a memory; Miranda had heard it before. She snatched desperately at that irrelevant strand of thought, concentrated hard on dredging up the memory, anything to crowd the fears from her mind. Chase. Chase. Someone had said it. She tried to bring back the voice, to match it to the utterance of that name.

The memory hit her like a blow. It was Richard who'd said it. *I haven't seen my brother in years. We had a falling-out when my father died. But then, Chase was always the problem kid in the family. . . .*

Miranda's eyes flew open with the revelation. Was it possible? There'd been no resemblance, no hint of familial ties in that face. Richard had had blue eyes, light brown hair, a weathered face always on the verge of sunburn. This man called Chase was all darkness, all shadow. It was hard to believe they were brothers. But that would explain the man's coldness, his look of condemnation. He thought she'd murdered Richard, and repulsion was exactly what he would feel, coming face-to-face with his brother's killer.

Slowly she sank onto the cot. Lying there beneath the window she could catch glimpses of blue sky and cloud. August. It would be a hot day. Already her T-shirt was damp with sweat.

She closed her eyes and tried to imagine soaring like a sea gull in that bright blue sky, tried to picture the island far below her.

But all she could see were the accusing eyes of Chase Tremain.

3

He truly was the ugliest dog on earth.

Miss Lila St. John regarded her pet with a mixture of affection and pity. Sir Oscar Henry San Angelo III, otherwise known as Ozzie, was a rare breed known as a Portuguese Water Dog. Miss St. John was not quite clear as to the attributes of this particular breed. She suspected it was some sort of geneticist's joke. Her niece had presented the dog to her—"to keep you company, Auntie"—and Miss St. John had been trying to remember ever since what that niece could hold against her. Not that Ozzie was entirely without redeeming value. He didn't bite, didn't bother the cat. He was a passable watchdog. But he ate like a horse, twitched like a mouse and was absolutely unforgiving if you neglected to take him on his twice-daily walk. He would stand by the door and whine.

The way he was doing now.

Oh, Miss St. John knew that look. Even if she couldn't actually see the beast's eyes under all that fur, she knew what the look meant. Sighing, she opened the door. The black bundle of fur practically shot down the porch steps and took off for the woods. Miss St. John had no choice but to follow him, and so off into the woods she went.

It was a warm evening, one of those still, sweet twilights that seem kissed with midsummer magic. She would not be surprised to see something extraordinary tonight. A doe and fawn, perhaps, or a fox cub, or even an owl.

She moved steadily through the trees in pursuit of the dog. She noticed they were headed in a direct line toward Rose Hill Cottage, the Tremains' summer camp. Such a tragedy, Richard Tremain's death. She hadn't particularly liked the man, but theirs were the last two cottages on this lonely road, and on her walks here she had occasionally seen him through his window, his head bent in concentration at his desk. He'd always been polite to her, and deferential, but she'd suspected much of it was automatic and not, in any sense, true respect. He'd had no use for elderly women; he simply tolerated them.

But as for young women, well, she'd heard that was a different story.

It troubled her, these recent revelations about his death. Not so much the fact of his murder, but the identity of the one accused. Miss St. John had met Miranda Wood, had spoken to her on several occasions. On this small island, in the dead of winter, only green thumb fanatics braved the icy roads to attend meetings of the local garden club. That's where Miss St. John had met Miranda. They'd sat together during a lecture on triploid marigolds, and again at the talk on gloxinia cultivation. Miranda was polite and deferential, but genuinely so. A lovely girl, not a hint of dishonesty in her eyes. It seemed to Miss St. John that any woman who cared so passionately about flowers, about living, growing things, could simply not be a murderess.

It bothered her, all that cruel talk flying about town these days. Miranda Wood, a killer? It went against Miss St. John's instincts, and her instincts were always, always good.

Ozzie bounded through the last stand of trees and shot off toward Rose Hill Cottage. Miss St. John resignedly followed suit. That's when she saw the light flickering through the trees. It came from the Tremain cottage. Just as quickly, it vanished.

At once she froze as an eerie thought flashed to mind. *Ghosts?* Richard was the only one who ever used that cottage. *But he's dead.*

The rational side of her brain, the side that normally guided Miss St. John's day-to-day existence, took control. It must be one of the family, of course. Evelyn, perhaps, come to wrap up her husband's affairs.

Still, Miss St. John couldn't shake off her uneasiness.

She crossed the driveway and went up the front porch steps. "Hello?" she called. "Evelyn? Cassie?" There was no answer to her knock.

She tried to peer in the window, but it was dark inside. "Hello?" she called again, louder. She thought she heard, from somewhere in the cottage, a soft thud. Then—silence.

Ozzie began to bark. He danced around on the porch, his claws tip-tapping on the wood.

"Oh, hush!" snapped Miss St. John. "Sit!"

The dog whined, sat, and gave her a distinctly wounded look.

Miss St. John stood there a moment, listening for more sounds, but she heard nothing except the whap-whap of Ozzie's tail against the porch.

Perhaps she should call the police. She debated that move all the way back to her cottage. Once there, in her cheery little kitchen, the very idea seemed so silly, so alarmist. It was a good half-hour drive out here to the north shore. The local police would be reluctant to send a man all the way out here, and for what? A will-o'-the-wisp tale? Besides, what could there possibly be in Rose Hill Cottage that would interest any burglars?

"It's just my imagination. Or my failing eyesight. After all, when one's seventy-four, one has to expect the faculties to get a little screwy."

Ozzie walked in a tight circle, lay down and promptly went to sleep.

"Good Lord," said Miss St. John. "I'm talking to my dog now. What part of my brain will rot next?"

Ozzie, as usual, offered no opinion.

The courtroom was packed. Already, a dozen people had been turned away at the door, and this wasn't even a trial, just a bail review hearing, a formality required by law to be held forty-eight hours after arrest.

Chase, who sat in the second row with Evelyn and her father, suspected the proceedings would be brief. The facts were stark, the suspect's guilt indisputable. A few words by the judge, a bang of the gavel and they'd all be out of there.

And the murderess would slink back to her cell, where she belonged.

"Damned circus, that's what it is," growled Evelyn's father, Noah DeBolt. Silver haired and gravel throated, at sixty-six he was still as formidable as ever. Chase felt the automatic urge to sit up straight and mind his manners. One did not slouch in the presence of Noah DeBolt. One was always courteous and deferential, even if one was an adult.

Even if one was the chief of police, Chase noted, as Lorne Tibbetts stopped and politely tipped his hat at Noah.

The principals were settling in their places. The deputy D.A. from Bass Harbor was seated at his table, flipping through a sheaf of papers. Lorne and Ellis, representing half the local police force, sat off to the left, their uniformed spines ramrod straight, their hair neatly slicked down. They had even parted it on the same side. The defense attorney, a youngster wearing a suit that looked as if it cost twice his annual salary, was fussing with the catch on his leather briefcase.

"They should clear this place out," grunted Noah. "Who the hell let all these spectators in? Invasion of privacy, I call it."

"It's open to the public, Daddy," said Evelyn wearily.

"There's public, and then there's *public*. These people don't belong here. It's none of their damn business." Noah rose and waved for Lorne's attention, but the chief of police's brilliantined head was facing forward. Noah glanced around for the bailiff, but the man had disappeared through a side door. In frustration, Noah sat back down. "Don't know what this town's coming to," he muttered. "All these new people. No sense of what's proper anymore."

"Quiet, Daddy," murmured Evelyn. Then, fuming, she muttered, "Where are the twins? Why aren't they here? I want the judge to see them. Poor kids without a father."

Noah snorted. "They're full-grown adults. They won't impress anyone."

"There. I see them," said Chase, spotting Cassie and Phillip a few rows back. They must have slipped in later, with the other spectators.

So the audience is in place, he thought. *All we need now are the two main players. The judge. And the accused.*

As if on cue, a side door opened. The ape-size bailiff reappeared, his hand gripping the arm of the much smaller prisoner.

At his second glimpse of Miranda Wood, Chase was struck by how much paler she appeared than he remembered. And how much more fragile. The top of her head barely reached the bailiff's shoulder. She was dressed unobtrusively, in a blue skirt and a simple white blouse, an outfit no doubt chosen by her attorney to make her look innocent, which she did. Her hair was gathered back in a neat but trim ponytail. No wanton-woman looks here. Those lush chestnut highlights were carefully restrained by a plain rubber band. She wore no jewelry, no makeup. The pallor of those cheeks came without the artifice of face powder.

On her way to the defendant's table she looked once, and only once, at the crowd. Her gaze swept the room and came to rest on Chase. It was only a few seconds of eye contact, a glimpse of her brittle mask of composure. Pride, that's what he saw in her face. He could read it in her body language: the straight back, the chin held aloft. Everyone else in this room would see it, too, would resent that show of pride. The brazen murderess, they'd think. A woman without repentance, without shame. He wished *he* could feel that way about her. It would make her guilt seem all the more assured, her punishment all the more justified.

But he knew what lay beneath the mask. He'd seen it in those eyes two days before, when they'd gazed out at him through a one-way mirror. Fear, pure and simple. She was terrified.

And she was too proud to show it.

* * *

From the instant Miranda walked into the courtroom, none of it seemed real. Her feet, her legs felt numb. She was actually grateful for the firm grip of the bailiff's hand around her arm as they stepped in the side door. She caught a kaleidoscopic glimpse of all those faces in the audience—if that's what you called a courtroom full of spectators. What else could you call them? An audience here to watch her performance, an act in the theater of her life. Half of them had come to hang her; the other half were here to watch. As her gaze slowly swept the room she saw familiar faces. There were her colleagues from the *Herald:* Managing Editor Jill Vickery, looking every bit the sleek professional, and staff reporters Annie Berenger and Ty Weingardt, both of them dressed à la classic rumpled writer. It was hard to tell that they were—or had been—friends. They all wore such carefully neutral expressions.

As her gaze shifted, she took in a single friendly face in the crowd—old Mr. Lanzo, her next-door neighbor. He was mouthing the words *I'm with you, sweetie!* She found herself almost smiling back.

Then her gaze shifted again, to settle on Chase Tremain's stony face. The smile instantly died on her lips. Of all the faces in the room, his was the one that most made her feel like shrinking into some dark, unreachable crevice, anywhere to escape his gaze of judgment. The faces beside him were no less condemning. Evelyn Tremain, dressed in widow's black, looked like a pale death's mask. Next to Evelyn was her father, Noah DeBolt, town patriarch, a man who with one steely look could wither the spirit of any who dared offend him. He was now aiming that poisonous gaze at Miranda.

The tug of the bailiff's hand redirected Miranda toward the defendant's table. Meekly she sat beside her attorney, who greeted her with a stiff nod. Randall Pelham was Ivy League and impeccably dressed for the part, but all Miranda could think of when she saw his face was how young he looked. He made her feel, at twenty-nine, positively middle-aged. Still, she'd had little choice in the matter. There were only two attorneys in practice on Shepherd's Island. The other was Les Hardee, a man with experience, a fine reputation and a fee to match. Unfortunately, Hardee's client list happened to include the names DeBolt and Tremain.

Randall Pelham had no such conflict of interest. He didn't have many clients, either. As the new kid in town, he was ready and willing to represent anyone, even the local murderess.

She asked softly, "Are we okay, Mr. Pelham?"

"Just let me do the talking. You sit there and look innocent."

"I am innocent."

To which Randall Pelham offered no response.

"All rise for His Honor Herbert C. Klimenko," said the bailiff. Everyone stood.

The sound of shuffling feet announced the arrival of Judge Klimenko, who creaked behind the bench and sank like a bag of old bones into his chair. He fumbled around in his pockets and finally managed to perch a pair of bifocals on his nose.

"They brought him out of retirement," someone whispered in the front row. "You know, they say he's senile."

"They also say he's deaf!" shot back Judge Klimenko. With that, he slammed down the gavel. "Court is now in session."

The hearing convened. She followed her attorney's advice and let him do the talking. For forty-five minutes she didn't say a word as two men, one she barely knew, one she knew not at all, argued the question of her freedom. They weren't here to decide guilt or innocence. That was for the trial. The issue to be settled today was more immediate: should she be set free pending that trial?

The deputy D.A. ticked off a list of reasons the accused should remain incarcerated. Weight of evidence. Danger to the community. Undeniable flight risk. The savage nature of the crime, he declared, pointed to the defendant's brutal nature. Miranda could not believe that this monster he kept referring to was *her*. *Is that what they all think of me?* she wondered, feeling the gaze of the audience on her back. *That I'm evil? That I would kill again?*

Only when she was asked, twice, to stand for Judge Klimenko's decision did her attention shift back to the present. Trembling, she rose to her feet and gazed up at the pair of eyes peering down at her over bifocals.

"Bail is set at one hundred thousand dollars cash or two hundred thousand dollars secured property." The gavel slammed down. "Court dismissed."

Miranda was stunned. Even as the audience milled around behind her, she stood frozen in despair.

"It's the best I could do," Pelham whispered.

It might as well have been a million. She would never be able to raise it.

"Come on, Ms. Wood," said the bailiff. "Time to go back."

In silence she let herself be escorted across the room, past the gazes of all those prying eyes. Only for a second did she pause, to glance back over her shoulder at Chase Tremain. As their gazes locked she thought she saw, for an instant, a flicker of something she hadn't seen before. Compassion. Just as quickly, it was gone.

Fighting tears, she turned and followed the bailiff through the side door.

Back to jail.

"That will keep her locked away," said Evelyn.

"A hundred thousand?" Chase shook his head. "It doesn't seem out of reach."

"Not for us, maybe. But for someone like her?" Evelyn snorted. The look of satisfaction on her flawlessly made-up face was not becoming. "No. No, I think Ms. Miranda Wood will be staying right where she belongs. Behind bars."

"She hasn't budged an inch," said Lorne Tibbetts.

"We've been questioning her for a week straight now and she sticks to that story like glue."

"It doesn't matter," said Evelyn. "Facts are facts. She can't refute them."

They were sitting outside, on Evelyn's veranda. At midmorning they'd been driven from the house by the heat; the sun streaming in the windows had turned the rooms into ovens. Chase had forgotten about these hot August days. In his memory, Maine was forever cool, forever immune to the miseries of summer. So much for childhood memories. He poured another glass of iced tea and handed the pitcher over to Tibbetts.

"So what do you think, Lorne?" asked Chase. "You have enough to convict?"

"Maybe. There are holes in the evidence."

"What holes?" demanded Evelyn.

Chase thought, *my sister-in-law is back to her old self again. No more hysterics since that day at the police station.* She looked cool and in control, which is how he'd always remembered her from their childhood. Evelyn the ice queen.

"There's the matter of the fingerprints," said Tibbetts.

"What do you mean?" asked Chase. "Weren't they on the knife?"

"That's the problem. The knife handle was wiped clean. Now, that doesn't make a lot of sense to me. Here's this crime of passion, see? She uses her own knife. Pure impulse. So why does she bother to wipe off the fingerprints?"

"She must be brighter than you think," Evelyn said, sniffing. "She's already got you confused."

"Anyway, it doesn't go along with an impulse killing."

"What other problems do you have with the case?" asked Chase.

"The suspect herself. She's a tough nut to crack."

"Of course she is. She's fighting for her life," said Evelyn.

"She passed the polygraph."

"She submitted to one?" asked Chase.

"She insisted on it. Not that it would've hurt her case if she flunked. It's not admissible evidence."

"So why should it change *your* mind?" asked Evelyn.

"It doesn't. It just bothers me."

Chase stared off toward the sea. He, too, was bothered. Not by the facts, but by his own instincts.

Logic, evidence, told him that Miranda Wood was the killer. Why did he have such a hard time believing it?

The doubts had started a week ago, in that police station hallway. He'd watched the whole interrogation. He'd heard her denials, her lame explanations. He hadn't been swayed. But when they'd come face-to-face in the hall, and she'd looked him straight in the eye, he'd felt the first stirrings of doubt. Would a murderess meet his gaze so unflinchingly? Would she face an accuser with such bald courage? Even when Evelyn had appeared, Miranda hadn't ducked for cover. Instead, she'd said the unexpected. *He loved you. I want you to know that.* Of all the things a murderess might have said, that was the most startling. It was an act of kindness, an honest attempt to comfort the widow. It earned her no points, no stars in court. She could simply have walked past, ignoring Evelyn, leaving her to her grief. Instead, Miranda had reached out in pity to the other woman.

Chase did not understand it.

"There's no question but that the weight of the evidence is against her," said Tibbetts. "Obviously, that's what the judge thought. Just look at the bail he set. He knew she'd never come up with that kind of cash. So she won't be walking out anytime soon. Unless she's been hiding a rich uncle somewhere."

"Hardly," said Evelyn. "A woman like that could only come from the wrong side of the tracks."

Wrong side of the tracks, thought Chase. Meaning poor. But not trash. He'd been able to see that through the one-way mirror. Trash was cheap, easily bent, easily bought. Miranda Wood was none of those.

A car marked Shepherd's Island Police pulled up in the driveway.

Tibbetts sighed. "Geez, they just won't leave me alone. Even on my day off."

Ellis Snipe, spindly in his cop's uniform, climbed out. His boots crunched toward them across the gravel. "Hey, Lorne," he called up to the veranda. "I figured you was here."

"It's Saturday, Ellis."

"Yeah, I know. But we sort of got us a problem."

"If it's that washroom again, just call the plumber. I'll okay the work order."

"No, it's that—" Ellis glanced uneasily at Evelyn. "It's that Miranda Wood woman."

Tibbetts rose to his feet and went over to the veranda railing. "What about her?"

"You know that hundred thousand bail they set?"

"Yeah."

"Well, someone paid it."

"What?"

"Someone's paid it. We just got the order to release her."

There was a long silence on the veranda. Then, in a low voice laced with venom, Evelyn said, *"Who* paid it?"

"Dunno," said Ellis. "Court says it was anonymous. Came through some Boston lawyer. So what do we do, huh, Lorne?"

Tibbetts let out a deep breath. He rubbed his neck, shifted his weight back and forth a few times. Then he said. "I'm sorry, Evelyn."

"Lorne, you can't do this!" she cried.

"I don't have a choice." He turned back to the other cop. "You got the court order, Ellis. Let her walk."

"I don't understand," said Miranda, staring in bewilderment at her attorney. "Who would do this for me?"

"A friend, obviously" was Randall Pelham's dry response. "A very *good* friend."

"But I don't have any friends with that kind of money. No one with a hundred thousand to spare."

"Well, someone's putting up the bail. My advice is, don't look a gift horse in the mouth."

"If I just knew who it was—"

"It's been handled through some Boston attorney who says his client wishes to stay anonymous."

"Why?"

"Maybe the donor's embarrassed."

To be helping a murderess, she thought.

"It's his—or her—right to remain anonymous. I say, take it. The alternative is to stay in jail. Not exactly the most comfortable spot to be in."

She let out a deep breath. "No, it isn't." In fact, it had been horribly bleak in that cell. She'd spent the past week staring at the window, longing for the simple pleasure of a walk by the sea. Or a decent meal. Or just the warmth of the sunshine on her face. Now it was all within reach.

"I wish I knew who to thank," she said softly.

"Not possible, Miranda. I say, just accept the favor." He snapped his briefcase shut.

Suddenly he irritated her, this kid barely out of braces, so smart and snazzy in his gray suit. Randall Pelham, Esquire.

"The arrangements are made. You can leave this afternoon. Will you be staying at your house?"

She paused, shuddering at the memory of Richard's body in her bed. The house had since been cleaned, courtesy of a housekeeping service. Her neighbor Mr. Lanzo had arranged it all, had told her the place looked fine now. It would be as if nothing had happened in that bedroom. There would be no signs of violence at all.

Except in her memory.

But where else could she go?

She nodded. "I—I suppose I'll go home."

"You know the drill, right? Don't leave the county. Bass Harbor's as far as you can go. Stay in touch at all times. And don't, I repeat don't, go around discussing the case. My job's tough enough as it is."

"And we wouldn't want to tax your abilities, would we?" she said under her breath.

He didn't seem to hear the comment. Or maybe he was ignoring her. He strode out of the cell, then turned to gaze at her. "We can still try a plea bargain."

She looked him in the eye. "No."

"That way we could limit the damage. You could walk out of here in ten years instead of twenty-five."

"I didn't kill him."

For a moment Pelham returned her gaze. With a shrug of impatience, he turned. "Plea bargain," he said. "That's my advice. Think about it."

She *did* think about it, all afternoon as she sat in that stark cell waiting for the release papers.

But as soon as she stepped out of the building and walked, as a free woman, into the sunshine, all thoughts of trading away even ten years of her life seemed unimaginable. She stood there on the sidewalk, gazing up at the sky, inhaling the sweetest air she'd ever breathed in her life.

She decided to walk the mile to her house.

By the time she came within sight of her front yard, her cheeks were flushed, her muscles pleasantly tired. The house looked the same as it always had, shingled cottage, trim lawn—which someone had obviously watered in her absence—brick walkway, a hedge of hydrangea bushes sprouting fluffy white clouds of flowers. Not a large house, but it was hers.

She started up the walkway.

Only when she'd mounted the porch steps did she see the vicious words someone had soaped on her front window. She halted, stung by the cruelty of the message.

Killer.

In sudden fury she swiped at the glass with her sleeve. The accusing words dissolved into soapy streaks. Who could have written such a horrible thing? Surely none of her neighbors. Kids. Yes, that's who it must have been. A bunch of punks. Or summer people.

As if that made it easier to dismiss. No one much cared what the summer people thought. The ones who lived on the island year round—those were the ones whose opinions counted. The ones you had to face every day.

She paused at the front door, almost afraid to go in. At last she reached for the knob and entered.

Inside, to her relief, everything seemed orderly, just the way things should be. A bill, made out by the Conscientious Cleaners Company, lay on the end table. "Complete cleaning," read the work order. "Special attention to the master bedroom. Remove stains." The work order was signed by her neighbor, Mr. Lanzo, bless him. Slowly she made a tour of inspection. She glanced in the kitchen, the bathroom, the spare bedroom. Her bedroom she left for last, because it was the most painful to confront. She stood in the doorway, taking in the neatly made bed, the waxed floor, the spotless area rug. No signs of murder, no signs of death. Just a sunny bedroom with plain farmhouse furniture. She stood there, taking it all in, not budging even when the phone rang in the living room. After a while the ringing stopped.

She went into the bedroom and sat on the bed. It seemed like a bad dream now, what she'd seen here. She thought, *If I just concentrate hard enough, I'll wake up. I'll find it was a nightmare.* Then she stared down at the floor and saw, by the foot of the bed, a brown stain in the oak planks.

At once she rose and left the room.

She walked into the living room just as the phone rang again. Automatically she picked up the receiver. "Hello?"

"Lizzie Borden took an ax and gave her mother forty whacks. When she saw what she had done, she gave her father forty-one!"

Miranda dropped the receiver. In horror she backed away, staring at the dangling earpiece. The caller was laughing now. She could hear the giggles, cruel and childlike, emanating from the receiver. She scrambled forward, grabbed the earpiece and slammed it down on the cradle.

The phone rang again.

She picked it up.

"Lizzie Borden took an ax—"

"Stop it!" she screamed. "Leave me alone!"

She hung up and again the phone rang.

This time she didn't answer it. In tears, she ran out the kitchen door and into the garden. There she sank into a heap on the lawn. Birds chirped overhead. The smell of warm soil and flowers drifted sweetly in the afternoon. She buried her face in the grass and cried.

Inside, the phone kept on ringing.

4

Miranda stood alone and unnoticed outside the cemetery gates. Through the wrought-iron grillwork she could see the mourners grouped about the freshly dug grave. It was a large gathering, as befitted a respected member of the community. *Respected, perhaps,* she added to herself. *But was he beloved?* Did any among them, including his wife, truly love him? *I thought I did. Once. . . .*

The voice of Reverend Marriner was barely a murmur. Much was lost in the rustle of the lilac branches overhead. She strained to hear the words. "Loving husband . . . always be missed . . . cruel tragedy . . . Lord, forgive . . ."

Forgive.

She whispered the word, as though it were a prayer that could somehow pull her from the jaws of guilt. But who would forgive her?

Certainly not anyone in that gathering of mourners.

She recognized almost every face there. Among them were her neighbors, her colleagues from the newspaper, her friends. *Make that former friends,* she thought with bitterness. Then there were those too lofty to have made her acquaintance, the ones who moved in social circles to which Miranda had never gained entrance.

She saw the grim but dry-eyed Noah DeBolt, Evelyn's father. There was Forrest Mayhew, president of the local bank, attired in his regulation gray suit and tie. In a category all to herself was Miss Lila St. John, the local flower and garden nut, looking freeze-dried at the eternal age of seventy-four. And then, of course, there were the Tremains. They formed a tragic tableau, poised beside the open grave. Evelyn stood between her son and Chase Tremain, as though she needed both men to steady her. Her daughter, Cassie, stood apart, almost defiantly so. Her flowered peach dress was in shocking contrast to the background of grays and blacks.

Yes, Miranda knew them all. And they knew her.

By all rights she should be standing there with them. She had once been Richard's friend; she owed it to him to say goodbye. She should follow her heart, consequences be damned.

But she lacked the courage.

So she remained on the periphery, a lone and voiceless exile, watching as they laid to rest the man who had once been her lover.

She was still there when it was over, when the mourners began to depart in a slow and steady procession through the gates. She saw their startled glances, heard the gasps, the murmurs of "Look, it's her." She met their gazes calmly. To flee would have seemed an act of cowardice. *I may not be brave,* she thought, *but I am not a coward.* Most of them quickly passed by, averting their eyes. Only Miss Lila St. John returned Miranda's gaze, and the look she gave her was neither friendly nor unfriendly. It was merely thoughtful. For an instant Miranda thought she saw a flicker of a smile in those searching eyes, and then Miss St. John, too, moved on.

A sharp intake of breath made Miranda turn.

The Tremains had halted by the gate. Slowly Evelyn raised her hand and pointed it at Miranda. "You have no right," she whispered. "No right to be here."

"Mom, forget it," said Phillip, tugging her arm. "Let's just go home."

"She doesn't belong here."

"Mom—"

"Get her away from here!" Evelyn lunged toward Miranda, her hands poised to claw.

At once Chase stepped between the two women. He pulled Evelyn against him, trapping her hands in his. "Evelyn, don't! I'll take care of it, okay? I'll talk to her. Just go home. Please." He glanced at the twins. "Phillip, Cassie! Come on, take your mother home. I'll be along later."

The twins each took an arm and Evelyn allowed herself to be led away. But when they reached their car she turned and yelled, "Don't let the bitch fool you, Chase! She'll twist you around, the way she did Richard!"

Miranda stumbled back a step, physically reeling from the impact of those accusing words. She felt the gate against her back swing away, found herself grabbing at it for support. The cold wrought iron felt like the only solid thing she could cling to and she held on for dear life. The squeal of the gate hinges suddenly pierced her cloud of confusion. She found she was standing in a clump of daisies, that the others had gone, and that she and Chase Tremain were the only people remaining in the cemetery.

He was watching her. He stood a few feet away, as though wary of approaching her. As though she was some sort of dangerous animal. She could see the suspicion in his dark eyes, the tension of his pose. How aristocratic he looked today, so remote, so untouchable in that charcoal suit. The jacket showed off to perfection his wide shoulders and narrow waist. Tailored, of course. A real Tremain wouldn't consider any off-the-rack rag.

Still, she had trouble believing this man, with his Gypsy eyes and his jet black hair, was a Tremain.

For a year she had gazed up at those portraits in the newspaper building. They'd hung on the wall opposite her desk, five generations of Tremain men, all of them ruddy faced and blue eyed. Richard's portrait, just as blue eyed, had fit right in. Hang a portrait of Chase Tremain on that same wall and it would look like a mistake.

"Why did you come here, Ms. Wood?" he asked.

She raised her chin. "Why shouldn't I?"

"It's inappropriate, to say the least."

"It's very appropriate. I cared about him. We were—we were friends."

"Friends?" His voice rose in mocking disbelief. "Is that what you call it?"

"You don't know anything about it."

"I know that you were more than friends. What shall we call your relationship, Ms. Wood? An affair? A romance?"

"Stop it."

"A hot little tumble on the boss's couch?"

"Stop it, damn you! It wasn't like that!"

"No, of course not. You were just *friends.*"

"All right! All right. . . ." She looked away, so he wouldn't see her tears. Softly she said, "We were lovers."

"At last. A word for it."

"And friends. Most of all, friends. I wish to God it had stayed that way."

"So do I. At least he'd still be alive."

She stiffened. Turning back to him she said, "I didn't kill him."

He sighed. "Of course you didn't."

"He was already dead. I found him—"

"In your house. In your bed."

"Yes. In my bed."

"Look Ms. Wood. I'm not the judge and jury. Don't waste your breath with me. I'm just here to tell you to stay away from the family. Evelyn's gone through enough hell. She doesn't need constant reminders. If we need to, we'll get a restraining order to keep you away. One false move and you'll be back in jail. Right where you belong."

"You're all alike," she said. "You Tremains and DeBolts. All cut from the same fancy silk. Not like the rest of us, who can be shoved out of sight. Right where we belong."

"It's not a matter of which cloth we're cut from. It's a matter of cold-blooded murder." He took a step toward her. She didn't move. She couldn't; her back was against the gate. "What happened, exactly?" he said, moving closer. "Did Richard break some sacred promise? Refuse to leave his wife? Or did he just come to his senses and decide he was walking out on you?"

"That's not what happened."

"So what did happen?"

"I walked out on *him!*"

Chase gazed down at her, skepticism shadowing every line of his face. "Why?"

"Because it was over. Because it was all wrong, everything between us. I wanted to get away. I'd already left the paper."

"He fired you?"

"I quit. Look in the files, Mr. Tremain. You'll find my letter of resignation. Dated two weeks ago. I was going to leave the island. Head somewhere I wouldn't have to see him every day. Somewhere I wouldn't be constantly reminded of what a disaster I'd made of things."

"Where were you planning to go?"

"It didn't matter. Just away." She looked off, past the gravestones. Far beyond the cemetery lay the sea. She could catch glimpses of it through the trees. "I grew up just fifty miles from here. Right across the water. This bay is my home. I've always loved it. Yet all I could think about was getting away."

She turned to look at him. "I was already free of him. Halfway back to happiness. Why should I kill Richard?"

"Why was he in your house?"

"He insisted on meeting me. I didn't want to see him. So I left and went for a walk. When I came back, I found him."

"Yes, I've heard your version. At least your story's consistent."

"It's also the truth."

"Truth, fiction." He shrugged. "In your case it all blends together, doesn't it?" Abruptly he turned and headed up the cemetery drive.

"What if it's *all* truth?" she called after him.

"Stay away from the family, Ms. Wood!" he yelled over his shoulder. "Or I'll have to call in Lorne Tibbetts."

"Just for a moment, consider the possibility that I didn't kill him! That someone else did!"

He was still walking away.

"Maybe it's someone you know!" she shouted. "Think about it! Or do you already know and you want me to take the blame? Tell me, Mr. Tremain! Who *really* killed your brother?"

That brought Chase to a sudden halt. He knew he should keep walking. He knew it was a mistake to engage the woman in any more of this insane dialogue. It *was* insane. Or she was insane. Yet he couldn't break away, not yet. What she'd just said had opened up too many frightening possibilities.

Slowly he turned to face her. She stood absolutely still, her gaze fixed on him. The afternoon sun washed her head with a coppery glow. All that beautiful hair seemed to overwhelm her face. She looked surprisingly fragile in that black dress, as though a strong gust might blow her away.

Was it possible? he wondered. Could this woman really have picked up a knife? Raised the blade over Richard's body? Plunged it down with so much rage, so much strength, that the tip had pierced straight through to his spine?

Slowly he moved toward her. "If you didn't kill him," he said, "who did?"

"I don't know."

"That's a pretty disappointing answer."

"He had enemies—"

"Angry enough to kill him?"

"He ran a newspaper. He knew things about certain people in this town. And he wasn't afraid to print the truth."

"Which people? What sort of scandal are we talking about?"

He saw her hesitate, wondered if she was dredging up some new lie.

"Richard was writing an article," she said. "About a local developer named Tony Graffam. He runs a company called Stone Coast Trust. Richard said he had proof of fraud—"

"My brother had paid reporters on his staff. Why would he bother to do his own writing?"

"It was a personal crusade of his. He was set on ruining Stone Coast. He needed just one last piece of evidence. Then he was going to print."

"And did he?"

"No. The article was supposed to appear two weeks ago. It never did."

"Who stopped it?"

"I don't know. You'd have to talk to Jill Vickery."

"The managing editor?"

Miranda nodded. "She knew the article was in the works and she wasn't crazy about the idea. Richard was the driving force behind the story. He was even willing to risk a libel suit. In fact, Tony Graffam has already threatened to sue."

"So we have one convenient suspect. Tony Graffam. Anyone else?"

She hesitated. "Richard wasn't a popular man."

"*Richard?*" He shook his head. "I doubt that. I was the brother with the popularity problem."

"Two months ago he cut salaries at the *Herald.* Laid off a third of the staff."

"Ah. So we have more suspects."

"He hurt people. Families—"

"Including his own."

"You don't know how hard it is these days! How desperate people are for work. Oh, he talked a good story. About how sorry he was to be laying people off. How it hurt him just as much as it hurt everyone else. It was *garbage.* I heard him talking about it later, to his accountant. He said, 'I cut the deadwood, just as you advised.' Deadwood. Those employees had been with the *Herald* for years. Richard had the money. He could have carried the loss."

"He was a businessman."

"Right. That's exactly what he was." Her hair, tossed by the wind, was like flames dancing. She was a wild and blazing fire, full of anger at him, at Richard, at the Tremains.

"So we've added to the pool of suspects," he said. "All those poor souls who lost their jobs. And their families. Why don't we toss in Richard's children? His father-in-law? His wife?"

"Yes! Why not Evelyn?"

Chase snorted in disgust. "You're very good, you know that? All that smoke and mirrors. But you haven't convinced me. I hope the jury is just as smart. I hope to hell they see through you and make you pay."

She looked at him mutely, all the fire, all the spirit suddenly drained from her body.

"I've already paid," she whispered. "I'll pay for the rest of my life. Because I'm guilty. Not of killing him. I didn't kill him." She swallowed and looked away. He could no longer see her face, but he could hear the anguish in her voice. "I'm guilty of being stupid. And naive. Guilty of having faith in the wrong man. I really thought I loved your brother. But that was before I knew him. And then, when I did know him, I tried to walk away. I wanted to do it while we were still . . . friends."

He saw her hand come up and stroke quickly across her face. It suddenly struck him how very brave she was. Not brazen, as he'd first thought upon seeing her today, but truly, heartbreakingly courageous.

She raised her head again, her gaze drawing level to his. The tears she'd tried to wipe away were still glistening on her lashes. He had a sudden, crazy yearning to touch her face, to wipe away the wetness of those tears. And with that yearning came another, just as insane, a man's hunger to know the taste of her lips, the softness of her hair. At once he took a step back, as though retreating from some dangerous flame. He thought, *I can see why you fell for her, Richard. Under different circumstances I might have fallen for her myself.*

"Oh, hell," she muttered in disgust. "What does it matter now, what I felt? To you or to anyone else?" Without looking back she left him and started up the driveway. Her abrupt departure seemed to leave behind an unfillable vacuum.

"Ms. Wood!" he yelled. She kept walking. He called out, "Miranda!" She stopped. "I have one question for you," he said. "Who bailed you out?"

Slowly she turned and looked at him. "You tell me," she said.

And then she walked away.

It was a long walk to the newspaper building. It took Miranda past familiar streets and storefronts, past people she knew. That was the worst part. She felt them staring at her through the shop windows. She saw them huddle in groups and whisper to each other. No one came right out and said anything to her face. They didn't have to. *All I lack,* she thought, *is a scarlet letter sewn on my chest. M for murderess.*

She kept her gaze fixed straight ahead and walked up Limerock Street. The *Herald* building stood before her, a brick-and-slate haven against all those watching eyes. She ducked through the double glass doors, into the newsroom.

Inside, all activity came to a dead halt.

She felt assaulted by all those startled looks.

"Hello, Miranda," said a cool voice.

Miranda turned. Jill Vickery, the managing editor, glided out of the executive office. She hadn't changed clothes since the funeral. On dark-haired, ivory-skinned Jill, the color black looked quite elegant.

Her short skirt hissed against her stockings as she clipped across the floor.

"Is there something I can do for you?" Jill asked politely.

"I—I came to get my things."

"Yes, of course." Jill shot a disapproving glance at the other employees, who were still gawking. "Are we all so efficient that we've no more work to do?"

At once everyone redirected their attention to their jobs.

Jill looked at Miranda. "I've already taken the liberty of cleaning out your desk. It's all in a box downstairs."

Miranda was so grateful for Jill's simple civility she scarcely registered annoyance that her desk had been coldbloodedly emptied of her belongings. She said, "I've also a few things in my locker."

"They should still be there. No one's touched it." There was a silence. "Well," said Jill, a prelude to escape from a socially awkward situation. "I wish you luck. Whatever happens." She started back toward her office.

"Jill?" called Miranda.

"Yes?"

"I was wondering about that article on Tony Graffam. Why it didn't run."

Jill looked at her with frank puzzlement. "Why does it matter?"

"It just does."

Jill shrugged. "It was Richard's decision. He pulled the story."

"Richard's? But he was working on it for months."

"I can't tell you his reasons. I don't know them. He just pulled it. And anyway, I don't think he ever wrote the story."

"But he told me it was nearly finished."

"I've checked his files." Jill turned and walked toward her office. "I doubt he ever got beyond the research stage. You know how he was, Miranda. The master of overstatement."

Miranda stared after her in bewilderment. The master of overstatement. It hurt to admit it, but yes, there was a lot of truth in that label.

People were staring at her again.

She headed down the stairwell and pushed into the women's lounge. There she found Annie Berenger, lacing up running shoes. Annie was dressed in her usual rumpled-reporter attire—baggy drawstring pants, wrinkled cotton shirt. The inside of her locker looked just as disorderly, a mound of wadded-up clothes, towels and books.

Annie glanced up and tossed her head of gray-streaked hair in greeting. "You're back."

"Just to clean out my things." Miranda found the cardboard box with her belongings stuffed under one of the benches. She dragged it out and carried it to her locker.

"I saw you at the funeral," said Annie. "That took guts, Mo."

"I'm not sure guts is the word for it."

Annie shoved her locker door shut and breathed a sigh of relief. "Comfortable at last. I just had to change out of that funeral getup. Can't think in those stupid high heels. Cuts the blood supply to my brain." She finished lacing up her running shoe. "So what's going to happen next? With you, I mean."

"I don't know. I refuse to think beyond a day or two." Miranda opened her locker and began to throw things into the box.

"Rumor has it you have friends in high places."

"What?"

"Someone bailed you out, right?"

"I don't know who it was."

"You must have an idea. Or is this your lawyer's advice, to plead ignorance?"

Miranda gripped the locker door. "Don't, Annie. Please."

Annie cocked her head, revealing all the lines and freckles of too many summers in the sun. "I'm being a jerk, aren't I? Sorry. It's just that Jill assigned me to the trial. I don't like having to drag an old colleague across the front page." She watched as Miranda emptied the locker and shut the door. "So. Can I get a statement from you?"

"I didn't do it."

"I've already heard that one."

"Want to earn a Pulitzer?" Miranda turned, squarely faced her. "Help me find out who killed him."

"You'll have to give me a lead, first."

"I don't have one."

Annie sighed. "That's the problem. Whether or not you did it, you're still the obvious suspect."

Miranda picked up the box and headed up the stairs. Annie trailed behind her.

"I thought real reporters went after the truth," said Miranda.

"This reporter," said Annie, "is basically lazy and angling for early retirement."

"At your age?"

"I turn forty-seven next month. I figure that's a good age to retire. If I can just get Irving to pop the question, it'll be a life of bonbons and TV soaps."

"You'd hate it."

"Oh, yeah." Annie laughed. "I'd be just miserable."

They walked into the newsroom. At once Miranda felt all those gazes turn her way. Annie, oblivious to their audience, went to her desk, threw her locker keys in her drawer and pulled out a pack of cigarettes. "You happen to have a light?" she asked Miranda.

"You always ask me, and I never have one."

Annie turned and yelled, "Miles!"

The summer intern sighed resignedly and tossed her a cigarette lighter. "Just give it back," he said.

"You're too young to smoke, anyway," snapped Annie.

"So were you once, Berenger."

Annie grinned at Miranda. "I love these boy wonders. They're so damn petulant."

Miranda couldn't help smiling. She sat on the desktop and looked at her ex-colleague. As always, Annie wore a wreath of cigarette smoke. It was part addiction, part prop, that cigarette. Annie had earned her reporter's stripes in a Boston newsroom where the floor was said to be an inch deep in cigarette butts.

"You do believe me, don't you?" asked Miranda softly. "You don't really think . . ."

Annie looked her straight in the eye. "No. I don't. And I was kidding about being lazy," said Annie. "I've been digging. I'll come up with something. It's not like I'm doing it out of friendship or anything. I mean, I could find out things that could hurt you. But it's what I have to do."

Miranda nodded. "Then start with this."

"What?"

"Find out who bailed me out."

Annie nodded. "A reasonable first step."

The back office door swung open. Jill Vickery came out and glanced around the newsroom. "Marine distress call. Sailboat's taking on water. Who wants the story?"

Annie slunk deep in her chair.

Miles sprang to his feet. "I'll take it."

"Coast Guard's already on the way. Hire a launch if you have to. Go on, get going. You don't want to miss the rescue." Jill turned and looked at Annie. "Are you busy at the moment?"

Annie shrugged. "I'm always busy."

Jill nodded toward Miles. "He'll need help. Go with the kid." She turned back to her office.

"I can't."

Jill stopped, turned to confront Annie. "Are you refusing my assignment?"

"Yeah. Sort of."

"On what grounds?"

Annie blew out a long, lazy puff of smoke. "Seasickness."

"I knew she'd confuse you, Chase. I just knew it. You don't understand her the way I do."

Chase looked up from the porch chair where he'd been brooding for
the past hour. He saw that Evelyn had changed out of her black dress
and was now wearing an obscenely bright lime green. He knew he
should feel sorry for his sister-in-law, but at the moment Evelyn looked
more in need of a stiff drink than of pity. He couldn't help comparing
her to Miranda Wood. Miranda, with her ill-fitting black dress and her
windblown hair, so alone on that cemetery hillside. He wondered if
Richard ever knew how much damage he'd done to her, or if he'd ever
cared.

"You haven't said a word since you got home," complained Evelyn.
"What is going on with you?"

"Just how well did you know Miranda Wood?" he asked.

She sat down and fussily arranged the folds of her green dress. "I've
heard things. I know she grew up in Bass Harbor. Went to some—
some state university. Had to do it all on scholarship. Couldn't afford it
otherwise. Really, not a very good family."

"Meaning what?"

"Mill workers."

"Ah. Dregs of the earth."

"What is the matter with you, Chase?"

He rose to his feet. "I need to take a walk."

"Oh. I'll go with you." She jumped to her feet, instantly wreaking
havoc on all those nicely arranged folds of her dress.

"No. I'd like to be alone for a while. If you don't mind."

Evelyn looked as if she minded very much, but she managed to cover
it gracefully. "I understand, Chase. We all need to mourn in our own
way."

He felt a distinct sense of relief as he walked away from that front
porch. The house had started to feel oppressive, as though the weight
of all those memories had crowded out the breathable air. For a half
hour he walked aimlessly. Only as his feet carried him closer to town
did he begin to move with a new sense of purpose.

He headed straight for the newspaper building.

He was greeted by Jill Vickery, the sleekly attractive managing editor. It was just like Richard to surround himself with gorgeous women.

Chase had met her earlier that day, at the funeral. Then, as now, she played the part of the professional to the hilt.

"Mr. Tremain," she said, offering her hand. "What a pleasure to see you again. May I show you around?"

"I was just wondering . . ." He glanced around the newsroom, which was currently occupied by only a bare-bones staff: the layout man arranging ads, another one staring at a computer screen, and that sloppy reporter puffing on a cigarette as she talked on the phone.

"Yes?" asked Jill.

"If I could go over some of my brother's files."

"Business or personal files?"

"Both."

She hesitated, then led him into the back office and through a door labeled Richard Tremain, Owner and Publisher. "These aren't all his files, you understand. He kept most of them here, but some he kept at home or at the cottage."

"You mean Rose Hill?"

"Yes. He liked to work out there, on occasion." She pointed to the desk. "The key's in the top drawer. Please let me know if you take anything."

"I wasn't planning to."

She paused, as though uncertain whether to trust him. But what choice did she have? He was, after all, the publisher's brother. At last she turned and left.

Chase waited for the door to shut, then he unlocked the file cabinet. He flipped immediately to the W's.

He found a file on Miranda Wood.

Chase carried it to the desk and spread it open. It appeared to be a routine personnel record. The employment application was dated one year ago, when Miranda was twenty-eight. Her address was listed as 18 Willow Street. In the attached photograph she was smiling; it was the face of a confident young woman with her whole life ahead of her. It almost hurt to see how happy she looked. Her university record was outstanding. If anything, she was overqualified for her job as copy editor. Under the question "Why do you want this job?" she had written, "I grew up near Penobscot Bay. I want, more than anything, to live and work in the place I've always called home." He flipped through the pages and scanned the semiannual employee evaluation, filled out by Jill Vickery. It was excellent. He turned to the last page.

There was a letter of resignation, dated two weeks ago.

* * *

To: Richard Tremain, Publisher, *Island Herald.*

Dear Mr. Tremain,

I hereby notify you of my resignation from my position as copy editor. My reasons are personal. I would greatly appreciate a letter of reference, as I plan to seek employment elsewhere.

That was all. No explanations, no regrets. Not even a hint of recrimination.

So she told me the truth, he thought. *She really did walk off the job.*

"Mr. Tremain?" It was Jill Vickery, back again. "Are you looking for anything in particular? Maybe I can help you."

"Maybe you can."

She came in and gracefully settled into the chair across from him. Her gaze at once took in the file on the desk. "I see you have Miranda's employee record."

"Yes. I'm trying to understand what happened. Why she did it."

"I think you should know she was here just a short while ago."

"In the building?"

"She came to collect her things. I'm glad you two avoided a, uh . . . unexpected encounter."

He nodded. "So am I."

"Let me say this, Mr. Tremain. I'm very sorry about your brother. He was a wonderful man, an exceptional writer. He truly believed in the power of the printed word. We're going to miss him."

It was a canned speech, but she delivered it with such sincerity he was almost convinced she meant it. Jill Vickery certainly had the PR down flat.

"I understand Richard had a story in the pipeline," he said. "Something about a company called Stone Coast Trust. You familiar with it?"

Jill sighed. "Why does this particular article keep coming up?"

"Someone else interested?"

"Miranda Wood. She just asked about it. I told her that as far as I know, the story was never written. At least, I never saw it."

"But it was scheduled to run?"

"Until Richard canceled it."

"Why?"

She sat back and smoothly flicked her hair off her face. "I wouldn't know. I suspect he didn't have enough evidence to go to print."

"What, exactly, is the story on Stone Coast Trust?"

"Small-town stuff, really. Not very interesting to outsiders."

"Try me."

"It had to do with developers' rights. Stone Coast has been buying up property on the north shore. Near Rose Hill Cottage, as a matter of fact, so you know how lovely it is up there. Pristine coastline, trees. Tony Graffam—he's president of Stone Coast—claimed he was out to preserve the area. Then we heard rumors of a high-class development in the works. And then, a month ago, the zoning on those lots was abruptly changed from conservation to resort. It's now wide open to development."

"That's all there is to the article?"

"In a nutshell. May I ask the reason for your interest?"

"It was something Miranda Wood told me. About other people having motives to kill my brother."

"In this case, she's stretching the point." Jill rose to her feet. "But one can hardly blame her for trying. She hasn't much else to grab onto."

"You think she'll be convicted?"

"I wouldn't want to hazard a guess. But from what my news staff tells me, it sounds likely."

"You mean that reporter? Annie something?"

"Annie Berenger. Yes, she's assigned to the story."

"Can I talk to her?"

Jill frowned. "Why?"

He shook his head. "I don't know. I guess I'm just trying to understand who this Miranda Wood really is. Why she would kill." He sat back, ran his hand through his hair. "I still can't quite fit the pieces together. I thought, maybe someone who's been watching the case—someone who knew her personally . . ."

"Of course. I understand." The words were sympathetic but her eyes were indifferent. "I'll send Annie in to talk to you."

She left. A moment later Annie Berenger appeared.

"Come in," said Chase. "Have a seat."

Annie shut the door and sat in the chair across from him. She looked like a reporter: frizzy red hair streaked with gray, sharp eyes, wrinkled slacks. She also reeked of cigarettes. It brought back memories of his father. All she needed was a splash of whiskey on her breath. A good old newsman's smell.

She was watching him with clear suspicion. "Boss lady says you want to talk about Miranda."

"You knew her pretty well?"

"The word is *know*. Present tense. Yes, I do."

"What do you think of her?"

Her mouth twitched into a smile. "This is your own private investigation?"

"Call it my quest for the truth. Miranda Wood denies killing my brother. What do you think?"

Annie lit a cigarette. "You know, I used to cover the police beat in Boston."

"So you're familiar with murder."

"In a manner of speaking." Leaning back, she thoughtfully exhaled a cloud of smoke. "Miranda had the motive. Oh, we all knew about the affair. It's hard to hide something like that in this newsroom. I tried to, well, advise her against it. But she follows her heart, you know? And it got her into trouble. That's not to say she did it. Killed him." Annie flicked off an ash. "I don't think she did."

"Then who did?"

Annie shrugged.

"You think it's tied to the Tony Graffam story?"

Annie's eyebrow shot up. "You dig stuff up fast. Must run in the family, that newsman's nose."

"Miranda Wood says Richard had a story about to break. True?"

"He said he did. I know he was writing it. He had a few more details to check before it went to print."

"What details?"

"Financial data, about Stone Coast Trust. Richard had just got his hands on some account information."

"Why didn't the article get to print?"

"Honest opinion?" Annie snorted. "Because Jill Vickery didn't want to risk a libel suit."

Chase frowned. "But Jill says the article doesn't exist. That Richard never wrote it."

Annie blew out a last breath of smoke and stubbed out her cigarette in the ashtray. "Here's a piece of wisdom for you, Mr. T," she said. She looked him in the eye. "Never trust your editor."

Did the article exist or didn't it?

Chase spent the next hour searching the files in Richard's office. He found nothing under *G* for Graffam or *S* for Stone Coast Trust. He tried a few more headings, but none of them panned out. Did Richard keep the file at home?

It was late afternoon when he finally returned to the house. To his relief, Evelyn and the twins were out. He had the place to himself. He went straight into Richard's home office and continued his search for the Graffam file.

He didn't find it. Yet Miranda claimed it existed. So did Annie Berenger.

Something strange was going on, something that added to all his doubts about Miranda's guilt. He mentally played back all the holes in the prosecution's case. The lack of fingerprints on the murder weapon. The fact she had passed the polygraph test. And the woman herself— proud, unyielding in her protestations of innocence.

He gave up trying to talk himself out of his next move. There was no way around it. Not if he wanted to know more. Not if he wanted to shake these doubts.

He had to talk to Miranda Wood.

He pulled on his windbreaker and headed out into the dusk.

Five blocks later he turned onto Willow Street. It was just the way he'd remembered it, a tidy, middle-class neighborhood with inviting front porches and well-tended lawns. Through the fading light he could just make out the address numbers. A few more houses to go. . . .

Farther up the street a screen door slammed shut. He saw a woman come down her porch steps and start toward him along the sidewalk. He recognized her silhouette, the thick cloud of hair, the slim figure clad in jeans. She'd taken only a few steps when she spotted him and stopped dead in her tracks.

"I have to talk to you," he said.

"I made a promise, remember?" she answered. "Not to go near you or your family. Well, I'm keeping that promise." She turned and started to walk away.

"This is different. I have to ask you about Richard."

She kept walking.

"Will you listen to me?"

"That's how I got into this mess!" she shot back over her shoulder. "Listening to a Tremain!"

He watched in frustration as she headed swiftly up the street. It was useless to pursue her. She was already a block away now, and by the set of her shoulders he could tell she wasn't going to change her mind. In fact, she had just stepped off the sidewalk and was crossing the street, as though to put the width of the road between them.

Forget her, he thought. *If she's too stubborn to listen, let her go to jail.*

Chase turned and had started in the opposite direction when a car drove past. He would scarcely have noticed it except for one detail: its headlights were off. A few paces was all it took for Chase to register that fact. He stopped, turned. Far ahead, Miranda's slender figure was crossing the street.

By then the car had moved halfway down the block.

The driver'll see her in time, he thought. *He has to see her.*

The car's engine suddenly revved up in a threatening growl of power. Tires screeched. The car leaped forward in a massive blur of steel and smoke, and roared ahead through the shadows.

It was aiming straight for Miranda.

5

The headlights sprang on, trapping its insubstantial victim in a blaze of light.

"Look out!" Chase shouted.

Miranda whirled and found her eyes flooded with a terrible, blinding brightness. Even as the car shot closer and those lights threatened to engulf her, she was paralyzed by disbelief, by the detached sense of certainty that this was not really happening. She had no time to reason it out. An instant before that ton of steel could slam into her body, her reflexes took over. She flung herself sideways, out of the path of the onrushing headlights.

Suddenly she was flying, suspended for an eternity in the summer darkness as death rushed past her in a roar of wind and light.

And then she was lying on the grass.

She didn't know how long she had been there. She knew only that the grass was damp, that her head hurt and that gentle hands were stroking her face. Someone called her name, again and again. It was a voice she knew, a voice she thought, in that confused moment, she must have known all her life. Its very timbre seemed to blanket her with the warmth of safety.

Again he called her name, and this time she heard panic in his voice. *He's afraid. Why?*

She opened her eyes and dazedly focused on his face. That's when she registered exactly who he was. All illusion of safety fell away.

"Don't." She brushed his hand aside. "Don't touch me."

"Lie still."

"I don't need you!" She struggled to sit up, but found herself unable to move under his restraining hands. He had her pinned by her shoulders to the grass.

"Look," he said, his voice maddeningly reasonable. "You took a mean tumble. You might have broken something—"

"I said, don't touch me!" Defiantly she shoved him away and sat up. Pure rage propelled her to her knees. Then, as the night wavered before her eyes, she found herself sinking back to the grass. There she sat and clutched her spinning head. "Oh, God," she groaned. "Why can't you just—just go away and leave me alone."

"Not on your life," came the answer, grim and resolute.

To her amazement she was suddenly, magically lifted up into the air. Through her anger she had to admit it felt good to be carried, good to be held, even if the man holding her was Chase Tremain. She was floating, borne like a featherweight through the darkness. *Toward what?* she wondered with sudden apprehension.

"That's enough," she protested. "Let me down."

"Only a few more steps."

"I hope you get a hernia."

"Keep up the damn wiggling and I will."

He swept her up the porch steps and in the front door. With unerring instinct he carried her straight to the bedroom and managed to flick on the wall switch. The room—the bed—sprang into view. The bed where she'd found Richard. Though the blood was gone, the mattress new and unstained, this room would always remind her of death. She hadn't slept here since that night, would never sleep here again.

She shuddered against him. "Please," she whispered, turning her face against his chest. "Not here. Not this room."

For a moment he paused, not understanding. Then, gently he answered, "Whatever you say, Miranda."

He carried her back to the living room and lowered her onto the couch. She felt the cushions sag as he sat beside her. "Does anything hurt?" he asked. "Your back? Your neck?"

"My shoulder, a little. I think I fell on it."

She flinched at the touch of his hands. Carefully he maneuvered her arm, checking its range of motion. She was scarcely aware of the occasional twinges he evoked from her muscles. Her attention was too acutely focused on the face gazing down at her. Once again she was struck by how unlike Richard he was. It wasn't just the blackness of his hair and eyes. It was his calmness under fire, as though he held any emotions he might be feeling under tight rein. This was not a man who'd easily reveal himself, or his secrets, to anyone.

"It seems all right," he said, straightening. "Still, I'd better call a doctor. Who do you see?"

"Dr. Steiner."

"Steiner? Is that old goat still in practice?"

"Look, I'm okay. I don't need to see him."

"Let's just be on the safe side." He reached for the telephone.

"But Dr. Steiner doesn't make house calls," she protested. "He never has."

"Then tonight," Chase said grimly, dialing the phone, "I guess we're going to make history."

Lorne Tibbetts poured himself a cup of coffee and turned to look at Chase. "What I want to know is, what in blazes are you doing here?"

Chase, leaning over Miranda's kitchen table, wearily rubbed his face. "To tell you the truth, Lorne," he muttered, "I don't know."

"Oh."

"I guess I thought I could . . . figure things out. Make sense of what's happened."

"That's our job, Chase. Not yours."

"Yeah, I know. But—"

"You don't think I'm doing a good job?"

"I just get this feeling there's more than meets the eye. Now I know there is."

"You mean that car?" Lorne shrugged. "Doesn't prove a thing."

"He was *aiming* for her. I saw it. As soon as she stepped into the street he hit the gas."

"He?"

"He, she. It was dark. I didn't see the driver. Just the license plate. And the taillights. Big car, American. I'm pretty sure."

"Color?"

"Dark. Black, maybe blue."

Lorne nodded. "You're not a bad witness, Chase."

"What do you mean?"

"I had Ellis check on that license number. Matches a brown '88 Lincoln, registered to an island resident."

"Who?"

"Mr. Eddie Lanzo. Ms. Wood's next-door neighbor."

Chase stared at him. "Her neighbor? Have you brought him in yet?"

"The car was stolen, Chase. You know how it is around here. Folks leave their keys in the ignition. We found the car over by the pier."

Chase sat back, stunned. "So the driver's untraceable," he said. "That makes it even more likely he was trying to kill her."

"It just means it was some crazy kid out for a joyride. Got his hands on that wheel, got a little overwhelmed by all that power, pushed too hard on the gas pedal."

"Lorne, he was out to kill her."

Lorne sat down and looked him in the eye. "And what are you out to do?"

"Learn the truth."

"You don't believe she did it?"

"I've been hearing some things, Lorne. Other names, other motives. Tony Graffam, for instance."

"We've looked into that. Graffam was off the island when your brother was killed. I have half a dozen witnesses who'll say so."

"He could have hired someone."

"Graffam was in big enough trouble with that north shore development. Charges of bribing the land planning commission. That article would've simply been the last nail in the coffin. Anyway, how does this tie in with what happened tonight? Why would he go after Miranda Wood?"

Chase fell silent at that question. He couldn't see a motive, either. Other people in town might dislike Miranda, but who would go to the trouble of killing her?

"Maybe we're looking at this the wrong way," said Chase. "Let's ask a more basic question. Who put up the bail money? Someone wanted her out so badly he put up a hundred thousand dollars."

"A secret admirer?"

"In jail she's safe. Out here she's a sitting duck. You have any idea who bailed her out, Lorne?"

"No."

"The money could be traced."

"A lawyer handled the transfer of funds. All cash. Came from some Boston account. Only the bank knows the account holder's identity. And they aren't talking."

"Subpoena the bank. Get the name on that account."

"It'll take time."

"Do it, Lorne. Before something else happens."

Lorne went to the sink and rinsed his coffee cup. "I still don't see why you're getting into this," he said.

Chase himself didn't know the answer. Just this morning he'd wanted Miranda Wood put behind bars. Now he wasn't sure what he wanted. That innocent face, her heartfelt denials of guilt had him thoroughly confused.

He looked around the kitchen, thinking it didn't *look* like the kitchen of a murderess. Plants hung near the window, obviously well tended and well loved. The wallpaper had dainty wildflowers scattered across an eggshell background. Tacked to the refrigerator were snapshots of two little towheaded boys—nephews, maybe?—a schedule of the local garden club meetings and a shopping list. At the bottom of the list was written "cinnamon tea." Was that the sort of beverage a murderess would drink? He couldn't picture Miranda holding a knife in one hand and a cup of herbal tea in the other.

Chase looked around as Dr. Steiner shuffled into the kitchen. Some things on the island never changed, and this old grouch was one of them. He looked exactly the same as Chase remembered from his boyhood, right down to the wrinkled brown suit and the alligator medical bag. "All this to-do," the doctor said disapprovingly. "For nothin' but a muscle strain."

"You sure about that?" asked Chase. "She was sort of dazed for a minute. Right after it happened."

"I looked her over good. She's fine, neurologically speaking. You just keep an eye on her tonight, young man. Make sure she doesn't get into trouble. You know, headache, double vision, confusion—"

"I can't."

"Can't what?"

"I can't stay and watch her. It's awkward. Considering . . ."

"No kidding," muttered Lorne.

"She's not my responsibility," said Chase. "What do I do?"

Dr. Steiner grunted and turned for the kitchen door. "You figure it out. By the way," he said, pausing in the doorway, "I don't do house calls." The door slammed shut.

Chase turned to find Lorne looking at him. "What?"

"Nothing," said Lorne. He reached for his hat. "I'm going home."

"And what the hell am I supposed to do?"

"That," said Lorne with an I-told-you-so look, "is your problem."

Miranda lay on the living-room couch and stared at the ceiling. She could hear voices from the kitchen, the sound of the door opening and closing. She wondered what Chase had told them, whether Tibbetts believed any of it. She herself couldn't believe what had happened. But all she had to do was close her eyes and it came back to her: the roar of the car engine, the twin headlights rushing at her.

Who hates me so much they want me dead?

It wasn't hard to come up with an answer. The Tremain family. Evelyn and Phillip and Cassie. . . .

And Chase.

No, that wasn't possible. His shout of warning had saved her life. If not for him, she would be lying right now on a slab in Ben LaPorte's Funeral Home.

That thought made her shudder. Hugging herself, she burrowed deeper into the couch cushions, seeking some safe little nook in which to hide. She heard the kitchen door open and shut again, then footsteps creaked into the living room and approached the couch. She looked up and saw Chase.

Weariness was what she read in his eyes, and uncertainty, as though he hadn't quite made up his mind what should be done next. Or what should be said next. He'd shed his windbreaker. His chambray shirt was the comfortably faded blue of a well-worn, well-loved garment. That shirt reminded her of her father, of how it used to feel to nestle her face against his shoulder, of those wondrous childhood scents of laundry soap and pipe tobacco and safety. That was what she saw in that faded blue shirt, what she longed for.

What she'd never find with this man.

Chase sat in the armchair. A prudent distance away, she noted. *Keeping me at arm's length.*

"Feeling better?" he asked.

"I'll be fine." She kept her voice like his—detached, neutral. She added, "You can leave if you want."

"No. Not yet. I'll wait here awhile, if that's okay. Until Annie gets here."

"Annie?"

"I didn't know who else to call. She said she'd be over to spend the night. You should have someone here to keep an eye on you. Make sure you don't slide into a coma or something."

She gave a tired laugh. "A coma would feel pretty good right now."

"That's not very funny."

She looked up at the ceiling. "You're right. It isn't."

There was a long silence.

Finally he said, "That wasn't an accident, Miranda. He was trying to kill you."

She didn't answer. She lay there fighting back the sob swelling in her throat. *Why should it matter to you?* she thought. *You, of all people.*

"Maybe you haven't heard," he said. "The car belonged to your neighbor. Mr. Lanzo."

She looked at him sharply. "Eddie Lanzo would never hurt me! He's the only one who's stood by me. My one friend in this town."

"I didn't say it was him. Lorne thinks the driver stole Mr. Lanzo's car. They found it abandoned by the pier."

"Poor Eddie," she murmured. "Guess that's the last time he leaves his keys in the car."

"So if it wasn't Eddie, who does want you dead?"

"I can make a wild guess." She looked at him. "So can you."

"Are you referring to Evelyn?"

"She hates me. She has every right to hate me. So do her children." She paused. "So do you."

He was silent.

"You still think I killed him. Don't you?"

Sighing, he raked his fingers through his hair. "I don't know what to think anymore. About you, about anyone. All I can be sure of is what I saw tonight. It's all tied in, this whole bloody mess. It has to be."

He looks so tired, so confused, she thought. *Almost as confused as I am.*

"Maybe you should move out of here for a few days," he said. "Until things get sorted out."

"Where would I go?"

"You must have friends."

"I did." She looked away. "At least, I thought I did. But everything's changed. I pass them on the street and they don't even say hello. Or they cross to the other side. Or they pretend they don't see me. That's the worst of all. Because I begin to think I don't exist." She looked at him. "It's a very small town, Chase. You either fit in, or you don't belong. And there's no way a murderess could ever fit in." She lay back against the cushions and stared at the ceiling. "Besides, this is my house. *My* house. I saved like crazy for the down payment. I won't leave it. It's not much, but at least it's mine."

"I can understand that. It's a nice house."

He sounded sincere enough, but his words struck her as patronizing. The lord of the manor extolling the charms of the shepherd's hovel.

Suddenly annoyed, she sat up. The abrupt movement made the room spin. She clutched her head for a moment, waiting for the spell to pass.

"Look, let's be straight with each other," she muttered through her hands. "It's only a two-bedroom cottage. The basement's damp, the water pipes screech and there's a leak in the kitchen roof. It's not Chestnut Street."

"To be honest," he said quietly, "I never felt at home on Chestnut Street."

"Why not? You were raised there."

"But it wasn't really a home. Not like this house."

Puzzled, she looked up at him. It struck her then how rough around the edges he seemed, a dark, rumpled stranger hulking in her mauve armchair. No, this man didn't quite fit on Chestnut Street. He belonged on the docks, or on the windswept deck of a schooner, not in some stuffy Victorian parlor.

"I'm supposed to believe you'd prefer a cottage on Willow Street to the family mansion?"

"I guess it does sound—I don't know. Phony. But it's true. Know where I spent most of my time as a kid? In the turret, playing around all the trunks and the old furniture. That was the only place in the house where I felt comfortable. The one room no one else cared to visit."

"You sound like the family outcast."

"In a way, I was."

She laughed. "I thought all Tremains were, by definition, *in.*"

"One can have the family name and still not be part of the family. Or didn't you ever feel that way?"

"No, I was always very much part of my family. What there was of it." Her gaze drifted to the spinet piano, where the framed photo of her father was displayed. It was a grainy shot, one of the few she still had of him, taken with her old Kodak Brownie. He was grinning at her over the hood of his Chevy, a bald little gnome of a man dressed in blue overalls. She found herself smiling back at the image.

"Your father?" asked Chase.

"Yes. Stepfather, really. But he was every bit as wonderful as any real father."

"I hear he worked for the mill."

She frowned at him. It disturbed her that Chase was obviously acquainted with that detail of her life. A detail that was none of his business. "Yes," she said. "Both my parents did. What else have you heard about me?"

"It's not that I've been checking up on you."

"But you have, haven't you? You and your family have probably run my name through some computer. Criminal check. Family history. Credit report—"

"We've done no such thing."

"Personal life. All the hot and juicy details."

"Where would I find those?"

"Try my police record." In irritation she rose from the couch and moved to the fireplace. There she stood focused on the clock over the mantelpiece. "It's getting late, Mr. Tremain. Annie should be here any minute. You're free to leave, so why don't you?"

"Why don't you sit back down? It makes me nervous, having you up and about."

"I make *you* nervous?" She turned to him. "You hold all the cards. You know everything about me. What my parents did for a living. Where I went to school. Who I slept with. I don't like that."

"Were there that many?"

His retort struck her like a physical blow. She could think of no response to such a cruel question. She was reduced to staring at him in speechless fury.

"Don't answer," he said. "I don't want to know. Your love life's none of my business."

"You're right. It's none of your damn business." She turned away, angrily clutching the mantelpiece with both hands. "No matter what you learn about me, it'll all fit right in with your image of the mill worker's daughter, won't it? Well, I'm not ashamed of where I came from. My parents made an honest living. They didn't have some trust fund to keep them in caviar. Like some families I know," she added, leaving no doubt by the tone of her voice just which family she was referring to.

He acknowledged the insult with a brief silence.

"I'm surprised you fell for Richard," he said. "Considering your attitude toward trust-funders."

"Before I knew Richard, I didn't *have* an attitude problem." She turned to confront him. "Then I got to know him. I saw what the money did to him. For him. He never had to struggle. He always had that green buffer to protect him. It made him careless. Immune to other people's pain." Her jaw came up in a pose of proud disdain. "Just like you."

"Now you're making the assumptions about me."

"You're a Tremain."

"I'm like you. I have a job, Miranda. I work."

"So did Richard. It kept him amused."

"Okay, maybe you're right about Richard. He didn't need to work. The *Herald* was more of a hobby to him, a reason to get up in the morning. And he got a kick out of telling his friends in Boston that he was a publisher. But that was Richard. You can't slap that rich-boy label on me because it won't stick. I was booted out of the family years ago. I don't have a trust fund and I don't own a mansion. But I do have a job that pays the bills. And, yes, keeps me *amused.*"

His anger was tightly controlled but evident all the same. *I've touched a nerve,* she thought. An acutely sensitive one. Chastened, she sat in a chair by the fireplace. "I guess—I guess I assumed a few too many things."

He nodded. "We both did."

In silence they gazed at each other across the room. A truce, however uneasy, had at last settled between them.

"You said you were booted out of the family. Why?" she asked.

"Simple. I got married."

She looked at him in puzzlement. He had said the words without emotion, with the tone of voice one used to describe the weather. "I take it she wasn't a suitable bride."

"Not according to my father."

"The wrong side of the tracks?"

"In a manner of speaking. My father, he was attuned to that sort of thing."

Naturally, she thought. "And was your father right? About those girls from the wrong side of the tracks?"

"That wasn't why we got divorced."

"Why did you?"

"Christine was too . . . ambitious."

"Hardly a flaw."

"It is when I'm just the rung on the social ladder she's trying to climb."

"Oh."

"And then we had some lean years. I was working all the time, and . . ." He shrugged. Another silence stretched between them.

"Richard never told me what kind of work you do."

He leaned back, the tension easing away from his face. Unexpectedly he laughed. "Probably because what I do struck him as so damn boring. My partners and I design office buildings."

"You're an architect?"

"Structural engineer. My architect partners do the creative work. I make sure the walls don't come crashing down."

An engineer. Not exactly a fluff career, she thought, but a real, honest job. Like her father had.

She shook her head. "It's strange. When I look at you, I can't quite believe you're his brother. I always assumed . . ."

"That we'd be a matched set? No, we were definitely different. In more ways than you'll ever know."

Yes, the more she knew about Chase, the less he seemed like a Tremain. And the more she thought she could like him.

"What did you ever see in my brother?" he asked.

His question, voiced so softly, was jarring all the same. It reminded her of the ghosts that still hovered in this house.

She sighed. "I saw what I wanted to see."

"Which was?"

"A man who needed me. A man I could play savior to."

"*Richard?*"

"Oh, it *seemed* as if he had everything going for him. But he also had this . . . this vulnerability. This need to be saved. From what, I don't know. Maybe himself."

"And you were going to save him."

She gave a bitter laugh. "I don't know. You don't think about these things. You just feel. And you fall into it. . . ."

"You mean you followed your heart."

She looked up at him. "Yes," she whispered.

"Didn't it seem wrong to you?"

"Of course it did!"

"But?"

Her whole body sagged with the weight of her unhappiness. "I couldn't . . . see my way out of it. I cared about him. I wanted to be there for him. And he'd string me along. He'd tell me things would work out, as long as we both had faith." She looked down at her hands, clasped together in her lap. "I guess I lost my faith first."

"In him? Or the situation?"

"Him. I began to see the flaws. It came out, after a while. How he manipulated people, used people. If he didn't need you, he'd ignore you. A user, that's what he was. An expert at making people do what he wanted."

"Then you broke it off. How did he react?"

"He couldn't believe it. I don't think anyone ever left *him*. He kept calling me, bothering me. And every day, at work, I'd have to face him. Pretend nothing was going on between us."

"Everyone knew, though."

She shrugged. "Probably. I'm not very good at hiding things. Annie knew, because I told her. And everyone else must have guessed." She sighed. The truth was, she hadn't cared at the time. Love, and then pain, had made her indifferent to public opinion.

They said nothing for a moment. She wondered what he thought of her now, whether any of it made a difference. Suddenly it mattered what he *did* think of her. He was scarcely more than a stranger, and a hostile one, but it mattered very much.

"You're not the first one, you know," he said. "There were other women."

It was a cruel revelation to spring on her, and Chase didn't know why he did it. He only knew that he wanted to give her a good, hard shaking. To shatter any rose-colored illusions she might still harbor about Richard. She might say the feelings were gone, but deep inside, might a few warm memories still linger?

He saw, by the look in her eyes, that his words had had their intended effect. Instantly he regretted the wounds he'd inflicted. Still, shouldn't she know? Shouldn't she be told just how naive she'd been?

"Were there many?" she asked softly.

"Yes."

She looked away, as though to hide the pain from view. "I—I think I knew that. Yes, I must have known that."

"It's just the way he was," said Chase. "He liked being admired. He was like that as a boy, too."

She nodded. And he realized, yes, she did know that about Richard. On some level she must have sensed his unquenchable thirst for admiration. And tried to satisfy it.

Chase had done damage enough. Here she was, demoralized and wounded. *And I pour on the salt.*

I should get out of here, leave her alone.

Where the hell was Annie Berenger?

Miranda seemed to shake herself back to life. She brushed her hair off her face, sat up and looked at him. So much torment in those eyes, he thought. And, at the same time, so much courage.

"You never told me why you're here," she said.

"The doctor thought someone should watch you—"

"No. I mean, why did you come in the first place?"

"Oh." He sat back. "I was at the *Herald* this afternoon. Talked to Jill Vickery, about the Stone Coast Trust article you mentioned. She says it was never written. That Richard never got that far with it."

Miranda shook her head. "I don't understand. I know he had at least a few pages written. I saw them on his desk, at the *Herald.*"

"Well, I couldn't find any article. I thought maybe you'd know where to look. Or maybe you'd have it."

She looked at him in bewilderment. "Why would I?"

"I assume Richard was a frequent visitor here."

"But he didn't bring his work. Have you checked the house?"

"It's not there."

She thought about it a moment. "Sometimes," she said, "he'd drive up to the north shore, to write. He had a cottage . . ."

"You mean Rose Hill. Yes, I suppose I should check there tomorrow."

Their gazes intersected, held. She said, "You're starting to believe me. Aren't you?"

He heard, in her voice, the stirring of hope—however faint. He found himself wanting to respond, to offer her some small scrap of a chance that he might believe her. It was hard *not* to believe her, especially when she looked at him that way, her gaze unwavering, those gray eyes bright and moist. They could rob a man of his common sense, those eyes, could sweep self-control right out from under him. They awakened other sensations as well, disturbing ones. She was sitting more than half a room away, but even at that distance her presence was like some heady perfume, impossible to ignore.

She asked again, softly, "Do you believe me?"

Abruptly he rose to his feet, determined to shake off the dangerous spell she was weaving around him. "No," he said. "I can't say that I do."

"But don't you see there's something more to this than just a—a crime of passion?"

"I admit, things don't feel quite right. But I'm not ready to believe you. Not by a long shot."

There was a knock on the door. Startled, Chase turned to see the door swing open and Annie Berenger poke her head in.

"Hello, cavalry's here," she called. She came in dressed in an old T-shirt and sweatpants. Blades of wet grass clung to her running shoes. "What's the situation?"

"I'm fine," said Miranda.

"But she needs watching," said Chase. "If there are any problems, Dr. Steiner's number is by the phone."

"Leaving already?" asked Annie.

"They'll be expecting me at home." He went to the door. There he paused and glanced back at Miranda.

She hadn't moved. She just sat there. He had the urge to say something comforting. To tell her that what he'd said earlier wasn't quite true. That he *was* starting to believe her. But he couldn't admit it to her; he could scarcely admit it to himself. And there was Annie, watching everything with her sharp reporter's eyes.

So he merely said, "Good night, Miranda. I hope you're feeling better. And Annie, thanks for the favor." Then he turned and walked out the door.

Outside, it took him a few seconds to accustom his eyes to the darkness. By the time he'd reached the edge of the front yard he could finally make out the walkway under his feet.

He could also see the silhouette of a man standing stoop-shouldered before him on the sidewalk.

Chase halted, instantly tense.

"She okay?" asked the man.

"Who are you?" demanded Chase.

"I could ask the same o' you," came the cranky reply.

"I'm . . . visiting," said Chase.

"So, is Mo gonna be all right, or what?"

"Mo? Oh, you mean Miranda. Yes, she'll be fine, Mr. . . ."

"Eddie Lanzo. Live next door. Like to keep an eye on her, y'know? Not good, a nice young woman livin' all by herself. And all these crazies runnin' around here, peekin' in windows. Not safe to be female these days."

"Someone's staying with her tonight, so you needn't worry."

"Yeah. Okay. Well, I won't bother her none, then." Eddie Lanzo turned to go back to his house. "Whole island's going to pot, I tell ya," he muttered. "Too many crazies. Last time I leave my keys in the car."

"Mr. Lanzo?" called Chase.

"Yeah?"

"Just a question. I was wondering if you were home the night Richard Tremain was killed?"

"Me?" Eddie snorted. "I'm always home."

"Did you happen to see or hear anything?"

"I already tol' Lorne Tibbetts. I go to bed at nine o'clock sharp, and that's it till morning."

"Then you're a sound sleeper? You didn't hear anything?"

"How can I with my hearing aid turned off?"

"Oh." Chase watched as the man shuffled back to his house, still muttering about Peeping Toms and car thieves. It somehow surprised Chase that a grouchy old geezer like Lanzo would show such concern about Miranda Wood. *A nice young woman,* Lanzo had called her.

What the hell does he know? thought Chase. *What do we ever know about anyone? People have their secrets. I have mine, Miranda Wood has hers.*

He turned and headed for Chestnut Street.

It was a twenty-minute walk, made invigorating by the brisk night air. When at last he stepped in the front door he found that, except for the lamp in the foyer, all the lights were out. Had no one else come home?

Then he heard Evelyn call out his name.

He found her sitting all alone in the darkened parlor. He could barely make out her shadow in the rocking chair. The dim glow of the street lamp through the window framed her silhouette.

"At last you're home," she said.

He started toward one of the lamps. "You need some light in here, Evelyn."

"No, Chase. Don't. I like the dark. I always have."

He paused, uncertain of what to say, what to do. He lingered in the shadows, watching her.

"I've been waiting for you," she murmured. "Where did you go, Chase?"

He paused. "To see Miranda Wood."

Her reaction was cold, dead silence. Even the creak of her rocking chair had stilled.

"She has you in her spell. Doesn't she?" Evelyn whispered.

"There's no spell. I just had some questions to ask her, about Richard." He sighed. "Look, Evelyn, it's been a long day for you. Why don't you go up and get some sleep?"

Still the figure did not move. She sat like a black statue against the window. "That night I called you," she said, "the night he died—I was hoping . . ."

"Yes?"

Another silence. Then, "I've always liked you, Chase. Since we were kids. I always hoped you'd be the one to propose. Not Richard, but you." The rocking chair began to creak again, softly. "But you never did."

"I was in love with Christine. Remember?"

"Oh, Christine." She hissed out the name in disgust. "She wasn't good enough for you. But you found that out."

"We were mismatched, that's all."

"So were Richard and I."

He didn't know what to say. He knew what she was leading up to, and he wanted to avoid that particular path of conversation. In all those years of growing up together he had never been able to picture himself and Evelyn DeBolt as a couple. Certainly she was attractive enough. And she was closer to his age than she was to Richard's. But he had seen, early on, that she had a talent for manipulating people, for twisting minds and hearts. The same talent Richard had possessed.

And yet, he felt so very sorry for her.

He said gently, "You're just tired, Evelyn. You've had a terrible week. But the worst of it's over now."

"No. The worst part is just beginning. The loneliness."

"You have your children—"

"You'll be leaving soon, won't you?"

"A few more days. I have to. I have a job in Greenwich."

"You could stay. Take over the *Herald.* Phillip's still too young to run it."

"I'd be a lousy publisher. You know that. And I don't belong here anymore. Not on this island."

For a moment they regarded each other through the shadows.

"So that's it, then," she whispered. "For us."

"I'm afraid so."

He saw the silhouette nod sadly.

"Will you be all right?"

"Fine." She gave a soft laugh. "I'll be just fine."

"Good night, Evelyn."

"Good night."

He left her sitting there by the window. Only as he moved toward the stairwell did he suddenly notice the sour odor lingering in the hall. An empty glass sat on the foyer table, near the telephone. He picked up the glass and sniffed it.

Whiskey.

We all have our secrets. Evelyn does, too.

He set the glass back down. Then, deep in thought, he climbed the stairs to bed.

6

"So where were you two last night?" Chase asked.

The twins, busy attacking sausage and eggs, simultaneously looked up at their uncle.

"I was over at Zach Brewer's," said Phillip. "You remember the Brewers, don't you? Over on Pearl Street."

"What little Phil really means is, he was checking out Zach's sister," said Cassie.

"At least I wasn't holed up in some cave, pining for a date."

"I wasn't pining for a date. I was busy."

"Oh, sure," snorted Phillip.

"Busy? Doing what?" asked Chase.

"I was over at the *Herald,* trying to get a handle on things," said Cassie. "You know, Dad left things such a mess. No written plans for succession. Not a clue as to which direction he wanted the paper to go. Editorially speaking."

"Let Jill Vickery take care of it," said Phillip with a shrug. "That's what we pay her for."

"I'd think at least you'd care, Phil. Seeing as you're the heir apparent."

"These transitions need to be handled gradually." Phil nonchalantly shoveled another forkful of eggs into his mouth.

"In the meantime, the *Herald* drifts around rudderless. I don't want it to be just another church and social rag. We should turn it into a muckraking journal. Shake things up along the coast, get people mad. The way Dad got 'em mad a few months ago."

"Got who mad?" asked Chase.

"Those stooges on the planning board. The ones who voted to re-zone the north shore. Dad made 'em out to look pretty greasy. I bet Jill was quaking in her shiny Italian shoes, waiting for that libel suit to pop."

"You seem to know a lot about what goes on at the *Herald*," said Chase.

"Of course. Second best tries harder."

She said it lightly, but Chase couldn't miss the note of resentment in her voice. He understood exactly how she felt. He, too, had been the second-best sibling, had spent his childhood trying harder, to no avail. Richard had been the anointed one. Just as Phillip was now.

The doorbell rang. "That'll be Granddad," said Phillip. "He's early."

Chase stood. "I'll get it."

Noah DeBolt was standing on the front porch. "Good morning, Chase. Is Evelyn ready for her appointment?"

"I think so. Come in, sir."

That "sir" was automatic. One simply didn't call this man by his first name. As Noah walked in the door, Chase marveled at the fact that the years hadn't stooped the shoulders in that tailored suit, nor softened the glare of those ice blue eyes.

Noah paused in the foyer and glanced critically around the house. "It's about time we made some changes in here. A new couch, new chairs. Evelyn's put up with this old furniture long enough."

"They're my mother's favorites," said Chase. "Antiques—"

"I know what the hell they are! Junk." Noah's gaze focused on the twins, who were staring at him through the doorway. "What, are you two still eating breakfast? Come on, it's eight-thirty! With the fees lawyers charge, we don't want to be late."

"Really, Mr. DeBolt," said Chase. "I can drive us all to the lawyer. You didn't have to bother—"

"Evelyn asked me to come," said Noah. "What my girl asks for, I deliver." He glanced up the stairs. Evelyn had just appeared on the landing. "Right, sweetheart?"

Head held high, Evelyn came down the stairs. It was the first Chase had seen of her since the night before. No tremor, no effects of whiskey were apparent this morning. She looked cool as aspic. "Hello, Daddy," she said.

Noah gave her a hug. "Now," he said softly, "let's go finish this unpleasant business."

They drove in Noah's Mercedes, Evelyn and her father in the front seat, Chase crammed in the back with the twins. How had Richard tolerated it all these years, he wondered, living in the same town with this bully of a father-in-law? But that was the price one paid for marrying Noah DeBolt's only daughter: eternal criticism, eternal scrutiny.

Now that Richard was dead, Noah was back in control of his daughter's life. He drove them to Les Hardee's office. He escorted Evelyn through the front door. He led her by the arm right up to the reception desk.

"Mrs. Tremain to see Les," said Noah. "We're here to review the will."

The receptionist gave them a strange look—something Chase could only read as panic—and pressed the intercom button. "Mr. Hardee," she said. "They're here."

Instantly Les Hardee popped out of his office. His suit and tie marked him as a dapper man; his sweating brow did not match the image. "Mr. DeBolt, Mrs. Tremain," he said, almost painfully. "I would have called you earlier, but I only just—That is to say, we . . ." He swallowed. "There seems to be a problem with the will."

"Nothing that can't be fixed," said Noah.

"Actually . . ." Hardee opened the conference-room door. "I think we should all sit down."

There was another man in the room. Hardee introduced them to Vernon FitzHugh, an attorney from Bass Harbor. FitzHugh looked like a working-class version of Hardee, articulate enough, but rough around the edges, the sort of guy who probably had had to sling hash to pay his way through law school. They all sat at the conference table, Hardee and FitzHugh at opposite ends.

"So what's this little problem with Richard's will?" asked Noah. "And what do you have to do with all this, Mr. FitzHugh?"

FitzHugh cleared his throat. "I'm afraid I'm the bearer of bad news. Or, in this case, a new will."

"What?" Noah turned to Hardee. "What's this garbage, Les? *You* were Richard's attorney."

"That's what I thought," said Hardee morosely.

"Then where did this other will come from?"

Everyone looked at FitzHugh.

"A few weeks ago," explained FitzHugh, "Mr. Tremain came to my office. He said he wanted to draw up a new will, superseding the will drawn up previously by Mr. Hardee. I advised him that Mr. Hardee was the one who should do it, but Mr. Tremain insisted I draw it up. So I honored his request. I would have brought it to your attention earlier, but I've been out of town for a few weeks. I didn't hear of Mr. Tremain's death until last night."

"This is bizarre," said Evelyn. "Why would Richard draw up a new will? How do we even know it was really him?"

"It was him," confirmed Hardee. "I recognize his signature."

There was a long silence.

"Well," said Evelyn. "Let's hear it, Les. What's been changed."

Hardee slipped on his glasses and began to read aloud. "I, Richard D. Tremain, being of sound mind and body—"

"Oh, skip the legal gobbledygook!" snapped Noah. "Get to the basics. What's different about the new will?"

Hardee looked up. "Most of it is unchanged. The house, joint accounts, contents therein, all go to Mrs. Tremain. There are generous trust accounts for the children, and a few personal items left to his brother."

"What about Rose Hill Cottage?" asked Noah.

Here Hardee shifted in his chair. "Perhaps I should just read it." He flipped ahead six pages and cleared his throat. "That parcel of land on the north shore comprising approximately forty acres, inclusive of the access road, as well as the structure known as Rose Hill Cottage, I bequeath to . . ." Here Hardee paused.

"What about Rose Hill?" pressed Evelyn.

Hardee took a deep breath. "I bequeath to my dear friend and companion, Miranda Wood."

"Like hell," said Noah.

On the street outside Hardee's office, Noah and Evelyn sat side by side in the car. Neither one spoke. Neither was comfortable with the silence. The others had chosen to walk home, much to Noah's relief. He needed this time alone with Evelyn.

Noah said softly, "Is there anything you want to tell me, Evelyn?"

"What do you mean, Daddy?"

"Anything at all. About Richard."

She looked at her father. "Am I supposed to say something?"

"You can tell me, you know. We're family, that's what matters. And family stick together. Against the whole world, if they have to."

"I don't know what you're talking about."

Noah looked into his daughter's eyes. They were the same shade of green as his wife's eyes had been. Here was the one link he had left to his darling Susannah. Here was the one person in the world he still cared about. She returned his gaze calmly, without even the tiniest flicker of uneasiness. Good. Good. She could hold her own against anyone. In that way, she truly was a DeBolt.

He said, "I'd do anything for you, Evelyn. Anything. All you have to do is ask."

She looked straight ahead. "Then take me home, Daddy."

He started the engine and turned the car toward Chestnut Street. She didn't say a word during the entire drive. She was a proud girl, his daughter. Though she'd never ask for it, she needed his help. And she'd get it.

Whatever it takes, he thought. *It'll be done.*

After all, Evelyn was his flesh and blood, and he couldn't let flesh and blood go to prison.

Even if she was guilty.

Her garden had always been her sanctuary. Here Miranda had planted hollyhocks and delphiniums, baby's breath and columbine. She hadn't bothered with color schemes or landscape drawings. She'd simply sunk plants into the earth, scattered seeds and let the jungle of vines and flowers take over her backyard. They'd been neglected this past week, poor things. A few days of no watering had left the blooms bedraggled. But now she was home and her babies looked happier. Strangely enough, *she* was happy, as well. Her back was warmed by the sun, her hands were working the rich loam. This was all she needed. Fresh air and freedom. *How long will I have it?*

She put that thought firmly aside and swung the pickax into the hardened earth. She'd turn a little more soil, expand the perennial bed another two feet. She leaned the pickax against the house and knelt to loosen up the clods, sift out the stones.

The sun was making her drowsy.

At last, unable to resist the promise of a nap, she stretched out on the lawn. There she lay, her hands and knees caked with soil, the grass cushioning her bare legs. A perfect summer day, just like the days she remembered from her childhood. She closed her eyes and thought about all those afternoons when her mother was still alive, when her father would stand at the barbecue, singing as he grilled hamburgers. . . .

"What a sharp game you play," said a voice.

Miranda sat up with a start and saw Chase standing at her white picket fence. He shoved open the gate and came into the yard. As he approached, it occurred to her how filthy she must look in her gardening shorts and T-shirt. Framed against the glare of sun and blue sky, Chase looked immaculate, untouchable. She squinted to see his expression, but all she could make out was a dark oval, the flutter of his windblown hair.

"You knew, didn't you?" he said.

She rose to her feet and clapped the dirt from her hands. "Knew what?"

"How did you manage it, Miranda? A few sweet whispers? Write me into the will and I'll be yours forever?"

"I don't know what you're talking about."

"I just came from our family attorney. We found a nasty surprise waiting for us. Two weeks ago Richard made out a new will. He left Rose Hill Cottage to you."

Her immediate reaction was stunned silence. In disbelief she stared at him.

"Nothing to say? No denials?"

"I never expected—"

"I think it's exactly what you expected."

"No!" She turned away, confused. "I never wanted a thing—"

"Oh, come on!" He reached for her arm and pulled her around to face him. "What was it, blackmail? A way to keep you quiet about the affair?"

"I don't know anything about a will! Or the cottage! Besides, how could he leave it to me? Doesn't it go to his wife? Evelyn owns half—"

"No, she doesn't."

"Why not?"

"Rose Hill came through my mother's family. An inheritance that went directly to Richard, so Evelyn had no claim on it. It was Richard's to pass on any way he chose. And he chose to give it to you."

She shook her head. "I don't know why."

"That cottage was the one place on this island he really cared about. The one place we both cared about."

"All right, then!" she cried. "*You* take it! It's yours. I'll sign a statement today, handing it over. I don't want it. All I want is to be left *alone.*" She stared straight up at his coldly immobile face. "And to never, ever see another Tremain for as long as I live."

She broke away and ran up the back porch steps, into the house. The screen door slammed shut behind her. She headed straight into the kitchen, where she suddenly halted. There was nowhere else to run. In agitation she went to the sink and turned on the faucet. There, surrounded by her beloved ferns, she scrubbed furiously at the dirt caked on her hands.

She was still scrubbing when the screen door opened, then softly swung shut again. For a long time he didn't say a word. She knew he was standing behind her, watching her.

"Miranda," he said.

Angrily she turned off the faucet. "Go away."

"I want to hear your side of it."

"Why? You wouldn't believe me. You don't *want* to believe me. But you know what? I don't care anymore." She grabbed a dish towel and blotted her hands. "I'll go to the lawyer's this afternoon. Sign a statement of refusal, or whatever it's called. I would never accept it. Anything I received from him would be tainted. Just like I'm tainted."

"You're wrong, Miranda. I do want to believe you."

She stood very still, afraid to turn, to look at him. She sensed his approach as he moved toward her across the kitchen. And still she couldn't turn, couldn't face him. She could only stare down at the clumps of wet garden dirt in the sink.

"But you can't, can you?" she said.

"The facts argue against it."

"And if I tell you the facts are misleading?" Slowly she turned and found he was right there, so close she could reach up and touch his face. "What then?"

"Then I'd be forced to trust my instincts. But in this particular case, my instincts are shot all to hell."

She stared at him, suddenly confused by the signals he was sending. By the signals her body was sending. He had her closed off from all retreat, her back pinned against the kitchen sink. She had to tilt her head up just to meet his gaze, and the view she had of him, towering above her, was more than a little frightening. Yet it wasn't fear that seemed to be pumping through her veins. It was the warm and unexpected pulse of desire.

She slid away and paced across the kitchen, as far as she could get from him and still be in the same room. "I meant what I said. About refusing all rights to Rose Hill Cottage. In fact, I think we should do it right now. Go to the lawyer."

"Is that really what you want?"

"I know I don't want anything of his. Anything to remind me of him."

"You'd give up the cottage, just like that?"

"It doesn't mean a thing to me. I've never even seen the place."

Chase looked surprised. "He never took you to Rose Hill?"

"No. Oh, he told me about it. But it was his own private retreat. Not the sort of place he'd share with me."

"You could be handing back a fortune in real estate, sight unseen."

"It's not my fortune. It never was."

He regarded her with narrowed eyes. "I can't figure you out. Every time I think I have, you throw me a curve ball."

"I'm not all that complicated."

"You managed to intrigue Richard."

"I was hardly the first woman to do that."

"But you're the first one who ever left him."

"And look where it got me." She gave a bitter laugh. "You may not believe this, but I used to think of myself as a person with high morals. I paid my taxes. Stopped at every red light. Followed all the rules." She turned and stared out the window. Softly she said, "Then I fell for your brother. Suddenly I didn't know what the rules were anymore. I was slipping around in strange territory. God, it scared me. At the same time I felt . . . exhilarated. And that scared me even more." She turned to him. "I'd give anything to turn back the clock. To feel . . . innocent again."

Slowly he came toward her. "Some things we can't recapture, Miranda."

"No." She stared down, her cheeks flushed with guilt. "Some things we lose forever."

His touch, so unexpected, made her flinch. It was the gentlest of strokes, just his hand tracing the curve of her cheek. Startled, she looked up to find a gaze so searching it left her nowhere to hide. She hated feeling so nakedly exposed but she found she could not break away. The hand cupping her face was warm and so very compelling.

Here I am, falling into the same old trap, she thought. *With Richard I lost my innocence. What will I lose to this man? My soul?*

She said, "I learned my lesson from your brother, Chase. I'm no longer fair game." She turned and walked away, into the living room.

"I'm not Richard."

She looked back. "It doesn't matter who you are. What matters is that I'm not the same dumb, trusting soul I used to be."

"He really hurt you, didn't he?" He was watching her from the kitchen threshold. His shoulders seemed to fill the doorway.

She didn't answer. She sank into an armchair and stared at her dirt-stained knees.

Chase studied her from across the room. All his anger toward her, which had built up since that morning in Les Hardee's office, suddenly evaporated. In its place was a fury toward Richard. Golden boy Richard, who had always gotten what he wanted. Richard the firstborn, the one with the classic Tremain fair hair and blue eyes, had bought everything he ever coveted with the coin of wit and charm. But once he'd attained his goal, he'd lose interest.

That was his pattern with women. Once, Richard had wanted Evelyn DeBolt, and he'd won her. He'd had to marry her, of course. You didn't play games with the only child of Noah DeBolt. But after the prize was his he'd grown bored with his wife. That was Richard, always coveting, never satisfied.

And here was the one woman, the one prize, he hadn't been able to keep. Such an unassuming female, thought Chase, feeling a strange ache in his throat. Was it pity or sympathy? He couldn't tell the difference.

He sat in the chair across from her. "You . . . seem to have recovered from last night."

"Just some sore muscles. That's all." She shrugged, as though she knew he couldn't possibly be interested. Whatever turmoil was swirling in her head, she kept it carefully concealed. "I sent Annie home this morning. I couldn't see the point of her staying."

"Safety's sake?"

"Safety from what?"

"What if it wasn't an accident?"

She looked up. "At the moment I'm not terrifically popular in this town. But I can't see one of our upstanding citizens turning hit-and-run driver."

"Still, one of our upstanding citizens did steal Mr. Lanzo's car."

"Poor Eddie." She shook her head. "It'll just reinforce his paranoia. Now he'll add car thieves to that list of crazies he imagines cruising the street."

"Yes, he mentioned that last night. Something about Peeping Toms."

She smiled. "Eddie grew up in Chicago. He never did shake those big-city jitters. He swears he spotted some mob car watching my . . ." She suddenly paused, frowning. "You know, I never paid much attention to his stories. But now that I think about it . . . ."

"When did he tell you about that car?"

"Maybe a month or two ago."

"Before Richard's murder, then."

"Yes. So it's probably not related." She sighed. "It's just poor, crazy Eddie." She stood. "I'll change clothes. I can't go to the lawyer looking like this."

"You really want to go right now?"

"I have to. Until I do, I won't feel clean. Or free of him."

"I'll call ahead, then." He glanced at his watch. "We can just make the ferry to Bass Harbor."

"Bass Harbor? I thought Les Hardee was Richard's lawyer."

"He is. But this last will was drawn up by some lawyer named Vernon FitzHugh. Do you know him?"

"No, thank God." She turned and headed up the hall. "Or you'd probably accuse Mr. FitzHugh and me of fraud." She vanished into the bedroom.

Chase watched the door swing shut behind her. "As a matter of fact," he muttered, "the thought did cross my mind."

Vernon FitzHugh was expecting them. What he didn't anticipate was the purpose of their visit.

"Have you really thought this through, Ms. Wood? This is prime real estate we're talking about. The north shore has just been rezoned for development. I expect your piece of property, in a few years, will be worth well over—"

"It should never have come to me," said Miranda. "It belongs to the Tremain family."

FitzHugh glanced uneasily at Chase, one of those sidelong looks that reveal so much. "Perhaps we should discuss this in private, Ms. Wood. If Mr. Tremain would care to wait outside . . ."

"No, I want him to stay. I want him to hear every word." She looked meaningfully at FitzHugh. "So he can't accuse us of collusion."

"Collusion?" FitzHugh, alarmed, sat up straight. "Mr. Tremain, you don't think I wanted to get involved in this, do you? It's a messy situation. Two lawyers, two wills. And then, the complicating circumstances of the client's death." He assiduously avoided looking at Miranda. "I'm just trying to carry out Mr. Tremain's instructions. Which are to ensure that Rose Hill Cottage goes to Ms. Wood."

"I don't want it," said Miranda. "I want to give it back."

FitzHugh looked troubled. He removed his glasses and set them on the desk. It seemed, with that one gesture, he simultaneously shed the role of the detached professional. Now he was speaking to her as a friend, an adviser. The flat accent of a working-class Mainer slipped into his voice. This man knew only too well what it was like to be poor. And here was this stubborn young woman, throwing away the promise of security.

"Richard Tremain," he began, "came to me with a request. I'm bound to honor it. It's not my job to decide whether you're innocent or guilty. I just want to see that the intent of the will is carried out. I made very sure that this was what he wanted, and he wanted that land to go to you. If you're convicted, then the point will be moot—you can't inherit. But let's say you're found innocent. Then Rose Hill goes to you, no question about it. Wait a few days, Ms. Wood. If this is really what you want, come back and I'll draw up the papers. But I won't do it today. I have to think of Mr. Tremain's last request. After all, he was my client."

"Why *did* he come to you?" Chase asked. "Mr. Hardee has been Richard's attorney for years."

FitzHugh studied Chase for a moment, weighing the man's motives. Coercion was what he suspected, the wealthy Tremain family putting pressure on this woman, this outsider, to surrender her inheritance. It wasn't right. Someone had to take the woman's side, even if she refused to stand up for herself.

"Richard Tremain came to me," FitzHugh said, "because he *didn't* want Les Hardee involved."

"Why not?"

"Mr. Hardee is also Noah DeBolt's attorney. I think Mr. Tremain was worried this would leak out to his father-in-law."

"And what a riot that would have caused," said Chase.

"Having met Mr. DeBolt this morning, yes, I can imagine there would've been fireworks."

Chase leaned forward, his gaze narrowing on the attorney. "The day Richard was here to change his will, how did he seem to you? I mean, his state of mind. People don't just walk in and change their wills for no good reason."

FitzHugh frowned. "Well, he seemed . . . upset. He didn't mention any fear of dying. Said he just wanted to straighten out his affairs. . . ." He glanced at Miranda and reddened at the unintentional double entendre.

Miranda flushed, as well, but she refused to shrink from his gaze. *I'm through with being punished,* she thought. *Through with cringing at the looks people give me.*

"You said he was upset. What do you mean?" asked Chase.

"He seemed angry."

"At whom?"

"We didn't discuss it. He just came in and said he didn't want the cottage to go to Mrs. Tremain."

"He was specific about Evelyn?"

"Yes. And he was concerned only about Rose Hill Cottage. Not the bank account or the other assets. I assumed it was because those other assets were joint marital property, and he couldn't redirect those. But Rose Hill was his, through inheritance. He could dispose of it as he wished." FitzHugh looked at Miranda. "And he wanted you to have it."

She shook her head. "Why?"

"I assume, because he cared about you. Giving you Rose Hill was his way of telling you how much."

In silence Miranda bowed her head. She knew both men were watching her. She wondered what expression she'd see in Chase's eyes. Cynicism? Disbelief? *You can't imagine that your brother would feel love, not just lust, for a woman like me?*

"So, Ms. Wood?" asked FitzHugh. "You agree this isn't a move you should make?"

She raised her head and looked across the desk at the attorney. "Draw up the papers. I want to do it now."

"Maybe you don't," said Chase quietly.

Miranda looked at him in disbelief. "What?"

"Mr. FitzHugh has brought up some points I hadn't considered. You should think about it, just for a few days." His gaze met Miranda's. She could see that he was baffled by something he'd heard here today.

"Are you saying I should keep Rose Hill Cottage?"

"All I'm saying is this. Richard had a reason for changing the will. Before we go changing things back, let's find out why he did it."

Vernon FitzHugh nodded. "My thoughts exactly," he said.

They exchanged scarcely a word on the ferry back to Shepherd's Island. Only when they'd driven off the pier and turned onto Shore Circle Road did Miranda stir from her silence. "Where are we going?" she asked.

"The north shore."

"Why?"

"I want you to see Rose Hill. It's only fair you know exactly what you're handing back to Evelyn."

"You enjoy this, don't you?" she said. "Running me around in circles. Playing your little mind games. One minute you say I'm stealing Tremain property. The next, you're trying to talk me into playing thief. What's the point of it all, Chase?"

"I'm bothered by what FitzHugh told us. That Richard wanted to keep the cottage away from Evelyn."

"But it *should* go to her."

"Rose Hill came from my mother's side. The Pruitts. Evelyn has no claim to it."

"He could have left it to you."

Chase laughed. "Not likely."

"Why not?"

"We weren't exactly the closest of brothers. I was lucky just to get his collection of rusty Civil War swords. No, he wanted Rose Hill to go to someone he loved. You were his first choice. Maybe his only choice."

"He didn't love me, Chase," she said softly. "Not really."

They drove north, winding past summer cottages, past granite cliffs jagged with pines, past stony beaches where waves broke into white foam. Gulls circled and swooped at the blue-gray sea.

"Why did you say that?" he asked. "About Richard not loving you?"

"Because I knew. I think I always knew. Oh, maybe he *thought* he loved me. But for Richard, love was a lot of moonlight and madness. A fever that eventually breaks. It was just a matter of time."

"That sounds like Richard. As a kid, he was always in pursuit of the never-ending high."

"Are all you Tremains like that?"

"Hardly. My father was married to his work."

"And what are you married to?"

He glanced at her. She was struck by the intensity of his gaze, the gaze of a man who's not afraid to tell the truth. "Nothing and no one. At least, not anymore. Not since Christine."

"Your wife?"

He nodded. "It didn't last very long. I was just a kid, really, only twenty. Doing my share of wild and crazy things. It was a handy way to get back at my father, and it worked."

"What happened to Christine?"

"She found out I wasn't going to inherit the Tremain fortune and she walked out. Smart girl. She, at least, was using her head."

He focused on the road, which he obviously knew well. Miranda noticed how easily he handled the curves, guiding the car skillfully around each treacherous bend. Whatever wildness he'd displayed in his youth had since been reined in. Here was a man in tight control of his life, his emotions, not a man in pursuit of the ephemeral moonlight and madness.

A twenty-minute drive brought them to the last stretch of paved road. The asphalt gave way to a dirt access road flanked by birch and pine. Rustic signs proclaimed the different camps hidden among the trees. Mom and Pop's. Brandywine Cottage. Sanity Camp. Here and there, dirt tracks led off to the dozen or so summer retreats of prominent island families, most of whom had held their cottages for generations.

The access road began to climb, winding a half mile up the contours of the hillside. They passed a stone marker labeled St. John's Wood. Then they came to the last sign, every bit as rustic as the others: Rose Hill. A final bend in the road took them through the last stand of trees, and then a broad, sloping field lay before them. It sat at the very crest of the hill—a weathered cottage facing north, to the sea. Vines of purple clematis clung lovingly about the veranda railings. Rosebushes, overgrown with weeds but still valiantly blooming, crouched like thorny sentinels beside the porch steps.

They parked in the gravel turnaround and stepped out into an afternoon fragrant with the scent of flowers and sun-warmed grass. For a moment Miranda stood motionless, her face turned to the sky. Not a cloud marred that perfect blue. A single gull, riding the wind off the hillside, drifted overhead.

"Come on," said Chase. "Let me show you inside."

He led her up the porch steps. "I haven't seen the place in at least ten years. I'm almost afraid to go in."

"Afraid of what?"

"The changes. Of what they might've done to it. But I guess that's how it is with your childhood home."

"Especially if you were happy there."

He smiled. "Exactly."

For a moment they stood and regarded the old porch swing, creaking back and forth in the breeze.

"Do you have a key?" she asked.

"There should be one under here." He crouched down beneath one of the windowsills. "There's this little crack in the wood where Mom always kept a spare key. . . ." He sighed and straightened. "Not anymore. Well, if the door's locked, maybe we can find a window open somewhere." Tentatively he reached for the knob. "How do you like that?" He laughed, pushing open the door. "It's not even locked."

As the door creaked open, the front room swung into view—a faded Oriental carpet stretched across the threshold, a stone fireplace, wide pine floors. Miranda stepped inside and suddenly halted in surprise.

At her feet lay a jumble of papers. A rolltop desk stood in the corner, its drawers wide open, their contents strewn across the floor. Books had been pulled off a nearby shelf and tossed haphazardly among the papers.

Chase stepped inside and came to a halt beside her. The screen door slammed shut.

"What the hell?" he said.

7

In silence they took in the ransacked desk, the scattered papers. Without a word Chase moved quickly toward the next room.

Miranda followed him into the kitchen. There were no signs of disturbance here. The pots and pans were hung on a beam rack, the flour and sugar canisters lined up neatly on the butcher block counters.

She was right on his heels as he headed for the stairs. They ran up the steps and looked first in the small guest bedroom. Everything appeared in order. Quickly Chase circled the room, opening closets, glancing in drawers.

"What are you looking for?" she asked.

He didn't answer. He moved across the hall, into the master bedroom.

Here double windows, flanked by lace curtains, faced the sea. A cream coverlet draped the four-poster bed. Motes of dust drifted in the sun-warmed stillness.

"Doesn't look like they touched this room, either," said Miranda.

Chase went to the dresser, picked up a silver hairbrush, and set it back down. "Obviously not."

"What on earth is going on here, Chase?"

He turned and glanced in frustration about the room. "This is crazy. They left the paintings on the walls. The furniture . . ."

"Nothing's missing?"

"Nothing valuable. At least, nothing your ordinary thief would go after." He opened a dresser drawer and glanced through the contents. He opened a second drawer and paused, staring inside. Slowly he withdrew a pair of women's panties. It was scarcely more than a few strips of black lace and silk. He pulled out a matching bra, equally skimpy, equally seductive.

He looked at Miranda, his gaze flat and unreadable. "Yours?" he asked quietly.

"I told you, I've never been here. They must belong to Evelyn."

He shook his head. "I don't think so."

"How would you know?"

"She never comes out here. Despises the rustic life, or so she claims."

"Well, they're not mine. I don't own anything like—like that."

"There's more inside here. Maybe you'll recognize something else."

She went to the dresser and pulled out an emerald-and-cream bra. "Well, it's obvious this isn't mine."

"How so?"

"This is a 36C. I'm . . ." She cleared her throat. "Not that big."

"Oh."

Quickly she turned away, before he could confirm her statement. Not that he hadn't had the chance to look. He had eyes, didn't he?

And he sees too damn much, she thought. She turned toward the window and stood with her back to Chase, all the while struggling to regain her composure. Outside, the fading light of day slanted across the treetops. A long summer dusk. In the field below there would be fireflies and the hum of insects in the grass. And the chill. Even on these August evenings there was always the chill that rose from the sea. She hugged herself and shivered.

His approach was gentle, silent. She couldn't hear him, but she knew, without looking, that he was right behind her.

Chase was standing so close, in fact, that he could smell the scent of her hair—clean and sweet and intoxicating. The fading daylight from the window brought out its glorious chestnut hues. He wanted to reach out and run his fingers through those shimmering strands, to bury his face in the tangled silk. A mistake, a mistake. He knew it before it happened, and yet he couldn't help himself.

She shivered at his touch. Just the tiniest tremble, the softest sigh. He ran his hands down her shoulders, down the cool smoothness of her bare arms. She didn't pull away. No, she leaned back, as though melting against him. He wrapped his arms around her, enfolding her in their warmth.

"When I was a boy," he whispered, "I used to think there were magical creatures in that field down there. Elves and fairies hiding among the toadstools. I'd see their lights flitting about at night. It was only fireflies, of course. But to a kid, they might have been anything. Elvish lanterns, Dragon lights. I wish . . ."

"What do you wish, Chase?"

He sighed. "That I still had some of that child inside me. That we could have known each other then. Before all this happened. Before . . ."

"Richard."

Chase fell silent. His brother would always be there, his life and his death like a darkness hovering over them. What could possibly thrive in such shadow? Not friendship; certainly not love. *Love?* No, what Chase felt, standing there behind her, hugging her slim, warm body to his, had far more to do with lust. *Well, what the hell. Maybe it runs in my family,* he thought, *in my tainted bloodline. This propensity for reckless, hopeless affairs. Richard had it. My mother had it. Is it my turn to succumb?*

Miranda shifted in his embrace, turned to face him. One look at that soft, upturned mouth and he was lost.

She tasted of summer and warmth and sweet amber honey. At the first touch of their lips he wanted more, more. He felt like a man who has fallen drunk at his first sip of nectar and now craves nothing else. His hands found their way into that silken mass of hair, were buried in it, lost in it. He heard her murmur, "please," and was too fevered to think it anything but a request for more. Only when she said it again, and then, "Chase, no," did he finally pull away.

They stared at each other. The confusion he felt was mirrored in her eyes. She retreated a step, nervously shoving back her hair.

"I shouldn't have let you do that," she said. "It was a mistake."

"Why?"

"Because you—you'll say I led you on. That's what you'll tell Evelyn, isn't it? You think it's how I got hold of Richard. Temptation. Seduction. It's what everyone else believes."

"But is it true?"

"You've just proved it. Get me alone in a room and look what happens! Another Tremain male bites the dust." Her voice took on a cold edge. "What I want to know is, who's really seducing whom?"

She's all motion, all skittishness, he thought. In another moment she would shatter and fly into pieces.

"Neither of us did any seducing, any tempting. It just happened, Miranda. The way it usually happens. Nature tugs on our strings and we can't always resist."

"This time I will. This time I know better. Your brother taught me a few things. The most important thing is not to be so damn gullible when it comes to men."

That last word was still hanging in the air between them when they heard footsteps thump onto the porch below. Someone rapped on the front door.

Chase turned and left the room.

Miranda, suddenly weak, leaned against the windowsill. She clutched it tightly, as though drawing strength from the wood. *Too close,* she thought. *I let down my guard, let him slip right past my defenses.*

She would have to be more careful. She would have to remind herself that Chase and Richard were variations on a theme, a theme that had already wreaked havoc on her life. She took a deep breath and slowly let it out, willing the turmoil, the confusion, to flow out of her body. *Back in control,* she thought. She released the sill. She stood straight. Then, with a new semblance of calmness, she followed Chase down the stairs.

He was in the front room with the visitor. Miranda recognized her old acquaintance from the garden club, Miss Lila St. John, local expert on flowering perennials. Miss St. John was dressed in her signature black dress. Summer or winter, she always wore black, set off with a touch of white lace here and there. Today it was a black walking dress of crinkled linen. It did not quite match her brown boots or her straw hat, but on Miss St. John it all seemed to look just right.

She turned at the sound of Miranda's footsteps. If she was surprised to see Miranda she didn't show it. She simply nodded, then turned her sharp gray eyes back to the ransacked desk. On the front porch a dog whined. Through the screen door Miranda saw what looked like a large black fur ball with a red tongue.

"It's all my fault, you know," said Miss St. John. "I can't believe I was such an imbecile."

"How is it your fault?" asked Chase.

"I sensed something was wrong last week. We were taking our walk, you see, Ozzie and I. We walk every evening around dusk. That's when the deer come out, the pests, though I do love to see them. Anyway, I saw a light through the trees, somewhere in this direction. I came up to the cottage and knocked on the door. No one answered, so I left." She shook her head. "I shouldn't have, you know. I should have looked into it. I *knew* it didn't feel right."

"Did you see a car?"

"If you were coming to loot the joint, would *you* park your car out front? Of course not. I know I'd park down the road a bit, in the trees. Then I'd sneak up here on foot."

It was hard to imagine Miss St. John doing any such thing.

"It's a good thing you didn't get involved," said Chase. "You could have gotten yourself killed."

"At my age, Chase, getting killed is not a major concern." She used her walking stick, a knobby affair with a duck's head handle, to prod among the papers on the floor. "Any idea what he was after?"

"Not a clue."

"Not valuables, obviously. That's a Limoges on that shelf over there, isn't it?"

Chase glanced sheepishly at the hand-painted vase. "If you say so."

Miss St. John turned to Miranda. "Have you any thoughts on the matter?"

Miranda found herself under the gaze of two very intense gray eyes. Miss St. John might be dismissed by many as little more than a charming eccentric, but Miranda could see the intelligence in that gaze. While their previous conversations had tended more toward delphiniums and daffodils, even then, Miss St. John had made her feel like some sort of new plant species under a magnifying glass. "I'm not sure I know what to think, Miss St. John," she said.

"Take a look at the mess. What does it tell you?"

Miranda glanced at the papers, the scattered books. Then her gaze shifted to the bookcases. Only a top shelf had been emptied. Two full bookcases were undisturbed. "He didn't look through all the books. So whoever broke in here must have been interrupted. By you, maybe."

"Or he found what he was looking for," said Chase.

Miss St. John turned to him. "And what might that be?"

"A guess?" Chase and Miranda glanced at each other. "The file on Stone Coast Trust," Chase ventured.

"Ah." Miss St. John's eyes took on a gleam of interest. "Your brother's little campaign against Tony Graffam. Yes, Richard seemed to do quite a bit of writing out here. At that desk, in fact. On my evening walks I'd see him through the window."

"Did you ever stop to talk to him? About what he was working on?"

"Oh, no. That's why we come out here, isn't it? To get away from all those prying townies." She glanced at Miranda. "I never saw *you* out here."

"I've never been here," she said, shifting uneasily under that thoughtful gaze. This matter-of-fact reference to her link with Richard had taken her by surprise. And yet, Miss St. John's bluntness was far preferable to the delicate avoidance with which so many others treated the subject.

Miss St. John bent down for a closer look at the papers. "He must have done a prodigious amount of work here, judging by this mess. What is all this, anyway?"

Chase bent and sifted through the papers. "Looks like a lot of old article files. . . . Financial records from the *Herald* . . . And here we've got a collection of local personality profiles. Why, here's one of you, Miss St. John."

"Me? But I was never interviewed for anything."

Chase grinned. "Must be the unauthorized version, then."

"Does it mention all my sexy secrets?"

"Well, let's just take a good look here—"

"Oh, *give* me the damn thing." Miss St. John snatched the page out of his hands and scanned the typewritten notes. She read them aloud. "Age seventy-four . . . holds title to lot number two, St. John's Wood, and cottage thereon . . . rabid member of local garden club." Here she glanced up huffily. "*Rabid?*" She continued reading. "Eccentric recluse, never married. Engaged once, to an Arthur Simoneau, killed in action . . . Normandy. . . ." Her voice trailed off. Slowly she sat down, still clutching the piece of paper in both hands.

"Oh, Miss St. John," said Miranda. "I'm sorry."

The elderly woman looked up, still shaken. "It . . . was a very long time ago."

"I can't believe he went digging into your personal life, without you even knowing about it. Why would he do that?"

"You're saying it was Richard?" asked Miss St. John.

"Well, these are his papers."

Miss St. John frowned at the page for a moment. "No," she said slowly. "I don't believe he wrote this. There's an error in here. It says my cottage lies in St. John's Wood. But it lies three feet over the line, on Tremain property. A surveyor's mistake from seventy years past. Richard knew that."

Chase frowned. "I never heard that, about your cottage."

"Yes, your family land goes past the second stone wall. It includes the entire access road. So, technically, all the rest of us are trespassers on your private road. Not that it ever mattered. It always felt like a giant family out here. But now . . ." She shook her head. "So many strangers on the island. All those tourists from *Massachusetts.*" She made it sound like an invasion from hell.

"Did Stone Coast Trust approach you?" Miranda asked her. "About selling St. John's Wood?"

"They approached everyone on this road. I, of course, refused. So did Richard. That effectively squelched the project. Without Rose Hill, Stone Coast would own a disconnected patchwork of little lots. But now . . ." Sadly she sighed. "I imagine Evelyn, at this very moment, has her pen poised over the sales contract."

"Actually, she does not," said Chase. "Rose Hill didn't go to Evelyn. Richard left the property to Miranda."

Miss St. John stared at them. "Now that," she said after a long pause, "is an entirely unexpected development."

"For me, as well," said Miranda.

While Miss St. John sat back in thought, Miranda and Chase gathered up the rest of the papers. They found more article files, a few miscellaneous clippings, an old financial report from the *Herald.* Obviously Richard had used the cottage as another office. Was this where he had stored his most sensitive papers? Miranda wondered about this when she came across a whole bundle of personality profiles. Like the page on Miss St. John, the information contained in these files was highly private.

In some cases it was downright shocking. She was startled to read that Forrest Mayhew, the local bank president, had been arrested for drunk driving in Boston. That town selectman George LaPierre, married thirty years, had been treated last year for syphilis. That Dr. Steiner—*her* doctor—was under investigation for medicare fraud.

She handed the papers to Chase. "Look at these! Richard was collecting dirt on everyone in town!"

"Here, what's this?" he asked. There was a yellow adhesive note attached to the back cover of the folder. On it was the handwritten scrawl, "Mr. T., do you want more? Let me know." It was signed "W.B.R."

"So Richard *didn't* write these," said Miranda. "This person W.B.R.—whoever he was—must've done the reporting."

"You have anyone on staff with those initials?"

"No. At least, not at the moment." She reached for a manila folder lying on the floor. "Look, there's another note from W.B.R." This time the note was paper-clipped to the top cover. "All I could get. Sorry—W.B.R."

"What's inside?" asked Miss St. John.

Miranda opened the file and stared. "This is it! The file on Stone Coast Trust!"

"Jackpot," said Chase.

"There's no profile of Tony Graffam. But here's his tax return. A list of bank account numbers and assets . . ." She nodded. "We hit pay dirt."

"I think not," said Miss St. John.

They both looked at her.

"If that file is so important, why did the burglar leave it here?"
In silence they considered that question.

"Maybe our burglar wasn't interested in Stone Coast Trust at all,"
said Miss St. John. "I mean, look at all this nasty information Richard's
been gathering. Snoopy reports on drunk driving. Medicare fraud.
Syphilis. George LaPierre, of all people! And at his age, too. These
files could destroy some fine reputations. Now, I tell you, isn't that a
motive for burglary?"

Or murder, thought Miranda. Why had Richard gathered such information in the first place? Was he planning an exposé on island resi-
dents? Or was there some darker reason? Coercion, for instance.
Blackmail.

"If someone broke in to steal his own file, then we can assume it's
now gone," said Chase. "Which means George LaPierre, Dr. Steiner,
all the others in this pile didn't do it."

"Not necessarily," said Miss St. John. "What if he broke in and
simply substituted a milder version? Mine, for instance. There's not a
thing in my profile that qualifies as scandalous. How do you know I
didn't come in here and destroy a far more venomous version?"

Chase smiled. "I will duly place you on the list of suspects, Miss St.
John."

"Don't you discount me, Chase Tremain. Age alone does not take
one out of the running. I have more up here—" she tapped her head
"—than that imbecile George LaPierre had in his prime. If he ever *had*
a prime."

"What you're saying, Miss St. John," said Miranda, "is that we can't
count out any name in this pile. Or any name *not* in this pile."

"Correct."

Miranda frowned at the books. "One thing doesn't make sense.
First, our burglar searches the desk. He throws around some papers,
looking for some incriminating file. Why would he then search the
bookcase? That's not the sort of place Richard would keep papers."

After a pause Miss St. John said, "You're right, of course. That
doesn't make sense."

"Well," said Chase, "I guess we should call Lorne. Though I'm not
sure he'd be much help at this point." He turned to the phone.

He'd already picked up the receiver when Miss St. John suddenly
said, "Wait. Perhaps you should hold off on that call." She was staring
at a loose page near her feet. Thoughtfully she picked up the paper
and smoothed it across her knee.

Frowning, Chase hung up the receiver. "Why?"

"This is a profile of Valerie Everhard. You remember her, Chase.

Our local librarian. And a married lady. According to this, Valerie has taken on a lover."

"So?"

"The man she's seeing is our chief of police." Miss St. John looked up and her eyes had lost all trace of humor. "Lorne Tibbetts."

"Why did he have these awful reports?" asked Miranda. "What was he planning to do with them?"

They were driving through darkness back to town. The fog had rolled in from the sea and curtained off all view beyond the dim haze of their headlights. Nothing seemed real in this mist, nothing seemed familiar. They were driving through a strange land, through a swirling cloud that seemed as if it would never lift.

"It doesn't sound like Richard," said Chase. "Snooping around in his neighbors' private lives. He committed enough sins of his own. If anyone was vulnerable to blackmail, it was Richard. Besides, who cares if Lorne is having a little fling with the librarian?"

"The librarian's husband?"

"Okay, but why would Richard care?"

She shook her head, unable to come up with an answer. "I wonder if any of these people knew about these files. Miss St. John didn't." She looked down at the papers on her lap and thought of the terrible secrets they contained. She had the sudden urge to shove the pile away, to throw off that unclean burden. "Chase?" she asked. "How do we know any of this is true?"

"We don't." He gave a short laugh. "And we can't exactly knock on George LaPierre's door and ask if he's had syphilis."

Miranda frowned at the note clipped to the folder. "I wonder who this is. This W.B.R. who got the information."

"The initials don't ring any bells?"

"None at all."

As the darkness flew past their windshield, Miranda thought of all the secrets revealed in these files. The banker's weakness for whiskey. The doctor's white-collar fraud. The husband and wife who conversed with their fists. All of it concealed beneath the glaze of respectability. *What private pains we nurse in silence.*

"Why *these* particular people?" she asked suddenly.

"Because they have the most to lose?" Chase suggested. "We're talking old island families here. LaPierre, Everhard, St. John. All of them respected names."

"Except for Tony Graffam."

"That's true. I guess he has a file in there, too . . ." He paused. "Wait. There's our link."

"What?"

"The north shore. You haven't lived here long enough to know all these families. But I grew up with them. I remember the summers I used to play with Toby LaPierre. And Daniel Steiner. And Valerie Everhard. Their families all have summer cottages out there."

"It could be coincidental."

"Or it could mean everything."

Chase frowned at the highway. The fog was thinning. "When we get back to your house," he said, "let's take a good look at those names. See if my hunch holds up."

An hour and a half later they sat at Miranda's dining table, the pages spread out before them. The remains of a hastily prepared supper—mushroom omelets and toast—had been pushed aside and they were now on their second cup of coffee. It was such a domestic scene, she thought with a twinge of longing, almost like newlyweds lingering at the dinner table. Except that the man sitting across from her could never, would never, fit into the picture. He was a temporary apparition, a visitor passing through her dining room.

She forced herself to focus on the sheet of paper, where he'd just checked off the final name.

"Okay, here's the list," said Chase. "Everyone in Richard's file. I'm almost certain they all own property on the north shore."

"Are any names missing?"

Chase sat back and mentally ticked off the camps along the access road. "There's Richard, of course. Then there's old man Sulaway's property, down the road. He's a retired lobsterman, sort of a recluse. And then there's Frenchman's Cottage. I think it was sold some years back. To hippies, I heard. They come up for the summers."

"So they'd be living there now."

"If they still own the place. But they're not from this area. I can't see Richard bothering to dig up information on them. And as for old Sully, well, an eighty-five-year-old sounds like a pretty unlikely victim for blackmail."

Blackmail. Miranda gazed at the papers on the table. "What was Richard thinking of?" she wondered. "What did he have against these people?"

"Something to do with the rezoning? Were any of these names on the land commission?"

"They couldn't have voted, anyway. They would've been disqualified.

You know, conflict of interest." She sat back. "Maybe our burglar was looking for something entirely different."

"Then the question is, did he—or she—find it?"

From somewhere in the house came a sound that made them both glance up. It was the soft tinkle of breaking glass.

Miranda jerked to her feet in alarm. At once Chase grabbed her hand, signaled her to be silent. Together they moved from the dining room into the living room. A quick glance around told them the windows were all intact. They paused for a moment, listening, but heard no other sounds. Chase started toward the bedrooms.

They were moving up the hall when they heard, louder this time, the distinct crash of shattering glass.

"That came from the cellar!" said Miranda.

Chase wheeled and headed back into the kitchen. He flicked on a wall switch and yanked open the cellar door. A single bare bulb shone over the narrow stairway. A strange mist seemed to swirl in the shadows, obscuring the bottom of the stairs. They had taken only two steps down when they both smelled smoke.

"You've got a fire in here!" said Chase, moving down the steps. "Where's your extinguisher?"

"I'll get it!" Miranda scrambled into the kitchen, pulled the extinguisher from the pantry shelf and dashed back down the cellar steps.

By now the smoke was thick enough to make her eyes burn. Through the whirling haze she saw the source: a bundle of flaming rags. Nearby, just beneath a shattered basement window, lay a red brick. At once she understood what had happened, and her panic gave way to fury. *How dare they smash my window? How dare they attack me in my own home?*

"Stay back!" Chase yelled, plunging forward through the smoke. His shoes crunched over broken glass as he crossed the concrete floor. He aimed the extinguisher; a stream of white shot out and hissed over the flames. A few sweeps of the nozzle and the fire faltered and died under a smothering blanket of powder. Only the smoke remained, a stinking pall that hung like a cloud around the bare light bulb.

"It's out!" said Chase. He was prowling the basement now, searching for new flames. He didn't notice that Miranda had gone rigid with fury, didn't see that she was staring, white-faced, at the broken glass on the floor.

"Why can't they leave me *alone?*" she cried.

Chase turned and looked at her with sudden intensity. He said, dead quiet, "You mean this has happened before?"

"Not—not this. But phone calls, really cruel ones. Again and again. And messages, written on my window."

"What sort of messages?"

"What you'd expect." She swallowed and looked away. "You know, to the local murderess."

He took a step toward her. "You know who's doing it?"

"I told myself it was just—just some kids. But kids, they wouldn't set fire to my house. . . ."

Chase glanced down at the brick, then up at the shattered window. "It's a crazy way to burn down a house," he said. He went to her, took her by the shoulders, gently rubbed her arms. She felt warmth in his touch, and strength. Courage. He framed her face with his hands and said quietly, "I'm going to call the police."

She nodded. Together they started up the steps to the kitchen. They were halfway up the stairs when the door above them suddenly slammed shut. An instant later the bolt squealed home.

"They've shut us in!" cried Miranda.

He dashed past her up the stairs and began pounding on the door. In frustration he threw himself against it. His shoulder slammed into the wood.

"It's solid!" said Miranda. "You can't break it down."

Chase groaned. "I think I just found that out."

Footsteps creaked across the floor overhead. Miranda froze, tracing with her gaze the intruder's movements.

"What's he doing?" she whispered.

As if in answer to her question, the single light bulb suddenly went out. The basement was plunged into darkness.

"Chase?" she cried.

"I'm here! Right here. Give me your hand."

She reached up blindly toward him; at once he found her wrist. "It's all right," he murmured, pulling her toward him, gathering her tightly against his chest. Just the unyielding support of that embrace was enough to take the edge off her panic. "We'll be okay," he murmured. "We just have to find a way out. We can't make it through the window. You have a cellar door? A coal hatch?"

"There's—there's an old loading hatch near the furnace. It opens to the side yard."

"All right. Let's see if we can get it open. Just move us in the right direction."

Together they felt their way down the steps, to the cellar floor. Shards of glass skittered before their feet as they inched their way through the darkness. It seemed like a journey across eternity, through a blackness so thick it might have been firm to the touch. At last

Miranda's extended hand touched pipes, then the cold, damp granite of the cellar wall.

"Which way to the hatch?" asked Chase.

"I think it's to the left."

Upstairs, the creaking moved across the floor, then a door slammed shut. *They've left the house,* Miranda thought in relief. *They're not going to hurt us.*

"I found the oil tank!" said Chase.

"Then the coal hatch should be just above. There are some steps—"

"Right here." He released her hand. Though she knew he was right beside her, that break in contact left her hovering at the edge of panic. If only she could see something, anything! She could hear Chase shoving up against the wood, could hear the crack and groan of the hatch as he struggled to swing it open. Straining to see through the darkness, she could make out, little by little, the vague outline of his head, then the gleam of sweat on his face. More details seemed to emerge out of darkness: the hulking shadow of the furnace, the oil tank, the reddish glint of the copper pipes. It was all visible now.

Too visible. Where was the light coming from?

With new apprehension she turned and stared up at the basement window. Reflected in the shattered glass was a flickering dance of orange light. Firelight. "Oh, my God," she whispered. "Chase . . ."

He turned and stared.

Even as they watched, the glow in the window shards leaped to a new and horrifying brilliance.

"We have to get out of here!" she cried.

He shoved against the hatch. "I can't get it open!"

"Here, let me help you!"

They both pushed up against the wood, pounded it with their bare fists. Already, smoke was swirling in through the broken window. Overhead, through the cracks in the floorboards, they could see the terrible glow of flames consuming the house above. Most of the heat was funneled up, toward the roof, but soon the timbers would give way. They would be trapped beneath falling debris.

The hatch was immovable.

Chase snatched up the fire extinguisher and began to pound it against the wood. "I'll keep trying to break through!" he yelled. "You get to the window—yell for help!"

Miranda scrambled over to the window. Smoke was billowing in, a thick, suffocating black cloud. She could barely reach the opening. She glanced around in panic for a crate, a chair, something to stand on. Nothing was in sight.

She screamed louder than she had ever screamed in her life.

Even then, she knew help wouldn't reach them in time. The basement window faced the back of the house, toward the garden. She was too far below the opening for her voice to carry any distance. She glanced up, at the floor beams. Already, the evil glow of heat shone through. She could hear the groan of the wood as it sagged. How long before those beams gave way? How long before she and Chase collapsed under that smothering blackness of smoke? The air had grown unbearably close.

It's already an oven, she thought. *And it will only get hotter. . . .*

8

Chase pounded desperately at the hatch. A board splintered, but the barrier held. "Someone's nailed it shut!" he yelled. "Keep calling for help!

She screamed, again and again, until her voice cracked, until she had almost no voice left.

She heard, in the distance, the sound of a dog barking, and Mr. Lanzo's far-off shouts. She tried to shout back. All she could manage was a pitifully weak cry. There was no answering call. Had she imagined the voice? Or couldn't he hear her?

Even if he did, would he track her screams to this small opening facing the garden? Safety lay so close, yet was so unreachable. If she stood on tiptoe she could actually poke her hand through the shards of broken glass, could feel the soil beneath her fingertips. Just inches away would be her beloved delphiniums, her newly planted violas. . . .

An image of her garden, of rich, moist earth and a freshly tilled flower bed suddenly flashed into her mind. Hadn't she just expanded that bed? Hadn't she used a pickax to break up the sod? The pickax— where did she leave it? She remembered laying it against the side of the house—

Near the cellar window.

With her bare fist she broke away the last shards of glass. Something warm ran down her arm. Blood, she thought with a strange sense of detachment. But no pain—she was too panicked to feel anything but the desperate need to escape the flames. She reached through the open window and ran her fingers along the outside wall. Nothing on the right, just the rough clapboard shingles above a granite foundation.

She shifted to the left side of the window, swept her hand along the outside frame and touched warm metal. The pickax head!

She gripped it so tightly her fingers cramped. Painfully she managed to slide the heavy iron head sideways, in front of the window. With a little wriggling she maneuvered first the sharp point, then the blade end, through the window opening.

The pick landed with a hard clang on the concrete floor.

Coughing and gasping, she dragged the tool into the blinding smoke. Already, flames were engulfing the floor-boards above her head. "Chase!" she cried. "Where are you?"

"I'm here!"

She started toward the sound of Chase's voice but halfway across she lost her bearings. The whole room seemed to be moving around her like some crazy circus ride. *I can't faint now,* she thought. *If I do, I'll never wake up.* Already her knees were giving way. How she needed a breath of fresh air, just one! She sank to the floor. The concrete felt blessedly damp and cool against her face.

"Miranda!"

The sound of Chase's voice seemed to jump-start some last internal surge of strength. She struggled back to her knees. "I can't—can't see you. . . ."

"I'll find you! Keep talking!"

"No, we'll both get lost! Stay by the hatch!" She began to crawl, moving in the direction of his voice, dragging the pickax behind her. The sound of the fire above them had grown to a roar. Fallen embers lay scattered and glowing on the concrete. Blinded by smoke, she put her hand on one and the pain that seared her skin brought a sob to her throat.

"I'm coming for you!" Chase shouted.

His voice seemed far away, as though he were calling from some distant room. She realized she was fading, and that the room had grown dark, and that this inferno was where she would die. She clawed her way forward, dragging herself and the pickax a few more precious inches.

"Miranda!" His voice seemed even more distant now, another world, another universe. And that seemed most terrible of all—that she would die without the comfort of his touch.

She reached out to drag herself one last time—

And found his hand. Instantly his fingers closed around her wrist and he hauled her close. His touch was like some wondrous restorative. She found the strength to rise once again to her knees.

"Here," she said with a cough, dragging the pickax toward him. "Will this work?"

"It has to!" He staggered to his feet. "Stay low," he commanded. "Keep your head down!"

She heard him grunt as he swung the pickax, heard the thunk of the metal slamming into the wood. Another swing, another blow. Splinters flew, raining into her hair. He was coughing, weaving. Against the backlight of flames she could see him struggle to stay on his feet.

He swung again.

The hatch gave way. A blast of cool air flew in through the jagged opening. The inrush of fresh oxygen was like throwing fuel on the fire. Everywhere, timbers seemed to explode into flame. Miranda dropped to the ground, her face buried in her arms. An ember fell hissing onto her head. She brushed it away, shuddering at the smell of her own burning hair.

Chase gasped in one last breath of air, then, grunting from the effort, he heaved the pickax against the wood.

The hatch flew apart.

Miranda felt herself yanked upward, through some long, dark tunnel. She could see no light at the other end, could see no end at all. There was just that black passage, the dizzying sense of motion, the clawlike grasp of fingers against her flesh.

Then, suddenly, there was the grass.

And there was Chase, cradling her in his arms, stroking her face, her hair.

She took in a breath. The rush of air into her lungs was almost painful. She coughed, drew in more air, more! She felt drunk on its sweetness.

The night was a whirlwind of noise, sirens, shouting voices and the crackle of fire. She gazed up in horror at the flames; they seemed to fill the heavens.

"Oh, God," she whispered. "My house . . ."

"We made it out," said Chase. "That's all that matters. We're alive."

She focused on his face. It was a mask of soot, lit by the hellish glow of the fire. They stared at each other, a look of shared wonder that they were both still breathing.

"Miranda," he murmured. He bent and pressed his lips to her forehead, her eyelids, her mouth. He tasted of smoke and sweat and desperation. All at once, they were both shaking and clutching each other in wild relief.

"Mo! Honey! You all right?"

Mr. Lanzo, dressed in his pajamas, scuttled toward them across the lawn. "I was afraid you were inside! Kept tellin' those idiot firemen I heard you screaming!"

"We're okay," Chase said. He took Miranda's face in his hands and kissed her. "We're fine."

Somewhere, a window shattered in the heat of the flames.

"Hey! You people move back!" a fireman yelled. "Everyone get back!"

Chase pulled Miranda to her feet. Together they retreated across Mr. Lanzo's lawn and onto the street. They watched as the fire hoses unleashed a torrent of spray. Water hissed onto the flames.

"Aw, honey," said Mr. Lanzo sadly. "It's too late. She's gone."

Even as he said it, the roof collapsed. Miranda watched in despair as a sheet of flame shot up, turning the night sky into a blazing dawn. *It's all gone,* she thought. *Everything I owned. I've lost it all.*

She wanted to scream out her fury, her anguish, but the violence of those flames held her in a trance. She could only watch as a strange numbness took hold.

"Ms. Wood?"

Slowly she turned.

Lorne Tibbetts was standing beside her. "What happened here?" he asked.

"What the hell do you *think* happened?" Chase shot back. "Someone torched her house. While we were in it."

Lorne looked at Miranda, who stared back at him with dazed eyes. He looked at the burning house, which had already collapsed into little more than a heap of firewood.

"You'd better come with me," he said. "I'll need a statement. From both of you."

"Now do you believe it?" asked Chase. "Someone's trying to kill her."

Lorne Tibbetts's gaze, in the best poker player tradition, revealed absolutely nothing. He began to doodle in the margin of his notepad. Nothing artistic there, not even a few healthy free-form loops. These were tight little triangles linked together like crystals. The geometric creation of a geometric mind. He clicked his pen a few times, then he turned and yelled, "Ellis?"

Ellis poked his head in the door. "Yo, Lorne."

"You finished with Ms. Wood?"

"Got it all down."

"Okay." Lorne rose to his feet and started out of the room.

"Wait," said Chase. "What happens now?"

"I talk to her. Ellis talks to you."

"You mean I have to tell it all over again?"

"It's the way we do things around here. Independent questioning. Routine police procedure." He tucked his shirt into his trousers, smoothed back his hair and walked out the door.

Ellis Snipe sat in Lorne's vacated seat and grinned at Chase. "Hey, Mr. T. How ya doing?"

Chase looked at that moronic, gap-toothed smile and wondered, *Was Mayberry ever this bad?*

"Why don't we start at the beginning," said Ellis.

"Which beginning?" Chase shot back.

Ellis looked confused. "Uh, you choose."

Chase sighed. He glanced at the door, wondering how Miranda was holding up. No matter what Dr. Steiner had said, a hospital bed was where she belonged. But the old quack had simply dressed her glass cuts, examined her lungs and declared hospitalization unnecessary. What Dr. Steiner had neglected to consider was her emotional state. She'd lost her house, her possessions; she was left with no sense of order to her life. What she needed was a safe place, a cocoon where no one could hurt her. . . .

"Uh, Mr. Tremain? You think you could maybe try and cooperate?"

Chase looked at Ellis. What was the point of fighting? he thought wearily. Ellis Snipe looked like the kind of robot who'd follow orders to the letter. If he had to, he'd sit there all night, waiting for Chase to talk.

For the second time that night Chase told the story. He took it back to the cottage, the evidence of a break-in, the secret files. This time he left out the information about Lorne Tibbetts and his fling with the librarian. Some things, he thought, should remain private.

Ellis wrote it all down in a weird, spidery script that couldn't possibly be produced by a normal personality.

When Chase was finished, Ellis asked one and only one question. "Was there anything in those secret files about me?"

"Not a thing," said Chase.

Ellis looked disappointed.

After Ellis had left, Chase sat alone at the table, wondering what came next. A third cop, another go-around with the story? The whole affair had taken on a surreal quality, like some never-ending night-mare. For ten minutes he waited for something to happen. Then, fed up with being ignored, he shoved his chair back and went in search of Miranda.

He found her in the same interrogation room where he'd first laid eyes on her over a week before. She was sitting alone. A smudge of soot blackened her cheek, and her hair was dusted with ash.

She gazed at him with a look of utter exhaustion. "The cop station from hell," she murmured.

He smiled. Then he saw her hand. It was encased in bandages. "Is it as serious as it looks?"

"The doctor just believes in doing a thorough job." She looked in wonder at the free-form sculpture of surgical gauze and tape. "I was afraid he'd amputate."

"A hand as nice as yours? I wouldn't have let him."

She tried to return the smile, but couldn't quite manage it.

"You have to leave the island," he said.

"I can't. The terms of my bail—"

"To hell with the bail terms! You can't wait around for the next accident, the next fire."

"I can't leave the county."

"This time you were lucky. Next time—"

"What am I *supposed* to do?" She looked at him in sudden anger. "Run and hide?"

"Yes."

"From *what?* I don't even know who's trying to kill me!" Her cry echoed in the stark room. At once she flushed, as though shamed by the sound of her own hysteria.

"If I leave, I'll never know what I'm running from," she said quietly. "Or if I'm still being hunted. What kind of life is that, Chase? Never knowing if I'm safe. Always waking up at night, listening for footsteps. Wondering if that creak on the stairs is someone coming for me. . . ." She shuddered and stared down at the table.

Lord, he thought. *How did I ever get involved with this woman? She's not my problem. I'm not her white knight. I should get up and walk right out of this room. Who would blame me?*

And then a voice inside him said, *I would.*

He pulled out a chair and sat across from her. She didn't look up. She just kept staring at the ugly tabletop.

"If you won't leave, then what are you going to do?"

She shrugged. It hurt him to see the hopelessness in that gesture. "Does it matter?"

"It matters to me."

"Why?" The look she gave him made him want to say things he knew he'd regret. That he cared whether she lived or died. He cared what happened to her. He cared too much.

He said, with unassailable logic, "Because what happened tonight is somehow tied in with Richard. The break-in at Rose Hill. The fire. And you."

She gave a dispirited laugh. "Yes, somewhere in all this mess, I seem to fit in. And I haven't the faintest idea why."

The door opened. Ellis said, "There you are, Mr. T. Lorne says you both can go. Says he can't think of any more questions."

I hope I never see this place again, thought Chase as they followed Ellis down the hall, into the front office. Lorne was sitting at one of the desks, talking on the phone. He glanced up as Chase and Miranda walked past, and motioned to them to wait.

"Oh, hell." Chase sighed. "He just thought of another question."

Lorne hung up and said to Ellis, "Bring the car around. We got us another call."

"Man, oh, man," Ellis whined as he headed out to the garage. "This is one heck of a Thursday night."

Lorne looked at Miranda. "You got a place to stay?"

"I'll drive her to the hotel," said Chase.

"I was thinking along the lines of someplace safer," Lorne said. "A friend's house, maybe?"

"There's always Mr. Lanzo," said Miranda.

"No, I'll take you over to Annie's house," said Chase. "At least *her* faculties are still intact."

"Yeah, that'd be better," said Lorne, reaching for his hat. "Considering."

"Considering what?" said Chase.

"The two empty gas cans we found over by Ms. Wood's house. Plus the two-by-fours nailed over the cellar hatch."

Miranda stared at him. There it was. Undeniable proof someone was trying to kill her. Her body seemed to sag against Chase. "Then you believe me," she whispered.

Lorne reached for his hat. "Well, I'll tell you what I believe, Ms. Wood. I do believe this is one of the weirdest nights we've ever had here on this island. And I do not like the trend."

"What else is going on?" asked Chase.

"An assault. On Miss Lila St. John, if you can believe it. She just called in the report."

"Someone attacked her?" said Chase, shocked. "Why?"

"She claims she tried to stop a break-in." Lorne, obviously skeptical, started for the door. "At Rose Hill Cottage."

* * *

"So," said Annie Berenger, pouring out three tall whiskeys. "Do I get to write all about the juicy details? Or is this baby-sitting job another gratis deal?"

"I thought you and Miranda were friends," said Chase.

"Oh, we are. But I'm a reporter, too." She handed Chase a glass. "It's my job to take advantage of the situation." She glanced at the closed door to the bathroom, where Miranda was showering. "You know, Chase, she looked pretty beat-up. Shouldn't she be in a hospital or something?"

"She'll be fine right here, Annie. As long as you keep your eagle eye on her."

"Terrific. What I always wanted to be. A mommy." She tossed back a quick slug of whiskey. "Oh, don't get me wrong. I like Miranda. I used to be a lot like her. About a century ago." She poured herself a second glass. "But women grow up fast these days. We have to. It's the men who age us. Take my boyfriend, Irving. Please. I've been waiting a year for him to pop the question. It's giving me gray hairs." She took a sip of whiskey, then turned and looked at Chase. "So how much trouble is she in?"

"It could get dangerous. Are you ready for that?"

"Ready?" She went to an end table and opened the drawer. Casually she pulled out a revolver. "Little souvenir I picked up in Boston. I'm a lousy shot, but sometimes I get lucky." She tossed the gun back into the drawer. "Good enough?"

"I'm impressed."

Annie laughed. "Men always are when they see my pistol's bigger than theirs." She glanced over her shoulder as the bathroom door opened. "Hi. Feeling better?"

"Just cleaner," said Miranda, walking barefoot into the living room. She was wearing one of Annie's huge T-shirts. It hung like a dress over her slim hips.

Annie held out a glass of whiskey. "Join us in a toast."

"To what?"

"Just drink it. We'll think of something."

Miranda came toward them and took the glass. She brought with her those fresh shower smells, the scent of flowers and soap and feminine warmth. Her hair, still damp, was a mass of unruly waves. The sight of her sent Chase's head swimming. Or was it the whiskey?

"So what happens now?" asked Annie.

Chase turned away and set his glass on the nearest table. "The police are handling it."

"Look, I've been covering that beat for five years. I wouldn't be too optimistic."

"Lorne's a bright guy. He can figure it out."

"But whose side is he on? I'm not saying Lorne's corrupt, or anything. But you did find that page about him and Valerie Everhard."

"A fling with the local librarian?" Chase shrugged. "I'd consider that only a minor scandal.

"Did you ask Lorne about it?"

"Yes. He didn't deny it. And he didn't seem bothered by it."

"Annie, did you know Richard had those files?" Miranda asked.

Annie shrugged. "We had a number of files on local personalities. Jill did the interviews, wrote the pieces. Every summer we'd run a few profiles. But nothing that'd make tongues twitter." She set her glass down. "Well, whatever was in those files, it's all up in smoke now. A pity you didn't have copies. You've lost your only clues."

"I don't think so," said Chase. "Those were the papers the burglar left behind. Whatever he's really after is still at Rose Hill."

"How do you know?"

"Because he went back there tonight."

"What he didn't count on," said Miranda, "was tangling with Miss Lila St. John. Again."

Annie shook her head and laughed. "That is one poor, unfortunate burglar."

Miss Lila St. John was, at that moment, holding a bag of ice to a nasty-looking goose egg on the back of her head. "What do you mean, did I get a good look at him?" she snapped. "Does it seem likely I got a look at him? Considering where he whacked me?"

"It was just a routine question, ma'am," whimpered Ellis.

"That is the problem with you police people. You are so tied up with your routine questions you never bother to think."

"Miss St. John," Lorne politely interjected, "allow me to rephrase Ellis's question. What, exactly, did you see?"

"Precious little."

"A figure? A face?"

"Just a light. I told you, I was sitting here reading. *Death Becomes You.*

"Excuse me?"

"The name of the book. It features a police detective with a genius IQ." She paused. "Obviously, a novel with no basis in reality."

Lorne let that one slide by. Miss St. John deserved a little leeway tonight. After all, a blow on the head—even a head as hard as hers—would make anyone cranky. "Go on," he said.

"Well, I put the book aside to make tea. And as I did, I happened to look out that window. It faces south, toward Rose Hill Cottage. That's when I saw the light."

"A car headlight?"

"No, much dimmer. A flashlight, I think. Moving through the woods. I knew it was headed for Rose Hill. That's all that lies in that direction. So I decided to check on it."

"Why didn't you call us?"

"Because it might simply have been one of the Tremains. Now, how would it look if I dragged you men all the way out here, just to confront the rightful owner?"

"The rightful owner seems to be in doubt."

"Let's not confuse ourselves with that issue. Anyway, I went out—"

"Alone?"

"If only! I would have been just fine if Ozzie hadn't followed me."

"Ozzie?" inquired Ellis.

As if on cue, an enormous black dog sauntered across the room and eyed Ellis.

"Yes, you certainly made a racket," said Miss St. John to the dog. "All that yowling and thrashing in the bushes. No wonder you never catch anything." She looked at Lorne. "It's *his* fault. He followed me up the road. Somewhere along the way I lost track of the light. I was trying to see through the dark and shoo off Ozzie at the same time. He was making such unattractive noises. I turned around and gave him a slap. And that's when he whacked me."

"Ozzie?" asked Ellis.

"No! The man. Or woman. It was dark, so I couldn't tell you which."

"Did you black out?"

"I'm not sure. Things got a little confused at that point. I remember being on my knees in the bushes. Hearing footsteps run away. And feeling mad as hell." She glared at Ozzie. "Yes, and I do mean at *you.*"

The dog, unperturbed, began to lick Lorne's brand-new boot. Gingerly, Lorne gave the dog a little shove. Ozzie, looking insulted, redirected his affectionate overtures toward a more agreeable target—Ellis's leg.

"Then you never saw your attacker?" Lorne asked.

"No, I can't say I did."

"What happened then?"

"I came back here. Oh, I got a little turned around in the dark, but I found my way back, eventually. And I called you."

"So the attack happened—when?"

"It would be about two hours ago."

About the same time the flames were consuming the last of Miranda Wood's house, thought Lorne. It seemed unlikely that the same culprit could have set fire to the house, then raced out here in time to knock Miss St. John on the head. Two crimes, two criminals. Too bad.

Lorne preferred simple solutions.

"Are you certain your attacker was headed for Rose Hill?" he asked.

"I know he was. And he'll be back."

"Why?"

"Because he didn't get what he wanted."

"You're referring to the scandal sheets?"

Miss St. John gave him a look of pure innocence. "Oh. You know about that?"

"Yes. And for your information, Miss St. John, I didn't come on to Valerie Everhard. She came on to me."

Ellis looked up from the dog now nuzzling his knee.

"What was that about Valerie Everhard?"

"Never mind," snapped Lorne and Miss St. John simultaneously.

"There was a report on me, too," said Miss St. John with a faint note of pride. "As well as almost everyone on this road. I had no idea Richard Tremain was such a busybody."

"Any idea why?"

"I'll give the man the benefit of the doubt and attribute it to mere curiosity. As opposed to less benign motives."

Blackmail was what she meant. Lorne couldn't see that such a scheme made much sense. First of all, none of those secrets was particularly nasty. Embarrassing, perhaps, but nothing that couldn't be lived down. And that included his own penchant for married librarians. Second, the would-be victims ranged from the moderately well-to-do Forrest Mayhew to the outright cash-strapped Gordimers. Why blackmail a family that can scarcely pay their grocery bills?

Unless money was not the sought-after payment.

He wondered about this all the way back to town. Wondered why Richard Tremain would want those secrets. Wondered if he was even the one who'd collected them in the first place. The cottage, after all, had been open to others in the family. Cassie. Phillip.

Evelyn.

No, not Evelyn, he thought. She wouldn't dirty her hands in this filth.

"You and Valerie Everhard," Ellis muttered as he drove. "I never woulda guessed."

"Look, I felt sorry for her," said Lorne. "She needed some male attention."

"Oh." Ellis kept staring straight ahead at the road and nodding to himself.

"What the hell's that supposed to mean?" Lorne demanded.

"Oh, I was just thinking."

"About what?"

"How awful sorry you must be feeling for that woman right now."

"Valerie Everhard?"

"No." said Ellis. "The widow Tremain."

"It's a matter of loyalty, Chase," said Noah. "To the family. To your brother. To the people who *matter.*"

Chase said nothing. He simply continued slicing his ham, albeit with more concentrated vigor than usual. He knew they were all watching him. Noah and Evelyn. The twins. They were waiting for him to respond. But he kept on slicing that meat, mangling it, really, into smaller and smaller pieces.

"Never mind, Daddy," said Evelyn. "Can't you see? He's so wrapped up with that witch, he can't see the trap he's—"

"Please, Evelyn." Chase set down his knife.

"She's twisted you around, Chase! She has a talent for that! Among other things. But you can't be bothered with the facts anymore. No, all you want to believe are her lies."

"I want to believe the truth," he said quietly.

"The truth is, she's a whore."

"Evelyn," cut in Noah. "That is quite enough."

Evelyn turned on her father. "Whose side are you on?"

"You know damn well I'm on your side. I always have been."

"Then why don't you back me up?"

"Because this conversation doesn't become you. You've forgotten all I taught you about dignity. Pride."

"Well, *excuse me,* Daddy. It's not every day one's husband gets murdered." She glanced around at the sideboard. "Where's that wine? It's not too early for a drink."

"You will get over the murder. You'll get beyond it. And you will remember who you are."

"Who I am?" She rose to her feet. "Who I am is more of an embarrassment every day." She shoved her chair back against the table and left the room.

There was a long silence.

"She does have a point, Chase," said Noah, sounding quite reasonable. "The family should stick together. No matter what attractions this Miranda Wood person offers, don't you think it's best you stand by us?"

"What attraction *does* she offer?" asked Cassie.

"That's irrelevant," snapped Chase.

Noah raised an eyebrow. "Is it?"

Chase met Noah's gaze with a look of sheer indifference. Which, at that moment, wasn't at all what he was feeling. He had plenty of feelings when it came to Miranda Wood, and indifference wasn't one of them. All night he'd dreamt about her. He'd awakened sweating, remembering the fire, feeling once again the panic of not being able to find her in that well of smoke and flames. He'd drop back to sleep, only to sink yet again into the same nightmare. Some time during his fitful tossing and turning, he'd come to several realizations. That he was incapable of logical thought where Miranda Wood was concerned. That the attraction he felt for her was growing more dangerous every day.

And that, no matter what his instincts told him, the weight of evidence still pointed to her guilt.

This morning he'd risen from bed exhausted but absolutely clear-headed. He knew what he had to do. He had to put some distance between them. As he should have done from the very beginning.

He said, "You don't have to worry, Noah. I don't plan to see her again."

"I always thought you were the smarter Tremain," said Noah. "I was right."

Chase shrugged. "Not really a flattering comment. Considering how little you thought of Richard."

Noah glanced at the twins. "You two! Don't you have something better to do?"

"Not really," said Phillip.

"Well, clear the table, then. Go on."

"It's not as if we didn't know," said Cassie.

Noah frowned at her. "Know what?"

"That you and Dad didn't get along."

"For that matter, young lady, he didn't get along with you, either."

"Normal father-daughter disagreements. Not like you two, always at each other's throats. All that yelling and name-calling—"

"That's enough!" Noah's face had turned an ugly red. He rose partway out of his chair, his gaze targeted on his insolent granddaughter. "The day you were born, Cassandra, I took one look at you and I said, 'Watch out for that one. She's going to be trouble.'"

"Yes, it runs in our family, doesn't it?"

Instantly Phillip was on his feet, tugging at Noah's arm. "Come on, Granddad. Let's go outside, you and me. Walk around the block. I wanted to tell you about my year at Harvard—"

"Damn nursery for snooty rich boys."

"Just a walk, Granddad. It'll do you good."

Noah harrumphed and shoved his chair against the table. "Let's go, then. Hell, I could use the fresh air."

The two men walked out, slamming the front door behind them.

Cassie looked at Chase and smiled ironically. "One big happy family."

"What was that you said? About Noah and Richard."

"They despised each other. You knew that."

"Despised wasn't the word that came to mind. Disliked, maybe. You know, the usual rivalry between father and son-in-law."

"This wasn't just your usual rivalry." Cassie began to slice her ham into dainty pieces. For the first time Chase found himself actually seeing his niece. Before, she'd always seemed lost from view, the colorless sister skulking in the shadow of her brother. Now he took a new and closer look, and what he saw was a young woman with a square jaw and eyes like a ferret's. The resemblance to Noah was startling. No wonder the old man didn't get along with her. He probably saw too much of himself in that face. She looked him straight in the eye. No squirming, no discomfort, just that steady gaze.

"What did they argue about? Noah and your father?"

"Anything. Everything. Oh, they never let it get beyond these walls. Dad was weird that way. We could all be screaming at each other in this house, but once we stepped out the door he insisted we look like the perfect family. It was so phony. In public Dad and Noah would make like old buddies. And all the time there was that rivalry between them."

"Over your mother?"

"Of course. Noah's darling. And Dad could never be a good enough husband." She snorted. "Not that he tried very hard."

Chase paused, wondering how to phrase his next question. "Did you know your father was having . . . affairs?"

"He's been at it for years," Cassie said with a wave of her hand. "Lots of women."

"Which ones?"

She shrugged. "I figured that was his business."

"You two weren't very close, were you?"

"Daughters just weren't his thing, Uncle Chase. While I was working my butt off, getting straight A's, he was planning for Phillip's Harvard education. Grooming him to take over the *Herald.*"

"Phillip doesn't seem exactly thrilled by the prospect."

"You noticed that? Dad never did." She took a few bites of ham, then gave Chase a thoughtful look. "And what was the problem between *you* two?"

"Problem?" He resisted the urge to look away, to avoid her gaze. She would probably know immediately that he was hiding something. As it was, she'd probably already detected the flicker of discomfort in his eyes.

"The last time I saw you, Uncle Chase, I was ten years old. That was at Grandpa Tremain's funeral. Now, Greenwich isn't that far away. But you never came back for a visit, not once."

"Lives get complicated. You know how it is, Cassie."

She gave him a searching look, then said, "It's not easy, is it? Being the ignored sibling in the family?"

Damn this sharp-eyed brat, he thought. He gathered up his empty dishes and rose to his feet.

"You don't think she did it. Do you?" Cassie asked. They didn't have to mention names. They both knew exactly what they were talking about.

"I haven't decided," he said. He carried the dishes toward the kitchen. In the doorway he stopped. "By the way, Cassie," he said. "I called here last night about seven, to say I wouldn't be home for dinner. No one answered the phone. Where was your mother?"

"I really wouldn't know." Cassie picked up a slice of toast and calmly began to spread marmalade on it. "You'd have to ask her."

Chase drove directly to Rose Hill. No detours, no little side trips to pick up suspected murderesses. He had no intention of being distracted by Miranda Wood today. What he needed was a dose of cool-headed logic, and that meant keeping his distance. Today he had other things on his mind, the first item being: Who kept trying to break in to the cottage, and what was he searching for?

The answer lay somewhere in Rose Hill.

So that was where he headed. He drove with the window rolled down, the salt air whistling past his cheek. It brought back all those summer days of his childhood, riding with his mother along this very road, the smell of the sea in his face, the cry of the gulls echoing off the cliffs. How she had loved this drive! His mother had been a daredevil behind the wheel, screeching around these curves, laughing as the wind tangled her dark hair. They'd both laughed a lot those days, and he'd wondered if anyone else in the world had a mother so wild, so beautiful. So free.

Her death had left him devastated.

If only, before she'd died, she'd told him the truth.

He turned onto the access road and bumped along past all the old camp signs, past the cottages of families whose kids he'd once played with. Good memories, bad memories—they all returned as he drove up that road. He remembered twirling in the tire swing until he was so dizzy he threw up. Kissing buck-toothed Lucy Baylor behind the water tower. Hearing that awful crash of a breaking window and knowing it was *his* baseball they'd find lying in the shattered glass. The memories were so vivid he didn't notice that he'd already rounded the last bend and was just now turning onto the gravel driveway.

There was a car parked in front of the cottage.

He pulled up beside it and climbed out. He saw no sign of the driver. Could their burglar have turned desperate enough to pay a visit in broad daylight?

He hurried up the porch steps and was startled to hear the whistling of a kettle from the kitchen. Who the hell would be brazen enough to not only break in, but also make himself right at home? He shoved open the door and came face-to-face with the guilty party.

"I've just made some tea," said Miranda. She gave him a tight smile, not unfriendly, just nervous. Perhaps afraid. She nodded down at the tea tray she was carrying. "Would you like some?"

Chase glanced around the room, at the books arranged in neat piles on the floor. The desk had been cleared, the drawers' contents emptied into a series of cardboard boxes. Slowly his gaze shifted and took in the three bookcases. One was already two-thirds empty.

"We spent the morning going through Richard's papers," Miranda explained. "I'm afraid we haven't turned up anything yet, but—"

He shook his head. "We?"

"Miss St. John and I."

"Is she here?"

"She went back to her house, to feed Ozzie."

Their gazes met. *I try to stay away from you,* he thought, *and damn it, here you are. Here we are, alone in this house.*

The possibilities flooded his mind. Temptation, enemy of reason, danced its devil dance, the way it did every time he was in the same room with her. He thought of Richard, thought of her, thought of the two of them together. It hurt. Maybe that's why he chose to think of it. To quell the rising need he felt when he looked at her now.

"She—Miss St. John—thought it made sense to get started without you," Miranda said in a rush, as though suddenly frantic to fill the silence. "We didn't know when you'd get here, and we didn't want to call the house. I suppose we're trespassing, in a way, but . . ." Her voice trailed off.

"Technically speaking," he said after a pause, "you are."

She set down the tea tray, then straightened to face him. Her nervousness was gone. In its place was calm determination. "Maybe so. But it's what I have to do. We can search together. Or we can search separately. But I am going to search." She raised her chin, met his gaze without flinching. "So, Chase. Which way shall it be?"

9

His gaze was neutral, as unrevealing as that blank wall behind him. More revealing to Miranda was her acute sense of disappointment. She'd hoped to see at least a trace of gladness in his eyes, that he'd be pleased to find her here today. What she hadn't expected was this . . . indifference. *So that's how it is between us,* she thought. *What's happened since I saw you last? What did Evelyn say to you? That's it, isn't it? They've gotten to you. Richard's family. Your family.*

He shrugged. "It does make sense, I suppose. Working together."

"Of course it does."

"And you've already gotten off to a good start, I see."

In silence she poured a cup of tea, then carried it to the bookcase. There she calmly continued the task she'd been working on earlier— pulling down the books, riffling through the pages for any loose papers. She felt him watching her, sensed his gaze like a prickling in her back. "You can start on the other bookcase," she said without looking at him.

"What have you found so far?"

"No surprises." She reached for another book. "Unless you count Richard's rather weird taste in reading material." She looked at a book jacket. *The Advanced Physics of Ocean Waves.* "This one, for instance. I never knew he was interested in physics."

"He wasn't. When it came to science, he was functionally illiterate."

She opened the cover. "Well, this *is* his book. I see someone's written him a dedication in the front. . . ." Glancing at the title page, she suddenly flushed.

"What is it?"

"You know the old saying?" Miranda murmured. "About not judging a book by its cover?"

Chase moved behind her and read over her shoulder. *"One Hundred and One Sexual Positions.* Fully illustrated?"

Miranda flipped open to a random page and instantly flushed. "They meant what they said about fully illustrated."

He reached around her to take the book. His breath grazed her neck; it left her skin tingling.

"Obviously a dummy jacket," said Chase. "I wonder how many other disguised books are in that stack?"

"I didn't really check," Miranda admitted. "I was looking for loose papers. I wasn't paying much attention to the books themselves."

Chase flipped to the title page and read aloud the handwritten dedication. "To my darling Richard. Can we try number forty-eight again? Love, M." Chase glanced at Miranda.

"I didn't give him that thing!" she protested.

"Then who's M?"

"Someone else. Not me."

He frowned at the dedication. "I wonder what number forty-eight is." He flipped to the page.

"Well?"

Chase took a discreet peek. "You don't want to know," he muttered and let the page riffle shut.

A slip of paper flew out and landed on the floor. They both stared at it in surprise. Chase was the first to snatch it up.

"Dearest love," he read aloud. "I'm thinking of you every day, every hour. I've given up caring about propriety or reputation or hellfire. There's only you and me and the time we have together. That, my darling, is my new definition of heaven." Chase glanced at her, one eyebrow raised in a cynical slant.

Miranda looked straight at him. "In case you're wondering," she said evenly, "I didn't write that note, either." In irritation she took the book and set it down on the nearest pile.

"Then I guess we'll just file it under 'interesting stuff,' " said Chase. "And continue with the rest of these books."

Miranda settled onto the rug. Chase sat in front of the other bookcase. They didn't touch, didn't look at each other. *Safer that way,* she thought. *For both of us.*

For half an hour they flipped through books, slapped them shut, threw clouds of dust in the air. Miranda was the one who found the next piece of the puzzle. It was tucked away in a financial ledger, in an envelope labeled Deductible Expenses.

"It's a receipt," she said, frowning at the slip of paper. "A month ago Richard paid four hundred dollars to this company."

"For what services?" asked Chase.

"It doesn't say. It's just made out to the Alamo Detective Agency in Bass Harbor."

"A detective agency? I wonder what Richard was after."

"Chase." She handed him the slip of paper. "Look at the name of the payee."

"William B. Rodell?" He glanced at her quizzically.

At least you're looking at me again, she thought. *At least we're connecting.* "Don't you remember?" she said. "That note attached to Richard's files."

Chase stared at the receipt, revelation suddenly brightening his dark features.

"Of course," he said softly. "William B. Rodell . . ."

W.B.R.

It was easy to see how the Alamo Detective Agency got its name. Willie Rodell was a good ol' boy transplant from San Antonio who split his time between Maine and Florida. Summertime was for Maine, and here he was, sitting behind his old steel desk, books and papers piled up in front of him like the battlements of a fort. The office was strictly a solo affair—one phone, one desk, one man. But what a man. Willie Rodell had enough flesh on his bones to fill the suits of two six-footers. *This must be what they mean by Texas-size,* thought Miranda.

"Yeah, I mighta done some work for Mr. Tremain now and again," said Rodell, leaning back in his equally Texas-size chair.

"Meaning you did or you didn't?" asked Chase.

"Well, you're holdin' one of my receipts there, so I guess it means I did."

"What sort of job?"

Willie shrugged. "Routine stuff."

"What *is* your routine stuff?"

"Mostly I do domestic affairs, if you catch my drift. Who's doin' what to whom, that sorta thing." His smirk rearranged the folds of his face into something vaguely obscene.

"But that's not the sort of thing you did for Richard, was it?"

"Nope. Though I hear tell there was more than enough dirt to dig in his particular case."

Cheeks burning, Miranda stared down fixedly at Willie's desk, a battle zone of broken pencils and twisted paper clips scattered among a bizarre assortment of magazines. *Hot Ladies. National Locksmith. Car and Driver.*

Chase got right to the point. "He hired you to compile files on his neighbors. Didn't he?"

Willie looked at him blandly. "Files?"

"We saw them, Mr. Rodell. They were among Richard's papers. Detailed reports on almost every resident along the access road. Each one containing sensitive information."

"Dirt sheets."

"That's right."

Willie shrugged. "I didn't write 'em."

"There was a note attached to one of the reports. It said, 'Want more? Let me know.' It was signed with the initials W.B.R." Chase reached over and plucked one of Willie's business cards from the desk. "Which just happens to be your initials."

"Helluva coincidence, hey?"

"He wanted dirt on his neighbors. Why?"

"He was snoopy?"

"So he paid you to write those reports."

"I told you, I didn't write 'em." Willie held up one fat hand. "Scout's honor."

"Then who did?"

"Dunno. But I admire his work."

Miranda, who'd been sitting quietly, focused on one of the magazines on the desk. *National Locksmith.* "You stole them," she said. She looked up at Willie's moonlike face. "That's what Richard hired you for. To steal those files from someone else."

Willie reached up and smoothed back a nonexistent strand of hair.

"You were paid to be a burglar," said Miranda. "What else were you paid for?"

"Look," said Willie, holding up both fat hands in a gesture of mock surrender. "Folks pay me to gather info, okay? That's all I do. Clients don't care how I get it, long as I get it."

"And where did you get those dirt sheets?" asked Chase.

"They were part of a bunch o' papers I sorta picked up."

"What else did you sort of pick up?"

"Financial records, bank statements. Hey, I didn't exactly *steal* 'em. I just, well, borrowed 'em for a few minutes. Long enough to run 'em through ol' man Xerox. Then I put 'em right back where I found 'em."

"The office of Stone Coast Trust," said Miranda.

Willie gave her a man-in-the-moon grin. "Betcha you're real good at Twenty Questions."

"So those were Tony Graffam's files," said Chase. "Not Richard's."

"Mr. T. didn't even know they existed till I handed 'em over. Thought for sure he was gonna want more. You know how it is. Get a taste of appetizer, you want the main course. Well, those papers were just the appetizer. I coulda got more."

"Why didn't you?"

"He fired me."

They frowned at him. "What?" said Miranda.

"That's right," said Willie. "Two days after I hand him those papers, he calls and says, thanks, he won't be needin' my services no more and how much do I owe you? That was that."

"Did he say why he fired you?"

"Nope. Just told me to keep it under my hat, and that he wasn't interested in Stone Coast no more."

"When was this?"

"Oh, about a week before he died."

"The same time he told Jill to kill the article," said Miranda. She looked at Chase. "Maybe he saw what Tony Graffam had on him. And decided to drop the whole investigation."

"But I looked over those papers, 'fore I handed 'em over," said Willie. "There wasn't any report on Tremain. Far as I could tell, wasn't nothin' in there to blackmail him with."

"Did you keep copies?"

"Mr. T. took it all. Didn't want loose papers floatin' around." Willie folded his hands behind his neck and stretched. Blots of sweat showed in his cavernous armpits. "Naw, I don't think it was the files. I think someone went and offered him a little, you know, incentive payment to forget the whole thing. So that's what he did."

"But Richard didn't need the money," said Miranda. "They couldn't bribe him."

"Sweetie, you can bribe just about anyone," said Willie, obviously an authority on such matters. "All it takes is the right price. And even a fella as rich as Tremain had his price."

"The lazy man's method of investigative journalism," said Chase. "Hire a thug to steal the evidence."

"I had no idea he'd do such a thing," said Miranda, gazing ahead in quiet disbelief. It was just after noon, a time when Main Street in Bass Harbor should have been bustling with tourists. Today, though, a cold summer drizzle had cooled the ardor of even the most inveterate sightseers. Miranda and Chase, hunched in their jackets, walked alone.

"And I thought it was just talent," she said softly. "The way he could pull a story together. Come up with evidence that surprised everyone. All that time he was paying someone to do the dirty work."

"It was just Richard's way," said Chase. "Meaning the easy way."

She looked at him. His hair, dampened by mist, was a cap of black, unruly waves. He stared straight ahead, his profile unrevealing. "Is that how he was as a boy?" she asked.

"He was good at finding shortcuts. For a few bucks he'd get someone to write his book report. Or help him cram for tests. He even found some idiot to finish his math homework for him." Chase grinned sheepishly. "Me."

"He bribed you into doing his homework?"

"It was more like, well, blackmail."

"What did he have on you?"

"Lots. Broken windows. Trampled flower beds. I was a pretty bad kid."

"But good at math, obviously."

Chase laughed. "When someone threatened exposure, I was good at a lot of things."

"And Richard took advantage of it."

"He was older. In a lot of ways, smarter. Everyone liked him, wanted to believe the best of him. And the worst of me." He shook his head. "I can see the same thing happening with his kids now. Phillip's the golden boy. And Cassie, she'll be trying all her life to match up."

"Will you be trying all *your* life to match up?"

He looked at her, then looked away. "No. I don't particularly care to make the same mistakes Richard did."

Meaning me, she thought.

The day suddenly seemed colder, darker. It was more than just her sagging spirits. The drizzle had turned to rain.

"Let's duck in someplace and get lunch," said Chase. "We've got another hour and a half till the ferry leaves."

They found a café tucked into an alley off Main Street. From the outside it seemed an unassuming little place with a name to match: Mary Jane's. It was the whiff of rich coffee and grilled meat that finally drew them in. Nothing fancy served here, just good plain food, roast chicken and red potatoes and crisp green beans, accompanied by freshly brewed coffee. Miranda's spirits might be sagging, but her appetite was in fine shape. She moved on to a slice of peach pie and a third round of coffee. A good thing she didn't normally react to stress by overeating. By now she'd be twenty pounds overweight.

"In a way," said Chase, "I'm relieved to learn the truth about those files."

"Relieved to learn Richard paid for an out-and-out burglary?"

"At least he wasn't the one snooping on his neighbors. The one planning blackmail."

She set down her fork. "Yes, I suppose you could talk yourself into thinking that breaking into Stone Coast Trust was somehow, well, morally correct."

"I'm not saying it was. But I can see how Richard might justify it. He's seen the coast eaten away by development. Then it hits close to home and he figures it's time to play dirty. Find out what you can about the developer. Steal a few files, financial records. Throw it back in the other guy's face."

"But he didn't. That's the strange part. He paid Rodell to steal those files. Then, after he gets hold of them, he drops the whole crusade. Kills the article, fires Rodell." She paused, and added softly, "And changes his will."

Chase frowned. "I don't see how that's related."

"The timing fits. Maybe he found something in those papers that got him angry at Evelyn. Made him decide to keep her from ever getting Rose Hill."

"You think there was a file on Evelyn? We didn't see one."

"He might've destroyed it. Or it could have been taken from the cottage. After his death."

They both fell silent at the implications of that statement. Who but Evelyn herself would bother to take such a file?

"This is crazy," said Chase. "Why would Evelyn steal it? It was her own damn cottage. She could walk in and out without anyone raising an eyebrow." He reached for his coffee cup, took a deliberate sip. "I can't see her breaking in and trashing the place."

You can't see her killing anyone, either. Can you? she thought. She wondered about Chase and his sister-in-law. Was their relationship merely cordial? Or did it run deeper than that? He'd stubbornly resisted the possibility that Evelyn might be guilty of wrongdoing, be it theft or murder. Miranda could understand why. Evelyn was a beautiful woman.

Now a free woman.

There was, after all, an appealing tidiness to a match between Chase and Evelyn. It would keep the money in the family, the same last name on the checkbook. Everyone would slip into their new roles with a minimum of muss and fuss. Chase had spent his boyhood trying to live up to his brother's image. Now he could slip right into Richard's place. Much as Miranda hated to admit it, such a mating would have a certain symmetry, a social correctness.

Something I'd never be able to give him.

The waitress came by with the check. Miranda reached for it, but Chase snatched it up first. "I'll take care of it," he said.

Miranda took a few bills from her pocket and laid them on the table. "What's that for?" asked Chase.

"Call it pride," she said, rising to her feet, "but I always pay my way."

"With me you don't have to."

"I have to," she said flatly. "Especially with you." She grabbed her jacket and headed out the door.

He caught up with her outside. The rain had stopped but the sun had not yet emerged and the sky was a cold monochrome of gray. They walked side by side for a moment, not quite friends, not quite strangers.

"I'll be honest," he said. "I wasn't planning to see you today. Or ever again."

"It's a small town, Chase. It's hard to avoid a person here."

"I was going to drive back to Greenwich tomorrow."

"Oh." She lowered her eyes, willing herself not to feel disappointment. Or hurt. All those emotions she'd vowed never to feel for another Tremain. The emotions she was feeling now.

"But I've been thinking," he said.

Those four words made her halt and look up at him. *He's watching me, waiting for me to reveal myself. Give myself away as beguiled and bedazzled.*

Which, damn it, I am.

"I've been thinking," he said, "of staying a few more days. Just to clear up those questions about Richard."

She said nothing.

"Anyway, that's why I'm staying in town. It's the only reason."

Her chin came up. "Did I imply otherwise?"

"No." He let out a breath. "No, you didn't."

They walked on, another block, another silence.

"You'll be looking for the same answers, I expect," he said.

"I don't have much choice, do I? It's my future. My freedom."

"Look, I know it makes sense, in a way, for you and I to work together. But it's not exactly . . ."

"Seemly," she finished for him. "That's what you mean, isn't it? That it's embarrassing for you to be consorting with a woman like me."

"I didn't say that."

"Never mind, Chase." In irritation she turned and continued walking. "You're right, of course. We can't work together. Because we don't really trust each other. Do we?"

He didn't answer. He simply walked beside her, his hands thrust deep in his pockets. And that, more than anything he could have said, was what hurt her most.

They might not trust each other. They might not want anything to do with each other. But the simple fact was, if they wanted answers, the cottage was where they both had to look. So when Miranda pulled into the gravel driveway of Rose Hill the next morning she was not surprised to see Chase's car already parked there. Ozzie was sprawled on the front porch, looking dejected. He managed a few halfhearted wags of his tail as she came up the steps, but when he saw she wasn't going to invite him inside he flopped back down into a whimpering imitation of a shag rug.

Miss St. John and Chase had already gone through the second bookcase. The place was looking more and more like a disaster zone, with cardboard boxes filled with papers, books precariously stacked in towers, empty coffee cups and dirty spoons littering the end tables.

"I see you started without me," said Miranda, careful to avoid looking at Chase. He was just as carefully avoiding her gaze. "What have you found?"

"Odds and ends," said Miss St. John, thoughtfully eyeing them both. "Shopping lists, receipts. Another love note from M. And a few quite literate college term papers."

"Phillip's?"

"Cassandra's. She must have done some writing out here. A few of the books are hers, as well."

Miranda picked up a bundle of papers and glanced through the titles. "A political analysis of the Boer conflict." "Doom foretold: the French colonialists in Vietnam." "The media and presidential politics." All were authored by Cassandra Tremain.

"A smart cookie," said Miss St. John. "A pity that slick brother of hers always steals the spotlight."

Miranda dug deeper in the box and pulled out the latest note from M. It was typewritten.

I waited till midnight—you never came. Did you forget? I wanted to call, but I'm always afraid she'll pick up the phone. She has you every weekend, every night, every holiday. I get the dregs.

How can you say you love me, when you leave me here, waiting for you? I'm worth more than this. I really am.

Quietly Miranda let the note flutter back into the box. Then she went to the window and stood staring out, toward the sea. Pity stirred inside her, for the woman who had written that note, for the pain she'd suffered. *The price we both paid for loving the wrong man.*

"Miranda?" Chase asked. "Is something wrong?"

"No." She cleared her throat and turned to him. "I'm fine. So . . . where should I start looking?"

"You could help me finish with this shelf. I'm finding papers here and there, so it's going slower than I expected."

"Yes, of course." She went to the shelf, pulled out a book and sat on the floor beside him. Not too close, not too far. *Neither friends nor enemies,* she thought. Just two people sharing the same rug, the same purpose. *For that, we don't even have to like each other.*

For an hour they flipped through pages, brushed away dust. Most of the books, it seemed, hadn't been opened in ages. There were old postcards dated twenty years earlier, addressed to Chase's mother. There was a hand-scrawled list of bird species sighted at Rose Hill, and a library notice from twelve years before, still stuck in the overdue book. Over the years, so many bits and pieces of the Tremain and Pruitt families had ended up on these shelves. It took time to sort out the vital from the trivial.

An oversize atlas of the state of Maine provided the next clue. Chase pulled it off the shelf and glanced in the front cover. Then he turned and called, "Miss St. John? You ever heard of a place called Hemlock Heights?"

"No. Why?"

"There's a map of it tucked in here." Chase pulled the document out of the atlas and spread it out on the rug. It was a collection of six photocopied pages taped together to form a site map. The pages looked fairly fresh. Property lines had been sketched in, and the lots were labeled by number. At the top was the development's name: Hemlock Heights. "I wonder if Richard was thinking of investing in real estate."

Miss St. John crouched down for a closer look. "Wait. This looks rather familiar. Isn't this our access road? And this lot at the end—lot number one. That's Rose Hill. I recognized that little jag up the mountain."

Chase nodded. "You're right. That's exactly what this is. Here's St. John's Wood. And the stone wall."

"It's the Stone Coast Trust map," said Miranda. "See? Most of the lots are labeled Sold."

"Good heavens," said Miss St. John. "I had no idea so many of the camps have changed hands. There are only four of us who haven't sold out to Tony Graffam."

"What kind of offer did he make for St. John's Wood?" asked Miranda.

"It was a very good price at the time. When I refused to sell he bumped it up even higher. That was a year ago. I couldn't understand why the offer was so generous. You see, this was all conservation land. These old camps were grandfathered in, built before the days of land commissions. The cottages were allowed to stand, but you couldn't develop any of it. From a commercial standpoint the land was worthless. Then suddenly it's all been rezoned for development. And now I'm sitting on a gold mine." She looked at the other unsold lots on the map. "So is old Sulaway. And the hippies in Frenchman's Cottage."

"And Tony Graffam," said Miranda.

"But what if the zoning decision was a sham?" said Chase. "What if there were payoffs? If that fact became public knowledge . . ."

"My guess is, there'd be such protest, the zoning would be reversed," said Miss St. John. "And Mr. Graffam would be the proud owner of a lot of worthless property."

"But it's worthless to him right now, Miss St. John," said Miranda, studying the map. "Graffam needs that access road to get to his lots. And you said the road belongs—belonged—to Richard."

"Yes, we keep coming back to that, don't we?" said Chase softly. "That link between Richard and Stone Coast Trust. The link that refuses to go away. . . ." He stood, clapping the dust from his trousers. "Maybe it's time we paid a visit to our neighbors."

"Which ones?" asked Miranda.

"Sulaway and the hippies. The other two on this road who didn't sell. Let's find out if Graffam put any pressure to bear. Like a blackmail note or two."

"He didn't try to blackmail Miss St. John," pointed out Miranda. "And she didn't sell."

"Ah, but my property's scarcely worth the effort," said Miss St. John. "I'm just a tiny patch off to the side. And as for trying to blackmail me, well, you saw for yourself he doesn't have a thing on me worth mentioning. Not that I wouldn't mind generating a whiff of scandal at my age."

"The others could be more vulnerable," said Chase. "Old Sulaway, for instance. We should at least talk to him."

"A good idea," said Miss St. John. "Since you thought of it, Chase, *you* do it."

Chase laughed. "You are a coward, Miss St. John."

"No, I'm just too old for the aggravation."

Without warning, Chase reached for Miranda's hand and with one smooth motion pulled her up in an arc that almost, but not quite, ended in his arms. She reached out to steady herself and found her palms pressing against his chest. At once she stepped back.

"Is this a request for me to come along?" she said.

"It's more along the lines of a plea. To help me soften up old Sulaway."

"Does he need softening up?"

"Let's just say he hasn't taken kindly to me since I batted a baseball through his window. And that was twenty-five years ago."

Miranda laughed in disbelief. "You sound like you're afraid of him. Both of you."

"Obviously she's never met old Sulaway," said Miss St. John.

"Is there something I should know about him?"

Chase and Miss St. John glanced at each other.

"Just be careful when you walk into his front yard," said Miss St. John. "Give him lots of warning. And be ready to get out of there fast."

"Why? Does he have a dog or something?"

"No. But he does have a shotgun."

10

"You're that boy who broke my window!" yelled Homer Sulaway. "Yeah, I recognize you." He stood on the front porch, his skinny arms looped around a rifle, his lobsterman's dungarees rolled up at the ankles. Chase had told Miranda the man was eighty-five. The toothless, prune-faced apparition on that porch looked about a century older. "You two go on, now! Leave me alone. Can't afford to fix no more broken windows."

"But I paid for it, remember?" said Chase. "Had to mow lawns for six months, but I did pay for it."

"Damn right," said Sully. "Or I'd 'a got it outta your old man's hide."

"Can we talk to you, Mr. Sulaway?"

"What about?"

"Stone Coast Trust. I wanted to know if—"

"Not interested." Sully turned and shuffled back across the porch.

"Mr. Sulaway, I have a young lady here who'd like to ask—"

"Don't have no use for young ladies. Or old ladies, either." The screen door slammed shut behind him.

There was a silence. "Well," muttered Chase. "The old boy's definitely mellowed."

"I think he's afraid," said Miranda. "That's why he's not talking to us."

"Afraid of what?"

"Let's find out." She approached the cottage and called, "Mr. Sulaway? All we want to know is, are they trying to blackmail you? Has Stone Coast threatened you in some way?"

"Those are lies they're spreading!" Sulaway yelled through the screen door. "Vicious lies! Not true, any of it!"

"That's not what Tony Graffam says."

The door flew open and Sully stormed out onto the porch. "What's Graffam got to say about me? What's he tellin' people now?"

"We could stand out here and yell about it. Or we could talk in private. Which do you prefer?"

Sulaway glanced around, as though searching for watchers in the woods. Then he snapped, "Well? You two need an engraved invitation, or what?"

They followed him inside. Sully's kitchen was a dark little space, the windows closed in by trees, every shelf and countertop crammed full with junk and knickknacks. Newspapers were stacked in piles about the floor. The kitchen table was about the only unoccupied surface. They sat around it, in old ladder-back chairs that look dangerously close to collapse.

"Your brother's the one they was really pressurin'," Sully told Chase. "But Richard, he wasn't about to give in, no sir. He tells us, we gotta stick together. Says we can't sell, no matter how many letters they send us, how many lies they tell." Sully shook his head. "Didn't do no good. Just about everybody on this road went and signed on Graffam's dotted line, just like that. And Richard, look what went and happened to him. Hear he got himself poked with a knife."

Miranda saw Chase glance in her direction. Old Sully was so out of touch he didn't realize he was sitting with the very woman accused of plunging that knife into Richard Tremain.

"You said something about a letter," said Chase. "Telling you to sell. Did Graffam send it?"

"Wasn't signed. I hear none of 'em were."

"So Richard got a letter, as well?"

"I figure. So did Barretts down the way. Maybe everyone did. People wouldn't talk about 'em."

"What did the letter say? The one you got?"

"Lies. Mean, wicked lies. . . ."

"And the one they sent Richard?"

Sully shrugged. "I wasn't privy to that."

Miranda glanced around the kitchen with its overflowing shelves. A pack rat, this Mr. Sulaway was. He kept things, junk and treasure both. She said, "Do you still have that letter?"

Sully hunched his shoulders, like a hermit crab about to retreat into its shell. He grunted. "Maybe."

"May we see it?"

"I dunno." He sighed, rubbed his face. "I dunno."

"We know they're lies, Mr. Sulaway. We just want to see what tactics they're using. We have to stop Graffam before he does any more damage."

For a moment Sully sat hunched and silent. Miranda thought he might not have heard what she said. But then he creaked to his feet and shuffled over to the kitchen counter. From the flour canister he pulled out a folded sheet of paper. He handed it to Miranda.

She laid it flat on the table.

"What really happened to Stanley? The Lula M knows. So do we."

Below those cryptic words was a handwritten note, penciled in. "Sell, Sully."

"Who's Stanley?" asked Miranda.

Sully had shrunk into his chair and was staring down at his leathery hands.

"Mr. Sulaway?"

The answer came out in a whisper. "My brother."

"What does that note refer to?"

"It was a long time ago. . . ." Sully wiped his eyes, as though to clear away some mist clouding his vision. "Just an accident," he murmured. "Happens all the time out there. The sea, you can't trust her. Can't turn yer back on her. . . ."

"What happened to Stanley?" asked Miranda gently.

"Got . . . got his boot caught in the trap line. Pulled him clean over the side. Water's cold in December. It'll freeze yer blood. I was aboard the *Sally M,* didn't see it." He turned, stared at the window. The trees outside seemed to close in upon the house, shutting it off from light, from warmth.

They waited.

He said softly. "I was the one found him. Draggin' in the water off *Lula*'s stern. I cut him loose . . . hauled him aboard . . . brought him to port." He shuddered. "That was it. Long time ago, fifty years. Maybe more. . . ."

"And this note?"

"It's a lie, got spread around after . . ."

"After what?"

"After I married Jessie." He paused. "Stanley's wife."

There it is, thought Miranda. The secret. The shame.

"Mr. Sulaway?" asked Chase quietly. "What did they have on Richard?"

Sully shook his head. "Didn't tell me."

"But they did have something?"

"Whatever it was, it didn't make him sell. Had a hard head, your brother. That's what got him in the end."

"Why didn't *you* sell, Mr. Sulaway?" Miranda asked.

The old man turned to her. "Because I won't," he said. She saw in his eyes the look of a man who's been backed into the last corner of his life. "Ain't no way they can scare me. Not now."

"Can't they?"

He shook his head. "I got cancer."

"Do you think he killed his brother?" asked Miranda.

They were walking along the road, through the dappled shade of pine and birch. Chase had his hands in his pockets, a frown on his brow. "What does it matter now, whether he did it or not?"

Yes, what did it matter? she wondered. The old man was about to face his final judgment. Innocent or guilty, he'd already lived fifty years with the consequences.

"It's hard to believe Graffam was able to dig up that story," said Miranda. "He's a newcomer to the island. What he had on Sully was fifty years old. How did Graffam find out about it?"

"Hired investigator?"

"And he used the name 'Sully' in that note. Remember? Only a local person would use that nickname."

"So he had a local informant. Someone with his finger on the island's pulse."

"Or someone in the business of knowing what goes on in this town," she added, thinking of Willie B. Rodell and the Alamo Detective Agency.

They came to a sign that read Harmony House.

"Used to be called Frenchman's Cottage," said Chase. "Until the hippies bought it." Down a rutted road they walked. They heard the tinkle of wind chimes before they saw the cottage. The sound floated through the trees, dancing on the breeze. The chimes were of iridescent glass, sparkling as they swayed from the porch overhang. The cottage door hung wide open.

"Anyone home?" called Chase.

At first only the wind chimes answered. Then, faintly, they heard the sound of laughter, approaching voices. Through the trees they saw them—two men and a woman, walking toward them.

None of the three was wearing a stitch.

The trio, spotting unexpected visitors, didn't seem in the least perturbed. The woman had wild hair generously streaked with gray, and an expression of placid indifference. The two men flanking her were equally shaggy and serene. One of the men, silver haired and weathered, seemed to be the official spokesperson. As his two companions went into the cottage, he came forward with his hand held out in greeting.

"You've found Harmony House," he said. "Or is this just a fortunate accident?"

"It's on purpose," said Chase, shaking the man's hand. "I'm Chase Tremain, Richard's brother. He owned Rose Hill Cottage, up the road."

"Ah, yes. The place with the weird vibes."

"Weird?"

"Vanna feels it whenever she gets close. Disharmonic waves. Tremors of dissonance."

"I must have missed it."

"Meat eaters usually do." The man looked at Miranda. He had pale blue eyes and a gaze that was far too direct for comfort. "Does my natural state bother you?"

"No," she said. "It's just that I'm not used to . . ." Her gaze drifted downward, then snapped back to his face.

The man looked at her as though she were a creature to be pitied. "How far we've fallen from Eden," he said, sighing. He went to the porch railing and grabbed a sarong that had been hanging out to dry. "But the first rule of hospitality," he said, wrapping the cloth around his waist, "is to make your guests comfortable. So we'll just cover the family jewels." He motioned them into the cottage.

Inside, the woman, Vanna, now also draped in a sarong, sat cross-legged beneath a stained glass window. Her eyes were closed; her hands lay palm up on her knees. The other man knelt at a low table, rolling what appeared to be brown rice sushi. Potted plants were everywhere, thick as weeds. They blended right in with the Indonesian hangings, the dangling crystals, the smell of incense. The whole effect was jarred only by the fax machine in the corner.

Their host, who went by the surprisingly mundane name of Fred, poured rose hip tea and offered them carob cookies. They came to Maine every summer, he said, to reconnect with the earth. New York was purgatory, a place with one foot in hell. False people, false values. They worked there only because it kept them in touch with the common folk. Plus, they needed the income. For most of the year they tolerated the sickness of city life, breathing in the toxins, poisoning their bodies with refined sugars. Summers were for cleansing. And that was why they came here, why they left their jobs for two months every year.

"What *are* your jobs?" asked Miranda.

"We own the accounting firm of Nickels, Fay and Bledsoe. I'm Nickels."

"I'm Fay," said the man rolling sushi.

The woman, undoubtedly Bledsoe, continued to meditate in silence.

"So you see," said Fred Nickels, "there is no way we can be persuaded to sell. This land is a connection to our mother."

"Was it hers?" asked Chase.

"Mother Earth owns everything."

Chase cleared his throat. "Oh."

"We refuse to sell. No matter how many of those ridiculous letters they send us—"

Both Miranda and Chase sat up straight. "Letters?" they said simultaneously.

"We three have lived together for fifteen years. Perfect sexual harmony. No jealousy, no friction. All our friends know it. So it would hardly upset us to have our arrangement announced to the world."

"Is that what the letters threatened to do?" asked Miranda.

"Yes. 'Expose your deviant life-style' was the phrase, I think."

"You're not the only ones to get a letter," said Chase. "My hunch is, everyone on this road—everyone who didn't want to sell—got one in the mail."

"Well, they threatened the wrong people here. Deviant life-styles are exactly what we wish to promote. Am I right, friends?"

The man with the sushi looked up and said, "Ho."

"He agrees," said Fred.

"Was the letter signed?" asked Miranda.

"No. It was postmarked Bass Harbor, and it came to our house in New York."

"When?"

"Three, four months ago. It advised us to sell the camp. It didn't say to whom, specifically. But then we got the offer from Mr. Graffam, so I assumed he was behind it. I had Stone Coast Trust checked out. A few inquiries here and there, just to find out what I was dealing with. My sources say there's money involved. Graffam's just a front for a silent investor. My bet is it's organized crime."

"What would they want with Shepherd's Island?" asked Chase.

"New York's getting uncomfortable for 'em. Hotdog D.A.'s and all that. I think they're moving up the coast. And the north shore's just the foothold they'd want. Tourist industry's already booming up here. And look at this place! Ocean. Forest. No crime. Tell me some poor schlump from the city wouldn't pay good money to stay at a resort right here."

"Did you ever meet Graffam?"

"He paid us a visit, to talk land deal. And we told him, in no uncertain terms, to—" Fred stopped, grinned "—fornicate with himself. I'm not sure he knew the meaning of the word."

"What kind of man is he?" asked Miranda.

Fred snorted. "Slick. Dumb. I mean, we're talking *really* stupid. The IQ of an eggplant. What idiot names a development Hemlock Heights? Might as well call it Poison Oak Estates." He shook his head. "I can't believe he got those other suckers to sell." He laughed. "You should meet him, Tremain. Tell me if you don't agree he's a throwback to our paramecium ancestors."

"A paramecium," said the woman, Bledsoe, briefly opening her eyes, "is far more advanced."

"Unfortunately," said Fred, "I'm afraid the rezoning is a fait accompli. Soon we'll be surrounded. Condos here, a Dunkin' Donuts there. The Cape Codification of Shepherd's Island." He paused. "And you know what? *That's* when we'll sell! My God, what a profit! We could buy a whole damn county up in the Allagash."

"The project could still be stopped," said Miranda. "They won't get their hands on Rose Hill. And the zoning could be reversed."

"Not a chance," said Fred. "We're talking tax income here. Conservation land brings in zilch for the island. But a nice little tourist resort? Hey, I'm a CPA. I know the powers of the almighty buck."

"There are people who'll fight it."

"Makes no difference." Fred sniffed appreciatively at his rose hip tea. The edges of his sarong had slipped apart and he sat with thighs naked. Incense smoke wafted about his grizzled head. "They can scream, protest. Lay their bodies before the bulldozers. But it's hopeless. There are things people just can't stop."

"A cynical answer," said Miranda.

"For cynical times."

"Well, they can't buy Rose Hill," said Miranda, rising to her feet. "And if organized crime's behind these purchases, you can bet the island will fight back. People here don't take well to mobsters. They don't take to outsiders, period."

Fred gazed up at her with a smile. "But *you* are an outsider, aren't you, Ms. Wood?"

"I'm not from this island. I came here a year ago."

"Yet they accepted *you.*"

"No, they didn't." Miranda turned toward the door. She stood there for a moment, staring through the screen. Outside, the trees were swaying under a canopy of blue sky. "They never accepted me," she said softly. "And you know what?" She let out a long sigh of resignation. "I've only now come to realize it. They never will."

There was a third car parked in the driveway at Rose Hill.

They saw it as they walked up the last bend of the road—a late-model Saab with a gleaming burgundy finish. A glance through the car window revealed a spotless interior, not even a loose business card or candy wrapper on the leather upholstery.

The screen door squealed open and Miss St. John came out on the porch. "There you are," she said. "We have a visitor. Jill Vickery."

Of course, thought Miranda. Who else would manage to keep such an immaculate car?

Jill was standing amidst all the books, holding a box in her arms. She glanced at Miranda with a look of obvious surprise, but made no comment about her presence. "Sorry to pop in unannounced," she said. "I had to get a few records. Phillip and I are meeting the accountant tomorrow. You know, working out any tax problems for the transfer of the *Herald.*"

Chase frowned. "You found the financial records here?"

"Just last month's worth. I couldn't find them back in the office, so I figured he'd brought them out here to work on. I was right."

"Where were they?" asked Chase. "We've combed all through his files. I never saw them."

"They were upstairs. The nightstand drawer." How she knew where to look was something she didn't bother to explain. She glanced around the front room. "You've certainly torn the place apart. What are you looking for? Hidden treasure?"

"Any and all files on Stone Coast Trust," said Chase.

"Yes, Annie mentioned you were dogging that angle. Personally, I think it's a dead end." Coolly she turned to look at Miranda. "And how are things going for you?" It was merely a polite question, carrying neither warmth nor concern.

"Things are . . . difficult," said Miranda.

"I can imagine. I hear you're staying with Annie these days."

"Only temporarily."

Jill flashed her one of those ironic smiles. "It's rather inconvenient, actually. The trial was going to be Annie's story. And now you're living with her. I'll have to pull her off it. Objective reporting and all."

"No one at the *Herald* could possibly be objective," Chase pointed out.

"I suppose not." Jill shifted the box in her arms. "Well, I'd better be going. Let you get on with your search."

"Ms. Vickery?" called Miss St. John. "I wonder if you could shed some light on an item we found here."

"Yes?"

"It's a note, from someone named M." Miss St. John handed her the slip of paper. "Miranda here didn't write it. Do you know who did?"

Jill read the note without any apparent emotion, not even a twitch of her perfect eyebrow. Miranda thought, *If only I had an ounce of her style, her poise.*

"It's not dated. So . . ." Jill looked up. "I can think of several possibilities. None of them had that particular initial. But M could stand for a nickname. Or just the word *me.*"

"Several possibilities?"

"Yes." Jill glanced uneasily at Miranda. "Richard, he . . . had his attractions. Especially for the female summer interns. There was that one we had last year. Before you were hired, Miranda. Her name was Chloe something or other. Couldn't write worth a damn, but she was good decoration. And she picked up interviews no one else could get, which drove poor Annie up a wall." Jill looked again at the note. "This was typed on a manual typewriter. See? The *e* loop's smudged, key needs to be cleaned. If I remember right, Chloe always worked on an old manual. The only one in the office who couldn't compose on a computer keyboard." She gave the note back to Miss St. John. "It could have been her."

"Whatever happened to Chloe?" asked Chase.

"What you'd expect to happen. Some hot and heavy flirting. A few fireworks. And then, just another broken heart."

Miranda felt her throat tighten, her face flush. None of them was looking directly at her, but she knew she was the focus of their attention, as surely as if they were staring. She went to the window and found herself gripping the curtain, fighting to keep her head erect, her spine straight. Another broken heart. It made her feel like some object on an assembly line, just another stupid, gullible woman. It's what they thought of her.

It's what she thought of herself.

Jill again shifted her box of papers. "I'd better get back to the office or the mice will play." She went to the door then stopped. "Oh, I almost forgot to tell you, Chase. Annie just heard the news."

"What news?" asked Chase.

"Tony Graffam's back in town."

Miranda didn't react. She heard Jill go down the porch steps, heard the Saab's engine roar to life, the tires crunch away across the gravel. She felt Chase and Miss St. John's gaze on her back. They were watching her in silence, an unbearable, pitying silence.

She pushed open the screen door and fled from the cottage.

Halfway across the field Chase caught up to her. He grabbed her arm and pulled her around to face him. "Miranda—"

"Leave me alone!"

"You can't run away from it—"

"If only I could!" she cried. "Jill said it! I'm just another broken heart. Another dumb woman who got exactly what she deserved."

"You didn't deserve it."

"Damn you, Chase, don't feel sorry for me! I can't stand that, either." She broke free and started to turn away. He pulled her back. This time he held on, got a tight grip on each wrist. She found herself staring into his dark, inescapable eyes.

"I don't feel sorry for you," he shot back. "You don't get my pity, Miranda. Because you're too good for it. You've got more going for you than any woman I've met. Okay, you're naive. And gullible. We all start out that way. You've learned from it, fine. You should. You want to kick yourself, and maybe it's well deserved. But don't overdo it. Because I think Richard fell just as hard for you as you fell for him."

"Is that supposed to make me feel better?"

"I'm not trying to make you feel better. I'm just telling you what I think."

"Right." Her laughter was self-mocking. "That I'm one notch above a bimbo?" Again she tried to pull free. Again he held her tight.

"No," he said quietly. "What I'm saying is this. I know you're not the first. I know Richard had a lot of women. I've met a few of them through the years. Some of them were gorgeous. Some of them were talented, even brilliant. But out of all those women—and they were, each and every one of them, exceptional—you're the only one I could see him really falling for."

"Out of all those *gorgeous* women?" She shook her head and laughed. "Why me?"

Quietly he said, "Because you're the one *I'd* fall for."

At once she went still. He stared down at her, his dark hair stirring in the wind, his face awash in sunlight. She heard her own quick breaths, heard her heartbeat pounding in her ears. He released her wrists. She didn't move, even when his arms circled behind her, even as he drew her hard against him. She scarcely had the breath to whimper before he settled his mouth firmly on hers.

At the first touch of his lips she was lost. The sun seemed to spin overhead, a dizzying view of brightness against a field of blue. And then there was only him, all rough edges and shadows, his dark head blotting out the sky, his mouth stealing away her breath. She wavered for an instant between resistance and surrender. Then she found herself reaching up and around his neck, opening her lips to his eager assault, pressing more eagerly against the bite of his teeth. She drank him in, his taste, his warmth. Through the roaring in her ears she heard his low groans of satisfaction and need, ever more need. How quickly she had yielded, how easily she had fallen—the woman mastered first by one brother, and now the other.

The day's unbearable brightness seemed to flood her eyes as she pulled away. Her cheeks were blazing. The buzz of insects in the field and the rustle of grass in the wind were almost lost in the harsh sound of her own breathing.

"I won't be passed around, Chase," she said. "I won't."

Then she turned and stalked across the field. She headed back to the cottage, her feet stirring the perfume of sun-warmed grass. She knew he was following somewhere behind, but this time he made no attempt to catch up. She walked alone, and the brightness of the afternoon, the dancing wildflowers, the floating haze of dandelion fuzz only seemed to emphasize her own wretchedness.

Miss St. John was standing on the porch. With scarcely a nod to the other woman, Miranda walked right past her and into the cottage. Inside, she went straight to the bookcase, grabbed another armful of books from the shelf and sat on the floor. She was single-mindedly flipping through the pages when she heard footsteps come up the porch.

"It's not a good time for an argument, Chase," she heard Miss St. John say.

"I'm not planning to argue."

"You have that look in your eye. For heaven's sake, cool down. Stop. Take a deep breath."

"With all due respect, Miss St. John, you're *not* my mother."

"All right, I'm not your mother!" Miss St. John snapped. As she stomped away down the steps, she muttered, "But I can see when a man sorely needs my advice!"

The screen door slapped shut. Chase stood just inside the threshold, gazing at Miranda. "You took it the wrong way," he said.

Miranda looked up at him. "Did I?"

"What happened between you and Richard is a separate issue. A dead issue. It has nothing to do with you and me."

She snapped the book shut. "It has everything to do with you and me."

"But you make it sound like I'm just—just picking up the affair where he left off."

"Okay, maybe it's not that bald. Maybe you're not even aware you're doing it." She reached for another book and stubbornly focused on the pages as she flipped through it. "But we both know Richard was the golden boy of the family. The one who had it all, inherited everything. You were the Tremain who didn't even get a decent trust fund. Well, if you can't inherit a newspaper or a fortune, at least you can inherit your brother's cast-off mistress. Or, gee, maybe even his wife. Just think. Evelyn wouldn't even have to go to the trouble of changing her last name."

"Are you finished?"

"Definitely."

"Good. Because I don't think I can stand here and listen to that garbage any longer. First of all, I'm not in the least bit interested in my sister-in-law. I never was. When Richard married her, I had to stop myself from sending him my condolences. Second, I don't give a damn who gets the *Herald*. I sure as hell never wanted the job. The paper was Richard's baby, from the start. And third—" He paused and took a deep breath, as though drawing the courage to say what had to be said. "Third," he said quietly, "I'm not a Tremain."

She looked up at him sharply. "What are you saying? You're Richard's brother, aren't you?"

"His half brother."

"You mean . . ." She stared into those Gypsy eyes, saw herself reflected in irises dark as coals.

Chase nodded. "My father knew. I don't think Mother ever told him, exactly. She didn't have to. He could just look at me and see it." He smiled, a bitter, ironic smile. "Funny that I myself never did. All the time I was growing up, I didn't understand why I couldn't match up to Richard. No matter how hard I tried, he was the one who got Dad's attention. My mother tried to make up for it. She was my very best friend, right up until she died. And then it was just the three of us." He sank into a chair and rubbed his forehead, as though trying to massage away the memories.

"When did you learn?" Miranda asked softly. "That he wasn't your father?"

"Not until years later, when Dad was dying. He had one of those cliché deathbed confessions. Only he didn't tell *me*. He told Richard. Even at the very end, Richard was the privileged one." Wearily Chase leaned back, his head pressed against the cushions, his gaze focused on the ceiling. "Later they read the will. I couldn't understand why I'd been essentially cut out. Oh, he left me enough to get me started in business. But that was it. I thought it had to do with my marriage, the fact Dad had opposed it from the start. I was hurt, but I accepted it. My wife didn't. She got in a shouting match with Richard, started yelling that it wasn't fair. Richard lost his cool and let it all out. The big secret. The fact his brother was a bastard."

"Is that when you left the island?"

He nodded. "I came back once or twice, to humor my wife. After we got divorced it seemed like my last link to this place had been cut. So I stayed away. Until now."

They fell silent. He seemed lost in bad memories, old hurts. *No wonder I could never find any hint of Richard in his face,* she thought. *He's not a Tremain at all. He's his own man, the sort of man Richard could never be.*

The sort of man I could love.

He felt her studying him, sensed she was reaching out to him. Abruptly he rose to his feet and moved with studied indifference toward the screen door. There he stood looking out at the field. "Maybe you were right," he said.

"About what?"

"That what happened between you and Richard is still hanging over us."

"And if it is?"

"Then this is a mistake. You, me. It's the wrong reason to get involved."

She looked down, unwilling to reveal, even to the stiffly turned back, the hurt in her eyes. "Then we shouldn't, should we?" she murmured.

"No." He turned to face her. She found her gaze drawn, almost against her will, to meet his. "The truth is, Miranda, we have too many reasons not to. What's happened between us has been . . ." He shrugged. "It was an attraction, that's all."

That's all. Nothing, really, in the larger context of life. Not something you risked your heart on.

"Still . . ." he said.

"Yes?" She looked up with a sudden, insane leap of hope.

"We can't walk away from each other. Not with all that's happened. Richard's death. The fire." He gestured about the book-strewn room. "And this."

"You don't trust me. Yet you want my help?"

"You're the only one with stakes high enough to see this through."

She gave a tired laugh. "You got that part right." She wrapped her arms around herself. "So, what comes next?"

"I'll go have a talk with Tony Graffam."

"Shall I come?"

"No. I want to check him out on my own. In the meantime, you can finish up here. There's still the upstairs."

Miranda gazed around the room, at the dusty piles of books, the stacks of papers, and she shook her head. "If I just knew what I was looking for. What the burglar was looking for."

"I have a hunch it's still here somewhere."

"Whatever *it* is."

Turning, Chase pushed open the door. "When you find it, you'll know."

11

Fred Nickels had said Tony Graffam was slick and dumb. He was right on both counts. Graffam wore a silk suit, a tie in blinding red paisley and a gold pinkie ring. The office, like the man, was all flash, little substance: plush carpet, spanking new leather chairs, but no secretary, no books on the shelves, no papers on the desk. The wall had only one decoration—a map of the north shore of Shepherd's Island. It was not labeled as such, but Chase needed only a glance at the broad, curving bay to recognize the coastline.

"I tell you, it's a witch-hunt!" Graffam complained. "First the police, now you." He stayed behind his desk, refusing to emerge even to shake hands, as though clinging to the polished barrier for protection. In agitation he slid his fingers through his tightly permed hair. "You think I'd go and waste someone? Just like that? And for what, a piece of property? Do I look dumb?"

Chase politely declined to answer that question. He said, "You were pressing an offer for Rose Hill Cottage, weren't you?"

"Well, of course. It's the prime lot up there."

"And my brother refused to sell."

"Look, I'm sorry about your brother. Tragedy, a real tragedy. Not that he and I were on good terms, you understand. I couldn't deal with him. He had a closed mind when it came to the project. I mean, he actually went and got hostile. I don't know why. It's only business, right?"

"But I was under the impression this wasn't a business deal, at all. Stone Coast Trust is billed as a conservation project."

"And that's exactly what it is. I offered your brother top dollar for that land, more than Nature Conservancy would've paid. Plus, he would've retained lifetime use of the family cottage. An incredible deal."

"Incredible."

"With the addition of Rose Hill, we could extend the park all the way back to the hillside. It would add elevation. Views. Access."

"Access?"

"For maintenance, of course. You know, for the hiking trails. Decent footpaths, so everyone could enjoy a taste of nature. Even the handicapped. I mean, mobility impaired."

"You thought of everything."

Graffam smiled. "Yes. We did."

"Where does Hemlock Heights come in?"

Graffam paused. "Excuse me?"

"Hemlock Heights. That is, I believe, the name of your planned development."

"Well, nothing was *planned*—"

"Then why did you apply for rezoning? And how much did you pay to bribe the land commission?"

Graffam's face had gone rigid. "Let me repeat myself, Mr. Tremain. Stone Coast Trust was formed to protect the north shore. I admit, we might have to develop a parcel here and there, just to maintain the trust. But sometimes we have to compromise. We have to do things we'd rather not."

"Does that include blackmail?"

Graffam sat up sharply. "What?"

"I'm talking about Fred Nickels. And Homer Sulaway. The names should be familiar to you."

"Yes, of course. Two of the property owners. They declined my offer."

"Someone sent them nasty letters, telling them to sell."

"You think I sent them?"

"Who else? Four people turned you down. Two of them got threatening letters. And a third—my brother—winds up dead."

"That's what you're leading up to, isn't it? Trying to make it look like I had something to do with his death."

"Is that what I said?"

"Look, I've taken enough heat on this deal. A year of putting up with this—this small-town crap. I've turned handsprings to make this project work, but I'm not going to be his fall guy."

Chase stared at Graffam in confusion. What was the man babbling about? Whose fall guy?

"I was out of state when it happened. I have witnesses who'll swear to that."

"Who are you working for?" Chase cut in.

Graffam's jaw suddenly snapped shut. Slowly he sat back, his expression hardening to stone.

"So you have a backer," said Chase. "Someone who's put up the money. Someone who's doing the dirty work. Who are you fronting for? The mob?"

Graffam said nothing.

"You're scared, Graffam. I can tell."

"I don't have to answer any of your questions."

Chase pressed the attack. "My brother was set to blow the whistle on Stone Coast, wasn't he? So you sent him one of your threatening letters. But then you found out he couldn't be blackmailed. Or bought off. So what did you do? Pay someone to take care of the problem?"

"Meaning murder?" Graffam burst out laughing. "Come on, Tremain. A broad killed him. We both know that. Dangerous creatures, broads. Tick 'em off and they get ideas. They see red, grab a kitchen knife and that's it. Even the cops agree. It was a broad. She had the motive."

"And you had a lot of money to lose. So did your backer. Richard already had his hands on your account numbers. He traced your invisible partner. He could have exposed the deal—"

"But he didn't. He killed the article, remember? I had it on good authority it was gonna stay dead. So why should we go after him?"

Chase fell silent. That's what Jill had said, that Richard was the one who'd canceled the article, called off the crusade. It was the one detail that didn't make sense. Why had Richard backed down?

Did he back down? Or had Jill Vickery lied?

He brooded over that last possibility as he left Graffam's office and walked to the car. What did he know about Jill, really? Only that she'd been with the *Herald* for five years, that she kept it running smoothly. That she was bright, stylish and underpaid. She could land a better job anywhere on the East Coast. Why had she chosen to stay with this Podunk paper and work for slave wages?

He'd planned to return at once to Rose Hill Cottage. Instead, he drove to the *Herald*.

He found the office manned only by a skeleton crew: the summer intern, tapping at a computer keyboard, and the layout tech, stooped over a drawing table. Chase walked past them, into Richard's office, and went straight to the file cabinet.

He found Jill Vickery's employment file right where it should be. He sat at the desk and opened the folder.

Inside was a neatly typed résumé, three pages, all the right names and jobs. B.A., Bowdoin, 1977. Masters, Columbia, 1979. Stints on the city desk, *San Francisco Chronicle;* then obits, *San Diego Union;* police beat, *San Jose Times;* op-ed editor, *Portland Press Herald.* A solid résumé.

So why does she end up here?

Something about that résumé bothered him. Something that didn't seem quite right. It was enough to make him reach for the phone and dial the *Portland Press Herald,* her previous employer. He spoke to the current op-ed editor, a woman who vaguely recalled a Jill Vickery. It had been a while back, though.

Chase next called the *San Jose Times.* This time there was some uncertainty, a lot of yelling around the city room, asking if anyone remembered a reporter named Jill Vickery from seven years before. Someone yelled, wasn't there a Jill on the police beat years back? That was good enough for Chase. He hung up and considered letting it drop.

Still, that résumé. What was it that bothered him?

The obits. *San Diego Union.* That didn't make sense. Obits was the coal mine equivalent of the newspaper business. You worked your way up from there. Why had she gone from the city desk in San Francisco to a bottom-of-the-barrel position?

He dialed the *San Diego Union.* No one named Jill Vickery had ever worked there.

Ditto for San Francisco.

Half the résumé was a fraud. Was it just a case of padding a thin work history? And what was she doing during those eight years between college and her job with the *San Jose Times?*

Once again he reached for the phone. This time he called Columbia University, Department of Journalism. In any given year, how many students could possibly graduate with a master's degree? And how many of these students would have the first name Jill?

There was only one in 1979, they told him. But it wasn't a Jill Vickery who'd graduated. It was a Jill Westcott.

Once again, he called the *San Diego Union.* This time he asked about a Jill Westcott. This time they remembered the name. We'll fax you the article, they said.

A few minutes later it slid out of the fax machine, sharp and clear.

A photo of Jill Westcott, now named Jill Vickery. And with it was a tale of cold-blooded murder.

*   *   *

Miranda sat in the fading light of day and stared listlessly at her surroundings. She'd spent the afternoon rummaging through the bathroom and two bedrooms. Now she was hot, dusty and discouraged. Nothing of substance had turned up, only innocuous bits of paper—store receipts, a ten-year-old postcard from Spain, another typewritten note from M.

. . . I am not the weak little nothing I used to be. I can live without you quite nicely, and I intend to do so. I don't need your pity. I am not like the others, those women with minds the size of walnut shells. What I want to know, what I don't understand, is what attracts you to creatures like that? Is it the jiggling flesh? The cow-eyed worship? Well, it doesn't mean a thing. It's empty devotion. Without your money, you wouldn't rate a second glance from those bimbos. I'm the only one who doesn't give a damn how much you have in the bank. And now you've lost me.

The bitterness, the pain of that letter seemed to rub off on her own mood. She put it back in the drawer, buried it among the silky underclothes. Another woman's lingerie. Another woman's anguish.

By the time she'd straightened up the room again the afternoon had slid toward twilight. She didn't turn on the lamp. It was soothing, the veil of semidarkness, the chirp of crickets through the open window. From the field came that indefinable scent of evening—the mist from the sea, the cooling grasses. She went to a chair by the window, sat down and leaned her head back to rest. So many doubts, so many worries weighed upon her. Always, looming over every tentative moment of joy, was that threat of prison. There were times, during these past few days of freedom, that she had almost been able to push the thought from mind. But in the moments like this, when the silence was deep and she was alone in her fears, the image of prison bars seemed to close around her. *How many years will they keep me? Ten, twenty, a lifetime?*

I would rather die.

She shuddered back to alertness.

Downstairs, the screen door had softly squealed open.

"Chase?" she called. "Is that you?" There was silence. She rose from the chair and went to the top of the stairs. "Chase?"

She heard the screen door softly tap shut, then there was nothing, only the distant chirp of crickets from the fields.

Her first instinct was to reach for the light switch. Just in time she stopped herself. Darkness was her friend. It would hide her, protect her.

She shrank away from the stairs. Trembling, she stood with her back pressed against the wall and listened. No new sounds drifted up from the first floor. All she heard was the hammering of her own heartbeat. Her palms were slick. Every nerve ending was scraped raw with fear.

There it was—a footstep. In the kitchen. An image shot through her mind. The cabinets, the drawers. The knives.

Her breath was coming in tight gasps. She shrank farther from the stairs, her thoughts flying frantically toward escape. Two upstairs bedrooms, plus a bathroom. And screens on all the windows. Could she make it through in time?

From below came more footsteps. The intruder had moved out of the kitchen. He was approaching the stairs.

Miranda fled into the master bedroom. Darkness obscured her path; she collided with a nightstand. A lamp wobbled, fell over. The clatter as it crashed to the floor was all the intruder needed to direct him toward this bedroom.

In panic she dashed to the window. Through the darkness she saw a portion of gently sloping roof. From there it would be a twenty-foot drop to the ground. The sash was already up. Only the screen stood between her and freedom. She shoved at it—and it refused to push free. Only then did she see that the screen had been nailed to the window frame.

Frantic now, she began to kick at the steel mesh, sobbing as each blow met resistance. Again and again she kicked, and each time the wire sagged outward, but held.

A footstep creaked on the stairway.

She aimed a last desperate kick at the mesh.

The window frame splintered, and the whole screen fell away and thudded to the ground. At once she scrambled over the sill and dropped down onto the ledge of roof. There she hesitated, torn between the solid comfort of shingles beneath her feet and the free-fall of escape. She couldn't see what lay directly below. The rosebushes? She grabbed hold of the roof and lowered her body over the edge. For a few seconds she clung there, steeling herself for the impact.

She let go.

The night air rushed up at her. The fall seemed endless, a hurtling downward through space and darkness.

Her feet slammed into the ground. Instantly her legs buckled, and she fell sprawling to the gravel. For a moment she lay there as the sky whirled overhead like a kaleidoscope of stars. A frantic burst of adrenaline had masked all the sensation of pain. Her legs could be shattered. She wouldn't have felt it. She knew only that she had to escape, had to run.

She staggered to her feet and began to stumble down the road. She rounded the bend of the driveway—

And was instantly blinded by a pair of headlights leaping at her from the darkness. Instinctively she raised her arms to shield her eyes against the onslaught. She heard the car's brakes lock, heard gravel fly under the skidding tires. The door swung open.

"Miranda?"

With a sob of joy she stumbled forward into Chase's arms. "It's you," she cried. "Thank God it's you."

"What is it?" he whispered, pulling her close against him. "Miranda, what's happened?"

She clung to the solid anchor of his chest. "He's there—in the cottage—"

"Who?"

Suddenly, through the darkness, they both heard it: the slam of the back door, the thrash of running footsteps through the brush.

"Get in the car!" ordered Chase, "Lock the doors!"

"What?"

He gave her a push. "Just do it!"

"Chase!" she yelled.

"I'll be back!"

Stunned, she watched him melt into the night, heard his footsteps thud away. Her instinct was to follow him, to stay close in case he needed her. But already she'd lost sight of him and could make out nothing but the towering shadows of trees against the starry sky, and beneath them, a darkness so thick it seemed impenetrable.

Do what he says!

She climbed into the car, locked the doors and felt instantly useless. While she sat here in safety Chase could be fighting for his life.

And what good will I do him?

She pushed open the door and scrambled out of the car, around to the rear.

In the trunk she found a tire iron. It felt heavy and solid in her grasp. It would even the odds against any opponent. Any unarmed opponent, she was forced to amend.

She turned, faced the forest. It loomed before her, a wall of shadow and formless threat.

Somewhere in that darkness Chase was in danger.

She gripped the tire iron more tightly and started off into the night.

*   *   *

The crash of footsteps, through the underbrush alerted Chase that his quarry had shifted direction. Chase veered right, in pursuit of the sound. Branches thrashed his face, bushes clawed at his trousers. The darkness was so dense under the trees that he felt like a blind man stumbling through a landscape of booby traps.

At least his quarry would be just as blind. *But maybe not as helpless,* he thought, ducking under a pine branch. *What if he's armed? What if I'm being led into a trap?*

It's a risk I have to take.

The footsteps moved to the left of him. By slivers of starlight filtering through the trees Chase caught a glimpse of movement. That was all he could make out, shadow moving through shadow. Heedless of the branches whipping his face he plunged ahead and found himself snagged in brambles. The shadow zigzagged, flitting in and out of the cover of trees. Chase pulled free of the thicket and resumed his pursuit. He was gaining. He could hear, through the pounding of his heart, the hard breathing of his quarry. The shadow was just ahead, just beyond the next curtain of branches.

Chase mustered a last burst of speed and broke through, into a clearing. There he came to a halt.

His quarry had vanished. There was no movement, no sound, only the whisper of wind through the treetops. A flutter of shadow off to his right made him whirl around. Nothing there. He halted in confusion as he heard the crackle of underbrush to his left. He turned, listening for footsteps, trying to locate his quarry. Was that breathing, somewhere close by? No, the wind . . .

Again, that crackle of twigs. He moved forward, one step, then another.

Too late he felt the rush of air, the hiss of the branch as it swung its arc toward his head.

The blow pitched him forward. He reached out to cushion the fall, felt the bite of pine needles, the slap of wet leaves as he scraped across the forest floor. He tried to cling to consciousness, to order his body to rise to its feet and face the enemy. It refused to obey. Already he saw the darkness thicken before his eyes. He wanted to curse, to rail in fury at his own helplessness. But all he could manage was a groan.

Pain. The pounding of a jackhammer in his head. Chase ordered it to stop, demanded it stop, but it kept beating away at his brain.

"He's coming around," said a voice.

Then another voice, softer, fearful. "Chase? Chase?"

He opened his eyes and saw Miranda gazing down at him. The lamp-light shimmered in her tumbled hair, washed like liquid gold across her cheek. Just the sight of her seemed to quiet the aching in his head. He struggled to remember where he was, how he had gotten there. An image of darkness, the shadow of trees, still lingered.

Abruptly he tried to sit up, and caught a spinning view of other people, other faces in the room.

"No," said Miranda. "Don't move. Just lie still."

"Someone—someone out there—"

"He's gone. We've already searched the woods," said Lorne Tibbetts.

Chase settled back on the couch. He knew where he was now. Miss St. John's cottage. He recognized the chintz fabric, the jungle of plants. And the dog. The panting black mop sat near one end of the couch, watching him. Or was it? With all that hair, who could say if the beast even had eyes? Slowly Chase's gaze shifted to the others in the room. Lorne. Ellis. Miss St. John. And Dr. Steiner, wielding his trusty penlight.

"Pupils look fine. Equal and reactive," said Dr. Steiner.

"Take that blasted thing away," Chase groaned, batting at the penlight.

Dr. Steiner snorted. "Can't do much damage to a head as hard as his." He set a bottle of pills on the end table. "For the headache. May make you a little drowsy, but it'll cut the pain." He snapped his bag shut and headed for the door. "Call me in the morning. But not too early. And may I remind you—all of you—I do not, repeat, do *not* make house calls!" The door slammed shut behind him.

"What wonderful bedside manner," moaned Chase.

"You remember anything?" asked Lorne.

Chase managed to sit up. The effort sent a bolt of pain into his skull. At once he dropped his head into his hands.

"Not a damn thing," he mumbled.

"Didn't see his face?"

"Just a shadow."

Lorne paused. "You sure there was someone there?"

"Hey, I didn't imagine the headache." Chase grabbed the pill bottle, fumbled the cap off and gulped two tablets down, dry. "Someone hit me."

"A man? Woman?" pressed Lorne.

"I never saw him. Her. Whatever."

Lorne turned to Miranda. "He was unconscious when you found him?"

"Coming around. I heard his groans."

"Pardon me for asking, Ms. Wood. But can I see that tire iron you were carrying?"

"What?"

"The tire iron. You had it earlier."

Miss St. John sighed. "Don't be ridiculous, Lorne."

"I'm just being thorough. I have to look at it."

Without a word Miranda fetched the tire iron from the porch and brought it back to Lorne. "No blood, no hair," she said tightly. "I wasn't the one who hit him."

"No, I guess not," said Lorne.

"Jill Vickery," Chase muttered.

Lorne glanced at him. "Who?"

The pain in Chase's head suddenly gave way to a clear memory of that afternoon. "It's not her real name. Check with the San Diego police, Lorne. It may or may not tie in. But you'll find she has an arrest record."

"For what?"

Chase raised his head. "She killed her lover."

They all stared at him.

"*Jill?*" said Miranda. "When did you find this out?"

"This afternoon. It happened ten, eleven years ago. She was acquitted. Justifiable homicide. She claimed he'd threatened her life."

"How does this fit in with anything else?" asked Lorne.

"I'm not sure. All I know is, half her job résumé was pure fiction. Maybe Richard found out. If he did—and confronted her . . ."

Lorne turned to Miss St. John. "I need to use your telephone."

"In the kitchen."

Lorne spent only a few minutes on the phone. He emerged from the kitchen shaking his head. "Jill Vickery's at home. Says she was home all evening."

"It's only a half-hour drive to town," said Miss St. John. "She could have made it, barely."

"Assuming her car was right nearby. Assuming she could slip right behind the wheel and take off." He looked at Ellis. "You checked up and down the road?"

Ellis nodded. "No strange cars. No one saw nothin'."

"Well," said Lorne, "whoever it was, I don't think he'll be back." He reached for his hat. "Take my advice, Chase. Don't drive anywhere tonight. You're in no shape to get behind a wheel."

Chase gave a tired laugh. "I wasn't planning to."

"I can take him up to the cottage," said Miranda. "I'll keep an eye on him."

Lorne paused and looked first at Miranda, then at Chase. If he had doubts about the arrangement, he didn't express them. He simply said, "You do that, Ms. Wood. You keep a *good* eye on him." Motioning to Ellis, he opened the door. "We'll be in touch."

12

Light spilled from the hallway across the pine floor of the bedroom. Miranda pulled down the coverlet and said, "Come on, lie down. Doctor's orders."

"To hell with doctors. That doctor, anyway," growled Chase. He sat on the side of the bed and gave his head a shake, as though to clear it. "I'm okay. I feel fine."

She regarded his battered, unshaven face. "You look like a truck ran over you."

"The brutal truth!" He laughed. "Are you always so damn honest?"

There was a silence. "Yes," she said quietly. "As a matter of fact, I am."

He looked up at her. *What do you see in my eyes?* she wondered. *Sincerity? Or lies, bald, dangerous lies?*

It's still not there, is it? Trust. There'll always be that doubt between us.

She sat beside him on the bed. "Tell me everything you learned today. About Jill."

"Only what I read in the press file from San Diego." He reached down and began to pull off his shoes. "The trial got a fair amount of coverage. You know, sex, violence. Circulation boosters."

"What happened?"

"The defense claimed she was an emotionally battered woman. That she was young, naive, vulnerable. That her boyfriend was an abusive alcoholic who regularly beat her up. The jury believed it."

"What did the prosecution say?"

"That Jill had a lifelong hatred of men. That she used them, manipulated them. And when her lover tried to leave her, she flew into a rage.

Both sides agreed on the facts of the killing. That while her lover was passed out drunk she picked up a gun, put it to his head and pulled the trigger." Exhausted, Chase lay back on the pillows. The pills were taking effect. His eyelids were already drifting shut. "That was ten years ago," he said. "An era Jill conveniently left behind when she came to Maine."

"Did Richard know all this?"

"If he bothered to check, he did. Only the last half of her résumé was true. Richard may have been so dazzled by the whole package he didn't bother to confirm much beyond the last job or two. Or he may have found out the truth only recently. Who knows?"

Miranda sat thinking, trying to picture Jill as she must have been ten years ago. Young, vulnerable. Afraid.

Like me.

Or was the prosecution's description a more accurate image? A man hater, a woman of twisted passions?

That's how they'll try to portray me. As a killer. And some people will believe it.

Chase had fallen asleep.

For a moment she sat beside him, listening to his slow and even breaths, wondering if he could ever learn to trust her. If she could ever be more to him than just a piece of the puzzle—the puzzle of his brother's death.

She rose and pulled the coverlet over his sleeping form. He didn't move. Gently she smoothed back his hair, stroked the beard-roughened cheek. Still he didn't move.

She left him and went downstairs. The boxes of papers confronted her, other bits and pieces of that puzzle. She separated them into files. Article files. Financial records. Personal notes from M, as well as from other, unidentified women. The miscellaneous debris of a man's life. How little she had known Richard! What a vast part of him he had kept private, even from his family. That's why he had so jealously guarded this north shore retreat.

In the fabric of his life, I was just a single, unimportant thread. Will I ever stop hurting from that?

She rose and checked the doors, the windows. Then she went back upstairs, to the master bedroom.

Chase was still asleep. She knew she should use the other room, the other bed, but tonight she didn't want to lie alone in the darkness. She wanted warmth and safety and the comfort of knowing Chase was nearby.

She had promised to look after him tonight. What better place to watch over him than in the same bed?

She lay down beside him, not close but near enough to imagine his warmth seeping toward her through the sheets.

Sometime during the night the dreams came.

A man, a lover, was holding her. Protecting her. Then she looked up at his face and saw he was a stranger. She pulled away, began to run. She found she was in a crowd of people. She began to search for a familiar face, a pair of arms she could reach out to, but they were all strangers, all strangers.

And then there he was, standing far beyond her reach. She cried out to him, held her hands out for him to grab. He moved toward her and her hands connected with warm and solid flesh. She heard him say, "I'm here, Miranda. Right here. . . ."

And he was.

Through the semidarkness she saw the gleam of his face, the twin shadows of his eyes. His gaze was so still, so very quiet. Her breath caught as he took her face in his hands. Slowly he pressed his lips to hers. That one touch sent a shudder of pleasure through her body. They stared at each other and the night seemed filled with the sounds of their breathing.

Again, he kissed her.

Again, that wave of pleasure. It crested to a wanting for more, more. Her sleep-drugged body awoke, alive with hunger. She pressed hard against him, willing their bodies to meld, their warmth to mingle, but that frustrating barrier of clothes still lay between them.

He reached for her T-shirt. Slowly he pulled it up and over her head, let it drop from the bed. She was not so patient. Already she was undoing his buttons, sliding back his shirt, fumbling at his belt buckle. No words were spoken; none were needed. The soft whispers, the whimpers, the moans said more than any words could have.

So did his hands. His fingers slid across, between, inside all the warm and secret places of her body. They teased her, inflamed her, brought her to the very edge of release. Then, with knowing cruelty, they abandoned her, leaving her unsatisfied. She reached out to him, silently pleading for more.

He grasped her hips and willingly thrust into her again, but this time not with his fingers.

She cried out, a sound of joy, of delight.

At the first ripple of her climax he let his own needs take over. Needs that made him drive deep inside her, again and again. As her last wave of pleasure washed through her, he found his own cresting, breaking. He rode it to the very end and collapsed, sweating and triumphant, into her welcoming arms.

And so they fell asleep.

Chase was the first to awaken. He found his arms looped around her, his face buried in the sweet-smelling strands of her hair. She was curled up on her side, facing away from him, the silky skin of her back pressed against his chest. The memory of their lovemaking was at once so vivid he felt his body respond with automatic desire. And why not, with this woman in his arms? She was life and lust and honeyed warmth. She was everything a woman should be.

And I'm treading on dangerous ground.

He pulled away and sat up. Morning light shone through the window, onto her pillow. So innocent she looked, so untouched by evil. It occurred to him that Jill Vickery once must have looked as pure.

Before she shot her lover.

Dangerous women. How could you tell them from the innocents?

He left the bed and went straight to the shower. Wash the magical spell away, he thought. Wash away the desire, the craving for Miranda Wood. She was like a sickness in his blood, making him do insane things.

Last night, for instance.

They had simply fallen into it, he told himself. A physical act, that was all, a chance collision of two warm bodies.

He watched her sleep as he dressed. With each layer of clothes he felt more protected, more invulnerable. But when she stirred and opened her eyes and smiled at him, he realized how thin his emotional armor really was.

"How are you feeling this morning?" she asked softly.

"Much better, thanks. I think I can drive myself back to town."

There was a silence. Her smile faded as she took in the fact he was already dressed. "You're leaving?"

"Yes. I just wanted to make sure you got out of here safely."

She sat up. Hugging the sheets to her chest, she watched him for a moment, as though trying to understand what had gone wrong between them. At last she said, "I'll be fine. You don't have to wait around."

"I'll stay. Until you get dressed."

A shrug was her response, as if it didn't matter to her one way or the other. *Good,* he thought. *No sticky emotions over last night. We're both too smart for that.*

He started to leave, then stopped. "Miranda?"

"Yes?"

He turned to look at her. She was still hugging her knees, still every bit as bewitching. To see her there could break any man's heart. He said, "It's not that I don't think you're a wonderful woman. It's just that . . ."

"Don't worry about it, Chase," she said flatly. "We both know it won't work."

He wanted to say, "I'm sorry," but somehow it seemed too lame, too easy. They were both adults. They had both made a mistake.

There was nothing more to be said.

"It's not as if any of this is incriminating," said Annie, flipping through the notes from M that were arrayed on her kitchen table. "Just your routine desperate-woman language. Darling. If you'd only see me. If only this, if only that. It's pathetic, but it's not murderous. It doesn't tell us that M—whoever she is—killed him."

"You're right." Miranda sighed, leaning back in the kitchen chair. "And it doesn't seem to tie in with Jill at all."

"Sorry. The only M around here is you. I'd say these letters could cause you more damage than good."

"Jill said there was a summer intern a year ago. A woman who got involved with Richard."

"Chloe? Ancient history. I can't imagine she'd sneak back to town just to kill an ex-lover. Besides, there's no M in her name."

"The M could stand for a nickname. A name only Richard used for her."

"Muffin? Marvelous?" Laughing, Annie rose to her feet. "I think we're beating a dead horse. And I'm going to be late." She went to the closet and pulled out a warm-up jacket. "Irving hates to be kept waiting."

Miranda glanced with amusement at Annie's attire: a torn T-shirt, scruffy running shoes and sweatpants. "Irving likes the casual look?"

"Irving *is* the casual look." Annie slung her purse over her shoulder. "We're sanding the deck this week. Loads of fun."

"Will I ever get to meet this boat bum of yours?"

Annie grinned. "Soon as I can drag him to shore. I mean, the yachting season's gotta end one of these days." She waved. "See ya."

After Annie had left, Miranda scrounged together a salad and sat down at the kitchen table for a melancholy dinner. Irving and his boat didn't sound like much in the way of companionship, but at least Annie had someone to keep her company. Someone to keep away the loneliness.

Once, Miranda hadn't minded being alone. She'd even enjoyed the silence, the peace of a house all to herself. Now she craved the simple presence of another human being. Even a dog would be nice. She'd have to think about getting one, a large one. A dog wouldn't desert her the way most of her friends had. The way Chase had.

She set down her fork, her appetite instantly gone. Where was he now? Probably sitting in that house on Chestnut Street, surrounded by all the other Tremains. He'd have Evelyn and the twins to keep him company. He wouldn't be alone or lonely. He would be just fine without her.

In anger she rose to her feet and slid the remains of her salad into the trash. Then she started for the door, determined to get outside, to run around the block, anything to escape the house.

At the front door she halted. A visitor stood on the porch, hand poised to ring the bell.

"Jill," whispered Miranda.

This was not the cool, unflappable Jill she knew. This Jill was white-faced and brittle.

"Annie's not here right now," said Miranda. "She . . . should be back any minute."

"You're the one I came to see." Without warning Jill slipped right past into the living room and shut the door behind her.

"I—I was just on my way out." Miranda edged slowly for the door.

Jill took a sidestep, blocking her way. For a moment she stood there, regarding Miranda. "It's not as if I haven't been punished," she said softly. "I've done everything I could to put it behind me. Everything. I've worked like a madwoman these last five years. Built the *Herald* into a real newspaper. You think Richard knew what he was doing? Of course not! He relied on me. *Me.* Oh, he never admitted it, but he let me run the show. Five years. And now you've ruined it for me. You've already got the police shoveling up old dirt. You think the Tremains will keep me on? Now that they know? Now that everyone knows?"

"I wasn't the one. I didn't tell Lorne."

"You're the reason it's all come up! You and your pathetic denials! Why don't you just admit you killed him? And leave the rest of us out of it."

"But I didn't kill him."

Jill began to pace the room. "I've sinned, you've sinned. Everyone has. We're all equal. What sets us apart is how we live with our sins. I've done the best I could. And now I find it's not good enough. Not good enough to erase what happened. . . ."

"Did Richard know? About San Diego?"

"No. I mean, yes, in the end. He found out. But it didn't matter to him—"

"It didn't matter that you killed a man?"

"He understood the circumstances. Richard was good that way." She let out a shaky laugh. "After all, he himself wasn't above a little sinning."

Miranda paused, gathered the courage for her next question. "You had an affair with him, didn't you?"

Jill's response was a careless shrug. "It didn't mean anything. It was years ago. You know, the new girl on the block. He got over it." She snapped her fingers. "Just like that. We stayed friends. We understood each other." She stopped pacing and turned to look at Miranda. "Now Lorne wants to know where I was the night Richard was killed. He's asking *me* to come up with an alibi! You're casting the blame all around, aren't you? To hell with who gets hurt. You just want off the hook. Well, sometimes that's not possible." She moved closer, her gaze fixed on Miranda, like a cat's on a bird. Softly she said, "Sometimes we have to pay for our sins. Whether it's an indiscreet affair. Or murder. We pay for it. I did. Why can't you?"

They stared at each other, caught in a binding fascination for each other's transgressions, each other's pain. *Killer and victim,* thought Miranda. *That's what I see in her eyes. Is that what you see in mine?*

The telephone rang, shattering the silence.

The sound seemed to rattle Jill. At once she turned and reached for the door. There she stopped. "You think you're the exception, Miranda. You think you're untouchable. Just wait. In a few years, when you're my age, you'll know just how vulnerable you are. We all are."

She walked out, closing the door behind her.

At once Miranda slid the bolt home.

The phone had stopped ringing. Miranda stared at it, wondering if it had been Chase, praying that he would call again.

The phone remained silent.

She began to pace the living room, hoping Chase, Annie, *anyone* would call. Starved for the sound of a human voice, she turned on the TV. Mindless entertainment, that's what she needed. For a half hour she sat on the couch among Annie's discarded socks and sweatshirts, flicking nervously between channels. Opera. Basketball. Game show. Opera again. In frustration she flicked it back to basketball.

Something clattered in the next room.

Startled, she left the couch and went into the kitchen. There she found herself staring down at a plastic saucer rolling around and around on its side across the linoleum floor. It collapsed, shuddered and fell still. Had it tumbled off the drainboard? She looked up at the sink and noticed, for the first time, that the window was wide open.

That's not the way I left it.

Slowly she backed away. The gun—Annie's gun. She had to get it.

In panic she turned to make a dash for the living room—

And found her head brutally trapped, her mouth covered by a wad of cloth. She flailed blindly against her captor, against the fumes burning her nose, her throat, but found her arms wouldn't work right. Her legs seemed to slide away from her, dissolving into some bottomless hole. She felt herself falling, caught a glimpse of the light as it receded into an impossibly high place. She tried to reach out for it but found her arms had gone numb.

The light wavered, shrank.

And then it winked out, leaving only the darkness.

Phillip was banging away at the piano. Rachmaninoff, Chase thought wearily. Couldn't the boy choose something a little more sedate? Mozart, for instance, or Haydn. Anything but this Russian thunder.

Chase headed out to the veranda, hoping to escape the racket, but the sound of the piano seemed to pound right through the walls. Resignedly he stood at the railing and stared toward the harbor. Already sunset. The sea had turned to red flame.

He wondered what Miranda was doing.

Wondered if he'd ever stop wondering.

This morning, when they'd driven off in their separate cars, their separate ways, he'd known their relationship had gone as far as it could. To go any further would require a level of trust he wasn't ready to give her. Their amateur detective work had come to a dead end; for now they had no reason to see each other. It was time to let the pros take over. The police, at least, would be objective. They wouldn't be swayed by emotions or hormones.

They still believed Miranda was guilty.

"Uncle Chase?" Cassie pushed through the screen door and came out to join him. "You can't stand the music, either, I see."

He smiled. "Don't tell your brother."

"It's not that he's a bad musician. He's just . . . loud." She leaned against one of the posts and looked up at the sky, at the first stars winking in the gathering darkness.

"Think you could do me a favor?" she asked.

"What's that?"

"When Mom gets home, will you talk to her? About the *Herald.*"

"What about it?"

"Well, with all that's come up—about Jill Vickery, I mean—it's beginning to look like we'll need a strong hand on the helm. We all know Dad groomed Phillip to be the designated heir. And he's a bright kid— I'm not putting him down or anything. But the fact is, Phillip's just not that interested."

"He hasn't said much about it, one way or the other."

"Oh, he won't say anything. He'll never admit the truth. That he's not crazy about the job." She paused, then said with steel in her voice, "But I am."

Chase frowned at his niece. Not yet twenty, and she had the look of a woman who knew exactly what she wanted in life. "You think you have what it takes?"

"It's in my blood! I've been involved from the time I could put pen to paper. Or fingers to keyboard. I know how that office works. I can write, edit, lay out ads, drive the damn delivery truck. I can *run* that paper. Phillip can't."

Chase remembered Cassie's term papers, the ones he'd glanced through at the cottage. They weren't just the chewing up and spitting out of textbook facts, but thoughtful, critical analyses.

"I think you'd do a terrific job," he said. "I'll talk to your mother."

"Thanks, Uncle Chase. I'll remember to mention your name when I get my Pulitzer." Grinning, she turned to go back into the house.

"Cassie?"

"Yes?"

"What do you think of Jill Vickery?"

Cassie frowned at the change of subject. "You mean as a managing editor? She was okay. Considering what she got paid, we were lucky to keep her."

"I mean, on a personal level."

"Well, that's hard to say. You never really get to know Jill. She's like a closed book. I never had any idea about that stuff in San Diego."

"Do you think she had an affair with your father?"

Cassie shrugged. "Didn't they all?"

"Do you think she was hurt by it?"

Cassie thought this over for a moment. "I think, if she was, she got over it. Jill's a tough cookie. That's the way I'd like to be." She turned and went into the house.

Phillip was still playing Rachmaninoff.

Chase stood and watched the last glow of sunset fade from the sea. He thought about Jill Vickery, about Miranda, about all the women Richard had hurt, including his own wife, Evelyn.

We're lousy, we Tremain men, he thought. *We use women, then we hurt them.*

Am I any different?

In frustration he slapped the porch railing. *Yes, I am. I would be. If only I could trust her.*

Phillip's pounding on the piano had become unbearable.

Chase left the porch, walked down the steps and headed for his car.

He would talk to her one last time. He would look her in the eye and ask her if she was guilty. Tonight he would get his answer. Tonight he would decide, once and for all, if Miranda Wood was telling the truth.

No one answered Annie's front door.

The lights were on inside, and Chase could hear the TV. He rang the bell, knocked, called out Miranda's name. Still there was no answer. At last he tried the knob and found the door was unlocked. He poked his head inside.

"Miranda? Annie?"

The living room was deserted. A basketball game, unwatched, was playing out its last minute on the TV. A pair of Annie's socks lay draped over the back of the sofa. Everything seemed perfectly normal, yet not quite right. He stood there for a moment, as though expecting the former occupants of the room to magically reappear and confront him.

The basketball game went into its fifteen-second countdown. A last-ditch throw, across the court. Basket. The crowd cheered.

Chase crossed the room, into the kitchen, and halted.

Here things were definitely not right. A chair lay toppled on its side. On the floor a saucer lay upside down. Though the kitchen window was wide open, an odor hung in the room, something vaguely sharp, medicinal.

Quickly he searched the rest of the house. He found neither Miranda nor Annie.

With growing panic he hurried outside and glanced up and down the street. Except for the far-off barking of a dog, the evening was still.

No, not quite. Was that the sound of a car engine running? If seemed muffled or distant. He circled around the house and saw a small detached garage in back. The door was shut. The sound of the car engine, though still muffled, seemed closer.

He started toward the garage. Then, out of the corner of his eye, he sighted a flicker of movement. He turned just in time to spy a shadow slipping away, blending into the darkness.

This time, you bastard, Chase thought, *you don't get away from me.*

Chase sprinted off in pursuit.

He heard his quarry dodge left, toward a thick hedge of bushes. Chase, too, veered left, scrambled over a low stone wall and broke into a sprint.

The fleeing shadow burst through the hedge and made a sharp right, into a neighboring yard littered with garden tools. Chase, intent on capture, didn't notice his quarry had swept up a rake. It came flying at him through the darkness.

Chase ducked. Tines first, it flew over his head, then clattered into a wheelbarrow behind him. Chase leaped back to his feet.

His quarry grabbed a pickax, flung it.

Again Chase dodged. He heard the whoosh of air as the lethal weapon looped past. By the time he'd recovered his balance the figure was off and running again, toward a stand of trees.

He'll be lost in the shadows! thought Chase. He mustered a final burst of speed, drew within reach. His quarry was tired. He could hear the other man's ragged breaths. Chase launched himself forward, grabbed a handful of shirt and held on.

His quarry, instead of trying to pull free, spun around and charged like a bull.

Chase was flung backward, into a tree. The shock lasted only an instant. Rage, not pain, was his first response. Shoving away from the tree, he flung himself at his attacker. Both men fell off balance, went skidding across the wet leaves. The attacker punched, and the blow caught Chase in the belly. With a new strength born of fury, Chase slammed his fist blindly at the squirming shadow. The man groaned, tried to lash out. Chase hit him again. And again.

The man went limp.

Chase rolled away from the body. For a moment he sat there, catching his breath, wincing at the pain in his knuckles. The other man was still alive—he could hear him breathing. Chase grabbed the inert figure by the legs and dragged him across the leaf-strewn lawn, toward a faint pool of light from a distant porch lamp. There he knelt to see who his prisoner was. In disbelief he stared at the face, now revealed.

It was Noah DeBolt. Evelyn's father.

13

The steady growl of an engine slowly penetrated Chase's numbed awareness. The car in the garage . . . the closed door . . .

That's when the realization hit him. He lurched to his feet.

Miranda.

He sprinted across the yard to the garage. A cloud of fumes assailed him as he pushed through the door. Miranda's car was parked inside, its engine still running. In panic, he flung open the car door.

Miranda lay sprawled across the front seat.

He switched off the ignition. Coughing, choking, he dragged her roughly out of the car, out of the garage. It terrified him how lifeless she felt in his arms. He carried her to the lawn and laid her down on the grass.

"Miranda!" he yelled. He shook her hard, so hard her whole body shuddered. "Wake up," he pleaded. "Damn you, Miranda. Don't you give up on me. Wake up!"

Still she didn't move.

In panic he slapped her face. The brutality of that blow, the sting of her flesh against his, shocked him. He laid his ear to her breast. Her heart was beating. And there it was—a breath!

She groaned, moved her head.

"Yes!" he shouted. "Come on. Come on." She sank back into unconsciousness. He didn't want to do it, but he had no choice. He slapped her again.

This time she moved her hand, a reflexive gesture to ward off the savage blows. "No," she moaned.

"Miranda, it's me! Wake up." He brushed back her hair, gently took her face in his hands and kissed her forehead, her temples. "Please, Miranda," he whispered. "Look at me."

Slowly she opened her eyes. They were dazed and full of confusion. At once she lashed out blindly, as though still fighting for her life.

"No, it's me!" he cried. He held her, hugged her tightly against him. Her frantic thrashing grew weaker. He felt the panic melt from her body until she lay quietly in his arms.

"It's all over," he whispered. "All over."

She pulled away and stared up at him with a look of bewilderment. "Who . . ."

"It was Noah."

"Evelyn's *father?*"

Chase nodded. "He's the one who's been trying to kill you."

"You have no right to hold me, Lorne. You understand? *No right.*" Noah, his face bruised an ugly purple, stared at his accusers. Through the closed door came the sounds of the police station: the clack of a typewriter, the ringing phone, the voices of patrolmen headed out for night duty. But here, in the back room, there was dead silence.

Quietly Lorne said, "You're not in any position to pull rank, Noah. So talk to us."

"I don't have to say a thing," said Noah. "Not until Les Hardee gets here."

Lorne sighed. "Legally speaking, yeah, you're right. But it would sure make things easy if you'd just tell us why you tried to kill her."

"I didn't. I went to her house to talk to her. I heard the car running in the garage. I thought maybe she was trying to kill herself. I started to go in, to check on it. Then Chase showed up. I guess I panicked. That's why I ran."

"That's all you were doing there? Just paying Ms. Wood a visit?"

Noah gave him an icy nod.

"In a getup like that?" Lorne nodded at Noah's black shirt and trousers.

"What I wear happens to be my concern."

"Chase says differently. He says you dragged her in the garage, left her there and started the car."

Noah snorted. "Chase has a little trouble being objective. Especially where Miranda Wood is concerned. Besides, *he* attacked *me.* Who the hell's got the bruises, anyway? Look at my face. Look at it!"

"Seems to me you both got some pretty good bruises," said Lorne.

"Self-defense," claimed Noah. "I had to fight back."

"Chase thinks you're the one who's been going after her. That you set fire to her house. Drove at her with a stolen car. And what about tonight? Was that supposed to be a convenient little suicide?"

"She's got him all twisted around. Got him taking her side. The side of a murderer—"

"Who's the guilty party here, Noah?"

Noah, sensing he'd said too much already, said abruptly, "I'm not going to talk till Les gets here."

In frustration Lorne crumpled his paper coffee cup in his fist. "Okay," he said, dropping into a chair. "We can wait. As long as it takes, Noah. As long as it takes."

"It's not going to stick," said Miranda. "I know it won't."

They sat huddled together on a bench in the intake area. Ellis Snipe had brought them coffee and cookies. Perhaps it was his way of personally atoning for the ordeal the police had put them through. So many questions, so many reports to be filed. And then, halfway through the interrogation, Dr. Steiner had shown up, called in by Lorne to check on her condition. In the guise of a medical exam, he had practically assaulted her with his stethoscope. *Breathe deep, damn it! Gotta check your lungs. You think I like making all these house calls? This keeps up, you two will have to put me on retainer!*

The questions, the demands, had left her exhausted. It was all she could manage, to sit propped up against Chase's shoulder. Waiting— for what? For Noah to confess? For the police to tell her the nightmare was over?

She knew better than that.

"He'll get out of it," she said. "He'll find a way."

"This time he won't," said Chase.

"But I never saw his face. I can barely remember what happened. What can they charge him with? Trespassing?" Miranda shook her head. "This is Noah DeBolt we're talking about. In this town, a DeBolt can get away with murder."

"Not Richard's murder."

She stared at him. "You think he killed Richard? His own son-in-law?"

"It's starting to fall together, Miranda. Remember what that lawyer FitzHugh told us? The real reason Richard gave Rose Hill to you? It was to keep the land out of Evelyn's control."

"I don't see what you're getting at."

"Who's the one person in the world Evelyn listens to? Trusts? Her *father.* Noah could have talked her into selling the land."

"You think this is all for control of Rose Hill? That's not much of a motive for murder."

"But the threat of bankruptcy is. If his investment collapsed, Noah would be left holding acres of land he could never develop. Worthless land."

"The north shore? Then you think Noah was the money behind Stone Coast Trust."

"Which makes Tony Graffam nothing but a front man. A patsy, really. My guess is, Richard found out. He had those financial records from Stone Coast, remember? The account numbers, the tax returns. I think he matched one of those accounts to Noah."

"Richard could have ruined him right then and there," she pointed out. "All he had to do was run the story in the *Herald*. But he canceled it."

"It's the way their relationship worked, Richard and Noah. They were always out to cut each other down. But not in public, *never* in public. It was a private rivalry, just between them. That's why Richard didn't print the article. It would've exposed his own father-in-law. And brought the family's dirty linen out into the public eye."

Miranda shook her head. "We'll never prove it. Not after Noah's lawyer gets through with the smoke and mirrors. You've been away from this island too long, Chase. You've forgotten how it is. The DeBolts, they're the equivalent of gods in this town."

"Not any longer."

"Then there's the matter of evidence. How do you prove he killed Richard?" She sighed, an admission of defeat. "No, *I'm* the convenient suspect. The one they'll convict." She sat back wearily. "The one they'll put away."

"That won't happen, Miranda. I won't let it happen."

Their gazes met. For the first time she saw what she'd been longing to see in his eyes. Trust. "Then you think I'm telling the truth."

"I know you're telling the truth." He touched her face. As his hand stroked down the curve of her cheek she closed her eyes and felt herself melting, flowing like warm liquid against him. "I think I've known it all along. But I was afraid to admit it. Afraid to consider the other possibilities. . . ."

"It wasn't me, Chase. It wasn't." She slid into his arms and there she found warmth and courage, all the courage she'd somehow lost in these past soul-battering days. *Believe me,* she thought. *Never stop believing me.*

They were still locked in that embrace when Evelyn Tremain walked in the station door.

Miranda felt Chase stiffen against her, heard his sharp intake of breath. Slowly she raised her head and turned to see Evelyn and the DeBolt family attorney, Les Hardee, standing a few feet away.

"So it's come to this, has it?" Evelyn said quietly.

Chase said nothing.

"Where is my father?" said Evelyn.

"In the room down the hall," said Chase. "He's talking to Lorne."

"Without me?" cut in the attorney. He headed swiftly down the hall, muttering, "A clear violation of rights. . . ."

Evelyn hadn't moved. She was still staring at them. "What sort of lies are you spreading about my father, Chase?"

Slowly Chase stood to face her. "Only the truth, Evelyn. It may be hard to take, but you'll have to accept it."

"The *truth?*" Evelyn let out a disbelieving laugh. "An officer calls me, tells me my father's been arrested for assault. Assault? *Noah De-Bolt?* Who's lying, Chase? My father? You?" She looked at Miranda. "Or someone else?"

"Lorne will explain the charges. You'd better talk to him."

"Because you won't? Is that it? Oh, Chase." She shook her head. "You've turned your back on your own family. We love you. And look how you hurt us." She turned, faced the corridor. Softly she said, "I just hope Lorne has the good sense to know the truth when he hears it." Taking a deep breath, she started down the hall.

"Wait here," Chase said to Miranda.

"What are you going to do?"

He didn't answer. He just kept walking away, in pursuit of Evelyn.

Stunned, Miranda watched him vanish around the corner. She heard a door open, then close behind him, shutting her out. She wondered what was going on in that room, what words were being exchanged, what deals forged. She had no doubt there *would* be deals, declarations of Noah's innocence. His attorney would do his best to twist the story around, make it seem like some crazy misunderstanding. Somehow they'd manage to make Miranda look like the guilty party.

Please, Chase, she thought. *Don't let them sway you. Don't start doubting me again.*

She stared down the hall and waited.

And she feared the worst.

"The charges are preposterous," said Evelyn. "My father's never broken a law in his life. Why, if he gets too much change back from a clerk, he'll go across town to return it. How can you accuse him of assault, much less attempted murder?"

"Mr. Tremain here has the bruises to prove it," said Lorne.

"So does my client!" cut in Les Hardee. "All that proves is, they traded blows in the dark. A case of mistaken identity. Two men blindly duking it out. At the very worst, you can accuse my client of idiotic behavior."

"Thanks a lot, Les," grunted Noah.

"The point is," said Hardee, "you can't hold him. The damage—" he glanced at Chase's bruised face, then at Noah's face, even more bruised "—appears to be mutual. And as for that nonsense about trying to kill Miranda Wood, well, where's your evidence? She was facing a jail term. Of course she was depressed. Of course she'd consider suicide."

"What about the fire?" pointed out Chase. "The car that almost ran her down? I was there, I saw it. *Someone's* trying to kill her."

"Not Mr. DeBolt."

"Does he have alibis?"

"Do *you* have evidence?" Hardee shot back. He turned to Lorne. "Look, let's call a halt to this farce. I'll take the responsibility. Release Mr. DeBolt."

Lorne sighed. "I can't."

Evelyn and Hardee stared at the diminutive chief of police.

"I'm afraid there is evidence," said Lorne, almost apologetically. "Ellis found a bottle of chloroform behind the garage. That kind of argues against suicide, doesn't it?"

"Nothing to do with me," said Noah.

"Then here's some more evidence," cut in Chase. It was time to gamble, time to shoot the wad. He was going to make a guess here; he only hoped it was the right one. "You know that money from the Bank of Boston? That hundred thousand dollars used to bail out Miranda Wood? Well, I had a banker friend of mine slip into the computer. Match that money transfer to an account."

"What?" Lorne turned to Chase in surprise. "You know who paid the bail?"

"Yes." *Here goes,* thought Chase. "Noah DeBolt."

It was Evelyn who reacted first, with a rage that transformed her face into an ugly mask. The look was directed at her father. "You did *what?*"

Noah said nothing. His silence was all Chase needed to back up his hunch. Right on target.

"It can be officially confirmed," said Chase. "Yes, it was your father who paid the bail."

Evelyn was still staring at Noah. "You let her out?"

Noah's head drooped. In an instant he'd been transformed into a very old, very tired-looking man. "I did it for you," he whispered.

"For me? For *me?*" Evelyn laughed. "What other favors have you done for me, Daddy?"

"It was for you. Everything was for you—"

"You crazy old man," muttered Evelyn. "You must be going senile."

"No." Noah's head shot up. "I would've done anything, don't you see? I was protecting you! My little girl—"

"Protecting me from what?"

"From yourself. From what you did. . . ."

Evelyn turned away in disgust. "I don't know what the hell he's raving about."

"Don't turn your back on me, young lady!"

"You can see he needs a doctor, Lorne. Try a psychiatrist."

"This is the thanks I get!" Noah roared. "For keeping you out of *prison?*"

Instant silence. Evelyn, white-faced, turned to confront her father. "Prison? For what?"

"Richard." Noah, his rage suddenly spent, sank slowly back against the chair. Softly he said, "For Richard."

"You thought . . . that I—" Evelyn shook her head. "Why? You knew it was that—that bitch!"

Noah merely looked away. With that one gesture he gave his answer. An answer that lifted a weight so heavy from Chase's soul he felt he was floating. It was a burden he could only now acknowledge had been there all along, the burden of proof. With that one gesture, the last blot of suspicion was washed away.

"You know Miranda's innocent," said Chase.

Noah dropped his head in his hands. "Yes," he whispered.

"How?" cut in Lorne.

"Because I had her followed. Oh, I knew about the affair. I knew what he was up to. I'd had enough of it! I wasn't going to see him hurt Evelyn again. So I hired a man, told him to watch her. To follow her, take photos. Catch 'em in the act. I wanted Evelyn to know, once and for all, what a bastard she'd married."

"And the night he was killed, you had Miranda under surveillance?" asked Lorne.

Noah nodded.

"What did your man see?"

"Of the murder? Nothing. He was busy following the woman. She left the house, walked to the beach. Sat there for an hour or so. Then she went home. By then my son-in-law was already dead."

Exactly what she said, thought Chase. *It was all the truth, right down to the last detail.*

"Then your man never saw the killer?" said Lorne.

"No."

"But you assumed your daughter . . ."

Noah shrugged. "It seemed . . . a logical guess. He had it coming. All these years of hurting her. You think he didn't deserve it? You think she wasn't justified?"

"But I didn't do it," said Evelyn.

Her words went ignored.

"Why did you bail out Miranda Wood?" asked Lorne.

"I thought if she went to trial, if her story held together, there was a chance they'd start to look at other suspects."

"You mean Evelyn."

"Better to have it over and done with!" blurted out Noah. "If there was an accident, that would end it. No more questions. No more suspects."

"So you wanted her out of jail," said Chase. "Out on the street, where you could reach her."

"That's enough, Noah!" cut in Hardee. "You don't have to answer these questions."

"Damn you, Les!" snapped Evelyn. "You should have told him that earlier!" She looked at her father, her expression a mixture of pity and disgust. "Let me set your mind at rest, Daddy. I didn't kill Richard. The fact you thought I did only shows how little you know me. Or I you."

"I'm sorry about this, Evelyn," said Lorne quietly. "But now I'm going to have to ask you a few questions."

Evelyn turned to him. Her chin came up, a gesture of stubborn pride, newfound strength. For the first time in all the years he'd known her Chase felt a spark of admiration for his sister-in-law.

"Ask away, Lorne," she said. "You're the cop. And I guess I'm now your prime suspect."

Chase didn't stay to hear the rest. He left the room and headed down the hall to find Miranda. *Now it can be proved. It was true, every word you said.* They could start from the beginning, he thought. He suddenly strode ahead with new hope, new anticipation. The shadow of murder was gone, and they had a chance to do it over, to do it right.

He rounded the corner eagerly, expecting to see her sitting on the bench.

The bench was empty.

He went over to the clerk, who was typing out Noah's arrest report. "Did you see where she went?"

The clerk glanced up. "You mean Ms. Wood?"

"Yes."

"She left the station. About, oh, twenty minutes ago."

"Did she say where she was going?"

"Nope. Just got up and walked out."

In frustration Chase turned to the door. *You never make it easy for me, do you?* he thought. Then he pushed through the door and headed out into the night.

All day Ozzie had been restless. Last night, all that frantic running around and police activity had driven the beast nearly mad with excitement. A day later and the agitation still hadn't worn off. He was all nerved up, clawing at the door, whining and tip-tapping back and forth across the wood floor.

Maybe it's my fault, Miss St. John thought, gazing in disgust at her hysterical dog. *Maybe my mood has simply rubbed off on him.*

Ozzie crouched at the front door like a discarded fur coat, staring pitifully at his mistress.

"You," said Miss St. John, "are a tyrant."

Ozzie merely whimpered.

"Oh, all right," said Miss St. John. "Out, out!" She opened the door. The dog bounded out into the twilight.

Miss St. John followed the beast down the gravel driveway. Ozzie was dancing along, his fur bouncing like black corkscrews. Truly an ugly animal, thought Miss St. John, the same thought that occurred to her on every walk. That he was worth several thousand dollars for his pedigree alone only went to show you the worthlessness of pedigrees, be they for dogs or people. But what Ozzie lacked in beauty he made up in energy. Already he was trotting far ahead and veering up the path, toward Rose Hill.

Miss St. John, feeling more like dog than mistress, followed him.

The cottage was dark. Chase and Miranda had left that morning and now the place stood deserted and forlorn. A pity. Such charming cottages should not go empty, especially not in the summertime.

She climbed the steps and peered through the window. Shadows of furniture huddled within. The books were back in the shelves. She could see the gleam of their spines lined up against the wall. Though they'd combed those books and papers thoroughly, she still wondered whether they had missed something. Some small, easily overlooked item that held the answers to Richard Tremain's death.

The door was locked, but she knew where the key was kept. What harm would there be in another little visit? She'd always felt just a bit proprietary when it came to Rose Hill. After all, she'd played near here almost every day as a child. And as an adult she'd made a point of keeping an eye on the cottage, as a favor to the Tremains.

Ozzie seemed happy enough, padding about in the yard.

Miss St. John retrieved the key from the planter, unlocked the door and went inside.

It seemed very still, very sad in that living room. She turned on all the lamps and wandered about, her gaze combing the nooks and crannies of the furniture. They'd already made a search of those places. There was no point repeating it.

She went through the kitchen, through the upstairs bedrooms, came back down again. No hunches, no revelations.

She was turning to leave when her gaze swept past the area rug, set right in front of the door. That's when a memory struck her, of a scene from *Tess of the D'Urbervilles*. A confessional note, slipped under the closed door, only to be pushed accidentally under the adjacent rug. A note that was never found because it lay hidden from view.

So vivid was that image that when she bent and pulled up the edge of the rug she was not at all startled to see a sealed envelope lying there.

The note was from M. The intended recipient had never found it, never read it.

. . . This pain is alive, like a creature gnawing at my organs. It won't die. It refuses to die. You put it there, you planted it, you gave the embryo all those years of nourishment.

And then you walked away.

You say you are doing me a kindness. You say it is better to break off now, because, if it goes on longer, it will only hurt more. You don't know what it is to hurt. Once you claimed to be love's walking wounded. Once, I thought to save you.

You were the serpent I hugged to my breast.

Now you say you've found a new savior. You think she'll make you happy. But she won't. It will be the same with her as it was with the others. You'll decide she isn't perfect. No one who's ever loved you, really loved you, has ever been good enough for you.

But you're getting old, flabby, and still you think that somewhere there's a young and perfect woman just longing to make love to your wrinkled old carcass.

She doesn't know you the way I do. I've had years to learn all your dirty little secrets. Your conceits and lies and cruelty. You'll use her, the way you've used all the others. And then she'll be tossed on the heap with the rest of us, another woman terribly hurt.

You should suffer where you've sinned. A good clean slice—

Miss St. John, still clutching the letter, abruptly left Rose Hill and hurried home.

With shaking hands she made two phone calls. The first was to Lorne Tibbetts.

The second was to Miranda Wood.

14

Miranda was near the point of exhaustion by the time she climbed up Annie's porch steps. It had been only a ten-minute walk from the police station, but the distance she had traveled had been emotional, not physical. Sitting alone on that bench, shut out from the fancy deal-making between attorneys and cops, she'd come to the sad realization that Noah DeBolt would never be charged with any crime worse than trespassing. That she, Miranda, was too convenient a suspect to be let off the hook. And that Chase, by walking down the corridor, by joining Evelyn and Noah behind that closed door, had made his choice.

Didn't they say that crisis brought families together? Well, the arrest of patriarch Noah DeBolt was one hell of a crisis. The family would rally.

Miranda was not, could never be, part of that family.

She stepped in the front door. Annie was still not home. Silence hung like a shroud over the house. When the phone suddenly rang, the sound was almost shocking to her ears.

She picked up the receiver.

"Miranda?" came a breathless voice.

"Miss St. John? Is something wrong?"

"Are you home alone?" was Miss St. John's bizarre reply.

"Well, yes, at the moment—"

"I want you to lock the door. Do it now."

"No, everything's all right. They've arrested Noah DeBolt—"

"Listen to me! I found another letter, at Rose Hill. That's what she was after, don't you see? The reason she kept going to the cottage! To get back all her letters!"

"Whose letters?"

"M."

"But Noah DeBolt—"

"This has nothing to do with Noah! It was a crime of passion, Miranda. The classic motive. Let me read you the letter. . . ."

Miranda listened.

By the time Miss St. John had finished, Miranda's hands were numb from clutching the receiver.

"I've already called the police," said Miss St. John. "They've sent a man to pick up Jill Vickery. Until then, keep your doors locked. It's a sick letter, Miranda, written by a sick woman. If she comes to the house, *don't let her in.*"

Miranda hung up.

At once she missed the sound of a human voice, any voice, even one transmitted through telephone wires. *Annie, come home. Please.*

She stared at the phone, wondering if she should call someone. But who? It was only as she stood there, thinking, that she noticed several days' mail mounded haphazardly by the telephone, some of it threatening to spill over onto the floor. A half-dozen household bills mingled with ad circulars and magazines. Annie's bookkeeping must be as sloppy as her housekeeping, she thought, straightening the pile. Only then did she notice the newsletter from the alumni association of Tufts University—Annie's old alma mater. It lay at the edge of the table, four photocopied pages stapled together, personal notes from the class of '68, with a mass-mailing label on front. Of no particular interest to Miranda—except for one detail.

It was addressed to Margaret Ann Berenger.

You're the only M I know, Annie had said.

And all the time, she'd known another.

It doesn't mean she's the one.

Miranda stood staring at that label. Margaret Ann Berenger. Where was the proof, where was the link between Annie and all those letters from M?

It suddenly occurred to her. A *typewriter.*

A manual model, Jill had said, with an *e* hammer in need of cleaning. It would be a large item, difficult to hide. A quick check of all the closets, all the cabinets, confirmed that there was no manual typewriter in the house. Could it be in the garage?

No, she'd been in the garage. It was barely large enough to hold a car, much less store household items.

She checked, anyway. No typewriter.

She went back into the house, her mind racing. By now Jill might already be under arrest. Annie would hear of it in no time, would know the search for the real M was on. Her first move would be to get rid of the incriminating typewriter, if she hadn't already done so. It was the one piece of evidence that could link Annie to Richard's murder.

It could prove my innocence. I have to find it, before she destroys it. I have to get it to the police.

There was one more place she had to look.

She ran from the house and got into her car.

Moments later she pulled up in front of the *Herald* building. It was dark inside. The latest issue had just been put to bed. No one would be working late tonight, so she'd have the building to herself.

She let herself in the front door with her key—the key she'd never gotten around to turning in. With a twinge of irony she remembered that it was Richard who'd told her to keep it. He was certain he could talk her into returning to the job.

Well, here she was, back again.

She moved up the aisle of desks and went straight to Annie's. She flicked on the lamp. The top drawer was unlocked. Among the jumble of pens and paper clips she found some loose keys. Which one would open Annie's locker? She gathered them all up and headed down the stairwell and into the women's room.

She turned on the light. A flowered couch, mauve wallpaper, Victorian prints sprang into view. Jill's decorative touch couldn't disguise the fact it was a closed-in dungeon of a room, without a single window. Miranda moved to the bank of lockers. There were six of them, extra wide to accommodate employees' heavy coats and boots during the winter months. She knew which one belonged to Annie. It had the sticker that said I've Got PMS. What's Your Excuse?

She inserted the first key into the lock. It didn't turn.

She tried the second key, then the third. The lock popped open.

She swung open the door and frowned at the contents. On the top shelf were mittens, a pair of old running shoes, a wool scarf.

On the bottom shelf a sweater lay draped over a towel-wrapped bundle. Miranda took out the bundle. The object inside was heavy. She unwrapped the towel, revealed the contents.

It was an old blue-green Olivetti with pica type.

She slid in a scrap of paper and with shaking hands typed the name Margaret Ann Berenger. The *e* loop was smudged.

An overwhelming sense of relief, almost euphoria, at once washed over her. Quickly she shut the locker and rewrapped the typewriter. As she gathered it up in her arms, a puff of air blew past her cheek. That was all the warning she had, that soft whisper of wind through the door as it opened and shut behind her.

Miranda turned.

The intruder stood in the doorway, her hair a mass of windblown waves, her face utterly devoid of emotion.

Miranda said softly, "Annie."

In silence Annie's gaze settled on the typewriter in Miranda's arms.

"I thought you were with Irving," said Miranda.

Annie's gaze slowly rose once again to meet Miranda's. Sadness now filled those eyes, a look of pain that seemed to spill from her very soul. *Why did I never see it before?* thought Miranda.

"There is no Irving," said Annie.

Miranda shook her head in confusion.

"There never was an Irving. I made him up. All the dates, all those evenings out. You see, I'd drive to the harbor. Park there and just sit. Hours, sometimes." Annie took a deep breath and, shuddering, let it out. "I couldn't take the pity, Miranda. All that sympathy for an old maid."

"I never thought that—"

"Of course you did. You all did. Then there was Richard. I wouldn't give him the satisfaction of knowing that—" Her voice broke. She wiped her hand across her eyes.

Slowly Miranda set the typewriter down on the bench. "Knowing what, Annie?" she asked softly. "How badly he hurt you? How alone you really were?"

A shudder racked Annie's body.

"He hurt us both," said Miranda. "Every woman he ever touched. Every woman who ever loved him. He hurt us all."

"Not the way he hurt me!" Annie cried. The echo of her pain seemed to reverberate endlessly against those stark walls. "Five years of my life, Miranda. That's what I gave him. Five years of secrets. I was forty-two when we met. I still had time for a baby. A few short years left. I kept hoping, waiting for him to make up his mind. To leave Evelyn." She wiped her eyes again, smearing a streak of mascara and tears across her cheek. "Now it's too late for me. It was my last chance and he took it from me. He *stole* it from me. And then he ended it." She shook her head, laughing through her tears. "He said he was only trying to be kind. That he didn't want me to waste any more years on him. Then he said the thing that hurt me most of all. He said, 'It was just your fantasy, Annie. I never really loved you the way you thought I did.' " The look she gave Miranda was the gaze of a tortured animal's. "Five years, and he tells me that. What he didn't tell me was the truth.

He'd found someone younger. You." There was no hostility, no anger in her voice, only quiet resignation. "I never blamed you, Miranda. You didn't know. You were just another victim. He would have left you, the way he left us all."

"You're right, Annie. We were all his victims."

"I'm sorry. I'm so sorry, Miranda." Annie slid her hand into her jacket pocket. "But someone has to suffer for it." Slowly she withdrew the gun.

Miranda stared at the barrel, now pointed at her chest. She wanted to argue, to plead, anything to make Annie lower the gun. But her voice had frozen in her throat. She could only stare at the black circle of the barrel and wonder if she would feel the bullet.

"Come, Miranda. Let's go."

Miranda shook her head. "Where—where are we going?"

Annie opened the door and gestured for Miranda to move first. "Up the stairs. To the roof."

No one was home.

Chase circled around Annie's house to the garage and found that the car was gone. Miranda must have returned, then left again. He was standing in the driveway, wondering where to look next, when he heard the phone ringing inside the house. He ran up the porch steps and into the living room to answer the call.

It was Lorne Tibbetts. "Is Miranda there?" he asked.

"No, I'm looking for her."

"What about Annie Berenger?"

"Not here, either."

"Okay," said Lorne. "I want you to leave the house, Chase. Do it right now."

Chase was stunned by the unexpected command. He said, "I'm waiting for Miranda to show up."

He heard Lorne turn and say something to Ellis. Then, "Look, we got evidence snowballing down here. If Annie Berenger shows up first, you keep things nice and casual, okay? Don't rattle her. Just calmly leave the house. Ellis is on his way over."

"What the hell's going on?"

"We think we know who M is. And it's not Jill Vickery. Now get out of there." Lorne hung up.

If it isn't Jill Vickery . . .

Chase went to the end table and opened the drawer. Annie's gun was missing.

He slammed the drawer shut.

Where are you, Miranda?

The next thought sent him running outside to his car. There might still be time to find them. He'd missed Miranda by only five, maybe ten minutes. They couldn't have gone far, not yet. If he circled around town, kept his eyes open, he might be able to find her car.

If they were still in the area.

I can't lose you. Now that we can prove your innocence. Now that we have a chance together.

He swung the car around. With tires screeching, he raced back toward town.

"Go on. Up the last flight."

Miranda paused, her foot on the next step. "Please, Annie . . ."

"Keep moving."

Miranda turned to face her. They were already on the third-floor landing. One more flight and then the door to the roof. Once she'd marveled at the beauty of this stairwell, at the carved mahogany banister, the gleaming wood finish. Now it had become a spiral death trap. She gripped the railing, drawing strength from the unyielding support of solid wood.

"Why are you doing this?" she asked.

"Go on. Go!"

"We were friends once—"

"Until Richard."

"But I didn't know! I had no idea you were in love with him! If only you'd told me."

"I never told anyone. I couldn't. It was his idea, you see. Keep it quiet, keep it our little secret. He said he wanted to protect me."

Then I'm the only one left who knows, thought Miranda. *The only one still alive.*

"Move," said Annie. "Up the stairs."

Miranda didn't budge. She looked Annie in the eye. Quietly she said, "Why don't you just shoot me now? Right here. If that's what you're going to do anyway."

"It's your choice." Calmly Annie raised the gun. "I'm not afraid of killing. They say that it's hardest the first time you do it. And you know what? It wasn't really hard at all. All I had to do was think about how much he hurt me. The knife seemed to move all by itself. I was just a witness."

"I'm not Richard. I never meant to hurt you."

"But you will, Miranda. You know the truth."

"So do the police. They found that letter, Annie. The last one you wrote."

Annie shook her head. "They arrested Jill tonight. But you're still the one they'll blame. Because they'll find the typewriter in your car. What a clever girl you'll seem, making up all those letters, planting them in the cottage. Throwing suspicion on poor innocent Jill. But then the guilt caught up with you. You got depressed. You knew jail was inevitable. So you chose the easy way out. You climbed to the roof of the newspaper building. And you jumped."

"I won't do it."

Annie gripped the gun with both hands and pointed it at Miranda's chest. "Then you'll die here. I had to kill you, you see. I found you planting the typewriter in Jill's office. You had a gun. You ordered me into the stairwell. I tried to grab the gun and it went off. A tidy end for everyone involved." Slowly she cocked back the pistol hammer. "Or would you rather it be the roof?"

I have to buy time, thought Miranda. *Have to wait for a chance, any chance, to escape.*

She turned and gazed up at the last flight of stairs.

"Go on," said Annie.

Miranda began to climb.

Fourteen steps, each one a fleeting eternity. Fourteen lifetimes, passing, gone. Frantically she tried to visualize the roof, the layout, the avenues of escape. She'd been up there only once, when the news staff had gathered for a group photo. She recalled a flat stretch of asphalt, punctuated by three chimneys, a heating duct, a transformer shed. Four stories down—that would be the drop. Would it kill her? Or was it just high enough to leave her crippled on the sidewalk, a helpless mound of broken bones, to be dispatched with a few blows by Annie?

The door to the roof loomed just above. If she could just get through that door and barricade it, she might be able to buy time, to scream for help.

Only a few steps more.

She stumbled and fell forward, catching herself on the stairs.

"Get up," said Annie.

"My ankle—"

"I said, get up!"

Miranda sat on the step and reached down to massage her foot. "I think I sprained it."

Annie took a step closer. "Then crawl if you have to! But get up those stairs!"

Miranda, her back braced firmly against the step, her legs wound up tight, calmly kept rubbing her ankle. And all the time she thought, *Closer, Annie. Come closer* . . .

Annie moved up another step. She was standing just below Miranda now, the gun frighteningly close. "I can't wait. Your time's run out." She raised the gun to Miranda's face.

That's when Miranda raised her foot—in a vicious, straight-out kick that thudded right into Annie's stomach. It sent Annie toppling backward down the stairs, to sprawl on the third-floor landing. But even as she fell she never released the gun. There was no opportunity to wrestle away the weapon. Annie was already rising to her knees, gun in hand. Her aim swept up toward her prey.

Miranda yanked open the rooftop door and dashed through just as Annie fired. She heard the bullet splinter the door, felt wood chips fly, sting her face. There was no latch, no way to bolt the door shut. So little time, so little time! Fourteen steps and Annie would be on the roof.

Miranda glanced wildly about her, could make out in the darkness the silhouette of chimneys, crates, other unidentifiable shapes.

Footsteps thudded up the stairs.

In panic Miranda took off into the shadows and slipped behind a transformer shed. She heard the door fly open, heard it bang shut again.

Then she heard Annie's voice, calling through the darkness. "There's nowhere to run, Miranda. Nowhere to go but straight down. Wherever you are, I'll find you. . . ."

Chase spotted it from a block away: Miranda's old Dodge, parked in front of the *Herald* building. He pulled up behind it and climbed out. A glance through the window told him the car was unoccupied. Miranda—or whoever had driven it here—must be in the building.

He rattled the front door to the *Herald*. It was locked. Through the glass he saw a lamp burning on one of the desks. Someone had to be inside. He banged on the door and called, "Miranda?" There was no answer.

He rattled the door again, then started around to the back of the building. There had to be another way in, an unlocked window or a loading door. He had circled the corner and was moving down one of the alleys when he heard it. Gunfire.

It came from somewhere inside the building.

"Miranda?" he yelled.

He wasted no more time searching for unlocked entrances. He grabbed a trash can from the alley, carried it around to the front of the building and hurled it through the window. Glass shattered, flying like hail across the desks inside. He kicked in the last jagged fragments, scrambled over the sill and dropped onto a carpet littered with razor-like shards. At once he was running past the desks, moving straight for the back of the building. With every step he took he grew more terrified of what he might find. Images of Miranda raced through his head. He shoved through the first door and confronted the deserted print shop. Newspapers—the next issue—were bundled and stacked against the walls. No Miranda.

He turned, moved down the hall to the women's lounge. Again, that surge of terror as he pushed through the door.

Again, no Miranda.

He turned and headed straight into the women's rest room, pushing open stall doors. No one there.

Ditto for the men's room.

Where the hell had that gunshot come from?

He ran back into the hall and started up the stairwell. Two more floors to search. Offices on the second floor, storage and news file rooms on the third. Somewhere up there he'd find her.

Just let me find you alive.

Miranda hugged the side of the transformer shed and listened for the sound of footsteps. Except for the hammering of her own heart she heard nothing, not even the softest crunch of shoes on asphalt. *Where is she? Which way is she moving?*

Quickly Miranda glanced to either side of her. Her eyes had began to adjust to the darkness. She could make out, to the left, a jumble of crates. Right beside them were the handrails of a fire escape. A way off the roof! If she could just make it to that edge, without being seen.

Where was Annie?

She had to risk a look. She crouched down and slowly inched toward the corner. What she saw made her pull back at once in panic.

Annie was moving straight toward the transformer shed.

Miranda's instinct told her to run, to attempt a final dash for freedom. Logic told her she'd never make it. Annie was already too close.

In desperation she scrabbled for a few bits of gravel near her feet. She flung it high overhead, aiming blindly for the opposite end of the roof. She heard it clatter somewhere off in the darkness.

For a few terrifying seconds she listened for sounds—any sounds. Nothing.

Again she edged around the corner of the transformer. Annie was following the sound, toward the opposite edge of the roof, stalking slowly toward one of the chimneys. A few steps farther. One more . . .

Now was her chance—her only one! Miranda ran.

Her footsteps sounded like drumbeats across the asphalt roof. Even before she reached the fire escape she heard the first gunshot, heard the whine of the bullet as it hurtled past. No time to think, only move! She scrambled for the fire escape, swung her leg over onto the first metal rung.

Another gunshot exploded.

The bullet's impact was like a punch in the shoulder. Its force sent her toppling sideways, over the roof's edge. She caught a dizzying view of the night sky, then felt herself falling, falling. Instinctively she reach up, clawed blindly for a handhold. As she tumbled over the edge of the fire escape landing, her left hand closed around cold steel—the railing. Even as her legs slipped away, dangling beneath her like dead weights, her grip held. She tried to reach up with the other arm but it wouldn't seem to obey her commands. She could only raise it to shoulder height, and then her hand closed only weakly around the outside edge of the landing. For a second she clung there, her feet hanging uselessly. Then she managed to brace one foot against the brick face of the building. *Still alive, still here!* she thought. *If I can just pull myself over the rail—get back onto the landing . . .*

The flicker of a shadow moving just above made her freeze. Slowly she lifted her gaze and stared into the gun barrel. Annie was standing at the roof's edge, aiming directly at Miranda's head.

"Now," said Annie softly. "Let go of the fire escape."

"No. No—"

"Just open your fingers. Lean back. A fast and easy way to die."

"It won't work. They'll find out! They'll know you did it!"

"Jump, Miranda. *Jump.*"

Miranda stared down at the ground. It was so far away, so very far.

Annie swung one leg over the roof's edge, aimed her heel at Miranda's hand gripping the rail and stamped down.

Miranda screamed. Still she held on.

Annie raised her heel, stamped again, then again, each blow crushing Miranda's left hand.

The pain was unbearable. Miranda's grip loosened. She lost her foothold, was left dangling free. Her left hand, throbbing in agony, could stand the abuse no longer. Her right hand, already weak and growing numb from the bullet wound, didn't have the strength to hold her weight. She gazed up in despair as Annie raised her heel and prepared to stamp down one last time.

The blow never fell.

Instead, Annie's body was jerked up and backward, like a puppet whose strings have been yanked all at once. She let out an unearthly screech of rage, of disbelief. And then there was a thud as her body, hurled aside, slammed onto the rooftop.

An instant later Chase appeared at the roof's edge. He leaned over and grabbed her left wrist. "Take my other hand! Take it!" he yelled.

Bracing her feet against the brick wall, Miranda managed to raise her right arm. "I can't . . . can't reach you. . . ."

"Come on, Miranda!" He leaned farther, his body stretching over the edge. "You have to do it! I need both your hands! Just reach up, that's all! I'll grab it, darling. Please!"

Darling. That single word, one she'd never heard before on his lips, seemed to spark some new source of strength deep inside her. She took a breath and strained toward the heavens. *That's as far as I can go,* she thought in despair. *No farther.*

That's when his hand closed around her wrist. At once she was held in a grip so tight she never feared, even for an instant, that she would fall. He dragged her up and up, over the roof's edge.

Only then did her strength give out. She had no need of it now, not when Chase was here to lend her his. She tumbled into his arms.

No tree had ever felt so solid, so unbendable. Nothing, no one could hurt her in the fortress of those arms. He said, "My God, Miranda, I thought—"

Instantly he fell silent.

A pistol hammer clicked back.

They both spun around to see Annie standing a few feet away. She wobbled on unsteady legs. With both hands she clutched the gun.

"It's too late, Annie," said Chase. "The police know. They have your final letter. They know you killed Richard. Even now they're looking for you. It's over."

Annie slowly lowered the gun. "I know," she whispered. She took a deep breath and looked up at the sky. "I loved you," she said to the heavens. "Damn you, Richard. *I loved you!*" she screamed.

Then she raised the gun, put the barrel in her mouth and calmly pulled the trigger.

15

This time the ministrations of cranky Dr. Steiner were insufficient. Only a hospital—and a surgeon—would do. An emergency ferry run was ordered and Miranda was loaded aboard the *Jenny B* with Dr. Steiner in attendance. The hospital in Bass Harbor was alerted to an incoming patient: gunshot wound to the right shoulder, patient conscious and oriented, blood pressure stable, bleeding under control. The *Jenny B* pulled away from the dock with two passengers, a crew of three and a corpse.

Chase wasn't aboard.

He was at that moment fidgeting in a chair in Lorne Tibbett's back office, answering a thousand and one questions. A command performance. A woman, after all, was dead; an investigation was called for; and as Lorne so succinctly put it, the choice was between talk or jail. All the time Chase sat there, he was wondering about the *Jenny B*. Had it reached Bass Harbor yet? Was Miranda stable?

Would Lorne ever finish with the damn questions?

It was two in the morning when Chase finally walked out of the police station. The night was warm, warm for Maine, anyway, but he felt chilled as he walked to his car. No more ferries to Bass Harbor tonight. He was stranded on the island until morning. At least he knew that Miranda was out of danger. A phone call to the hospital had told him she was resting comfortably, and was expected to recover.

Now he wondered where to go, where to sleep.

Not Chestnut Street. He could never sleep under Evelyn's roof again, not after the damage he'd done to the DeBolt family. No, tonight he felt rootless, cut off from the DeBolts, from the Tremains,

from the legacy of his rich and haughty past. He felt born anew.
Cleansed.

He got in the car and drove to Rose Hill.

The cottage felt cold, devoid of life or spirit, as if any joy that had
ever existed within had long since fled. Only the bedroom held any
warmth. This was where he and Miranda had made love. Here the
memory of that night, that one night, still lingered.

He lay on the bed and tried to conjure up the memory of her scent,
her softness, but it was like trying to catch your own reflection in water.
Every time you reach out to hold it, it slips from your grasp.

The way Miranda had slipped from his grasp.

She's not one of us, Evelyn had once said. *She's not our kind of
people.*

Chase thought of Noah, of Richard, of Evelyn. Of his own father.
And he thought, *Evelyn's right. Miranda's not our kind of people.*

She's far better.

"Happy endings," said Miss St. John, "are not automatic. Sometimes
one has to work for them."

Chase took the advice, and the cup of coffee she handed him, in
silence. The advice was something he already knew. Hadn't experience
taught him that happy endings were what you found in fairy tales, not
real life? Hadn't his own marriage proved the point?

*But this time it will be different. I'll make it different. If only I could be
certain I'm the one she wants.*

He sipped his cup of coffee and absentmindedly scratched Ozzie's
wild black mop of hair. He didn't know why he was petting the beast,
except that Ozzie seemed so damn appreciative. A glance at his watch
told Chase he had plenty of time to catch the twelve-o'clock ferry to
Bass Harbor. To Miranda.

All night he'd lain sleepless in bed, wondering about their chances,
their future. The specter of his brother couldn't be so easily dispelled.
Just a few short weeks ago Richard had been the man she loved, or
thought she loved. Richard had taken her innocence, used her, nearly
destroyed her. *And now here I am, another Tremain. After what Richard
did to her, why should she trust me?*

Events, emotions had moved at lightning speed these past few days.
A week ago he had called her a murderess. Only hours ago he had
come to accept her innocence as gospel truth. She had every right to
resent him, to never forgive him for the things he'd once said to her. So
many cruel and terrible words had passed between them. Could love,
real love, grow from such poisoned beginnings?

He wanted to believe it could. He had to believe it could.

But those doubts kept tormenting him.

When Miss St. John had come knocking at the cottage door at ten o'clock with an offer of coffee and a morning chat, he'd almost welcomed the intrusion, though he suspected her invitation was inspired by more than neighborly kindness. Word of the night's goings-on must already be buzzing about town. Miss St. John, with her mile-long antennae, had no doubt picked up the signals and was probably curious as hell.

Now that she'd been brought up to date, she was going to offer an opinion, whether he wanted to hear it or not.

"Miranda's a lovely woman, Chase," she said. "A very kind woman."

"I know" was all he could answer.

"But you have doubts."

He sighed, a breath that seemed weighted with pain and uncertainty. "After all that's happened . . ."

"People are entitled to make mistakes, Chase. Miranda made one with your brother. It wasn't a terrible sort of mistake. It had nothing to do with cruelty or bad intentions. It had only to do with love. With misjudgment. The mistake was real. But the emotions were the right ones."

"But you don't understand," he said, looking up at her. "My doubts have nothing to do with her. It's *me*, whether she can forgive me. For being a Tremain. For being this symbol of everything, everyone who's ever hurt her."

"I think Miranda's the one who's searching for forgiveness."

He shook his head. "What should I forgive *her* for?"

"You have to answer that."

He sat in silence for a moment, rubbing the ugly head of that ugly dog. *What do I forgive you for? For showing me the real meaning of innocence. For making me question every stuffy notion I was brought up to believe in. For making me realize I've been an idiot.*

For making me fall in love with you.

With sudden determination he put down his coffee cup and rose to his feet. "I'd better get going," he said. "I've got a ferry to catch."

"And then what happens?" asked Miss St. John, walking him to the door.

Smiling, he took her hand—the hand of a very wise woman. "Miss St. John," he said, "when I find out, you'll be the first to know."

She waved as he headed out to his car. "I'll count on it!" she yelled.

Chase drove like a crazy man to the ferry landing. He arrived an hour early, only to find a long line of cars already waiting to board.

Rather than risk missing the sail, he decided to leave his car and board as a foot passenger.

Two hours later he walked off onto the dock in Bass Harbor. No taxis here; he had to hitch a ride to the hospital. By the time he strode up to the patient information desk, it was already two-thirty.

"Miranda Wood," said the volunteer, setting down the phone receiver, "was discharged an hour ago."

"What?"

"That's what the floor nurse said. The patient left with Dr. Steiner."

Chase felt ready to punch the desk in frustration. "Where did they go?" he snapped.

"I wouldn't know, sir. You could ask upstairs, at the nurses' station, second floor."

Chase was about to head for the stairwell when he suddenly glanced up at the wall clock. "Miss—what time does the ferry return to Shepherd's Island?" he asked.

"I think the last one leaves at three o'clock."

Twenty minutes.

He hurried outside and glanced up and down the street for a taxi, a bus, anything on wheels that might take him to the landing. They *had* to be at the landing. Where else would she and Dr. Steiner go, except back to the island?

It was the last ferry of the day and he'd never catch it in time.

Happy endings are not automatic. Sometimes one has to work for them.

Okay, damn it, he thought. I'm ready to work. I'm ready to do anything it takes to make this turn out right.

He took off at a sprint down the street. It was two miles to the ferry landing.

He ran every step of the way.

The deckhand yelled, "All aboard!" and the engines of the *Jenny B* growled to life.

Standing at the rail, Miranda stared out over the gray-green expanse of Penobscot Bay. So many islands in the distance, so many places in the world to run to. Soon she'd be on her way, leaving memories, good and bad, behind her. There was just this one last journey to Shepherd's Island, to tie up all those loose ends, and then she could turn her back on this place forever. It was a departure she'd planned weeks ago, before Richard's murder, before the horrors of her arrest.

Before Chase.

"I still say it was an idiotic idea, young lady," said Dr. Steiner, hunched irritably on a bench beside her. "Checking out just like that.

What if you start to bleed again? What if you get an infection? I can't handle those complications! I tell you, I'm getting too old for this business. Too old!"

"I'll be just fine, Doc," she said, her gaze focused on the bay. "Really," she said softly, "I'll be just fine. . . ."

Dr. Steiner began to mutter to himself, a grumpy monologue about disobedient patients and how hard it was to be a doctor these days. Miranda scarcely listened. She had too many other things on her mind.

A quiet exit, some time alone—yes, all in all, it was better this way. Seeing Chase again would be too confusing. What she needed was escape, a chance to analyze what she really felt form him. Love? She thought so. Yes, she was *sure* of it. But she'd been wrong before, terribly wrong. *I don't want to make the same mistake, suffer the same consequences.*

And yet . . .

She gripped the railing and gazed off moodily at the islands. The wind had come up and it whistled across the water, blew its cold salt breath against her face.

I do love him, she thought. *I know I do.*

But it's not enough to make a future. Too much stood in the way. The ghost of Richard. The shadow of mistrust. And always, always, those metaphorical train tracks on whose wrong side she'd grown up. It shouldn't make a difference, but then, she was merely Miranda Wood. Perhaps, to a Tremain, it made *all* the difference.

"Bow line's free!" called the deckhand.

The engines of the *Jenny B* throttled up. Slowly she pivoted to starboard, to face the far-off green hillock that was Shepherd's Island. The deckhand strode the length of the boat and released the stern line. Just as it slipped free there came a shout from the dock.

"Wait! Hold the boat!"

"We're full up!" yelled the deckhand. "Catch the next one."

"I said *hold up!*"

"Too late!" barked the deckhand. Already the *Jenny B* was pulling away from the dock.

It was the deckhand's sharp and sudden oath that made Miranda turn to look. She saw, far astern, a figure racing toward the end of the pier. He took a flying leap across the growing gap of water and landed with only inches to spare on the deck of the *Jenny B*.

"Son of a gun," marveled the deckhand. "Are you nuts?"

Chase scrambled to his feet. "Have to talk to someone—one of your passengers—"

"Man, you must want to talk *real* bad."

Chase took a calming breath and glanced around the deck. His gaze stopped at Miranda. "Yeah," he said softly. "Real bad."

Miranda, caught standing against the rail, could only stare in astonishment as Chase walked toward her. The other passengers were all watching, waiting to see what would happen next.

"Young man," snapped Dr. Steiner. "If you sprained your ankle, don't expect me to fix it. You two and all your damn fool stunts."

"My ankle's fine," said Chase, his gaze never leaving Miranda. "I just want to talk to your patient. If it's all right with her."

Miranda gave a laugh of disbelief. "After a leap like that, how could I refuse?"

"Let's go up front." Chase reached for her hand. "For this, I don't need an audience."

They walked to the bow and stood by the rail. Here the salt wind flew at them unremittingly, whipping at their clothes, their hair. Above, gulls swooped and circled, airborne companions of the plodding *Jenny B.*

Chase said, "They told me you checked out early. You should have stayed in the hospital."

Miranda hugged herself against the wind and stared down at the water. "I couldn't lie in that bed another day. Not with so many things hanging over me."

"But it's over, Miranda."

"Not yet. There's still that business with the police. And I have to settle with my lawyer."

"That can wait."

"But I can't." She raised her head and faced the wind. "I want to leave this place. As soon as I can. Any way I can."

"Where are you going?"

"I don't know. I've thought about heading west. Jill Vickery walked away from her past. Maybe I can, too."

There was a long silence. "Then you're not staying on the island," he said.

"No. There's nothing here for me now. I'll be getting the insurance money from the house. It will be enough to get me out of here. To go some place where they don't know me, or Richard, or anything that happened."

The water broke before the bow of the *Jenny B* and the spray flew up, misting their faces.

"It's not an easy thing," she said, "living in a town where they'll always wonder about you. I understand now why Jill Vickery left San

Diego. She wanted to wash away the guilt. She wanted to get back her innocence. That's what I want back, Chase. My innocence."

"You never lost it."

"Yes, I did. That's what you thought. What you'll always think of me."

"I know better now. I have no more questions, Miranda. No more doubts."

She shook her head. Sadly she turned away. "It's not as easy as that, to bury the past."

"Okay, so it's not." He pulled her around to face him. "It's never easy, Miranda. Love. Life. You know, just this morning, Miss St. John said a very wise thing to me. She said happy endings aren't automatic. You have to work for them." He reached up and framed her face in his hands. "Don't you think this happy ending is worth working for?"

"But I don't know if I believe in them anymore. Happy endings."

"Neither did I. But I'm beginning to change my mind."

"You'll always be wondering about me, Chase. About whether you can trust me—"

"No, Miranda. That's the one thing I'll *never* wonder about."

He kissed her then, a sweet and gentle joining that spoke not of passion but of hope. That one touch of his lips seemed to rinse away the terrible grime of guilt, of remorse, that had stained her soul.

The renewal of innocence. That's what he offered; that's what she found in his arms.

It seemed only a short time later when the gulls suddenly burst forth into a wild keening, a raucous announcement that land was close at hand. The couple standing at the bow did not stir from each other's arms. Even when the boat's whistle blew, even when the *Jenny B* glided into the harbor, they would still be standing there.

Together.

WHISTLEBLOWER

Prologue

Branches whipped his face, and his heart was pounding so hard he thought his chest would explode, but he couldn't stop running. Already, he could hear the man gaining on him, could almost imagine the bullet slicing through the night and slamming into his back. Maybe it already had. Maybe he was trailing a river of blood; he was too numb with terror to feel anything now, except the desperate hunger to live. The rain was pouring down his face, icy, blinding sheets of it, rattling on the dead leaves of winter. He stumbled through a pool of darkness and found himself sprawled flat on his belly in the mud. The sound of his fall was deafening. His pursuer, alerted by the sharp crack of branches, altered course and was now headed straight for him. The thud of a silencer, the zing of a bullet past his cheek, told him he'd been spotted. He forced himself to his feet and made a sharp right, zigzagging back toward the highway. Here in the woods, he was a dead man. But if he could flag down a car, if he could draw someone's attention, he might have a chance.

A crash of branches, a coarse oath, told him his pursuer had stumbled. He'd gained a few precious seconds. He kept running, moving only by an instinctive sense of direction. There was no light to guide his way, nothing except the dim glow of the clouds in the night sky. The road had to be just ahead. Any second now, his feet would hit pavement.

And then what? What if there's no car to flag down, no one to help me?

Then, through the trees ahead, he saw a faint flickering, two watery beams of light.

With a desperate burst of speed, he sprinted toward the car. His lungs were on fire, his eyes blinded by the lash of branches and rain. Another bullet whipped past him and thudded into a tree trunk, but the gunman behind him had suddenly lost all importance. All that mattered was those lights, beckoning him through the darkness, taunting him with the promise of salvation.

When his feet suddenly hit the pavement, he was shocked. The lights were still ahead, bobbing somewhere beyond the trees. Had he missed the car? Was it already moving away, around a curve? No, there it was, brighter now. It was coming this way. He ran to meet it, following the bend of the road and knowing all the time that here in the open, he was an easy target. The sound of his shoes slapping the wet road filled his ears. The lights twisted toward him. At that instant, he heard the gun fire a third time. The force of the impact made him stumble to his knees, and he was vaguely aware of the bullet tearing through his shoulder, of the warmth of his own blood dribbling down his arm, but he was oblivious to pain. He could focus only on staying alive. He struggled back to his feet, took a stumbling step forward . . .

And was blinded by the onrush of headlights. There was no time to throw himself out of the way, no time even to register panic. Tires screamed across the pavement, throwing up a spray of water.

He didn't feel the impact. All he knew was that he was suddenly lying on the ground and the rain was pouring into his mouth and he was very, very cold.

And that he had something to do, something important.

Feebly, he reached into the pocket of his windbreaker, and his fingers curled around the small plastic cylinder. He couldn't quite remember why it mattered so much, but it was still there and he was relieved. He clutched it tightly in his palm.

Someone was calling to him. A woman. He couldn't see her face through the rain, but he could hear her voice, hoarse with panic, floating through the buzz in his head. He tried to speak, tried to warn her that they had to get away, that death was waiting in the woods. But all that came out was a groan.

1

Three miles out of Redwood Valley, a tree had fallen across the road, and with the heavy rains and backed-up cars, it took Catherine Weaver nearly three hours to get past the town of Willits. By then it was already ten o'clock and she knew she wouldn't reach Garberville till midnight. She hoped Sarah wouldn't sit up all night waiting for her. But knowing Sarah, there'd be a supper still warm in the oven and a fire blazing in the hearth. She wondered how pregnancy suited her friend. Wonderfully, of course. Sarah had talked about this baby for years, had chosen its name—Sam or Emma—long before it was conceived. The fact she no longer had a husband was a minor point. "You can only wait around so long for the right father," Sarah had said. "Then you have to take matters into your own hands.

And she had. With her biological clock furiously ticking its last years away, Sarah had driven down to visit Cathy in San Francisco and had calmly selected a fertility clinic from the yellow pages. A liberal-minded one, of course. One that would understand the desperate longings of a thirty-nine-year-old single woman. The insemination itself had been a coolly clinical affair, she'd said later. Hop on the table, slip your feet into the stirrups, and five minutes later, you were pregnant. Well, almost. But it was a simple procedure, the donors were certifiably healthy, and best of all, a woman could fulfill her maternal instincts without all that foolishness about marriage.

Yes, the old marriage game. They'd both suffered through it. And after their divorces, they'd both carried on, albeit with battle scars.

Brave Sarah, thought Cathy. *At least she has the courage to go through with this on her own.*

The old anger washed through her, still potent enough to make her mouth tighten. She could forgive her ex-husband Jack for a lot of things. For his selfishness. His demands. His infidelity. But she could never forgive him for denying her the chance to have a child. Oh, she could have gone against his wishes and had a baby anyway, but she'd wanted him to want one as well. So she'd waited for the time to be right. But during their ten years of marriage, he'd never been "ready," never felt it was the "right time."

What he should have told her was the truth: that he was too self-centered to be bothered with a baby.

I'm thirty-seven years old, she thought. *I no longer have a husband. I don't even have a steady boyfriend. But I could be content, if only I could hold my own child in my arms.*

At least Sarah would soon be blessed.

Four months to go and then the baby was due. Sarah's baby. Cathy had to smile at that thought, despite the rain now pouring over her windshield. It was coming down harder now; even with the wipers thrashing at full speed, she could barely make out the road. She glanced at her watch and saw it was already eleven-thirty; there were no other cars in sight. If she had engine trouble out here, she'd probably have to spend the night huddled in the backseat, waiting for help to arrive.

Peering ahead, she tried to make out the road's dividing line and saw nothing but a solid wall of rain. This was ridiculous. She really should have stopped at that motel in Willits, but she hated the thought of being only fifty miles from her goal, especially when she'd already driven so far.

She spotted a sign ahead: Garberville, 10 Miles. So she was closer than she'd thought. Twenty-five miles more, then there'd be a turnoff and a five-mile drive through dense woods to Sarah's cedar house. The thought of being so close fueled her impatience. She fed the old Datsun some gas and sped up to forty-five miles an hour. It was a reckless thing to do, especially in these conditions, but the thought of a warm house and hot chocolate was just too tempting.

The road curved unexpectedly; startled, she jerked the wheel to the right and the car slid sideways, tobogganing wildly across the rain-slicked pavement. She knew enough not to slam on the brakes. Instead, she clutched the wheel, fighting to regain control. The tires skidded a few feet, a heart-stopping ride that took her to the very edge of the road. Just as she thought she'd clip the trees, the tires gripped the pavement. The car was still moving twenty miles an hour, but at least it was headed in a straight line. With clammy hands, she managed to negotiate the rest of the curve.

What happened next caught her completely by surprise. One instant she was congratulating herself for averting disaster, the next, she was staring ahead in disbelief.

The man had appeared out of nowhere. He was crouched in the road, captured like a wild animal in the glare of her headlights. Reflexes took over. She slammed on the brakes, but it was already too late. The screech of her tires was punctuated by the thud of the man's body against the hood of her car.

For what seemed like eternity, she sat frozen and unable to do anything but clutch the steering wheel and stare at the windshield wipers skating back and forth. Then, as the reality of what she'd just done sank in, she shoved the door open and dashed out into the rain.

At first she could see nothing through the downpour, only a glistening strip of blacktop lit by the dim glow of her taillights. *Where is he?* she thought frantically. With water streaming past her eyes, she traced the road backward, struggling to see in the darkness. Then, through the pounding rain, she heard a low moan. It came from somewhere off to the side, near the trees.

Shifting direction, she plunged into the shadows and sank ankle-deep in mud and pine needles. Again she heard the moan, closer now, almost within reach.

"Where are you?" she screamed. "Help me find you!"

"Here . . ." The answer was so weak she barely heard it, but it was all she needed. Turning, she took a few steps and practically stumbled over his crumpled body in the darkness. At first, he seemed to be only a confusing jumble of soaked clothes, then she managed to locate his hand and feel for his pulse. It was fast but steady, probably steadier than her own pulse, which was skipping wildly. His fingers suddenly closed over hers in a desperate grip. He rolled against her and struggled to sit up.

"Please! Don't move!" she said.

"Can't—can't stay here—"

"Where are you hurt?"

"No time. Help me. Hurry—"

"Not till you tell me where you're hurt!"

He reached out and grabbed her shoulder in a clumsy attempt to rise to his feet. To her amazement, he managed to pull himself halfway up. For an instant they wobbled against each other, then his strength seemed to collapse and they both slid to their knees in the mud. His breathing had turned harsh and irregular and she wondered about his injuries. If he was bleeding internally he could die within minutes. She had to get him to a hospital now, even if it meant dragging him back to the car.

"Okay. Let's try again," she said, grabbing his left arm and draping it around her neck. She was startled by his gasp of agony. Immediately she released him. His arm left a sticky trail of warmth around her neck. *Blood.*

"My other side's okay," he grunted. "Try again."

She shifted to his right side and pulled his arm over her neck. If she weren't so frantic, it would have struck her as a comical scene, the two of them struggling like drunkards to stand up. When at last he was on his feet and they stood swaying together in the mud, she wondered if he even had the strength to put one foot in front of the other. She certainly couldn't move them both. Though he was slender, he was also a great deal taller than she'd expected, and much more than her five-foot-five frame could support.

But something seemed to compel him forward, a kindling of some hidden reserves. Even though their soaked clothes, she could feel the heat of his body and could sense the urgency driving him onward. A dozen questions formed in her head, but she was breathing too hard to voice them. Her every effort had to be concentrated on getting him to the car, and then to a hospital.

Gripping him around the waist, she latched her fingers through his belt. Painfully they made their way to the road, struggling step by step. His arm felt taut as wire over her neck. It seemed everything about him was wound up tight. There was something desperate about the way his muscles strained to move forward. His urgency penetrated right through to her skin. It was a panic as palpable as the warmth of his body, and she was suddenly infected with his need to flee, a need made more desperate by the fact they could move no faster than they already were. Every few feet she had to stop and shove back her dripping hair just to see where she was going. And all around them, the rain and darkness closed off all view of whatever danger pursued.

The taillights of her car glowed ahead like ruby eyes winking in the night. With every step the man grew heavier and her legs felt so rubbery she thought they'd both topple in the road. If they did, she wouldn't have the strength to haul him back up again. Already, his head was sagging against her cheek and water trickled from his rain-matted hair down her neck. The simple act of putting one foot in front of the other was so automatic that she never even considered dropping him on the road and backing the car to him instead. And the taillights were already so close, just beyond the next veil of rain.

By the time she'd guided him to the passenger side, her arm felt
ready to fall off. With the man on the verge of sliding from her grasp,
she barely managed to wrench the door open. She had no strength left
to be gentle; she simply shoved him inside.

He flopped onto the front seat with his legs still hanging out. She
bent down, grabbed his ankles, and heaved them one by one into the
car, noting with a sense of detachment that no man with feet this big
could possible be graceful.

As she slid into the driver's seat, he made a feeble attempt to raise
his head, then let it sink back again. "Hurry," he whispered.

At the first turn of the key in the ignition, the engine sputtered and
died. Dear God, she pleaded. Start. *Start!* She switched the key off,
counted slowly to three, and tried again. This time the engine caught.
Almost shouting with relief, she jammed it into gear and made a tire-
screeching takeoff toward Garberville. Even a town that small must
have a hospital or, at the very least, an emergency clinic. The question
was: could she find it in this downpour? And what if she was wrong?
What if the nearest medical help was in Willits, the other direction?
She might be wasting precious minutes on the road while the man bled
to death.

Suddenly panicked by that thought, she glanced at her passenger. By
the glow of the dashboard, she was that his head was still flopped back
against the seat. He wasn't moving.

"Hey! Are you all right?" she cried.

The answer came back in a whisper. "I'm still here."

"Dear God. For a minute I thought . . ." She looked back at the
road, her heart pounding. "There's got to be a clinic somewhere—"

"Near Garberville—there's a hospital—"

"Do you know how to find it?"

"I drove past it—fifteen miles . . ."

If he drove here, where's his car? she thought. "What happened?" she
asked. "Did you have an accident?"

He started to speak but his answer was cut off by a sudden flicker of
light. Struggling to sit up, he turned and stared at the headlights of
another car far behind them. His whispered oath made her look sideways in alarm.

"What is it?"

"That car."

She glanced in the rearview mirror. "What about it?"

"How long's it been following us?"

"I don't know. A few miles. Why?"

The effort of keeping his head up suddenly seemed too much for him, and he let it sink back down with a groan. "Can't think," he whispered. "Christ, I can't think . . ."

He's lost too much blood, she thought. In a panic, she shoved hard on the gas pedal. The car seemed to leap through the rain, the steering wheel vibrating wildly as sheets of spray flew up from the tires. Darkness flew at dizzying speed against their windshield. *Slow down, slow down! Or I'll get us both killed.*

Easing back on the gas, she let the speedometer fall to a more manageable forty-five miles per hour. The man was struggling to sit up again.

"Please, keep your head down!" she pleaded.

"That car—"

"It's not there anymore."

"Are you sure?"

She looked at the rearview mirror. Through the rain, she saw only a faint twinkling of light, but nothing as definite as headlights. "I'm sure," she lied and was relieved to see him slowly settle back again. *How much farther?* she thought. *Five miles? Ten?* And then the next thought forced its way into her mind: *He might die before we get there.*

His silence terrified her. She needed to hear his voice, needed to be reassured that he hadn't slipped into oblivion. "Talk to me," she urged. "Please."

"I'm tired. . . ."

"Don't stop. Keep talking. What—what's your name?"

The answer was a mere whisper: "Victor."

"Victor. That's a great name. I like that name. What do you do, Victor?"

His silence told her he was too weak to carry on any conversation. She couldn't let him lose consciousness! For some reason it suddenly seemed crucial to keep him awake, to keep him in touch with a living voice. If that fragile connection was broken, she feared he might slip away entirely.

"All right," she said, forcing her voice to remain low and steady. "Then *I'll* talk. You don't have to say a thing. Just listen. Keep listening. My name is Catherine. Cathy Weaver. I live in San Francisco, the Richmond district. Do you know the city?" There was no answer, but she sensed some movement in his head, a silent acknowledgment of her words. "Okay," she went on, mindlessly filling the silence. "Maybe you don't know the city. It really doesn't matter. I work with an independent film company. Actually, it's Jack's company. My ex-husband. We make horror films. Grade B, really, but they turn a profit. Our last one was *Reptilian.* I did the special-effects makeup. Really gruesome stuff. Lots of green scales and slime . . ." She laughed—it was a strange, panicked sound. It had an unmistakable note of hysteria.

She had to fight to regain control.

A wink of light made her glance up sharply at the rearview mirror. A pair of headlights was barely discernible through the rain. For a few seconds she watched them, debating whether to say anything to Victor. Then, like phantoms, the lights flickered off and vanished.

"Victor?" she called softly. He responded with an unintelligible grunt, but it was all she needed to be reassured that he was still alive. That he was listening. *I've got to keep him awake,* she thought, her mind scrambling for some new topic of conversation. She'd never been good at the glib sort of chitchat so highly valued at filmmakers' cocktail parties. What she needed was a joke, however stupid, as long as it was vaguely funny. *Laughter heals.* Hadn't she read it somewhere? That a steady barrage of comedy could shrink tumors? *Oh sure,* she chided herself. *Just make him laugh and the bleeding will miraculously stop. . . .*

But she couldn't think of a joke, anyway, not a single damn one. So she returned to the topic that had first come to mind: her work.

"Our next project's slated for January. *Ghouls.* We'll be filming in Mexico, which I hate, because the damn heat always melts the makeup. . . ."

She looked at Victor but saw no response, not even a flicker of movement. Terrified that she was losing him, she reached out to feel for his pulse and discovered that his hand was buried deep in the pocket of his windbreaker. She tried to tug it free, and to her amazement he reacted to her invasion with immediate and savage resistance. Lurching awake, he blindly lashed at her, trying to force her away.

"Victor, it's all right!" she cried, fighting to steer the car and protect herself at the same time. "It's all right! It's me, Cathy. I'm only trying to help!"

At the sound of her voice, his struggles weakened. As the tension eased from his body, she felt his head settle slowly against her shoulder. "Cathy," he whispered. It was a sound of wonder, of relief. "Cathy . . ."

"That's right. It's only me." Gently, she reached up and brushed back the tendrils of his wet hair. She wondered what color it was, a concern that struck her as totally irrelevant but nonetheless compelling. He reached for her hand. His fingers closed around hers in a grip that was surprisingly strong and steadying. *I'm still here,* it said. *I'm warm and alive and breathing.* He pressed her palm to his lips. So tender was the gesture, she was startled by the roughness of his unshaven jaw against her skin. It was a caress between strangers, and it left her shaken and trembling.

She returned her grip to the steering wheel and shifted her full attention back to the road. He had fallen silent again, but she couldn't ignore the weight of his head on her shoulder or the heat of his breath in her hair.

The torrent eased to a slow but steady rain, and she coaxed the car to fifty. The Sunnyside Up cafe whipped past, a drab little box beneath a single streetlight, and she caught a glimpse of Victor's face in the brief glow of light. She saw him only in profile: a high forehead, sharp nose, a jutting chin, and then the light was gone and he was only a shadow breathing softly against her. But she'd seen enough to know she'd never forget that face. Even as she peered through the darkness, his profile floated before her like an image burned into her memory.

"We have to be getting close," she said, as much to reassure herself as him. "Where a cafe appears, a town is sure to follow." There was no response. "Victor?" Still no response. Swallowing her panic, she sped up to fifty-five.

Though they'd passed the Sunnyside Up over a mile ago, she could still make out the streetlight winking on and off in her mirror. It took her a few seconds to realize it wasn't just one light she was watching but two, and that they were moving—a pair of headlights, winding along the highway. Was it the same car she'd spotted earlier?

Mesmerized, she watched the lights dance like twin wraiths among the trees, then, suddenly, they vanished and she saw only darkness. A ghost? she wondered irrationally. Any instant she expected the lights to rematerialize, to resume their phantom twinkling in the woods. She was watching the mirror so intently that she almost missed the road sign:

Garberville, Pop, 5,750
Gas—Food—Lodging

A half mile later streetlights appeared, glowing a hazy yellow in the drizzle; a flatbed truck splashed by, headed in the other direction. Though the speed limit had dropped to thirty-five, she kept her foot firmly on the gas pedal and for once in her life prayed for a police car to give chase.

The *Hospital* road sign seemed to leap out at her from nowhere. She braked and swerved onto the turnoff. A quarter mile away, a red *Emergency* sign directed her up a driveway to a side entrance. Leaving Victor in the front seat, she ran inside, through a deserted waiting room, and cried to a nurse sitting at her desk: "Please, help me! I've got a man in my car. . . ."

The nurse responded instantly. She followed Cathy outside, took one look at the man slumped in the front seat, and yelled for assistance.

Even with the help of a burly ER physician, they had difficulty pulling Victor out of the car. He had slid sideways, and his arm was wedged under the emergency hand brake.

"Hey, Miss!" the doctor barked at Cathy. "Climb in the other side and free up his arm!"

Cathy scrambled to the driver's seat. There she hesitated. She would have to manipulate his injured arm. She took his elbow and tried to unhook it from around the brake, but discovered his wristwatch was snagged in the pocket of his windbreaker. After unsnapping the watchband, she took hold of his arm and lifted it over the brake. He responded with a groan of pure agony. The arm slid limply toward the floor.

"Okay!" said the doctor. "Arm's free! Now, just ease him toward me and we'll take it from there."

Gingerly, she guided Victor's head and shoulders safely past the emergency brake. Then she scrambled back outside to help load him onto the wheeled stretcher. Three straps were buckled into place. Everything became a blur of noise and motion as the stretcher was wheeled through the open double doors into the building.

"What happened?" the doctor barked over his shoulder at Cathy.

"I hit him—on the road—"

"When?"

"Fifteen—twenty minutes ago."

"How fast were you driving?"

"About thirty-five."

"Was he conscious when you found him?"

"For about ten minutes—then he sort of faded—"

A nurse said: "Shirt's soaked with blood. He's got broken glass in his shoulder."

In that mad dash beneath harsh fluorescent lights, Cathy had her first clear look at Victor, and she saw a lean, mud-streaked face, a jaw tightly squared in pain, a broad forehead matted damply with light brown hair. He reached out to her, grasping for her hand.

"Cathy—"

"I'm here, Victor."

He held on tightly, refusing to break contact. The pressure of his fingers in her flesh was almost painful. Squinting through the pain, he focused on her face. "I have to—have to tell you—"

"Later!" snapped the doctor.

"No, wait!" Victor was fighting to keep her in view, to hold her beside him. He struggled to speak, agony etching lines on his face.

Cathy bent close, drawn by the desperation of his gaze. "Yes, Victor," she whispered, stroking his hair, longing to ease his pain. This link between their hands, their gazes, felt forged in timeless steel. "Tell me."

"We can't delay!" barked the doctor. "Get him in the room."

All at once, Victor's hand was wrenched away from her as they whisked him into the trauma suite, a nightmarish room of stainless steel and blindingly bright lights. He was lifted onto the surgical table.

"Pulse 110," said a nurse. "Blood pressure eight-five over fifty!"

The doctor ordered, "Let's get two IVs in. Type and cross six units of blood. And get hold of a surgeon. We're going to need help. . . ."

The machine-gun fire of voices, the metallic clang of cabinets and IV poles and instruments was deafening. No one seemed to notice Cathy standing in the doorway, watching in horrified fascination as a nurse pulled out a knife and began to tear off Victor's bloody clothing. With each rip, more and more flesh was exposed, until the shirt and windbreaker were shredded off, revealing a broad chest thickly matted with tawny hair. To the doctors and nurses, this was just another body to labor over, another patient to be saved. To Cathy, this was a living, breathing man, a man she cared about, if only because they had shared those last harrowing moments. The nurse shifted her attention to his belt, which she quickly unbuckled. With a few firm tugs, she peeled off his trousers and shorts and threw them into a pile with the other soiled clothing. Cathy scarcely noticed the man's nakedness, or the nurses and technicians shoving past her into the room. Her shocked gaze had focused on Victor's left shoulder, which was oozing fresh blood onto the table. She remembered how his whole body had resonated with pain when she'd grabbed that shoulder; only now did she understand how much he must have suffered.

A sour taste flooded her throat. She was going to be sick.

Struggling against the nausea, she somehow managed to stumble away and sink into a nearby chair. There she sat for a few minutes, oblivious to the chaos whirling around her. Looking down, she noted with instinctive horror the blood on her hands.

"There you are," someone said. A nurse had just emerged from the trauma room, carrying a bundle of the patient's belongings. She motioned Cathy over to a desk. "We'll need your name and address in case the doctors have any more questions. And the police will have to be notified. Have you called them?"

Cathy shook her head numbly. "I—I guess I should. . . ."

"You can use this phone."

"Thank you."

It rang eight times before anyone answered. The voice that greeted her was raspy with sleep. Obviously, Garberville provided little late-night stimulation, even for the local police. The desk officer took down Cathy's report and told her he'd be in touch with her later, after they'd checked the accident scene.

The nurse had opened Victor's wallet and was flipping through the various ID cards for information. Cathy watched her fill in the blanks on a patient admission form: *Name: Victor Holland. Age: 41. Occupation: Biochemist. Next of kin: Unknown.*

So that was his full name. Victor Holland. Cathy stared down at the stack of ID cards and focused on what appeared to be a security pass for some company called Viratek. A color photograph showed Victor's quietly sober face, its green eyes gazing straight into the camera. Even if she had never seen his face, this was exactly how she would have pictured him, his expression unyielding, his gaze unflinchingly direct. She touched her palm, where he had kissed her. She could still recall how his beard had stung her flesh.

Softly, she asked, "Is he going to be all right?"

The nurse continued writing. "He's lost a lot of blood. But he looks like a pretty tough guy. . . ."

Cathy nodded, remembering how, even in his agony, Victor had somehow dredged up the strength to keep moving through the rain. Yes, she knew just how tough a man he was.

The nurse handed her a pen and the information sheet. "If you could write your name and address at the bottom. In case the doctor has any more questions."

Cathy fished out Sarah's address and phone number from her purse and copied them onto the form. "My name's Cathy Weaver. You can get hold of me at this number."

"You're staying in Garberville?"

"For three weeks. I'm just visiting."

"Oh. Terrific way to start a vacation, huh?"

Cathy sighed as she rose to leave. "Yeah. Terrific."

She paused outside the trauma room, wondering what was happening inside, knowing that Victor was fighting for his life. She wondered if he was still conscious, if he would remember her. It seemed important that he *did* remember her.

Cathy turned to the nurse. "You will call me, won't you? I mean, you'll let me know if he . . ."

The nurse nodded. "We'll keep you informed."

Outside, the rain had finally stopped and a belt of stars twinkled through a parting in the clouds. To Cathy's weary eyes, it was an exhilarating sight, that first glimpse of the storm's end. As she drove out of the hospital parking lot, she was shaking from fatigue. She never noticed the car parked across the street or the brief glow of the cigarette before it was snuffed out.

2

Barely a minute after Cathy left the hospital, a man walked into the emergency room, sweeping the smells of a stormy night in with him through the double doors. The nurse on duty was busy with the new patient's admission papers. At the sudden rush of cold air, she looked up to see a man approach her desk. He was about thirty-five, gaunt-faced, silent, his dark hair lightly feathered by gray. Droplets of water sparkled on his tan Burberry raincoat.

"Can I help you, sir?" she asked, focusing on his eyes, which were as black and polished as pebbles in a pond.

Nodding, he said quietly, "Was there a man brought in a short time ago? Victor Holland?"

The nurse glanced down at the papers on her desk. That was the name. Victor Holland. "Yes," she said. "Are you a relative?"

"I'm his brother. How is he?"

"He just arrived, sir. They're working on him now. If you'll wait, I can check on how he's doing—" She stopped to answer the ringing telephone. It was a technician calling with the new patient's laboratory results. As she jotted down the numbers, she noticed out of the corner of her eye that the man had turned and was gazing at the closed door to the trauma room. It suddenly swung open as an orderly emerged carrying a bulging plastic bag streaked with blood. The clamor of voices spilled from the room:

"Pressure up to 110 over 70!"

"OR says they're ready to go."

"Where's that surgeon?"

"On his way. He had car trouble."

"Ready for X rays! Everyone back!"

Slowly the door closed, muffling the voices. The nurse hung up just as the orderly deposited the plastic bag on her desk. "What's this?" she asked.

"Patient's clothes. They're a mess. Should I just toss 'em?"

"I'll take them home," the man in the raincoat cut in. "Is everything here?"

The orderly flashed the nurse an uncomfortable glance. "I'm not sure he'd want to . . . I mean, they're kind of . . . uh, dirty. . . ."

The nurse said quickly, "Mr. Holland, why don't you let us dispose of the clothes for you? There's nothing worth keeping in there. I've already collected his valuables." She unlocked a drawer and pulled out a sealed manila envelope labeled: Holland, Victor. Contents: Wallet, Wristwatch. "You can take these home. Just sign this receipt."

The man nodded and signed his name: David Holland. "Tell me," he said, sliding the envelope in his pocket. "Is Victor awake? Has he said anything?"

"I'm afraid not. He was semiconscious when he arrived."

The man took this information in silence, a silence that the nurse found suddenly and profoundly disturbing. "Excuse me, Mr. Holland?" she asked. "How did you hear your brother was hurt? I didn't get a chance to contact any relatives. . . ."

"The police called me. Victor was driving my car. They found it smashed up at the side of the road."

"Oh. What an awful way to be notified."

"Yes. The stuff of nightmares."

"At least someone was able to get in touch with you." She sifted through the sheaf of papers on her desk. "Can we get your address and phone number? In case we need to reach you?"

"Of course." The man took the ER papers, which he quickly scanned before scrawling his name and phone number on the blank marked Next of Kin. "Who's this Catherine Weaver?" he asked, pointing to the name and address at the bottom of the page.

"She's the woman who brought him in."

"I'll have to thank her." He handed back the papers.

"Nurse?"

She looked around and saw that the doctor was calling to her from the trauma room doorway. "Yes?"

"I want you to call the police. Tell them to get in here as soon as possible."

"They've been called, Doctor. They know about the accident—"

"Call them again. This is no accident."

"What?"

"We just got the X rays. The man's got a bullet in his shoulder."

"A *bullet?*" A chill went through the nurse's body, like a cold wind sweeping in from the night. Slowly, she turned toward the man in the raincoat, the man who'd claimed to be Victor Holland's brother. To her amazement, no one was there. She felt only a cold puff of night air, and then she saw the double doors quietly slide shut.

"Where the hell did he go?" the orderly whispered.

For a few seconds she could only stare at the closed doors. Then her gaze dropped and she focused on the empty spot on her desk. The bag containing Victor Holland's clothes had vanished.

"Why did the police call again?"

Cathy slowly replaced the telephone receiver. Even though she was bundled in a warm terry-cloth robe, she was shivering. She turned and stared across the kitchen at Sarah. "That man on the road—they found a bullet in his shoulder."

In the midst of pouring tea, Sarah glanced up in surprise. "You mean—someone *shot* him?"

Cathy sank down at the kitchen table and gazed numbly at the cup of cinnamon tea that Sarah had just slid in front of her. A hot bath and a soothing hour of sitting by the fireplace had made the night's events seem like nothing more than a bad dream. Here in Sarah's kitchen, with its chintz curtains and its cinnamon and spice smells, the violence of the real world seemed a million miles away.

Sarah leaned toward her. "Do they know what happened? Has he said anything?"

"He just got out of surgery." She turned and glanced at the telephone. "I should call the hospital again—"

"No. You shouldn't. You've done everything you possibly can." Sarah gently touched her arm. "And your tea's getting cold."

With a shaking hand, Cathy brushed back a strand of damp hair and settled uneasily in her chair. A bullet in his shoulder, she thought. Why? Had it been a random attack, a highway gunslinger blasting out the car window at a total stranger? She'd read about it in the newspapers, the stories of freeway arguments settled by the pulling of a trigger.

Or had it been a deliberate attack? Had Victor Holland been targeted for death?

Outside, something rattled and clanged against the house. Cathy sat up sharply. "What was that?"

"Believe me, it's not the bogeyman," said Sarah, laughing. She went to the kitchen door and reached for the bolt.

"Sarah!" Cathy called in panic as the bolt slid open. "Wait!"

"Take a look for yourself." Sarah opened the door. The kitchen light swung across a cluster of trash cans sitting in the carport. A shadow slid to the ground and scurried away, trailing food wrappers across the driveway. "Raccoons," said Sarah. "If I don't tie the lids down, those pests'll scatter trash all over the yard." Another shadow popped its head out of a can and stared at her, its eyes glowing in the darkness. Sarah clapped her hands and yelled, "Go on, get lost!" The raccoon didn't budge. "Don't you have a home to go to?" At last, the raccoon dropped to the ground and ambled off into the trees. "They get bolder every year," Sarah sighed, closing the door. She turned and winked at Cathy. "So take it easy. This isn't the big city."

"Keep reminding me." Cathy took a slice of banana bread and began to spread it with sweet butter. "You know, Sarah, I think it'll be a lot nicer spending Christmas with you than it ever was with old Jack."

"Uh-oh. Since we're now speaking of ex-husbands—" Sarah shuffled over to a cabinet "—we might as well get in the right frame of mind. And tea just won't cut it." She grinned and waved a bottle of brandy.

"Sarah, you're not drinking alcohol, are you?"

"It's not for *me.*" Sarah set the bottle and a single wine glass in front of Cathy. "But I think *you* could use a nip. After all, it's been a cold, traumatic night. And here we are, talking about turkeys of the male variety."

"Well, since you put it that way . . ." Cathy poured out a generous shot of brandy. "To the turkeys of the world," she declared and took a sip. It felt just right going down.

"So how *is* old Jack?" asked Sarah.

"Same as always."

"Blondes?"

"He's moved on to brunettes."

"It took him only a year to go through the world's supply of blondes?"

Cathy shrugged. "He might have missed a few."

They both laughed then, light and easy laughter that told them their wounds were well on the way to healing, that men were now creatures to be discussed without pain, without sorrow.

Cathy regarded her glass of brandy. "Do you suppose there *are* any good men left in the world? I mean, shouldn't there be *one* floating around somewhere? Maybe a mutation or something? One measly decent guy?"

"Sure. Somewhere in Siberia. But he's a hundred-and-twenty years old."

"I've always liked older men."

They laughed again, but this time the sound wasn't as lighthearted. So many years had passed since their college days together, the days when they had *known*, had never doubted, that Prince Charmings abounded in the world.

Cathy drained her glass of brandy and set it down. "What a lousy friend I am. Keeping a pregnant lady up all night! What time is it, anyway?"

"Only two-thirty in the morning."

"Oh, Sarah! Go to bed!" Cathy went to the sink and began wetting a handful of paper towels.

"And what are you going to do?" Sarah asked.

"I just want to clean up the car. I didn't get all the blood off the seat."

"I already did it."

"What? When?"

"While you were taking a bath."

"Sarah, you idiot."

"Hey, I didn't have a miscarriage or anything. Oh, I almost forgot." Sarah pointed to a tiny film canister on the counter. "I found that on the floor of your car."

Cathy shook her head and sighed. "It's Hickey's."

"Hickey! Now *there's* a waste of a man."

"He's also a good friend of mine."

"That's all Hickey will ever be to a woman. A *friend*. So what's on the roll of film? Naked women, as usual?"

"I don't even want to know. When I dropped him off at the airport, he handed me a half-dozen rolls and told me he'd pick them up when he got back. Guess he didn't want to lug 'em all the way to Nairobi."

"Is that where he went? Nairobi?"

"He's shooting 'gorgeous ladies of Africa' or something." Cathy slipped the film canister into her bathrobe pocket. "This must've dropped out of the glove compartment. Gee. I hope it's not pornographic."

"Knowing Hickey, it probably is."

They both laughed at the irony of it all. Hickman Von Trapp, whose only job it was to photograph naked females in erotic poses, had absolutely no interest in the opposite sex, with the possible exception of his mother.

"A guy like Hickey only goes to prove my point," Sarah said over her shoulder as she headed up the hall to bed.

"What point is that?"

"There really *are* no good men left in the world!"

It was the light that dragged Victor up from the depths of unconsciousness, a light brighter than a dozen suns, beating against his closed eyelids. He didn't want to wake up; he knew, in some dim, scarcely functioning part of his brain, that if he continued to struggle against this blessed oblivion he would feel pain and nausea and something else, something much, much worse: terror. Of what, he couldn't remember. Of death? No, no, this was death, or as close as one could come to it, and it was warm and black and comfortable. But he had something important to do, something that he couldn't allow himself to forget. He tried to think, but all he could remember was a hand, gentle but somehow strong, brushing his forehead, and a voice, reaching to him softly in the darkness.

My name is Catherine. . . .

As her touch, her voice, flooded his memory, so too did the fear. Not for himself (he was dead, wasn't he?) but for her. Strong, gentle Catherine. He'd seen her face only briefly, could scarcely remember it, but somehow he knew she was beautiful, the way a blind man knows, without benefit of vision, that a rainbow or the sky or his own dear child's face is beautiful. And now he was afraid for her.

Where are you? he wanted to cry out.

"He's coming around," said a female voice (not Catherine's, it was too hard, too crisp) followed by a confusing rush of other voices.

"Watch that IV!"

"Mr. Holland, hold still. Everything's going to be all right—"

"I said, watch the IV!"

"Hand me that second unit of blood—"

"Don't move, Mr. Holland—"

Where are you, Catherine? The shout exploded in his head. Fighting the temptation to sink back into unconsciousness, he struggled to lift his eyelids. At first, there was only a blur of light and color, so harsh he felt it stab through his sockets straight to his brain. Gradually the blur took the shape of faces, strangers in blue, frowning down at him. He tried to focus but the effort made his stomach rebel.

"Mr. Holland, take it easy," said a quietly gruff voice. "You're in the hospital—the recovery room. They've just operated on your shoulder. You just rest and go back to sleep. . . ."

No. No, I can't, he tried to say.

"Five milligrams of morphine going in," someone said, and Victor felt a warm flush creep up his arm and spread across his chest.

"That should help," he heard. "Now, sleep. Everything went just fine. . . ."

You don't understand, he wanted to scream. *I have to warn her*—It was the last conscious thought he had before the lights once again were swallowed by the gentle darkness.

Alone in her husbandless bed, Sarah lay smiling. No, laughing! Her whole body seemed filled with laughter tonight. She wanted to sing, to dance. To stand at the open window and shout out her joy! It was all hormonal, she'd been told, this chemical pandemonium of pregnancy, dragging her body on a roller coaster of emotions. She knew she should rest, she should work toward serenity, but tonight she wasn't tired at all. Poor exhausted Cathy had dragged herself up the attic steps to bed. But here was Sarah, still wide awake.

She closed her eyes and focused her thoughts on the child resting in her belly. *How are you, my love? Are you asleep? Or are you listening, hearing my thoughts even now?*

The baby wiggled in her belly, then fell silent. It was a reply, secret words shared only between them. Sarah was almost glad there was no husband to distract her from this silent conversation, to lie here in jealousy, an outsider. There was only mother and child, the ancient bond, the mystical link.

Poor Cathy, she thought, riding those roller coaster emotions from joy to sadness for her friend. She knew Cathy yearned just as deeply for a child, but eventually time would snatch the chance away from her. Cathy was too much of a romantic to realize that the man, the circumstances, might never be right. Hadn't it taken Cathy ten long years to finally acknowledge that her marriage was a miserable failure? Not that Cathy hadn't tried to make it work. She had tried to the point of developing a monumental blind spot to Jack's faults, primarily his selfishness. It was surprising how a woman so bright, so intuitive, could have let things drag on as long as she did. But that was Cathy. Even at thirty-seven she was open and trusting and loyal to the point of idiocy.

The clatter of gravel outside on the driveway pricked Sarah's awareness. Lying perfectly still, she listened and for a moment heard only the familiar creak of the trees, the rustle of branches against the shake roof. Then—there it was again. Stones skittering across the road, and then the faint squeal of metal. Those raccoons again. If she didn't shoo them off now, they'd litter garbage all over the driveway.

Sighing, she sat up and hunted in the darkness for her slippers.

Shuffling quietly out of her bedroom, she navigated instinctively down
the hallway and into the kitchen. Her eyes found the night too comfortable; she didn't want to assault them with light. Instead of flipping
on the carport switch, she grabbed the flashlight from its usual spot on
the kitchen shelf and unlocked the door.

Outside, moonlight glowed dimly through the clouds. She pointed
the flashlight at the trash cans, but her beam caught no raccoon eyes,
no telltale scattering of garbage, only the dull reflection of stainless
steel. Puzzled, she crossed the carport and paused next to the Datsun
that Cathy had parked in the driveway.

That was when she noticed the light glowing faintly inside the car.
Glancing through the window, she saw that the glove compartment was
open. Her first thought was that it had somehow fallen open by itself or
that she or Cathy had forgotten to close it. Then she spotted the road
maps strewn haphazardly across the front seat.

With fear suddenly hissing in her ear, she backed away, but terror
made her legs slow and stiff. Only then did she sense that someone was
nearby, waiting in the darkness; she could feel his presence, like a chill
wind in the night.

She wheeled around for the house. As she turned, the beam of her
flashlight swung around in a wild arc, only to freeze on the face of a
man. The eyes that stared down at her were as slick and as black as
pebbles. She scarcely focused on the rest of his face: the hawk nose,
the thin, bloodless lips. It was only the eyes she saw. They were the
eyes of a man without a soul.

"Hello, Catherine," he whispered, and she heard, in his voice, the
greeting of death.

Please, she wanted to cry out as she felt him wrench her hair backward, exposing her neck. *Let me live!*

But no sound escaped. The words, like his blade, were buried in her
throat.

Cathy woke up to the quarreling of blue jays outside her window, a
sound that brought a smile to her lips for it struck her as somehow
whimsical, this flap and flutter of wings across the panes, this maniacal
crackling of feathered enemies. So unlike the morning roar of buses
and cars she was accustomed to. The blue jays' quarrel moved to the
rooftop, and she heard their claws scratching across the shakes in a
dance of combat. She trailed their progress across the ceiling, up one
side of the roof and down the other. Then, tired of the battle, she
focused on the window.

Morning sunlight cascaded in, bathing the attic room in a soft haze.

Such a perfect room for a nursery! She could see all the changes Sarah had already made here—the Jack-and-Jill curtains, the watercolor animal portraits. The very prospect of a baby sleeping in this room filled her with such joy that she sat up, grinning, and hugged the covers to her knees. Then she glanced at her watch on the nightstand and saw it was already nine-thirty—half the morning gone!

Reluctantly, she left the warmth of her bed and poked around in her suitcase for a sweater and jeans. She dressed to the thrashing of blue jays in the branches, the battle having moved from the roof to the treetops. From the window, she watched them dart from twig to twig until one finally hoisted up the feathered version of a white flag and took off, defeated. The victor, his authority no longer in question, gave one last screech and settled back to preen his feathers.

Only then did Cathy notice the silence of the house, a stillness that magnified her every heartbeat, her every breath.

Leaving the room, she descended the attic steps and confronted the empty living room. Ashes from last night's fire mounded the grate. A silver garland drooped from the Christmas tree. A cardboard angel with glittery wings winked on the mantelpiece. She followed the hallway to Sarah's room and frowned at the rumpled bed, the coverlet flung aside. "Sarah?"

Her voice was swallowed up in the stillness. How could a cottage seem so immense? She wandered back through the living room and into the kitchen. Last night's teacups still sat in the sink. On the windowsill, an asparagus fern trembled, stirred by a breeze through the open door.

Cathy stepped out into the carport where Sarah's old Dodge was parked. "Sarah?" she called.

Something skittered across the roof. Startled, Cathy looked up and suddenly laughed as she heard the blue jay chattering in the tree above—a victory speech, no doubt. Even the animal kingdom had its conceits.

She started to head back into the house when her gaze swept past a stain on the gravel near the car's rear tire. For a few seconds she stared at the blot of rust-brown, unable to comprehend its meaning. Slowly, she moved alongside the car, her gaze tracing the stain backward along its meandering course.

As she rounded the rear of the car, the driveway came into full view. The dried rivulet of brown became a crimson lake in which a single swimmer lay open-eyed and still.

The blue jay's chatter abruptly ceased as another sound rose up and filled the trees. It was Cathy, screaming.

                              *   *   *

"Hey, mister. Hey, mister."

Victor tried to brush off the sound but it kept buzzing in his ear, like a fly that can't be shooed away.

"Hey, mister. You awake?"

Victor opened his eyes and focused painfully on a wry little face stubbled with gray whiskers. The apparition grinned, and darkness gaped where teeth should have been. Victor stared into that foul black hole of a mouth and thought: *I've died and gone to hell.*

"Hey, mister, you got a cigarette?"

Victor shook his head and barely managed to whisper: "I don't think so."

"Well, you got a dollar I could borrow?"

"Go away," groaned Victor, shutting his eyes against the daylight. He tried to think, tried to remember where he was, but his head ached and the little man's voice kept distracting him.

"Can't get no cigarettes in this place. Like a jail in here. Don't know why I don't just get up and walk out. But y'know, streets are cold this time of year. Been rainin' all night long. Least in here it's warm. . . ."

Raining all night long . . . Suddenly Victor remembered. The rain. Running and running through the rain.

Victor's eyes shot open. "Where am I?"

"Three East. Land o' the bitches."

He struggled to sit up and almost gasped from the pain. Dizzily, he focused on the metal pole with its bag of fluid dripping slowly into the plastic intravenous tube, then stared at the bandages on his left shoulder. Through the window, he saw that the day was already drenched in sunshine. "What time is it?"

"Dunno. Nine o'clock, I guess. You missed breakfast."

"I've got to get out of here." Victor swung his legs out of bed and discovered that, except for a flimsy hospital gown, he was stark naked. "Where's my clothes? My wallet?"

The old man shrugged. "Nurse'd know. Ask her."

Victor found the call button buried among the bed sheets. He stabbed it a few times, then turned his attention to peeling off the tape affixing the IV tube to his arm.

The door hissed open and a woman's voice barked, *"Mr. Holland! What do you think you're doing?"*

"I'm getting out of here, that's what I'm doing," said Victor as he stripped off the last piece of tape. Before he could pull the IV out, the nurse rushed across the room as fast as her stout legs could carry her and slapped a piece of gauze over the catheter.

"Don't blame me, Miss Redfern!" screeched the little man.

"Lenny, go back to your own bed this instant! And as for you, Mr. Holland," she said, turning her steel-blue eyes on Victor, "you've lost too much blood." Trapping his arm against her massive biceps, she began to retape the catheter firmly in place.

"Just get me my clothes."

"Don't argue, Mr. Holland. You have to stay."

"Why?"

"Because you've got an IV, that's why!" she snapped, as if the plastic tube itself was some sort of irreversible condition.

"I want my clothes."

"I'd have to check with the ER. Nothing of yours came up to the floor."

"Then call the ER, damn you!" At Miss Redfern's disapproving scowl, he added with strained politeness, *"If* you don't mind."

It was another half hour before a woman showed up from the business office to explain what had happened to Victor's belongings.

"I'm afraid we—well, we seem to have . . . lost your clothes, Mr. Holland," she said, fidgeting under his astonished gaze.

"What do you mean, *lost?"*

"They were—" she cleared her throat "—er, stolen. From the emergency room. Believe me, this has never happened before. We're really very sorry about this, Mr. Holland, and I'm sure we'll be able to arrange a purchase of replacement clothing. . . ."

She was too busy trying to make excuses to notice that Victor's face had frozen in alarm. That his mind was racing as he tried to remember, through the blur of last night's events, just what had happened to the film canister. He knew he'd had it in his pocket during the endless drive to the hospital. He remembered clutching it there, remembered flailing senselessly at the woman when she'd tried to pull his hand from his pocket. After that, nothing was clear, nothing was certain. *Have I lost it?* he thought. *Have I lost my only evidence?*

". . . While the money's missing, your credit cards seem to be all there, so I guess that's something to be thankful for."

He looked at her blankly. "What?"

"Your valuables, Mr. Holland." She pointed to the wallet and watch she'd just placed on the bedside table. "The security guard found them in the trash bin outside the hospital. Looks like the thief only wanted your cash."

"And my clothes. Right."

The instant the woman left, Victor pressed the button for Miss Redfern. She walked in carrying a breakfast tray. "Eat, Mr. Holland," she said. "Maybe your behavior's all due to hypoglycemia."

"A woman brought me to the ER," he said. "Her first name was Catherine. I have to get hold of her."

"Oh, look! Eggs and Rice Krispies! Here's your fork—"

"Miss Redfern, will you forget the damned Rice Krispies!"

Miss Redfern slapped down the cereal box. "There is no need for profanity!"

"I have to find that woman!"

Without a word, Miss Redfern spun around and marched out of the room. A few minutes later she returned and brusquely handed him a slip of paper. On it was written the name Catherine Weaver followed by a local address.

"You'd better eat fast," she said. "There's a policeman coming over to talk to you."

"Fine," he grunted, stuffing a forkful of cold, rubbery egg in his mouth.

"And some man from the FBI called. He's on his way, too."

Victor's head jerked up in alarm. "The FBI? What was his name?"

"Oh, for heaven's sake, how should I know? Something Polish, I think."

Staring at her, Victor slowly put down his fork. "Polowski," he said softly.

"That sounds like it. Polowski." She turned and headed out of the room. "The FBI indeed," she muttered. "Wonder what he did to get *their* attention. . . ."

Before the door had even swung shut behind her, Victor was out of bed and tearing at his IV. He scarcely felt the sting of the tape wrenching the hair off his arm; he had to concentrate on getting the hell out of this hospital before Polowski showed up. He was certain the FBI agent had set him up for that ambush last night, and he wasn't about to wait around for another attack.

He turned and snapped at his roommate, "Lenny, where are your clothes?"

Lenny's gaze traveled reluctantly to a cabinet near the sink. "Don't got no other clothes. Besides, they wouldn't fit you, mister . . ."

Victor yanked open the cabinet door and pulled out a frayed cotton shirt and a pair of baggy polyester pants. The pants were too short and about six inches of Victor's hairy legs stuck out below the cuffs, but he had no trouble fastening the belt. The real trouble was going to be finding a pair of size twelve shoes. To his relief, he discovered that the cabinet also contained a pair of Lenny's thongs. His heels hung at least an inch over the back edge, but at least he wouldn't be barefoot.

"Those are mine!" protested Lenny.

"Here. You can have this." Victor tossed his wristwatch to the old man. "You should be able to hock that for a whole new outfit."

Suspicious, Lenny put the watch up against his ear. "Piece of junk. It's not ticking."

"It's quartz."

"Oh. Yeah. I knew that."

Victor pocketed his wallet and went to the door. Opening it just a crack, he peered down the hall toward the nurses' station. The coast was clear. He glanced back at Lenny. "So long, buddy. Give my regards to Miss Redfern."

Slipping out of the room, Victor headed quietly down the hall, away from the nurses' station. The emergency stairwell door was at the far end, marked by the warning painted in red: Alarm Will Sound If Opened. He walked steadily towards it, willing himself not to run, not to attract attention. But just as he neared the door, a familiar voice echoed in the hall.

"Mr. Holland! You come back here this instant!"

Victor lunged for the door, slammed against the closing bar, and dashed into the stairwell.

His footsteps echoed against the concrete as he pounded down the stairs. By the time he heard Miss Redfern scramble after him into the stairwell, he'd already reached the first floor and was pushing through the last door to freedom.

"Mr. Holland!" yelled Miss Redfern.

Even as he dashed across the parking lot, he could still hear Miss Redfern's outraged voice echoing in his ears.

Eight blocks away he turned into a K Mart, and within ten minutes had bought a shirt, blue jeans, underwear, socks and a pair of size-twelve tennis shoes, all of which he paid for with his credit card. He tossed Lenny's old clothes into a trash can.

Before emerging back outside, he peered through the store window at the street. It seemed like a perfectly normal mid-December morning in a small town, shoppers strolling beneath a tacky garland of Christmas decorations, a half-dozen cars waiting patiently at a red light. He was just about to step out the door when he spotted the police car creeping down the road. Immediately he ducked behind an undressed mannequin and watched through the nude plastic limbs as the police car made its way slowly past the K Mart and continued in the direction of the hospital. They were obviously searching for someone. Was he the one they wanted?

He couldn't afford to risk a stroll down Main Street. There was no way of knowing who else besides Polowski was involved in the double cross.

It took him at least an hour on foot to reach the outskirts of town, and by then he was so weak and wobbly he could barely stand. The surge of adrenaline that had sent him dashing from the hospital was at last petering out. Too tired to take another step, he sank onto a boulder at the side of the highway and halfheartedly held out his thumb. To his immense relief, the next vehicle to come along—a pickup truck loaded with firewood—pulled over. Victor climbed in and collapsed gratefully on the seat.

The driver spat out the window, then squinted at Victor from beneath an Agway Seeds cap. "Goin' far?"

"Just a few miles. Oak Hill Road."

"Yep. I go right past it." The driver pulled back onto the road. The truck spewed black exhaust as they roared down the highway, country music blaring from the radio.

Through the plucked strains of guitar music, Victor heard a sound that made him sit up sharply. A siren. Whipping his head around, he saw a patrol car zooming up fast behind them. *That's it,* thought Victor. *They've found me. They're going to stop this truck and arrest me. . . .*

But for what? For walking away from the hospital? For insulting Miss Redfern? Or had Polowski fabricated some charge against him?

With a sense of impending doom, he waited for the patrol car to overtake them and start flashing its signal to pull over. In fact, he was so certain they *would* be pulled over that when the police car sped right past them and roared off down the highway, he could only stare ahead in amazement.

"Must be some kinda trouble," his companion said blandly, nodding at the rapidly vanishing police car.

Victor managed to clear his throat. "Trouble?"

"Yep. Don't get much of a chance to use that siren of theirs but when they do, boy oh boy, do they go to town with it."

With his heart hammering against his ribs, Victor sat back and forced himself to calm down. He had nothing to worry about. The police weren't after him, they were busy with some other concern. He wondered what sort of small-town catastrophe could warrant blaring sirens. Probably nothing more exciting than a few kids out on a joyride.

By the time they reached the turnoff to Oak Hill Road, Victor's pulse had settled back to normal. He thanked the driver, climbed out, and began the trek to Catherine Weaver's house. It was a long walk, and the road wound through a forest of pines. Every so often he'd pass a mailbox along the road and, peering through the trees, would spot a house. Catherine's address was coming up fast.

What on earth should he say to her? Up till now he'd concentrated only on reaching her house. Now that he was almost there, he had to come up with some reasonable explanation for why he'd dragged himself out of a hospital bed and trudged all this way to see her. A simple *thanks for saving my life* just wouldn't do it. He had to find out if she had the film canister. But she, of course, would want to know why the damn thing was so important.

You could tell her the truth.

No, forget that. He could imagine her reaction if he were to launch into his wild tale about viruses and dead scientists and double-crossing FBI agents. *The FBI is out to get you? I see. And who else is after you, Mr. Holland?* It was so absurdly paranoid he almost felt like laughing. No, he couldn't tell her any of it or he'd end up right back in a hospital, and this time in a ward that would make Miss Redfern's Three East look like paradise.

She didn't need to know any of it. In fact, she was better off igno-rant. The woman had saved his life, and the last thing he wanted to do was put her in any danger. The film was all he wanted from her. After today, she'd never see him again.

He was so busy debating what to tell her that he didn't notice the police cars until well after he'd rounded the road's bend. Suddenly he froze, confronted by three squad cars—probably the entire police fleet of Garberville—parked in front of a rustic cedar house. A half-dozen neighbors lingered in the gravel driveway, shaking their heads in disbe-lief. Good God, had something happened to Catherine?

Swallowing the urge to turn and flee, Victor propelled himself for-ward, past the squad cars and through the loose gathering of onlook-ers, only to be stopped by a uniformed officer.

"I'm sorry, sir. No one's allowed past this point."

Dazed, Victor stared down and saw that the police had strung out a perimeter of red tape. Slowly, his gaze moved beyond the tape, to the old Datsun parked near the carport. Was that Catherine's car? He tried desperately to remember if she'd driven a Datsun, but last night it had been so dark and he'd been in so much pain that he hadn't both-ered to pay attention. All he could remember was that it was a compact model, with scarcely enough room for his legs. Then he noticed the faded parking sticker on the rear bumper: Parking Permit, Studio Lot A.

I work for an independent film company, she'd told him last night.

It was Catherine's car.

Unwillingly, he focused on the stained gravel just beside the Datsun, and even though the rational part of him knew that that peculiar brick red could only be dried blood, he wanted to deny it. He wanted to believe there was some other explanation for that stain, for this ominous gathering of police.

He tried to speak, but his voice sounded like something dragged up through gravel.

"What did you say, sir?" the police officer asked.

"What—what happened?"

The officer shook his head sadly. "Woman was killed here last night. Our first murder in ten years."

"Murder?" Victor's gaze was still fixed in horror on the bloodstained gravel. "But—*why?*"

The officer shrugged. "Don't know yet. Maybe robbery, though I don't think he got much." He nodded at the Datsun. "Car was the only thing broken into."

If Victor said anything at that point, he never remembered what it was. He was vaguely aware of his legs carrying him back through the onlookers, past the three police cars, toward the road. The sunshine was so brilliant it hurt his eyes and he could barely see where he was going.

I killed her, he thought. *She saved my life and I killed her. . . .*

Guilt slashed its way to his throat and he could scarcely breathe, could barely take another step for the pain. For a long time he stood there at the side of the road, his head bent in the sunshine, his ears filled with the sound of blue jays, and mourned a woman he'd never known.

When at last he was able to raise his head again, rage fueled the rest of his walk back to the highway, rage against Catherine's murderer. Rage at himself for having put her in such danger. It was the film the killer had been searching for, and he'd probably found it in the Datsun. If he hadn't, the house would have been ransacked, as well.

Now what? thought Victor. He dismissed the possibility that his briefcase—with most of the evidence—might still be in his wrecked car. That was the first place the killer would have searched. Without the film, Victor was left with no evidence at all. It would all come down to his word against Viratek's. The newspapers would dismiss him as nothing more than a disgruntled ex-employee. And after Polowski's double cross, he couldn't trust the FBI.

At that last thought, he quickened his pace. The sooner he got out of Garberville, the better. When he got back to the highway, he'd hitch another ride. Once safely out of town, he could take the time to plan his next move.

He decided to head south, to San Francisco.

3

From the window of his office at Viratek, Archibald Black watched the limousine glide up the tree-lined driveway and pull to a stop at the front entrance. Black snorted derisively. The cowboy was back in town, damn him. And after all the man's fussing about the importance of secrecy, about keeping his little visit discreet, the idiot had the gall to show up in a limousine—with a uniformed driver, no less.

Black turned from the window and paced over to his desk. Despite his contempt for the visitor, he had to acknowledge the man made him uneasy, the way all so-called men of action made him uneasy. Not enough brains behind all that muscle. Too much power in the hands of imbeciles, he thought. Is this an example of who we have running the country?

The intercom buzzed. "Mr. Black?" said his secretary. "A Mr. Tyrone is here to see you."

"Send him in, please," said Black, smoothing the scorn from his expression. He was wearing a look of polite deference when the door opened and Matthew Tyrone walked into the office.

They shook hands. Tyrone's grip was unreasonably firm, as though he was trying to remind Black of their relative positions of power. His bearing had all the spit and polish of an ex-marine, which Tyrone was. Only the thickening waist betrayed the fact that Tyrone's marine days had been left far behind.

"How was the flight from Washington?" inquired Black as they sat down.

"Terrible service. I tell you, commercial flights aren't what they used to be. To think the average American pays good money for the privilege."

"I imagine it can't compare with Air Force One."

Tyrone smiled. "Let's get down to business. Tell me where things stand with this little crisis of yours."

Black noted Tyrone's use of the word *yours*. *So now it's my problem,* he thought. Naturally. That's what they meant by deniability: When things go wrong, the other guy gets the blame. If any of this leaked out, Black's head would be the one to fall. But then, that's why this contract was so lucrative—because he—meaning Viratek—was willing to take that risk.

"We've recovered the documents," said Black. "And the film canisters. The negatives are being developed now."

"And your two employees?"

Black cleared his throat. "There's no need to take this any further."

"They're a risk to national security."

"You can't just kill them off!"

"Can't we?" Tyrone's eyes were a cold, gun-metal gray. An appropriate color for someone who called himself "the Cowboy." You didn't argue with anyone who had eyes like that. Not if you had an instinct for self-preservation.

Black dipped his head deferentially. "I'm not accustomed to this sort of . . . business. And I don't like dealing with your man Savitch."

"Mr. Savitch has performed well for us before."

"He killed one of my senior scientists!"

"I assume it was necessary."

Black looked down unhappily at his desk. Just the thought of that monster Savitch made him shudder.

"Why, exactly, did Martinique go bad?"

Because he had a conscience, thought Black. He looked at Tyrone. "There was no way to predict it. He'd worked in commercial R and D for ten years. He'd never presented a security problem before. We only found out last week that he'd taken classified documents. And then Victor Holland got involved. . . ."

"How much does Holland know?"

"Holland wasn't involved with the project. But he's clever. If he looked over those papers, he might have pieced it together."

Now Tyrone was agitated, his fingers drumming the desktop. "Tell me about Holland. What do you know about him?"

"I've gone over his personnel file. He's forty-one years old, born and raised in San Diego. Entered the seminary but dropped out after a year. Went on to Stanford, then MIT. Doctorate in biochemistry. He was with Viratek for four years. One of our most promising researchers."

"What about his personal life?"

"His wife died three years ago of leukemia. Keeps pretty much to himself these days. Quiet kind of guy, likes classical jazz. Plays the saxophone in some amateur group."

Tyrone laughed. "Your typical nerd scientist." It was just the sort of moronic comment an ex-marine like Tyrone would make. It was an insult that grated on Black. Years ago, before he created Viratek Industries, Black too had been a research biochemist.

"He should be a simple matter to dispose of," said Tyrone. "Inexperienced. And probably scared." He reached for his briefcase. "Mr. Savitch is an expert on these matters. I suggest you let him take care of the problem."

"Of course." In truth, Black didn't think he had any choice. Nicholas Savitch was like some evil, frightening force that, once unleashed, could not be controlled.

The intercom buzzed. "Mr. Gregorian's here from the photo lab," said the secretary.

"Send him in." Black glanced at Tyrone. "The film's been developed. Let's see just what Martinique managed to photograph."

Gregorian walked in carrying a bulky envelope. "Here are those contact prints you requested," he said, handing the bundle across the desk to Black. Then he cupped his hand over his mouth, muffling a sound suspiciously like laughter.

"Yes, Mr. Gregorian?" inquired Black.

"Nothing, sir."

Tyrone cut in, "Well, let's see them!"

Black removed the five contact sheets and lay them out on the desk for everyone to see. The men stared.

For a long time, no one spoke. Then Tyrone said, "Is this some sort of joke?"

Gregorian burst out laughing.

Black said, "What the hell is this?"

"Those are the negatives you gave me, sir," Gregorian insisted. "I processed them myself."

"These are the photos you got back from Victor Holland?" Tyrone's voice started soft and rose slowly to a roar. "Five rolls of *naked women?*"

"There's been a mistake," said Black. "It's the wrong film—"

Gregorian laughed harder.

"Shut up!" yelled Black. He looked at Tyrone. "I don't know how this happened."

"Then the roll we want is still out there?"

Black nodded wearily.

Tyrone reached for the phone. "We need to clean things up. Fast."

"Who are you calling?" asked Black.

"The man who can do the job," said Tyrone as he punched in the numbers. "Savitch."

In his motel room on Lombard Street, Victor paced the avocado-green carpet, wracking his brain for a plan. Any plan. His well-organized scientist's mind had already distilled the situation into the elements of a research project. Identify the problem: someone is out to kill me. State your hypothesis: Jerry Martinique uncovered something dangerous and he was killed for it. Now they think I have the information—and the evidence. Which I don't. Goal: Stay alive. Method: *Any damn way I can!*

For the last two days, his only strategy had consisted of holing up in various cheap motel rooms and pacing the carpets. He couldn't hide out forever. If the feds were involved, and he had reason to believe they were, they'd soon have his credit card charges traced, would know exactly where to find him.

I need a plan of attack.

Going to the FBI was definitely out. Sam Polowski was the agent Victor had contacted, the one who'd arranged to meet him in Garberville. No one else should have known about that meeting. Sam Polowski had never shown up.

But someone else had. Victor's aching shoulder was a constant reminder of that near-disastrous rendezvous.

I could go to the newspapers. But how would he convince some skeptical reporter? Who would believe his stories of a project so dangerous it could kill millions? They would think his tale was some fabrication of a paranoid mind.

And I am not paranoid.

He paced over to the TV and switched it on to the five o'clock news. A perfectly coiffed anchorwoman smiled from the screen as she read a piece of fluff about the last day of school, happy children, Christmas vacation. Then her expression sobered. Transition. Victor found himself staring at the TV as the next story came on.

"And in Garberville, California, there have been no new leads in the murder investigation of a woman found slain Wednesday morning. A houseguest found Sarah Boylan, 39, lying in the driveway, dead of stab wounds to the neck. The victim was five months pregnant. Police say they are puzzled by the lack of motive in this terrible tragedy, and at the present time there are no suspects. Moving on to national news . . ."

No, no, no! Victor thought. She wasn't pregnant. Her name wasn't Sarah. It's a mistake. . . .

Or was it?

My name is Catherine, she had told him.

Catherine Weaver. Yes, he was sure of the name. He'd remember it till the day he died.

He sat on the bed, the facts spinning around in his brain. Sarah. Cathy. A murder in Garberville.

When at last he rose to his feet, it was with a swelling sense of urgency, even panic. He grabbed the hotel room phone book and flipped to the *W*s. He understood now. The killer had made a mistake. If Cathy Weaver was still alive, she might have that roll of film—or know where to find it. Victor had to reach her.

Before someone else did.

Nothing could have prepared Cathy for the indescribable sense of gloom she felt upon returning to her flat in San Francisco. She had thought she'd cried out all her tears that night in the Garberville motel, the night after Sarah's death. But here she was, still bursting into tears, then sinking into deep, dark meditations. The drive to the city had been temporarily numbing. But as soon as she'd climbed the steps to her door and confronted the deathly silence of her second-story flat, she felt overwhelmed once again by grief. And bewilderment. Of all the people in the world to die, why Sarah?

She made a feeble attempt at unpacking. Then, forcing herself to stay busy, she surveyed the refrigerator and saw that her shelves were practically empty. It was all the excuse she needed to flee her apartment. She pulled a sweater over her jeans and, with a sense of escape, walked the four blocks to the neighborhood grocery store. She bought only the essentials, bread and eggs and fruit. Enough to tide her over for a few days, until she was back on her feet and could think clearly about any sort of menu.

Carrying a sack of groceries in each arm, she walked through the gathering darkness back to her apartment building. The night was chilly, and she regretted not wearing a coat. Through an open window, a woman called, "Time for dinner!" and two children playing kickball in the street turned and scampered for home.

By the time Cathy reached her building, she was shivering and her arms were aching from the weight of the groceries. She trudged up the steps and, balancing one sack on her hip, managed to pull out her keys and unlock the security door. Just as she swung through, she heard footsteps, then glimpsed a blur of movement rushing toward her from the side. She was swept through the doorway, into the building. A grocery bag tumbled from her arms, spilling apples across the floor. She stumbled forward, catching herself on the wood banister. The door slammed shut behind her.

She spun around, ready to fight off her attacker.

It was Victor Holland.

"You!" she whispered in amazement.

He didn't seem so sure of *her* identity. He was frantically searching her face, as though trying to confirm he had the right woman. "Cathy Weaver?"

"What do you think you're—"

"Where's your apartment?" he cut in.

"What?"

"We can't stand around out here."

"It's—it's upstairs—"

"Let's go." He reached for her arm but she pulled away.

"My groceries," she said, glancing down at the scattered apples.

He quickly scooped up the fruit, tossed it in one of the bags, and nudged her toward the stairs. "We don't have a lot of time."

Cathy allowed herself to be herded up the stairs and halfway down the hall before she stopped dead in her tracks. "Wait a minute. You tell me what this is all about, Mr. Holland, and you tell me right now or I don't move another step!"

"Give me your keys."

"You can't just—"

"Give me your keys!"

She stared at him, shocked by the command. Suddenly she realized that what she saw in his eyes was panic. They were the eyes of a hunted man.

Automatically she handed him her keys.

"Wait here," he said. "Let me check the apartment first."

She watched in bewilderment as he unlocked her door and cautiously eased his way inside. For a few moments she heard nothing. She pictured him moving through the flat, tried to estimate how many seconds each room would require for inspection. It was a small flat, so why was he taking so long?

Slowly she moved toward the doorway. Just as she reached it, his head popped out. She let out a little squeak of surprise. He barely caught the bag of groceries as it slipped from her grasp.

"It's okay," he said. "Come on inside."

The instant she stepped over the threshold, he had the door locked and bolted behind her. Then he quickly circled the living room, closing the drapes, locking windows.

"Are you going to tell me what's going on?" she asked, following him around the room.

"We're in trouble."

"You mean *you're* in trouble."

"No. I mean *we*. Both of us." He turned to her, his gaze clear and steady. "Do you have the film?"

"What are you talking about?" she asked, utterly confused by the sudden shift of conversation.

"A roll of film. Thirty-five millimeter. In a black plastic container. Do you have it?"

She didn't answer. But an image from that last night with Sarah had already taken shape in her mind: a roll of film on the kitchen counter. Film she'd thought belonged to her friend Hickey. Film she'd slipped into her bathrobe pocket and later into her purse. But she wasn't about to reveal any of this, not until she found out why he wanted it. The gaze she returned to him was purposefully blank and unrevealing.

Frustrated, he forced himself to take a deep breath, and started over. "That night you found me—on the highway—I had it in my pocket. It wasn't with me when I woke up in the hospital. I might have dropped it in your car."

"Why do you want this roll of film?"

"I need it. As evidence—"

"For what?"

"It would take too long to explain."

She shrugged. "I've got nothing better to do at the moment—"

"Damn it!" He stalked over to her. Taking her by the shoulders, he forced her to look at him. "Don't you understand? That's why your friend was killed! The night they broke into your car, they were looking for that film!"

She stared at him, a look of sudden comprehension and horror. "Sarah . . ."

"Was in the wrong place at the wrong time. The killer must have thought she was *you.*"

Cathy felt trapped by his unrelenting gaze. And by the inescapable threat of his revelation. Her knees wobbled, gave way. She sank into the nearest chair and sat there in numb silence.

"You have to get out of here," he said. "Before they find you. Before they figure out you're the Cathy Weaver they're looking for."

She didn't move. She couldn't move.

"Come on, Cathy. There isn't much time!"

"What was on that roll of film?" she asked softly.

"I told you. Evidence. Against a company called Viratek."

She frowned. "Isn't—isn't that the company you work for?"

"Used to work for."

"What did they do?"

"They're involved in some sort of illegal research project. I can't tell you the particulars."

"Why not?"

"Because I don't know them. I'm not the one who gathered the evidence. A colleague—a friend—passed it to me, just before he was killed."

"What do you mean by killed?"

"The police called it an accident. I think otherwise."

"You're saying he was murdered over a research project?" She shook her head. "Must have been dangerous stuff he was working on."

"I know this much. It involves biological weapons. Which makes the research illegal. And incredibly dangerous."

"Weapons? For what government?"

"Ours."

"I don't understand. If this is a federal project, that makes it all legal, right?"

"Not by a long shot. People in high places have been known to break the rules."

"How high are we talking about?"

"I don't know. I can't be sure of anyone. Not the police, not the Justice Department. Not the FBI."

Her eyes narrowed. The words she was hearing sounded like paranoid ravings. But the voice—and the eyes—were perfectly sane. They were sea-green, those eyes. They held an honesty, a steadiness that should have been all the assurance she needed.

It wasn't. Not by a long shot.

Quietly she said, "So you're telling me the FBI is after you. Is that correct?"

Sudden anger flared in his eyes, then just as quickly, it was gone. Groaning, he sank onto the couch and ran his hands through his hair. "I don't blame you for thinking I'm nuts. Sometimes I wonder if I'm all there. I thought if I could trust anyone, it'd be you. . . ."

"Why me?"

He looked at her. "Because you're the one who saved my life. You're the one they'll try to kill next."

She froze. No, no, this was insane. Now he was pulling her into his delusion, making her believe in his nightmare world of murder and conspiracy. She wouldn't let him! She stood up and started to walk away, but his voice made her stop again.

"Cathy, think about it. Why was your friend Sarah killed? Because they thought she was *you.* By now they've figured out they killed the wrong woman. They'll have to come back and do the job right. Just in case you know something. In case you have evidence—"

"This is crazy!" she cried, clapping her hands over her ears. "No one's going to—"

"They already have!" He whipped out a scrap of newspaper from his shirt pocket. "On my way over here, I happened to pass a newsstand. This was on the front page." He handed her the piece of paper.

She stared in bewilderment at the photograph of a middle-aged woman, a total stranger. "San Francisco woman shot to death on front doorstep," read the accompanying headline.

"This has nothing to do with me," she said.

"Look at her name."

Cathy's gaze slid to the third paragraph, which identified the victim. Her name was Catherine Weaver.

The scrap of newsprint slipped from her grasp and fluttered to the floor.

"There are three Catherine Weavers in the San Francisco phone book," he said. "That one was shot to death at nine o'clock this morning. I don't know what's happened to the second. She might already be dead. Which makes you next on the list. They've had enough time to locate you."

"I've been out of town—I only got back an hour ago—"

"Which explains why you're still alive. Maybe they came here earlier. Maybe they decided to check out the other two women first."

She shot to her feet, suddenly frantic with the need to flee. "I have to pack my things—"

"No. Let's just get the hell out of here."

Yes, do what he says! an inner voice screamed at her.

She nodded. Turning, she headed blindly for the door. Halfway there, she halted. "My purse—"

"Where is it?"

She headed back, past a curtained window. "I think I left it by the—"

Her next words were cut off by an explosion of shattering glass. Only the closed curtains kept the shards from piercing her flesh. Pure reflex sent Cathy diving to the floor just as the second gun blast went off. An instant later she found Victor Holland sprawled on top of her, covering her body with his as the third bullet slammed into the far wall, splintering wood and plaster.

The curtains shuddered, then hung still.

For a few seconds Cathy was paralyzed by terror, by the weight of Victor's body on hers. Then panic took hold. She squirmed free, intent on fleeing the apartment.

"Stay down!" Victor snapped.

"They're trying to kill us!"

"Don't make it easy for them!" He dragged her back to the floor. "We're getting out. But not through the front door."

"How—"

"Where's your fire escape?"

"My bedroom window."

"Does it go to the roof?"

"I'm not sure—l think so—"

"Then let's move it."

On hands and knees they crawled down the hall, into Cathy's unlit bedroom. Beneath the window they paused, listening. Outside, in the darkness, there was no sound. Then, from downstairs in the lobby, came the tinkle of breaking glass.

"He's already in the building!" hissed Victor. He yanked open the window. "Out, out!"

Cathy didn't need to be prodded. Hands shaking, she scrambled out and lowered herself onto the fire escape. Victor was right behind her.

"Up," he whispered. "To the roof."

And then what? she wondered, climbing the ladder to the third floor, past Mrs. Chang's flat. Mrs. Chang was out of town this week, visiting her son in New Jersey. The apartment was dark, the windows locked tight. No way in there.

"Keep going," said Victor, nudging her forward.

Only a few more rungs to go.

At last, she pulled herself up and over the edge and onto the asphalt roof. A second later, Victor dropped down beside her. Potted plants shuddered in the darkness. It was Mrs. Chang's rooftop garden, a fragrant mélange of Chinese herbs and vegetables.

Together, Victor and Cathy weaved their way through the plants and crossed to the opposite edge of the roof, where the next building abutted theirs.

"All the way?" said Cathy.

"All the way."

They hopped onto the adjoining roof and ran across to the other side, where three feet of emptiness separated them from the next building. She didn't pause to think of the perils of that leap, she simply flung herself across the gap and kept running, aware that every step took her farther and farther from danger.

On the roof of the fourth building, Cathy finally halted and stared over the edge at the street below. End of the line. It suddenly occurred to her that it was a very long drop to the ground below. The fire escape looked as sturdy as a Tinkertoy.

She swallowed. "This probably isn't a good time to tell you this, but—"

"Tell me what?"

"I'm afraid of heights."

He clambered over the edge. "Then don't look down."

Right, she thought, slithering onto the fire escape. *Don't look down.* Her palms were so slick with sweat she could barely grip the rungs. Suddenly seized by an attack of vertigo, she froze there, clinging desperately to that flimsy steel skeleton.

"Don't stop now!" Victor whispered up to her. "Just keep moving!"

Still she didn't move. She pressed her face against the rung, so hard she felt the rough edge bite into her flesh.

"You're okay, Cathy!" he said. "Come on."

The pain became all-encompassing, blocking out the dizziness, even the fear. When she opened her eyes again, the world had steadied. On rubbery legs, she descended the ladder, pausing on the third floor landing to wipe her sweaty palms on her jeans. She continued downward, to the second-floor landing. It was still a good fifteen-foot drop to the ground. She unlatched the extension ladder and started to slide it down, but it let out such a screech that Victor immediately stopped her.

"Too noisy. We have to jump!"

"But—"

To her astonishment, he scrambled over the railing and dropped to the ground. "Come on!" he hissed from below. "It's not that far. I'll catch you."

Murmuring a prayer, she lowered herself over the side and let go.

To her surprise he did catch her—but held on only for a second. The bullet wound had left his injured shoulder too weak to hold on. They both tumbled to the ground. She landed smack on top of him, her legs astride his hips, their faces inches apart. They stared at each other, so stunned they could scarcely breathe.

Upstairs, a window slid open and someone yelled, "Hey, you bums! If you don't clear out this instant, I'm calling the cops!"

Instantly Cathy rolled off Victor, only to stagger into a trash can. The lid fell off and slammed like a cymbal against the sidewalk.

"That's it for rest stops," Victor grunted and scrambled to his feet. *"Move it."*

They took off at a wild dash down the street, turned up an alley, and kept running. It was a good five blocks before they finally stopped to catch their breath. They glanced back.

The street was deserted.

They were safe!

Nicholas Savitch stood beside the neatly made bed and surveyed the room. It was every inch a woman's room, from the closet hung with a half-dozen simple but elegant dresses, to the sweetly scented powders and lotions lined up on the vanity table. It took only a single circuit around the room to tell him about the woman whose bedroom this was. She was slim, a size seven dress, size six-and-a-half shoe. The hairs on the brush were brown and shoulder-length. She owned only a few pieces of jewelry, and she favored natural scents, rosewater and lavender. Her favorite color was green.

Back in the living room, he continued to gather information. The woman subscribed to the Hollywood trade journals. Her taste in music, like her taste in books, was eclectic. He noticed a scrap of newspaper lying on the floor. He picked it up and glanced at the article. Now this was interesting. The death of Catherine Weaver I had not gone unnoticed by Catherine Weaver III.

He pocketed the article. Then he saw the purse, lying on the floor near the shattered window.

Bingo.

He emptied the contents on the coffee table. Out tumbled a wallet, checkbook, pens, loose change, and . . . an address book. He opened it to the *B*s. There he found the name he was looking for: Sarah Boylan.

He now knew this was the Catherine Weaver he'd been seeking. What a shame he'd wasted his time hunting down the other two.

He flipped through the address book and spotted a half dozen or so San Francisco listings. The woman may have been clever enough to slip away from him this time. But staying out of sight was a more difficult matter. And this little book, with its names of friends and relatives and colleagues, could lead him straight to her.

Somewhere in the distance, a police siren was wailing.

It was time to leave.

Savitch took the address book and the woman's wallet and headed out the door. Outside, his breath misted in the cold air as he walked at a leisurely pace down the street.

He could afford to take his time.

But for Catherine Weaver and Victor Holland, time was running out.

4

There was no time to rest. They jogged for the next six blocks, miles and miles, it seemed to Cathy. Victor moved tirelessly, leading her down side streets, avoiding busy intersections. She let him do the thinking and navigating. Her terror slowly gave way to numbness and a disorienting sense of unreality. The city itself seemed little more than a dreamscape, asphalt and streetlights and endless twists and turns of concrete. The only reality was the man striding close beside her, his gaze alert, his movements swift and sure. She knew he too must be afraid, but she couldn't see his fear.

He took her hand; the warmth of that grasp, the strength of those fingers, seemed to flow into her cold, exhausted limbs.

She quickened her pace. "I think there's a police substation down that street," she said. "If we go a block or two further—"

"We're not going to the police."

"What?" She stopped dead, staring at him.

"Not yet. Not until I've had a chance to think this through."

"Victor," she said slowly. "Someone is trying to kill us. Trying to kill *me*. What do you mean, you need time to *think this through?*"

"Look, we can't stand around talking about it. We have to get off the streets." He grabbed her hand again. "Come on."

"Where?"

"I have a room. It's only a few blocks away."

She let him drag her only a few yards before she mustered the will to pull free. "Wait a minute. Just *wait.*"

He turned, his face a mask of frustration, and confronted her. "Wait for what? For that maniac to catch up? For the bullets to start flying again?"

"For an explanation!"

"I'll explain it all. When we're safe."

She backed away. "Why are you afraid of the police?"

"I can't be sure of them."

"Do you have a reason to be afraid? What have you done?"

With two steps he closed the gap between them and grabbed her hard by the shoulders. "I just pulled you out of a death trap, remember? The bullets were going through your window, not mine!"

"Maybe they were aimed at you!"

"Okay!" He let her go, let her back away from him. "You want to try it on your own? Do it. Maybe the police'll be a help. Maybe not. But I can't risk it. Not until I know all the players behind this."

"You—you're letting me go?"

"You were never my prisoner."

"No." She took a breath—it misted in the cold air. She glanced down the street, toward the police substation. "It's . . . the reasonable thing to do," she muttered, almost to reassure herself. "That's what they're there for."

"Right."

She frowned, anticipating what lay ahead. "They'll ask a lot of questions."

"What are you going to tell them?"

She looked at him, her gaze unflinchingly meeting his. "The truth."

"Which'll be at best, incomplete. And at worst, unbelievable."

"I have broken glass all over my apartment to prove it."

"A drive-by shooting. Purely random."

"It's their job to protect me."

"What if they don't think you need protection?"

"I'll tell them about you! About Sarah."

"They may or may not take you seriously."

"They have to take me seriously! Someone's trying to kill me!" Her voice, shrill with desperation, seemed to echo endlessly through the maze of streets.

Quietly he said, "I know."

She glanced back toward the substation. "I'm going."

He said nothing.

"Where will you be?" she asked.

"On my own. For now."

She took two steps away, then stopped. "Victor?"

"I'm still here."

"You did save my life. Thank you."

He didn't respond. She heard his footsteps slowly walk away. She stood there thinking, wondering if she was doing the right thing. Of course she was. A man afraid of the police—with a story as paranoid as his was—had to be dangerous.

But he saved my life.

And once, on a rainy night in Garberville, she had saved his.

She replayed all the events of the last week. Sarah's murder, never explained. The other Catherine Weaver, shot to death on her front doorstep. The film canister that Sarah had retrieved from the car, the one Cathy had slipped into her bathrobe pocket . . .

Victor's footsteps had faded.

In that instant she realized she'd lost the only man who could help her find the answers to all those questions, the one man who'd stood by her in her darkest moment of terror. The one man she knew, by some strange intuition, she could trust. Facing that deserted street, she felt abandoned and utterly friendless. In sudden panic, she whirled around and called out: "Victor!"

At the far end of the block, a silhouette stopped and turned. He seemed an island of refuge in that crazy, dangerous world. She started toward him, her legs moving her faster and faster, until she was running, yearning for the safety of his arms, the arms of a man she scarcely knew. Yet it didn't feel like a stranger's arms gathering her to his chest, welcoming her into his protective embrace. She felt the pounding of his heart, the grip of his fingers against her back, and something told her that this was a man she could depend upon, a man who wouldn't fold when she needed him most.

"I'm right here," he murmured. "Right here." He stroked through her windblown hair, his fingers burying deep in the tangled strands. She felt the heat of his breath against her face, felt her own quick and shuddering response. And then, all at once, his mouth hungrily sought hers and he was kissing her. She responded with a kiss just as desperate, just as needy. Stranger though he was, he had been there for her and he was still here, his arms sheltering her from the terrors of the night.

She burrowed her face against his chest, longing to press ever deeper, ever closer. "I don't know what to do! I'm so afraid, Victor, and I don't know what to do. . . ."

"We'll work this out together. Okay?" He cupped her face in his hands and tilted it up to his. "You and I, we'll beat this thing."

She nodded. Searching his eyes, connecting with that rock-solid gaze, she found all the assurance she needed.

A wind gusted down the street. She shivered in its wake. "What do we do first?" she whispered.

"First," he said, pulling off his windbreaker and draping it over her shoulders, "We get you warmed up. And inside." He took her hand. "Come on. A hot bath, a good supper, and you'll be operating on all cylinders again."

It was another five blocks to the Kon-Tiki Motel. Though not exactly a five-star establishment, the Kon-Tiki was comfortingly drab and anonymous, one of a dozen on motel row. They climbed the steps to Room 214, overlooking the half-empty parking lot. He unlocked the door and motioned her inside.

The rush of warmth against her cheeks was delicious. She stood in the center of that utterly charmless space and marveled at how good it felt to be safely surrounded by four walls. The furnishings were spare: a double bed, a dresser, two nightstands with lamps, and a single chair. On the wall was a framed print of some nameless South Pacific island. The only luggage she saw was a cheap nylon bag on the floor. The bedcovers were rumpled, recently napped in, the pillows punched up against the headboard.

"Not much," he said. "But it's warm. And it's paid for." He turned on the TV. "We'd better keep an eye on the news. Maybe they'll have something on the Weaver woman."

The Weaver woman, she thought. *It could have been me.* She was shivering again, but now it wasn't from the cold. Settling onto the bed she stared numbly at the TV, not really seeing what was on the screen. She was more aware of *him.* He was circling the room, checking the windows, fiddling with the lock on the door. He moved quietly, efficiently, his silence a testimony to the dangers of their situation. Most men she knew began to babble nonsense when they were scared; Victor Holland simply turned quiet. His mere presence was overwhelming. He seemed to fill the room.

He moved to her side. She flinched as he took her hands and gently inspected them, palm side up. Looking down, she saw the bloodied scratches, the flakes of rust from the fire escape embedded in her skin.

"I guess I'm a mess," she murmured.

He smiled and stroked her face. "You could use some washing up. Go ahead. I'll get us something to eat."

She retreated into the bathroom. Through the door she could hear the drone of the TV, the sound of Victor's voice ordering a pizza over the phone. She ran hot water over her cold, numb hands. In the mirror over the sink she caught an unflattering glimpse of herself, her hair a tangled mess, her chin smudged with dirt. She washed her face, rubbing new life, new circulation into those frigid cheeks. Glancing down, she noticed Victor's razor on the counter. The sight of that blade cast her situation into a new focus—a frightening one. She picked up the razor, thinking how lethal that blade looked, how vulnerable she would be tonight. Victor was a large man, at least six foot two, with powerful arms. She was scarcely five foot five, a comparative weakling. There was only one bed in the next room. She had come here voluntarily. What would he assume about her? That she was a willing victim? She thought of all the ways a man could hurt her, kill her. It wouldn't take a razor to finish the job. Victor could use his bare hands. *What am I doing here?* she wondered. *Spending the night with a man I scarcely know?*

This was not the time to have doubts. She'd made the decision. She had to go by her instincts, and her instincts told her Victor Holland would never hurt her.

Deliberately she set down the razor. She would have to trust him. She was afraid not to.

In the other room, a door slammed shut. Had he left?

Opening the door a crack, she peered out. The TV was still on. There was no sign of Victor. Slowly she emerged, to find she was alone. She began to circle the room, searching for clues, anything that would tell her more about the man. The bureau drawers were empty, and so was the closet. Obviously he had not moved into this room for a long stay. He'd planned only one night, maybe two. She went to the nylon bag and glanced inside. She saw a clean pair of socks, an unopened package of underwear, and a day-old edition of the *San Francisco Chronicle*. All it told her was that the man kept himself informed and he traveled light.

Like a man on the run.

She dug deeper and came up with a receipt from an automatic teller machine. Yesterday he'd tried to withdraw cash. The machine had printed out the message: *Transaction cannot be completed. Please contact your bank.* Why had it refused him the cash? she wondered. Was he overdrawn? Had the machine been out of order?

The sound of a key grating in the lock caught her by surprise. She glanced up as the door swung open.

The look he gave her made her cheeks flush with guilt. Slowly she rose to her feet, unable to answer that look of accusation in his eyes.

The door swung shut behind him.

"I suppose it's a reasonable thing for you to do," he said. "Search my things."

"I'm sorry. I was just . . ." She swallowed. "I had to know more about you."

"And what terrible things have you dug up?"

"Nothing!"

"No deep dark secrets? Don't be afraid. Tell me, Cathy."

"Only . . . only that you had trouble getting cash out of your account."

He nodded. "A frustrating state of affairs. Since by my estimate I have a balance of six thousand dollars. And now I can't seem to touch it." He sat down in the chair, his gaze still on her face. "What else did you learn?"

"You—you read the newspaper."

"So do a lot of people. What else?"

She shrugged. "You wear boxer shorts."

Amusement flickered in his eyes. "Now we're getting personal."

"You . . ." She took a deep breath. "You're on the run."

He looked at her a long time without saying a word.

"That's why you won't go to the police," she said. "Isn't it?"

He turned away, gazing not at her but at the far wall. "There are reasons."

"Give me one, Victor. One good reason is all I need and then I'll shut up."

He sighed. "I doubt it."

"Try me. I have every reason to believe you."

"You have every reason to think I'm paranoid." Leaning forward, he ran his hands over his face. "Lord, sometimes *I* think I must be."

Quietly she went to him and knelt down beside his chair. "Victor, these people who are trying to kill me—who are they?"

"I don't know."

"You said it might involve people in high places."

"It's just a guess. It's a case of federal money going to illegal research. Deadly research."

"And federal money has to be doled out by someone in authority."

He nodded. "This is someone who's bent the rules. Someone who could be hurt by a political scandal. He just might try to protect himself by manipulating the Bureau. Or even your local police. That's why I won't go to them. That's why I left the room to make my call."

"When?"

"While you were in the bathroom. I went to a pay phone and called the police. I didn't want it traced."

"You just said you don't want them involved."

"This call I had to make. There's a third Catherine Weaver in that phone book. Remember?"

A third victim on the list. Suddenly weak, she sat down on the bed. "What did you say?" she asked softly.

"That I had reason to think she might be in danger. That she wasn't answering her phone."

"You tried it?"

"Twice."

"Did they listen to you?"

"Not only did they listen, they demanded to know my name. That's when I picked up the cue that something must already have happened to her. At that point I hung up and hightailed it out of the booth. A call can be traced in seconds. They could've had me surrounded."

"That makes three," she whispered. "Those two other women. And me."

"They have no way of finding you. Not as long as you stay away from your apartment. Stay out of—"

They both froze in panic.

Someone was knocking on the door.

They stared at each other, fear mirrored in their eyes. Then, after a moment's hesitation, Victor said: "Who is it?"

"Domino's," called a thin voice.

Cautiously, Victor eased open the door. A teenage boy stood outside, wielding a bag and a flat cardboard box.

"Hi!" chirped the boy. "A large combo with the works, two Cokes and extra napkins. Right?"

"Right." Victor handed the boy a few bills. "Keep the change," he said and closed the door. Turning, he gave Cathy a sheepish look. "Well," he admitted. "Just goes to show you. Sometimes a knock at the door really is just the pizza man."

They both laughed, a sound not of humor but of frayed nerves. The release of tension seemed to transform his face, melted his wariness to warmth. Erase those haggard lines, she thought, and he could almost be called a handsome man.

"I tell you what," he said. "Let's not think about this mess right now. Why don't we just get right down to the really important issue of the day. Food."

Nodding, she reached out for the box. "Better hand it over. Before I eat the damn bedspread."

While the ten o'clock news droned from the television set, they tore into the pizza like two ravenous animals. It was a greasy and utterly satisfying banquet on a motel bed. They scarcely bothered with conversation—their mouths were too busy devouring cheese and pepperoni. On the TV, a dapper anchorman announced a shakeup in the mayor's office, the resignation of the city manager, news that, given their current situation, seemed ridiculously trivial. Scarcely thirty seconds were devoted to that morning's killing of Catherine Weaver I; as yet, no suspects were in custody. No mention was made of any second victim by the same name.

Victor frowned. "Looks like the other woman didn't make it to the news."

"Or nothing's happened to her." She glanced at him questioningly. "What if the second Cathy Weaver is all right? When you called the police, they might've been asking you routine questions. When you're on edge, it's easy to—"

"Imagine things?" The look he gave her almost made her bite her tongue.

"No," she said quietly. "Misinterpret. The police can't respond to every anonymous call. It's natural they'd ask for your name."

"It was more than a request, Cathy. They were champing at the bit to interrogate me."

"I'm not doubting your word. I'm just playing devil's advocate. Trying to keep things level and sane in a crazy situation."

He looked at her long and hard. At last he nodded. "The voice of a rational woman," he sighed. "Exactly what I need right now. To keep me from jumping at my own shadow."

"And remind you to eat." She held out another slice of pizza. "You ordered this giant thing. You'd better help me finish it."

The tension between them instantly evaporated. He settled onto the bed and accepted the proffered slice. "That maternal look becomes you," he noted wryly. "So does the pizza sauce."

"What?" She swiped at her chin.

"You look like a two-year-old who's decided to fingerpaint her face."

"Good grief, can you hand me the napkins?"

"Let me do it." Leaning forward, he gently dabbed away the sauce. As he did, she studied his face, saw the laugh lines creasing the corners of his eyes, the strands of silver intertwined with the brown hair. She remembered the photo of that very face, pasted on a Viratek badge. How somber he'd looked, the unsmiling portrait of a scientist. Now he appeared young and alive and almost happy.

Suddenly aware that she was watching him, he looked up and met her gaze. Slowly his smile faded. They both went very still, as though seeing, in each other's eyes, something they had not noticed before. The voices on the television seemed to fade into a far-off dimension.

She felt his fingers trace lightly down her cheek. It was only a touch, but it left her shivering.

She asked, softly, "What happens now, Victor? Where do we go from here?"

"We have several choices."

"Such as?"

"I have friends in Palo Alto. We could turn to them."

"Or?"

"Or we could stay right where we are. For a while."

Right where we are. In this room, on this bed. She wouldn't mind that. Not at all.

She felt herself leaning toward him, drawn by a force against which she could offer no resistance. Both his hands came up to cradle her face, such large hands, but so infinitely gentle. She closed her eyes, knowing that this kiss, too, would be a gentle one.

And it was. This wasn't a kiss driven by fear or desperation. This was a quiet melting together of warmth, of souls. She swayed against him, felt his arms circle behind her to pull her inescapably close. It was a dangerous moment. She could feel herself tottering on the edge of total surrender to this man she scarcely knew. Already, her arms had found their way around his neck and her hands were roaming through the silver-streaked thickness of his hair.

His kisses dropped to her neck, exploring all the tender rises and hollows of her throat. All the needs that had lain dormant these past few years, all the hungers and desires, seemed to stir inside her, awakening at his touch.

And then, in an instant, the magic slipped away. At first she didn't understand why he suddenly pulled back. He sat bolt upright. The expression on his face was one of frozen astonishment. Bewildered, she followed his gaze and saw that he was focused on the television set behind her. She turned to see what had captured his attention.

A disturbingly familiar face stared back from the screen. She recognized the Viratek logo at the top, the straight-ahead gaze of the man in the photo. Why on earth would they be broadcasting Victor Holland's ID badge?

". . . Sought on charges of industrial espionage. Evidence now links Dr. Holland to the death of a fellow Viratek researcher, Dr. Gerald Martinique. Investigators fear the suspect has already sold extensive research data to a European competitor. . . ."

Neither one of them seemed able to move from the bed. They could only stare in disbelief at the newscaster with the Ken doll haircut. The station switched to a commercial break, raisins dancing crazily on a field, proclaiming the wonders of California sunshine. The lilting music was unbearable.

Victor rose to his feet and flicked off the television.

Slowly he turned to look at her. The silence between them grew agonizing.

"It's not true," he said quietly. "None of it."

She tried to read those unfathomable green eyes, wanting desperately to believe him. The taste of his kisses were still warm on her lips. The kisses of a con artist? *Is this just another lie? Has everything you've told me been nothing but lies? Who and what are you, Victor Holland?*

She glanced sideways, at the telephone on the bedside stand. It was so close. One call to the police, that's all it would take to end this nightmare.

"It's a frame-up," he said. "Viratek's releasing false information."

"Why?"

"To corner me. What easier way to find me than to have the police help them?"

She edged toward the phone.

"Don't, Cathy."

She froze, startled by the threat in his voice.

He saw the instant fear in her eyes. Gently he said, "Please. Don't call. I won't hurt you. I promise you can walk right out that door if you want. But first listen to me. Let me tell you what happened. Give me a chance."

His gaze was steady and absolutely believable. And he was right beside her, ready to stop her from making a move. Or to break her arm, if need be. She had no other choice. Nodding, she settled back down on the bed.

He began to pace, his feet tracing a path in the dull green carpet.

"It's all some—some incredible lie," he said. "It's crazy to think I'd kill him. Jerry Martinique and I were the best of friends. We both worked at Viratek. I was in vaccine development, he was a microbiologist. His specialty was viral studies. Genome research."

"You mean—like chromosomes?"

"The viral equivalent. Anyway, Jerry and I, we helped each other through some bad times. He'd gone through a painful divorce and I . . ." He paused, his voice dropping. "I lost my wife three years ago. To leukemia."

So he'd been married. Somehow it surprised her. He seemed like the sort of man who was far too independent to have ever said, "I do."

"About two months ago," he continued, "Jerry was transferred to a new research department. Viratek had been awarded a grant for some defense project. It was top security—Jerry couldn't talk about it. But I could see he was bothered by something that was going on in that lab. All he'd say to me was, 'They don't understand the danger. They don't know what they're getting into.' Jerry's field was the alteration of viral genes. So I assume the project had something to do with viruses as weapons. Jerry was fully aware that those weapons are outlawed by international agreement."

"If he knew it was illegal, why did he take part in it?"

"Maybe he didn't realize at first what the project was áiming for. Maybe they sold it to him as purely defensive research. In any event, he got upset enough to resign from the project. He went right to the top—the founder of Viratek. Walked into Archibald Black's office and threatened to go public if the project wasn't terminated. Four days later he had an accident." Anger flashed in Victor's eyes. It wasn't directed at her, but the fury in that gaze was frightening all the same.

"What happened to him?" she asked.

"His wrecked car was found at the side of the road. Jerry was still inside. Dead, of course." Suddenly, the anger was gone, replaced by overwhelming weariness. He sank onto the bed. "I thought the accident investigation would blow everything into the open. It was a farce. The local cops did their best, but then some federal transportation "expert" showed up on the scene and took over. He said Jerry must've fallen asleep at the wheel. Case closed. That's when I realized just how deep this went. I didn't know who to go to, so I called the FBI in San Francisco. Told them I had evidence."

"You mean the film?" asked Cathy.

Victor nodded. "Just before he was killed, Jerry told me about some duplicate papers he'd stashed away in his garden shed. After the . . . accident, I went over to his house. Found the place ransacked. But they never bothered to search the shed. That's how I got hold of the evidence, a single file and a roll of film. I arranged a meeting with one of the San Francisco agents, a guy named Sam Polowski. I'd already talked to him a few times on the phone. He offered to meet me in Garberville. We wanted to keep it private, so we agreed to a spot just outside of town. I drove down, fully expecting him to show. Well, someone showed up, all right. Someone who ran me off the road." He paused and looked straight at her. "That's the night you found me."

The night my whole life changed, she thought.

"You have to believe me," he said.

She studied him, her instincts battling against logic. The story was just barely plausible, halfway between truth and fantasy. But the man looked solid as stone.

Wearily she nodded. "I do believe you, Victor. Maybe I'm crazy. Or just gullible. But I do."

The bed shifted as he sat down beside her. They didn't touch, yet she could almost feel the warmth radiating between them.

"That's all that matters to me right now," he said. "That you know, in your heart, I'm telling the truth."

"In my heart?" She shook her head and laughed. "My heart's always been a lousy judge of character. No, I'm guessing. I'm going by the fact you kept me alive. By the fact there's another Cathy Weaver who's now dead . . ."

Remembering the face of that other woman, the face in the newspaper, she suddenly began to shake. It all added up to the terrible truth. The gun blasts into her apartment, the other dead Cathy. And Sarah, poor Sarah.

She was gulping in shaky breaths, hovering on the verge of tears.

She let him take her in his arms, let him pull her down on the bed beside him. He murmured into her hair, gentle words of comfort and reassurance. He turned off the lamp. In darkness they held each other, two frightened souls joined against a terrifying world. She felt safe there, tucked away against his chest. This was a place where no one could hurt her. It was a stranger's arms, but from the smell of his shirt to the beat of his heart, it all seemed somehow familiar. She never wanted to leave that spot, ever.

She trembled as his lips brushed her forehead. He was stroking her face now, her neck, warming her with his touch. When his hand slipped beneath her blouse, she didn't protest. Somehow it seemed so natural, that that hand would come to lie at her breast. It wasn't the touch of a marauder, it was simply a gentle reminder that she was in safekeeping.

And yet, she found herself responding. . . .

Her nipple tingled and grew taut beneath his cupping hand. The tingling spread, a warmth that crept to her face and flushed her cheeks. She reached for his shirt and began to unbutton it. In the darkness she was slow and clumsy. By the time she finally slid her hand under the fabric, they were both breathing hard and fast with anticipation.

She brushed through the coarse mat of hair, stroking her way across that broad chest. He took in a sharp breath as her fingers skimmed a delicate circle around his nipple.

If playing with fire had been her intention, then she had just struck the match.

His mouth was suddenly on hers, seeking, devouring. The force of his kiss pressed her onto her back, trapping her head against the pillows. For a dizzy eternity she was swimming in sensations, the scent of male heat, the unyielding grip of his hands imprisoning her face. Only when he at last drew away did they both come up for air.

He stared down at her, as though hovering on the edge of temptation.

"This is crazy," he whispered.

"Yes. Yes, it is—"

"I never meant to do this—"

"Neither did I."

"It's just that you're scared. We're both scared. And we don't know what the hell we're doing."

"No." She closed her eyes, felt the unexpected bite of tears. "We don't. But I *am* scared. And I just want to be held. Please, Victor. Hold me, that's all. Just hold me."

He pulled her close, murmuring her name. This time the embrace was gentle, without the fever of desire. His shirt was still unbuttoned, his chest bared. And that's where she lay her head, against that curling nest of hair. Yes, he was right, so wise. They were crazy to be making love when they both knew it was fear, nothing else, that had driven their desire. And now the fever had broken.

A sense of peace fell over her. She curled up against him. Exhaustion robbed them both of speech. Her muscles gradually fell limp as sleep tugged her into its shadow. Even if she tried to, she could not move her arms or legs. Instead she was drifting free, like a wraith in the darkness, floating somewhere in a warm and inky sea.

Vaguely she was aware of light sliding past her eyelids.

The warmth encircling her body seemed to melt away. No, she wanted it back, wanted *him* back! An instant later she felt him shaking her.

"Cathy. Come on, wake up!"

Through drowsy eyes she peered at him. "Victor?"

"Something's going on outside."

She tumbled out of bed and followed him to the window. Through a slit in the curtains she spotted what had alarmed him: a patrol car, its radio crackling faintly, parked by the motel registration door. At once she snapped wide awake, her mind going over the exits from their room. There was only one.

"Out, now!" he ordered. "Before we're trapped."

He eased open the door. They scrambled out onto the walkway. The frigid night air was like a slap in the face. She was already shivering, more from fear than from the cold. Running at a crouch, they moved along the walkway, away from the stairs, and ducked past the ice machine.

Below, they heard the lobby door open and the voice of the motel manager: "Yeah, that'll be right upstairs. Gee, he sure seemed like a nice-enough guy. . . ."

Tires screeched as another patrol car pulled up, lights flashing.

Victor gave her a push. *"Go!"*

They slipped into a breezeway and scurried through, to the other side of the building. No stairways there! They climbed over the walkway railing and dropped into the parking lot.

Faintly they heard a banging, then the command: "Open up! This is the police."

At once they were sprinting instinctively for the shadows. No one spotted them, no one gave chase. Still they kept running, until they'd left the Kon-Tiki Motel blocks and blocks behind them, until they were so tired they were stumbling.

At last Cathy slowed to a halt and leaned back against a doorway, her breath coming out in clouds of cold mist. "How did they find you?" she said between gasps.

"It couldn't have been the call. . . ." Suddenly he groaned. "My credit card! I had to use it to pay the bill."

"Where now? Should we try another motel?"

He shook his head. "I'm down to my last forty bucks. I can't risk a credit card again."

"And I left my purse at the apartment. I—I'm not sure I want to—"

"We're not going back for it. They'll be watching the place."

They. Meaning the killers.

"So we're broke," she said weakly.

He didn't answer. He stood with his hands in his pockets, his whole body a study in frustration. "You have friends you can go to?"

"I think so. Uh, no. She's out of town till Friday. And what would I tell her? How would I explain you?"

"You can't. And we can't handle any questions right now."

That leaves out most of my friends, she thought. Nowhere to go, no one to turn to. Unless . . .

No, she'd promised herself never to sink that low, never to beg for *that* particular source of help.

Victor glanced up the street. "There's a bus stop over there." He reached in his pocket and took out a handful of money. "Here," he said. "Take it and get out of the city. Go visit some friends on your own."

"What about you?"

"I'll be okay."

"Broke? With everyone after you?" She shook her head.

"I'll only make things more dangerous for you." He pressed the money into her hand.

She stared down at the wad of bills, thinking: *This is all he has. And he's giving it to me.* "I can't," she said.

"You have to."

"But—"

"Don't argue with me." The look in his eyes left no alternative.

Reluctantly she closed her fingers around the money.

"I'll wait till you get on the bus. It should take you right past the station."

"Victor?"

He silenced her with a single look. Placing both hands on her shoulders, he stood her before him. "You'll be fine," he said. Then he pressed a kiss to her forehead. For a moment his lips lingered, and the warmth of his breath in her hair left her trembling. "I wouldn't leave you if I thought otherwise."

The roar of a bus down the block made them both turn.

"There's your limousine," he whispered. "Go." He gave her a nudge. "Take care of yourself, Cathy."

She started toward the bus stop. Three steps, four. She slowed and came to a halt. Turning, she saw that he had already edged away into the shadows.

"Get on it!" he called.

She looked at the bus. *I won't do it,* she thought.

She turned back to Victor. "I know a place! A place we can both stay!"

"What?"

"I didn't want to use it but—"

Her words were drowned out as the bus wheezed to the stop, then roared away.

"It's a bit of a walk," she said. "But we'd have beds and a meal. And I can guarantee no one would call the police."

He came out of the shadows. "Why didn't you think of this earlier?"

"I did think of it. But up till now, things weren't, well . . . desperate enough."

"Not desperate enough," he repeated slowly. He moved toward her, his face taut with incredulity. "Not *desperate* enough? Hell, lady. I'd like to know exactly what kind of crisis would qualify!"

"You have to understand, this is a last resort. It's not an easy place for me to turn to."

His eyes narrowed in suspicion. "This place is beginning to sound worse and worse. What are we talking about? A flophouse?"

"No, it's in Pacific Heights. You could even call the place a mansion."

"Who lives there? A friend?"

"Quite the opposite."

His eyebrow shot up. "An enemy?"

"Close." She let out a sigh of resignation. "My ex-husband."

5

"Jack, open up! Jack!" Cathy banged again and again on the door of the formidable Pacific Heights home. There was no answer. Through the windows they saw only darkness.

"Damn you, Jack!" She gave the door a slap of frustration. "Why aren't you *ever* home when I need you?"

Victor glanced around at the neighborhood of elegant homes and neatly trimmed shrubbery. "We can't stand around out here all night."

"We're not going to," she muttered. Crouching on her knees, she began to dig around in a red-brick planter.

"What are you doing?"

"Something I swore I'd never do." Her fingers raked the loamy soil, searching for the key Jack kept buried under the geraniums. Sure enough, there it was, right where it had always been. She rose to her feet, clapping the dirt off her hands. "But there are limits to my pride. Threat of death being one of them." She inserted the key and felt a momentary dart of panic when it didn't turn. But with a little jiggling, the lock at last gave way. The door swung open to the faint gleam of a polished wood floor, a massive bannister.

She motioned Victor inside. The solid thunk of the door closing behind them seemed to shut out all the dangers of the night. Cloaked in the darkness, they both let out a sigh of relief.

"Just what kind of terms are you on with your ex-husband?" Victor asked, following her blindly through the unlit foyer.

"Speaking. Barely."

"He doesn't mind you wandering around his house?"

"Why not?" She snorted. "Jack lets half the human race wander through his bedroom. The only prerequisite being XX chromosomes."

She felt her way into the pitch-dark living room and flipped on the light switch. There she froze in astonishment and stared at the two naked bodies intertwined on the polar bear rug.

"Jack!" she blurted out.

The larger of the two bodies extricated himself and sat up. "Hello, Cathy!" He raked his hand through his dark hair and grinned. "Seems like old times."

The woman lying next to him spat out a shocking obscenity, scrambled to her feet, and stormed off in a blur of wild red hair and bare bottom toward the bedroom.

"That's Lulu," yawned Jack, by way of introduction.

Cathy sighed. "I see your taste in women hasn't improved."

"No, sweetheart, my taste in women hit a high point when I married you." Unmindful of his state of nudity, Jack rose to his feet and re-garded Victor. The contrast between the two men was instantly appar-ent. Though both were tall and lean, it was Jack who possessed the striking good looks, and he knew it. He'd always known it. Vanity wasn't a label one could ever pin on Victor Holland.

"I see you brought a fourth," said Jack, giving Victor the once-over. "So, what'll it be, folks? Bridge or poker?"

"Neither," said Cathy.

"That opens up all *sorts* of possibilities."

"Jack, I need your help."

He turned and looked at her with mock incredulity. *"No!"*

"You know damn well I wouldn't be here if I could avoid it!"

He winked at Victor. "Don't believe her. She's still madly in love with me."

"Can we get serious?"

"Darling, you never did have a sense of humor."

"Damn you, Jack!" Everyone had a breaking point and Cathy had reached hers. She couldn't help it; without warning she burst into tears. "For once in your life will you *listen* to me?"

That's when Victor's patience finally snapped. He didn't need a de-gree in psychology to know this Jack character was a first-class jerk. Couldn't he see that Cathy was exhausted and terrified? Up till this moment, Victor had admired her for her strength. Now he ached at the sight of her vulnerability.

It was only natural to pull her into his arms, to ease her tear-streaked face against his chest. Over her shoulder, he growled out an oath that impugned not only Jack's name but that of Jack's mother as well.

The other man didn't seem to take offense, probably because he'd been called far worse names, and on a regular basis. He simply crossed his arms and regarded Victor with a raised eyebrow. "Being protective, are we?"

"She needs protection."

"From what, pray tell?"

"Maybe you haven't heard. Three days ago, someone murdered her friend Sarah."

"Sarah . . . Boylan?"

Victor nodded. "Tonight, someone tried to kill Cathy."

Jack stared at him. He looked at his ex-wife. "Is this true? What he's saying?"

Cathy, wiping away tears, nodded.

"Why didn't you tell me this to begin with?"

"Because you were acting like an ass to begin with!" she shot back.

Down the hall came the *click-click* of high-heeled shoes. "She's absolutely right!" yelled a female voice from the foyer. "You *are* an ass, Jack Zuckerman!" The front door opened and slammed shut again. The thud seemed to echo endlessly through the mansion.

There was a long silence.

Suddenly, through her tears, Cathy laughed. "You know what, Jack? I *like* that woman."

Jack crossed his arms and gave his ex-wife the critical once-over. "Either I'm going senile or you forgot to tell me something. Why haven't you gone to the police? Why bother old Jack about this?"

Cathy and Victor glanced at each other.

"We can't go to the police," Cathy said.

"I assume this has to do with *him?*" He cocked a thumb at Victor.

Cathy let out a breath. "It's a complicated story. . . ."

"It must be. If you're afraid to go to the police."

"I can explain it," said Victor.

"Mm-hm. Well." Jack reached for the bathrobe lying in a heap by the polar bear rug. "Well," he said again, calmly tying the sash. "I've always enjoyed watching creativity at work. So let's have it." He sat down on the leather couch and smiled at Victor. "I'm waiting. It's showtime."

Special Agent Sam Polowski lay shivering in his bed, watching the eleven o'clock news. Every muscle in his body ached, his head pounded, and the thermometer at his bedside read an irrefutable 101 degrees. So much for changing flat tires in the pouring rain. He wished he could get his hands on the joker who'd punched that nail in his tire while he was grabbing a quick bite at that roadside cafe. Not only had the culprit managed to keep Sam from his appointment in Garberville, thereby shredding the Viratek case into confetti, Sam had also lost track of his only contact in the affair: Victor Holland. And now, the flu.

Sam reached over for the bottle of aspirin. To hell with the ulcer. His head hurt. And when it came to headaches, there was nothing like Mom's time-tested remedy.

He was in the midst of gulping down three tablets when the news about Victor Holland flashed on the screen.

". . . New evidence links the suspect to the murder of fellow Viratek researcher, Dr. Gerald Martinique. . . ."

Sam sat up straight in bed. "What the hell?" he growled at the TV. Then he grabbed the telephone.

It took six rings for his supervisor to answer. "Dafoe?" Sam said. "This is Polowski."

"Do you know what time it is?"

"Have you seen the late-night news?"

"I happen to be in bed."

"There's a story on Viratek."

A pause. "Yeah, I know. I cleared it."

"What's with this crap about industrial espionage? They're making Holland out to be a—"

"Polowski, drop it."

"Since when did he become a murder suspect?"

"Look, just consider it a cover story. I want him brought in. For his own good."

"So you sic him with a bunch of trigger-happy cops?"

"I said drop it."

"But—"

"You're off the case." Dafoe hung up.

Sam stared in disbelief at the receiver, then at the television, then back at the receiver.

Pull me off the case? He slammed the receiver down so hard the bottle of aspirin tumbled off the nightstand.

That's what you think.

"I think I've heard about enough," said Jack, rising to his feet. "I want this man out of my house. And I want him out now."

"Jack, please!" said Cathy. "Give him a chance—"

"You're buying this ridiculous tale?"

"I believe him."

"Why?"

She looked at Victor and saw the clear fire of honesty burning in his eyes. "Because he saved my life."

"You're a fool, babycakes." Jack reached for the phone. "You yourself saw the TV. He's wanted for murder. If you don't call the police, I will."

But as Jack picked up the receiver, Victor grabbed his arm. "No," he said. Though his voice was quiet, it held the unmistakable note of authority.

The two men stared at each other, neither willing to back down.

"This is more than just a case of murder," said Victor. "This is deadly research. The manufacture of illegal weapons. This could reach all the way to Washington."

"Who in Washington?"

"Someone in control. Someone with the federal funds to authorize that research."

"I see. Some lofty public servant is out knocking off scientists. With the help of the FBI."

"Jerry wasn't just any scientist. He had a conscience. He was a whistleblower who would've taken this to the press to stop that research. The political fallout would've been disastrous, for the whole administration."

"Wait. Are we talking Pennsylvania Avenue?"

"Maybe."

Jack snorted. "Holland, I *make* Grade B horror films. I don't live them."

"This isn't a film. This is real. Real bullets, real bodies."

"Then that's all the more reason I want nothing to do with it." Jack turned to Cathy. "Sorry, sweetcakes. It's nothing personal, but I detest the company you keep."

"Jack," she said. "You have to help us!"

"You, I'll help. Him—no way. I draw the line at lunatics and felons."

"You heard what he said! It's a frame-up!"

"You are so gullible."

"Only about you."

"Cathy, it's all right," said Victor. He was standing very still, very calm. "I'll leave."

"No, you won't." Cathy shot to her feet and stalked over to her ex-husband. She stared him straight in the eye, a gaze so direct, so accusing, he seemed to wilt right down into a chair. "You owe it to me, Jack. You owe me for all the years we were married. All the years I put into *your* career, *your* company, *your* idiotic flicks. I haven't asked for anything. You have the house. The Jaguar. The bank account. I never asked because I didn't want to take a damn thing from this marriage except my own soul. But now I'm asking. This man saved my life tonight. If you ever cared about me, if you ever loved me, even a little, then you'll do me this favor."

"Harbor a criminal?"

"Only until we figure out what to do next."

"And how long might that take? Weeks? Months?"

"I don't know."

"Just the kind of definite answer I like."

Victor said, "I need time to find out what Jerry was trying to prove. What it is Viratek's working on—"

"You had one of his files," said Jack. "Why didn't you read the blasted thing?"

"I'm not a virologist. I couldn't interpret the data. It was some sort of RNA sequence, probably a viral genome. A lot of the data was coded. All I can be sure of is the name: Project Cerberus."

"Where is all this vital evidence now?"

"I lost the file. It was in my car the night I was shot. I'm sure they have it back."

"And the film?"

Victor sank into a chair, his face suddenly lined by weariness. "I don't have it. I was hoping that Cathy . . ." Sighing, he ran his hands through his hair. "I've lost that, too."

"Well," said Jack. "Give or take a few miracles, I'd say this puts your chances at just about zero. And I'm known as an optimist."

"I know where the film is," said Cathy.

There was a long silence. Victor raised his head and stared at her. "What?"

"I wasn't sure about you—not at first. I didn't want to tell you until I could be certain—"

Victor shot to his feet. *"Where is it?"*

She flinched at the sharpness of his voice. He must have noticed how startled she was—his next words were quiet but urgent. "I need that film, Cathy. Before they find it. Where is it?"

"Sarah found it in my car. I didn't know it was yours! I thought it was Hickey's."

"Who's Hickey?"

"A photographer—a friend of mine—"

Jack snorted. "Hickey. Now *there's* a ladies' man."

"He was in a rush to get to the airport," she continued. "At the last minute he left me with some rolls of film. Asked me to take care of them till he got back from Nairobi. But all his film was stolen from my car."

"And my roll?" asked Victor.

"It was in my bathrobe pocket the night Sarah—the night she—" She paused, swallowing at the mention of her friend. "When I got back here, to the city, I mailed it to Hickey's studio."

"Where's the studio?"

"Over on Union Street. I mailed it this afternoon—"

"So it should be there sometime tomorrow." He began to pace the room. "All we have to do is wait for the mail to arrive."

"I don't have a key."

"We'll find a way in."

"Terrific," sighed Jack. "Now he's turning my ex-wife into a burglar."

"We're only after the film!" said Cathy.

"It's still breaking and entering, sweetie."

"You don't have to get involved."

"But you're asking me to harbor the breakers and enterers."

"Just one night, Jack. That's all I'm asking."

"That sounds like one of *my* lines."

"And your lines always work, don't they?"

"Not this time."

"Then here's another line to chew on: 1988. Your federal tax return. Or lack of one."

Jack froze. He glowered at Victor, then at Cathy. "That's below the belt."

"Your most vulnerable spot."

"I'll get around to filing—"

"More words to chew on. Audit. IRS. Jail."

"Okay, okay!" Jack threw his arms up in surrender. "God, I *hate* that word."

"What, *jail?*"

"Don't laugh, babycakes. The word could soon apply to all of us." He turned and headed for the stairs.

"Where are you going?" Cathy demanded.

"To make up the spare beds. Seems I have houseguests for the night. . . ."

"Can we trust him?" Victor asked after Jack had vanished upstairs.

Cathy sank back on the couch, all the energy suddenly drained from her body, and closed her eyes. "We have to. I can't think of anywhere else to go. . . ."

She was suddenly aware of his approach, and then he was sitting beside her, so close she could feel the overwhelming strength of his presence. He didn't say a word, yet she knew he was watching her.

She opened her eyes and met his gaze. So steady, so intense, it seemed to infuse her with new strength.

"I know it wasn't easy for you," he said. "Asking Jack for favors."

She smiled. "I've always wanted to talk tough with Jack." Ruefully she added, "Until tonight, I've never quite been able to pull it off."

"My guess is, talking tough isn't in your repertoire."

"No, it isn't. When it comes to confrontation, I'm a gutless wonder."

"For a gutless wonder, you did pretty well. In fact, you were magnificent."

"That's because I wasn't fighting for me. I was fighting for you."

"You don't consider yourself worth fighting for?"

She shrugged. "It's the way I was raised. I was always told that sticking up for yourself was unladylike. Whereas sticking up for other people was okay."

He nodded gravely. "Self-sacrifice. A fine feminine tradition."

That made her laugh. "Spoken like a man who knows women well."

"Only two women. My mother and my wife."

At the mention of his dead wife, she fell silent. She wondered what the woman's name was, what she'd looked like, how much he'd loved her. He must have loved her a great deal—she'd heard the pain in his voice earlier that evening when he'd mentioned her death. She felt an unexpected stab of envy that this unnamed wife had been so loved. What Cathy would give to be as dearly loved by a man! Just as quickly she suppressed the thought, appalled that she could be jealous of a dead woman.

She turned away, her face tinged with guilt. "I think Jack will go along," she said. "Tonight, at least."

"That was blackmail, wasn't it? That stuff about the tax return?"

"He's a careless man. I just reminded him of his oversight."

Victor shook his head. "You are amazing. Jumping along rooftops one minute, blackmailing ex-husbands the next."

"You're so right," said Jack, who'd reappeared at the bottom of the stairs. "She is an amazing woman. I can't wait to see what she'll do next."

Cathy rose wearily to her feet. "At this point I'll do anything." She slipped past Jack and headed up the stairs. "Anything I have to to stay alive."

The two men listened to her footsteps recede along the hall. Then they regarded each other in silence.

"Well," said Jack with forced cheerfulness. "What's next on the agenda? Scrabble?"

"Try solitaire," said Victor, hauling himself off the couch. He was in no mood to share pleasantries with Jack Zuckerman. The man was slick and self-centered and he obviously went through women the way most men went through socks. Victor had a hard time imagining what Cathy had ever seen in the man. That is, aside from Jack's good looks and obvious wealth. There was no denying the fact he was a classic hunk, with the added attraction of money thrown in. Maybe it was that combination that had dazzled her.

A combination I'll certainly never possess, he thought.

He crossed the room, then stopped and turned. "Zuckerman?" he asked. "Do you still love your wife?"

Jack looked faintly startled by the question. "Do I still love her? Well, let me see. No, not exactly. But I suppose I have a sentimental attachment, based on ten years of marriage. And I respect her."

"Respect her? You?"

"Yes. Her talents. Her technical skill. After all, she's my number-one makeup artist."

That's what she meant to him. An asset he could use. *Thinking of himself, the jerk.* If there was anyone else Victor could turn to, he would. But the one man he would've trusted—Jerry—was dead. His other friends might already be under observation. Plus, they weren't in the sort of tax brackets that allowed private little hideaways in the woods. Jack, on the other hand, had the resources to spirit Cathy away to a safe place. Victor could only hope the man's sentimental attachment was strong enough to make him watch out for her.

"I have a proposition," said Victor.

Jack instantly looked suspicious. "What might that be?"

"I'm the one they're really after. Not Cathy. I don't want to make things any more dangerous for her than I already have."

"Big of you."

"It's better if I go off on my own. If I leave her with you, will you keep her safe?"

Jack shifted, looked down at his feet. "Well, sure. I guess so."

"Don't guess. Can you?"

"Look, we start shooting a film in Mexico next month. Jungle scenes, black lagoons, that sort of stuff. Should be a safe-enough place."

"That's next month. What about now?"

"I'll think of something. But first you get yourself out of the picture. Since you're the reason she's in danger in the first place."

Victor couldn't disagree with that last point. *Since the night I met her I've caused her nothing but trouble.*

He nodded. "I'm out of here tomorrow."

"Good."

"Take care of Cathy. Get her out of the city. Out of the country. Don't wait."

"Yeah. Sure."

Something about the way Jack said it, his hasty, whatever-you-say tone, made Victor wonder if the man gave a damn about anyone but himself. But at this point Victor had no choice. He had to trust Jack Zuckerman.

As he climbed the stairs to the guest rooms, it occurred to him that, come morning, it would be goodbye. A quiet little bond had formed between them. He owed his life to her and she to him. That was the sort of link one could never break.

Even if we never see each other again.

In the upstairs hall, he paused outside her closed door. He could hear her moving around the room, opening and closing drawers, squeaking bedsprings.

He knocked on the door. "Cathy?"

There was a pause. Then, "Come in."

One dim lamp lit the room. She was sitting on the bed, dressed in a ridiculously huge man's shirt. Her hair hung in damp waves to her shoulders. The scent of soap and shampoo permeated the shadows. It reminded him of his wife, of the shower smells and feminine sweetness. He stood there, pierced by a sense of longing he hadn't felt in over a year, longing for the warmth, the love, of a woman. Not just any woman. He wasn't like Jack, to whom a soft body with the right equipment would be sufficient. What Victor wanted was the heart and soul; the package they came wrapped in was only of minor importance.

His own wife Lily hadn't been beautiful; neither had she been unattractive. Even at the end, when the ravages of illness had left her shrunken and bruised, there had been a light in her eyes, a gentle spirit's glow.

The same glow he'd seen in Catherine Weaver's eyes the night she'd saved his life. The same glow he saw now.

She sat with her back propped up on pillows. Her gaze was silently expectant, maybe a little fearful. She was clutching a handful of tissues. *Why were you crying?* he wondered.

He didn't approach; he stood just inside the doorway. Their gazes locked together in the gloom. "I've just talked with Jack," he said.

She nodded but said nothing.

"We both agree. It's better that I leave as soon as possible. So I'll be taking off in the morning."

"What about the film?"

"I'll get it. All I need is Hickey's address."

"Yes. Of course." She looked down at the tissues in her fist.

He could tell she wanted to say something. He went to the bed and sat down. Those sweet woman smells grew intoxicating. The neckline of her oversized shirt sagged low enough to reveal a tempting glimpse of shadow. He forced himself to focus on her face.

"Cathy, you'll be fine. Jack said he'd watch out for you. Get you out of the city."

"Jack?" What sounded like a laugh escaped her throat.

"You'll be safer with him. I don't even know where I'll be going. I don't want to drag you into this—"

"But you already have. You've dragged me in over my head, Victor. What am I supposed to do now? I can't just—just sit around and wait for you to fix things. I owe it to Sarah—"

"And I owe to it you not to let you get hurt."

"You think you can hand me over to Jack and make everything be fine again? Well, it won't be fine. Sarah's dead. Her baby's dead. And somehow it's not just your fault. It's mine as well."

"No, it's not. Cathy—"

"It is my fault! Did you know she was lying there in the driveway all night? In the rain. In the cold. There she was, dying, and I slept through the whole damn thing. . . ." She dropped her face in her hands. The guilt that had been tormenting her since Sarah's death at last burst through. She began to cry, silently, ashamedly, unable to hold back the tears any longer.

Victor's response was automatic and instinctively male. He pulled her against him and gave her a warm, safe place to cry. As soon as he felt her settle into his arms, he knew it was a mistake. It was too perfect a fit. She felt as if she belonged there, against his heart, felt that if she ever pulled away there would be left a hole so gaping it could never be filled. He pressed his lips to her damp hair and inhaled her heady scent of soap and warm skin. That gentle fragrance was enough to drown a man with need. So was the softness of her face, the silken luster of that shoulder peeking out from beneath the shirt. And all the time he was stroking her hair, murmuring inane words of comfort, he was thinking: *I have to leave her. For her sake I have to abandon this woman. Or I'll get us both killed.*

"Cathy," he said. It took all the willpower he could muster to pull away. He placed his hands on her shoulders, made her look at him.

Her gaze was confused and brimming with tears. "We have to talk about tomorrow."

She nodded and swiped at the tears on her cheeks.

"I want you out of the city, first thing in the morning. Go to Mexico with Jack. Anywhere. Just keep out of sight."

"What will you do?"

"I'm going to take a look at that roll of film, see what kind of evidence it has."

"And then?"

"I don't know yet. Maybe I'll take it to the newspapers. The FBI is definitely out."

"How will I know you're all right? How do I reach you?"

He thought hard, fighting the distraction of her scent, her hair. He found himself stroking the bare skin of her shoulder, marveling at how smooth it felt beneath his fingers.

He focused on her face, on the look of worry in her eyes. "Every other Sunday I'll put an ad in the Personals. *Los Angeles Times.* It'll be addressed to, let's say, Cora. Anything I need to tell you will be there."

"Cora." She nodded. "I'll remember."

They looked at each other, a silent acknowledgment that this parting had to be. He cupped her face and pressed a kiss to her mouth. She barely responded; already, it seemed, she had said her goodbyes.

He rose from the bed and started for the door. There he couldn't resist asking, one more time: "You'll be all right?"

She nodded, but it was too automatic. The sort of nod one gave to dismiss an unimportant question. "I'll be fine. After all, I'll have Jack to watch over me."

He didn't miss the faint note of irony in her reply. Jack, it seemed, didn't inspire confidence in either of them. *What's my alternative? Drag her along with me as a moving target?*

He gripped the doorknob. No, it was better this way. He'd already ripped her life apart; he wasn't going to scatter the pieces as well.

As he was leaving, he took one last backward glance. She was still huddled on the bed, her knees drawn up to her chest. The oversized shirt had slid off one bare shoulder. For a moment he thought she was crying. Then she raised her head and met his gaze. What he saw in her eyes wasn't tears. It was something far more moving, something pure and bright and beautiful.

Courage.

In the pale light of dawn, Savitch stood outside Jack Zuckerman's house. Through the fingers of morning mist, Savitch studied the curtained windows, trying to picture the inhabitants within. He wondered who they were, in which room they slept, and whether Catherine Weaver was among them.

He'd find out soon.

He pocketed the black address book he'd taken from the woman's apartment. The name C. Zuckerman and this Pacific Heights address had been written on the inside front cover. Then the Zuckerman had been crossed out and replaced with Weaver. She was a divorcée, he concluded. Under Z, he'd found a prominent listing for a man named Jack, with various phone numbers and addresses, both foreign and domestic. Her ex-husband, he'd confirmed, after a brief chat with another name listed in the book. Pumping strangers for information was a simple matter. All it took was an air of authority and a cop's ID. The same ID he was planning to use now.

He gave the house one final perusal, taking in the manicured lawns and shrubbery, the trellis with its vines of winter-dormant wisteria. A successful man, this Jack Zuckerman. Savitch had always admired men of wealth. He gave his jacket a final tug to assure himself that the shoulder holster was concealed. Then he crossed the street to the front porch and rang the doorbell.

6

At first light, Cathy awakened. It wasn't a gentle return but a startling jerk back to consciousness. She was instantly aware that she was not in her own bed and that something was terribly wrong. It took her a few seconds to remember exactly what it was. And when she did remember, the sense of urgency was so compelling she rose at once from bed and began to dress in the semidarkness. *Have to be ready to run . . .*

The creak of floorboards in the next room told her that Victor was awake as well, probably planning his moves for the day. She rummaged through the closet, searching for things he might need in his flight. All she came up with was a zippered nylon bag and a raincoat. She searched the dresser next and found a few men's socks. She also found a collection of women's underwear. *Damn Jack and all his women,* she thought with sudden irritation and slammed the drawer shut. The thud was still resonating in the room when another sound echoed through the house.

The doorbell was ringing.

It was only seven o'clock, too early for visitors or deliverymen. Suddenly her door swung open. She turned to see Victor, his face etched with tension.

"What should we do?" she asked.

"Get ready to leave. Fast."

"There's a back door—"

"Let's go."

They hurried along the hall and had almost reached the top of the stairs when they heard Jack's sleepy voice below, grumbling: "I'm coming, dammit! Stop that racket, I'm coming!"

The doorbell rang again.

"Don't answer it!" hissed Cathy. "Not yet—"

Jack had already opened the door. Instantly Victor snatched Cathy back up the hall, out of sight. They froze with their backs against the wall, listening to the voices below.

"Yeah," they heard Jack say. "I'm Jack Zuckerman. And who are you?"

The visitor's voice was soft. They could tell only that it was a man.

"Is that so?" said Jack, his voice suddenly edged with panic. "You're with the *FBI,* you say? And what on earth would the *FBI* want with my *ex-wife?*"

Cathy's gaze flew to Victor. She read the frantic message in his eyes: *Which way out?*

She pointed toward the bedroom at the end of the hall. He nodded. Together they tiptoed along the carpet, all the time aware that one misstep, one loud creak, might be enough to alert the agent downstairs.

"Where's your warrant?" they heard Jack demand of the visitor. "Hey, wait a minute! You can't just barge in here without a court order or something!"

No time left! thought Cathy in panic as she slipped into the last room. They closed the door behind them.

"The window!" she whispered.

"You mean jump?"

"No." She hurried across the room and gingerly eased the window open. "There's a trellis!"

He glanced down dubiously at the tangled vines of wisteria. "Are you sure it'll hold us?"

"I know it will," she said, swinging her leg over the sill. "I caught one of Jack's blondes hanging off it one night. And believe me, she was a *big* girl." She glanced down at the ground far below and felt a sudden wave of nausea as the old fear of heights washed through her. "God," she muttered. "Why do we always seem to be hanging out of windows?"

From somewhere in the house came Jack's outraged shout: "You can't go up there! You haven't shown me your warrant!"

"Move!" snapped Victor.

Cathy lowered herself onto the trellis. Branches clawed her face as she scrambled down the vine. An instant after she landed on the dew-soaked grass, Victor dropped beside her.

At once they were on their feet and sprinting for the cover of shrubbery. Just as they rolled behind the azalea bushes, they heard a second-floor window slide open, and then Jack's voice complaining loudly: "I know my rights! This is an illegal search! I'm going to call my lawyer!"

Don't let him see us! prayed Cathy, burrowing frantically into the bush. She felt Victor's body curl around her back, his arms pulling her tightly to him, his breath hot and ragged against her neck. For an eternity they lay shivering in the grass as mist swirled around them.

"You see?" they heard Jack say. "There's no one here but me. Or would you like to check the garage?"

The window slid shut.

Victor gave Cathy a little push. "Go," he whispered. "The end of the hedge. We'll run from there."

On hands and knees she crawled along the row of azalea bushes. Her soaked jeans were icy and her palms scratched and bleeding, but she was too numbed by terror to feel any pain. All her attention was focused on moving forward. Victor was crawling close behind her. When she felt him bump up against her hip, it occurred to her what a ridiculous view he had, her rump swaying practically under his nose.

She reached the last bush and stopped to shove a handful of tangled hair off her face. "That house next?" she asked.

"Go for it!"

They both took off like scared rabbits, dashing across the twenty yards of lawn between houses. Once they reached the cover of the next house, they didn't stop. They kept running, past parked cars and early-morning pedestrians. Five blocks later, they ducked into a coffee shop. Through the front window, they glanced out at the street, watching for signs of pursuit. All they saw was the typical Monday morning bustle: the stop-and-go traffic, the passersby bundled up in scarves and over-coats.

From the grill behind them came the hiss and sizzle of bacon. The smell of freshly brewed coffee wafted from the counter burner. The aromas were almost painful; they reminded Cathy that she and Victor probably had a total of forty dollars between them. Damn it, why hadn't she begged, borrowed or stolen some cash from Jack?

"What now?" she asked, half hoping he'd suggest blowing the rest of their cash on breakfast.

He scanned the street. "Let's go on."

"Where?"

"Hickey's studio."

"Oh." She sighed. Another long walk, and all on an empty stomach.

Outside, a car passed by bearing the bumper sticker: Today is the First Day of the Rest of Your Life.

Lord, I hope it gets better than this, she thought. Then she followed Victor out the door and into the morning chill.

Field Supervisor Larry Dafoe was sitting at his desk, pumping away at his executive power chair. Upper body strength, he always said, was the key to success as a man. Bulk out those muscles *pull!,* fill out that size forty-four jacket *pull!,* and what you got was a pair of shoulders that'd impress any woman, intimidate any rival. And with this snazzy 700-buck model, you didn't even have to get out of your chair.

Sam Polowski watched his superior strain at the system of wires and pulleys and thought the device looked more like an exotic instrument of torture.

"What you gotta understand," gasped Dafoe, "is that there are other *pull!* issues at work here. Things you know nothing about."

"Like what?" asked Polowski.

Dafoe released the handles and looked up, his face sheened with a healthy sweat. "If I was at liberty to tell you, don't you think I already would've?"

Polowski looked at the gleaming black exercise handles, wondering whether he'd benefit from an executive power chair. Maybe a souped-up set of biceps was what he needed to get a little respect around this office.

"I still don't see what the point is," he said. "Putting Victor Holland in the hot seat."

"The point," said Dafoe, "is that you don't call the shots."

"I gave Holland my word he'd be left out of this mess."

"He's *part* of the mess! First he claims he has evidence, then he pulls a vanishing act."

"That's partly my fault. I never made it to the rendezvous."

"Why hasn't he tried to contact you?"

"I don't know." Polowski sighed and shook his head. "Maybe he's dead."

"Maybe we just need to find him." Dafoe reached for the exercise handles. "Maybe you need to get to work on the Lanzano file. Or maybe you should just go home. You look terrible."

"Yeah. Sure." Polowski turned. As he left the office, he could hear Dafoe once again huffing and puffing. He went to his desk, sat down and contemplated his collection of cold capsules, aspirin and cough syrup. He took a double dose of each. Then he reached in his briefcase and pulled out the Viratek file.

It was his own private collection of scrambled notes and phone numbers and news clippings. He sifted through them, stopping to ponder

once again the link between Holland and the woman Catherine
Weaver. He'd first seen her name on the hospital admission sheet, and
had later been startled to hear of her connection to the murdered
Garberville woman. Too many coincidences, too many twists and turns.
Was there something obvious here he was missing? Might the woman
have an answer or two?

He reached for the telephone and dialed the Garberville police department. They would know how to reach their witness. And maybe
she would know how to find Victor Holland. It was a long shot but Sam
Polowski was an inveterate horseplayer. He had a penchant for long
shots.

The man ringing his doorbell looked like a tree stump dressed in a
brown polyester suit. Jack opened the door and said, "Sorry, I'm not
buying today."

"I'm not selling anything, Mr. Zuckerman," said the man. "I'm with
the FBI."

Jack sighed. "Not again."

"I'm Special Agent Sam Polowski. I'm trying to locate a woman
named Catherine Weaver, formerly Zuckerman. I believe she—"

"Don't you guys ever know when to quit?"

"Quit what?"

"One of your agents was here this morning. Talk to him!"

The man frowned. "One of _our_ agents?"

"Yeah. And I just might register a complaint against him. Barged
right in here without a warrant and started tramping all over my
house."

"What did he look like?"

"Oh, I don't know! Dark hair, terrific build. But he could've used a
course in charm school."

"Was he about my height?"

"Taller. Skinnier. Lots more hair."

"Did he give you his name? It wasn't Mac Braden, was it?"

"Naw, he didn't give me any name."

Polowski pulled out his badge. Jack squinted at the words: Federal
Bureau of Investigation. "Did he show you one of these?" asked
Polowski.

"No. He just asked about Cathy and some guy named Victor Holland. Whether I knew how to find them."

"Did you tell him?"

"That jerk?" Jack laughed. "I wouldn't bother to give him the time
of day. I sure as hell wasn't going to tell him about—" Jack paused and

cleared his throat. "I wasn't going to tell him anything. Even if I knew. Which I don't."

Polowski slipped his badge into his pocket, all the time gazing steadily at Jack. "I think we should talk, Mr. Zuckerman."

"What about?"

"About your ex-wife. About the fact she's in big trouble."

"That," sighed Jack, "I already know."

"She's going to get hurt. I can't fill you in on all the details because I'm still in the dark myself. But I do know one woman's already been hit. Your wife—"

"My ex-wife."

"Your ex-wife could be next."

Jack, unconvinced, merely looked at him.

"It's your duty as a citizen to tell me what you know," Polowski reminded him.

"My duty. Right."

"Look, cooperate, and you and me, we'll get along just fine. Give me grief, and I'll give *you* grief." Polowski smiled. Jack didn't. "Now, Mr. Zuckerman. Hey, can I call you Jack? Jack, why don't you tell me where she is? Before it's too late. For both of you."

Jack scowled at him. He drummed his fingers against the door frame. He debated. At last he stepped aside. "As a law-abiding citizen, I suppose it is my duty." Grudgingly, he waved the man in. "Oh, just come in, Polowski. I'll tell you what I know."

The window shattered, raining slivers into the gloomy space beyond.

Cathy winced at the sound. "Sorry, Hickey," she said under her breath.

"We'll make it up to him," said Victor, knocking off the remaining shards. "We'll send him a nice fat check. You see anyone?"

She glanced up and down the alley. Except for a crumpled newspaper tumbling past the trash cans, nothing moved. A few blocks away, car horns blared, the sounds of another Union Street traffic jam.

"All clear," she whispered.

"Okay." Victor draped his windbreaker over the sill. "Up you go."

He gave her a lift to the window. She clambered through and landed among the glass shards. Seconds later, Victor dropped down beside her.

They were standing in the studio dressing room. Against one wall hung a rack of women's lingerie; against the other were makeup tables and a long mirror.

Victor frowned at a cloud of peach silk flung over one of the chairs. "What kind of photos does your friend take, anyway?"

"Hickey specializes in what's politely known as 'boudoir portraits.' "

Victor's startled gaze turned to a black lace negligee hanging from a wall hook. "Does that mean what I think it means?"

"What do you think it means?"

"You know."

She headed into the next room. "Hickey insists it's not pornography. It's tasteful erotic art. . . ." She stopped in her tracks as she came face-to-face with a photo blowup on the wall. Naked limbs—eight, maybe more—were entwined in a sort of human octopus. Nothing was left to the imagination. Nothing at all.

"Tasteful," Victor said dryly.

"That must be one of his, uh, commercial assignments."

"I wonder what product they were selling."

She turned and found herself staring at another photograph. This time it was two women, drop-dead gorgeous and wearing not a stitch.

"Another commercial assignment?" Victor inquired politely over her shoulder.

She shook her head. "Don't ask."

In the front room they found a week's worth of mail piled up beneath the door slot, darkroom catalogues and advertising flyers. The roll of film Cathy had mailed the day before was not yet in the mound.

"I guess we just sit around and wait for the postman," she said.

He nodded. "Seems like a safe-enough place. Any chance your friend keeps food around?"

"I seem to remember a refrigerator in the other room."

She led Victor into what Hickey had dubbed his "shooting gallery." Cathy flipped the wall switch and the vast room was instantly illuminated by a dazzling array of spotlights.

"So this is where he does it," said Victor, blinking in the sudden glare. He stepped over a jumble of electrical cords and slowly circled the room, regarding with humorous disbelief the various props. It was a strange collection of objects: a genuine English phone booth, a street bench, an exercise bicycle. In a place of honor sat a four-poster bed. The ruffled coverlet was Victorian; the handcuffs dangling from the bedposts were not.

Victor picked up one of the cuffs and let it fall again. "Just how good a friend *is* this Hickey guy, anyway?"

"None of this stuff was here when he shot me a month ago."

"He photographed *you?*" Victor turned and stared at her.

She flushed, imagining the images that must be flashing through his mind. She could feel his gaze undressing her, posing her in a sprawl across that ridiculous four-poster bed. With the handcuffs, no less.

"It wasn't like—like these other photos," she protested. "I mean, I just did it as a favor. . . ."

"A favor?"

"It was a purely *commercial* shot!"

"Oh."

"I was fully dressed. In overalls, as a matter of fact. I was supposed to be a plumber."

"A lady plumber?"

"I was an emergency stand-in. One of his models didn't show up that day, and he needed someone with an ordinary face. I guess that's me. Ordinary. And it really was just my face."

"And your overalls."

"Right."

They looked at each other and burst out laughing.

"I can guess what you were thinking," she said.

"I don't even want to *tell* you what I was thinking." He turned and glanced around the room. "Didn't you say there was some food around here?"

She crossed the room to the refrigerator. Inside she found a shelf of film plus a jar of sweet pickles, some rubbery carrots and half a salami. In the freezer they discovered real treasures: ground Sumatran coffee and a loaf of sourdough bread.

Grinning, she turned to him. "A feast!"

They sat together on the four-poster bed and gnawed on salami and half-frozen sourdough, all washed down with cups of coffee. It was a bizarre little picnic, paper plates with pickles and carrots resting in their laps, the spotlights glaring down like a dozen hot suns from the ceiling.

"Why did you say that about yourself?" he asked, watching her munch a carrot.

"Say what?"

"That you're ordinary. So ordinary that you get cast as the lady plumber?"

"Because I am ordinary."

"I don't think so. And I happen to be a pretty good judge of character."

She looked up at a wall poster featuring one of Hickey's super models. The woman stared back with a look of glossy confidence. "Well, I certainly don't measure up to *that.*"

"That," he said, "is pure fantasy. *That* isn't a real woman, but an amalgam of makeup, hairspray and fake eyelashes."

"Oh, I know that. That's my job, turning actors into some moviegoer's fantasy. Or nightmare, as the case may be." She reached into the jar and fished out the last pickle. "No, I really meant *underneath* it all. Deep inside, I *feel* ordinary."

"I think you're quite extraordinary. And after last night, I should know."

She gazed down, at the limp carrot stretched out like a little corpse across the paper plate. "There was a time—I suppose there's always that time, for everyone, when we're still young, when we feel special. When we feel the world's meant just for us. The last time I felt that way was when I married Jack." She sighed. "It didn't last long."

"Why did you marry him?"

"I don't know. Dazzle? I was only twenty-three, a mere apprentice on the set. He was the director." She paused. "He was *God.*"

"He impressed you, did he?"

"Jack can be very impressive. He can turn on the power, the charisma, and just overwhelm a gal. Then there was the champagne, the suppers, the flowers. I think what attracted him to me was that I didn't immediately fall for him. That I wasn't swooning at his every look. He thought of me as a challenge, the one he finally conquered." She gave him a rueful look. "That accomplished, he moved onto bigger and better things. That's when I realized that I wasn't particularly special. That I'm really just a perfectly ordinary woman. It's not a bad feeling. It's not as if I go through life longing to be someone different, someone special."

"Then who do you consider special?"

"Well, my grandmother. But she's dead."

"Venerable grandmothers always make the list."

"Okay, then. Mother Teresa."

"She's on everyone's list."

"Kate Hepburn. Gloria Steinem. My friend Sarah . . ." Her voice faded. Looking down, she added softly: "But she's dead, too."

Gently he took her hand. With a strange sense of wonder she watched his long fingers close over hers and thought about how the strength she felt in that grasp reflected the strength of the man himself. Jack, for all his dazzle and polish, had never inspired a fraction of the confidence she now felt in Victor. No man ever had.

He was watching her with quiet sympathy. "Tell me about Sarah," he said.

Cathy swallowed, trying to stem the tears. "She was absolutely lovely. I don't mean in *that* way." She nodded at the photo of Hickey's picture-perfect model. "I mean, in an inner sort of way. It was this look in her eyes. A perfect calmness. As though she'd found exactly what she wanted while all the rest of us were still grubbing around for lost treasure. I don't think she was born like that. She came to it, all by herself. In college, we were both pretty unsure of ourselves. Marriage certainly didn't help either of us. My divorce—it was nothing short of devastating. But Sarah's divorce only seemed to make her stronger. Better able to take care of herself. When she finally got pregnant, it was exactly as she planned it. There wasn't a father, you see, just a test tube. An anonymous donor. Sarah used to say that the primeval family unit wasn't man, woman and child. It was just woman and child. I thought she was brave, to take that step. She was a lot braver than I could ever be. . . ." She cleared her throat. "Anyway, Sarah *was* special. Some people simply are."

"Yes," he said. "Some people are."

She looked up at him. He was staring off at the far wall, his gaze infinitely sad. What had etched those lines of pain in his face? She wondered if lines so deep could ever be erased. There were some losses one never got over, never accepted.

Softly she asked, "What was your wife like?"

He didn't answer at first. She thought: *Why did I ask that? Why did I have to bring up such terrible memories?*

He said, "She was a kind woman. That's what I'll always remember about her. Her kindness." He looked at Cathy and she sensed it wasn't sadness she saw in those eyes, but acceptance.

"What was her name?"

"Lily. Lillian Dorinda Cassidy. A mouthful for such a tiny woman." He smiled. "She was about five foot one, maybe ninety pounds sopping wet. It used to scare me, how small she always seemed. Almost breakable. Especially toward the end, when she'd lost all that weight. It seemed as if she'd shrunk down to nothing but a pair of big brown eyes."

"She must have been young when she died."

"Only thirty-eight. It seemed so unfair. All her life, she'd done everything right. Never smoked, hardly ever touched a glass of wine. She even refused to eat meat. After she was diagnosed, we kept trying to figure out how it could've happened. Then it occurred to us what might have caused it. She grew up in a small town in Massachusetts. Directly downwind from a nuclear power plant."

"You think that was it?"

"One can never be sure. But we asked around. And we learned that, just in her neighborhood, at least twenty families had someone with leukemia. It took four years and a class-action suit to force an investigation. What they found was a history of safety violations going back all the way to the plant's opening."

Cathy shook her head in disbelief. "And all those years they allowed it to operate?"

"No one knew about it. The violations were hushed up so well even the federal regulators were kept in the dark."

"They shut it down, didn't they?"

He nodded. "I can't say I got much satisfaction, seeing the plant finally close. By that time Lily was gone. And all the families, well, we were exhausted by the fight. Even though it sometimes felt as though we were banging our heads against a wall, we knew it was something we had to do. *Somebody* had to do it, for all the Lilys of the world." He looked up, at the spotlights shining above. "And here I am again, still banging my head against walls. Only this time, it feels like the Great Wall of China. And the lives at stake are yours and mine."

Their gazes met. She sat absolutely still as he lightly stroked down the curve of her cheek. She took his hand, pressed it to her lips. His fingers closed over hers, refusing to release her hand. Gently he tugged her close. Their lips met, a tentative kiss that left her longing for more.

"I'm sorry you were pulled into this," he murmured. "You and Sarah and those other Cathy Weavers. None of you asked to be part of it. And somehow I've managed to hurt you all."

"Not you, Victor. You're not the one to blame. It's this windmill you're tilting at. This giant, dangerous windmill. Anyone else would have dropped his lance and fled. You're still going at it."

"I didn't have much of a choice."

"But you did. You could have walked away from your friend's death. Turned a blind eye to whatever's going on at Viratek. That's what Jack would have done."

"But I'm not Jack. There are things I can't walk away from. I'd always be thinking of the Lilys. All the thousands of people who might get hurt."

At the mention once again of his dead wife, Cathy felt some unbreachable barrier form between them—the shadow of Lily, the wife she'd never met. Cathy drew back, at once aching from the loss of his touch.

"You think that many people could die?" she asked.

"Jerry must have thought so. There's no way to predict the outcome. The world's never seen the effects of all-out biological warfare. I like to think it's because we're too smart to play with our own self-destruction. Then I think of all the crazy things people have done over the years and it scares me. . . ."

"Are viral weapons that dangerous?"

"If you alter a few genes, make it just a little more contagious, raise the kill ratio, you'd end up with a devastating strain. The research alone is hazardous. A single slip-up in lab security and you could have millions of people accidentally infected. And no means of treatment. It's the kind of worldwide disaster a scientist doesn't want to think about."

"Armageddon."

He nodded, his gaze frighteningly sane. "If you believe in such a thing. That's exactly what it'd be."

She shook her head. "I don't understand why these things are allowed."

"They aren't. By international agreement, they're outlawed. But there's always some madman lurking in the shadows who wants that extra bit of leverage, that weapon no one else has."

A madman. That's what one would have to be, to even think of unleashing such a weapon on the world. She thought of a novel she'd read, about just such a plague, how the cities had lain dead and decaying, how the very air had turned poisonous. But those were only the nightmares of science fiction. This was real.

From somewhere in the building came the sound of whistling.

Cathy and Victor both sat up straight. The melody traveled along the hall, closer and closer, until it stopped right outside Hickey's door. They heard a rustling, then the slap of magazines hitting the floor.

"It's here!" said Cathy, leaping to her feet.

Victor was right behind her as she hurried into the front room. She spotted it immediately, sitting atop the pile: a padded envelope, addressed in her handwriting. She scooped it up and ripped the envelope open. Out slid the roll of film. The note she'd scribbled to Hickey fluttered to the floor. Grinning in triumph, she held up the canister. "Here's your evidence!"

"We hope. Let's see what we've got on the roll. Where's the darkroom?"

"Next to the dressing room." She handed him the film. "Do you know how to process it?"

"I've done some amateur photography. As long as I've got the chemicals I can—" He stopped and glanced over at the desk.

The phone was ringing.

Victor shook his head. "Ignore it," he said and turned for the darkroom.

As they left the reception room, they heard the answering machine click on. Hickey's voice, smooth as silk, spoke on the recording. "This is the studio of Hickman Von Trapp, specializing in tasteful and artistic images of the female form. . . ."

Victor laughed. "Tasteful?"

"It depends on your taste," said Cathy as she followed him up the hall.

They had just reached the darkroom when the recording ended and was followed by the message beep. An agitated voice rattled from the speaker. "Hello? Hello, Cathy? If you're there, answer me, will you? There's an FBI agent looking for you—some guy named Polowski—"

Cathy stopped dead. "It's Jack!" she said, turning to retrace her steps toward the front room.

The voice on the speaker had taken on a note of panic. "I couldn't help it—he made me tell him about Hickey. Get out of there now!"

The message clicked off just as Cathy grabbed the receiver. "Hello? *Jack?*"

She heard only the dial tone. He'd already hung up. Hands shaking, she began to punch in Jack's phone number.

"There's no time!" said Victor.

"I have to talk to him—"

He grabbed the receiver and slammed it down. "Later! We have to get out of here!"

She nodded numbly and started for the door. There she halted. "Wait. We need money!" She turned back to the reception desk and searched the drawers until she found the petty cash box. Twenty-two dollars was all it contained. "Always keep just enough for decent coffee beans," Hickey used to say. She pocketed the money. Then she reached up and yanked one of Hickey's old raincoats from the door hook. He wouldn't miss it. And she might need it for concealment. "Okay," she said, slipping on the coat. "Let's go."

They paused only a second to check the corridor. From another suite came the faint echo of laughter. Somewhere above, high heels clicked across a wooden floor. With Victor in the lead, they darted down the hall and out the front door.

The midday sun seemed to glare down on them like an accusing eye. Quickly they fell into step with the rest of the lunch crowd, the businessmen and artists, the Union Street chic. No one glanced their way. But even with people all around her, Cathy felt conspicuous. As though, in this bright cityscape of crowds and concrete, she was the focus of the painter's eye.

She huddled deeper into the raincoat, wishing it were a mantle of invisibility. Victor had quickened his pace, and she had to run to keep up.

"Where do we go now?" she whispered.

"We've got the film. Now I say we head for the bus station."

"And then?"

"Anywhere." He kept his gaze straight ahead. "As long as it's out of this city."

7

That pesky FBI agent was ringing his doorbell again.

Sighing, Jack opened the front door. "Back already?"

"Damn right I'm back." Polowski stamped in and shoved the door closed behind him. "I want to know where to find 'em next."

"I told you, Mr. Polowski. Over on Union Street there's a studio owned by Mr. Hickman—"

"I've been to Von Whats-his-name's studio."

Jack swallowed. "You didn't find them?"

"You knew I wouldn't. You warned 'em, didn't you?"

"Really, I don't know why you're harassing me. I've tried to be—"

"They left in a hurry. The door was wide open. Food was still lying around. They left the empty cash box just sitting on the desk."

Jack drew himself up in outrage. "Are you calling my ex-wife a petty thief?"

"I'm calling her a desperate woman. And I'm calling you an imbecile for screwing things up. Now where is she?"

"I don't know."

"Who would she turn to?"

"No one I know."

"Think harder."

Jack stared down at Polowski's turgid face and marveled that any human being could be so unattractive. Surely the process of natural selection would have dictated against such unacceptable genes?

Jack shook his head. "I honestly don't know."

It was the truth, and Polowski must have sensed it. After a moment of silent confrontation, he backed off. "Then maybe you can tell me this. Why did you warn them?"

"It—it was—" Jack shrugged helplessly. "Oh, I don't know! After you left, I wasn't sure I'd done the right thing. I wasn't sure whether to trust you. *He* doesn't trust you."

"Who?"

"Victor Holland. He thinks you're in on some conspiracy. Frankly, the man struck me as just the slightest bit paranoid."

"He has a right to be. Considering what's happened to him so far." Polowski turned for the door.

"Now what happens?"

"I keep looking for them."

"Where?"

"You think I'd tell *you?*" He stalked out. "Don't leave town, Zucker-man," he snapped over his shoulder. "I'll be back to see you later."

"I don't think so," Jack muttered softly as he watched the other man lumber back to his car. He looked up and saw there wasn't a cloud in the sky. Smiling to himself, he shut the door.

It would be sunny in Mexico, as well.

Someone had left in a hurry.

Savitch strolled through the rooms of the photo studio, which had been left unlocked. He noted the scraps of a meal on the four-poster bed: crumbs of sourdough bread, part of a salami, an empty pickle jar. He also took note of the coffee cups: there were two of them. Interesting, since Savitch had spotted only one person leaving the studio, a squat little man in a polyester suit. The man hadn't been there long. Savitch had observed him climb into a dark green Ford parked at a fifteen-minute meter. The meter still had three minutes remaining.

Savitch continued his tour of the studio, eyeing the tawdry photos, wondering if this wasn't another waste of his time. After all, every other address he'd pulled from the woman's black book had turned up no sign of her. Why should Hickman Von Trapp's address be any different?

Still, he couldn't shake the instinct that he was getting close. Clues were everywhere. He read them, put them together. Today, this studio had been visited by two hungry people. They'd entered through a broken window in the dressing room. They'd eaten scraps taken from the refrigerator. They (or the man in the polyester suit) had emptied the petty cash box.

Savitch completed his tour and returned to the front room. That's when he noticed the telephone message machine blinking on and off.

He pressed the play button. The string of messages seemed endless. The calls were for someone named Hickey—no doubt the Hickman Von Trapp of the address book. Savitch lazily circled the room, half listening to the succession of voices. Business calls for the most part, inquiring about appointments, asking when proofs would be ready and would he like to do the shoot for *Snoop* magazine? Near the door, Savitch halted and stooped down to sift through the pile of mail. It was boring stuff, all addressed to Von Trapp. Then he noticed, off to the side, a loose slip of paper. It was a note, addressed to Hickey.

"Feel awful about this, but someone stole all those rolls of film from my car. This was the only one left. Thought I'd get it to you before it's lost, as well. Hope it's enough to save your shoot from being a complete waste—"

It was signed "Cathy."

He stood up straight. Catherine Weaver? It had to be! The roll of film—where the hell was the roll of film?

He rifled through the mail, searching, searching. He turned up only a torn envelope with Cathy Weaver's return address. The film was gone. In frustration, he began to fling magazines across the room. Then, in mid-toss, he froze.

A new message was playing on the recorder.

"Hello? Hello, Cathy? If you're there, answer me, will you? There's an FBI agent looking for you—some guy named Polowski. I couldn't help it—he made me tell him about Hickey. Get out of there now!"

Savitch stalked over to the answering machine and stared down as the mechanism automatically whirred back to the beginning. He replayed it.

Get out of there now!

There was now no doubt. Catherine Weaver had been here, and Victor Holland was with her. But who was this agent Polowski and why was he searching for Holland? Savitch had been assured that the Bureau was off the case. He would have to check into the matter.

He crossed over to the window and stared out at the bright sunshine, the crowded sidewalks. So many faces, so many strangers. Where, in this city, would two terrified fugitives hide? Finding them would be difficult, but not impossible.

He left the suite and went outside to a pay phone. There he dialed a Washington, D.C., number. He wasn't fond of asking the Cowboy for help, but now he had no choice. Victor Holland had his hands on the evidence, and the stakes had shot sky-high.

It was time to step up the pursuit.

* * *

The clerk yelled, "Next window, please!" and closed the grate.

"Wait!" cried Cathy, tapping at the pane. "My bus is leaving right now!"

"Which one?"

"Number 23 to Palo Alto—"

"There's another at seven o'clock."

"But—"

"I'm on my dinner break."

Cathy stared helplessly as the clerk walked away. Over the PA system came the last call for the Palo Alto express. Cathy glanced around just in time to see the Number 23 roar away from the curb.

"Service just ain't what it used to be," an old man muttered behind her. "Get there faster usin' yer damn thumb."

Sighing, Cathy shifted to the next line, which was eight-deep and slow as molasses. The woman at the front was trying to convince the clerk that her social security card was an acceptable ID for a check.

Okay, Cathy thought. *So we leave at seven o'clock. That puts us in Palo Alto at eight. Then what? Camp in a park? Beg a few scraps from a restaurant? What does Victor have in mind. . . ?*

She glanced around and spotted his broad back hunched inside one of the phone booths. Whom could he possibly be calling? She saw him hang up and run his hand wearily through his hair. Then he picked up the receiver and dialed another number.

"Next!" Someone tapped Cathy on the shoulder. "Go ahead, Miss."

Cathy turned and saw that the ticket clerk was waiting. She stepped to the window.

"Where to?" asked the clerk.

"I need two tickets to . . ." Cathy's voice suddenly faded.

"Where?"

Cathy didn't speak. Her gaze had frozen on a poster tacked right beside the ticket window. The words Have You Seen This Man? appeared above an unsmiling photo of Victor Holland. And at the bottom were listed the charges: Industrial espionage and murder. If you have any information about this man, please contact your local police or the FBI.

"Lady, you wanna go somewhere or not?"

"What?" Cathy's gaze jerked back to the clerk, who was watching her with obvious annoyance. "Oh. Yes, I'm—I'd like two tickets. To Palo Alto." Numbly she handed over a fistful of cash. "One way."

"Two to Palo Alto. That bus will depart at 7:00, Gate 11."

"Yes. Thank you . . ." Cathy took the tickets and turned to leave the line. That's when she spotted the two policemen, standing just inside the front entrance. They seemed to be scanning the terminal, searching—for what?

In a panic, her gaze shot to the phone booth. It was empty. She stared at it with a sense of abandonment. *You left me! You left me with two tickets to Palo Alto and five bucks in my pocket!*

Where are you, Victor?

She couldn't stand here like an idiot. She had to do something, had to move. She pulled the raincoat tightly around her shoulders and forced herself to stroll across the terminal. *Don't let them notice me,* she prayed. *Please. I'm nobody. Nothing.* She paused at a chair and picked up a discarded *San Francisco Chronicle.* Then, thumbing through the Want Ads, she sauntered right past the two policemen. They didn't even glance at her as she went out the front entrance.

Now what? she wondered, pausing amidst the confusion of a busy sidewalk. Automatically she started to walk and had taken only half a dozen steps down the street when she was wrenched sideways, into an alley.

She reeled back against the trash cans and almost sobbed with relief. "Victor!"

"Did they see you?"

"No. I mean, yes, but they didn't seem to care—"

"Are you sure?" She nodded. He turned and slapped the wall in frustration. "What the hell do we do now?"

"I have the tickets."

"We can't use them."

"How are we going to get out of town? Hitchhike? Victor, we're down to our last five dollars!"

"They'll be watching every bus that leaves. And they've got my face plastered all over the damn terminal!" He slumped back against the wall and groaned. *"Have you seen this man?* God, I looked like some two-bit gangster."

"It wasn't the most flattering photo."

He managed to laugh. "Have you *ever* seen a flattering wanted poster?"

She leaned back beside him, against the wall. "We've got to get out of this city, Victor."

"Amend that. *You've* got to get out."

"What's that supposed to mean?"

"The police aren't looking for you. So *you* take that bus to Palo Alto. I'll put you in touch with some old friends. They'll see you make it somewhere safe."

"No."

"Cathy, they've probably got my mug posted in every airport and car rental agency in town! We've spent almost all our money for those bus tickets. I say you use them!"

"I'm not leaving you."

"You don't have a choice."

"Yes I do. I choose to stick to you like glue. Because you're the only one I feel safe with. The only one I can count on!"

"I can move faster on my own. Without you slowing me down." He looked off, toward the street. "Hell, I don't even *want* you around."

"I don't believe that."

"Why should I care what you believe?"

"Look at me! Look at me and say that!" She grabbed his arm, willing him to face her. "Say you don't want me around!"

He started to speak, to repeat the lie. She knew then that it *was* a lie; she could see it in his eyes. And she saw something else in that gaze, something that took her breath away.

He said, "I don't—I won't have you—"

She just stood there, looking up at him, waiting for the truth to come.

What she didn't expect was the kiss. She never remembered how it happened. She only knew that all at once his arms were around her and she was being swept up into some warm and safe and wonderful place. It started as an embrace more of desperation than passion, a coming together of two terrified people. But the instant their lips met, it became something much more. This went beyond fear, beyond need. This was a souls' joining, one that wouldn't be broken, even after this embrace was over, even if they never touched again.

When at last they drew apart and stared at each other, the taste of him was still fresh on her lips.

"You see?" she whispered. "I was right. You do want me around. You do."

He smiled and touched her cheek. "I'm not a very good liar."

"And I'm not leaving you. You need me. You can't show your face, but I can! I can buy bus tickets, run errands—"

"What I really need," he sighed, "is a new face." He glanced out at the street. "Since there's no plastic surgeon handy, I suggest we hoof it over to the BART station. It'll be crowded at this hour. We might make it to the East Bay—"

"God, I'm such an *idiot!*" she groaned. "A new face is exactly what you need!" She turned toward the street. "Come on. There isn't much time. . . ."

"Cathy?" He followed her up the alley. They both paused, scanning the street for policemen. There were none in sight. "Where are we going?" he whispered.

"To find a phone booth."

"Oh. And who are we calling?"

She turned and the look she gave him was distinctly pained. "Someone we both know and love."

Jack was packing his suitcase when the phone rang. He considered not answering it, but something about the sound, an urgency that could only have been imagined, made him pick up the receiver. He was instantly sorry he had.

"Jack?"

He sighed. "Tell me I'm hearing things."

"Jack, I'm going to talk fast because your phone might be tapped—"

"You don't say."

"I need my kit. The whole shebang. And some cash. I swear I'll pay it all back. Get it for me right now. Then drop it off where we shot the last scene of *Cretinoid.* You know the spot."

"Cathy, you wait a minute! I'm in trouble enough as it is!"

"One hour. That's all I can wait."

"It's rush hour! I can't—"

"It's the last favor I'll ask of you." There was a pause. Then, softly, she added, "Please."

He let out a breath. "This is the absolute last time, right?"

"One hour, Jack. I'll be waiting."

Jack hung up and stared at his suitcase. It was only half packed, but it would have to do. He sure as hell wasn't coming back *here* tonight.

He closed the suitcase and carried it out to the Jaguar. As he drove away it suddenly occurred to him that he'd forgotten to cancel his date with Lulu tonight.

No time now, he thought. I've got more important things on my mind—like getting out of town.

Lulu would be mad as a hornet, but he'd make it up to her. Maybe a pair of diamond ear studs. Yeah, that would do the trick.

Good old Lulu, so easy to please. Now there was a woman he could understand.

The corner of Fifth and Mission was a hunker-down, chew-the-fat sort of gathering place for the street folk. At five forty-five it was even busier than usual. Rumor had it the soup kitchen down the block was fixing to serve beef Bourguignonne, which, as those who remembered better days and better meals could tell you, was made with red wine.

No one passed up the chance for a taste of the grape, even if every drop of alcohol was simmered clean out of it. And so they stood around on the corner, talking of other meals they'd had, of the weather, of the long lines at the unemployment office.

No one noticed the two wretched souls huddled in the doorway of the pawnshop.

Lucky for us, thought Cathy, burying herself in the folds of the raincoat. The sad truth was, they were both beginning to fit right into this crowd. Just a moment earlier she'd caught sight of her own reflection in the pawnshop window and had almost failed to recognize the disheveled image staring back. *Has it been that long since I've combed my hair? That long since I've had a meal or a decent night's sleep?*

Victor looked no better. A torn shirt and two days' worth of stubble on his jaw only emphasized that unmistakable look of exhaustion. He could walk into that soup kitchen down the block and no one would look twice.

He's going to look a hell of a lot worse when I get through with him, she thought with a grim sense of humor.

If Jack ever showed up with the kit.

"It's 6:05," Victor muttered. "He's had an hour."

"Give him time."

"We're running out of time."

"We can still make the bus." She peered up the street, as though by force of will she could conjure up her ex-husband. But only a city bus barreled into view. *Come on, Jack, come on! Don't let me down this time. . . .*

"Will ya lookit that!" came a low growl, followed by general murmurs of admiration from the crowd.

"Hey, pretty boy!" someone called as the group gathered on the corner to stare. "What'd you have to push to get yerself wheels like that?"

Through the gathering of men, Cathy spied the bright gleam of chrome and burgundy. "Get away from my car!" demanded a querulous voice. "I just had her waxed!"

"Looks like Pretty Boy got hisself lost. Turned down the wrong damn street, did ya?"

Cathy leaped to her feet. "He's here!"

She and Victor pushed through the crowd to find Jack standing guard over the Jaguar's gleaming finish.

"Don't—don't touch her!" he snapped as one man ran a grimy finger across the hood. "Why can't you people go find yourselves a job or something?"

"A job?" someone yelled. "What's that?"

"Jack!" called Cathy.

Jack let out a sigh of relief when he spotted her. "This is the last favor. The absolute *last* favor—"

"Where is it?" she asked.

Jack walked around to the trunk, where he slapped away another hand as it stroked the Jaguar's burgundy flank. "It's right here. The whole kit and kaboodle." He swung out the makeup case and handed it over. "Delivered as promised. Now I gotta run."

"Where are you going?" she called.

"I don't know." He climbed back into the car. "Somewhere. Anywhere!"

"Sounds like we're headed in the same direction."

"God, I hope not." He started the engine and revved it up a few times.

Someone yelled: "So long, Pretty Boy!"

Jack gazed out dryly at Cathy. "You know, you really should do something about the company you keep. Ciao, sweetcakes."

The Jaguar lurched away. With a screech of tires, it spun around the corner and vanished into traffic.

Cathy turned and saw that every eye was watching her.

Automatically, Victor moved close beside her, one tired and hungry man facing a tired and hungry crowd.

Someone called out: "So who's the jerk in the Jag?"

"My ex-husband," said Cathy.

"Doin' a lot better than you are, honey."

"No kidding." She held up the makeup case and managed a careless laugh. "I ask the creep for my clothes, he throws me a change of underwear."

"Babe, now ain't that just the way it works?"

Already, the men were wandering away, regrouping in doorways, or over by the corner newsstands. The Jaguar was gone, and so was their interest.

Only one man stood before Cathy and Victor, and the look he gave them was distinctly sympathetic. "That's all he left you, huh? Him with that nice, fancy car?" He turned to leave, then glanced back at them. "Say, you two need a place to stay or somethin'? I got a lot of friends. And I hate to see a lady out in the cold."

"Thanks for the offer," said Victor, taking Cathy's hand. "But we've got a bus to catch."

The man nodded and shuffled away, a kind but unfortunate soul whom the streets had not robbed of decency.

"We have a half hour to get on that bus," said Victor, hurrying Cathy along. "Better get to work."

They were headed up the street, toward the cover of an alley, when Cathy suddenly halted. "Victor—"

"What's the matter?"

"Look." She pointed at the newsstand, her hand shaking.

Beneath the plastic cover was the afternoon edition of the *San Francisco Examiner*. The headline read: "Two Victims, Same Name. Police Probe Coincidence." Beside it was a photo of a young blond woman. The caption was hidden by the fold, but Cathy didn't need to read it. She could already guess the woman's name.

"Two of them," she whispered. "Victor, you were right. . . ."

"All the more reason for us to get out of town." He pulled on her arm. "Hurry."

She let him lead her away. But even as they headed down the street, even as they left the newsstand behind them, she carried that image in her mind: the photograph of a blond woman, the second victim.

The second Catherine Weaver.

Patrolman O'Hanley was a helpful soul. Unlike too many of his colleagues, O'Hanley had joined the force out of a true desire to serve and protect. The "Boy Scout" was what the other men called him behind his back. The epithet both annoyed and pleased him. It told him he didn't fit in with the rough-and-tumble gang on the force. It also told him he was above it all, above the petty bribe-taking and backbiting and maneuverings for promotion. He wasn't out to glorify the badge on his chest. What he wanted was the chance to pat a kid on the head, rescue an old granny from a mugging.

That's why he found this particular assignment so frustrating. All this standing around in the bus depot, watching for a man some witness *might* have spotted a few hours ago. O'Hanley hadn't noticed any such character. He'd eyeballed every person who'd walked in the door. A sorry lot, most of them. Not surprising since, these days, anyone with the cash to spare took a plane. By the looks of these folks, none of 'em could spare much more than pennies. Take that pair over there, huddled together in the waiting area. A father and daughter, he figured, and both of 'em down on their luck. The daughter was bundled up in an old raincoat, the collar pulled up to reveal only a mop of wind-blown hair. The father was an even sorrier sight, gaunt-faced, white-whiskered, about as old as Methuselah. Still, there was a remnant of pride in the old codger—O'Hanley could see it in the way the man held himself, stiff and straight. Must've been an impressive fellow in his younger years since he was still well over six feet tall.

The public speaker announced final boarding for number fourteen to Palo Alto.

The old man and his daughter rose to their feet.

O'Hanley watched with concern as the pair shuffled across the terminal toward the departure gate. The woman was carrying only one small case, but it appeared to be a heavy one. And she already had her hands full, trying to guide the old man in the right direction. But they were making progress, and O'Hanley figured they'd make it to the bus okay.

That is, until the kid ran into them.

He was about six, the kind of kid no mother wants to admit she produced, the kind of kid who gives all six-year-olds a bad name. For the last half hour the boy had been tearing around the terminal, scattering ashtray sand, tipping over suitcases, banging locker doors. Now he was running. Only this kid was doing it *backward.*

O'Hanley saw it coming. The old man and his daughter were crossing slowly toward the departure gate. The kid was scuttling toward them. Intersecting paths, inevitable collision. The kid slammed into the woman's knees; the case flew out of her grasp. She stumbled against her companion. O'Hanley, paralyzed, expected the codger to keel over. To his surprise, the old man simply caught the woman in his arms and handily set her back on her feet.

By now O'Hanley was hurrying to their aid. He got to the woman just as she'd regained her footing. "You folks okay?" he asked.

The woman reacted as though he'd slapped her. She stared up at him with the eyes of a terrified animal. "What?" she said.

"Are you okay? Looked to me like he hit you pretty hard."

She nodded.

"How 'bout you, Gramps?"

The woman glanced at her companion. It seemed to O'Hanley that there was a lot being said in that glance, a lot he wasn't privy to.

"We're both fine," the woman said quickly. "Come on, Pop. We'll miss our bus."

"Can I give you a hand with him?"

"That's mighty kind of you, officer, but we'll do fine." The woman smiled at O'Hanley. Something about that smile wasn't right. As he watched the pair shuffle off toward bus number fourteen, O'Hanley kept trying to figure it out. Kept trying to put his finger on what was wrong with that pair of travelers.

He turned away and almost tripped over the fallen case. The woman had forgotten it. He snatched it up and started to run for the bus. Too late; the number fourteen to Palo Alto was already pulling away. O'Hanley stood helplessly on the curb, watching the taillights vanish around the corner.

Oh, well.

He turned in the makeup case at Lost and Found. Then he stationed himself once again at the entrance. Seven o'clock already and still no sighting of the suspect Victor Holland.

O'Hanley sighed. What a waste of a policeman's time.

Five minutes out of San Francisco, aboard the number fourteen bus, the old man turned to the woman in the raincoat and said, "This beard is killing me."

Laughing, Cathy reached up and gave the fake whiskers a tug. "It did the trick, didn't it?"

"No kidding. We practically got a police escort to the getaway bus." He scratched furiously at his chin. "Geez, how do those actors stand this stuff, anyway? The itch is driving me up a wall."

"Want me to take it off?"

"Better not. Not till we get to Palo Alto."

Another hour, she thought. She sat back and gazed out at the highway gliding past the bus window. "Then what?" she asked softly.

"I'll knock on a few doors. See if I can dig up an old friend or two. It's been a long time, but I think there are still a few in town."

"You used to live there?"

"Years ago. Back when I was in college."

"Oh." She sat up straight. "A *Stanford* man."

"Why do you make it sound just a tad disreputable?"

"I rooted for the Bears, myself."

"I'm consorting with the arch enemy?"

Giggling, she burrowed against his chest and inhaled the warm, familiar scent of his body. "It seems like another lifetime. Berkeley and blue jeans."

"Football. Wild parties."

"Wild parties?" she asked. "You?"

"Well, *rumors* of wild parties."

"Frisbee. Classes on the lawn . . ."

"Innocence," he said softly.

They both fell silent.

"Victor?" she asked. "What if your friends aren't there any longer? Or what if they won't take us in?"

"One step at a time. That's how we have to take it. Otherwise it'll all seem too overwhelming."

"It already does."

He squeezed her tightly against him. "Hey, we're doing okay. We made it out of the city. In fact, we waltzed out right under the nose of a cop. I'd call that pretty damn impressive."

Cathy couldn't help grinning at the memory of the earnest young Patrolman O'Hanley. "All policemen should be so helpful."

"Or blind," Victor snorted. "I can't believe he called me *Gramps.*"

"When I set out to change a face, I do it right."

"Apparently."

She looped her arm through his and pressed a kiss to one scowling, bewhiskered cheek. "Can I tell you a secret?"

"What's that?"

"I'm crazy about older men."

The scowl melted away, slowly reformed into a dubious smile. "How much older are we talking about?"

She kissed him again, this time full on the lips. "Much older."

"Hm. Maybe these whiskers aren't so bad, after all." He took her face in his hands. This time he was the one kissing her, long and deeply, with no thought of where they were or where they were going. Cathy felt herself sliding back against the seat, into a space that was inescapable and infinitely safe.

Someone behind them hooted: "Way to go, Gramps!"

Reluctantly, they pulled apart. Through the flickering shadows of the bus, Cathy could see the twinkle in Victor's eyes, the gleam of a wry smile.

She smiled back and whispered, "Way to go, Gramps."

The posters with Victor Holland's face were plastered all over the bus station.

Polowski couldn't help a snort of irritation as he gazed at that unflattering visage of what he knew in his gut was an innocent man. A damn witchhunt, that's what this'd turned into. If Holland wasn't already scared enough, this public stalking would surely send him diving for cover, beyond the reach of those who could help him. Polowski only hoped it'd also be beyond the reach of those with less benign intentions.

With all these posters staring him in the face, Holland would've been a fool to stroll through this bus depot. Still, Polowski had an instinct about these things, a sense of how people behaved when they were desperate. If he were in Holland's shoes, a killer on his trail and a woman companion to worry about, he knew what *he'd* do—get the hell out of San Francisco. A plane was unlikely. According to Jack Zuckerman, Holland was operating on a thin wallet. A credit card would've been out of the question. That also knocked out a rental car. What was left? It was either hitchhike or take the bus.

Polowski was betting on the bus.

His last piece of info supported that hunch. The tap on Zuckerman's phone had picked up a call from Cathy Weaver. She'd arranged some sort of drop-off at a site Polowski couldn't identify at first. He'd spent a frustrating hour asking around the office, trying to locate someone who'd not only seen Zuckerman's forgettable film, *Cretinoid,* but could also pinpoint where the last scene was filmed. The Mission District, some movie nut file clerk had finally told him. Yeah, she was sure of it. The monster came up through the manhole cover right at the corner of Fifth and Mission and slurped down a derelict or two just before the hero smashed him with a crated piano. Polowski hadn't stayed to hear the rest; he'd made a run for his car.

By that time, it was too late. Holland and the woman were gone, and Zuckerman had vanished. Polowski found himself cruising down Mission, his doors locked, his windows rolled up, wondering when the local police were going to clean up the damn streets.

That's when he remembered the bus depot was only a few blocks away.

Now, standing among the tired and slack-jawed travelers at the bus station, he was beginning to think he'd wasted his time. All those wanted posters staring him in the face. And there was a cop standing over by the coffee machine, taking furtive sips from a foam cup.

Polowski strolled over to the cop. "FBI," he said, flashing his badge.

The cop—he was scarcely more than a boy—instantly straightened. "Patrolman O'Hanley, sir."

"Seeing much action?"

"Uh—you mean today?"

"Yeah. Here."

"No, sir." O'Hanley sighed. "Pretty much a bust. I mean, I could be out on patrol. Instead they got me hanging around here eyeballing faces."

"Surveillance?"

"Yes, sir." He nodded at the poster of Holland. "That guy. Everyone's hot to find him. They say he's a spy."

"Do they, now?" Polowski took a lazy glance around the room. "Seen anyone around here who looks like him?"

"Not a one. I been watching every minute."

Polowski didn't doubt it. O'Hanley was the kind of kid who, if you asked him to, would scrub the Captain's boots with a toothbrush. He'd do a good job of it, too.

Obviously Holland hadn't come through here. Polowski turned to leave. Then another thought came to mind, and he turned back to O'Hanley. "The suspect may be traveling with a woman," he said. He pulled out a photo of Cathy Weaver, one Jack Zuckerman had been persuaded to donate to the FBI. "Have you seen her come through here?"

O'Hanley frowned. "Gee. She sure does look like . . . Naw. That can't be her."

"Who?"

"Well, there was this woman in here 'bout an hour ago. Kind of a down and outer. Some little brat ran smack into her. I sort've brushed her off and sent her on her way. She looked a lot like this gal, only in a lot worse shape."

"Was she traveling alone?"

"She had an old guy with her. Her pop, I think."

Suddenly Polowski was all ears. That instinct again—it was telling him something. "What did this old man look like?"

"Real old. Maybe seventy. Had this bushy beard, lot of white hair."

"How tall?"

"Pretty tall. Over six feet . . ." O'Hanley's voice trailed off as his gaze focused on the wanted poster. Victor Holland was six foot three. O'Hanley's face went white. "Oh, God . . ."

"Was it him?"

"I—I can't be sure—"

"Come on, come on!"

"I just don't know . . . Wait. The woman, she dropped a makeup case! I turned it in at that window there—"

It took only a flash of an FBI badge for the clerk in Lost and Found to hand over the case. The instant Polowski opened the thing, he knew he'd hit pay dirt. It was filled with theatrical makeup supplies. Stenciled inside the lid was: Property of Jack Zuckerman Productions.

He slammed the lid shut. "Where did they go?" he snapped at O'Hanley.

"They—uh, they boarded a bus right over there. That gate. Around seven o'clock."

Polowski glanced up at the departure schedule. At seven o'clock, the number fourteen had departed for Palo Alto.

It took him ten minutes to get hold of the Palo Alto depot manager, another five minutes to convince the man this wasn't just another Prince-Albert-in-the-can phone call.

"The number fourteen from San Francisco?" came the answer. "Arrived twenty minutes ago."

"What about the passengers?" pressed Polowski. "You see any of 'em still around?"

The manager only laughed. "Hey, man. If you had a choice, would *you* hang around a stinking bus station?"

Muttering an oath, Polowski hung up.

"Sir?" It was O'Hanley. He looked sick. "I messed up, didn't I? I let him walk right past me. I can't believe—"

"Forget it."

"But—"

Polowski headed for the exit. "You're just a rookie," he called over his shoulder. "Chalk it up to experience."

"Should I call this in?"

"I'll take care of it. I'm headed there, anyway."

"Where?"

Polowski shoved open the station door. "Palo Alto."

8

The front door was answered by an elderly oriental woman whose command of English was limited.

"Mrs. Lum? Remember me? Victor Holland. I used to know your son."

"Yes, yes!"

"Is he here?"

"Yes." Her gaze shifted to Cathy now, as though the woman didn't want her second visitor to feel left out of the conversation.

"I need to see him," said Victor. "Is Milo here?"

"Milo?" At last here was a word she seemed to know. She turned and called out loudly in Chinese.

Somewhere a door squealed open and footsteps stamped up the stairs. A fortyish oriental man in blue jeans and chambray shirt came to the front door. He was a dumpling of a fellow, and he brought with him the vague odor of chemicals, something sharp and acidic. He was wiping his hands on a rag.

"What can I do for you?" he asked.

Victor grinned. "Milo Lum! Are you still skulking around in your mother's basement?"

"Excuse me?" Milo inquired politely. "Am I supposed to know you, sir?"

"Don't recognize an old horn player from the Out of Tuners?"

Milo stared in disbelief. "Gershwin? That can't be *you?*"

"Yeah, I know," Victor said with a laugh. "The years haven't been kind."

"I didn't want to say anything, but . . ."

"I won't take it personally. Since—" Victor peeled off his false beard "—the face isn't all mine."

Milo gazed down at the lump of fake whispers, hanging like a dead animal in Victor's grasp. Then he stared up at Victor's jaw, still blotchy with spirit gum. "This is some kind of joke on old Milo, right?" He stuck his head out the door, glancing past Victor at the sidewalk. "And the other guys are hiding out there somewhere, waiting to yell *surprise!* Aren't they? Some big practical joke."

"I wish it were a joke," said Victor.

Milo instantly caught the undertone of urgency in Victor's voice. He looked at Cathy, then back at Victor. Nodding, he stepped aside. "Come in, Gersh. Sounds like I have some catching up to do."

Over a late supper of duck noodle soup and jasmine tea, Milo heard the story. He said little; he seemed more intent on slurping down the last of his noodles. Only when the ever-smiling Mrs. Lum had bowed good-night and creaked off to bed did Milo offer his comment.

"When you get in trouble, man, you sure as hell do it right."

"Astute as always, Milo," sighed Victor.

"Too bad we can't say the same for the cops," Milo snorted. "If they'd just bothered to ask around, they would've learned you're harmless. Far as I know, you're guilty of only one serious crime."

Cathy looked up, startled. "What crime?"

"Assaulting the ears of victims unlucky enough to hear his saxophone."

"This from a piccolo player who practices with earplugs," observed Victor.

"That's to drown out extraneous noise."

"Yeah. Mainly your own."

Cathy grinned. "I'm beginning to understand why you called yourselves the Out of Tuners."

"Just some healthy self-deprecating humor," said Milo. "Something we needed after we failed to make the Stanford band." Milo rose, shoving away from the kitchen table. "Well, come on. Let's see what's on that mysterious roll of film."

He led them along the hall and down a rickety set of steps to the basement. The chemical tang of the air, the row of trays lined up on a stainless-steel countertop and the slow drip, drip of water from the faucet told Cathy she was standing in an enormous darkroom. Tacked on the walls was a jumble of photos. Faces, mostly, apparently snapped around the world. Here and there she spotted a newsworthy shot: soldiers storming an airport, protestors unfurling a banner.

"Is this your job, Milo?" she asked.

"I wish," said Milo, agitating the developing canister. "No, I just work in the ol' family business."

"Which is?"

"Shoes. Italian, Brazilian, leather, alligator, you name it, we import it." He cocked his head at the photos. "That's how I get my exotic faces. Shoe-buying trips. I'm an expert on the female arch."

"For that," said Victor, "he spent four years at Stanford."

"Why not? Good a place as any to study the fine feet of the fair sex." A timer rang. Milo poured out the developer, removed the roll of film, and hung it up to dry. "Actually," he said, squinting at the negatives, "it was my dad's dying request. He wanted a son with a Stanford degree. I wanted four years of nonstop partying. We both got our wishes." He paused and gazed off wistfully at his photos. "Too bad I can't say the same of the years since then."

"What do you mean?" asked Cathy.

"I mean the partying's long since over. Gotta earn those profits, keep up those sales. Never thought life'd come down to the bottom line. Whatever happened to all that rabble-rousing potential, hey, Gersh? We sort of lost it along the way. All of us, Bach and Ollie and Roger. The Out of Tuners finally stepped into line. Now we're all marching to the beat of the same boring drummer." He sighed and glanced at Victor. "You make out anything on those negatives?"

Victor shook his head. "We need prints."

Milo flipped off the lights, leaving only the red glow of the darkroom lamp. "Coming up."

As Milo laid out the photographic paper, Victor asked, "What happened to the other guys? They still around?"

Milo flipped the exposure switch. "Roger's VP at some multinational bank in Tokyo. Into silk suits and ties, the whole nine yards. Bach's got an electronics firm in San José."

"And Ollie?"

"What can I say about Ollie?" Milo slipped the first print into the bath. "He's still lurking around in that lab over at Stanford Med. I doubt he ever sees the light of day. I figure he's got some secret chamber in the basement where he keeps his assistant Igor chained to the wall."

"This guy I have to meet," said Cathy.

"Oh, he'd love you." Victor laughed and gave her arm a squeeze. "Seeing as he's probably forgotten what the female of the species looks like."

Milo slid the print into the next tray. "Yeah, Ollie's the one who never changed. Still the night owl. Still plays a mean clarinet." He glanced at Victor. "How's the sax, Gersh? You keeping it up?"

"Haven't played in months."

"Lucky neighbors."

"How did you ever get that name?" asked Cathy. "Gersh?"

"Because," said Milo, wielding tongs as he transferred another batch of prints between trays, "he's a firm believer in the power of George Gershwin to win a lady's heart. 'Someone to Watch Over Me,' wasn't that the tune that made Lily say . . ." Milo's voice suddenly faded. He looked at his friend with regret.

"You're right," said Victor quietly. "That was the tune. And Lily said yes."

Milo shook his head. "Sorry. Guess I still have a hard time remembering she's gone."

"Well, she is," said Victor, his voice matter-of-fact. Cathy knew there was pain buried in the undertones. But he hid it well. "And right now," Victor said, "we've got other things to think about."

"Yeah." Milo, chastened, turned his attention back to the prints he'd just developed. He fished them out and clipped the first few sheets on the line to dry. "Okay, Gersh. Tell us what's on this roll that's worth killing for."

Milo switched on the lights.

Victor stood in silence for a moment, frowning at the first five dripping prints. To Cathy, the data was meaningless, only a set of numbers and codes, recorded in an almost illegible hand.

"Well," grunted Milo. "That sure tells me a lot."

Victor's gaze shifted quickly from one page to the next. He paused at the fifth photo, where a column ran down the length of the page. It contained a series of twenty-seven entries, each one a date followed by the same three letters: EXP.

"Victor?" asked Cathy. "What does it mean?"

He turned to them. It was the look in his eyes that worried her. The stillness. Quietly he said, "We need to call Ollie."

"You mean tonight?" asked Milo. "Why?"

"This isn't just some experiment in test tubes and petri dishes. They've gone beyond that, to clinical trials." Victor pointed to the last page. "These are monkeys. Each one was infected with a new virus. A manmade virus. And in every case the results were the same."

"You mean this?" Milo pointed to the last column. "EXP?"

"It stands for expired," said Victor. "They all died."

* * *

Sam Polowski sat on a bench in the Palo Alto bus terminal and wondered: If I wanted to disappear, where would I go next? He watched a dozen or so passengers straggle off to board the 210 from San José, noting they were by and large the Birkenstock and backpack set. Probably Stanford students heading off for Christmas break. He wondered why it was that students who could afford such a pricey university couldn't seem to scrape up enough to buy a decent pair of jeans. Or even a decent haircut, for that matter.

At last Polowski rose and automatically dusted off his coat, a habit he'd picked up from his early years of hanging around the seamier side of town. Even if the grime wasn't actually visible, he'd always *felt* it was there, coating any surface he happened to brush against, ready to cling to him like wet paint.

He made one phone call—to Dafoe's answering machine, to tell him Victor Holland had moved on to Palo Alto. It was, after all, his responsibility to keep his supervisor informed. He was glad he only had to talk to a recording and not to the man himself.

He left the bus station and strolled down the street, heading Lord knew where, in search of a spark, a hunch. It was a nice-enough neighborhood, a nice-enough town. Palo Alto had its old professors' houses, its bookshops and coffee houses where university types, the ones with the beards and wire-rim glasses, liked to sit and argue the meaning of Proust and Brecht and Goethe. Polowski remembered his own university days, when, after being subjected to an hour of such crap from the students at the next table, he had finally stormed over to them and yelled, "Maybe Brecht meant it that way, maybe not. But can you guys answer this? *What the hell difference does it make?*"

This did not, needless to say, enhance his reputation as a serious scholar.

Now, as he paced along the street, no doubt in the footsteps of more serious philosophers, Polowski turned over in his head the question of Victor Holland. More specifically the question of where such a man, in his desperation, would hide. He stalked past the lit windows, the glow of TVs, the cars spilling from garages. Where in this warren of suburbia was the man hiding?

Holland was a scientist, a musician, a man of few but lasting friendships. He had a Ph.D. from MIT, a B.S. from Stanford. The university was right up the road. The man must know his way around here. Maybe he still had friends in the neighborhood, people who'd take him in, keep his secrets.

Polowski decided to take another look at Holland's file. Somewhere in the Viratek records, there had to be some employment reference, some recommendation from a Stanford contact. A friend Holland might turn to.

Sooner or later, he would have to turn to *someone.*

It was after midnight when Dafoe and his wife returned home. He was in an excellent mood, his head pleasantly abuzz with champagne, his ears still ringing with the heartwrenching aria from *Samson and Delilah.* Opera was a passion for him, a brilliant staging of courage and conflict and *amore,* a vision of life so much grander than the petty little world in which he found himself. It launched him to a plane of such thrilling intensity that even his own wife took on exciting new aspects. He watched her peel off her coat and kick off her shoes. Forty pounds overweight, hair streaked with silver, yet she had her attractions. *It's been three weeks. Surely she'll let me tonight.* . . .

But his wife ignored his amorous looks and wandered off to the kitchen. A moment later, the rumble of the automatic dishwasher announced another of her fits of housecleaning.

In frustration, Dafoe turned and stabbed the blinking button on his answering machine. The message from Polowski completely destroyed any amorous intentions he had left.

". . . Reason to believe Holland is in, or has just left, the Palo Alto area. Following leads. Will keep you informed. . . ."

Polowski, you half-wit. Is following orders so damn difficult?

It was 3:00 a.m. Washington time. An ungodly hour, but he made the phone call.

The voice that answered was raspy with sleep. "Tyrone here."

"Cowboy, this is Dafoe. Sorry to wake you."

The voice became instantly alert, all sleep shaken from it. "What's up?"

"New lead on Holland. I don't know the particulars, but he's headed south, to Palo Alto. May still be there."

"The university?"

"It is the Stanford area."

"That may be a very big help."

"Anything for an old buddy. I'll keep you posted."

"One thing, Dafoe."

"Yeah?"

"I can't have any interference. Pull all your people out. We'll take it from here."

Dafoe paused. "I might . . . have a problem."

"A problem?" The voice, though quiet, took on a razor's edge.

"It's, uh, one of my men. Sort of a wild card. Sam Polowski. He's got this Holland case under his skin, wants to go after him."

"There's such a thing as a direct order."

"At the moment, Polowski's unreachable. He's in Palo Alto, digging around in God knows what."

"Loose cannons. I don't like them."

"I'll pull him back as soon as I can."

"Do that. And keep it quiet. It's a matter of utmost security."

After Dafoe hung up, his gaze shifted automatically to the photo on the mantelpiece. It was a '68 snapshot of him and the Cowboy: two young marines, both of them grinning, their rifles slung over their shoulders as they stood ankle-deep in a rice paddy. It was a crazy time, when one's very life depended on the loyalty of buddies. When Semper Fi applied not only to the corps in general but to each other in particular. Matt Tyrone was a hero then, and he was a hero now. Dafoe stared at that smiling face in the photo, disturbed by the threads of envy that had woven into his admiration for the man. Though Dafoe had much to be proud of—a solid eighteen years in the FBI, maybe even a shot at assistant director somewhere in his stars, he couldn't match the heady climb of Matt Tyrone in the NSA. Though Dafoe wasn't clear as to exactly what position the Cowboy held in the NSA, he had heard that Tyrone regularly attended cabinet meetings, that he held the trust of the president, that he dealt in secrets and shadows and security. He was the sort of man the country needed, a man for whom patriotism was more than mere flag-waving and rhetoric; it was a way of life. Matt Tyrone would do more than die for his country; he'd live for it.

Dafoe couldn't let such a man, such a friend, down.

He dialed Sam Polowski's home phone and left a message on the recorder.

This is a direct order. You are to withdraw from the Holland case immediately. Until further notice you are on suspension.

He was tempted to add, *by special request from my friends in Washington,* but thought better of it. No room for vanity here. The Cowboy had said national security was at stake.

Dafoe had no doubt it truly was. He'd gotten the word from Matt Tyrone. And Matt Tyrone's authority came direct from the President himself.

"This does not look good. This does not look good at all."

Ollie Wozniak squinted through his wire-rim glasses at the twenty-four photographs strewn across Milo's dining table. He held one up for a closer look. Through the bottle-glass lens, one pale blue eye stared out, enormous. One only saw Ollie's eyes; everything else, hollow cheeks, pencil lips and baby-fine hair, seemed to recede into the background pallor. He shook his head and picked up another photo.

"You're right, of course," he said. "Some of these I can't interpret. I'd like to study 'em later. But these here are definitely raw mortality data. Rhesus monkeys, I suspect." He paused and added quietly, "I hope."

"Surely they wouldn't use people for this sort of thing," said Cathy.

"Not officially." Ollie put down the photo and looked at her. "But it's been done."

"Maybe in Nazi Germany."

"Here, too," said Victor.

"What?" Cathy looked at him in disbelief.

"Army studies in germ warfare. They released colonies of Serratia Marcescens over San Francisco and waited to see how far the organism spread. Infections popped up in a number of Bay Area hospitals. Some of the cases were fatal."

"I can't believe it," murmured Cathy.

"The damage was unintentional, of course. But people died just the same."

"Don't forget Tuskegee," said Ollie. "People died in those experiments, too. And then there was that case in New York. Mentally retarded kids in a state hospital who were deliberately exposed to hepatitis. No one died there, but the ethics were just as shaky. So it's been done. Sometimes in the name of humanity."

"Sometimes not," said Victor.

Ollie nodded. "As in this particular case."

"What exactly are we talking about here?" asked Cathy, nodding at the photos. "Is this medical research? Or weapons development?"

"Both." Ollie pointed to one of the photos on the table. "By all appearances, Viratek's engaged in biological weapons research. They've dubbed it Project Cerberus. From what I can tell, the organism they're working on is an RNA virus, extremely virulent, highly contagious, producing over eighty-percent mortality in its lab animal hosts. This photo here—" he tapped one of the pages "—shows the organism produces vesicular skin lesions on the infected subjects."

"Vesicular?"

"Blisterlike. That could be one route of transmission, the fluid in those lesions." He sifted through the pile and pulled out another page. "This shows the time course of the illness. The viral counts, periods of infectiousness. In almost every case the course is the same. The subject's exposed here." He pointed to Day One on the time graph. "Minor signs of illness here at Day Seven. Full-blown pox on Day Twelve. And here—" he tapped the graph at Day Fourteen "—the deaths begin. The time varies, but the result's the same. They all die."

"You used the word *pox,*" said Cathy.

Ollie turned to her, his eyes like blue glass. "Because that's what it is."

"You mean like chickenpox?"

"I wish it was. Then it wouldn't be so deadly. Almost everyone gets exposed to chickenpox as a kid, so most of us are immune. But this one's a different story."

"Is it a new virus?" asked Milo.

"Yes and no." He reached for an electron micrograph. "When I saw this I thought there was something weirdly familiar about all this. The appearance of the organism, the skin lesions, the course of illness. The whole damn picture. It reminded me of something I haven't read about in decades. Something I never dreamed I'd see again."

"You're saying it's an old virus?" said Milo.

"Ancient. But they've made some modifications. Made it more infectious. And deadlier. Which turns this into a real humdinger of a weapon, considering the millions of folks it's already killed."

"*Millions?*" Cathy stared at him. "What are we talking about?"

"A killer we've known for centuries. Smallpox."

"That's impossible!" said Cathy. "From what I've read, we conquered smallpox. It's supposed to be extinct."

"It was," said Victor. "For all practical purposes. Worldwide vaccination wiped it out. Smallpox hasn't been reported in decades. I'm not even sure they still make the vaccine. Ollie?"

"Not available. No need for it since the virus has vanished."

"So where did *this* virus come from?" asked Cathy.

Ollie shrugged. "Probably someone's closet."

"Come on."

"I'm serious. After smallpox was eradicated, a few samples of virus were kept alive in government labs, just in case someone needed it for future research. It's the scientific skeleton in the closet, so to speak. I'd assume those labs are top security. Because if any of the virus got out, there could be a major epidemic." He looked at the stack of photos. "Looks like security's already been breached. Someone obviously got hold of the virus."

"Or had it handed to them," said Victor. "Courtesy of the U.S. government."

"I find that incredible, Gersh," said Ollie. "This is a powderkeg experiment you're talking about. No committee would approve this sort of project."

"Right. That's why I think this is a maverick operation. It's easy to come up with a scenario. Bunch of hardliners cooking this up over at NSA. Or joint chiefs of staff. Or even the Oval Office. Someone says: 'World politics have changed. We can't get away with nuking the enemy. We need a new weapons option, one that'll work well against a Third World army. Let's find one.' And some guy in that room, some red, white and blue robot, will take that as the go-ahead. International law be damned."

"And since it's unofficial," said Cathy, "it'd be completely deniable."

"Right. The administration could claim it knew nothing."

"Sounds like Iran-Contra all over again."

"With one big difference," said Ollie. "When Iran-Contra fell apart, all you had were a few ruined political careers. If Project Cerberus goes awry, what you'll have is a few million dead people."

"But Ollie," said Milo. "I got vaccinated for smallpox when I was a kid. Doesn't that mean I'm safe?"

"Probably. Assuming the virus hasn't been altered too much. In fact, everyone over 35 is probably okay. But remember, there's a whole generation after us that never got the vaccine. Young adults and kids. By the time you could manufacture enough vaccine for them all, we'd have a raging epidemic."

"I'm beginning to see the logic of this weapon," said Victor. "In any war, who makes up the bulk of combat soldiers? Young adults."

Ollie nodded. "They'd be hit bad. As would the kids."

"A whole generation," Cathy murmured. "And only the old would be spared." She glanced at Victor and saw, mirrored in his eyes, the horror she felt.

"They chose an appropriate name," said Milo.

Ollie frowned. "What?"

"Cerberus. The three-headed dog of Hades." Milo looked up, visibly shaken. "Guardian of the dead."

It wasn't until Cathy was fast asleep and Milo had retired upstairs that Victor finally broached the subject to Ollie. It had troubled him all evening, had shadowed his every moment since they'd arrived at Milo's house. He couldn't look at Cathy, couldn't listen to the sound of her voice or inhale the scent of her hair without thinking of the terrible possibilities. And in the deepest hours of night, when it seemed all the world was asleep except for him and Ollie, he made the decision.

"I need to ask you a favor," he said.

Ollie gazed at him across the dining table, steam wafting up from his fourth cup of coffee. "What sort of favor?"

"It has to do with Cathy."

Ollie's gaze shifted to the woman lying asleep on the living room floor. She looked very small, very defenseless, curled up beneath the comforter. Ollie said, "She's a nice woman, Gersh."

"I know."

"There hasn't really been anyone since Lily. Has there?"

Victor shook his head. "I guess I haven't felt ready for it. There were always other things to think about. . . ."

Ollie smiled. "There are always excuses. I should know. People keep telling me there's a glut of unattached female baby boomers. I haven't noticed."

"And I never bothered to notice." Victor looked at Cathy. "Until now."

"What're you gonna do with her, Gersh?"

"That's what I need you for. I'm not the safest guy to hang around with these days. A woman could get hurt."

Ollie laughed. "Hell, a *guy* could get hurt."

"I feel responsible for her. And if something happened to her, I'm not sure I could ever . . ." He let out a long sigh and rubbed his bloodshot eyes. "Anyway, I think it's best if she leaves."

"For where?"

"She has an ex-husband. He'll be working down in Mexico for a few months. I think she'd be pretty safe."

"You're sending her to her ex-husband?"

"I've met him. He's a jerk, but at least she won't be alone down there."

"Does Cathy agree to this?"

"I didn't ask her."

"Maybe you should."

"I'm not giving her a choice."

"What if she wants the choice?"

"I'm not in the mood to take any crap, Okay? I'm doing this for her own good."

Ollie took off his glasses and cleaned them on the tablecloth. "Excuse me for saying this, Gersh, but if it was me, I'd want her nearby, where I could sort of keep an eye on her."

"You mean where I can watch her get killed?" Victor shook his head. "Lily was enough. I won't go through it with Cathy."

Ollie thought it over for a moment, then he nodded. "What do you want me to do?"

"Tomorrow I want you to take her to the airport. Buy her a ticket to Mexico. Let her use your name. Mrs. Wozniak. Make sure she gets safely off the ground. I'll pay you back when I can."

"What if she won't get on the plane? Do I just shove her aboard?"

"Do whatever it takes, Ollie. I'm counting on you."

Ollie sighed. "I guess I can do it. I'll call in sick tomorrow. That'll free up my day." He looked at Victor. "I just hope you know what you're doing."

So do I, thought Victor.

Ollie rose to his feet and tucked the envelope with the photos under his arm. "I'll get back to you in the morning. After I show these last two photos to Bach. Maybe he can identify what those grids are."

"If it's anything electronic, Bach'll figure it out."

Together they walked to the door. There they paused and regarded each other, two old friends who'd grown a little grayer and, Victor hoped, a little wiser.

"Somehow it'll all work out," said Ollie. "Remember. The system's there to be beaten."

"Sounds like the old Stanford radical again."

"It's been a long time." Grinning, Ollie gave Victor a clap on the back. "But we're still not too old to raise a little hell, hey, Gersh? See you in the morning."

Victor waved as Ollie walked away into the darkness. Then he closed the door and turned off all the lights.

In the living room he sat beside Cathy and watched her sleep. The glow of a streetlight spilled in through the window onto her tumbled hair. *Ordinary,* she had called herself. Perhaps, if she'd been a stranger he'd merely passed on the street, he might have thought so, too. A chance meeting on a rainy highway in Garberville had made it impossible for him to ever consider this woman ordinary. In her gentleness, her kindness, she was very much like Lily.

In other ways, she was very different.

Though he'd cared about his wife, though they'd never stopped being good friends, he'd found Lily strangely passionless, a pristine, spiritual being trapped by human flesh. Lily had never been comfortable with her own body. She'd undress in the dark, make love—the rare times they did—in the dark. And then, the illness had robbed her of what little desire she had left.

Gazing at Cathy, he couldn't help wondering what passions might lie harbored in her still form.

He cut short the speculation. What did it matter now? Tomorrow, he'd send her away. *Get rid of her,* he thought brutally. It was necessary. He couldn't think straight while she was around. He couldn't stay focused on the business at hand: exposing Viratek. Jerry Martinique had counted on him. Thousands of potential victims counted on him. He was a scientist, a man who prided himself on logic. His attraction to this particular woman was, in the grand scheme of things, clearly unimportant.

That was what the scientist in him said.

That problem finally settled, he decided to get some rest while he could. He kicked off his shoes and stretched out beside her to sleep. The comforter was large enough—they could share it. He climbed beneath it and lay for a moment, not touching her, almost afraid to share her warmth.

She whimpered in her sleep and turned toward him, her silky hair tumbling against his face.

This was more than he could resist. Sighing, he wrapped his arms around her and felt her curl up against his chest. It was their last night together. They might as well spend it keeping each other warm.

That was how he fell asleep, with Cathy in his arms.

Only once during the night did he awaken. He had been dreaming of Lily. They were walking together, in a garden of pure white flowers. She said absolutely nothing. She simply looked at him with profound sadness, as if to say, *Here I am, Victor. I've come back to you. Why doesn't that make you happy?* He couldn't answer her. So he simply took her in his arms and held her.

He'd awakened to find he was holding Cathy, instead.

Joy instantly flooded his heart, warmed the darkest corners of his soul. It took him by surprise, that burst of happiness; it also made him feel guilty. But there it was. And the joy was all too short-lived. He remembered that today she'd be going away.

Cathy, Cathy. What a complication you've become.

He turned on his side, away from her, mentally building a wall between them.

He concentrated on the dream, trying to remember what had happened. He and Lily had been walking. He tried to picture Lily's face, her brown eyes, her curly black hair. It was the face of the woman he'd been married to for ten years, a face he should know well.

But the only face he saw when he closed his eyes was that of Catherine Weaver.

It took Nicholas Savitch only two hours to pack his bags and drive down to Palo Alto. The word from Matt Tyrone was that Holland had slipped south to the Stanford area, perhaps to seek out old friends.

Holland was, after all, a Stanford man. Maybe not the red-and-white rah-rah Cardinals type, but a Stanford man nonetheless. These old school ties could run deep. It was only a guess on Savitch's part; he'd never gone beyond high school. His education consisted of what a hungry and ambitious boy could pick up on Chicago's south side. Mainly a keen, almost uncanny knack for crawling into another man's head, for sensing what a particular man would think and do in a given situation. Call it advanced street psychology. Without spending a day in college, Savitch had earned his degree.

Now he was putting it to use.

The *finder,* they called him. He liked that name. He grinned as he drove, his leather-gloved hands expertly handling the wheel. Nicholas Savitch, diviner of human souls, the hunter who could ferret a man out of deepest hiding.

In most cases it was a simple matter of logic. Even while on the run, most people conformed to old patterns. It was the fear that did it. It made them seek out their old comforts, cling to their usual habits. In a strange town, the familiar was precious, even if it was only the sight of those ubiquitous golden arches.

Like every other fugitive, Victor Holland would seek the familiar.

Savitch turned his car onto Palm Drive and pulled up in front of the Stanford Arch. The campus was silent; it was 2:00 a.m. Savitch sat for a moment, regarding the silent buildings, Holland's alma mater. Here, in his former stomping grounds, Holland would turn to old friends, revisit old haunts. Savitch had already done his homework. He carried, in his briefcase, a list of names he'd culled from the man's file. In the morning he'd start in on those names, knock on neighbors' doors, flash his government ID, ask about new faces in the neighborhood.

The only possible complication was Sam Polowski. By last report, the FBI agent was also in town, also on Holland's trail. Polowski was a dogged operator. It'd be messy business, taking out a Bureau man. But then, Polowski was only a cog, the way the Weaver woman was only a cog, in a much bigger wheel.

Neither of them would be missed.

9

In the cold, clear hours before dawn, Cathy woke up shaking, still trapped in the threads of a nightmare. She had been walking in a world of concrete and shadow, where doorways gaped and silhouettes huddled on street corners. She drifted among them, one among the faceless, taking refuge in obscurity, instinctively avoiding the light. No one pursued her; no attacker lunged from the alleys. The real terror lay in the unending maze of concrete, the hard echoes of the streets, the frantic search for a safe place.

And the certainty that she would never find it.

For a moment she lay in the darkness, curled up beneath a down comforter on Milo's living room floor. She barely remembered having crawled under the covers; it must have been sometime after three when she'd fallen asleep. The last she remembered, Ollie and Victor were still huddled in the dining room, discussing the photographs. Now there was only silence. The dining room, like the rest of the house, lay in shadow.

She turned on her back, and her shoulder thumped against something warm and solid. Victor. He stirred, murmuring something she couldn't understand.

"Are you awake?" she whispered.

He turned toward her and in his drowsiness enfolded her in his arms. She knew it was only instinct that drew him to her, the yearning of one warm body for another. Or perhaps it was the memory of his wife sleeping beside him, in his mind always there, always waiting to be held. For the moment, she let him cling to the dream. *While he's still half asleep, let him believe I'm Lily,* she thought. *What harm can there be? He needs the memory. And I need the comfort.*

She burrowed into his arms, into the safe spot that once had belonged to another. She took it without regard for the consequences, willing to be swept up into the fantasy of being, for this moment, the one woman in the world he loved. How good it felt, how protected and cared for. From the soap-and-sweat smell of his chest to the coarse fabric of his shirt, it was sanctuary. He was breathing warmly into her hair now, whispering words she knew were for another, pressing kisses to the top of her head. Then he trapped her face in his hands and pressed his lips to hers in a kiss so undeniably needy it ignited within her a hunger of her own. Her response was instinctive and filled with all the yearning of a woman too long a stranger to love.

She met his kiss with one just as deep, just as needy.

At once she was lost, whirled away into some grand and glorious vortex. He stroked down her face, her neck. His hands moved to the buttons of her blouse. She arched against him, her breasts suddenly aching to be touched. It had been so long, so long.

She didn't know how the blouse fell open. She knew only that one moment his fingers were skimming the fabric, and the next moment, they were cupping her flesh. It was that unexpected contact of skin on forbidden skin, the magic torment of his fingers caressing her nipple, that made any last resistance fall away. How many chances were left to them? How many nights together? She longed for so many more, an eternity, but this might be all they had. She welcomed it, welcomed him, with all the passion of a woman granted one last taste of love.

With a knowing touch, she slid her hands down his shirt, undoing buttons, stroking her way through the dense hair of his chest, to the top of his trousers. There she paused, feeling his startled intake of breath, knowing that he too was past retreat.

Together they fumbled at buttons and zippers, both of them suddenly feverish to be free. It all fell away in a tumult of cotton and lace. And when the last scrap of clothing was shed, when nothing came between them but the velvet darkness, she reached up and pulled him to her, on her.

It was a joyful filling, as if, in that first deep thrust within her, he also reached some long-empty hollow in her soul.

"Please," she murmured, her voice breaking into a whimper.

He fell instantly still. "Cathy?" he asked, his hands anxiously cupping her face. "What—"

"Please. Don't stop. . . ."

His soft laughter was all the reassurance she needed. "I have no intention of stopping," he whispered. "None whatsoever . . ."

And he didn't stop. Not until he had taken her with him all the way, higher and further than any man ever could, to a place beyond thought or reason. Only when release came, wave flooding upon wave, did she know how very high and far they had climbed.

A sweet exhaustion claimed them.

Outside, in the grayness of dawn, a bird sang. Inside, the silence was broken ónly by the sound of their breathing.

She sighed into the warmth of his shoulder. "Thank you."

He touched her face. "For what?"

"For making me feel . . . wanted again."

"Oh, Cathy."

"It's been such a long time. Jack and I, we—we stopped making love way before the divorce. It was me, actually. I couldn't bear having him . . ." She swallowed. "When you don't love someone anymore, when they don't love you, it's hard to let yourself be . . . touched."

He brushed his fingers down her cheek. "Is it still hard? Being touched?"

"Not by you. Being touched by you is like . . . being touched the very first time."

By the window's pale light she saw him smile. "I hope your very first time wasn't too awful."

Now she smiled. "I don't remember it very well. It was such a frantic, ridiculous thing on the floor of a college dorm room."

He reached out and patted the carpet. "I see you've come a long way."

"Haven't I?" she laughed. "But floors can be terribly romantic places."

"Goodness. A carpet connoisseur. How do dorm room and living room floors compare?"

"I couldn't tell you. It's been such a long time since I was eighteen." She paused, hovering on the edge of baring the truth. "In fact," she admitted, "it's been a long time since I've been with anyone."

Softly he said, "It's been a long time for both of us."

She let that revelation hang for a moment in the semidarkness. "Not—not since Lily?" she finally asked.

"No." A single word, yet it revealed so much. The three years of loyalty to a dead woman. The grief, the loneliness. How she wanted to fill that womanless chasm for him! To be his savior, and he, hers. Could she make him forget? No, not forget; she couldn't expect him ever to forget Lily. But she wanted a space in his heart for herself, a very large space designed for a lifetime. A space to which no other woman, dead or alive, could ever lay claim.

"She must have been a very special woman," she said.

He ran a strand of her hair through his fingers. "She was very wise, very aware. And she was kind. That's something I don't always find in a person."

She's still part of you, isn't she? She's still the one you love.

"It's the same sort of kindness I find in you," he said.

His fingers had slid to her face and were now stroking her cheek. She closed her eyes, savoring his touch, his warmth. "You hardly know me," she whispered.

"But I do. That night, after the accident, I survived purely on the sound of your voice. And the touch of your hand. I'd know them both, anywhere."

She opened her eyes and gazed at him. "Would you really?"

He pressed his lips to her forehead. "Even in my sleep."

"But I'm not Lily. I could never be Lily."

"That's true. You can't be. No one can."

"I can't replace what you lost."

"What makes you think that's what I want? Some sort of replacement? She was my wife. And yes, I loved her." By the way he said it, his answer invited no exploration.

She didn't try.

From somewhere in the house came the jingle of a telephone. After two rings it stopped. Faintly they heard Milo's voice murmuring upstairs.

Cathy sat up and reached automatically for her clothes. She dressed in silence, her back turned to Victor. A new modesty had sprung up between them, the shyness of strangers.

"Cathy," he said. "People do move on."

"I know."

"You've gotten over Jack."

She laughed, a small, tired sound. "No woman ever really gets over Jack Zuckerman. Yes, I'm over the worst of it. But every time a woman falls in love, really falls in love, it takes something out of her. Something that can never be put back."

"It also gives her something."

"That depends on who you fall in love with, doesn't it?"

Footsteps thumped down the stairs, creaked across the dining room. A wide-awake Milo stood in the doorway, his uncombed hair standing out like a brush. "Hey, you two!" he hissed. "Get up! Hurry."

Cathy rose to her feet in alarm. "What is it?"

"That was Ollie on the phone. He called to say some guy's in the area, asking questions about you. He's already been down to Bach's neighborhood."

"What?" Now Victor was on his feet and hurriedly stuffing his legs into his trousers.

"Ollie figures the guy'll be knocking around here next. Guess they know who your friends are."

"Who was asking the questions?"

"Claimed he was FBI."

"Polowski," muttered Victor, pulling his shirt on. "Has to be."

"You know him?"

"The same guy who set me up. The guy who's been tailing us ever since."

"How did he know we're here?" said Cathy. "No one could've followed us—"

"No one had to. They have my profile. They know I have friends here." Victor glanced at Milo. "Sorry, buddy. Hope this doesn't get you into trouble."

Milo's laugh was distinctly tense. "Hey, I didn't do nothin' wrong. Just harbored a felon." The bravado suddenly melted away. He asked, "Exactly what kind of trouble should I expect?"

"Questions," said Victor, quickly buttoning his shirt. "Lots of 'em. Maybe they'll even take a look around. Just keep cool, tell 'em you haven't heard from me. Think you can do it?"

"Sure. But I don't know about Ma—"

"Your Ma's no problem. Just tell her to stick to Chinese." Victor grabbed the envelope of photos and glanced at Cathy. "Ready?"

"Let's get out of here. Please."

"Back door," Milo suggested.

They followed him through the kitchen. A glance told them the way was clear. As he opened the door, Milo added, "I almost forgot. Ollie wants to see you this afternoon. Something about those photos."

"Where?"

"The lake. Behind the boathouse. You know the place."

They stepped out into the chill dampness of morning. Fog-borne silence hung in the air. *Will we ever stop running?* thought Cathy. *Will we never stop listening for footsteps?*

Victor clapped his friend on the shoulder. "Thanks, Milo. I owe you a big one."

"And one of these days I plan to collect!" Milo hissed as they slipped away.

Victor held up his hand in farewell. "See you around."

"Yeah," Milo muttered into the mist. "Let's hope not in jail."

The Chinese man was lying. Though the man betrayed nothing in his voice, no hesitation, no guilty waver, still Savitch knew this Mr. Milo Lum was hiding something. His eyes betrayed him.

He was seated on the living room couch, across from Savitch. Off to the side sat Mrs. Lum in an easy chair, smiling uncomprehendingly. Savitch might be able to use the old biddy; for now, it was the son who held his interest.

"I can't see why you'd be after him," said Milo. "Victor's as clean as they come. At least, he was when I knew him. But that was a long time ago."

"How far back?" asked Savitch politely.

"Oh, years. Yeah. Haven't seen him since. No, sir."

Savitch raised an eyebrow. Milo shifted on the couch, shuffled his feet, glanced pointlessly around the room.

"You and your mother live here alone?" Savitch asked.

"Since my dad died."

"No tenants? No one else lives here?"

"No. Why?"

"There were reports of a man fitting Holland's description in the neighborhood."

"Believe me, if Victor was wanted by the police, he wouldn't hang around here. You think I'd let a murder suspect in the house? With just me and my old Ma?"

Savitch glanced at Mrs. Lum, who merely smiled. The old woman had sharp, all-seeing eyes. A survivor's eyes.

It was time for Savitch to confirm his hunch. "Excuse me," he said, rising to his feet. "I had a long drive from the city. May I use your restroom?"

"Uh, sure. Down that hall."

Savitch headed into the bathroom and closed the door. Within seconds he'd spotted the evidence he was looking for. It was lying on the tiled floor: a long strand of brown hair. Very silky, very fine.

Catherine Weaver's shade.

It was all the proof he needed to proceed. He reached under his jacket for the shoulder holster and pulled out the semiautomatic. Then he gave his crisp white shirt a regretful pat. Messy business, interrogation. He would have to watch the bloodstains.

He stepped out into the hall, casually holding his pistol at his side. He'd go for the old woman first. Hold the barrel to her head, threaten to pull the trigger. There was an uncommonly strong bond between this mother and son. They would protect each other at all costs.

Savitch was halfway down the hall when the doorbell rang. He halted. The front door was opened and a new voice said, "Mr. Milo Lum?"

"And who the hell are you?" came Milo's weary reply.

"The name's Sam Polowski. FBI."

Every muscle in Savitch's body snapped taut. No choice now; he had to take the man out.

He raised his pistol. Soundlessly, he made his way down the hall toward the living room.

"Another one?" came Milo's peevish voice. "Look, one of your guys is already here—"

"What?"

"Yeah, he's back in the—"

Savitch stepped out and was swinging his pistol toward the front doorway when Mrs. Lum shrieked.

Milo froze. Polowski didn't. He rolled sideways just as the bullet thudded into the door frame, splintering wood.

By the time Savitch got off a second shot, Polowski was crawling somewhere behind the couch and the bullet slammed uselessly into the stuffing. That was it for chances—Polowski was armed.

Savitch decided it was time to vanish.

He turned and darted back up the hall, into a far bedroom. It was the mother's room; it smelled of incense and old-lady perfume. The window slid open easily. Savitch kicked out the screen, scrambled over the sill and sank heel-deep into the muddy flower bed. Cursing, he slogged away, trailing clumps of mud across the lawn.

He heard, faintly, "Halt! FBI!" but continued running.

He nursed his rage all the way back to the car.

Milo stared in bewilderment at the trampled pansies. "What the hell was that all about?" he demanded. "Is this some sort of FBI practical joke?"

Sam Polowski didn't answer; he was too busy tracking the footprints across the grass. They led to the sidewalk, then faded into the road's pebbly asphalt.

"Hey!" yelled Milo. "What's going on?"

Polowski turned. "I didn't really see him. What did he look like?"

Milo shrugged. "I dunno. Efrem Zimbalist-type."

"Meaning?"

"Tall, clean-cut, great build. Typical FBI."

There was a silence as Milo regarded Polowski's sagging belly.

"Well," amended Milo, "maybe not *typical* . . ."

"What about his face?"

"Lemme think. Brown hair? Maybe brown eyes?"

"You're not sure."

"You know how it is. All you white guys look alike to me."

An eruption of rapid Chinese made them both turn. Mrs. Lum had followed them out onto the lawn and was jabbering and gesticulating.

"What's she saying?" asked Polowski.

"She says the man was about six foot one, had straight dark brown hair parted on the left, brown eyes, almost black, a high forehead, a narrow nose and thin lips, and a small tattoo on his inside left wrist."

"Uh—is that all?"

"The tattoo read PJX."

Polowski shook his head in amazement. "Is she always this observant?"

"She can't exactly converse in English. So she does a lot of watching."

"Obviously." Polowski took out a pen and began to jot the information in a notebook.

"So who was this guy?" prodded Milo.

"Not FBI."

"How do I know *you're* FBI."

"Do I look like it?"

"No."

"Only proves my point."

"What?"

"If I wanted to pretend I was an agent, wouldn't I at least try to *look* like one? Whereas, if I *am* one, I wouldn't bother to try and look like one."

"Oh."

"Now." Polowski slid the notebook in his pocket. "You're still going to insist you haven't seen, or heard from, Victor Holland?"

Milo straightened. "That's right."

"And you don't know how to get in touch with him?"

"I have no idea."

"That's too bad. Because I could be the one to save his life. I've already saved yours."

Milo said nothing.

"Just why the hell do you think that guy was here? To pay a social visit? No, he was after information." Polowski paused and added, ominously, "And believe me, he would've gotten it."

Milo shook his head. "I'm confused."

"So am I. That's why I need Holland. He has the answers. But I need him alive. That means I need to find him before the other guy does. Tell me where he is."

Polowski and Milo looked at each other long and hard.

"I don't know," said Milo. "I don't know what to do."

Mrs. Lum was chattering again. She pointed to Polowski and nodded.

"Now what's she saying?" asked Polowski.

"She says you have big ears."

"For that, I can look in the mirror."

"What she means is, the size of your ears indicates sagacity."

"Come again?"

"You're a smart dude. She thinks I should listen to you."

Polowski turned and grinned at Mrs. Lum. "Your mother is a great judge of character." He looked back at Milo. "I wouldn't want anything to happen to her. Or you. You both have to get out of town."

Milo nodded. "On that particular point, we both agree." He turned toward the house.

"What about Holland?" called Polowski. "Will you help me find him?"

Milo took his mother by the arm and guided her across the lawn. Without even a backward look he said, "I'm thinking about it."

"It was those two photos. I just couldn't figure them out," said Ollie.

They were standing on the boathouse pier, overlooking the bed of Lake Lagunita. The lake was dry now, as it was every winter, drained to a reedy marsh until spring. They were alone, the three of them, sharing the lake with only an occasional duck. In the spring, this would be an idyllic spot, the water lapping the banks, lovers drifting in rowboats, here and there a poet lolling under the trees. But today, under black clouds, with a cold mist rising from the reeds, it was a place of utter desolation.

"I knew they weren't biological data," said Ollie. "I kept thinking they looked like some sort of electrical grid. So this morning, right after I left Milo's, I took 'em over to Bach's, down in San José. Caught him at breakfast."

"Bach?" asked Cathy.

"Another member of the Out of Tuners. Great bassoon player. Started an electronics firm a few years back and now he's working with the big boys. Anyway, the first thing he says as I walk in the door is, 'Hey, did the FBI get to you yet?' And I said, 'What?' and he says,

'They just called. For some reason they're looking for Gershwin. They'll probably get around to you next.' And that's when I knew I had to get you two out of Milo's house, stat."

"So what did he say about those photos?"

"Oh, yeah." Ollie reached into his briefcase and pulled out the photos. "Okay. This one here, it's a circuit diagram. An electronic alarm system. Very sophisticated, very secure. Designed to be breached by use of a keypad code, punched in at this point here. Probably at an entryway. You seen anything like it at Viratek?"

Victor nodded. "Building C-2. Where Jerry worked. The keypad's in the hall, right by the Special Projects door."

"Ever been inside that door?"

"No. Only those with top clearance can get through. Like Jerry."

"Then we'll have to visualize what comes next. Going by the diagram, there's another security point here, probably another keypad. Right inside the first door, they've stationed a camera system."

"You mean like a bank camera?" asked Cathy.

"Similar. Only I'd guess this one's being monitored twenty-four hours a day."

"They went first class, didn't they?" said Victor. "Two secured doors, plus inspection by a guard. Not to mention the guard at the outside gate."

"Don't forget the laser lattice."

"What?"

"This inner room here." Ollie pointed to the diagram's core. "Laser beams, directed at various angles. They'll detect movement of just about anything bigger than a rat."

"How do the lasers get switched off?"

"Has to be done by the security guard. The controls are on his panel."

"You can tell all this from the diagram?" asked Cathy. "I'm impressed."

"No problem." Ollie grinned. "Bach's firm designs security systems."

Victor shook his head. "This looks impossible. We can't get through all that."

Cathy frowned at him. "Wait a minute. What are you talking about? You aren't considering going into that building, are you?"

"We discussed it last night," said Victor. "It may be the only way—"

"Are you crazy? Viratek's out to kill us and you want to break *in*?"

"It's the proof we need," said Ollie. "You try going to the newspapers or the Justice Department and they'll demand evidence. You can bet Viratek's going to deny everything. Even if someone does launch an investigation, all Viratek has to do is toss the virus and, *proof!* your evidence is gone. No one can prove a thing."

"You have photos—"

"Sure. A few pages of animal data. The virus is never identified. And all that evidence could've been fabricated by, say, some disgruntled ex-employee."

"So what *is* proof? What do you need, another dead body? Victor's, for instance?"

"What we need is the virus—a virus that's supposed to be extinct. Just a single vial and the case against them is nailed shut."

"Just a single vial. Right." Cathy shook her head. "I don't know what I'm worried about. No one can get through those doors. Not without the keypad codes."

"Ah, but those we have!" Ollie flipped to the second photo. "The mysterious numbers. See, they finally make sense. Two sets of seven digits. Not phone numbers at all! Jerry was pointing the way through Viratek's top security."

"What about the lasers?" she pointed out, her agitation growing. They couldn't be serious! Surely they could see the futility of this mission. She didn't care if her fear showed; she had to be their voice of reason. "And then there's the guards," she said. "Two of them. Do you have a way past them? Or did Jerry also leave you the formula for invisibility?"

Ollie glanced uneasily at Victor. "Uh, maybe I should let you two discuss this first. Before we make any other plans."

"I thought I was part of all this," said Cathy. "Part of every decision. I guess I was wrong."

Neither man said a thing. Their silence only fueled Cathy's anger. She thought: *So you left me out of this. You didn't respect my opinion enough to ask me what I think, what I want.*

Without a word she turned and walked away.

Moments later, Victor caught up with her. She was standing on the dirt path, hugging herself against the cold. She heard his approach, sensed his uncertainty, his struggle to find the right words. For a moment he simply stood beside her, not speaking.

"I think we should run," she said. She gazed over the dry lake bed and shivered. The wind that swept across the reeds was raw and biting; it sliced right through her sweater. "I want to get away," she said. "I want to go somewhere warm. Some place where the sun's shining, where I can lie on a beach and not worry about who's watching me from the bushes. . . ." Suddenly reminded of the terrible possibilities, she turned and glanced at the oaks hulking behind them. She saw only the fluttering of dead leaves.

"I agree with you," said Victor quietly.

"You do?" She turned to him, relieved. "Let's go, Victor! Let's leave now. Forget this crazy idea. We can catch the next bus south—"

"This very afternoon. You'll be on your way."

"*I* will?" She stared at him, at first not willing to accept what she'd heard. Then the meaning of his words sank in. "You're not coming."

Slowly he shook his head. "I can't."

"You mean you won't."

"Don't you see?" He took her by the shoulders, as though to shake some sense into her. "We're backed into a corner. Unless we do something—I do something—we'll always be running."

"Then let's *run!*" She reached for him, her fingers clutching at his windbreaker. She wanted to scream at him, to tear away his cool mask of reason and get to the raw emotions beneath. They had to be there, buried deep in that logical brain of his. "We could go to Mexico," she said. "I know a place on the coast—in Baja. A little hotel near the beach. We could stay there a few months, wait until things are safer—"

"It'll never be safer."

"Yes, it will! They'll forget about us—"

"You're not thinking straight."

"I am. I'm thinking I want to stay alive."

"And that's exactly why I have to do this." He took her face in his hands, trapping it so she could look nowhere but at him. No longer was he the lover, the friend—his voice now held the cold, steady note of authority and she hated the sound of it. "I'm trying to keep you alive," he said. "With a future ahead of you. And the only way I can do that is to blow this thing wide open so the world knows about it. I owe it to you. And I owe it to Jerry."

She wanted to argue with him, to plead with him to go with her, but she knew it was useless. What he said was true. Running would only be a temporary solution, one that would give them a few sweet months of safety, but a temporary one just the same.

"I'm sorry, Cathy," he said softly. "I can't think of any other way—"

"—But to get rid of me," she finished for him.

He released her. She stepped back, and the sudden gulf between them left her aching. She couldn't bear to look at him, knowing that the pain she felt wouldn't be reflected in his eyes. "So how does it work?" she said dully. "Do I leave tonight? Will it be plane, train or automobile?"

"Ollie will drive you to the airport. I've asked him to buy you the ticket under his name—Mrs. Wozniak. He'll have to be the one to see you off. We thought it'd be safer if I didn't come along to the airport."

"Of course."

"That'll get you to Mexico. Ollie'll give you enough cash to keep you going for a while. Enough to get you anywhere you want to go from there. Baja. Acapulco. Or just hang around with Jack if you think that's best."

"Jack." She turned away, unwilling to show her tears. "Right."

"Cathy." She felt his hand on her shoulder, as though he wanted to turn her toward him, to pull her back one last time into his arms. She refused to move.

Footsteps approached. They both glanced around to see Ollie, standing a few feet away. "Ready to go?" he asked.

There was a long silence. Then Victor nodded. "She's ready."

"Uh, look," Ollie mumbled, suddenly aware that he'd stepped in at a bad time. "My car's over by the boathouse. If you want, I can, uh, wait for you there. . . ."

Cathy furiously dashed away her tears. "No," she said with sudden determination. "I'm coming."

Victor stood watching her, his gaze veiled by some cool, impenetrable mist.

"Goodbye, Victor," she said.

He didn't answer. He just kept looking at her through that terrible mist.

"If I—if I don't see you again . . ." She stopped, struggling to be just as brave, just as invulnerable. "Take care of yourself," she finished. Then she turned and followed Ollie down the path.

Through the car window, she glimpsed Victor, still standing on the lake path, his hands jammed in his pockets, his shoulders hunched against the wind. He didn't wave goodbye; he merely watched them drive away.

It was an image she'd carry with her forever, that last, fading view of the man she loved. The man who'd sent her away.

As Ollie turned the car onto the road, she sat stiff and silent, her fists balled in her lap, the pain in her throat so terrible she could scarcely breathe. Now he was behind them. She couldn't see him, but she knew he was still standing there, as unmoving as the oaks that surrounded him. *I love you,* she thought. *And I will never see you again.*

She turned to look out. He was a distant figure now, almost lost among the trees. In a gesture of farewell, she reached up and gently touched the window.

The glass was cold.

* * *

"I have to stop off at the lab," said Ollie, turning into the hospital parking lot. "I just remembered I left the checkbook in my desk. Can't get you a plane ticket without it."

Cathy nodded dully. She was still in a state of shock, still trying to accept the fact that she was now on her own. That Victor had sent her away.

Ollie pulled into a stall marked Reserved, Wozniak. "This'll only take a sec."

"Shall I come in with you?"

"You'd better wait in the car. I work with a very nosy bunch. They see me with a woman and they want to know everything. Not that there's ever anything to know." He climbed out and shut the door. "Be right back."

Cathy watched him stride away and vanish into a side entrance. She had to smile at the thought of Ollie Wozniak squiring around a woman—any woman. Unless it was someone with a Ph.D. who could sit through his scientific monologues.

A minute passed.

Outside, a bird screeched. Cathy glanced out at the trees lining the hospital driveway and spotted the jay, perched among the lower branches. Nothing else moved, not even the leaves.

She leaned back and closed her eyes.

Too little sleep, too much running, had taken its toll. Exhaustion settled over her, so profound she thought she would never again be able to move her limbs. *A beach,* she thought. *Warm sand. Waves washing at my feet . . .*

The jay's cry cut off in mid-screech. Only vaguely did Cathy register the sudden silence. Then, even through her half sleep, she sensed the shadowing of the window, like a cloud passing before the sun.

She opened her eyes. A face was staring at her through the glass.

Panic sent her lunging for the lock button. Before she could jam it down, the door was wrenched open. A badge was thrust up to her face.

"FBI!" the man barked. "Out of the car, please."

Slowly Cathy emerged, to stand weak-kneed against the door. *Ollie,* she thought, her gaze darting toward the hospital entrance. *Where are you?* If he appeared, she had to be ready to bolt, to flee across the parking lot and into the woods. She doubted the man with the badge would be able to keep up; his stubby legs and thick waist didn't go along with a star athlete.

But he must have a gun. If I bolt, would he shoot me in the back?

"Don't even think about it, Miss Weaver," the man said. He took her arm and gave her a nudge toward the hospital entrance. "Go on. Inside."

"But—"

"Dr. Wozniak's waiting for us in the lab."

Waiting didn't exactly describe Ollie's predicament. Bound and trussed would have been a better description. She found Ollie bent over double in his office, handcuffed to the foot of his desk, while three of his lab colleagues stood by gaping in amazement.

"Back to work, folks," said the agent as he herded the onlookers out of the office. "Just a routine matter." He shut the door and locked it. Then he turned to Cathy and Ollie. "I have to find Victor Holland," he said. "And I have to find him fast."

"Man," Ollie muttered into his chest. "This guy sounds like a broken record."

"Who are you?" demanded Cathy.

"The name's Sam Polowski. I work out of the San Francisco office." He pulled out his badge and slapped it on the desk. "Take a closer look if you want. It's official."

"Uh, excuse me?" called Ollie. "Could I maybe, possibly, get into a more comfortable position?"

Polowski ignored him. His attention was focused on Cathy. "I don't think I need to spell it out for you, Miss Weaver. Holland's in trouble."

"And you're one of his biggest problems," she retorted.

"That's where you're wrong." Polowski moved closer, his gaze unflinching, his voice absolutely steady. "I'm one of his hopes. Maybe his only hope."

"You're trying to kill him."

"Not me. Someone else, someone who's going to succeed. Unless I can stop it."

She shook her head. "I'm not stupid! I know about you. What you've been trying to—"

"Not me. The other guy." He reached for the telephone on the desk. "Here," he said, holding the receiver out to her. "Call Milo Lum. Ask him what happened at his house this morning. Maybe he'll convince you I'm on your side."

Cathy stared at the man, wondering what sort of game he was playing. Wondering why she was falling for it. *Because I want so much to believe him.*

"He's alone out there," said Polowski. "One man trying to buck the U.S. government. He's new to the game. Sooner or later he's going to slip, do something stupid. And that'll be it." He dialed the phone for her and again held out the receiver. "Go on. Talk to Lum."

She heard the phone ring three times, followed by Milo's answer "Hello? Hello?"

Slowly she took the receiver. "Milo?"

"Is that you? Cathy? God, I was hoping you'd call—"

"Listen, Milo. I need to ask you something. It's about a man named Polowski."

"I've met him."

"You *have?*" She looked up and saw Polowski nodding.

"Lucky for me," said Milo. "The guy's got the charm of an old shoe but he saved my life. I don't know what Gersh was talking about. Is Gersh around? I have to—"

"Thanks, Milo," she murmured. "Thanks a lot." She hung up.

Polowski was still looking at her.

"Okay," she said. "I want your side of it. From the beginning."

"You gonna help me out?"

"I haven't decided." She crossed her arms. "Convince me."

Polowski nodded. "That's just what I plan to do."

10

For Victor it was a long and miserable afternoon. After leaving the lake, he wandered around the campus for a while, ending up at last in the main quad. There in the courtyard, standing among the buildings of sandstone and red tile, Victor struggled to keep his mind on the business at hand: exposing Viratek. But his thoughts kept shifting back to Cathy, to that look she'd given him, full of hurt abandonment.

As if I'd betrayed her.

If she could just see the good sense in his actions. He was a scientist, a man whose life and work was ruled by logic. Sending her away was the logical thing to do. The authorities were closing in, the noose was growing ever tighter. He could accept the danger to himself. After all, he'd chosen to take on Jerry's battle, to see this through to the end.

What he hadn't chosen was to put Cathy in danger. *Now she's out of the mess and on her way to a safe place. One less thing to worry about. Time to put her out of my mind.*

As if I could.

He stared up at one of the courtyard's Romanesque arches and reminded himself, once again, of the wisdom of his actions. Still, the uneasiness remained. Where was she? Was she safe? She'd been gone only an hour and he missed her already.

He gave a shrug, as though by that gesture, he could somehow cast off the fears. Still they remained, constant and gnawing. He found a place under the eaves and huddled on the steps to wait for Ollie's return.

At dusk he was still waiting. By the last feeble light of day, he paced the stone courtyard. He counted and recounted the number of hours it should've taken Ollie to drive to San José Airport and return. He added in traffic time, red lights, ticket-counter delays. Surely three hours was enough. Cathy had to be on a plane by now, jetting for warmer climes.

Where was Ollie?

At the sound of the first footstep, he spun around. For a moment he couldn't believe what he was seeing, couldn't understand how she could be standing there, silhouetted beneath the sandstone archway. "Cathy?" he said in amazement.

She stepped out, into the courtyard. "Victor," she said softly. She started toward him, slowly at first, and then, in a jubilant burst of flight, ran toward his waiting arms. He swept her up, swung her around, kissed her hair, her face. He didn't understand why she was here but he rejoiced that she was.

"I don't know if I've done the right thing," she murmured. "I hope to God I have."

"Why did you come back?"

"I wasn't sure—I'm still not sure—"

"Cathy, what are you doing here?"

"You can't fight this alone! And he can help you—"

"Who can?"

From out of the twilight came another voice, gruff and startling. "*I* can."

At once Victor stiffened. His gaze shifted back to the arch behind Cathy. A man emerged and walked slowly toward him. Not a tall man, he had the sort of body that, in a weight-loss ad, would've been labeled Before. He came up to Victor and planted himself squarely on the courtyard stones.

"Hello, Holland," he said. "I'm glad we've finally met. The name is Sam Polowski."

Victor turned and looked in disbelief at Cathy. "Why?" he asked in quiet fury. "Just tell me that. *Why?*"

She reacted as though he'd delivered a physical blow. Tentatively she reached for his arm; he pulled away from her at once.

"He wants to help," she said, her voice wretched with pain. "*Listen to him!*"

"I'm not sure there's any point to listening. Not now." He felt his whole body go slack in defeat. He didn't understand it, would never understand it. It was over, the running, the scraping along on fear and hope. All because Cathy had betrayed him. He turned matter-of-factly to Polowski. "I take it I'm under arrest," he said.

"Hardly," said Polowski, nodding toward the archway. "Seeing as he's got my gun."

"What?"

"Hey, Gersh! Over here!" Ollie yelled. "See, I got him covered!"

Polowski winced. "Geez, do ya have to wave the damn thing?"

"Sorry," said Ollie.

"Now, does that convince you, Holland?" asked Polowski. "You think I'd hand my piece over to an idiot like him if I didn't want to talk to you?"

"He's telling the truth," insisted Cathy. "He gave the gun to Ollie. He was willing to take the risk, just to meet you face-to-face."

"Bad move, Polowski," said Victor bitterly. "I'm wanted for murder, remember? Industrial espionage? How do you know I won't just blow you away?"

" 'Cause I know you're innocent."

"That makes a difference, does it?"

"It does to me."

"Why?"

"You're caught up in something big, Holland. Something that's going to eat you up alive. Something that's got my supervisor doing backflips to keep me off the case. I don't like being pulled off a case. It hurts my delicate ego."

The two men gazed at each other through the gathering darkness, each sizing up the other.

At last Victor nodded. He looked at Cathy, a quiet plea for forgiveness, for not believing in her. When at last she came into his arms, he felt the world had suddenly gone right again.

He heard a deliberate clearing of a throat. Turning, he saw Polowski hold out his hand. Victor took it in a handshake that could very well be his doom—or his salvation.

"You've led me on a long, hard chase," said Polowski. "I think it's time we worked together."

"Basically," said Ollie, "what we have here is just your simple, everyday mission impossible."

They were assembled in Polowski's hotel room, a five-member team that Milo had just dubbed the "Older, Crazier Out of Tuners," or Old COOTS for short. On the table in the center of the room lay potato chips, beer and the photos detailing Viratek's security system. There was also a map of the Viratek compound, forty acres of buildings and wooded grounds, all of it surrounded by an electrified fence. They had been studying the photos for an hour now, and the job that lay before them looked hopeless.

"No easy way in," said Ollie, shaking his head. "Even if those keypad codes are still valid, you're faced with the human element of recognition. Two guards, two positions. No way they're gonna let you pass."

"There has to be a way," said Polowski. "Come on, Holland. You're the egghead. Use that creative brain of yours."

Cathy looked at Victor. While the others had tossed ideas back and forth, he had said very little. *And he's the one with the most at stake—his life,* she thought. It took incredible courage—or foolhardiness—even to consider such a desperate move. Yet here he was, calmly scanning the map as though he were planning nothing more dangerous than a Sunday drive.

He must have felt her gaze, for he slung his arm around her and tugged her close. Now that they were reunited, she savored every moment they shared, committed to memory every look, every caress. Soon he could be wrenched away from her. Even now he was making plans to enter what looked like a death trap.

He pressed a kiss to the top of her head. Then, reluctantly, he turned his attention back to the map.

"The electronics I'm not worried about," he said. "It's the human element. The guards."

Milo cocked his head toward Polowski. "I still say ol' J. Edgar here should get a warrant and raid the place."

"Right," snorted Polowski. "By the time that order gets through the judge and Dafoe and your Aunt Minnie's cousin, Viratek'll have that lab turned into a baby-milk factory. No, we need to get in on our own. Without anyone getting word of it." He looked at Ollie. "And you're sure this is the only evidence we'll need?"

Ollie nodded. "One vial should do it. Then we take it to a reputable lab, have them confirm it's smallpox, and your case is airtight."

"They'll have no way around it?"

"None. The virus is officially extinct. Any company caught playing with a live sample is, ipso facto, dead meat."

"I like that," said Polowski. "That ipso facto stuff. No fancy Viratek attorney can argue that one away."

"But first you gotta get hold of a vial," said Ollie. "And from where I'm standing, it looks impossible. Unless we're willing to try armed robbery."

For one frightening moment, Polowski actually seemed to give that thought serious consideration. "Naw," he conceded. "Wouldn't go over well in court."

"Besides which," said Ollie, "I refuse to shoot another human being. It's against my principles."

"Mine, too," said Milo.

"But theft," said Ollie, "that's acceptable."

Polowski looked at Victor. "A group with high moral standards."

Victor grinned. "Holdovers from the sixties."

"Sounds like we're back to the first option," said Cathy. "We have to steal the virus." She focused on the map of the compound, noting the electrified fence that circled the entire complex. The main road led straight to the front gate. Except for an unpaved fire road, labeled *not maintained,* no other approaches were apparent.

"All right," she said. "Assume you do get through the front gate. You still have to get past two locked doors, two separate guards and a laser grid. Come on."

"The doors are no problem," said Victor. "It's the two guards."

"Maybe a diversion?" suggested Milo. "How about we set a fire?"

"And bring in the town fire department?" said Victor. "Not a good idea. Besides, I've dealt with this night guard at the front gate. I know him. And he goes strictly by the book. Never leaves the booth. At the first hint of anything suspicious, he'll hit the alarm button."

"Maybe Milo could whip up a fake security pass," said Ollie. "You know, the way he used to fix us up with those fake drivers' licenses."

"He falsified IDs?" said Polowski.

"Hey, I just changed the age to twenty-one!" protested Milo.

"Made great passports, too," said Ollie. "I had one from the kingdom of Booga Booga. It got me right past the customs official in Athens."

"Yeah?" Polowski looked impressed. "So what about it, Holland? Would it work?"

"Not a chance. The guard has a master list of top-security employees. If he doesn't know the face, he'll do a double check."

"But he does let some people through automatically?"

"Sure. The bigwigs. The ones he recognizes on—" Victor suddenly paused and turned to stare at Cathy "—on sight. Lord. It just might work."

Cathy took one look at his face and immediately read his mind. "No," she said. "It's not that easy! I need to see the subject! I need molds of his face. Detailed photos from every angle—"

"But you *could* do it. You do it all the time."

"On film it works! But this is face-to-face!"

"It's at night, through a car window. Or through a video camera. If you could just make me pass for one of the exec's—"

"What are you talking about?" demanded Polowski.

"Cathy's a makeup artist. You know, horror films, special effects."

"This is different!" Cathy said. The difference being it was Victor's life on the line. No, he couldn't ask her to do this. If anything went wrong, she would be responsible. Having his death on her conscience would be more than she could live with.

She shook her head, praying he'd read the deadly earnestness in her gaze. "There's too much at stake," she insisted. "It's not as simple as— as filming *Slimelords!*"

"You did *Slimelords?*" asked Milo. "Terrific flick!"

"Besides," said Cathy, "it's not that easy, copying a face. I have to cast a mold, to get the features just right. For that I need a model."

"You mean the real guy?" asked Polowski.

"Right. The real guy. And I hardly think you're going to get some Viratek executive to sit down and let me slap plaster all over his face."

There was a long silence.

"That does present a problem," said Milo.

"Not necessarily."

They all turned and looked at Ollie.

"What are you thinking?" asked Victor.

"About this guy who works with me once in a while. Down in the lab . . ." Ollie looked up, and the grin on his face was distinctly smug. "He's a veterinarian."

The events of the past few weeks had weighed heavily on Archibald Black, so heavily, in fact, that he found it difficult to carry on with those everyday tasks of life. Just driving to and from his office at Viratek was an ordeal. And then, to sit down at his desk and face his secretary and pretend that nothing, absolutely nothing, was wrong— that was almost more than he could manage. He was a scientist, not an actor.

Not a criminal.

But that's what they would call him, if the experiments in C wing ever came to light. His instinct was to shut the lab down, to destroy the contents of those incubators. But Matthew Tyrone insisted the work continue. They were so close to completion. After all, Defense had underwritten the project, and Defense expected a product. This matter of Victor Holland was only a minor glitch, soon to be solved. The thing to do was carry on.

Easy for Tyrone to say, thought Black. *Tyrone had no conscience to bother him.*

These thoughts had plagued him all day. Now, as Black packed up his briefcase, he felt desperate to flee forever this teak-and-leather office, to take refuge in some safe and anonymous job. It was with a sigh of relief that he walked out the door.

It was dark when he pulled into his gravel driveway. The house, a saltbox of cedar and glass tucked among the trees, looked cold and empty and in need of a woman. Perhaps he should call his neighbor Muriel. She always seemed to appreciate an impromptu dinner together. Her snappy wit and green Jell-O salad almost made up for the fact she was 75. What a shame his generation didn't produce many Muriels.

He stepped out of his car and started up the path to the front door. Halfway there, he heard a soft *whht!* and almost simultaneously, a sharp pain stung his neck. Reflexively he slapped at it; something came away in his hands. In wonderment, he stared down at the dart, trying to understand where it had come from and how such a thing had managed to lodge in his neck. But he found he couldn't think straight. And then he found he was having trouble seeing, that the night had suddenly darkened to a dense blackness, that his legs were being sucked into some sort of quagmire. His briefcase slipped from his grasp and thudded to the ground.

I'm dying, he thought. And then, *Will anyone find me here?*

It was his last conscious thought before he collapsed onto the leaf-strewn path.

"Is he dead?"

Ollie bent forward and listened for Archibald Black's breathing. "He's definitely alive. But out cold." He looked up at Polowski and Victor. "Okay, let's move it. He'll be out for only an hour or so."

Victor grabbed the legs, Ollie and Polowski, the arms. Together they carried the unconscious man a few dozen yards through the woods, toward the clearing where the van was parked.

"You—you sure we got an hour?" gasped Polowski.

"Plus or minus," said Ollie. "The tranquilizer's designed for large animals, so the dose was only an estimate. And this guy's heavier than I expected." Ollie was panting now. "Hey, Polowski, he's slipping. Pull your weight, will ya?"

"I am! I think his right arm's heavier than his left."

The van's side door was already open for them. They rolled Black inside and slid the door closed. A bright light suddenly glared, but the unconscious man didn't even twitch.

Cathy knelt down at his side and critically examined the man's face.

"Can you do it?" asked Victor.

"Oh, I can do it," she said. "The question is, will you pass for him?" She glanced up and down the man's length, then back at Victor. "Looks about your size and build. We'll have to darken your hair, give you a widow's peak. I think you'll pass." She turned and glanced at Milo, who was already poised with his camera. "Take your photos. A few shots from every angle. I need lots of hair detail."

As Milo's strobe flashed again and again, Cathy donned gloves and an apron. She pointed to a sheet. "Drape him for me," she directed. "Everything but his face. I don't want him to wake up with plaster all over his clothes."

"Assuming he wakes up at all," said Milo, frowning down at Black's inert form.

"Oh, he'll wake up," said Ollie. "Right where we found him. And if we do the job right, Mr. Archibald Black will never know what hit him."

It was the rain that awakened him. The cold droplets pelted his face and dribbled into his open mouth. Groaning, Black turned over and felt gravel bite into his shoulder. Even in his groggy state it occurred to him that this did not make sense. Slowly he took stock of all the things that were not as they should be: the rain falling from the ceiling, the gravel in his bed, the fact he was still wearing his shoes . . .

At last he managed to shake himself fully awake. He found to his puzzlement that he was sitting in his driveway, and that his briefcase was lying right beside him. By now the rain had swelled to a downpour—he had to get out of the storm. Half crawling, half walking, Black managed to make it up the porch steps and into the house.

An hour later, huddled in his kitchen, a cup of coffee in hand, he tried to piece together what had happened. He remembered parking his car. He'd taken out his briefcase and apparently had managed to make it halfway up the path. And then . . . what?

A vague ache worried its way into his awareness. He rubbed his neck. That's when he remembered something strange had happened, just before he blacked out. Something associated with that ache in his neck.

He went to a mirror and looked. There it was, a small puncture in the skin. An absurd thought popped into his head: *Vampires.* Right.

Damn it, Archibald. You are a scientist. Come up with a rational explanation.

He went to the laundry hamper and fished out his damp shirt. To his alarm he spotted a droplet of blood on the lapel. Then he saw what had caused it: a common, everyday tailor's pin. It was still lodged in the collar, no doubt left there by the dry cleaners. There was his rational explanation. He'd been pricked by a collar pin and the pain had sent him into a faint.

In disgust, he threw the shirt down. First thing in the morning, he was going to complain to the Tidy Girl cleaners and demand they do his suit for free.

Vampires, indeed.

"Even with bad lighting, you'll be lucky if you pass," said Cathy.

She stood back and gave Victor a long, critical look. Slowly she walked around him, eyeing the newly darkened hair, the resculpted face, the new eye color. It was as close as she could make it, but it wasn't good enough. It would never be good enough, not when Victor's life was at stake.

"I think he's the spitting image," said Polowski. "What's the problem now?"

"The problem is, I suddenly realize it's a crazy idea. I say we call it off."

"You've been working on him all afternoon. You got it right down to the damn freckles on his nose. What else can you improve on?"

"I don't know. I just don't feel *good* about this!"

There was a silence as she confronted the four men.

Ollie shook his head. "Women's intuition. That's a dangerous thing to disregard."

"Well, here's *my* intuition," said Polowski. "I think it'll work. And I think it's our best option. Our chance to nail the case."

Cathy turned to Victor. "You're the one who'll get hurt. It's your decision." What she really wanted to say was, *Please. Don't do it. Stay with me. Stay alive and safe and mine.* But she knew, looking into his eyes, that he'd already made his decision, and no matter how much she might wish for it, he would never really be hers.

"Cathy," he said. "It'll work. You have to believe that."

"The only thing I believe," she said, "is that you're going to get killed. And I don't want to be around to watch it."

Without another word, she turned and walked out the door.

Outside, in the parking lot of the Rockabye Motel, she stood in the darkness and hugged herself. She heard the door shut, and then his footsteps moved toward her across the blacktop.

"You don't have to stay," he said. "There's still that beach in Mexico. You could fly there tonight, be out of this mess."

"Do you want me to go?"

A pause, then, "Yes."

She shrugged, a poor attempt at nonchalance. "All right. I suppose it all makes perfect sense. I've done my part."

"You saved my life. At the very least, I owe you a measure of safety."

She turned to him. "Is that what weighs most on your mind, Victor? The fact that you *owe* me?"

"What weighs most on my mind is that you might get caught in the crossfire. I'm prepared to walk through those doors at Viratek. I'm prepared to do a lot of stupid things. But I'm not prepared to watch you get hurt. Does that make any sense?" He pulled her against him, into a place that felt infinitely warm and safe. "Cathy, Cathy. I'm not crazy. I don't want to die. But I don't see any way around this. . . ."

She pressed her face against his chest, felt his heartbeat, so steady, so regular. She was afraid to think of that heart not beating, of those arms no longer alive to hold her. He was brave enough to go through with this crazy scheme; couldn't she somehow dredge up the same courage? She thought, *I've come this far with you. How could I dream of walking away? Now that I know I love you?*

The motel door opened, and light arced across the parking lot. "Gersh?" said Ollie. "It's getting late. If we want to go ahead, we'll have to leave now."

Victor was still looking at her. "Well?" he said. "Do you want Ollie to take you to the airport?"

"No." She squared her shoulders. "I'm coming with you."

"Are you sure that's what you want to do?"

"I'm never sure of anything these days. But on this I've decided. I'll stick it out." She managed a smile. "Besides, you might need me on the set. In case your face falls off."

"I need you for a hell of a lot more than that."

"Gersh?"

Victor reached out for Cathy's hand. She let him take it. "We're coming," he said. "Both of us."

"I'm approaching the front gate. One guard in the booth. No one else around. Copy?"

"Loud and clear," said Polowski.

"Okay. Here I go. Wish me luck."

"We'll be tuned in. Break a leg." Polowski clicked off the microphone and glanced at the others. "Well, folks, he's on his way."

To what? Cathy wondered. She glanced around at the other faces. There were four of them huddled in the van. They'd parked a half mile from Viratek's front gate. Close enough to hear Victor's transmissions, but too far away to do him much good. With the microphone link, they could mark his progress.

They could also mark his death.

In silence, they waited for the first hurdle.

"Evening," said Victor, pulling up at the gate.

The guard peered out through the booth window. He was in his twenties, cap on straight, collar button fastened. This was Pete Zahn, Mr. By-the-book Extraordinaire. If anyone was to cut the operation short, it would be this man. Victor made a brave attempt at a smile and prayed his mask wouldn't crack. It seemed an eternity, that exchange of looks. Then, to Victor's relief, the man smiled back.

"Working late, Dr. Black?"

"Forgot something at the lab."

"Must be important, huh? To make a special trip at midnight."

"These government contracts. Gotta be done on time."

"Yeah." The guard waved him through. "Have a nice night."

Heart pounding, Victor pulled through the gate. Only when he'd rounded the curve into the empty parking lot did he manage a sigh of relief. "First base," he said into the microphone. "Come on, guys. Talk to me."

"We're here," came the response. It was Polowski.

"I'm heading into the building—can't be sure the signal will get through those walls. So if you don't hear from me—"

"We'll be listening."

"I've got a message for Cathy. Put her on."

There was a pause, then he heard, "I'm here, Victor."

"I just wanted to tell you this. I'm coming back. I promise. Copy?"

He wasn't sure if it was just the signal's waiver, but he thought he heard the beginning of tears in her reply. "I copy."

"I'm going in now. Don't leave without me."

It took Pete Zahn only a minute to look up Archibald Black's license plate number. He kept a Rolodex in the booth, though he seldom referred to it as he had a good memory for numbers. He knew every executive's license by heart. It was his own little mind game, a test of his cleverness. And the plate on Dr. Black's car just didn't seem right.

He found the file card. The auto matched up okay: a gray 1991 Lincoln sedan. And he was fairly certain that *was* Dr. Black sitting in the driver's seat. But the license number was all wrong.

He sat back and thought about it for a while, trying to come up with all the possible explanations. That Black was simply driving a different auto. That Black was playing a joke on him, testing him.

That it hadn't been Archibald Black, at all.

Pete reached for the telephone. The way to find out was to call Black's home. It was after midnight, but it had to be done. If Black didn't answer the phone, then that must be him in the Lincoln. And if he *did* answer, then something was terribly wrong and Black would want to know about it.

Two rings. That's all it took before a groggy voice answered, "Hello?"

"This is Pete Zahn, night man at Viratek. Is this—is this Dr. Black?"

"Yes."

"Dr. *Archibald* Black?"

"Look, it's late! What is it?"

"I don't know how to tell you this, Dr. Black, but . . ." Pete cleared his throat. "Your double just drove through the gate. . . ."

"I'm through the front door. Heading up the hall to the security wing. In case anyone's listening." Victor didn't expect a reply, and he heard none. The building was a concrete monstrosity, designed to last forever. He doubted a radio signal would make it through these walls. Though he'd been on his own from the moment he'd entered the front gate, at least he'd had the comfort of knowing his friends were listening in on the progress. Now he was truly alone.

He moved at a casual pace to the locked door marked Authorized Personnel Only. A camera hung from the ceiling, its lens pointed straight at him. He pointedly ignored it and turned his attention to the security keypad mounted on the wall. The numbers Jerry had given him had gotten him through the front door; would the second combination get him through this one? His hands were sweating as he punched in the seven digits. He felt a dart of panic as a beep sounded and a message flashed on the screen: *Incorrect security code. Access denied.*

He could feel the sweat building up beneath the mask. Were the numbers wrong? Had he simply transposed two digits? He knew someone was watching him through the camera, wondering why he was taking so long. He took a deep breath and tried again. This time, he entered the digits slowly, deliberately. He braced himself for the warning beep. To his relief, it didn't go off.

Instead, a new message appeared. *Security code accepted. Please enter.*

He stepped through, into the next room.

Third hurdle, he thought in relief as the door closed behind him. Now for the home run.

Another camera, mounted in a corner, was pointed at him. Acutely conscious of that lens, he made his way across the room to the inner lab door. He turned the knob and a warning bell sounded.

Now what? he thought. Only then did he notice the red light glowing over the door, and the warning *Laser grid activated.* He needed a key to shut it off. He saw no other way to deactivate it, no way to get past it, into the room beyond.

It was time for desperate measures, time for a little chutzpah. He patted his pockets, then turned and faced the camera. "Hello?" He waved.

A voice answered over an intercom. "Is there a problem, Dr. Black?"

"Yes. I can't seem to find my keys. I must have left them at home. . . ."

"I can cut the lasers from here."

"Thanks. Gee, I don't know how this happened."

"No problem."

At once the red warning light shut off. Cautiously Victor tried the door; it swung open. He gave the camera a goodbye wave and entered the last room.

Inside, to his relief, there were no cameras anywhere—at least, none that he could spot. A bit of breathing space, he thought. He moved into the lab and took a quick survey of his surroundings. What he saw was a mind-numbing display of space-age equipment—not just the expected centrifuges and microscopes, but instruments he'd never seen before, all of them brand-new and gleaming. He headed through the decontamination chamber, past the laminar flow unit, and went straight to the incubators. He opened the door.

Glass vials tinkled in their compartments. He took one out. Pink fluid glistened within. The label read Lot #341. Active.

This must be it, he thought. This was what Ollie had told him to look for. Here was the stuff of nightmares, the grim reaper distilled to submicroscopic elements.

He removed two vials, fitted them into a specially padded cigarette case, and slipped it into his pocket. *Mission accomplished,* he thought in triumph as he headed back through the lab. All that lay before him was a casual stroll back to his car. Then the champagne . . .

He was halfway across the room when the alarm bell went off.

He froze, the harsh ring echoing in his ears.

"Dr. Black?" said the guard's voice over some hidden intercom. "Please don't leave. Stay right where you are."

Victor spun around wildly, trying to locate the speaker. "What's going on?"

"I've just been asked to detain you. If you'll hold on, I'll find out what—"

Victor didn't wait to hear the reason—he bolted for the door. Even as he reached it, he heard the whine of the lasers powering on, felt something slash his arm. He shoved through the first door, dashed across the anteroom and out the security door, into the hallway.

Everywhere, alarms were going off. The whole damn building had turned into an echo chamber of ringing bells. His gaze shot right, to the front entrance. No, not that way—the guard was stationed there.

He sprinted left, toward what he hoped was a fire exit. Somewhere behind him a voice yelled, "Halt!" He ignored it and kept running. At the end of the hall he slammed against the opening bar and found himself in a stairwell. No exit, only steps leading up and down. He wasn't about to be trapped like a rat in the basement. He headed up the stairs.

One flight into his climb, he heard the stairwell door slam open on the first floor. Again a voice commanded, "Halt or I'll shoot!"

A bluff, he thought.

A pistol shot exploded, echoing up the concrete stairwell.

Not a bluff. With new desperation, he pushed through the landing door, into the second-floor hallway. A line of closed doors stretched before him. Which one, which one? There was no time to think. He ducked into the third room and softly shut the door behind him.

In the semidarkness, he spotted the gleam of stainless steel and glass beakers. Another lab. Only this one had a large window, now shimmering with moonlight, looming over the far countertop.

From down the hall came the slam of a door being kicked open and the guard's shouted command: "Freeze!"

He was down to one last escape route. Victor grabbed a chair, raised it over his head, and flung it at the window. The glass shattered, raining moonlight-silvered shards into the darkness below. He scarcely bothered to look before he leapt. Bracing himself for the impact, he jumped from the window and landed in a tangle of shrubbery.

"Halt!" came a shout from above.

That was enough to jar Victor back to his feet. He sprinted off across a lawn, into the cover of trees. Glancing back, he saw no pursuing shadow. The guard wasn't about to risk his neck leaping out any window.

Got to make it out the gate . . .

Victor circled around the building, burrowing his way through bushes and trees to a stand of oaks. From there he could view the front gate, way off in the distance. What he saw made his heart sink.

Floodlights illuminated the entrance, glaring down on the four security cars blocking the driveway. Now a panel truck pulled up. The driver went around to the back and opened the doors. At his command two German shepherds leaped out and danced around, barking at his feet.

Victor backed away, stumbling deeper into the grove of oaks. *No way out,* he thought, glancing behind him at the fence, topped with coils of barbed wire. Already, the dogs' barking was moving closer. *Unless I can sprout wings and fly, I'm a dead man.* . . .

11

"Something's wrong!" Cathy cried as the first security car drove past. Polowski touched her arm. "Easy. It could be just a routine patrol."

"No. Look!" Through the trees, they spotted three more cars, all roaring down the road at top speed toward Viratek.

Ollie muttered a surprisingly coarse oath and reached for the microphone.

"Wait!" Polowski grabbed his hand. "We can't risk a transmission. Let him contact us first."

"If he's in trouble—"

"Then he already knows it. Give him a chance to make it out on his own."

"What if he's trapped?" said Cathy. "Are we just going to sit here?"

"We don't have a choice. Not if they've blockaded the front gate—"

"We *do* have a choice!" said Cathy, scrambling forward into the driver's seat.

"What the hell are you doing?" demanded Polowski.

"Giving him a fighting chance. If we don't—"

They all fell instantly silent as a transmission suddenly hissed over the receiver. "Looks like I got myself in a bind, guys. Don't see a way out. You copy?"

Ollie snatched up the microphone. "Copy, Gersh. What's your situation?"

"Bad."

"Specify."

"Front gate's blocked and lit up like a football field. Big time alarms going off. They just brought in the dogs—"

"Can you get over the fence?"

"Negative. It's electrified. Low voltage, but more than I can handle. You guys better hit the road without me."

Polowski grabbed the microphone and barked, "Did you get the stuff?"

Cathy turned and snapped: "Forget that! Ask him where he is. *Ask him!*"

"Holland?" said Polowski. "Where are you?"

"At the northeast perimeter. Fence goes all the way around. Look, get moving. I'll manage—"

"Tell him to head for the east fence!" Cathy said. "Near the midpoint!"

"What?"

"Just tell him!"

"Go to the east fence," Polowski said into the microphone. "Midpoint."

"I copy."

Polowski looked up at Cathy in puzzlement. "What the hell are you thinking of?"

"This is a getaway car, right?" she muttered as she turned on the engine. "I say we put it to its intended use!" She threw the van into gear and spun it around, onto the road.

"Hey, you're going the wrong way!" yelled Milo.

"No, I'm not. There's a fire road, just off to the left somewhere. There it is." She made a sharp turn, onto what was little more than a dirt track. They bounced along, crashing through tree branches and shrubs, a ride so violently spine-shaking it was all they could do to hang on.

"How did you find this *wonderful* road?" Polowski managed to ask.

"It was on the map. I saw it when we were studying the plans for Viratek."

"Is this a scenic route? Or does it go somewhere?"

"The east fence. Used to be the construction entrance for the compound. I'm hoping it's still clear enough to get through. . . ."

"And then what happens?"

Ollie sighed. "Don't ask."

Cathy steered around a bush that had sprung up in her path and ran head-on into a sapling. Her passengers tumbled to the floor. "Sorry," she muttered. Reversing gear, she spun them back on the road. "It should be just ahead. . . ."

A barrier of chain link suddenly loomed before them. Instantly she cut the lights. Through the darkness, they could hear dogs barking, moving in. Where was he?

Then they saw him, flitting through the moonlight. He was running. Somewhere off to the side, a man shouted and gunfire spat the ground.

"Brace yourselves!" yelled Cathy. She snapped on her seatbelt and gripped the steering wheel. Then she stepped on the gas.

The van jerked forward like a bronco, barreled through the underbrush, and slammed into the fence. The chain link sagged; electrical sparks hissed in the night. Cathy threw the gears into reverse, backed up, and hit the gas again.

The fence toppled; barbed wire scraped across the windshield.

"We're through!" said Ollie. He yanked open the sliding door and yelled: "Come on, Gersh! Come on!"

The running figure zigzagged across the grass. All around him, gunfire exploded. He made a last flying leap across the coil of barbed wire and stumbled.

"Come on, Gersh!"

Gunfire spattered the van.

Victor struggled back to his feet. They heard the rip of clothing, then he was reaching up to them, being dragged inside, to safety.

The door slammed shut. Cathy backed up, wheeled the van around and slammed on the gas pedal.

They leaped forward, bouncing through the bushes and across ruts. Another round of bullets pinged the van. Cathy was oblivious to it. She focused only on getting them back to the main road. The sound of gunfire receded. At last the trees gave way to a familiar band of blacktop. She turned left and gunned the engine, anxious to put as many miles as possible between them and Viratek.

Off in the distance, a siren wailed.

"We got company!" said Polowski.

"Which way now?" Cathy cried. Viratek lay behind them; the sirens were approaching from ahead.

"I don't know! Just get the hell out of here!"

As yet her view of the police cars was blocked by trees, but she could hear the sirens moving rapidly closer. *Will they let us pass? Or will they pull us over?*

Almost too late she spotted a clearing, off to the side. On sudden impulse she veered off the pavement, and the van bounced onto a stubbly field.

"Don't tell me," groaned Polowski. "Another fire road?"

"Shut up!" she snapped and steered straight for a clump of bushes.

With a quick turn of the wheel, she circled behind the shrubbery and cut her lights.

It was just in time. Seconds later, two patrol cars, lights flashing, sped right past the concealing bushes. She sat frozen, listening as the sirens faded in the distance. Then, in the darkness, she heard Milo say softly, "Her name is Bond. Jane Bond."

Half laughing, half crying, Cathy turned as Victor scrambled beside her, onto the front seat. At once she was in his arms, her tears wetting his shirt, her sobs muffled in the depths of his embrace. He kissed her damp cheeks, her mouth. The touch of his lips stilled her tremors.

From the back came the sound of a throat being cleared. "Uh, Gersh?" inquired Ollie politely. "Don't you think we ought to get moving?"

Victor's mouth was still pressed against Cathy's. Reluctantly he broke contact but his gaze never left her face. "Sure," he murmured, just before he pulled her back for another kiss. "But would somebody else mind driving . . . ?"

"Here's where things get dangerous," said Polowski. He was at the wheel now, as they headed south toward San Francisco. Cathy and Victor sat in front with Polowski; in the back of the van, Milo and Ollie lay curled up asleep like two exhausted puppies. From the radio came the soft strains of a country western song. The dials glowed a vivid green in the darkness.

"We've finally got the evidence," said Polowski. "All we need to hang 'em. They'll be desperate. Ready to try anything. From here on out, folks, it's going to be a game of cat and mouse."

As if it wasn't already, thought Cathy as she huddled closer to Victor. She longed for a chance to be alone with him. There had been no time for tearful reunions, no time for any confessions of love. They'd spent the last two hours on a harrowing journey down backroads, always avoiding the police. By now the break-in at Viratek would have been reported to the authorities. The state police would be on the lookout for a van with frontal damage.

Polowski was right. Things were only getting more dangerous.

"Soon as we hit the city," said Polowski, "we'll get those vials off to separate labs. Independent confirmation. That should wipe any doubts away. You know names we can trust, Holland?"

"Fellow alum back in New Haven. Runs the hospital lab. I can trust him."

"Yale? Great. That'll have clout."

"Ollie has a pal at UCSF. They'll take care of the second vial."

"And when those reports get back, I know a certain journalist who loves to have a little birdie chirp in his ear." Polowski gave the steering wheel a satisfied slap. "Viratek, you are dead meat."

"You enjoy this, don't you?" said Cathy.

"Workin' the right side of the law? I say it's good for the soul. It keeps your mind sharp and your feet on their toes. It helps you stay young."

"Or die young," said Cathy.

Polowski laughed. "Women. They just never understand the game."

"I don't understand it, at all."

"I bet Holland here does. He just had the adrenaline high of his life. Didn't you?"

Victor didn't answer. He was gazing ahead at the blacktop stretching before their headlights.

"Well, wasn't it a high?" asked Polowski. "To claw your way to hell and back again? To know you made it through on nothing much more than your wits?"

"No," said Victor quietly. "Because it's not over yet."

Polowski's grin faded. He turned his attention back to the road. "Almost," he said. "It's almost over."

They passed a sign: San Francisco: 12 Miles.

Four in the morning. The stars were mere pinpricks in a sky washed out by streetlights. In a North Beach doughnut shop, five weary souls had gathered around steaming coffee and cheese Danish. Only one other table was occupied, by a man with bloodshot eyes and shaking hands. The girl behind the counter sat with her nose buried in a paperback. Behind her, the coffee machine hissed out a fresh brew.

"To the Old Coots," said Milo, raising his cup. "Still the best ensemble around."

They all raised their cups. "To the Old Coots!"

"And to our newest and fairest member," said Milo. "The beautiful—the intrepid—"

"Oh, *please,*" said Cathy.

Victor wrapped his arm around her shoulder. "Relax and be honored. Not everyone gets into this highly selective group."

"The only requirement," said Ollie, "is that you have to play a musical instrument badly."

"But I don't play anything."

"No problem." Ollie fished out a piece of waxed paper from the pile of Danishes and wrapped it around his pocket comb. "Kazoo."

"Fitting," said Milo. "Since that was Lily's instrument."

"Oh." She took the comb. Lily's instrument. It always came back to *her,* the ghost who would forever be there. Suddenly the air of celebration was gone, as though swept away by the cold wind of dawn. She glanced at Victor. He was looking out the window, at the garishly lit streets. *What are you thinking? Are you wishing she was here? That it wasn't me being presented this silly kazoo, but her?*

She put the comb to her lips and hummed an appropriately out-of-tune version of "Yankee Doodle." Everyone laughed and clapped, even Victor. But when the applause was over, she saw the sad and weary look in his eyes. Quietly she set the kazoo down on the table.

Outside, a delivery truck roared past. It was 5:00 a.m.; the city was stirring.

"Well, folks," said Polowski, slapping down a dollar tip. "We got a hotshot reporter to roust outta bed. And then you and I—" he looked at Victor "—have a few deliveries to make. When's United leave for New Haven?"

"At ten-fifteen," said Victor.

"Okay. I'll buy you the plane tickets. In the meantime, you see if you can't grow yourself a new mustache or something." Polowski glanced at Cathy. "You're going with him, right?"

"No," she said, looking at Victor.

She was hoping for a reaction, any reaction. What she saw was a look of relief. And, strangely, resignation.

He didn't try to change her mind. He simply asked, "Where will you be going?"

She shrugged. "Maybe I should stick to our original plan. You know, head south. Hang out with Jack for a while. What do you think?"

It was his chance to stop her. His chance to say, *No, I want you around. I won't let you leave, not now, not ever.* If he really loved her, that's exactly what he would say.

Her heart sank when he simply nodded and said, "I think it's a good idea."

She blinked back the tears before anyone could see them. With an indifferent smile she looked at Ollie. "So I guess I'll need a ride. When are you and Milo heading home?"

"Right now, I guess," said Ollie, looking bewildered. "Seeing as our job's pretty much done."

"Can I hitch along? I'll catch the bus at Palo Alto."

"No problem. In fact, you can sit in the honored front seat."

"Long as you don't let her behind the wheel," grumbled Milo. "I want a nice, quiet drive home if you don't mind."

Polowski rose to his feet. "Then we're all set. Everyone's got a place to go. Let's do it."

Outside, on a street rumbling with early-morning traffic, with their friends standing only a few yards away, Cathy and Victor said their goodbyes. It wasn't the place for sentimental farewells. Perhaps that was all for the best. At least she could leave with some trace of dignity. At least she could avoid hearing, from his lips, the brutal truth. She would simply walk away and hold on to the fantasy that he loved her. That in their brief time together she'd managed to work her way, just a little, into his heart.

"You'll be all right?" he asked.

"I'll be fine. And you?"

"I'll manage." He thrust his hands in his pockets and looked off at a bus idling near the corner. "I'll miss you," he said. "But I know it doesn't make sense for us to be together. Not under the circumstances."

I would stay with you, she thought. *Under any circumstances. If I only knew you wanted me.*

"Anyway," he said with a sigh, "I'll let you know when things are safe again. When you can come home."

"And then?"

"And then we'll take it from there," he said softly.

They kissed, a clumsy, polite kiss, all the more hurried because they knew their friends were watching. There was no passion here, only the cool, dry lips of a man saying goodbye. As they pulled apart, she saw his face blur away through the tears.

"Take care of yourself, Victor," she said. Then, shoulders squared, she turned and walked toward Ollie and Milo.

"Is that it?" asked Ollie.

"That's it." Brusquely she rubbed her hand across her eyes. "I'm ready to go."

"Tell me about Lily," she said.

The first light of dawn was already streaking the sky as they drove past the boxy row homes of Pacifica, past the cliffs where sea waves crashed and gulls swooped and dove.

Ollie, his gaze on the road, asked: "What do you want to know?"

"What kind of woman was she?"

"She was a nice person," said Ollie. "And brainy. Though she never went out of her way to impress people, she was probably the smartest one of all of us. Definitely brighter than Milo."

"And a lot better-looking than Ollie," piped a voice from the back-seat.

"A real kind, real decent woman. When she and Gersh got married, I remember thinking, 'he's got himself a saint.' " He glanced at Cathy, suddenly noticing her silence. "Of course," he added quickly, "not every man *wants* a saint. I know I'd be happier with a lady who can be a little goofy." He flashed Cathy a grin. "Someone who might, say, crash a van through an electrified fence, just for kicks."

It was a sweet thing to say, a comment designed to lift her spirits. It couldn't take the edge off her pain.

She settled back and watched dawn lighten the sky. How she needed to get away! She thought about Mexico, about warm water and hot sand and the tang of fresh fish and lime. She would throw herself into working on that new film. Of course, Jack would be on the set, Jack with his latest sweetie pie in tow, but she could handle that now. Jack would never be able to hurt her again. She was beyond that now, beyond being hurt by any man.

The drive to Milo's house seemed endless.

When at last they pulled up in the driveway, the dawn had already blossomed into a bright, cold morning. Milo climbed out and stood blinking in the sunshine.

"So, guys," he said through the car window. "Guess here's where we go our separate ways." He looked at Cathy. "Mexico, right?"

She nodded. "Puerto Vallarta. What about you?"

"I'm gonna catch up with Ma in Florida. Maybe get a load of Disney World. Wanna come, Ollie?"

"Some other time. I'm going to go get some sleep."

"Don't know what you're missing. Well, it's been some adventure. I'm almost sorry it's over." Milo turned and headed up the walk to his house. On the front porch he waved and yelled, "See you around!" Then he vanished through the front door.

Ollie laughed. "Milo and his ma, together? Disney World'll never be the same." He reached for the ignition. "Next stop, the bus station. I've got just enough gas to get us there and—"

He didn't get a chance to turn the key.

A gun barrel was thrust in the open car window. It came to rest squarely against Ollie's temple.

"Get out, Dr. Wozniak," said a voice.

Ollie's reply came out in a bare croak. "What—what do you want?"

"Do it now." The click of the hammer being cocked was all the coaxing Ollie needed.

"Okay, okay! I'm getting out!" Ollie scrambled out and backed away, his hands raised in surrender.

Cathy, too, started to climb out, but the gunman snapped, "Not you! You stay inside."

"Look," said Ollie, "You can have the damn car! You don't need her—"

"But I do. Tell Mr. Holland I'll be in contact. Regarding Ms. Weaver's future." He went around and opened the passenger door. "You, into the driver's seat!" he commanded her.

"No. Please—"

The gun barrel dug into her neck. "Need I ask again?"

Trembling, she moved behind the wheel. Her knee brushed the car keys, still dangling from the ignition. The man slid in beside her. Though the gun barrel was still thrust against her neck, it was the man's eyes she focused on. They were black, fathomless. If any spark of humanity lurked in those depths, she couldn't see it.

"Start the engine," he said.

"Where—where are we going?"

"For a drive. Somewhere scenic."

Her thoughts were racing, seeking some means of escape, but she came up with nothing. That gun was insurmountable.

She turned on the ignition.

"Hey!" yelled Ollie, grabbing at the door. "You can't do this!"

Cathy screamed, "Ollie, no!"

The gunman had already shifted his aim out the window.

"Let her go!" yelled Ollie. "Let her—"

The gun went off.

Ollie staggered backward, his face a mask of astonishment.

Cathy lunged at the gunman. Pure animal rage, fueled by the instinct to survive, sent her clawing first for his eyes. At the last split second he flinched away. Her nails scraped down his cheek, drawing blood. Before he could shift his aim, she grabbed his wrist, wrenching desperately for control of the gun. He held fast. Not with all her strength could she keep the gun at bay, keep the barrel from turning toward her.

It was the last image she registered: that black hole, slowly turning until it was pointed straight at her face.

Something lashed at her from the side. Pain exploded in her head, shattering the world into a thousand slivers of light.

They faded, one by one, into darkness.

12

"Victor's here," said Milo.

It seemed to take Ollie forever to register their presence. Victor fought the urge to shake him to consciousness, to drag the words out of his friend's throat. He was forced to wait, the silence broken only by the hiss of oxygen, the gurgle of the suction tube. At last Ollie stirred and squinted through pain-glazed eyes at the three men standing beside his bed. "Gersh. I didn't—couldn't—" He stopped, exhausted by the effort just to talk.

"Easy, Ollie," said Milo. "Take it slow."

"Tried to stop him. Had a gun . . ." Ollie paused, gathering the strength to continue.

Victor listened fearfully for the next terrible words to come out. He was still in a state of disbelief, still hoping that what Milo had told him was one giant mistake, that Cathy was, at this very moment, on a bus somewhere to safety. Only two hours ago he'd been ready to board a plane for New Haven. Then he'd been handed a message at the United gate. It was addressed to passenger Sam Polowski, the name on his ticket. It had consisted of only three words: *Call Milo immediately.*

Passenger "Sam Polowski" never did board the plane.

Two hours, he thought in anguish. What have they done to her in those two long hours?

"This man—what did he look like?" asked Polowski.

"Didn't see him very well. Dark hair. Face sort of . . . thin."

"Tall? Short?"

"Tall."

"He drove off in your car?"

Ollie nodded.

"What about Cathy?" Victor blurted out, his control shattered. "He—didn't hurt her? She's all right?"

There was a pause that, to Victor, seemed like an eternity in hell. Ollie's gaze settled mournfully on Victor. "I don't know."

It was the best Victor could hope for. *I don't know.* It left open the possibility that she was still alive.

Suddenly agitated, he began to pace the floor. "I know what he wants," he said. "I know what I have to give him—"

"You can't be serious," said Polowski. "That's our evidence! You can't just hand it over—"

"That's exactly what I'm going to do."

"You don't even know how to contact him!"

"He'll contact *me.*" He spun around and looked at Milo. "He must've been watching your house all this time. Waiting for one of us to turn up. That's where he'll call."

"If he calls," said Polowski.

"He will." Victor touched his jacket pocket, where the two vials from Viratek still rested. "I have what he wants. He has what I want. I think we're both ready to make a trade."

The sun, glaring and relentless, was shining in her eyes. She tried to escape it, tried to close her lids tighter, to stop those rays from piercing through to her brain, but the light followed her.

"Wake up. *Wake up!*"

Icy water slapped her face. Cathy gasped awake, coughing, rivulets of water trickling from her hair. She struggled to make out the face hovering above her. At first all she saw was a dark oval against the blinding circle of light. Then the man moved away and she saw eyes like black agate, a slash of a mouth. A scream formed in her throat, to be instantly frozen by the cold barrel of a gun against her cheek.

"Not a sound." he said. "Got that?"

In silent terror she nodded.

"Good." The gun slid away from her cheek and was tucked under his jacket. "Sit up."

She obeyed. Instantly the room began to spin. She sat clutching her aching head, the fear temporarily overshadowed by waves of pain and nausea. The spell lasted for only a few moments. Then, as the nausea faded, she became aware of a second man in the room, a large, broad-shouldered man she'd never before seen. He sat off in a corner, saying nothing, but watching her every move. The room itself was small and windowless. She couldn't tell if it was day or night. The only furniture was a chair, a card table and the cot she was sitting on. The floor was a bare slab of concrete. *We're in a basement,* she thought. She heard no other sounds, either outside or in the building. Were they still in Palo Alto? Or were they a hundred miles away?

The man in the chair crossed his arms and smiled. Under different circumstances, she might have considered that smile a charming one. Now it struck her as frighteningly inhuman. "She seems awake enough," he said. "Why don't you proceed, Mr. Savitch?"

The man called Savitch loomed over her. "Where is he?"

"Who?" she said.

Her answer was met by a ringing slap to her cheek. She sprawled backwards on the cot.

"Try again," he said, dragging her back up to a sitting position. "Where is Victor Holland?"

"I don't know."

"You were with him."

"We—we split up."

"Why?"

She touched her mouth. The sight of blood on her fingers shocked her temporarily into silence.

"Why?"

"He—" She bowed her head. Softly she said, "He didn't want me around."

Savitch let out a snort. "Got tired of you pretty quick, did he?"

"Yes," she whispered. "I guess he did."

"I don't know why."

She shuddered as the man ran his finger down her cheek, her throat. He stopped at the top button of her blouse. *No,* she thought. *Not that.*

To her relief, the man in the chair suddenly cut in. "This is getting us nowhere."

Savitch turned to the other man. "You have another suggestion, Mr. Tyrone?"

"Yes. Let's try using her in a different way." Fearfully Cathy watched as Tyrone moved to the card table and opened a satchel. "Since we can't go to him," he said, "we'll have Holland come to us." He turned and smiled at her. "With your help, of course."

She stared at the cellular telephone he was holding. "I told you. I don't know where he is."

"I'm sure one of his friends will track him down."

"He's not stupid. He wouldn't come for me—"

"You're right. He's not stupid." Tyrone began to punch in a phone number. "But he's a man of conscience. And that's a flaw that's every bit as fatal." He paused, then said into the telephone, "Hello? Mr. Milo Lum? I want you to pass this message to Victor Holland for me. Tell him I have something of his. Something that won't be around much longer . . ."

"It's him!" hissed Milo. "He wants to make a deal."

Victor shot to his feet. "Let me talk to him—"

"Wait!" Polowski grabbed his arm. "We have to take this slow. Think about what we're—"

Victor pulled his arm free and snatched the receiver from Milo. "This is Holland," he barked into the phone. "Where is she?"

The voice on the other end paused, a silence designed to emphasize just who held the upper hand. "She's with me. She's alive."

"How do I know that?"

"You'll have to take my word for it."

"Word, hell! I want proof!"

Again there was a silence. Then, through the crackle of the line, came another voice, so tremulous, so afraid, it almost broke his heart. "Victor, it's me."

"Cathy?" He almost shouted with relief. "Cathy, are you all right?"

"I'm . . . fine."

"Where are you?"

"I don't know—I think—" She stopped. The silence was agonizing. "I can't be sure."

"He hasn't hurt you?"

A pause. "No."

She's not telling me the truth, he thought. *He's done something to her . . .*

"Cathy, I promise. You'll be all right. I swear to you I'll—"

"Let's talk business." The man was back on the line.

Victor gripped the receiver in fury. "If you hurt her, if you just touch her, I swear I'll—"

"You're hardly in a position to bargain."

Victor felt a hand grasp his arm. He turned and met Polowski's gaze. *Keep your head* was the message he saw. *Go along with him. Make a bargain. It's the only way to buy time.*

Nodding, Victor fought to regain control. When he spoke again, his voice was calm. "Okay. You want the vials, they're yours."

"Not good enough."

"Then I'll throw myself into the bargain. A trade. Is that acceptable?"

"Acceptable. You and the vials in exchange for her life."

An anguished cry of *"No!"* pierced the dialogue. It was Cathy, somewhere in the background, shouting, "Don't, Victor! They're going to—"

Through the receiver, Victor heard the thud of a blow, followed by soft moans of pain. All his control shattered. He was screaming now, cursing, begging, anything to make the man stop hurting her. The words ran together, making no sense. He couldn't see straight, couldn't think straight.

Again, Polowski took his arm, gave it a shake. Victor, breathing hard, stared at him through a gaze blurred by tears. Polowski's eyes advised: *Make the deal. Go on.*

Victor swallowed and closed his eyes. *Give me strength,* he thought. He managed to ask, "When do we make the exchange?"

"Tonight. At 2:00 a.m."

"Where?"

"East Palo Alto. The old Saracen Theater."

"But it's closed. It's been closed for—"

"It'll be open. Just you, Holland. I spot anyone else and the first bullet has her name on it. Clear?"

"I want a guarantee! I want to know she'll be—"

He was answered by silence. And then, seconds later, he heard a dial tone.

Slowly he hung up.

"Well? What's the deal?" demanded Polowski.

"At 2:00 a.m. Saracen Theater."

"Half an hour. That barely gives us time to set up a—"

"I'm going alone."

Milo and Polowski stared at him. "Like hell," said Polowski.

Victor grabbed his jacket from out of the closet. He gave the pocket a quick pat; the cigarette case was right where he'd left it. He turned and reached for the door.

"But Gersh!" said Milo. "He's gonna kill you!"

Victor paused in the doorway. "Probably," he said softly. "But it's Cathy's only chance. And it's a chance I have to take."

"He won't come," said Cathy.

"Shut up," Matt Tyrone snapped and shoved her forward.

As they moved down the glass-strewn alley behind the Saracen Theater, Cathy frantically searched her mind for some way to sabotage this fatal meeting. It *would* be fatal, not just for Victor, but for her, as well. The two men now escorting her through the darkness had no intention of letting her live. The best she could hope for was that Victor would survive. She had to do what she could to better his chances.

"He's already got his evidence," she said. "You think he'd give that up just for me?"

Tyrone glanced at Savitch. "What if she's right?"

"Holland's coming," said Savitch. "I know how he thinks. He's not going to leave the little woman behind." Savitch gave Cathy's cheek a deceptively gentle caress. "Not when he knows exactly what we'll do to her."

Cathy flinched away, repelled by his touch. *What if he really doesn't come?* she thought. *What if he does the sensible thing and leaves me to die?*

She wouldn't blame him.

Tyrone gave her a push up the steps and into the building. "Inside. Move."

"I can't see," she protested, feeling her way along a pitch-black passage. She stumbled over boxes, brushed past what felt like heavy drapes. "It's too dark—"

"Then let there be light," said a new voice.

The lights suddenly sprang on, so bright she was temporarily blinded. She raised her hand to shield her eyes. Through the glare she could make out a third man, looming before her. Beyond him, the floor seemed to drop away into a vast blackness.

They were standing on a theater stage. It was obvious no performer had trod these boards in years. Ragged curtains hung like cobwebs from the rafters. Panels of an old set, the ivy-hung battlements of a medieval castle, still leaned at a crazy tilt against the back wall, framed by a pair of mops.

Tyrone said, "Any problems, Dafoe?"

"None," said the new man. "I've reconned the building. One door at the front, one backstage. The emergency side doors are padlocked. If we block both exits, he's trapped."

"I see the FBI deserves its fine reputation."

Dafoe grinned and dipped his head. "I knew the Cowboy would want the very best."

"Okay, Ms. Weaver." Tyrone shoved Cathy forward, toward a chair placed directly under the spotlight. "Let's put you right where he can see you. Center stage."

It was Savitch who tied her to the chair. He knew exactly what he was doing. She had no hope of working her hands free from such tight, professional knots.

He stepped back, satisfied with his job. "She's not going anywhere," he said. Then, as an afterthought, he ripped off a strip of cloth tape and slapped it over her mouth. "So we don't have any surprises," he said.

Tyrone glanced at his watch. "Zero minus fifteen. Positions, gentlemen."

The three men slipped away into the shadows, leaving Cathy alone on the empty stage. The spotlight beating down on her face was hot as the midday sun. Already she could feel beads of sweat forming on her forehead. Though she couldn't see them, by their voices she could guess the positions of the three men. Tyrone was close by, Savitch was at the back of the theater, near the building's front entrance. And the man named Dafoe had stationed himself somewhere above, in one of the box seats. Three different lines of fire. No route of escape.

Victor, don't be a fool, she thought. *Stay away . . .*

And if he doesn't come? She couldn't bear to consider that possibility, either, for it meant he was abandoning her. It meant he didn't care enough even to make the effort to save her.

She closed her eyes against the spotlight, against the tears. *I love you. I could take anything, even this, if I only knew you loved me.*

Her hands were numb from the ropes. She tried to wriggle the bonds looser, but only succeeded in rubbing her wrists raw. She fought to remain calm, but with every minute that passed, her heart seemed to pound harder. A drop of sweat trickled down her temple.

Somewhere in the shadows ahead, a door squealed open and closed. Footsteps approached, their pace slow and deliberate. She strained to see against the spotlight's glare, but could make out only the hint of shadow moving through shadow.

The stage floorboards creaked behind her as Tyrone strolled out from the wings. "Stop right where you are, Mr. Holland," he said.

13

Another spotlight suddenly sprang on, catching Victor in its glare. He stood halfway up the aisle, a lone figure trapped in a circle of brilliance.

You came for me! she thought. *I knew, somehow I knew, that you would.* . . .

If only she could shout to him, warn him about the other two men. But the tape had been applied so tightly that the only sound she could produce was a whimper.

"Let her go," said Victor.

"You have something we want first."

"I said, *let her go!*"

"You're hardly in a position to bargain." Tyrone strolled out of the wings, onto the stage. Cathy flinched as the icy barrel of a gun pressed against her temple. "Let's see it, Holland," said Tyrone.

"Untie her first."

"I could shoot you both and be done with it."

"Is this what it's come to?" yelled Victor. "Federal dollars for the murder of civilians?"

"It's all a matter of cost and benefit. A few civilians may have to die now. But if this country goes to war, think of all the millions of Americans who'll be saved!"

"I'm thinking of the Americans you've already killed."

"Necessary deaths. But you don't understand that. You've never seen a fellow soldier die, have you, Holland? You don't know what a helpless feeling it is, to watch good boys from good American towns get cut to pieces. With this weapon, they won't have to. It'll be the enemy dying, not us."

"Who gave you the authority?"

"I gave myself the authority."

"And who the hell are *you?*"

"A patriot, Mr. Holland! I do the jobs no one else in the Administration'll touch. Someone says, 'Too bad our weapons don't have a higher kill ratio.' That's my cue to get one developed. They don't even have to ask me. They can claim total ignorance."

"So you're the fall guy."

Tyrone shrugged. "It's part of being a good soldier. The willingness to fall on one's sword. But I'm not ready to do that yet."

Cathy tensed as Tyrone clicked back the gun hammer. The barrel was still poised against her skull.

"As you can see," said Tyrone, "the cards aren't exactly stacked in her favor."

"On the other hand," Victor said calmly, "how do you know I've brought the vials? What if they're stashed somewhere, a publicity time bomb ticking away? Kill her now and you'll never find out."

Deadlock. Tyrone lowered the pistol. He and Victor faced each other for a moment. Then Tyrone reached into his pocket, and Cathy heard the click of a switchblade. "This round goes to you, Holland," he said as he cut the bindings. The sudden rush of circulation back into Cathy's hands was almost painful. Tyrone ripped the tape off her mouth and yanked her out of the chair. "She's all yours!"

Cathy scrambled off the stage. On unsteady legs, she moved up the aisle, toward the circle of the spotlight, toward Victor. He pulled her into his arms. Only by the thud of his racing heart did she know how close he was to panic.

"Your turn, Holland," called Tyrone.

"Go," Victor whispered to her. "Get out of here."

"Victor, he has two other men—"

"Let's have it!" yelled Tyrone.

Victor hesitated. Then he reached into his jacket and pulled out a cigarette case. "They'll be watching me," he whispered. "You move for the door. Go on. *Do it.*"

She stood paralyzed by indecision. She couldn't leave him to die. And she knew the other two gunmen were somewhere in the darkness, watching their every move.

"She stays where she is!" said Tyrone. "Come on, Holland. The vials!"

Victor took a step further, then another.

"No further!" commanded Tyrone.

Victor halted. "You want it, don't you?"

"Put it down on the floor."

Slowly Victor set the cigarette case down by his feet.

"Now slide it to me."

Victor gave the case a shove. It skimmed down the aisle and came to a rest in the orchestra pit.

Tyrone dropped from the stage.

Victor began to back away. Taking Cathy's hand, he edged her slowly up the aisle, toward the exit.

As if on cue, the click of pistol hammers being snapped back echoed through the theater. Reflexively, Victor spun around, trying to sight the other gunmen. It was impossible to see anything clearly against the glare of the spotlight.

"You're not leaving yet," said Tyrone, reaching down for the case. Gingerly he removed the lid. In silence he stared at the contents.

This is it, thought Cathy. *He has no reason to keep us alive, now that he has what he wants. . . .*

Tyrone's head shot up. "Double cross," he said. Then, in a roar, *"Double cross! Kill them!"*

His voice was still reverberating through the far reaches of the theater when, all at once, the lights went out. Blackness fell, so impenetrable that Cathy had to reach out to get her bearings.

That's when Victor pulled her sideways, down a row of theater seats.

"Stop them!" screamed Tyrone in the darkness.

Gunfire seemed to erupt from everywhere at once. As Cathy and Victor scurried on hands and knees along the floor, they could hear bullets thudding into the velvet-backed seats. The gunfire quickly became random, a blind spraying of the theater.

"Hold your fire!" yelled Tyrone. "Listen for them!"

The gunfire stopped. Cathy and Victor froze in the darkness, afraid to give away their position. Except for the pounding of her own pulse, Cathy heard absolute silence. *We're trapped. We make a single move and they'll know where we are.*

Scarcely daring to breathe, she reached back and pulled off her shoe. With a mighty heave, she threw it blindly across the theater. The clatter of the shoe's landing instantly drew a new round of gunfire. In the din of ricocheting bullets, Victor and Cathy scurried along the remainder of the row and emerged in the side aisle.

Again, the gunfire stopped.

"No way out, Holland!" yelled Tyrone. "Both doors are covered! It's just a matter of time. . . ."

Somewhere above, in a theater balcony, a light suddenly flickered on. It was Dafoe, holding aloft a cigarette lighter. As the flame leapt brightly, casting its terrible light against the shadows, Victor shoved Cathy to the floor behind a seat.

"I know they're here!" shouted Tyrone. "See 'em, Dafoe?"

As Dafoe moved the flame, the shadows shifted, revealing new forms, new secrets. "I'll spot 'em any second. Wait. I think I see—"

Dafoe suddenly jerked sideways as a shot rang out. The flame's light danced crazily on his face as he wobbled for a moment on the edge of the balcony. He reached out for the railing, but the rotten wood gave way under his weight. He pitched forward, his body tumbling into a row of seats.

"Dafoe!" screamed Tyrone. "Who the hell—"

A tongue of flame suddenly slithered up from the floor. Dafoe's lighter had set fire to the drapes! The flames spread quickly, dancing their way along the heavy velvet fabric, toward the rafters. As the first flames touched wood, the fire whooshed into a roar.

By the light of the inferno, all was revealed: Victor and Cathy, cowering in the aisle. Savitch, standing near the entrance, semiautomatic at the ready. And onstage, Tyrone, his expression demonic in the fire's glow.

"They're yours, Savitch!" ordered Tyrone.

Savitch aimed. This time there was no place for them to hide, no shadows to scurry off to. Cathy felt Victor's arm encircle her in a last protective embrace.

The gun's explosion made them both flinch. Another shot; still she felt no pain. She glanced at Victor. He was staring at her, as though unable to believe they were both alive.

They looked up to see Savitch, his shirt stained in a spreading abstract of blood, drop to his knees.

"Now's your chance!" yelled a voice. *"Move, Holland!"*

They whirled around to see a familiar figure silhouetted against the flames. Somehow, Sam Polowski had magically appeared from behind the drapes. Now he pivoted, pistol clutched in both hands, and aimed at Tyrone.

He never got a chance to squeeze off the shot.

Tyrone fired first. The bullet knocked Polowski backward and sent him sprawling against the smoldering velvet seats.

"Get out of here!" barked Victor, giving Cathy a push toward the exit. "I'm going back for him—"

"Victor, you can't!"

But he was on his way. Through the swirling smoke she could see him moving at a half crouch between rows of seats. *He needs help. And time's running out.* . . .

Already the air was so hot it seemed to sear its way into her throat. Coughing, she dropped to the floor and took in a few breaths of relatively smoke-free air. She still had time to escape. All she had to do was crawl up the aisle and out the theater door. Every instinct told her to flee now, while she had the chance.

Instead, she turned from the exit and followed Victor into the maelstrom.

She could just make out his figure, scrambling before a solid wall of fire. She raised her arm to shield her face against the heat. Squinting into the smoke, she crawled forward, moving ever closer to the flames. "Victor!" she screamed.

She was answered only by the fire's roar, and by a sound even more ominous: the creak of wood. She glanced up. To her horror she saw that the rafters were sagging and on the verge of collapse.

Panicked, she scurried blindly forward, toward where she'd last spotted Victor. He was no longer visible. In his place was a whirlwind of smoke and flame. Had he already escaped? Was she alone, trapped in this blazing tinderbox?

Something slapped against her cheek. She stared, at first uncomprehending, at the human hand dangling before her face. Slowly she followed it up, along the bloodied arm, to the lifeless eyes of Dafoe. Her cry of terror seemed to funnel into the fiery cyclone.

"Cathy?"

She turned at the sound of Victor's shout. That's when she saw him, crouching in the aisle just a few feet away. He had Polowski under the arms and was struggling to drag him toward the exit. But the heat and smoke had taken its toll; he was on the verge of collapse.

"The roof's about to fall!" she screamed.

"Get out!"

"Not without you!" She scrambled forward and grabbed Polowski's feet. Together they hauled their burden up the aisle, across carpet that was already alight with sparks. Step by step they neared the top of the aisle. Only a few yards to go!

"I've got him," gasped Victor. "Go—open the door—"

She rose to a half crouch and turned.

Matt Tyrone stood before her.

"Victor!" she sobbed.

Victor, his face a mask of soot and sweat, turned to meet Tyrone's gaze. Neither man said a word. They both knew the game had been played out. Now the time had come to finish it.

Tyrone raised his gun.

Just as he did, they heard the loud crack of splintering wood. Tyrone glanced up as one of the rafters sagged, spilling a shower of burning tinder.

That brief distraction was all the time Cathy needed. In an act of sheer desperation she lunged at Tyrone's legs, knocking him backward. The gun flew from his grasp and slid off beneath a row of seats.

At once Tyrone was back on his feet. He aimed a savage kick at her. The blow hit her in the ribs, an impact so agonizing she hadn't the breath to cry out. She simply sprawled in the aisle, stunned and utterly helpless to ward off any other blows.

Through the darkness gathering before her eyes, she saw two figures struggling. Victor and Tyrone. Framed against a sea of fire, they grappled for each other's throats. Tyrone threw a punch; Victor staggered back a few paces. Tyrone charged him like a bull. At the last instant Victor side-stepped him and Tyrone met only empty air. He stumbled and sprawled forward, onto the smoldering carpet. Enraged, he rose to his knees, ready to charge again.

The crack of collapsing timber made him glance skyward.

He was still staring up in astonishment as the beam crashed down on his head.

Cathy tried to cry out Victor's name but no sound escaped. The smoke had left her throat too parched and swollen. She struggled to her knees. Polowski was lying beside her, groaning. Flames were everywhere, shooting up from the floor, clambering up the last untouched drapes.

Then she saw him, stumbling toward her through that vision of hellfire. He grabbed her arm and shoved her toward the exit.

Somehow, they managed to tumble out the door, dragging Polowski behind them. Coughing, choking, they pulled him across the street to the far sidewalk. There they collapsed.

The night sky suddenly lit up as an explosion ripped through the theater. The roof collapsed, sending up a whoosh of flames so brilliant they seemed to reach to the very heavens. Victor threw his body over Cathy's as the windows in the building above shattered, raining splinters onto the sidewalk.

For a moment there was only the sound of the flames, crackling across the street. Then, somewhere in the distance, a siren wailed.

Polowski stirred and groaned.

"Sam!" Victor turned his attention to the wounded man. "How you doing, buddy?"

"Got . . . got one helluva stitch in my side. . . ."

"You'll be fine." Victor flashed him a tense grin. "Listen! Hear those sirens? Help's on the way."

"Yeah." Polowski, eyes narrowed in pain, stared up at the flame-washed sky.

"Thanks, Sam," said Victor softly.

"Had to. You . . . too damn stupid to listen . . ."

"We got her back, didn't we?"

Polowski's gaze shifted to Cathy. "We—we did okay."

Victor rubbed a hand across his smudged and weary face. "But we're back to square one. I've lost the evidence—"

"Milo . . ."

"It's all in there." Victor stared across at the flames now engulfing the old theater.

"Milo has it," whispered Sam.

"What?"

"You weren't looking. Gave it to Milo."

Victor sat back in bewilderment. "You mean you *took* them? You took the vials?"

Polowski nodded.

"You—you stupid son of a—"

"Victor!" said Cathy.

"He stole my bargaining chip!"

"He saved our lives!"

Victor stared down at Polowski.

Polowski returned a pained grin. "Dame's got a head on her shoulders," he murmured. "Listen to her."

The sirens, which had risen to a scream, suddenly cut off. Men's shouts at once sliced through the hiss and roar of the flames. A burly fireman loped over from the truck and knelt beside Polowski.

"What've we got here?"

"Gunshot wound," said Victor. "And a wise-ass patient."

The fireman nodded. "No problem, sir. We can handle both."

By the time they'd loaded Polowski into an ambulance, the Saracen Theater had been reduced to little more than a dying bonfire. Victor and Cathy watched the taillights of the ambulance vanish, heard the fading wail of the siren, the hiss of water on the flames.

He turned to her. Without a word he pulled her into his arms and held her long and hard, two silent figures framed against a sea of smoldering flames and chaos. They were both so weary neither knew which was holding the other up. Yet even through her exhaustion, Cathy felt the magic of that moment. It was eerily beautiful, that last sputtering glow, the reflections dancing off the nearby buildings. Beautiful and frightening and final.

"You came for me," she murmured. "Oh, Victor, I was so afraid you wouldn't. . . ."

"Cathy, you knew I would!"

"I *didn't* know. You had your evidence. You could have left me—"

"No, I couldn't." He buried a kiss in her singed hair. "Thank God I wasn't already on that plane. They'd have had you, and I'd have been two thousand miles away."

Footsteps crunched toward them across the glass-littered pavement. "Excuse me," a voice said. "Are you Victor Holland?"

They turned to see a man in a rumpled parka, a camera slung over his shoulder, watching them.

"Who are you?" asked Victor.

The man held out his hand. "Jay Wallace. *San Francisco Chronicle.* Sam Polowski called me, said there'd be some fireworks in case I wanted to check it out." He gazed at the last remains of the Saracen Theater and shook his head. "Looks like I got here a little too late."

"Wait. *Sam* called you? When?"

"Maybe two hours ago. If he wasn't my ex-brother-in-law, I'd a hung up on him. For days he's been dropping hints he had a story to spill. Never followed through, not once. I almost didn't come tonight. You know, it's a helluva long drive down here from the city."

"He told you about me?"

"He said you had a story to tell."

"Don't we all?"

"Some stories are better than others." The reporter glanced around, searching. "So where is Sam, anyway? Or didn't the Bozo show up?"

"That Bozo," said Victor, his voice tight with anger, "is a goddamn hero. Stick *that* in your article."

More footsteps approached. This time it was two police officers. Cathy felt Victor's muscles go taut as he turned to face them.

The senior officer spoke. "We've just been informed that a gunshot victim was taken to the ER. And that you were found on the scene."

Victor nodded. His look of tension suddenly gave way to one of overwhelming exhaustion. And resignation. He said, quietly, "I was present. And if you search that building, you'll find three more bodies."

"*Three?*" The two cops glanced at each other.

"Musta been some fireworks," muttered the reporter.

The senior officer said, "Maybe you'd better give us your name, sir."

"My name . . ." Victor looked at Cathy. She read the message in those weary eyes: *We've reached the end. I have to tell them. Now they'll take me away from you, and God knows when we'll see each other again. . . .*

She felt his hand tighten around hers. She held on, knowing with every second that passed that he would soon be wrenched from her grasp.

His gaze still focused on her face, he said, "My name is Victor Holland."

"Holland . . . Victor Holland?" said the officer. "Isn't that . . ."

And still Victor was looking at her. Until they'd clapped on the handcuffs, until he'd been pulled away, toward a waiting squad car, his gaze was locked on her.

She was left anchorless, shivering among the dying embers.

"Ma'am, you'll have to come with us."

She looked up, dazed, at the policeman. "What?"

"Hey, she doesn't have to!" cut in Jay Wallace. "You haven't charged her with anything!"

"Shut up, Wallace."

"I've had the court beat. I know her rights!"

Quietly Cathy said, "It doesn't matter. I'll come with you, officer."

"Wait!" said Wallace. "I wanna talk to you first! I got just a few questions—"

"She can talk to you later," snapped the policeman, taking Cathy by the arm. "*After* she talks to us."

The policemen were polite, even kind. Perhaps it was her docile acceptance of the situation, perhaps they could sense she was operating on her last meager reserves of strength. She answered all their questions. She let them examine the rope burns on her wrists. She told them about Ollie and Sarah and the other Catherine Weavers. And the whole time, as she sat in that room in the Palo Alto police station, she kept hoping she'd catch a glimpse of Victor. She knew he had to be close by. Were they, at that very moment, asking him these same questions?

At dawn, they released her.

Jay Wallace was waiting outside near the front steps. "I have to talk to you," he said as she walked out.

"Please. Not now. I'm tired. . . ."

"Just a few questions."

"I can't. I need to—to—" She stopped. And there standing on that cold and empty street, she burst into tears "I don't know what to do," she sobbed. "I don't know how to help him. How to reach him."

"You mean Holland? They've already taken him to San Francisco."

"What?" She raised her startled gaze to Wallace.

"An hour ago. The big boys from the Justice Department came down as an escort. I hear tell they're flying him straight to Washington. First-class treatment all the way."

She shook her head in bewilderment. "Then he's all right—he's not under arrest—"

"Hell, lady," said Wallace, laughing. "The man is now a genuine hero."

A hero. But she didn't care what they called him, as long as he was safe.

She took a deep breath of bitingly chill air. "Do you have a car, Mr. Wallace?" she asked.

"It's parked right around the corner."

"Then you can give me a ride."

"Where to?"

"To . . ." She paused, wondering where to go, where Victor would look for her. Of course. Milo's. "To a friend's house," she said. "I want to be there when Victor calls."

Wallace pointed the way to the car. "I hope it's a long drive," he said. "I got a lot of gaps to fill in before this story goes to press."

Victor didn't call.

For four days she sat waiting near the phone, expecting to hear his voice. For four days, Milo and his mother brought her tea and cookies, smiles and sympathy. On the fifth day, when she still hadn't heard from him, those terrible doubts began to haunt her. She remembered that day by the lake bed, when he'd tried to send her away with Ollie. She thought of all the words he could have said, but never had. True, he'd come back for her. He'd knowingly walked straight into a trap at the Saracen Theater. But wouldn't he have done that for any of his friends? That was the kind of man he was. She'd saved his life once. He remembered his debts, and he paid them back. It had to do with honor.

It might have nothing to do with love.

She stopped waiting by the phone. She returned to her flat in San Francisco, cleaned up the glass, had the windows replaced, the walls replastered. She took long walks and paid frequent visits to Ollie and Polowski in the hospital. Anything to stay away from that silent telephone.

She got a call from Jack. "We're shooting next week," he whined. "And the monster's in terrible shape. All this humidity! Its face keeps melting into green goo. Get down here and do something about it, will you?"

She told him she'd think about it.

A week later she decided. Work was what she needed. Green goo and cranky actors—it was better than waiting for a call that would never come.

She reserved a one-way flight from San José to Puerto Vallarta. Then she packed, throwing in her entire wardrobe. A long stay, that's what she planned, a long vacation.

But before she left, she would drive down to Palo Alto. She had promised to pay Sam Polowski one last visit.

14

(AP) Washington.

Administration spokesman Richard Jungkuntz repeated today that neither the President nor any of his staff had any knowledge of biological weapons research being conducted at Viratek Industries in California. Viratek's Project Cerberus, which involved development of genetically altered viruses, was clearly in violation of international law. Recent evidence, gathered by reporter Jay Wallace of the *San Francisco Chronicle,* has revealed that the project received funds directly authorized by the late Matthew Tyrone, a senior aide to the Secretary of Defense.

In today's Justice Department hearings, delayed four hours because of heavy snowstorms, Viratek president Archibald Black testified for the first time, promising to reveal, to the best of his knowledge, the direct links between the Administration and Project Cerberus. Yesterday's testimony, by former Viratek employee Dr. Victor Holland, has already outlined a disturbing tale of deception, cover-ups and possibly murder.

The Attorney General's office continues to resist demands by Congressman Leo D. Fanelli that a special prosecutor be appointed . . .

Cathy put down the newspaper and smiled across the hospital solarium at her three friends. "Well, guys. Aren't you lucky to be here in sunny California and not freezing your you-know-what's off in Washington."

"Are you kidding?" groused Polowski. "I'd give anything to be in on those hearings right now. Instead of hooked up to all these—these *doohickeys.*" He gave his intravenous line a tug, clanging a bottle against the pole.

"Patience, Sam," said Milo. "You'll get to Washington."

"Ha! Holland's already told 'em the good stuff. By the time they get around to hearing my testimony, it'll be back-page news."

"I don't think so," said Cathy. "I think it'll be front-page news for a long time to come." She turned and looked out the window at the sunshine glistening on the grass. *A long time to come.* That's how long it would be before she'd see Victor again. If ever. Three weeks had already passed since she'd last laid eyes on him. Via Jay Wallace in Washington, she'd heard that it was like a shark-feeding whenever Victor appeared in public, mobs of reporters and federal attorneys and Justice Department officials. No one could get near him.

Not even me, she thought.

It had been a comfort, having these three new friends to talk to. Ollie had bounced back quickly and was discharged—or kicked out, as Milo put it—a mere eight days after being shot. Polowski had had a rougher time of it. Post-operative infections, plus a bad case of smoke inhalation, had prolonged his stay to the point that every day was another trial of frustration for him. He wanted out. He wanted back on the beat.

He wanted a real, honest-to-God cheeseburger and a cigarette.

One more week, the doctors said.

At least there's an end to his waiting in sight, Cathy thought. *I don't know when I'll see or hear from Victor again.*

The silence was to be expected, Polowski had told her. Sequestration of witnesses. Protective custody. The Justice Department wanted an airtight case, and for that it would keep its star witness incommunicado. For the rest of them, depositions had been sufficient. Cathy had given her testimony two weeks before. Afterward, they'd told her she was free to leave town any time she wished.

Now she had a plane ticket to Mexico in her purse.

She was through with waiting for telephone calls, through with wondering whether he loved her or missed her. She'd been through this before with Jack, the doubts, the fears, the slow but inevitable realization that something was wrong. She knew enough not to be hurt again, not this way.

At least, out of all this pain, I've discovered three new friends. Ollie and Polowski and Milo, the most unlikely trio on the face of the earth.

"Look, Sam," said Milo, reaching into his backpack. "We brought ya something."

"No more hula-girl boxer shorts, okay? Caught hell from the nurses for that one."

"Naw. It's something for your lungs. To remind you to breathe deep."

"Cigarettes?" Polowski asked hopefully.

Milo grinned and held up his gift. "A kazoo!"

"I really needed one."

"You really do need it," said Ollie, opening up his clarinet case. "Seeing as we brought our instruments today and we weren't about to leave you out of this particular gig."

"You're not serious."

"What better place to perform?" said Milo, giving his piccolo a quick and loving rubdown. "All these sick, depressed patients lying around, in need of a bit of cheering up. Some good music."

"Some peace and quiet!" Polowski turned pleading eyes to Cathy. "They're not serious."

She looked him in the eye and took out her kazoo. "Dead serious."

"Okay, guys," said Ollie. "Hit it!"

Never before had the world heard such a rendering of "California, Here I Come!" And, if the world was lucky, never again. By the time they'd played the last note, nurses and patients had spilled into the solarium to check on the source of that terrible screeching.

"Mr. Polowski!" said the head nurse. "If your visitors can't behave—"

"You'll throw 'em out?" asked Polowski hopefully.

"No need," said Ollie. "We're packing up the pipes. By the way, folks, we're available for private parties, birthdays, cocktail hours. Just get in touch with our business manager—" at this, Milo smiled and waved "—to set up your own special performance."

Polowski groaned, "I want to go back to bed."

"Not yet," said the nurse. "You need the extra stimulation." Then, with a sly wink at Ollie, she turned and whisked out of the room.

"Well," said Cathy. "I think I've done my part to cheer you up. Now it's time I hit the road."

Polowski looked at her in astonishment. "You're leaving me with these lunatics?"

"Have to. I have a plane to catch."

"Where you going?"

"Mexico. Jack called to say they're shooting already. So I thought I'd get on down there and whip up a few monsters."

"What about Victor?"

"What about him?"

"I thought—that is—" Polowski looked at Ollie and Milo. Both men merely shrugged. "He's going to miss you."

"I don't think so." She turned once again to gaze out the window. Below, in the walkway, an old woman sat in a wheelchair, her wan face turned gratefully to the sun. Soon Cathy would be enjoying that very sunshine, somewhere on a Mexican beach.

By their silence, she knew the three men didn't know what to say. After all, Victor was their friend, as well. They couldn't defend or condemn him. Neither could she. She simply loved him, in ways that made her decision to leave all the more right. She'd been in love before, she knew that the very worst thing a woman can sense in a man is indifference.

She didn't want to be around to see it in Victor's eyes.

Gathering up her purse, she said, "Guys, I guess this is it."

Ollie shook his head. "I really wish you'd hang around. He'll be back any day. Besides, you can't break up our great little quartet."

"Sam can take my place on the kazoo."

"No way," said Polowski.

She planted a kiss on his balding head. "Get better. The country needs you."

Polowski sighed. "I'm glad somebody does."

"I'll write you from Mexico!" She slung her purse over her shoulder and turned. One step was all she managed before she halted in astonishment.

Victor was standing in the doorway, a suitcase in hand. He cocked his head. "What's this about Mexico?"

She couldn't answer. She just kept staring at him, thinking how unfair it was that the man she was trying so hard to escape should look so heartbreakingly wonderful.

"You got back just in time," said Ollie. "She's leaving."

"What?" Victor dropped his suitcase and stared at her in dismay. Only then did she notice his wrinkled clothes, the day-old growth of beard shadowing his face. The toe of a sock poked out from a corner of the closed suitcase.

"You can't be leaving," he said.

She cleared her throat. "It was unexpected. Jack needs me."

"Did something happen? Is there some emergency?"

"No, it's just that they're filming and, oh, things are a royal mess on the set. . . ." She glanced at her watch, a gesture designed to speed her escape. "Look, I'll miss my plane. I promise I'll give you a call when I get to—"

"You're not his only makeup artist."

"No, but—"

"He can do the movie without you."

"Yes, but—"

"Do you *want* to leave? Is that it?"

She didn't answer. She could only look at him mutely, the anguish showing plainly in her eyes.

Gently, firmly, he took her hand. "Excuse us, guys," he said to the others. "The lady and I are going for a walk."

Outside, leaves blew across the brown winter lawn. They walked beneath a row of oak trees, through patches of sun and shadow. Suddenly he stopped and pulled her around to face him.

"Tell me now," he said. "What gave you this crazy idea of leaving?"

She looked down. "I didn't think it made much difference to you."

"Wouldn't make a *difference?* Cathy, I was climbing the walls! Thinking of ways to get out of that hotel room and back to you! You have no idea how I worried. I wondered if you were safe—if this whole crazy mess was really over. The lawyers wouldn't let me call out, not until the hearings were finished. I did manage to sneak out and call Milo's house. No one answered."

"We were probably here, visiting Sam."

"And I was going crazy. They had me answering the same damn questions over and over again. And all I could think of was how much I missed you." He shook his head. "First chance I got, I flew the coop. And got snowed in for hours in Chicago. But I made it. I'm here. Just in time, it seems." Gently he took her by the shoulders. "Now. Tell me. Are you still flying off to Jack?"

"I'm not leaving for Jack. I'm leaving for *myself.* Because I know this won't work."

"Cathy, after what we've been through together, we can make *anything* work."

"Not—not this."

Slowly he let his hands drop, but his gaze remained on her face. "That night we made love," he said softly. "That didn't tell you something?"

"But it wasn't *me* you were making love to! You were thinking of Lily—"

"*Lily?*" He shook his head in bewilderment. "Where does she come in?"

"You loved her so much—"

"And you loved Jack once. Remember?"

"I fell out of love. You never did. No matter how much I try, I'll never measure up to her. I won't be smart enough or kind enough—"

"Cathy, stop."

"I won't be *her.*"

"I don't want you to be her! I want the woman who'll hang off fire escapes with me and—and drag me off the side of the road. I want the woman who saved my life. The woman who calls herself average. The woman who doesn't know just how extraordinary she really is." He took her face in his hands and tilted it up to his. "Yes, Lily was a wonderful woman. She was wise and kind and caring. But she wasn't you. And she and I—we weren't the perfect couple. I used to think it was my fault, that if I were just a better lover—"

"You're a wonderful lover, Victor."

"No. Don't you see, it's *you.* You bring it out in me. All the want and need." He pulled her face close to his and his voice dropped to a whisper. "When you and I made love that night, it was like the very first time for me. No, it was even better. Because I loved you."

"And I loved you," she whispered.

He pulled her into his arms and kissed her, his fingers burrowing deep into her hair. "Cathy, Cathy," he murmured. "We've been so busy trying to stay alive we haven't had time to say all the things we should have. . . ."

His arms suddenly stiffened as a startling round of applause erupted above them. They looked up. Three grinning faces peered down at them from a hospital balcony.

"Hit it, boys!" yelled Ollie.

A clarinet, piccolo and kazoo screeched into concert. The melody was doubtful. Still, Cathy thought she recognized the familiar strains of George Gershwin. "Someone to Watch Over Me."

Victor groaned. "I say we try this again, but with a different band. And no audience."

She laughed. "Mexico?"

"Definitely." He grabbed her hand and pulled her toward a taxi idling at the curb.

"But, Victor!" she protested. "What about our luggage? All my clothes—"

He cut her off with another kiss, one that left her dizzy and breathless and starved for more.

"Forget the luggage," she whispered. "Forget everything." Let's just go. . . ."

They climbed into the taxi. That's when the band on the hospital balcony abruptly switched to a new melody, one Cathy didn't at first recognize. Then, out of the muddy strains, the kazoo screeched out a solo that, for a few notes, was perfectly in tune. They were playing *Tannhäuser.* Wedding music!

"What the hell's that terrible noise?" asked the taxi driver.

"Music," said Victor, grinning down at Cathy. "The most beautiful music in the world."

She fell into his arms, and he held her there.

The taxi pulled away from the curb. But even as they drove away, even as they left the hospital far behind them, they thought they could hear it in the distance: the sound of Sam Polowski's kazoo, playing one last fading note of farewell.

NEVER SAY DIE

Prologue

1970

Laos–North Vietnam border

Thirty miles out of Muong Sam, they saw the first tracers slash the sky.

Pilot William "Wild Bill" Maitland felt the DeHavilland Twin Otter buck like a filly as they took a hit somewhere back in the fuselage. He pulled into a climb, instinctively opting for the safety of altitude. As the misty mountains dropped away beneath them, a new round of tracers streaked past, splattering the cockpit with flak.

"Damn it, Kozy. You're bad luck," Maitland muttered to his copilot. "Seems like every time we go up together, I taste lead."

Kozlowski went right on chomping his wad of bubble gum. "What's to worry?" he drawled, nodding at the shattered windshield. "Missed ya by at least two inches."

"Try one inch."

"Big difference."

"One extra inch can make a *hell* of a lot of difference."

Kozy laughed and looked out the window. "Yeah, that's what my wife tells me."

The door to the cockpit swung open. Valdez, the cargo kicker, his shoulders bulky with a parachute pack, stuck his head in. "What the hell's goin' on any—" He froze as another tracer spiraled past.

"Got us some mighty big mosquitoes out there," Kozlowski said and blew a huge pink bubble.

"What was that?" asked Valdez. "AK-47?"

"Looks more like .57-millimeter," said Maitland.

"They didn't say nothin' about no .57s. What kind of briefing did we get, anyway?"

Kozlowski shrugged. "Only the best your tax dollars can buy."

"How's our 'cargo' holding up?" Maitland asked. "Pants still dry?"

Valdez leaned forward and confided, "Man, we got us one weird passenger back there."

"So what's new?" Kozlowski said.

"I mean, this one's *really* strange. Got flak flyin' all 'round and he doesn't bat an eye. Just sits there like he's floatin' on some lily pond. You should see the medallion he's got 'round his neck. Gotta weigh at least a kilo."

"Come on," said Kozlowski.

"I'm tellin' you, Kozy, he's got a kilo of gold hangin' around that fat little neck of his. Who is he?"

"Some Lao VIP," said Maitland.

"That all they told you?"

"I'm just the delivery boy. Don't need to know any more than that." Maitland leveled the DeHavilland off at eight thousand feet. Glancing back through the open cockpit doorway, he caught sight of their lone passenger sitting placidly among the jumble of supply crates. In the dim cabin, the Lao's face gleamed like burnished mahogany. His eyes were closed, and his lips were moving silently. In prayer? wondered Maitland. Yes, the man was definitely one of their more interesting cargoes.

Not that Maitland hadn't carried strange passengers before. In his ten years with Air America, he'd transported German shepherds and generals, gibbons and girlfriends. And he'd fly them anywhere they had to go. If hell had a landing strip, he liked to say, he'd take them there—as long as they had a ticket. Anything, anytime, anywhere, was the rule at Air America.

"Song Ma River," said Kozlowski, glancing down through the fingers of mist at the lush jungle floor. "Lot of cover. If they got any more .57s in place, we're gonna have us a hard landing."

"Gonna be a hard landing anyhow," said Maitland, taking stock of the velvety green ridges on either side of them. The valley was narrow; he'd have to swoop in fast and low. It was a hellishly short landing strip, nothing but a pin scratch in the jungle, and there was always the chance of an unreported gun emplacement. But the orders were to drop the Lao VIP, whoever he was, just inside North Vietnamese territory. No return pickup had been scheduled; it sounded to Maitland like a one-way trip to oblivion.

"Heading down in a minute," he called over his shoulder to Valdez. "Get the passenger ready. He's gonna have to hit the ground running."

"He says that crate goes with him."

"What? I didn't hear anything about a crate."

"They loaded it on at the last minute. Right after we took on supplies for Nam Tha. Pretty heavy sucker. I might need some help."

Kozlowski resignedly unbuckled his seatbelt. "Okay," he said with a sigh. "But remember, I don't get paid for kickin' crates."

Maitland laughed. "What the hell *do* you get paid for?"

"Oh, lots of things," Kozlowski said lazily, ducking past Valdez and through the cockpit door. "Eatin'. Sleepin'. Tellin' dirty jokes—"

His last words were cut off by a deafening blast that shattered Maitland's eardrums. The explosion sent Kozlowski—or what was left of Kozlowski—flying backward into the cockpit. Blood spattered the control panel, obscuring the altimeter dial. But Maitland didn't need the altimeter to tell him they were going down fast.

"Kozy!" screamed Valdez, staring down at the remains of the copilot. *"Kozy!"*

His words were almost lost in the howling maelstrom of wind. The DeHavilland shuddered, a wounded bird fighting to stay aloft. Maitland, wrestling with the controls, knew immediately that he'd lost hydraulics. The best he could hope for was a belly flop on the jungle canopy.

He glanced back to survey the damage and saw, through a swirling cloud of debris, the bloodied body of the Lao passenger, thrown against the crates. He also saw sunlight shining through oddly twisted steel, glimpsed blue sky and clouds where the cargo door should have been. What the hell? Had the blast come from *inside* the plane?

He screamed to Valdez, "Bail out!"

The cargo kicker didn't respond; he was still staring in horror at Kozlowski.

Maitland gave him a shove. "Get the hell *out* of here!"

Valdez at last reacted. He stumbled out of the cockpit and into the morass of broken crates and rent metal. At the gaping cargo door he paused. "Maitland?" he yelled over the wind's shriek.

Their gazes met, and in that split second, they knew. They both knew. It was the last time they'd see each other alive.

"I'll be out!" Maitland shouted. *"Go!"*

Valdez backed up a few steps. Then he launched himself out the cargo door.

Maitland didn't glance back to see if Valdez's parachute had opened; he had other things to worry about.

The plane was sputtering into a dive.

Even as he reached for his harness release, he knew his luck had run out. He had neither the time nor the altitude to struggle into his parachute. He'd never believed in wearing one anyway. Strapping it on was like admitting you didn't trust your skill as a pilot, and Maitland knew—everyone knew—that he was the best.

Calmly he refastened his harness and grasped the controls. Through the shattered cockpit window he watched the jungle floor, lush and green and heartwrenchingly beautiful, swoop up to meet him. Somehow he'd always known it would end this way: the wind whistling through his crippled plane, the ground rushing toward him, his hands gripping the controls. This time he wouldn't be walking away. . . .

It was startling, this sudden recognition of his own mortality. An astonishing thought. *I'm going to die.*

And astonishment was exactly what he felt as the DeHavilland sliced into the treetops.

Vientiane, Laos

At 1900 hours the report came in that Air America Flight 5078 had vanished.

In the Operations Room of the U.S. Army Liaison, Colonel Joseph Kistner and his colleagues from Central and Defense Intelligence greeted the news with shocked silence. Had their operation, so carefully conceived, so vital to U.S. interests, met with disaster?

Colonel Kistner immediately demanded confirmation.

The command at Air America provided the details. Flight 5078, due in Nam Tha at 1500 hours, had never arrived. A search of the presumed flight path—carried on until darkness intervened—had revealed no sign of wreckage. But flak had been reported heavy near the border, and .57-millimeter gun emplacements were noted just out of Muong Sam. To make things worse, the terrain was mountainous, the weather unpredictable and the number of alternative nonhostile landing strips limited.

It was a reasonable assumption that Flight 5078 had been shot down.

Grim acceptance settled on the faces of the men gathered around the table. Their brightest hope had just perished aboard a doomed plane. They looked at Kistner and awaited his decision.

"Resume the search at daybreak," he said.

"That'd be throwing away live men after dead," said the CIA officer. "Come on, gentlemen. We all know that crew's gone."

Cold-blooded bastard, thought Kistner. But as always, he was right. The colonel gathered together his papers and rose to his feet. "It's not the men we're searching for," he said. "It's the wreckage. I want it located."

"And then what?"

Kistner snapped his briefcase shut. "We melt it."

The CIA officer nodded in agreement. No one argued the point. The operation had met with disaster. There was nothing more to be done.

Except destroy the evidence.

1

Present

Bangkok, Thailand

General Joe Kistner did not sweat, a fact that utterly amazed Willy Jane Maitland, since she herself seemed to be sweating through her sensible cotton underwear, through her sleeveless chambray blouse, all the way through her wrinkled twill skirt. Kistner looked like the sort of man who ought to be sweating rivers in this heat. He had a fiercely ruddy complexion, bulldog jowls, a nose marbled with spidery red veins, and a neck so thick, it strained to burst free of his crisp military collar. *Every inch the blunt, straight-talking, tough old soldier,* she thought. *Except for the eyes. They're uneasy. Evasive.*

Those eyes, a pale, chilling blue, were now gazing across the veranda. In the distance the lush Thai hills seemed to steam in the afternoon heat. "You're on a fool's errand, Miss Maitland," he said. "It's been twenty years. Surely you agree your father is dead."

"My mother's never accepted it. She needs a body to bury, General."

Kistner sighed. "Of course. The wives. It's always the wives. There were so many widows, one tends to forget—"

"*She* hasn't forgotten."

"I'm not sure what I can tell you. What I ought to tell you." He turned to her, his pale eyes targeting her face. "And really, Miss Maitland, what purpose does this serve? Except to satisfy your curiosity?"

That irritated her. It made her mission seem trivial, and there were few things Willy resented more than being made to feel insignificant. Especially by a puffed up, flat-topped warmonger. Rank didn't impress her, certainly not after all the military stuffed shirts she'd met in the past few months. They'd all expressed their sympathy, told her they couldn't help her and proceeded to brush off her questions. But Willy wasn't a woman to be stonewalled. She'd chip away at their silence until they'd either answer her or kick her out.

Lately, it seemed, she'd been kicked out of quite a few offices.

"This matter is for the Casualty Resolution Committee," said Kistner. "They're the proper channel to go—"

"They say they can't help me."

"Neither can I."

"We both know you can."

There was a pause. Softly, he asked, "Do we?"

She leaned forward, intent on claiming the advantage. "I've done my homework, General. I've written letters, talked to dozens of people—everyone who had anything to do with that last mission. And whenever I mention Laos or Air America or Flight 5078, your name keeps popping up."

He gave her a faint smile. "How nice to be remembered."

"I heard you were the military attaché in Vientiane. That your office commissioned my father's last flight. And that you personally ordered that final mission."

"Where did you hear *that* rumor?"

"My contacts at Air America. Dad's old buddies. I'd call them a reliable source."

Kistner didn't respond at first. He was studying her as carefully as he would a battle plan. "I may have issued such an order," he conceded.

"Meaning you don't remember?"

"Meaning it's something I'm not at liberty to discuss. This is classified information. What happened in Laos is an extremely sensitive topic."

"We're not discussing military secrets here. The war's been over for fifteen years!"

Kistner fell silent, surprised by her vehemence. Given her unassuming size, it was especially startling. Obviously Willy Maitland, who stood five-two, tops, in her bare feet, could be as scrappy as any six-foot marine, and she wasn't afraid to fight. From the minute she'd walked onto his veranda, her shoulders squared, her jaw angled stubbornly, he'd known this was not a woman to be ignored. She reminded him of that old Eisenhower chestnut, "It's not the size of the dog in the fight but the size of the fight in the dog." Three wars, fought in Japan, Korea and Nam, had taught Kistner never to underestimate the enemy.

He wasn't about to underestimate Wild Bill Maitland's daughter, either.

He shifted his gaze across the wide veranda to the brilliant green mountains. In a wrought-iron birdcage, a macaw screeched out a defiant protest.

At last Kistner began to speak. "Flight 5078 took off from Vientiane with a crew of three—your father, a cargo kicker and a copilot. Sometime during the flight, they diverted across North Vietnamese territory, where we assume they were shot down by enemy fire. Only the cargo kicker, Luis Valdez, managed to bail out. He was immediately captured by the North Vietnamese. Your father was never found."

"That doesn't mean he's dead. Valdez survived—"

"I'd hardly call the man's outcome 'survival.' "

They paused, a momentary silence for the man who'd endured five years as a POW, only to be shattered by his return to civilization. Luis Valdez had returned home on a Saturday and shot himself on Sunday.

"You left something out, General," said Willy. "I've heard there was a passenger. . . ."

"Oh. Yes," said Kistner, not missing a beat. "I'd forgotten."

"Who was he?"

Kistner shrugged. "A Lao. His name's not important."

"Was he with Intelligence?"

"That information, Miss Maitland, is classified." He looked away, a gesture that told her the subject of the Lao was definitely off-limits. "After the plane went down," he continued, "we mounted a search. But the ground fire was hot. And it became clear that if anyone *had* survived, they'd be in enemy hands."

"So you left them there."

"We don't believe in throwing lives away, Miss Maitland. That's what a rescue operation would've been. Throwing live men after dead."

Yes, she could see his reasoning. He was a military tactician, not given to sentimentality. Even now, he sat ramrod straight in his chair, his eyes calmly surveying the verdant hills surrounding his villa, as though eternally in search of some enemy.

"We never found the crash site," he continued. "But that jungle could swallow up anything. All that mist and smoke hanging over the valleys. The trees so thick, the ground never sees the light of day. But you'll get a feeling for it yourself soon enough. When are you leaving for Saigon?"

"Tomorrow morning."

"And the Vietnamese have agreed to discuss this matter?"

"I didn't tell them my reason for coming. I was afraid I might not get the visa."

"A wise move. They aren't fond of controversy. What *did* you tell them?"

"That I'm a plain old tourist." She shook her head and laughed. "I'm on the deluxe private tour. Six cities in two weeks."

"That's what one has to do in Asia. You don't confront the issues. You dance around them." He looked at his watch, a clear signal that the interview had come to an end.

They rose to their feet. As they shook hands, she felt him give her one last, appraising look. His grip was brisk and matter-of-fact, exactly what she expected from an old war dog.

"Good luck, Miss Maitland," he said with a nod of dismissal. "I hope you find what you're looking for."

He turned to look off at the mountains. That's when she noticed for the first time that tiny beads of sweat were glistening like diamonds on his forehead.

General Kistner watched as the woman, escorted by a servant, walked back toward the house. He was uneasy. He remembered Wild Bill Maitland only too clearly, and the daughter was very much like him. There would be trouble.

He went to the tea table and rang a silver bell. The tinkling drifted across the expanse of veranda, and seconds later, Kistner's secretary appeared.

"Has Mr. Barnard arrived?" Kistner asked.

"He has been waiting for half an hour," the man replied.

"And Ms. Maitland's driver?"

"I sent him away, as you directed."

"Good." Kistner nodded. "Good."

"Shall I bring Mr. Barnard in to see you?"

"No. Tell him I'm canceling my appointments. Tomorrow's, as well."

The secretary frowned. "He will be quite annoyed."

"Yes, I imagine he will be," said Kistner as he turned and headed toward his office. "But that's his problem."

A Thai servant in a crisp white jacket escorted Willy through an echoing, cathedral-like hall to the reception room. There he stopped and gave her a politely questioning look. "You wish me to call a car?" he asked.

"No, thank you. My driver will take me back."

The servant looked puzzled. "But your driver left some time ago."

"He couldn't have!" She glanced out the window in annoyance. "He was supposed to wait for—"

"Perhaps he is parked in the shade beyond the trees. I will go and look."

Through the French windows, Willy watched as the servant skipped gracefully down the steps to the road. The estate was vast and lushly planted; a car could very well be hidden in that jungle. Just beyond the driveway, a gardener clipped a hedge of jasmine. A neatly graveled path traced a route across the lawn to a tree-shaded garden of flowers and stone benches. And in the far distance, a fairy blue haze seemed to hang over the city of Bangkok.

The sound of a masculine throat being cleared caught her attention. She turned and for the first time noticed the man standing in a far corner of the reception room. He cocked his head in a casual acknowledgment of her presence. She caught a glimpse of a crooked grin, a stray lock of brown hair drooping over a tanned forehead. Then he turned his attention back to the antique tapestry on the wall.

Strange. He didn't look like the sort of man who'd be interested in moth-eaten embroidery. A patch of sweat had soaked through the back of his khaki shirt, and his sleeves were shoved up carelessly to his elbows. His trousers looked as if they'd been slept in for a week. A briefcase, stamped U.S. Army ID Lab, sat on the floor beside him, but he didn't strike her as the military type. There was certainly nothing disciplined about his posture. He'd seem more at home slouching at a bar somewhere instead of cooling his heels in General Kistner's marble reception room.

"Miss Maitland?"

The servant was back, shaking his head apologetically. "There must have been a misunderstanding. The gardener says your driver returned to the city."

"Oh, no." She looked out the window in frustration. "How do I get back to Bangkok?"

"Perhaps General Kistner's driver can take you back? He has gone up the road to make a delivery, but he should return very soon. If you wish, you can see the garden in the meantime."

"Yes. Yes, I suppose that'd be nice."

The servant, smiling proudly, opened the door. "It is a very famous garden. General Kistner is known for his collection of dendrobiums. You will find them at the end of the path, near the carp pond."

She stepped out into the steam bath of late afternoon and started down the gravel path. Except for the *clack-clack* of the gardener's hedge clippers, the day was absolutely still. She headed toward a stand of trees. But halfway across the lawn she suddenly stopped and looked back at the house.

At first all she saw was sunlight glaring off the marble facade. Then she focused on the first floor and saw the figure of a man standing at one of the windows. The servant, perhaps?

Turning, she continued along the path. But every step of the way, she was acutely aware that someone was watching her.

Guy Barnard stood at the French windows and observed the woman cross the lawn to the garden. He liked the way the sunlight seemed to dance in her clipped, honey-colored hair. He also liked the way she moved, the coltish swing of her walk. Methodically, his gaze slid down, over the sleeveless blouse and the skirt with its regrettably sensible hemline, taking in the essentials. Trim waist. Sweet hips. Nice calves. Nice ankles. Nice . . .

He reluctantly cut off that disturbing train of thought. This was not a good time to be distracted. Still, he couldn't help one last appreciative glance at the diminutive figure. Okay, so she was a touch on the scrawny side. But she had great legs. Definitely great legs.

Footsteps clipped across the marble floor. Guy turned and saw Kistner's secretary, an unsmiling Thai with a beardless face.

"Mr. Barnard?" said the secretary. "Our apologies for the delay. But an urgent matter has come up."

"Will he see me now?"

The secretary shifted uneasily. "I am afraid—"

"I've been waiting since three."

"Yes, I understand. But there is a problem. It seems General Kistner cannot meet with you as planned."

"May I remind you that I didn't request this meeting. General Kistner did."

"Yes, but—"

"I've taken time out of *my* busy schedule—" he took the liberty of exaggeration "—to drive all the way out here, and—"

"I understand, but—"

"At least tell me why he insisted on this appointment."

"You will have to ask him."

Guy, who up till now had kept his irritation in check, drew himself up straight. Though he wasn't a particularly tall man, he stood a full head taller than the secretary. "Is this how the general normally conducts business?"

The secretary merely shrugged. "I am sorry, Mr. Barnard. The change was entirely unexpected. . . ." His gaze shifted momentarily and focused on something beyond the French windows.

Guy followed the man's gaze. Through the glass, he saw what the man was looking at: the woman with the honey-colored hair.

The secretary shuffled his feet, a signal that he had other duties to attend to. "I assure you, Mr. Barnard," he said, "if you call in a few days, we will arrange another appointment."

Guy snatched up his briefcase and headed for the door. "In a few days," he said, "I'll be in Saigon."

A whole afternoon wasted, he thought in disgust as he walked down the front steps. He swore again as he reached the empty driveway. His car was parked a good hundred yards away, in the shade of a poinciana tree. The driver was nowhere to be seen. Knowing Puapong, the man was probably off flirting with the gardener's daughter.

Resignedly Guy trudged toward the car. The sun was like a broiler, and waves of heat radiated from the gravel road. Halfway to the car, he happened to glance at the garden, and he spotted the honey-haired woman, sitting on a stone bench. She looked dejected. No wonder; it was a long drive back to town, and Lord only knew when her ride would turn up.

What the hell, he thought, starting toward her. He could use some company.

She seemed to be deep in thought; she didn't look up until he was standing right beside her.

"Hi there," he said.

She squinted up at him. "Hello." Her greeting was neutral, neither friendly nor unfriendly.

"Did I hear you needed a lift back to town?"

"I have one, thank you."

"It could be a long wait. And I'm heading there anyway." She didn't respond, so he added, "It's really no trouble."

She gave him a speculative look. She had silver-gray eyes, direct, unflinching; they seemed to stare right through him. No shrinking violet, this one. Glancing back at the house, she said, "Kistner's driver was going to take me. . . ."

"I'm here. He isn't."

Again she gave him that look, a silent third degree. She must have decided he was okay, because she finally rose to her feet. "Thanks. I'd appreciate it."

Together they walked the graveled road to his car. As they approached, Guy noticed a back door was wide open and a pair of dirty brown feet poked out. His driver was sprawled across the seat like a corpse.

The woman halted, staring at the lifeless form. "Oh, my God. He's not—"

A blissful snore rumbled from the car.

"He's not," said Guy. "Hey. Puapong!" He banged on the car roof.

The man's answering rumble could have drowned out thunder.

"Hello, Sleeping Beauty!" Guy banged the car again. "You gonna wake up, or do I have to kiss you first?"

"What? What?" groaned a voice. Puapong stirred and opened one bloodshot eye. "Hey, boss. You back so soon?"

"Have a nice nap?" Guy asked pleasantly.

"Not bad."

Guy graciously gestured for Puapong to vacate the back seat. "Look, I hate to be a pest, but do you mind? I've offered this lady a ride."

Puapong crawled out, stumbled around sleepily to the driver's seat and sank behind the wheel. He shook his head a few times, then fished around on the floor for the car keys.

The woman was looking more and more dubious. "Are you sure he can drive?" she muttered under her breath.

"This man," said Guy, "has the reflexes of a cat. When he's sober."

"Is he sober?"

"Puapong! Are you sober?"

With injured pride, the driver asked, "Don't I look sober?"

"There's your answer," said Guy.

The woman sighed. "That makes me feel *so* much better." She glanced back longingly at the house. The Thai servant had appeared on the steps and was waving good-bye.

Guy motioned for the woman to climb in. "It's a long drive back to town."

She was silent as they drove down the winding mountain road. Though they both sat in the back seat, two feet apart at the most, she seemed a million miles away. She kept her gaze focused on the scenery.

"You were in with the general quite a while," he noted.

She nodded. "I had a lot of questions."

"You a reporter?"

"What?" She looked at him. "Oh, no. It was just . . . some old family business."

He waited for her to elaborate, but she turned back to the window.

"Must've been some pretty important family business," he said.

"Why do you say that?"

"Right after you left, he canceled all his appointments. Mine included."

"You didn't get in to see him?"

"Never got past the secretary. And Kistner's the one who asked to see *me.*"

She frowned for a moment, obviously puzzled. Then she shrugged. "I'm sure I had nothing to do with it."

And I'm just as sure you did, he thought in sudden irritation. Lord, why was the woman making him so antsy? She was sitting perfectly still, but he got the distinct feeling a hurricane was churning in that pretty head. He'd decided that she *was* pretty after all, in a no-nonsense sort of way. She was smart not to use any makeup; it would only cheapen that girl-next-door face. He'd never before had any interest in the girl-next-door type. Maybe the girl down the street or across the tracks. But this one was different. She had eyes the color of smoke, a square jaw and a little boxer's nose, lightly dusted with freckles. She also had a mouth that, given the right situation, could be quite kissable.

Automatically he asked, "So how long will you be in Bangkok?"

"I've been here two days already. I'm leaving tomorrow."

Damn, he thought.

"For Saigon."

His chin snapped up in surprise. "Saigon?"

"Or Ho Chi Minh City. Whatever they call it these days."

"Now that's a coincidence," he said softly.

"What is?"

"In two days, *I'm* leaving for Saigon."

"Are you?" She glanced at the briefcase, stenciled with U.S. Army ID Lab, lying on the seat. "Government affairs?"

He nodded. "What about you?"

She looked straight ahead. "Family business."

"Right," he said, wondering what the hell business her family was in. "You ever been to Saigon?"

"Once. But I was only ten years old."

"Dad in the service?"

"Sort of." Her gaze stayed fixed on some faraway point ahead. "I don't remember too much of the city. Lot of dust and heat and cars. One big traffic jam. And the beautiful women . . ."

"It's changed a lot since then. Most of the cars are gone."

"And the beautiful women?"

He laughed. "Oh, they're still around. Along with the heat and dust. But everything else has changed." He was silent a moment. Then, almost as an afterthought, he added, "If you get stuck, I might be able to show you around."

She hesitated, obviously tempted by his invitation. *Come on, come on, take me up on it,* he thought. Then he caught a glimpse of Puapong, grinning and winking wickedly at him in the rearview mirror.

He only hoped the woman hadn't noticed.

But Willy most certainly *had* seen Puapong's winks and grins and had instantly comprehended the meaning. *Here we go again,* she thought wearily. *Now he'll ask me if I want to have dinner and I'll say no I can't, and then he'll say, what about a drink? and I'll break down and say yes because he's such a damnably good-looking man. . . .*

"Look, I happen to be free tonight," he said. "Would you like to have dinner?"

"I can't," she said, wondering who had written this tired script and how one ever broke out of it.

"Then how about a drink?" He shot her a half smile and she felt herself teetering at the edge of a very high cliff. The crazy part was, he really *wasn't* a handsome man at all. His nose was crooked, as if, after managing to get it broken, he hadn't bothered to set it back in place. His hair was in need of a barber or at least a comb. She guessed he was somewhere in his late thirties, though the years scarcely showed except around his eyes, where deep laugh lines creased the corners. No, she'd seen far better-looking men. Men who offered more than a sweaty one-night grope in a foreign hotel.

So why is this guy getting to me?

"Just a drink?" he offered again.

"Thanks," she said. "But no thanks."

To her relief, he didn't press the issue. He nodded, sat back and looked out the window. His fingers drummed the briefcase. The mindless rhythm drove her crazy. She tried to ignore him, just as he was trying to ignore her, but it was hopeless. He was too imposing a presence.

By the time they pulled up at the Oriental Hotel, she was ready to leap out of the car. She practically did.

"Thanks for the ride," she said, and slammed the door shut.

"Hey, wait!" called the man through the open window.

"I never caught your name!"

"Willy."

"You have a last name?"

She turned and started up the hotel steps. "Maitland," she said over her shoulder.

"See you around, Willy Maitland!" the man yelled.

Not likely, she thought. But as she reached the lobby doors, she couldn't help glancing back and watching the car disappear around the corner. That's when she realized she didn't even know the man's name.

Guy sat on his bed in the Liberty Hotel and wondered what had compelled him to check into this dump. Nostalgia, maybe. Plus cheap government rates. He'd always stayed here on his trips to Bangkok, ever since the war, and he'd never seen the need for a change until now. Certainly the place held a lot of memories. He'd never forget those hot, lusty nights of 1973. He'd been a twenty-year-old private on R and R; she'd been a thirty-year-old army nurse. Darlene. Yeah, that was her name. The last he'd seen of her, she was a chain-smoking mother of three and about fifty pounds overweight. What a shame. The woman, like the hotel, had definitely gone downhill.

Maybe I have, too, he thought wearily as he stared out the dirty window at the streets of Bangkok. How he used to love this city, loved the days of wandering through the markets, where the colors were so bright they hurt the eyes; loved the nights of prowling the back streets of Pat Pong, where the music and the girls never quit. Nothing bothered him in those days—not the noise or the heat or the smells.

Not even the bullets. He'd felt immune, immortal. It was always the *other* guy who caught the bullet, the other guy who got shipped home in a box. And if you thought otherwise, if you worried too long and hard about your own mortality, you made a lousy soldier.

Eventually, he'd become a lousy soldier.

He was still astonished that he'd survived. It was something he'd never fully understand: the simple fact that he'd made it back alive.

Especially when he thought of all the other men on that transport plane out of Da Nang. Their ticket home, the magic bird that was supposed to deliver them from all the madness.

He still had the scars from the crash. He still harbored a mortal dread of flying.

He refused to think about that upcoming flight to Saigon. Air travel, unfortunately, was part of his job, and this was just one more plane he couldn't avoid.

He opened his briefcase, took out a stack of folders and lay down on the bed to read. The file he opened first was one of dozens he'd brought with him from Honolulu. Each contained a name, rank, serial

number, photograph and a detailed history—as detailed as possible—
of the circumstances of disappearance. This one was a naval airman,
Lieutenant Commander Eugene Stoddard, last seen ejecting from his
disabled bomber forty miles west of Hanoi. Included was a dental chart
and an old X-ray report of an arm fracture sustained as a teenager.
What the file left out were the nonessentials: the wife he'd left behind,
the children, the questions.

There were always questions when a soldier was missing in action.

Guy skimmed the pages, made a few mental notes and reached for
another file. These were the most likely cases, the men whose stories
best matched the newest collection of remains. The Vietnamese government was turning over three sets, and Guy's job was to confirm the
skeletons were non-Vietnamese and to give each one a name, rank and
serial number. It wasn't a particularly pleasant job, but one that had to
be done.

He set aside the second file and reached for the next.

This one didn't contain a photograph; it was a supplementary file,
one he'd reluctantly added to his briefcase at the last minute. The
cover was stamped Confidential, then, a year ago, restamped Declassified. He opened the file and frowned at the first page.

Code Name: Friar Tuck
Status: Open (Current as of 10/85)
File Contains:
  1. Summary of Witness Reports
  2. Possible Identities
  3. Search Status

Friar Tuck. A legend known to every soldier who'd fought in Nam.
During the war, Guy had assumed those tales of a rogue American
pilot flying for the enemy were mere fantasy.

Then, a few weeks ago, he'd learned otherwise.

He'd been at his desk at the Army Lab when two men, representatives of an organization called the Ariel Group, had appeared in his
office. "We have a proposition," they'd said. "We know you're visiting
Nam soon, and we want you to look for a war criminal." The man they
were seeking was Friar Tuck.

"You've got to be kidding." Guy had laughed. "I'm not a military
cop. And there's no such man. He's a fairy tale."

In answer, they'd handed him a twenty-thousand-dollar check—"for
expenses," they'd said. There'd be more to come if he brought the
traitor back to justice.

"And if I don't want the job?" he'd asked.

"You can hardly refuse" was their answer. Then they'd told Guy exactly what they knew about him, about his past, the thing he'd done in the war. A brutal secret that could destroy him, a secret he'd kept hidden away behind a wall of fear and self-loathing. They told him exactly what he could expect if it came to light. The hard glare of publicity. The trial. The jail cell.

They had him cornered. He took the check and awaited the next contact.

The day before he left Honolulu, this file had arrived special delivery from Washington. Without looking at it, he'd slipped it into his brief-case.

Now he read it for the first time, pausing at the page listing possible identities. Several names he recognized from his stack of MIA files, and it struck him as unfair, this list. These men were missing in action and probably dead; to brand them as possible traitors was an insult to their memories.

One by one, he went over the names of those voiceless pilots suspected of treason. Halfway down the list, he stopped, focusing on the entry "William T. Maitland, pilot, Air America." Beside it was an asterisk and, below, the footnote: "Refer to File #M-70-4163, Defense Intelligence. (Classified.)"

William T. Maitland, he thought, trying to remember where he'd heard the name. Maitland, Maitland.

Then he thought of the woman at Kistner's villa, the little blonde with the magnificent legs. I'm here on family business, she'd said. For that she'd consulted General Joe Kistner, a man whose connections to Defense Intelligence were indisputable.

See you around, Willy Maitland.

It was too much of a coincidence. And yet . . .

He went back to the first page and reread the file on Friar Tuck, beginning to end. The section on Search Status he read twice. Then he rose from the bed and began to pace the room, considering his options. Not liking any of them.

He didn't believe in using people. But the stakes were sky-high, and they were deeply, intensely personal. *How many men have their own little secrets from the war?* he wondered. *Secrets we can't talk about? Secrets that could destroy us?*

He closed the file. The information in this folder wasn't enough; he needed the woman's help.

But am I cold-blooded enough to use her?

Can I afford not to? whispered the voice of necessity.

It was an awful decision to make. But he had no choice.

It was 5:00 p.m., and the Bong Bong Club was not yet in full swing. Up onstage, three women, bodies oiled and gleaming, writhed together like a trio of snakes. Music blared from an old stereo speaker, a relentlessly primitive beat that made the very darkness shudder.

From his favorite corner table, Siang watched the action, the men sipping drinks, the waitresses dangling after tips. Then he focused on the stage, on the girl in the middle. She was special. Lush hips, meaty thighs, a pink, carnivorous tongue. He couldn't define what it was about her eyes, but she had *that look.* The numeral 7 was pinned on her G-string. He would have to inquire later about number seven.

"Good afternoon, Mr. Siang."

Siang looked up to see the man standing in the shadows. It never failed to impress him, the size of that man. Even now, twenty years after their first meeting, Siang could not help feeling he was a child in the presence of this giant.

The man ordered a beer and sat down at the table. He watched the stage for a moment. "A new act?" he asked.

"The one in the middle is new."

"Ah, yes, very nice. Your type, is she?"

"I will have to find out." Siang took a sip of whiskey, his gaze never leaving the stage. "You said you had a job for me."

"A small matter."

"I hope that does not mean a small reward."

The man laughed softly. "No, no. Have I ever been less than generous?"

"What is the name?"

"A woman." The man slid a photograph onto the table. "Her name is Willy Maitland. Thirty-two years old. Five foot two, dark blond hair cut short, gray eyes. Staying at the Oriental Hotel."

"American?"

"Yes."

Siang paused. "An unusual request."

"There is some . . . urgency."

Ah. The price goes up, thought Siang. "Why?" he asked.

"She departs for Saigon tomorrow morning. That leaves you only tonight."

Siang nodded and looked back at the stage. He was pleased to see that the girl in the middle, number seven, was looking straight at him. "That should be time enough," he said.

* * *

Willy Maitland was standing at the river's edge, staring down at the swirling water.

From across the dining terrace, Guy spotted her, a tiny figure leaning at the railing, her short hair fluffing in the wind. From the hunch of her shoulders, the determined focus of her gaze, he got the impression she wanted to be left alone. Stopping at the bar, he picked up a beer—Oranjeboom, a good Dutch brand he hadn't tasted in years. He stood there a moment, watching her, savoring the touch of the frosty bottle against his cheek.

She still hadn't moved. She just kept gazing down at the river, as though hypnotized by something she saw in the muddy depths. He moved across the terrace toward her, weaving past empty tables and chairs, and eased up beside her at the railing. He marveled at the way her hair seemed to reflect the red and gold sparks of sunset.

"Nice view," he said.

She glanced at him. One look, utterly uninterested, was all she gave him. Then she turned away.

He set his beer on the railing. "Thought I'd check back with you. See if you'd changed your mind about that drink."

She stared stubbornly at the water.

"I know how it is in a foreign city. No one to share your frustrations. I thought you might be feeling a little—"

"Give me a break," she said, and walked away.

He must be losing his touch, he thought. He snatched up his beer and followed her. Pointedly ignoring him, she strolled along the edge of the terrace, every so often flicking her hair off her face. She had a cute swing to her walk, just a little too frisky to be considered graceful.

"I think we should have dinner," he said, keeping pace. "And maybe a little conversation."

"About what?"

"Oh, we could start off with the weather. Move on to politics. Religion. My family, your family."

"I assume this is all leading up to something?"

"Well, yeah."

"Let me guess. An invitation to your room?"

"Is that what you think I'm trying to do?" he asked in a hurt voice. "Pick you up?"

"Aren't you?" she said. Then she turned and once again walked away.

This time he didn't follow her. He didn't see the point. Leaning back against the rail, he sipped his beer and watched her climb the steps to the dining terrace. There, she sat down at a table and retreated behind a menu. It was too late for tea and too early for supper. Except for a dozen boisterous Italians sitting at a nearby table, the terrace was empty. He lingered there a while, finishing off the beer, wondering what his next approach should be. Wondering if anything would work. She was a tough nut to crack, surprisingly fierce for a dame who barely came up to his shoulder. A mouse with teeth.

He needed another beer. And a new strategy. He'd think of it in a minute.

He headed up the steps, back to the bar. As he crossed the dining terrace, he couldn't help a backward glance at the woman. Those few seconds of inattention almost caused him to collide with a well-dressed Thai man moving in the opposite direction. Guy murmured an automatic apology. The other man didn't answer; he walked right on past, his gaze fixed on something ahead.

Guy took about two steps before some inner alarm went off in his head. It was pure instinct, the soldier's premonition of disaster. It had to do with the eyes of the man who'd just passed by.

He'd seen that look of deadly calm once before, in the eyes of a Vietnamese. They had brushed shoulders as Guy was leaving a popular Da Nang nightclub. For a split second their gazes had locked. Even now, years later, Guy still remembered the chill he'd felt looking into that man's eyes. Two minutes later, as Guy had stood waiting in the street for his buddies, a bomb ripped apart the building. Seventeen Americans had been killed.

Now, with a growing sense of alarm, he watched the Thai stop and survey his surroundings. The man seemed to spot what he was looking for and headed toward the dining terrace. Only two of the tables were occupied. The Italians sat at one, Willy Maitland at the other. At the edge of the terrace, the Thai paused and reached into his jacket.

Reflexively, Guy took a few steps forward. Even before his eyes registered the danger, his body was already reacting. Something glittered in the man's hand, an object that caught the bloodred glare of sunset. Only then could Guy rationally acknowledge what his instincts had warned him was about to happen.

He screamed, "Willy! Watch out!"

Then he launched himself at the assassin.

2

_____

At the sound of the man's shout, Willy lowered her menu and turned. To her amazement, she saw it was the crazy American, toppling chairs as he barreled across the cocktail lounge. What was that lunatic up to now?

In disbelief, she watched him shove past a waiter and fling himself at another man, a well-dressed Thai. The two bodies collided. At the same instant, she heard something hiss through the air, felt an unexpected flick of pain in her arm. She leapt up from her chair as the two men slammed to the ground near her feet.

At the next table, the Italians were also out of their chairs, pointing and shouting. The bodies on the ground rolled over and over, toppling tables, sending sugar bowls crashing to the stone terrace. Willy was lost in utter confusion. What was happening? Why was that idiot fighting with a Thai businessman?

Both men staggered to their feet. The Thai kicked high, his heel thudding squarely into the other man's belly. The American doubled over, groaned and landed with his back propped up against the terrace wall.

The Thai vanished.

By now the Italians were hysterical.

Willy scrambled through the fallen chairs and shattered crockery and crouched at the man's side. Already a bruise the size of a golf ball had swollen his cheek. Blood trickled alarmingly from his torn lip. "Are you all right?" she cried.

He touched his cheek and winced. "I've probably looked worse."

She glanced around at the toppled furniture. "Look at this mess! I hope you have a good explanation for— What are you doing?" she demanded as he suddenly gripped her arm. "Get your hands off me!"

"You're bleeding!"

"What?" She followed the direction of his gaze and saw that a shocking blotch of red soaked her sleeve. Droplets splattered to the flagstones.

Her reaction was immediate and visceral. She swayed dizzily and sat down smack on the ground, right beside him. Through a cottony haze, she felt her head being shoved down to her knees, heard her sleeve being ripped open. Hands probed gently at her arm.

"Easy," he murmured. "It's not bad. You'll need a few stitches, that's all. Just breathe slowly."

"Get your hands off me," she mumbled. But the instant she raised her head, the whole terrace seemed to swim. She caught a watery view of mass confusion. The Italians chattering and shaking their heads. The waiters staring openmouthed in horror. And the American watching her with a look of worry. She focused on his eyes. Dazed as she was, she registered the fact that those eyes were warm and steady.

By now the hotel manager, an effete Englishman wearing an immaculate suit and an appalled expression, had appeared. The waiters pointed accusingly at Guy. The manager kept clucking and shaking his head as he surveyed the damage.

"This is dreadful," he murmured. "This sort of behavior is simply not tolerated. Not on *my* terrace. Are you a guest? You're not?" He turned to one of the waiters. "Call the police. I want this man arrested."

"Are you all blind?" yelled Guy. "Didn't any of you see he was trying to kill her?"

"What? What? Who?"

Guy poked around in the broken crockery and fished out the knife. "Not your usual cutlery," he said, holding up the deadly looking weapon. The handle was ebony, inlaid with mother of pearl. The blade was razor sharp. "This one's designed to be thrown."

"Oh, rubbish," sputtered the Englishman.

"Take a look at her arm!"

The manager turned his gaze to Willy's blood-soaked sleeve. Horrified, he took a stumbling step back. "Good God. I'll—I'll call a doctor."

"Never mind," said Guy, sweeping Willy off the ground. "It'll be faster if I take her straight to the hospital."

Willy let herself be gathered into Guy's arms. She found his scent strangely reassuring, a distinctly male mingling of sweat and after-shave. As he carried her across the terrace, she caught a swirling view of shocked waiters and curious hotel guests.

"This is embarrassing," she complained. "I'm all right. Put me down."

"You'll faint."

"I've never fainted in my life!"

"It's not a good time to start." He got her into a waiting taxi, where she curled up in the back seat like a wounded animal.

The emergency-room doctor didn't believe in anesthesia. Willy didn't believe in screaming. As the curved suture needle stabbed again and again into her arm, she clenched her teeth and longed to have the lunatic American hold her hand. If only she hadn't played tough and sent him out to the waiting area. Even now, as she fought back tears of pain, she refused to admit, even to herself, that she needed any man to hold her hand. Still, it would have been nice. It would have been wonderful.

And I still don't know his name.

The doctor, whom she suspected of harboring sadistic tendencies, took the final stitch, tied it off and snipped the silk thread. "You see?" he said cheerfully. "That wasn't so bad."

She felt like slugging him in the mouth and saying, *You see? That wasn't so bad, either.*

He dressed the wound with gauze and tape, then gave her a cheerful slap—on her wounded arm, of course—and sent her out into the waiting room.

He was still there, loitering by the reception desk. With all his bruises and cuts, he looked like a bum who'd wandered in off the street. But the look he gave her was warm and concerned. "How's the arm?" he asked.

Gingerly she touched her shoulder. "Doesn't this country believe in Novocaine?"

"Only for wimps," he observed. "Which you obviously aren't."

Outside, the night was steaming. There were no taxis available, so they hired a *tuk-tuk,* a motorcycle-powered rickshaw, driven by a toothless Thai.

"You never told me your name," she said over the roar of the engine.

"I didn't think you were interested."

"Is that my cue to get down on my knees and beg for an introduction?"

Grinning, he held out his hand. "Guy Barnard. Now do I get to hear what the Willy's short for?"

She shook his hand. "Wilone."

"Unusual. Nice."

"Short of Wilhelmina, it's as close as a daughter can get to being William Maitland, Jr."

He didn't comment, but she saw an odd flicker in his eyes, a look of sudden interest. She wondered why. The *tuk-tuk* puttered past a *klong*, its stagnant waters shimmering under the streetlights.

"Maitland," he said casually. "Now that's a name I seem to remember from the war. There was a pilot, a guy named Wild Bill Maitland. Flew for Air America. Any relation?"

She looked away. "Just my father."

"No kidding! You're Wild Bill Maitland's kid?"

"You've heard the stories about him, have you?"

"Who hasn't? He was a living legend. Right up there with Earthquake Magoon."

"That's about what he was to me, too," she muttered. "Nothing but a legend."

There was a pause in their exchange, and she wondered if Guy Barnard was shocked by the bitterness in her last statement. If so, he didn't show it.

"I never actually met your old man," he said. "But I saw him once, on the Da Nang airstrip. I was working ground crew."

"With Air America?"

"No. Army Air Cav." He sketched a careless salute. "Private First Class Barnard. You know, the real scum of the earth."

"I see you've come up in the world."

"Yeah." He laughed. "Anyway, your old man brought in a C-46, engine smoking, fuel zilch, fuselage so shot up you could almost see right through her. He sets her down on the tarmac, pretty as you please. Then he climbs out and checks out all the bullet holes. Any other pilot would've been down on his knees kissing the ground. But your dad, he just shrugs, goes over to a tree and takes a nap." Guy shook his head. "Your old man was something else."

"So everyone tells me." Willy shoved a hank of wind-blown hair off her face and wished he'd stop talking about her father. That's how it'd been, as far back as she could remember. When she was a child in Vientiane, at every dinner party, every cocktail gathering, the pilots would invariably trot out another Wild Bill story. They'd raise toasts to his nerves, his daring, his crazy humor, until she was ready to scream. All those stories only emphasized how unimportant she and her mother were in the scheme of her father's life.

Maybe that's why Guy Barnard was starting to annoy her.

But it was more than just his talk about Bill Maitland. In some odd, indefinable way, Guy reminded her too much of her father.

The *tuk-tuk* suddenly hit a bump in the road, throwing her against Guy's shoulder. Pain sliced through her arm and her whole body seemed to clench in a spasm.

He glanced at her, alarmed. "Are you all right?"

"I'm—" She bit her lip, fighting back tears. "It's really starting to hurt."

He yelled at the driver to slow down. Then he took Willy's hand and held it tightly. "Just a little while longer. We're almost there. . . ."

It was a long ride to the hotel.

Up in her room, Guy sat her down on the bed and gently stroked the hair off her face. "Do you have any painkillers?"

"There's—there's some aspirin in the bathroom." She started to rise to her feet. "I can get it."

"No. You stay right where you are." He went into the bathroom, came back out with a glass of water and the bottle of aspirin. Even through her cloud of pain, she was intensely aware of him watching her, studying her as she swallowed the tablets. Yet she found his nearness strangely reassuring. When he turned and crossed the room, the sudden distance between them left her feeling abandoned.

She watched him rummage around in the tiny refrigerator. "What are you looking for?"

"Found it." He came back with a cocktail bottle of whiskey, which he uncapped and handed to her. "Liquid anesthesia. It's an old-fashioned remedy, but it works."

"I don't like whiskey."

"You don't have to like it. By definition, medicine's not supposed to taste good."

She managed a gulp. It burned all the way down her throat. "Thanks," she muttered. "I think."

He began to walk a slow circle, surveying the plush furnishings, the expansive view. Sliding glass doors opened onto a balcony. From the Chaophya River flowing just below came the growl of motorboats plying the waters. He wandered over to the nightstand, picked up a rambutan from the complimentary fruit basket and peeled off the prickly shell. "Nice room," he said, thoughtfully chewing the fruit. "Sure beats my dive—the Liberty Hotel. What do you do for a living, anyway?"

She took another sip of whiskey and coughed. "I'm a pilot."

"Just like your old man?"

"Not exactly. I fly for the paycheck, not the excitement. Not that the pay's great. No money in flying cargo."

"Can't be too bad if you're staying here."

"I'm not paying for this."

His eyebrows shot up. "Who is?"

"My mother."

"Generous of her."

His note of cynicism irritated her. What right did he have to insult her? Here he was, this battered vagabond, eating *her* fruit, enjoying *her* view. The *tuk-tuk* ride had tossed his hair in all directions, and his bruised eye was swollen practically shut. Why was she even putting up with this jerk?

He was watching her with curiosity. "So what else is Mama paying for?" he asked.

She looked him hard in the eye. "Her own funeral arrangements," she said, and was satisfied to see his smirk instantly vanish.

"What do you mean? Is your mother dead?"

"No, but she's dying." Willy gazed out the window at the lantern lights along the river's edge. For a moment they seemed to dance like fireflies in a watery haze. She swallowed; the lights came back into focus. "God," she sighed, wearily running her fingers through her hair. "What the hell am I doing here?"

"I take it this isn't a vacation."

"You got that right."

"What is it, then?"

"A wild-goose chase." She swallowed the rest of the whiskey and set the tiny bottle down on the nightstand. "But it's Mom's last wish. And you're always supposed to grant people their dying wish." She looked at Guy. "Aren't you?"

He sank into a chair, his gaze locked on her face. "You told me before that you were here on family business. Does it have to do with your father?"

She nodded.

"And that's why you saw Kistner today?"

"We were hoping—I was hoping—that he'd be able to fill us in about what happened to Dad."

"Why go to Kistner? Casualty resolution isn't his job."

"But Military Intelligence is. In 1970, Kistner was stationed in Laos. He was the one who commissioned my father's last flight. And after the plane went down, he directed the search. What there was of a search."

"And did Kistner tell you anything new?"

"Only what I expected to hear. That after twenty years, there's no point pursuing the matter. That my father's dead. And there's no way to recover his remains."

"It must've been tough hearing that. Knowing you've come all this way for nothing."

"It'll be hard on my mother."

"And not on you?"

"Not really." She rose from the bed and wandered out onto the balcony, where she stared down at the water. "You see, I don't give a damn about my father."

The night was heavy with the smells of the river. She knew Guy was watching her; she could feel his gaze on her back, could imagine the shocked expression on his face. Of course, he would be shocked; it was appalling, what she'd just said. But it was also the truth.

She sensed, more than heard, his approach. He came up beside her and leaned against the railing. The glow of the river lanterns threw his face into shadow.

She stared down at the shimmering water. "You don't know what it's like to be the daughter of a legend. All my life, people have told me how brave he was, what a hero he was. God, he must have loved the glory."

"A lot of men do."

"And a lot of women suffer for it."

"Did your mother suffer?"

She looked up at the sky. "My mother . . ." She shook her head and laughed. "Let me tell you about my mother. She was a nightclub singer. All the best New York clubs. I went through her scrapbook, and I remember some reviewer wrote, 'Her voice spins a web that will trap any audience in its magic.' She was headed for the moon. Then she got married. She went from star billing to a—a footnote in some man's life. We lived in Vientiane for a few years. I remember what a trouper she was. She wanted so badly to go home, but there she was, scraping the store shelves for decent groceries. Laughing off the hand grenades. Dad got the glory. But she's the one who raised me." Willy looked at Guy. "That's how the world works. Isn't it?"

He didn't answer.

She turned her gaze back to the river. "After Dad's contract ended with Air America, we tried it for a while in San Francisco. He worked for a commuter airline. And Mom and I, well, we just enjoyed living in a town without mortars and grenades going off. But . . ." She sighed. "It didn't last. Dad got bored. I guess he missed the old adrenaline high. And the glory. So he went back."

"They got divorced?"

"He never asked for one. And Mom wouldn't hear of it anyway. She loved him." Willy's voice dropped. "She still loves him."

"He went back to Laos alone, huh?"

"Signed up for another two years. Guess he preferred the company of danger junkies. They were all like that, those A.A. pilots—all volunteers, not draftees—all of 'em laughing death in the face. I think flying was the only thing that gave them a rush, made them feel alive. Must've been the ultimate high for Dad. Dying."

"And here you are, over twenty years later."

"That's right. Here I am."

"Looking for a man you don't give a damn about. Why?"

"It's not me asking the questions. It's my mother. She's never wanted much. Not from me, not from anyone. But this was something she had to know."

"A dying wish."

Willy nodded. "That's the one nice thing about cancer. You get some time to tie up the loose ends. And my father is one hell of a big loose end."

"Kistner gave you the official verdict—your father's dead. Doesn't that tie things up?"

"Not after all the lies we've been told."

"Who's lied to you?"

She laughed. "Who hasn't? Believe me, we've made the rounds. We've talked to the Joint Casualty Resolution Committee. Defense Intelligence. The CIA. They all had the same advice—drop it."

"Maybe they have a point."

"Maybe they're hiding the truth."

"Which is?"

"That Dad survived the crash."

"What's your evidence?"

She studied Guy for a moment, wondering how much to tell him. Wondering why she'd already told him as much as she had. She knew nothing about him except that he had fast reflexes and a sense of humor. That his eyes were brown, and his grin distinctly crooked. And that, in his own rumpled way, he was the most attractive man she'd ever met.

That last thought was as jolting as a bolt of lightning on a clear summer's day. But he *was* attractive. There was nothing she could specifically point to that made him that way. Maybe it was his self-assurance, the confident way he carried himself. *Or maybe it's the damn whiskey,* she thought. That's why she was feeling so warm inside, why her knees felt as if they were about to buckle.

She gripped the steel railing. "My mother and I, we've had, well, *hints* that secrets have been kept from us."

"Anything concrete?"

"Would you call an eyewitness concrete?"

"Depends on the eyewitness."

"A Lao villager."

"He saw your father?"

"No, that's the whole point—he didn't."

"I'm confused."

"Right after the plane went down," she explained, "Dad's buddies printed up leaflets advertising a reward of two kilos of gold to anyone who brought in proof of the crash. The leaflets were dropped along the border and all over Pathet Lao territory. A few weeks later a villager came out of the jungle to claim the reward. He said he'd found the wreckage of a plane, that it had crashed just inside the Vietnam border. He described it right down to the number on the tail. And he swore there were only two bodies on board, one in the cargo hold, another in the cockpit. The plane had a crew of *three.*"

"What did the investigators say about that?"

"We didn't hear this from them. We learned about it only after the classified report got stuffed into our mailbox, with a note scribbled 'From a friend.' I think one of Dad's old Air America buddies got wind of a cover-up and decided to let the family know about it."

Guy was standing absolutely still, like a cat in the shadows. When he spoke, she could tell by his voice that he was very, very interested.

"What did your mother do then?" he asked.

"She pursued it, of course. She wouldn't give up. She hounded the CIA. Air America. She got nothing out of them. But she did get a few anonymous phone calls telling her to shut up."

"Or?"

"Or she'd learn things about Dad she didn't want to know. Embarrassing things."

"Other women? What?"

This was the part that made Willy angry. She could barely bring herself to talk about it. "They implied—" She let out a breath. "They implied he was working for the other side. That he was a traitor."

There was a pause. "And you don't believe it," he said softly.

Her chin shot up. "Hell, no, I don't believe it! Not a word. It was just their way to scare us off. To keep us from digging up the truth. It wasn't the only stunt they pulled. When we kept asking questions, they stopped release of Dad's back pay, which by then was somewhere in the tens of thousands. Anyway, we floundered around for a while, trying to get information. Then the war ended, and we thought we'd finally hear the answers. We watched the POWs come back. It was tough on Mom, seeing all those reunions on TV. Hearing Nixon talk about our brave men finally coming home. Because hers didn't. But we were surprised to hear of one man who did make it home—one of the crew members on Dad's plane."

Guy straightened in surprise. "Then there *was* a survivor?"

"Luis Valdez, the cargo kicker. He bailed out as the plane was going down. He was captured almost as soon as he hit the ground. Spent the next five years in a North Vietnamese prison camp."

"Doesn't that explain the missing body? If Valdez bailed out—"

"There's more. The very day Valdez flew back to the States, he called us. I answered the phone. I could hear he was scared. He'd been warned by Intelligence not to talk to anyone. But he thought he owed it to Dad to let us know what had happened. He told us there was a passenger on that flight, a Lao who was already dead when the plane went down. And that the body in the cockpit was probably Kozlowski, the copilot. That still leaves a missing body."

"Your father."

She nodded. "We went back to the CIA with this information. And you know what? They denied there was any passenger on that plane, Lao or otherwise. They said it carried only a shipment of aircraft parts."

"What did Air America say?"

"They claim there's no record of any passenger."

"But you had Valdez's testimony."

She shook her head. "The day after he called, the day he was supposed to come see us, he shot himself in the head. Suicide. Or so the police report said."

She could tell by his long silence that Guy was shocked. "How convenient," he murmured.

"For the first time in my life, I saw my mother scared. Not for herself, but for me. She was afraid of what might happen, what they might do. So she let the matter drop. Until . . ." Willy paused.

"There was something else?"

She nodded. "About a year after Valdez died—I guess it was around '76—a funny thing happened to my mother's bank account. It picked up an extra fifteen thousand dollars. All the bank could tell her was that the deposit had been made in Bangkok. A year later, it happened again, this time, around ten thousand."

"All that money, and she never found out where it came from?"

"No. All these years she's been trying to figure it out. Wondering if one of Dad's buddies, or maybe Dad himself—" Willy shook her head and sighed. "Anyway, a few months ago, she found out she had cancer. And suddenly it seemed very important to learn the truth. She's too sick to make this trip herself, so she asked me to come. And I'm hitting the same brick wall she hit twenty years ago."

"Maybe you haven't gone to the right people."

"Who *are* the right people?"

Quietly, Guy shifted toward her. "I have connections," he said softly. "I could find out for you."

Their hands brushed on the railing; Willy felt a delicious shock race through her whole arm. She pulled her hand away.

"What sort of connections?"

"Friends in the business."

"Exactly what *is* your business?"

"Body counts. Dog tags. I'm with the Army ID Lab."

"I see. You're in the military."

He laughed and leaned sideways against the railing. "No way. I bailed out after Nam. Went back to college, got a master's in stones and bones. That's physical anthropology, emphasis on Southeast Asia. Anyway, I worked a while in a museum, then found out the army paid better. So I hired on as a civilian contractor. I'm still sorting bones, only these have names, ranks and serial numbers."

"And that's why you're going to Vietnam?"

He nodded. "There are new sets of remains to pick up in Saigon and Hanoi."

Remains. Such a clinical word for what was once a human being.

"I know a few people," he said. "I might be able to help you."

"Why?"

"You've made me curious."

"Is that all it is? Curiosity?"

His next move startled her. He reached out and brushed back her short, tumbled hair. The brief contact of his fingers seemed to leave her whole neck sizzling. She froze, unable to react to this unexpectedly intimate contact.

"Maybe I'm just a nice guy," he whispered.

Oh, hell, he's going to kiss me, she thought. *He's going to kiss me and I'm going to let him, and what happens next is anyone's guess. . . .*

She batted his hand away and took a panicked step back. "I don't believe in nice guys."

"Afraid of men?"

"I'm not afraid of men. But I don't trust them, either."

"Still," he said with an obvious note of laughter in his voice, "you let me into your room."

"Maybe it's time to let you out." She stalked across the room and yanked open the door. "Or are you going to be difficult?"

"Me?" To her surprise, he followed her to the door. "I'm never difficult."

"I'll bet."

"Besides, I can't hang around tonight. I've got more important business."

"Really."

"Really." He glanced at the lock on her door. "I see you've got a heavy-duty dead bolt. Use it. And take my advice—don't go out on the town tonight."

"Darn! That was next on my agenda."

"Oh, and in case you need me—" he turned and grinned at her from the doorway "—I'm staying at the Liberty Hotel. Call anytime."

She started to snap, *Don't hold your breath.* But before she could get out the words, he'd left.

She was staring at a closed door.

3

Tobias Wolff swiveled his wheelchair around from the liquor cabinet and faced his old friend. "If I were you, Guy, I'd stay the hell out of it."

It had been five years since they'd last seen each other. Toby still looked as muscular as ever—at least from the waist up. Fifteen years' confinement to a wheelchair had bulked out those shoulders and arms. Still, the years had taken their inevitable toll. Toby was close to fifty now, and he looked it. His bushy hair, cut Beethoven style, was almost entirely gray. His face was puffy and sweating in the tropical heat. But the dark eyes were as sharp as ever.

"Take some advice from an old Company man," he said, handing Guy a glass of Scotch. "There's no such thing as a coincidental meeting. There are only planned encounters."

"Coincidence or not," said Guy, "Willy Maitland could be the break I've been waiting for."

"Or she could be nothing but trouble."

"What've I got to lose?"

"Your life?"

"Come on, Toby! You're the only one I can trust to give me a straight answer."

"It was a long time ago. I wasn't directly connected to the case."

"But you were in Vientiane when it happened. You must remember something about the Maitland file."

"Only what I heard in passing, none of it confirmed. Hell, it was like the Wild West out there. Rumors flying thicker'n the mosquitoes."

"But not as thick as you covert-action boys."

Toby shrugged. "We had a job to do. We did it."

"You remember who handled the Maitland case?"

"Had to be Mike Micklewait. I know he was the case officer who debriefed that villager—the one who came in for the reward."

"Did Micklewait think the man was on the level?"

"Probably not. I know the villager never got the reward."

"Why wasn't Maitland's family told about all this?"

"Hey, Maitland wasn't some poor dumb draftee. He was working for Air America. In other words, CIA. That's a job you don't talk about. Maitland knew the risks."

"The family deserved to hear about any new evidence." Guy thought about the surreptitious way Willy and her mother *had* learned of it.

Toby laughed. "There was a secret war going on, remember? We weren't even supposed to be in Laos. Keeping families informed was at the bottom of anyone's priority list."

"Was there some other reason it was hushed up? Something to do with the passenger?"

Toby's eyebrows shot up. "Where did you hear that rumor?"

"Willy Maitland. She heard there was a Lao on board. Everyone's denying his existence, so my guess is he was a very important person. Who was he?"

"I don't know." Toby wheeled around and looked out the open window of his apartment. From the darkness came the sounds and smells of the Bangkok streets. Meat sizzling on an open-air grill. Women laughing. The rumble of a *tuk-tuk.* "There was a hell of a lot going on back then. Things we never talked about. Things we were even ashamed to talk about. What with all the agents and counteragents and generals and soldiers of fortune, you could never really be sure who was running the place. Everyone was pulling strings, trying to get rich quick. I couldn't wait to get the hell out." He slapped the wheelchair in anger. "And this is where I end up. Great retirement." Sighing, he leaned back and stared out at the night. "Let it be, Guy," he said softly. "If you're right—if someone's out to hit Maitland's kid—then this is too hot to handle."

"Toby, that's the point! *Why* is the case so hot? Why, after all these years, would Maitland's brat be making them nervous? What do they think she'll find out?"

"Does she know what she's getting into?"

"I doubt it. Anyway, nothing'll stop this dame. She's a chip off the old block."

"Meaning she's trouble. How're you going to get her to work with you?"

"That's the part I haven't figured out yet."

"There's always the Romeo approach."

Guy grinned. "I'll keep it in mind."

In fact, that was precisely the tactic he'd been considering all evening. Not because he was so sure it would work, but because she was an attractive woman and he couldn't help wondering what she was really like under that tough-gal facade.

"Alternatively," Toby said, "you could try telling her the truth. That you're not after her. You're after the three million bounty."

"Two million."

"Two million, three million, what's the difference? It's a lot of dough."

"And I could use a lot of help," Guy said with quiet significance.

Toby sighed. "Okay," he said, at last wheeling around to look at him. "You want a name, I'll give you one. May or may not help you. Try Alain Gerard, a Frenchman, living these days in Saigon. He used to have close ties with the Company, knew all the crap going on in Vientiane."

"Ex-Company and living in Saigon? Why haven't the Vietnamese kicked him out?"

"He's useful to them. During the war he made his money exporting, shall we say, raw pharmaceuticals. Now he's turned humanitarian in his old age. U.S. trade embargoes cut the Viets off from Western markets. Gerard brings in medical supplies from France, antibiotics, X-ray film. In return, they let him stay in the country."

"Can I trust him?"

"He's ex-Company."

"Then I can't trust him."

Toby grunted. "You seem to trust me."

"You're different."

"That's only because I owe you, Barnard. Though I often think you should've left me to burn in that plane." Toby kneaded his senseless thighs. "No one has much use for half a man."

"Doesn't take legs to make a man, Toby."

"Ha. Tell that to Uncle Sam." Using his powerful arms, Toby shifted his weight in the chair. "When're you leaving for Saigon?"

"Tomorrow morning. I moved my flight up a few days." Guy's palms were already sweating at the thought of boarding that Air France plane. He tossed back a mind-numbing gulp of Scotch. "Wish I could take a boat instead."

Toby laughed. "You'd be the first boat person going *back* to Vietnam. Still scared to fly, huh?"

"White knuckles and all." He set his glass down and headed for the door. "Thanks for the drink. And the tip."

"I'll see what else I can do for you," Toby called after him. "I still might have a few contacts in-country. Maybe I can get 'em to watch over you. And the woman. By the way, is anyone keeping an eye on her tonight?"

"Some buddies of Puapong's. They won't let anyone near her. She should get to the airport in one piece."

"And what happens then?"

Guy paused in the doorway. "We'll be in Saigon. Things'll be safer there."

"In Saigon?" Toby shook his head. "Don't count on it."

The crowd at the Bong Bong Club had turned wild, the men drunkenly shouting and groping at the stage as the girls, dead-eyed, danced on. No one took notice of the two men huddled at a dark corner table.

"I am disappointed, Mr. Siang. You're a professional, or so I thought. I fully expected you to deliver. Yet the woman is still alive."

Stung by the insult, Siang felt his face tighten. He was not accustomed to failure—or to criticism. He was glad the darkness hid his burning cheeks as he set his glass of vodka down on the table. "I tell you, this could not be predicted. There was interference—a man—"

"Yes, an American, so I've been told. A Mr. Barnard."

Siang was startled. "You've learned his name?"

"I make it a point to know everything."

Siang touched his bruised face and winced. This Mr. Barnard certainly had a savage punch. If they ever crossed paths again, Siang would make him pay for this humiliation.

"The woman leaves for Saigon tomorrow," said the man.

"Tomorrow?" Siang shook his head. "That does not leave me enough time."

"You have tonight."

"Tonight? Impossible." Siang had, in fact, already spent the past four hours trying to get near the woman. But the desk clerk at the Oriental had stood watch like a guard dog over the passkeys, the hotel security officer refused to leave his post near the elevators, and a bellboy kept strolling up and down the hall. The woman had been untouchable. Siang had briefly considered climbing up the balcony, but his approach was hampered by two vagrants camped on the riverbank beneath her window. Though hostile-looking, the tramps had posed no real threat to a man like Siang, but he hadn't wanted to risk a foolish, potentially messy scene.

And now his professional reputation was at stake.

"The matter grows more urgent," said the man. "This must be done soon."

"But she leaves Bangkok tomorrow. I can make no guarantees."

"Then do it in Saigon. Whether you finish it here or there, *it has to be done.*"

Siang was stunned. "Saigon? I cannot return—"

"We'll send you under Thai diplomatic cover. A cultural attaché, perhaps. I'll decide and arrange the entry papers accordingly."

"Vietnamese security is tight. I will not be able to bring in any—"

"The diplomatic pouch goes out twice a week. Next drop is in three days. I'll see what weapons I can slip through. Until then, you'll have to improvise."

Siang fell silent, wondering how it would feel to once again walk the streets of Saigon. And he wondered about Chantal. How many years had it been since he'd seen her? Did she still hate him for leaving her behind? Of course, she would; she never forgot a grudge. Somehow, he'd have to work his way back into her affections. He didn't think that would be too difficult. Life in the new Vietnam must be hard these days, especially for a woman. Chantal liked her comforts; for a few precious luxuries, she might do anything. Even sell her soul.

She was a woman he could understand.

He looked across the table. "There will be expenses."

The man nodded. "I can be generous. As you well know."

Already Siang was making a mental list of what he'd need. Old clothes—frayed shirts and faded trousers—so he wouldn't stand out in a crowd. Cigarettes, soap and razor blades for bartering favors on the streets. And then he'd need a few special gifts for Chantal. . . .

He nodded. The bargain was struck.

"One more thing," said the man as he rose to leave.

"Yes?"

"Other . . . parties seem to be involved. The Company, for instance. I wouldn't want to pull that particular tiger's tail. So keep bloodshed to a minimum. Only the woman dies. No one else."

"I understand."

After the man had left, Siang sat alone at the corner table, thinking. Remembering Saigon. Had it really been fifteen years? His last memories of the city were of panicked faces, of hands clawing frantically at a helicopter door, of the roar of chopper blades and the swirl of dust as the rooftops fell away.

Siang took a deep swallow of vodka and stood to leave. Just then, whistles and applause rose from the crowd gathered around the dance stage. A lone girl stood brown and naked in the spotlight. Around her waist was wrapped an eight-foot boa constrictor. The girl seemed to shudder as the snake slithered down between her thighs. The men shouted their approval.

Siang grinned. Ah, the Bong Bong Club. Always something new.

Saigon

From the rooftop garden of the Rex Hotel, Willy watched the bicycles thronging the intersection of Le Loi and Nguyen Hue. A collision seemed inevitable, only a matter of time. Riders whisked through at breakneck speed, blithely ignoring the single foolhardy pedestrian inching fearfully across the street. Willy was so intent on silently cheering the man on that she scarcely registered the monotonous voice of her government escort.

"And tomorrow, we will take you by car to see the National Palace, where the puppet government ruled in luxury, then on to the Museum of History, where you will learn about our struggles against the Chinese and the French imperialists. The next day, you will see our lacquer factory; where you can buy many beautiful gifts to bring home. And then—"

"Mr. Ainh," Willy said with a sigh, turning at last to her guide. "It all sounds very fascinating, this tour you've planned. But have you looked into my other business?"

Ainh blinked. Though his frame was chopstick thin, he had a cherubic face made owlish by his thick glasses. "Miss Maitland," he said in a hurt voice, "I have arranged a private car! And many wonderful meals."

"Yes, I appreciate that, but—"

"You are unhappy with your itinerary?"

"To be perfectly honest, I don't really care about a tour. I want to find out about my father."

"But you have paid for a tour! We must provide one."

"I paid for the tour to get a visa. Now that I'm here, I need to talk to the right people. You can arrange that for me, can't you?"

Ainh shifted nervously. "This is a . . . a complication. I do not know if I can . . . that is, it is not what I . . ." He drifted into helpless silence.

"Some months ago, I wrote to your foreign ministry about my father. They never wrote back. If you could arrange an appointment . . ."

"How many months ago did you write?"

"Six, at least."

"You are impatient. You cannot expect instant results."

She sighed. "Obviously not."

"Besides, you wrote the Foreign Ministry. I have nothing to do with them. I am with the Ministry of Tourism."

"And you folks don't communicate with each other, is that it?"

"They are in a different building."

"Then maybe—if it's not too much trouble—you could take me to their building?"

He looked at her bleakly. "But then who will take the tour?"

"Mr. Ainh," she said with gritted teeth, *"cancel the tour."*

Ainh looked like a man with a terrible headache. Willy almost felt sorry for him as she watched him retreat across the rooftop garden. She could imagine the bureaucratic quicksand he would have to wade through to honor her request. She'd already seen how the system operated—or, rather, how it didn't operate. That afternoon, at Ton Son Nhut Airport, it had taken three hours in the suffocating heat just to run the gauntlet of immigration officials.

A breeze swept the terrace, the first she'd felt all afternoon. Though she'd showered only an hour ago, her clothes were already soaked with sweat. Sinking into a chair, she gazed off at the skyline of Saigon, now painted a dusty gold in the sunset. Once, this must have been a glorious town of tree-lined boulevards and outdoor cafés where one could while away the afternoons sipping coffee.

But after its fall to the North, Saigon slid from the dizzy impudence of wealth to the resignation of poverty. The signs of decay were everywhere, from the chipped paint on the old French colonials to the skeletons of buildings left permanently unfinished. Even the Rex Hotel, luxurious by local standards, seemed to be fraying at the edges. The terrace stones were cracked. In the fish pond, three listless carp drifted like dead leaves. The rooftop swimming pool had bloomed an unhealthy shade of green. A lone Russian tourist sat on the side and dangled his legs in the murky water, as though weighing the risks of a swim.

It occurred to Willy that her immediate situation was every bit as murky as that water. The Vietnamese obviously believed in a proper channel for everything, and without Ainh's help, there was no way she could navigate *any* channel, proper or otherwise.

What then? she thought wearily. *I can't do this alone. I need help. I need a guide. I need—*

"Now *there's* a lady who looks down on her luck," said a voice.

She looked up to see Guy Barnard's tanned face framed against the sunset. Her instant delight at seeing someone familiar—even *him*—only confirmed the utter depths of despair to which she'd sunk.

He flashed her a smile that could have charmed the habit off a nun. "Welcome to Saigon, capital of fallen dreams. How's it goin', kid?"

She sighed. "You need to ask?"

"Nope. I've been through it before, running around like a headless chicken, scrounging up seals of approval for every piddly scrap of paper. This country has got bureaucracy down to an art."

"I could live without the pep talk, thank you."

"Can I buy you a beer?"

She studied that smile of his, wondering what lay behind it. Suspecting the worst.

Seeing her weaken, he called for two beers, then dropped into a chair and regarded her with rumpled cheerfulness.

"I thought you weren't due in Saigon till Wednesday," she said.

"Change of plans."

"Pretty sudden, wasn't it?"

"Flexibility happens to be one of my virtues." He added, ruefully, "Maybe my only virtue."

The bartender brought over two frosty Heinekens. Guy waited until the man left before he spoke again.

"They brought in some new remains from Dak To," he said.

"MIAs?"

"That's what I have to find out. I knew I'd need a few extra days to examine the bones. Besides—" he took a gulp of beer "—I was getting bored in Bangkok."

"Sure."

"No, I mean it. I was ready for a change of scenery."

"You left the fleshpot of the East to come here and check out a few dead soldiers?"

"Believe it or not, I take my job seriously." He set the bottle down on the table. "Anyway, since I happen to be in town, maybe I could help you out. Since you probably need it."

Something about the way he looked at her, head cocked, teeth agleam in utter self-assurance, irritated her. "I'm doing okay," she said.

"Are you, now? So when's your first official meeting?"

"Things are being arranged."

"What sorts of things?"

"I don't know. Mr. Ainh's handling the details, and—"

"Mr. Ainh? You don't mean your *tour guide?*" He burst out laughing.

"Just why is that so funny?" she demanded.

"You're right," Guy said, swallowing his laughter. "It's not funny. It's pathetic. Do you want an advance look in my crystal ball? Because I can tell you exactly what's going to happen. First thing in the morning, your guide will show up with an apologetic look on his face."

"Why apologetic?"

"Because he'll tell you the ministry is closed for the day. After all, it's the grand and glorious holiday of July 18."

"Holiday? What holiday?"

"Never mind. He'll make something up. Then he'll ask if you wouldn't rather see the lacquer factory, where you can buy many beautiful gifts to bring home. . . ."

Now she was laughing. Those were, in fact, Mr. Ainh's exact words.

"Then, the following day, he'll come up with some other reason you can't visit the ministry. Say, they're all sick with the swine flu or there's a critical shortage of pencil erasers. *But*—you can visit the National Palace!"

She stopped laughing. "I think I'm beginning to get your point."

"It's not that the man's deliberately sabotaging your plans. He simply knows how hopeless it is to untangle this bureaucracy. All he wants is to do his own little job, which is to be a tour guide and file innocuous reports about the nice lady tourist. Don't expect more from him. The poor guy isn't paid enough for what he already does."

"I'm not helpless. I can always start knocking on a few doors myself."

"Yeah, but *which* doors? And where are they hidden? And do you know the secret password?"

"Guy, you're making this country sound like a carnival funhouse."

"*Fun* is not the operative word here."

"What *is* the operative word?"

"*Chaos.*" He pointed down at the street, where pedestrians and bicycles swarmed in mass anarchy. "See that? That's how this government works. It's every man for himself. Ministries competing with ministries, provinces with provinces. Every minor official protecting his own turf. Everyone scared to move an inch without a nod from the powers that be." He shook his head. "Not a system for the faint of heart."

"That's one thing I've never been."

"Wait till you've been sitting in some sweatbox of a 'reception' area for five hours. And your belly hurts from the bad water. And the closest bathroom is a hole in the—"

"I get the picture."

"Do you?"

"What are you suggesting I do?"

Smiling, he sat back. "Hang around with me. I have a contact here and there. Not in the Foreign Ministry, I admit, but they might be able to help you."

He wants something, she thought. *What is it?* Though his gaze was unflinching, she sensed a new tension in his posture, saw in his eyes the anticipation rippling beneath the surface.

"You're being awfully helpful. Why?"

He shrugged. "Why not?"

"That's hardly an answer."

"Maybe at heart I'm still the Boy Scout helping old ladies cross the street. Maybe I'm a nice guy."

"Maybe you could tell me the truth."

"Have you always had this problem trusting men?"

"Yes, and don't change the subject."

For a moment, he didn't speak. He sat drumming his fingers against the beer bottle. "Okay," he admitted. "So I fibbed a little. I was never a Boy Scout. But I meant it about helping you out. The offer stands."

She didn't say a thing. For Guy, that silence, that look of skepticism, said it all. The woman didn't trust him. But why not, when he'd sounded his most sincere? He wondered what had made her so mistrustful. Too many hard knocks in life? Too many men who'd lied to her?

Well, watch out, baby, 'cause this one's no different, he thought with a twinge of self-disgust.

He just as quickly shook off the feeling. The stakes were too high to be developing a conscience. Especially at his age.

Now he'd have to tell another lie. He'd been lying a lot lately. It didn't get any easier.

"You're right," he said. "I'm not doing this out of the kindness of my heart."

She didn't look surprised. That annoyed him. "What do you expect in return?" she asked, her eyes hard on his, "Money?" She paused. "Sex?"

That last word, flung out so matter-of-factly, made his belly do a tiny loop-the-loop. Not that he hadn't already thought about that particular subject. He'd thought about it a lot ever since he'd met her. And now that she was sitting only a few feet away, watching him with those unyielding eyes, he was having trouble keeping certain images out of his head. Briefly he considered the possibility of throwing a little sex into the deal, but he just as quickly discarded the idea. He felt low enough as it was.

He calmly reached for the Heineken. The frostiness had gone out of the bottle. "No," he said. "Sex isn't part of the bargain."

"I see." She bit her lip. "Then it's money."

He gave a nod.

"I think you should know that I don't have any. Not for you, anyway."

"It's not *your* money I'm after."

"Then whose?"

He paused, willing his expression to remain bland. His voice dropped to a murmur. "Have you ever heard of the Ariel Group?"

"Never."

"Neither had I. Until two weeks ago, when I was contacted by two of their representatives. They're a veterans' organization, dedicated to bringing our MIAs home—alive. Even if it means launching a Rambo operation."

"I see," she said, her lips tightening. "We're talking about paramilitary kooks."

"That's what I thought—at first. I was about to kick 'em out of my office when they pulled out a check—a very generous one, I might add. Twenty thousand. For expenses, they said."

"Expenses? What are they asking you to do?"

"A little moonlighting. They knew I was scheduled to fly in-country. They wanted me to conduct a small, private search for MIAs. But they aren't interested in skeletons and dog tags. They're after flesh and blood."

"Live ones? You don't really think there are any, do you?"

"They do. And they only have to produce one. A single living MIA to back up their claims. With the publicity that'd generate, Washington would be forced to take action."

He fell silent as the waiter came by to collect the empty beer bottles. Only when the man had left did Willy ask softly, "And where do I come in?"

"It's not you. It's your father. From what you've told me, there's a chance—a small one, to be sure—that he's still alive. If he is, I can help you find him. I can help you bring him home."

His words, uttered so quietly, so confidently, made Willy fall still. Guy could tell she was trying to read his face, trying to figure out what he wasn't telling her. And he wasn't telling her a lot.

"What do you get out of this?" she asked.

"You mean besides the pleasure of your company?"

"You said there was money involved. Since I'm not paying you, I assume someone else is. The Ariel Group? Are they offering you more than just expenses?"

"Move to the head of the class."

"How much?"

"For an honest to God live one? Two million."

"Two million *dollars?*"

He squeezed her hand, hard. "Keep it down, will you? This isn't exactly public information."

She dropped her voice to a whisper. "You're serious? Two million?"

"That's their offer. Now you think about *my* offer. Work with me, and we could both come out ahead. You'd get your father back. I'd pick up a nice little retirement fund. A win-win situation." He grinned, knowing he had her now. She'd be stupid to refuse. And Willy Maitland was definitely not stupid. "I think you'll agree," he said. "It's a match made in heaven."

"Or hell," she muttered darkly. She sat back and gave him a look of pure cast iron. "You're nothing but a bounty hunter."

"If that's what you want to call me."

"I could call you quite a few things. None of them flattering."

"Before you start calling me names, maybe you should think about your options. Which happen to be pretty limited. The way I see it, you can go it alone, which so far hasn't gotten you a helluva lot of mileage. Or—" he leaned forward and beamed her his most convincing smile "—you could work with me."

Her mouth tightened. "I don't work with mercenaries."

"What've you got against mercenaries?"

"Just a minor matter—principle."

"It's the money that bothers you, isn't it? The fact that I'm doing it for cash and not out of the goodness of my heart."

"This isn't some big-game hunt! We're talking about *men.* Men whose families have wiped out their savings to pay worthless little Rambos like you! I know those families. Some of them are still hanging in, twisting around on that one shred of hope. And you know as well as I do that those soldiers aren't sitting around in some POW camp, waiting to be rescued. They're *dead.*"

"You think *your* old man's alive."

"He's a different story."

"Right. And every one of those five hundred other MIAs could be another 'different story.' "

"*I* happen to have evidence!"

"But you don't have the smarts it takes to find him." Guy leaned forward, his gaze hard on hers. In the last night of sunset, her face seemed alight with fire, her cheeks glowing a beautiful dusky red. "If he's alive, you can't afford to screw up this chance. And you may get only one chance to find him. Because I'll tell you now, the Vietnamese won't let you back in the country for another deluxe tour. Admit it, Willy. You need me."

"No," she shot back. "You need *me*. Without my help, how are you going to cash in on your 'live one'?"

"How're *you* going to find him?"

She was the one leaning forward now, so close, he almost pulled back in surprise. "Don't underestimate me, sleazeball," she muttered.

"And don't overestimate yourself, Junior. It's not easy finding answers in this country. No one, nothing's ever what it seems here. A flicker in the eye, a break in the voice can mean all the difference in the world. You *need* a partner. And, hey, I'm not unreasonable. I'll even think about splitting the reward with you. Say, ten percent. That's money you never expected, just to let me—"

"I don't give a damn about the money!" She rose sharply to her feet. "Go get rich off someone else's old man." She spun around and walked away.

"Won't you even think about it?" he yelled.

She just kept marching away across the rooftop garden, oblivious to the curious glances aimed her way.

"Take it from me, Willy! You need me!"

A trio of Russian tourists, their faces ruddy from a few rounds of vodka, glanced up as she passed. One of the men raised his glass in a drunken salute. "Maybe you like Russian man better?" he shouted.

She didn't even break her stride. But as she walked away, every guest on that rooftop heard her answer, which came floating back with disarming sweetness over her shoulder.

"Go to hellski."

4

Guy watched her storm away, her chambray skirt snapping smartly about those fabulous legs. Annoyed as he was, he couldn't help laughing when he heard that comeback to the Russian.

Go to hellski. He laughed harder. He was still laughing as he wandered over to the bar and called for another Heineken. The beer was so cold, it made his teeth ache.

"For a fellow who's just gotten the royal heave-ho," said a voice, obviously British, "you seem to be in high spirits."

Guy glanced at the portly gentleman hunched next to him at the bar. With those two tufts of hair on his bald head, he looked like a horned owl. China blue eyes twinkled beneath shaggy eyebrows.

Guy shrugged. "Win some, lose some."

"Sensible attitude. Considering the state of womanhood these days." The man hoisted a glass of Scotch to his lips. "But then, I could have predicted she'd be a no go."

"Sounds like an expert talking."

"No, I sat behind her on the plane. Listened to some oily Frenchman ooze his entire repertoire all over her. Smashing lines, I have to say, but she didn't fall for it." He squinted at Guy. "Weren't *you* on that flight out of Bangkok?"

Guy nodded. He didn't remember the man, but then, he'd spent the entire flight white-knuckling his armrest and gulping down whiskey. Airplanes did that to him. Even nice big 747s with nice French stewardesses. It never failed to astonish him that the wings didn't fall off.

At the other end of the garden, the trio of Russians had started to sing. Not, unfortunately, in the same key. Maybe not even the same song. It was hard to tell.

"Never would've guessed it," the Englishman said, glancing over at the Russians. "I still remember the Yanks drinking at that very table. Never would've guessed there'd be Russians sitting there one day."

"When were you here?"

"Sixty-eight to '75." He held out a pudgy hand in greeting. "Dodge Hamilton, *London Post.*"

"Guy Barnard. Ex-draftee." He shook the man's hand. "Reporter, huh? You here on a story?"

"I was." Hamilton looked mournfully at his Scotch. "But it's fallen through."

"What has? Your interviews?"

"No, the concept. I called it a sentimental journey. Visit to old friends in Saigon. Or, rather, to one friend in particular." He took a swallow of Scotch. "But she's gone."

"Oh. A woman."

"That's right, a woman. Half the human race, but they might as well be from Mars for all I understand the sex." He slapped down the glass and motioned for another refill. The bartender resignedly shoved the whole bottle of Scotch over to Hamilton. "See, the story I had in mind was the search for a lost love. You know, the sort of copy that sells papers. My editor went wild about it." He poured the Scotch, recklessly filling the glass to the brim. "Ha! Lost love! I stopped by her old house today, over on Rue Catinat. Or what used to be Rue Catinat. Found her brother still living there. But it seems my old love ran away with some new love. A sergeant. From Memphis, no less."

Guy shook his head in sympathy. "A woman has a right to change her mind."

"One day after I left the country?"

There wasn't much a man could say to that. But Guy couldn't blame the woman. He knew how it was in Saigon—the fear, the uncertainty. No one knowing if there'd be a slaughter and everyone expecting the worst. He'd seen the news photos of the city's fall, recognized the look of desperation on the faces of the Vietnamese scrambling aboard the last choppers out. No, he couldn't blame a woman for wanting to get out of the country, any way she could.

"You could still write about it," Guy pointed out. "Try a different angle. How one woman escaped the madness. The price of survival."

"My heart's not in it any longer." Hamilton gazed sadly around the rooftop. "Or in this town. I used to love it here! The noise, the smells. Even the whomp of the mortar rounds. But Saigon's changed. The spirit's flown out of it. The funny part is, this hotel looks exactly the same. I used to stand at this very bar and hear your generals whisper to each other, 'What the hell are we doing here?' I don't think they ever quite figured it out." He laughed and took another gulp of Scotch. "Memphis. Why would she want to go to Memphis?"

He was muttering to himself now, some private monologue about women causing all the world's miseries. An opinion with which Guy could almost agree. All he had to do was think about his own miserable love life and he, too, would get the sudden, blinding urge to get thoroughly soused.

Women. All the same. Yet, somehow, all different.

He thought about Willy Maitland. She talked tough, but he could tell it was an act, that there was something soft, something vulnerable beneath that hard-as-nails surface. Hell, she was just a kid trying to live up to her old man's name, pretending she didn't need a man when she did. He had to admire her for that: her pride.

She was smart to turn down his offer. He wasn't sure he had the stomach to go through with it anyway. Let the Ariel Group tighten his noose. He'd lived with his skeletons long enough; maybe it was time to let them out of the closet.

I should just do my job, he thought. Go to Hanoi, pick up a few dead soldiers, fly them home.

And forget about Willy Maitland.

Then again . . .

He ordered another beer. Drank it while the debate raged on in his head. Thought about all the ways he could help her, about how much she needed *someone's* help. Considered doing it not because he was being forced into it, but because he wanted to. *Out of the goodness of my heart?* Now that was a new concept. No, he'd never been a Boy Scout. Something about those uniforms, about all that earnest goodliness and godliness, had struck him as faintly ridiculous. But here he was, Boy Scout Barnard, ready to offer his services, no strings attached.

Well, maybe a few strings. He couldn't help fantasizing about the possibilities. He thought of how it would be, taking her up to his room. Undressing her. Feeling her yield beneath him. He swallowed hard and reached automatically for the Heineken.

"No doubt about it," Hamilton muttered. "I tell you, it's all their fault."

"Hmm?" Guy turned. "Whose fault?"

"Women, of course. They cause more trouble than they're worth."

"You said it, pal." Guy sighed and lifted the beer to his lips. "You said it."

*   *   *

Men. They cause more trouble than they're worth, Willy thought as she viciously wound her alarm clock.

A bounty hunter. She should have guessed. Warning bells should have gone off in her head the minute he so generously offered his help. *Help.* What a laugh. She thought of all the solicitation letters she and her mother had received, all the mercenary groups who'd offered, for a few thousand dollars, to provide just such worthless help. There'd been the MIA Search Fund, the Men Alive Committee, Operation Chestnut—Let's Pull 'Em Out Of The Fire! had been *their* revolting slogan. How many grieving families had invested their hopes and savings on such futile dreams?

She stripped down to a tank top and flopped onto the bed. A decent night's sleep, she could tell, was another futile dream. The mattress was lumpy, and the pillow seemed to be stuffed with concrete. Not that it mattered. How could she get any rest with that damned disco music vibrating through the walls? At 8:00 the first driving drumbeats had announced the opening of Dance Night at the Rex Hotel. *Lord,* she thought, *what good is communism if it can't even stamp out disco?*

It occurred to her that, at that very minute, Guy Barnard was probably loitering downstairs in that dance hall, checking out the action. Sometimes she thought that was the real reason men started wars—it was an excuse to run away from home and check out the action.

What do I care if he's down there eyeing the ladies? The man's scum. He's not worth a second thought.

Still, she had to admit he had a certain tattered charm. Nice straight teeth and a dazzling smile and eyes that were brown as a wolf's. A woman could get in trouble for the sake of those eyes. *And heaven knows, I don't need that kind of trouble.*

Someone knocked on the door. She sat up straight and called out, "Who is it?"

"Room service."

"There must be a mistake. I didn't order anything."

There was no response. Sighing, she pulled on a robe and padded over to open the door.

Guy grinned at her from the darkness. "Well?" he inquired. "Have you thought about it?"

"Thought about what?" she snapped back.

"You and me. Working together."

She laughed in disbelief. "Either you're hard of hearing or I didn't make myself clear."

"That was two hours ago. I figured you might have changed your mind."

"I will *never* change my mind. Good *night.*" She slammed the door, shoved the bolt home and stepped back, seething.

There was a tapping on her window. She yanked the curtain aside and saw Guy smiling through the glass.

"Just one more question," he called.

"What?"

"Is that answer final?"

She jerked the curtain closed and stood there, waiting to see where he'd turn up next. Would he drop down from the ceiling? Pop up like a jack-in-the-box through the floor?

What was that rustling sound?

Glancing down sharply, she saw a piece of paper slide under the door. She snatched it up and read the scrawled message. "Call me if you need me."

Ha! she thought, ripping the note to pieces. "The day I need you is the day hell freezes over!" she yelled.

There was no answer. And she knew, without even looking, that he had already walked away.

Chantal gazed at the bottle of champagne, the tins of caviar and foie gras, and the box of chocolates, and she licked her lips. Then she said, "How dare you show up after all these years."

Siang merely smiled. "You have lost your taste for champagne? What a pity. It seems I shall have to drink it all myself." He reached for the bottle. Slowly, he untwisted the wire. The flight from Bangkok had jostled the contents; the cork shot out, spilling pale gold bubbles all over the earthen floor. Chantal gave a little sob. She appeared ready to drop to her knees and lap up the precious liquid. He poured champagne into one of two fluted glasses he'd brought all the way from Bangkok. One could not, after all, drink champagne from a teacup. He took a sip and sighed happily. "Taittinger. Delightful."

"Taittinger?" she whispered.

He filled the second glass and set it on the rickety table in front of her. She kept staring at it, watching the bubbles spiral to the surface.

"I need help," he said.

She reached for the glass, put it to her trembling lips, tasted the rim, then the contents. He could almost see the bubbles sliding over her tongue, slipping down that fine, long throat. Even if the rest of her was sagging, she still had that beautiful throat, slender as a stalk of grass. A legacy from her Vietnamese mother. Her Asian half had held up over the years; the French half hadn't done so well. He could see the freckles, the fine lines tracing the corners of her greenish eyes.

She was no longer merely tasting the champagne; she was guzzling. Greedily, she drained the last drop from her glass and reached for the bottle.

He slid it out of her reach. "I said I need your help."

She wiped her chin with the back of her hand. "What kind of help?"

"Not much."

"Ha. That's what you always say."

"A pistol. Automatic. Plus several clips of ammunition."

"What if I don't have a pistol?"

"Then you will find me one."

She shook her head. "This is not the old days. You don't know what it's like here. Things are difficult." She paused, looking down at her slightly crepey hands. "Saigon is a hell."

"Even hell can be made comfortable. I can see to that."

She was silent. He could read her mind almost as easily as if her eyes were transparent. She gazed down at the treasures he'd brought from Bangkok. She swallowed, her mouth still tingling with the taste of champagne. At last she said, "The gun. What do you want it for?"

"A job."

"Vietnamese?"

"American. A woman."

A spark flickered in Chantal's eyes. Curiosity. Maybe jealousy. Her chin came up. "Your lover?"

He shook his head.

"Then why do you want her dead?"

He shrugged. "Business. My client has offered generous compensation. I will split it with you."

"The way you did before?" she shot back.

He shook his head apologetically. "Chantal, Chantal." He sighed. "You know I had no choice. It was the last flight out of Saigon." He touched her face; it had lost its former silkiness. That French blood again: it didn't hold up well under years of harsh sunlight. "This time, I promise. You'll be paid."

She sat there looking at him, looking at the champagne. "What if it takes me time to find a gun?"

"Then I'll improvise. And I will need an assistant. Someone I can trust, someone discreet." He paused. "Your cousin, is he still in need of money?"

Their gazes met. He gave her a slow, significant smile. Then he filled her glass with champagne.

"Open the caviar," she said.

"I need your help," said Willy.

Guy, dazed and still half-asleep, stood in his doorway, blinking at the morning sunlight. He was uncombed, unshaven and wearing only a towel—a skimpy one at that. She tried to stay focused on his face, but her gaze kept dropping to his chest, to that mat of curly brown hair, to the scar knotting the upper abdomen.

He shook his head in disbelief. "You couldn't have told me this last night? You had to wait till the crack of dawn?"

"Guy, it's eight o'clock."

He yawned. "No kidding."

"Maybe you should try going to bed at a decent hour."

"Who says I didn't?" He leaned carelessly in the doorway and grinned. "Maybe sleep didn't happen to be on my agenda."

Dear God. Did he have a woman in his room? Automatically, Willy glanced past him into the darkened room. The bed was rumpled but unoccupied.

"Gotcha," he said, and laughed.

"I can see you're not going to be any help at all." She turned and walked away.

"Willy! Hey, come on." He caught her by the arm and pulled her around. "Did you mean it? About wanting my help?"

"Forget it. It was a lapse in judgment."

"Last night, hell had to freeze over before you'd come to me for help. But here you are. What made you change your mind?"

She didn't answer right off. She was too busy trying not to notice that his towel was slipping. To her relief, he snatched it together just in time and fastened it more securely around his hips.

At last she shook her head and sighed. "You were right. It's all going exactly as you said it would. No official will talk to me. No one'll answer my calls. They hear I'm coming and they all dive under their desks!"

"You could try a little patience. Wait another week."

"Next week's no good, either."

"Why?"

"Haven't you heard? It's Ho Chi Minh's birthday."

Guy looked heavenward. "How could I forget?"

"So what should I do?"

For a moment, he stood there thoughtfully rubbing his unshaven chin. Then he nodded. "Let's talk about it."

Back in his room, she sat uneasily on the edge of the bed while he dressed in the bathroom. The man was a restless sleeper, judging by the rumpled sheets. The blanket had been kicked off the bed entirely, the pillows punched into formless lumps by the headboard. Her gaze settled on the nightstand, where a stack of files lay. The top one was labeled Operation Friar Tuck. Declassified. Curious, she flipped open the cover.

"It's the way things work in this country," she heard him say through the bathroom door. "If you want to get from point A to point B, you don't go in a straight line. You walk two steps to the left, two to the right, turn and walk backward."

"So what should I do now?"

"The two-step. Sideways." He came out, dressed and freshly shaved. Spotting the open file on the nightstand, he calmly closed the cover. "Sorry. Not for public view," he said, sliding the stack of folders into his briefcase. Then he turned to her. "Now. Tell me what else is going on."

"What do you mean?"

"I get the feeling there's something more. It's eight o'clock in the morning. You can't have battled the bureaucracy this early. What really made you change your mind about me?"

"Oh, I haven't changed my mind about *you*. You're still a mercenary." Her disgust seemed to hang in the air like a bad odor.

"But now you're willing to work with me. Why?"

She looked down at her lap and sighed. Reluctantly she opened her purse and pulled out a slip of paper. "I found this under my door this morning."

He unfolded the paper. In a spidery hand was written "Die Yankee." Just seeing those two words again made her angry. A few minutes ago, when she'd shown the message to Mr. Ainh, his only reaction was to shake his head in regret. At least Guy was an American; surely *he'd* share her sense of outrage.

He handed the note back to her. "So?"

" '*So?*' " She stared at him. "I get a death threat slipped under my door. The entire Vietnamese government hides at the mention of my name. Ainh practically *commands* me to tour his stupid lacquer factory. And that's all you can say? 'So?' "

Clucking sympathetically, he sat down beside her. *Why does he have to sit so close?* she thought. She tried to ignore the tingling in her leg as it brushed against his, struggled to sit perfectly straight though his weight on the mattress was making her sag toward him.

"First of all," he explained, "this isn't necessarily a personal death threat. It could be merely a political statement."

"Oh, is *that* all," she said blandly.

"And think of the lacquer factory as a visit to the dentist. You don't want to go, but everyone thinks you should. And as for the elusive Foreign Ministry, you wouldn't learn a thing from those bureaucrats anyway. Speaking of bureaucrats, where's your baby-sitter?"

"You mean Mr. Ainh?" She sighed. "Waiting for me in the lobby."

"You have to get rid of him."

"I wish."

"We can't have him around." Rising, Guy took her hand and pulled her to her feet. "Not where we're going."

"Where *are* we going?" she demanded, following him out the door.

"To see a friend. I think."

"Meaning he might not see us?"

"Meaning I can't be sure he's a friend."

She groaned as they stepped into the elevator. "Terrific."

Down in the lobby, they found Ainh by the desk, waiting to ambush her. "Miss Maitland!" he called. "Please, you must hurry. We have a very busy schedule today."

Willy glanced at Guy, who simply shrugged and looked off in another direction. Drat the man, he was leaving it up to her. "Mr. Ainh," she said, "about this little tour of the lacquer factory—"

"It will be quite fascinating! But they do not take dollars, so if you wish to exchange for dong, I can—"

"I'm afraid I don't feel up to it," she said flatly.

Ainh blinked in surprise. "You are ill?"

"Yes, I . . ." She suddenly noticed that Guy was shaking his head. "Uh, no, I'm not. I mean—"

"What she means," said Guy, "is that I offered to show her around. You know—" he winked at Ainh "—a little *personal* tour."

"P-personal?" Flushing, Ainh glanced at Willy. "But what about *my* tour? It is all arranged! The car, the sight-seeing, a special lunch—"

"I tell you what, pal," said Guy, bending toward him conspiratorially. "Why don't *you* take the tour?"

"I have been on the tour," Ainh said glumly.

"Ah, but that was work, right? This time, why don't you take the day off, both you and the driver. Go see the sights of Saigon. And enjoy Ms. Maitland's lunch. After all, it's been paid for."

Ainh suddenly looked interested. "A free lunch?"

"And a beer." Guy slipped a few dollars into the man's breast pocket and patted the flap. "On me." He took Willy's arm and directed her across the lobby.

"But, Miss Maitland!" Ainh called out bleakly.

"Boy, what a blast you two guys're gonna have!" Guy sounded almost envious. "Air-conditioned car. Free lunch. No schedule to tie you down."

Ainh followed them outside, into a wall of morning heat so thick, it made Willy draw a breath of surprise. "Miss Maitland!" he said in desperation. "This is *not* the way it is supposed to be done!"

Guy turned and gave the man a solemn pat on the shoulder. "That, Mr. Ainh, is the whole idea."

They left the poor man standing alone on the steps, staring after them.

"What do you think he'll do?" whispered Willy.

"I think," said Guy, moving her along the crowded sidewalk, "he's going to enjoy a free lunch."

She glanced back and saw that Mr. Ainh had, indeed, disappeared into the hotel. She also noticed they were being followed. A street urchin, no more than twelve years old, caught up and danced around on the hot pavement.

"Lien-xo?" he chirped, dark eyes shining in a dirty face. They tried to ignore him, but the boy skipped along beside them, chattering all the way. His shirt hung in tatters; his feet were stained an apparently permanent brown. He pointed at Guy. *"Lien-xo?"*

"No, not Russian," said Guy. "Americanski."

The boy grinned. "Americanski? Yes?" He stuck out a smudgy hand and whooped. "Hello, Daddy!"

Resigned, Guy shook the boy's hand. "Yeah, it's nice to meet you too."

"Daddy rich?"

"Sorry. Daddy poor."

The boy laughed, obviously thinking that a grand joke. As Guy and Willy continued down the street, the boy hopped along at their side, shooing all the other urchins who had joined the procession. It was a tattered little parade marching through a sea of confusion. Bicycles whisked by, a multitude of wheels. And on the sidewalks, merchants squatted beside their meager collections of wares.

The boy tugged on Guy's arm. "Hey, Daddy. You got cigarette?"

"No," said Guy.

"Come on, Daddy. I do you favor, keep the beggars away."

"Oh, all right." Guy fished a pack of Marlboro cigarettes from his shirt pocket and handed the boy a cigarette.

"Guy, how could you?" Willy protested. "He's just a kid!"

"Oh, he's not going to smoke it," said Guy. "He'll trade it for something else. Like food. See?" He nodded at the boy, who was busy wrapping his treasure in a grimy piece of cloth. "That's why I always pack a few cartons when I come. They're handy when you need a favor." He turned and frowned up at one of the street signs. "Which, come to think of it, we do." He beckoned to the boy. "Hey, kid, what's your name?"

The boy shrugged.

"They must call you something."

"Other Americanski, he say I look like Oliver."

Guy laughed. "Probably meant Oliver Twist. Okay, Oliver. I got a deal for you. You do us a favor."

"Sure thing, Daddy."

"I'm looking for a street called Rue des Voiles. That's the old name, and it's not on the map. You know where it is?"

"Rue des Voiles? Rue des Voiles . . ." The boy scrunched up his face. "I think that one they call Binh Tan now. Why you want to go there? No stores, nothing to see."

Guy took out a thousand-dong note. "Just get us there."

The boy snapped up the money. "Okay, Daddy. You wait. Promise, you wait!" The boy trotted off down the street. At the corner, he glanced back and yelled again for good measure, "You wait!"

A minute later, he reappeared, trailed by a pair of bicycle-driven cyclos. "I find you the best. Very fast," said Oliver.

Guy and Willy stared in dismay at the two drivers. One smiled back toothlessly; the other was wheezing like a freight train.

Guy shook his head. "Where on earth did he dig up these fossils?" he muttered.

Oliver pointed proudly to the two old men and grinned. "My uncles!"

A voice behind the door said, "Go away."

"Mr. Gerard?" Guy called. There was no answer, but the man was surely lurking near the door; Willy could almost feel him crouched silently on the other side. Guy reached for the knocker fashioned after some grotesque face—either a horned lion or a goat with teeth—that hung on the door like a brass wart. He banged it a few times. "Mr. Gerard!"

Still no answer.

"It's important! We have to talk to you!"

"I said, go away!"

Willy muttered, "Do you suppose it's just possible he doesn't want to talk to us?"

"Oh, he'll talk to us." Guy banged on the door again. "The name's Guy Barnard!" he yelled. "I'm a friend of Toby Wolff."

The latch slid open. One pale eye peeped out through a crack in the door. The eye flicked back and forth, squinting first at Guy, then at Willy. The voice attached to the eye hissed, "Toby Wolff is an idiot."

"Toby Wolff is also calling in his chips."

The eye blinked. The door opened a fraction of an inch wider, the slit revealing a bald, crablike little man. "Well?" he snapped. "Are you just going to stand there?"

Inside, the house was dark as a cave, all the curtains drawn tightly over the windows. Guy and Willy followed the crustacean of a Frenchman down a narrow hallway. In the shadows, Gerard's outline was barely visible, but Willy could hear him just ahead of her, scuttling across the wood floor.

They emerged into what appeared to be a large sitting room. Slivers of light shimmered through worn curtains. In the suffocating darkness hulked vaguely discernible furniture.

"Sit, sit," ordered Gerard. Guy and Willy moved toward a couch, but Gerard snapped, "Not *there!* Can't you see that's a genuine Queen Anne?" He pointed at a pair of massive rosewood chairs. "Sit there." He settled into a brocade armchair by the window. With his arms crossed and his knobby knees jutting out at them, he looked like a disagreeable pile of bones. "So what does Toby want from me now?" he demanded.

"He said you could pass us some information."

Gerard snorted. "I am not in the business."

"You used to be."

"No longer. The stakes are too high."

Willy glanced thoughtfully around the room, noting in the shadows the soft gleam of ivory, the luster of fine old china. She suddenly realized they were surrounded by a treasure trove of antiques. Even the house was an antique, one of Saigon's lovely old French colonials, laced with climbing vines. By law it belonged to the state. She wondered what the Frenchman had done to keep such a home.

"It has been years since I had any business with the Company," said Gerard, "I know nothing that could possibly help you now."

"Maybe you do," said Guy. "We're here about an old matter. From the war."

Gerard laughed. "These people are perpetually at war! Which enemy? The Chinese? The French? The Khmer Rouge?"

"You know which war," Guy said.

Gerard sat back. *"That* war is over."

"Not for some of us," said Willy.

The Frenchman turned to her. She felt him studying her, measuring her significance. She resented being appraised this way. Deliberately she returned his stare.

"What's the girl got to do with it?" Gerard demanded.

"She's here about her father. Missing in action since 1970."

Gerard shrugged. "My business is imports. I know nothing about missing soldiers."

"My father wasn't a soldier," said Willy. "He was a pilot for Air America."

"Wild Bill Maitland," Guy added.

The sudden silence in the room was thick enough to slice. After a long pause, Gerard said softly, "Air America."

Willy nodded. "You remember him?"

The Frenchman's knobby fingers began to tap the armrest. "I knew of them, the pilots. They carried goods for me on occasion. At a price."

"Goods?"

"Pharmaceuticals," said Guy.

Gerard slapped the armrest in irritation. "Come, Mr. Barnard, we both know what we're talking about! Opium. I don't deny it. There was a war going on, and there was money to be made. So I made it. Air America happened to provide the most reliable delivery service. The pilots never asked questions. They were good that way. I paid them what they were worth. In gold."

Again there was a silence. It took all Willy's courage to ask the next question. "And my father? Was he one of the pilots you paid in gold?"

Alain Gerard shrugged. "Would it surprise you?"

Somehow, it wouldn't, but she tried to imagine what all those old family friends would say, the ones who'd thought her father a hero.

"He was one of the best," said Gerard.

She looked up. "The best?" She felt like laughing. "At what? Running drugs?"

"Flying. It was his calling."

"My father's calling," she said bitterly, "was to do whatever he wanted. With no thought for anyone else."

"Still," insisted Gerard, "he was one of the best."

"The day his plane went down . . ." said Guy. "Was he carrying something of yours?"

The Frenchman didn't answer. He fidgeted in his chair, then rose and went to the window, where he fussed prissily with the curtains.

"Gerard?" Guy prodded.

Gerard turned and looked at them. "Why are you here? What purpose do these questions serve?"

"I have to know what happened to him," said Willy.

Gerard turned to the window and peered out through a slit in the curtains. "Go home, Miss Maitland. Before you learn things you don't want to know."

"What things?"

"Unpleasant things."

"He was my father! I have a right—"

"A right?" Gerard laughed. "He was in a war zone! He knew the risks. He was just another man who did not come back alive."

"I want to know why. I want to know what he was doing in Laos."

"Since when does *anyone* know what they were really doing in Laos?" He moved around the room, covetously touching his precious treasures. "You cannot imagine the things that went on in those days. Our secret war. Laos was the country we didn't talk about. But we were all there. Russians, Chinese, Americans, French. Friends and enemies, packed into the same filthy bars of Vientiane. Good soldiers, all of us, out to make a living." He stopped and looked at Willy. "I still do not understand that war."

"But you knew more than most," said Guy. "You were working with Intelligence."

"I saw only part of the picture."

"Toby Wolff suggested you took part in the crash investigation."

"I had little to do with it."

"Then who was in charge?"

"An American colonel by the name of Kistner."

Willy looked up in surprise. "*Joseph* Kistner?"

"Since promoted to general," Guy noted softly.

Gerard nodded. "He called himself a military attaché."

"Meaning he was really CIA."

"Meaning any number of things. I was liaison for French Intelligence, and I was told only the minimum. That was the way the colonel worked, you see. For him, information was power. He shared very little of it."

"What do you know about the crash?"

Gerard shrugged. "They called it a 'routine loss' Hostile fire. A search was called at the insistence of the other pilots, but no survivors were found. After a day, Colonel Kistner put out the order to melt any wreckage. I don't know if the order was ever executed."

Willy shook her head. "Melt?"

"That's jargon for destroy," explained Guy. "They do it whenever a plane goes down during a classified mission. To get rid of the evidence."

"But my father wasn't flying a classified mission. It was a routine supply flight."

"They were *all* listed as routine supply flights," said Gerard.

"The cargo manifest listed aircraft parts," said Guy. "Not a reason to melt the plane. What was really on that flight?"

Gerard didn't answer.

"There was a passenger," Willy said. "They were carrying a passenger."

Gerard's gaze snapped toward her. "Who told you this?"

"Luis Valdez, Dad's cargo kicker. He bailed out as the plane went down."

"You spoke to this man Valdez?"

"It was only a short phone call, right after he was released from the POW camp."

"Then . . . he is still alive?"

She shook her head. "He shot himself the day after he got back to the States."

Gerard began to pace around the room again, touching each piece of furniture. He reminded her of a greedy gnome fingering his treasures.

"Who was the passenger, Gerard?" asked Guy.

Gerard picked up a lacquer box, set it back down again.

"Military? Intelligence? What?"

Gerard stopped pacing. "He was a phantom, Mr. Barnard."

"Meaning you don't know his name?"

"Oh, he had many names, many faces. A rumor always does. Some said he was a general. Or a prince. Or a drug lord." Turning, he stared out the curtain slit, a shriveled silhouette against the glow of light. "Whoever he was, he represented a threat to someone in a high place."

Someone in a high place. Willy thought of the intrigue that must have swirled in Vientiane, 1970. She thought of Air America and Defense Intelligence and the CIA. Who among all those players would have felt threatened by this one unnamed Lao?

"Who do *you* think he was, Mr. Gerard?" she asked.

The silhouette at the window shrugged. "It makes no difference now. He's dead. Everyone on that plane is dead."

"Maybe not all of them. My father—"

"Your father has not been seen in twenty years. And if I were you, I would leave well enough alone."

"But if he's alive—"

"If he's alive, he may not wish to be found." Gerard turned and looked at her, his expression hidden against the backglow of the window. "A man with a price on his head has good reason to stay dead."

5

She stared at him. "A price? I don't understand."

"You mean no one has told you about the bounty?"

"Bounty for what?"

"For the arrest of Friar Tuck."

She fell instantly still. An image took shape in her mind: words typed on a file folder. *Operation Friar Tuck. Declassified.* She turned to Guy. "You know what he's talking about, don't you. Who's Friar Tuck?"

Guy's expression was unreadable, as if a mask had fallen over his face. "It's nothing but a story."

"But you had his file in your room."

"It's just a nickname for a renegade pilot. A legend—"

"Not just a legend," insisted Gerard. "He was a real man, a traitor. Intelligence does not offer two-million-dollar bounties for mere legends."

Willy's gaze shot back to Guy. She wondered how he had the nerve—the gall—to meet her eyes. *You knew,* she thought. *You bastard. All the time, you knew.* Rage had tightened her throat almost beyond speech.

She barely managed to force out her next question, which she directed at Alain Gerard. "You think this—this renegade pilot is my father?"

"Intelligence thought so."

"Based on what evidence? That he could fly planes? The fact that he's not here to defend himself?"

"Based on the timing, the circumstances. In July 1970, William Maitland vanished from the face of the earth. In August of the same year, we heard the first reports of a foreign pilot flying for the enemy. Running weapons and gold."

"But there were hundreds of foreign pilots in Laos! Friar Tuck could have been a Frenchman, a Russian, a—"

"This much we did know—he was American."

She raised her chin. "You're saying my father was a traitor."

"I am telling you this only because it's something you should know. If he's alive, this is the reason he may not want to be found. You think you are on some sort of rescue mission, Miss Maitland, but you may be sadly mistaken. Your father could go home to a jail cell."

In the silence that followed, she turned her gaze to Guy. He still hadn't said a word; that alone proved his guilt. *Who do you work for?* she wondered. *The CIA? The Ariel Group? Or your lying, miserable self?*

She couldn't stand the sight of him. Even being in the same room with him made her recoil in disgust.

She rose. "Thank you, Mr. Gerard. You've told me things I needed to hear. Things I didn't expect."

"Then you agree it's best you drop the matter?"

"I don't agree. You think my father's a traitor. Obviously you're not the only one who thinks so. But you're all wrong."

"And how will you prove it?" Gerard snorted. "Tell me, Miss Maitland, how will you perform this grand miracle after twenty years?"

She didn't have an answer. The truth was, she didn't know what her next move would be. All she knew was that she would have to do it alone.

Her spine was ramrod straight as she followed Gerard back down the hall. The whole time, she was intensely aware of Guy moving right behind her. *I knew I couldn't trust him,* she thought. *From the very beginning I knew it.*

No one said a word until they reached the front door. There Gerard paused. Quietly he said, "Mr. Barnard? You will relay a message to Toby Wolff?"

Guy nodded. "Certainly. What's the message?"

"Tell him he has just called in his last chip." Gerard opened the front door. Outside, the sunshine was blinding. "There will be no more from me."

She made it scarcely five steps before her rage burst through.

"You lied to me. You scum, you were *using* me!"

The look on his face was the only answer Willy needed. It was written there clearly; the acknowledgment, the guilt.

"You knew about Friar Tuck. About the bounty. You weren't after just any 'live one,' were you? You were after a particular man—my father!"

Guy gave a shrug as though, now that the truth was out, it hardly mattered.

"How was this 'deal' with me supposed to work?" she pressed on. "Tell me, I'm curious. Were you going to turn him in the instant we found him—and my part of the deal be damned? Or were you going to humor me awhile, give me a chance to get my father home, let him step off the plane and onto American soil before you had him arrested? What was the plan, Guy? What *was* it?"

"There was no plan."

"Come on. A man like you always has a plan."

He looked tired. Defeated. "There was no plan."

She stared straight up at him, her fists clenching, unclenching. "I bet you had plans for that two million dollars. I bet you knew exactly how you were going to spend it. Every penny. And all you had to do was put my father away. You bastard." She should have slugged him right then and there. Instead, she walked away.

"Sure, I could use two million bucks!" he yelled. "I could use a lot of things! But I didn't want to use *you!*"

She kept walking. It took him only a few quick strides to catch up to her.

"Willy. Dammit, will you listen?"

"To what? More of your lies?"

"No. The truth."

"The truth?" She laughed. "Since when have you bothered with the truth?"

He grabbed her arm and pulled her around to face him. "Since right now."

"Let me go."

"Not until you hear me out."

"Why should I believe anything you say?"

"Look, I admit it. I knew about Friar Tuck. About the reward. And—"

"And you knew my father was on their list."

"Yes."

"Then why didn't you tell me?"

"I would have. I was going to."

"It was all worked out from the beginning, wasn't it? Use me to track down my father."

"I thought about it. At first."

"Oh, you're low, Guy. You're really scraping bottom. Does money mean so much to you?"

"I wasn't doing it for the money. I didn't have a choice. They backed me into it."

"Who?"

"The Ariel Group. I told you—two weeks ago they showed up in my office. They knew I was headed back to Nam. What I didn't tell you was the real reason they wanted me to work for them. They weren't tracking MIAs. They were tracking an old war criminal."

"Friar Tuck."

He nodded. "I told them I wasn't interested. They offered me money. A lot of it. I got a little interested. Then they made me an offer I couldn't refuse."

"Ah," she said with disdain.

"Not money . . ." he protested.

"Then what's the payoff?"

He ran his hand through his hair and let out a tired breath. "Silence."

She frowned, not understanding. He didn't say a thing, but she could see in his eyes some deep, dark agony. "Then that's it," she finally whispered. "Blackmail. What do they have on you, Guy? What are you hiding?"

"It's not—" he swallowed "—something I can talk about."

"I see. It must be pretty damn shocking. Which is no big surprise, I guess. But it still doesn't justify what you tried to do to me." She turned and walked away in disgust.

The road shimmered in the midmorning heat. Guy was right on her heels, like a stray dog that refused to be left behind. And he wasn't the only stray following her. The slap of bare feet announced the reappearance of Oliver, who skipped along beside her, chirping, "You want cyclo ride? It is very hot day! A thousand dong—I get you ride!"

She heard the squeak of wheels, the wheeze of an out-of-breath driver. Now Oliver's uncles had joined the procession.

"Go away," she said. "I don't want a ride."

"Sun very hot, very strong today. Maybe you faint. Once I see Russian lady faint." Oliver shook his head at the memory. "It was very bad sight."

"Go *away!*"

Undaunted, Oliver turned to Guy. "How about you, Daddy?"

Guy slapped a few bills into Oliver's grubby hand. "There's a thousand. Now scram."

Oliver vanished. Unfortunately, Guy wasn't so easily brushed off. He followed Willy into the town marketplace, past stands piled high with melons and mangoes, past counters where freshly butchered meat gathered flies.

"I was going to tell you about your father," Guy said. "I just wasn't sure how you'd take it."

"I'm not afraid of the truth."

"Sure you are! You're trying to protect him. That's why you keep ignoring the evidence."

"He wasn't a traitor!"

"You still love him, don't you?"

She turned sharply and walked away. Guy was right beside her. "What's wrong?" he said. "Did I hit a nerve?"

"Why should I care about him? He walked out on us."

"And you still feel guilty about it."

"Guilty?" She stopped. "Me?"

"That's right. Somewhere in that little-girl head of yours, you still blame yourself for his leaving. Maybe you had a fight, the way kids and dads always do, and you said something you shouldn't have. But before you had the chance to make up, he took off. And his plane went down. And here you are, twenty years later, still trying to make it up to him."

"Practicing psychiatry without a license now?"

"It doesn't take a shrink to know what goes on in a kid's head. I was fourteen when *my* old man walked out. I never got over being abandoned, either. Now I worry about my own kid. And it hurts."

She stared at him, astonished. "You have a child?"

"In a manner of speaking." He looked down. "The boy's mother and I, we weren't married. It's not something I'm particularly proud of."

"Oh."

"Yeah."

You walked out on them, she thought. *Your father left you. You left your son. The world never changes.*

"He wasn't a traitor," she insisted, returning to the matter at hand. "He was a lot of things—irresponsible, careless, insensitive. But he wouldn't turn against his own country."

"But he's on that list of suspects. If he's not Friar Tuck himself, he's probably connected somehow. And it's got to be a dangerous link. That's why someone's trying to stop you. That's why you're hitting brick walls wherever you turn. That's why, with every step you take, you're being followed."

"What!" In reflex, she turned to scan the crowd.

"Don't be so obvious." Guy grabbed her arm and dragged her to a pharmacy window. "Man at two o'clock," he murmured, nodding at a reflection in the glass. "Blue shirt, black trousers."

"Are you sure?"

"Absolutely. I just don't know who he's working for."

"He looks Vietnamese."

"But he could be working for the Russians. Or the Chinese. They both have a stake in this country."

Even as she started at the reflection, the man in the blue shirt melted into the crowd. She knew he was still lingering nearby; she could feel his gaze on her back.

"What do I do, Guy?" she whispered. "How do I get rid of him?"

"You can't. Just keep in mind he's there. That you're probably under constant surveillance. In fact, we seem to be under the surveillance of a whole damn army." At least a dozen faces were now reflected there, all of them crowded close and peering curiously at the two foreigners. In the back, a familiar figure kept bouncing up and down, waving at them in the glass.

"Hello, Daddy!" came a yell.

Guy sighed. "We can't even get rid of *him.*"

Willy stared hard at Guy's reflection. And she thought, *But I can get rid of you.*

Major Nathan Donnell of the Casualty Resolution team had shocking red hair, a booming voice and a cigar that stank to high heaven. Guy didn't know which was worse—the stench of that cigar or the odor of decay emanating from the four skeletons on the table. Maybe that's why Nate smoked those rotten cigars; they masked the smell of death.

The skeletons, each labeled with an ID number, were laid out on separate tarps. Also on the table were four plastic bags containing the personal effects and various other items found with the skeletons. After twenty or more years in this climate, not much remained of these bodies except dirt-encrusted bones and teeth. At least that much was left; sometimes fragments were all they had to work with.

Nate was reading aloud from the accompanying reports. In that grim setting, his resonant voice sounded somehow obscene, echoing off the walls of the Quonset hut. "Number 784-A, found in jungle, twelve klicks west of Camp Hawthorne. Army dog tag nearby—name, Elmore Stukey, Pfc."

"The tag was lying nearby?" Guy asked. "Not around the neck?"

Nate glanced at the Vietnamese liaison officer, who was standing off to the side. "Is that correct? It wasn't around the neck?"

The Vietnamese man nodded. "That is what the report said."

"Elmore Stukey," muttered Guy, opening the man's military medical record. "Six foot two, Caucasian, perfect teeth." He looked at the skeleton. Just a glance at the femur told him the man on the table couldn't have stood much taller than five-six. He shook his head. "Wrong guy."

"Cross off Stukey?"

"Cross off Stukey. But note that someone made off with his dog tag."

Nate let out a morbid laugh. "Not a good sign."

"What about these other three?"

"Oh, those." Nate flipped to another report. "Those three were found together eight klicks north of LZ Bird. Had that U.S. Army helmet lying close by. Not much else around."

Guy focused automatically on the relevant details: pelvic shape, configuration of incisors. "Those two are females, probably Asian," he noted. "But that one . . ." He took out a tape measure, ran it along the dirt-stained femur. "Male, five foot nine or thereabouts. Hmm. Silver fillings on numbers one and two." He nodded. "Possible."

Nate glanced at the Vietnamese liaison officer. "Number 786-A. I'll be flying him back for further examination."

"And the others?"

"What do you think, Guy?"

Guy shrugged. "We'll take 784-A, as well. Just to be safe. But the two females are yours."

The Vietnamese nodded. "We will make the arrangements," he said, and quietly withdrew.

There was a silence as Nate lit up another cigar, shook out the match. "Well, you sure made quick work of it. I wasn't expecting you here till tomorrow."

"Something came up."

"Yeah?" Nate's expression was thoughtful through the stinking cloud of smoke. "Anything I can help you with?"

"Maybe."

Nate nodded toward the door. "Come on. Let's get out of here. This place gives me the creeps."

They walked outside and stood in the dusty courtyard of the old military compound. Barbed wire curled on the wall above them. A rattling air conditioner dripped water from a window of the Quonset hut.

"So," said Nate, contentedly puffing on his cigar. "Is this business or personal?"

"Both. I need some information."

"Not classified, I hope."

"You tell me."

Nate laughed and squinted up at the barbed wire. "I may not tell you anything. But ask anyway."

"You were on the repatriation team back in '73, right?"

"Seventy-three through '75. But my job didn't amount to much. Just smiled a lot and passed out razors and toothbrushes. You know, a welcome-home handshake for returning POWs."

"Did you happen to shake hands with any POWs from Tuyen Quan?"

"Not many. Half a dozen. That was a pretty miserable camp. Had an outbreak of typhoid near the end. A lot of 'em died in captivity."

"But not all of them. One of the POWs was a guy named Luis Valdez. Remember him?"

"Just the name. And only because I heard he shot himself the day after he got home. I thought it was a crying shame."

"Then you never met him?"

"No, he went through closed debriefing. Totally separate channel. No outside contact."

Guy frowned, wondering about that closed debriefing. Why had Intelligence shut Valdez off from the others?

"What about the other POWs from Tuyen Quan?" asked Guy. "Did anyone talk about Valdez? Mention why he was kept apart?"

"Not really. Hey, they were a pretty delirious bunch. All they could talk about was going home. Seeing their families. Anyway, I don't think any of them knew Valdez. The camp held its prisoners two to a cell, and Valdez's cellmate wasn't in the group."

"Dead?"

"No. Refused to get on the plane. If you can believe it."

"Didn't want to fly?"

"Didn't want to go home, period."

"You remember his name?"

"Hell, yes. I had to file a ten-page report on the guy. Lassiter. Sam Lassiter. Incident got me a reprimand."

"What happened?"

"We tried to drag him aboard. He kept yelling that he wanted to stay in Nam. And he was this big blond Viking, you know? Six foot four, kicking and screaming like a two-year-old. Should've seen the Vietnamese, laughing at it all. Anyway, the guy got loose and tore off into the crowd. At that point, we figured, what the hell. Let the jerk stay if he wants to."

"Then he never went home?"

Nate blew out a cloud of cigar smoke. "Never did. For a while, we tried to keep tabs on him. Last we heard, he was sighted over in Cantho, but that was a few years ago. Since then he could've moved on. Or died." Nate glanced around at the barren compound. "Nuts—that's my diagnosis. Gotta be nuts to stay in this godforsaken country."

Maybe not, thought Guy. *Maybe he didn't have a choice.*

"What happened to the other guys from Tuyen?" Guy asked. "After they got home?"

"They had the usual problems. Post-traumatic-stress reaction, you know. But they adjusted okay. Or as well as could be expected."

"All except Valdez."

"Yeah. All except Valdez." Nate flicked off a cigar ash. "Couldn't do a thing for him, or for wackos like Lassiter. When they're gone, they're gone. All those kids—they were too young for that war. Didn't have their heads together to begin with. Whenever I think of Lassiter and Valdez, it makes me feel pretty damn useless."

"You did what you could."

Nate nodded. "Well, I guess we're good for something." Nate sighed and looked over at the Quonset hut. "At least 786-A's finally going home."

The Russians were singing again. Otherwise it was a pleasant enough evening. The beer was cold, the bartender discreetly attentive. From his perch at the rooftop bar, Guy watched the Russkies slosh another round of Stolichnaya into their glasses. They, at least, seemed to be having a good time; it was more than he could say for himself.

He had to come up with a plan, and fast. Everything he'd learned, from Alain Gerard that morning and from Nate Donnell that afternoon, had backed up what he'd already suspected: that Willy Maitland was in over her pretty head. He was convinced that the attack in Bangkok hadn't been a robbery attempt. Someone was out to stop her. Someone who didn't want her rooting around in Bill Maitland's past. The CIA? The Vietnamese? Wild Bill himself?

That last thought he discarded as impossible. No man, no matter how desperate, would send someone to attack his own daughter.

But what if it had been meant only as a warning? A scare tactic?

All the possibilities, all the permutations, were giving Guy a headache. Was Maitland alive? What was his connection to Friar Tuck? Were they one and the same man?

Why was the Ariel Group involved?

That was the other part of the puzzle—the Ariel Group. Guy mentally replayed that visit they'd paid him two weeks ago. The two men who'd appeared in his office had been unremarkable: clean shaven, dark suits, nondescript ties, the sort of faces you'd forget the instant they walked out your door. Only when they'd presented the check for twenty thousand dollars did he sit up and take notice. Whoever they were, they had cash to burn. And there was more money waiting—a lot more—if only he'd do them one small favor: locate a certain pilot known as Friar Tuck. "Your patriotic duty," they'd called it. The man was a traitor, a red-blooded American who'd gone over to the other side. Still, Guy had hesitated. It wasn't his kind of job. He wasn't a bounty hunter.

That's when they'd played their trump card.

Ariel, Ariel. He kept mulling over the name. Something Biblical. Lionlike men. Odd name for a vets organization. If that's what they were.

Ariel wasn't the only group hunting the elusive Friar Tuck. The CIA had a bounty on the man. For all Guy knew, the Vietnamese, the French and the men from Mars were after the pilot, as well.

And at the very eye of the hurricane was naive, stubborn, impossible Willy Maitland.

That she was so damnably attractive only made things worse. She was a maddening combination of toughness and vulnerability, and he'd been torn between using her and protecting her. Did any of that make sense?

The rhythmic thud of disco music drifted up from a lower floor. He considered heading downstairs to find some willing dance partner and trample a few toes. As he took another swallow of beer, a familiar figure passed through his peripheral vision. Turning, he saw Willy head for a table near the railing. He wondered if she'd consider joining him for a drink.

Obviously not, he decided, seeing how determinedly she was ignoring him. She stared off at the night, her back rigid, her gaze fixed somewhere in the distance. A strand of tawny hair slid over her cheek, and she tucked it behind her ear, a tight little gesture that made him think of a schoolmarm.

He decided to ignore her, too. But the more fiercely he tried to shove all thought of her from his mind, the more her image seemed to burn into his brain. Even as he focused his gaze on the bartender's dwindling bottle of Stolichnaya, he felt her presence, like a crackling fire radiating somewhere behind him.

What the hell. He'd give it one more try.

He shoved to his feet and strode across the rooftop.

Willy sensed his approach but didn't bother to look up, even when he grabbed a chair, sat down and leaned across the table.

"I still think we can work together," he said.

She sniffed. "I doubt it."

"Can't we at least talk about it?"

"I don't have a thing to say to you, Mr. Barnard."

"So it's back to Mr. Barnard."

Her frigid gaze met his across the table. "I could call you something else. I could call you a—"

"Can we skip the sweet talk? Look, I've been to see a friend of mine—"

"You have friends? Amazing."

"Nate was part of the welcome-home team back in '75. Met a lot of returning POWs. Including the men from Tuyen Quan."

Suddenly she looked interested. "He knew Luis Valdez?"

"No. Valdez was routed through classified debriefing. No one got near him. But Valdez had a cellmate in Tuyen Quan, a man named Sam Lassiter. Nate says Lassiter didn't go home."

"He died?"

"He never left the country."

She leaned forward, her whole body suddenly rigid with excitement. "He's still here in Nam?"

"Was a few years ago anyway. In Cantho. It's a river town in the Delta, about a hundred and fifty kilometers southwest of here."

"Not very far," she said, her mind obviously racing. "I could leave tomorrow morning . . . get there by afternoon . . ."

"And just how are you going to get there?"

"What do you mean, how? By car, of course."

"You think Mr. Ainh's going to let you waltz off on your own?"

"That's what bribes are for. Some people will do anything for a buck. Won't they?"

He met her hard gaze with one equally unflinching. "Forget the damn money. Don't you see someone's trying to use *both* of us? I want to know why." He leaned forward, his voice soft, coaxing. "I've made arrangements for a driver to Cantho first thing in the morning. We can tell Ainh I've invited you along for the ride. You know, just another tourist visiting the—"

She laughed. "You must think I have the IQ of a turnip. Why should I trust you? Bounty hunter. Opportunist. *Jerk.*"

"Lovely evening, isn't it?" cut in a cheery voice.

Dodge Hamilton, drink in hand, beamed down at them. He was greeted with dead silence.

"Oh, dear. Am I intruding?"

"Not at all," Willy said with a sigh, pulling a chair out for the ubiquitous Englishman. No doubt he wanted company for his misery, and she would do fine. They could commiserate a little more about his lost story and her lost father.

"No, really, I wouldn't dream of—"

"I insist." Willy tossed a lethal glance at Guy. "Mr. Barnard was just leaving."

Hamilton's gaze shifted from Guy to the offered chair. "Well, if you insist." He settled uneasily into the chair, set his glass down on the table and looked at Willy. "What I wanted to ask you, Miss Maitland, is whether you'd consent to an interview."

"Me? Why on earth?"

"I decided on a new focus for my Saigon story—a daughter's search for her father. Such a touching angle. A sentimental journey into—"

"Bad idea," Guy said, cutting in.

"Why?" asked Hamilton.

"It . . . has no passion," he improvised. "No romance. No excitement."

"Of course, there's excitement. A missing father—"

"Hamilton." Guy leaned forward. "No."

"He's asking *me,*" Willy said. "After all, it's about my father."

Guy's gaze swung around to her. "Willy," he said quietly, "think."

"I'm thinking a little publicity might open a few doors."

"More likely it'd close doors. The Vietnamese hate to hang out their dirty laundry. What if they know what happened to your father, and it wasn't a nice ending? They're not going to want the details all over the London papers. It'd be much easier to throw you out of the country."

"Believe me," said Hamilton, "I can be discreet."

"A discreet reporter. Right," Guy muttered.

"Not a word would be printed till she's left the country."

"The Vietnamese aren't dumb. They'd find out what you were working on."

"Then I'll give them a cover story. Something to throw them off the track."

"Excuse me . . ." Willy said politely.

"The matter's touchier than you realize, Hamilton," Guy said.

"I've covered delicate matters before. When I say something's off the record, I keep it off the record."

Willy rose to her feet. "I give up. I'm going to bed."

Guy looked up. "You can't go to bed. We haven't finished talking."

"You and I have definitely finished talking."

"What about tomorrow?"

"What about my story?"

"Hamilton," she said, "if it's dirty laundry you're looking for, why don't you interview *him?*" She pointed to Guy. Then she turned and walked away.

Hamilton looked at Guy. "What dirty laundry do you have?"

Guy merely smiled.

He was still smiling as he crumpled his beer can in his bare hands.

Lord, deliver me from the jerks of the world, Willy thought wearily as she stepped into the elevator. The doors slid closed. *Above all, deliver me from Guy Barnard.*

Leaning back, she closed her eyes and waited for the elevator to creep down to the fourth floor. It moved at a snail's pace, like everything else in this country. The stale air was rank with the smell of liquor and sweat. Through the creak of the cables she could hear a faint squeaking, high in the elevator shaft. Bats. She'd seen them the night before flapping over the courtyard. Wonderful. Bats and Guy Barnard. Could a girl ask for anything more?

If only there was some way she could have the benefit of his insider's knowledge without having to put up with *him.* The man was clever and streetwise, and he had those shadowy but all-important connections. Too bad he couldn't be trusted. Still, she couldn't help wondering what it would be like to take him up on his offer. Just the thought of working cheek to cheek with the man made her stomach dance a little pirouette of excitement. An ominous sign. The man was getting to her.

Oh, she'd been in love before; she knew how unreasonable hormones could be, how much havoc they could wreak, cavorting in a deprived female body.

I just won't think about him. It's the wrong time, the wrong place, the wrong situation.

And definitely the wrong man.

The elevator groaned to a halt, and the doors slid open to the deserted outdoor walkway. The night trembled to the distant beat of disco music as she headed through the shadows to her room. The entire fourth floor seemed abandoned this evening, all the windows unlit, the curtains drawn. She whirled around in fright as a chorus of shrieks echoed off the building and spiraled up into the darkness. Beyond the walkway railing, the shadows of bats rose and fluttered like phantoms over the courtyard.

Her hands were still shaking when she reached her door, and it took a moment to find the key. As she rummaged in her purse, a figure glided into her peripheral vision. Some sixth sense—a premonition of danger—made her turn.

At the end of the walkway, a man emerged from the shadows. As he passed beneath the glow of an outdoor lamp, she saw slick black hair and a face so immobile it seemed cast in wax. Then something else drew her gaze. Something in his hand. He was holding a knife.

She dropped her purse and ran.

Just ahead, the walkway turned a corner, past a huge air-conditioning vent. If she kept moving, she would reach the safety of the stairwell.

The man was yards behind. Surely the purse was what he wanted. But as she tore around the corner, she heard his footsteps thudding in pursuit. Oh, God, he wasn't after her money.

He was after her.

The stairwell lay ahead at the far end of the walkway. Just one flight down was the dance hall. She'd find people there. Safety . . .

With a desperate burst of speed, she sprinted forward. Then, through a fog of panic, she saw that her escape route was cut off.

Another man had appeared. He stood in the shadows at the far end of the walkway. She couldn't see his expression; all she saw was the faint gleam of his face.

She halted, spun around. As she did, something whistled past her cheek and clattered onto the walkway. A knife. Automatically, she snatched it up and wielded it in front of her.

Her gaze shifted first to one man, then the other. They were closing in.

She screamed. Her cry mingled with the dance music, echoed off the buildings and funneled up into the night. A wave of startled bats fluttered up through the darkness. *Can't anyone hear me?* she thought in desperation.

She cast another frantic look around, searching for a way out. In front of her, beyond the railing, lay a four-story drop to the courtyard. Just behind her, sunk into a square expanse of graveled roof, was the enormous air-conditioning vent. Through the rusted grating she saw its giant fan blades spinning like a plane's propeller. The blast of warm air was so powerful it made her skirt billow.

The men moved in for the kill.

6

She had no choice. She scrambled over the railing and dropped onto the grating. It sagged under her weight, lowering her heart-stoppingly close to the deadly blades. A rusted fragment crumbled off into the fan; the clatter of metal was deafening.

She inched her way over the grate, heading for a safe island of rooftop. It was only a few steps across, but it felt like miles of tightrope suspended over oblivion. Her legs were trembling as she finally stepped off the grate. It was a dead end; beyond lay a sheer drop. And a crumbling expanse of grating was all that separated her from the killers.

The two men glanced around in frustration, searching for a safe way to reach her. There was no other route; they would have to cross the vent. But the grating had barely supported her weight; these men were far heavier. She looked at the deadly whirl of the blades. They wouldn't risk it, she thought.

But to her disbelief, one of the men climbed over the railing and eased himself onto the vent. The mesh sagged but held. He stared at her over the spinning blades, and she saw in his eyes the impassive gaze of a man who'd simply come to do his job.

Trapped, she thought. Dear God, I'm trapped!

She screamed again, but her cry of terror was lost in the fan's roar.

He was halfway across, his knife poised. She clutched her knife and backed away to the very edge of the roof. She had two choices: a four-story drop to the pavement below, or hand-to-hand combat with an experienced assassin. Both prospects seemed equally hopeless.

She crouched, knife in trembling hand, to slash, to claw—anything to stay alive. The man took another step. The blade moved closer.

Then gunfire ripped the night.

Willy stared in bewilderment as the killer clutched his belly and looked down at his bloody hand, his face a mask of astonishment. Then, like a puppet whose strings have been cut, he crumpled. As dead weight hit the weakened grating, Willy closed her eyes and cringed.

She never saw his body fall through. But she heard the squeal of metal, felt the wild shuddering of the fan blades. She collapsed to her knees, retching into the darkness below.

When the heaving finally stopped, she forced her head up.

Her other attacker had vanished.

Across the courtyard, on the opposite walkway, something gleamed. The barrel of a gun being lowered. A small face peering at her over the railing. She struggled to make sense of why the boy was there, why he had just saved her life. Stumbling to her feet, she whispered, "Oliver?"

The boy merely put a finger to his lips. Then, like a ghost, he slipped away into the darkness.

Dazed, she heard shouts and the thud of approaching footsteps.

"Willy! Are you all right?"

She turned and saw Guy. And she heard the panic in his voice.

"Don't move! I'll come get you."

"No!" she cried. "The grate—it's broken—"

For a moment, he studied the spinning blades. Then, glancing around, he spotted a workman's ladder propped beneath a broken window. He dragged it to the railing, hoisted it over and slid it horizontally across the broken grate. Then he eased himself over the railing, carefully stepped onto a rung and extended his arm to Willy. "I'm right here," he said. "Put your left foot on the ladder and grab my hand. I won't let you fall, I swear it. Come on, sweetheart. Just reach for my hand."

She couldn't look down at the fan blades. She looked across them at Guy's face, tense and gleaming with sweat. At his hand, reaching for her. And in that instant she knew, without a shred of doubt, that he would catch her. That she could trust him with her life.

She took a breath for courage, then took the step forward, over the whirling blades.

Instantly his hand locked over hers. For a split second she teetered. Guy's rigid grasp steadied her. Slowly, jerkily, she lunged forward onto the rung where he balanced.

"I've got you!" he yelled as he swept her into his arms, away from the yawning vent. He swung her easily over the railing onto the walkway, then dropped down beside her. He pulled her into the safety of his arms.

"It's all right," he murmured over and over into her hair. "Everything's all right. . . ."

Only then, as she felt his heart pounding against hers, did she realize how terrified he'd been for her.

She was shaking so hard she could barely stand on her own two legs. It didn't matter. She knew the arms now wrapped around her would never let her fall.

They both stiffened as a harsh command was issued in Vietnamese. The people gathered about them quickly stepped aside to let a policeman through. Willy squinted as a blinding light shone in her eyes. The flashlight's beam shifted and froze on the air-conditioning vent. From the spectators came a collective gasp of horror.

"Dear God," she heard Dodge Hamilton whisper. "What a bloody mess."

Mr. Ainh was sweating. He was also hungry and tired, and he needed badly to use the toilet. But all these concerns would have to wait. He had learned that much from the war: patience. *Victory comes to those who endure.* This was what he kept saying to himself as he sat in his hard chair and stared down at the wooden table.

"We have been careless, Comrade." The minister's voice was soft, no more than a whisper; but then, the voice of power had no need to shout.

Slowly Ainh raised his head. The man sitting across from him had eyes like smooth, sparkling river stones. Though the face was wrinkled and the hair hung in silver wisps as delicate as cobwebs, the eyes were those of a young man—bold and black and brilliant. Ainh felt their gaze slice through him.

"The death of an American tourist would be most embarrassing," said the minister.

Ainh could only nod in meek agreement.

"You are certain Miss Maitland is uninjured?"

Ainh cleared his throat. Nodded again.

The minister's voice, so soft just a moment before, took on a razor's edge. "This Barnard fellow—he prevented an international incident, something our own people seem incapable of."

"But we had no warning, no reason to think this would happen."

"The attack in Bangkok—was that not a warning?"

"A robbery attempt! That's what the report—"

"And reports are never wrong, are they?" The minister's smile was disconcertingly bland. "First Bangkok. Then tonight. I wonder what our little American tourist has gotten herself into."

"The two attacks may not be connected."

"Everything, Comrade, is connected." The minister sat very still, thinking. "And what about Mr. Barnard? Are he and Miss Maitland—" the minister paused delicately "—involved?"

"I think not. She called him a . . . what is that American expression? A *jerk.*"

The minister laughed. "Ah. Mr. Barnard has trouble with the ladies!"

There was a knock on the door. An official entered, handed a report to the minister and respectfully withdrew.

"There is progress in the case?" inquired Ainh.

The minister looked up. "Of a sort. They were able to piece together fragments of the dead man's identity card. It seems he was already well-known to the police."

"Then that explains it!" said Ainh. "Some of these thugs will do anything for a few thousand dong."

"This was no robbery." The minister handed the report to Ainh. "He has connections to the old regime."

Ainh scanned the page. "I see mention only of a woman cousin—a factory worker." He paused, then looked up in surprise. "A mixed blood."

The minister nodded. "She is being questioned now. Shall we look in on her?"

Chantal was slouched on a wooden bench, aiming lethal glares at the policeman in charge of questioning.

"I have done nothing!" she spat out. "Why should I want anyone dead? An American bitch, you say? What, do you think I am crazy? I have been home all night! Talk to the old man who lives above me! Ask him who's been playing my radio all night! Ask him why he's been beating on my ceiling, the old crank! Oh, but I could tell you stories about *him.*"

"You accuse an old man?" said the policeman. "*You* are the counter-revolutionary! You and your cousin!"

"I hardly know my cousin."

"You were working together."

Chantal snorted. "I work in a factory. I have nothing to do with him."

The policeman swung a bag onto the table. He took out the items, placed them in front of her. "Caviar, Champagne. Pâté. We found these in your cupboards. How does a factory worker afford these things?"

Chantal's lips tightened, but she said nothing.

The policeman smiled. He gestured to a guard and Chantal, rigidly silent, was led from the room.

The policeman then turned respectfully to the minister, who, along with Ainh, was watching the proceedings. "As you can see, Minister Tranh, she is uncooperative. But give us time. We will think of a way to—"

"Let her go," said the minister.

The policeman looked startled. "I assure you, she can be made to talk."

Minister Tranh smiled. "There are other ways to get information. Release her. Then wait for the fly to drift back to the honeypot."

The policeman left, shaking his head. But, of course, he would do as ordered. After all, Minister Tranh had far more experience in such matters. Hadn't the old fox honed his skills on years of wartime espionage?

For a long time, the minister sat thinking. Then he picked up the champagne bottle and squinted at the label. "Ah. Taittinger." He sighed. "A favorite from my days in Paris." Gently he set the bottle back down and looked at Ainh. "I sense that Miss Maitland has blundered into something dangerous. Perhaps she is asking too many questions. Stirring up dragons from the past."

"You mean her father?" Ainh shook his head. "That is a very old dragon."

To which the minister said softly, "But perhaps not a vanquished one."

A large black cockroach crawled across the table. One of the guards slapped it with a newspaper, brushed the corpse onto the floor and calmly went on writing. Above him, a ceiling fan whirred in the heat, fluttering papers on the desk.

"Once again, Miss Maitland," said the officer in charge. "Tell me what happened."

"I've told you everything."

"I think you have left something out."

"Nothing. I've left nothing out."

"Yes, you have. There was a gunman."

"I saw no gunman."

"We have witnesses. They heard a shot. Who fired the gun?"

"I told you, I didn't see anyone. The grating was weak—he fell through."

"Why are you lying?"

Her chin shot up. "Why do you insist I'm lying?"

"Because we both know you are."

"Lay off her!" Guy cut in. "She's told you everything she knows."

The officer turned, looked at Guy. "You will kindly remain silent, Mr. Barnard."

"And you'll cut out the Gestapo act! You've been questioning her for two hours now. Can't you see she's exhausted?"

"Perhaps it is time you left."

Guy wasn't about to back down. "She's an American. You can't hold her indefinitely!"

The officer looked at Willy, then at Guy. He gave a nonchalant shrug. "She will be released."

"When?"

"When she tells the truth." Turning, he walked out.

"Hang in," Guy muttered. "We'll get you out of here yet." He followed the officer into the next room, slamming the door behind him.

The arguing went on for ten minutes. She could hear them shouting behind the door. At least Guy still had the strength to shout; she could barely hold her head up.

When Guy returned at last, she could see from his look of disgust that he'd gotten nowhere. He dropped wearily onto the bench beside her and rubbed his eyes.

"What do they want from me?" she asked. "Why can't they just leave me alone?"

"I get the feeling they're waiting for something. Some sort of approval. . . ."

"Whose?"

"Hell if I know."

A rolled-up newspaper whacked the table. Willy looked over and saw the guard flick away another dead roach. She shuddered.

It was midnight.

At 1:00 a.m., Mr. Ainh appeared, looking as sallow as an old bed sheet. Willy was too numb to move from the bench. She simply sat there, propped against Guy's shoulder, and let the two men do the talking.

"We are very sorry for the inconvenience," said Ainh, sounding genuinely contrite. "But you must understand—"

"*Inconvenience?*" Guy snapped. "Ms. Maitland was nearly killed earlier tonight, and she's been kept here for three hours now. What the hell's going on?"

"The situation is . . . unusual. A robbery attempt—on a foreigner, no less—well . . ." He shrugged helplessly.

Guy was incredulous. "You're calling this an attempted *robbery?*"

"What would you call it?"

"A cover-up."

Ainh shuffled uneasily. Turning, he exchanged a few words in Vietnamese with the guard. Then he gave Willy a polite bow. "The police say you are free to leave, Miss Maitland. On behalf of the Vietnamese government, I apologize for your most unfortunate experience. What happened does not in any way reflect on our high regard and warm feelings for the American people. We hope this will not spoil the remainder of your visit."

Guy couldn't help a laugh. "Why should it? It was just a little murder attempt."

"In the morning," Ainh went on quickly, "you are free to continue your tour."

"Subject to what restrictions?" Guy asked.

"No restrictions." Ainh cleared his throat and made a feeble attempt to smile. "Contrary to your government propaganda, Mr. Barnard, we are a reasonable people. We have nothing to hide."

To which Guy answered flatly, "Or so it seems."

"I don't get it. First they run you through the wringer. Then they hand you the keys to the country. It doesn't make sense."

Willy stared out the taxi window as the streets of Saigon glided past. Here and there, a lantern flickered in the darkness. A noodle vendor huddled on the sidewalk beside his steaming cart. In an open doorway, a beaded curtain shuddered, and in the dim room beyond, sleeping children could be seen, curled up like kittens on their mats.

"Nothing makes sense," she whispered. "Not this country. Or the people. Or anything that's happened. . . ."

She was trembling. The horror of everything that had happened that night suddenly burst through the numbing dam of exhaustion. Even Guy's arm, which had magically materialized around her shoulders, couldn't keep away the unnamed terrors of the night.

He pulled her against his chest, and only when she inhaled that comfortable smell of fatigue, felt the slow and steady beat of his heart, did her trembling finally stop. He kept whispering, "It's all right, Willy. I won't let anything happen to you." She felt his kiss, gentle as rain, on her forehead.

When the driver stopped in front of the hotel, Guy had to coax her out of the car. He led her through the nightmarish glare of the lobby. He was the pillar that supported her in the elevator. And it was his arm that guided her down the shadowed walkway and past the air-conditioning vent, now ominously silent. He didn't even ask her if she wanted his company for the night; he simply opened the door to his room, led her inside and sat her down on his bed. Then he locked the door and slid a chair in front of it.

In the bathroom, he soaked a washcloth with warm water. Then he came back out, sat down beside her on the bed and gently wiped her smudged face. Her cheeks were pale. He had the insane urge to kiss her, to breathe some semblance of life back into her body. He knew she wouldn't fight him; she didn't have the strength. But it wouldn't be right, and he wasn't the kind of man who'd take advantage of the situation, of her.

"There," he murmured, brushing back her hair. "All better."

She stirred and gazed up at him with wide, stunned eyes. "Thank you," she whispered.

"For what?"

"For . . ." She paused, searching for the right words. "For being here."

He touched her face. "I'll be here all night. I won't leave you alone. If that's what you want."

She nodded. It hurt him to see her look so tired, so defeated. *She's getting to me,* he thought. *This isn't supposed to happen. This isn't what I expected.*

He could see, from the brightness of her eyes, that she was trying not to cry. He slid his arm around her shoulders.

"You'll be safe, Willy," he whispered into the softness of her hair. "You'll be going home in the morning. Even if I have to strap you into that plane myself, you'll be going home."

She shook her head. "I can't."

"What do you mean, you can't?"

"My father . . ."

"Forget him. It isn't worth it."

"I made a promise. . . ."

"All you promised your mother was an answer. Not a body. Not some official report, stamped and certified. Just a simple answer. So give her one. Tell her he's dead, tell her he died in the crash. It's probably the truth."

"I can't lie to her."

"You have to." He took her by the shoulders, forcing her to look at him. "Willy, someone's trying to kill you. They've flubbed it twice. But what happens the third time? The fourth?"

She shook her head. "I'm not worth killing. I don't know anything!"

"Maybe it's not what you know. It's what you might find out."

Sniffling, she looked up in bewilderment. "That my father's dead? Or alive? What *difference* does it make to anyone?"

He sighed, a sound of overwhelming weariness. "I don't know. If we could talk to Oliver, find out who he works for—"

"He's just a kid!"

"Obviously not. He could be sixteen, seventeen. Old enough to be an agent."

"For the Vietnamese?"

"No. If he was one of theirs, why'd he vanish? Why did the police keep hounding you about him?"

She huddled on the bed, her confusion deepening. "He saved my life. And I don't even know why."

There it was again, that raw edge of vulnerability, shimmering in her eyes. She might be Wild Bill Maitland's brat, but she was also a woman, and Guy was having a hard time concentrating on the problem at hand. Why was someone trying to kill her?

He was too tired to think. It was late, she was so near, and there was the bed, just waiting.

He reached up and gently stroked her face. She seemed to sense immediately what was about to happen. Even though her whole body remained stiff, she didn't fight him. The instant their lips met, he felt a shock leap through her, through him, as though they'd both been hit by some glorious bolt of lightning. *My God,* he thought in surprise. *You wanted this as much as I did. . . .*

He heard her murmur, "No," against his mouth, but he knew she didn't mean it, so he went on kissing her until he knew that if he didn't stop right then and there, he'd do something he really didn't want to do.

Oh, yes I do, he thought with sudden abandon. *I want her more than I've wanted any other woman.*

She put her hand against his chest and murmured another "No," this one fainter. He would have ignored it, too, had it not been for the look in her eyes. They were wide and confused, the eyes of a woman pushed to the brink by fear and exhaustion. This wasn't the way he wanted her. Maddening as she could be, he wanted the living, breathing, *real* Willy Maitland in his arms.

He released her. They sat on the bed, not speaking for a while, just looking at each other with a shared sense of quiet astonishment.

"Why—why did you do that?" she asked weakly.

"You looked like you needed a kiss."

"Not from you."

"From someone, then. It's been a while since you've been kissed. Hasn't it?"

She didn't answer, and he knew he'd guessed the truth. *Hell, what a waste,* he thought, his gaze dropping briefly to that perfect little mouth. He managed a disinterested laugh. "That's what I thought."

Willy stared at his grinning face and wondered, *Is it so obvious?* Not only hadn't she been kissed in a long time, she hadn't *ever* been kissed like *that.* He knew exactly how to do it; he'd probably had years of practice with other women. For some insane reason, she found herself wondering how she compared, found herself hating every woman he'd ever kissed before her, hating even more every woman he'd kiss after her.

She flung herself down on the bed and turned her back on him. "Oh, leave me alone!" she cried. "I can't deal with this! I can't deal with you. I'm tired. I just want to sleep."

He didn't say anything. She felt him smooth her hair. It was nothing more than a brush of his fingers, but somehow, that one touch told her that he wouldn't leave, that he'd be there all night, watching over her. He rose from the bed and switched off the lamp. She lay very still in the darkness, listening to him move around the room. She heard him check the windows, then the door, testing how firmly the chair was wedged against it. Then, apparently satisfied, he went into the bathroom, and she heard water running in the sink.

She was still awake when he came back to bed and stretched out beside her. She lay there, worrying that he'd kiss her again and hoping desperately that he would.

"Guy?" she whispered.

"Yes?"

"I'm scared."

He reached for her through the darkness. Willingly, she let him pull her against his bare chest. He smelled of soap and safety. Yes, that's what it was. Safety.

"It's okay to be scared," he whispered. "Even if you are Wild Bill Maitland's kid."

As if she had a choice, she thought as she lay in his arms. The sad part was, she'd never wanted to be the daughter of a legend. What she'd wanted from Wild Bill wasn't valor or daring or the reflected glory of a hero.

What she'd wanted most of all was a father.

* * *

Siang crouched motionless in a stinking mud puddle and stared up the road at Chantal's building. Two hours had passed and the man was still there by the curb. Siang could see his vague form huddled in the darkness. A police agent, no doubt, and not a very good one. Was that a snore rumbling in the night? Yes, Siang thought, definitely a snore. How fortunate that surveillance was always relegated to those least able to withstand its monotony.

Siang decided to make his move.

He withdrew his knife. Noiselessly he edged out of the alley and circled around, slipping from shadow to shadow along the row of hootches. Barely five yards from his goal, he froze as the man's snores shuddered and stopped. The shadow's head lifted, shaking off sleep.

Siang closed in, yanked the man's head up by the hair and slit the throat.

There was no cry, only a gurgle, and then the hiss of a last breath escaping the dead man's lungs. Siang dragged the body around to the back of the building and rolled it into a drainage ditch. Then he slipped through an open window into Chantal's flat.

He found her asleep. She awakened instantly as he clapped his hand over her mouth.

"You!" she ground out through his fingers. "Damn you, you got me in trouble!"

"What did you tell the police?"

"Get away from me!"

"What did you tell them?"

She batted away his hand. "I didn't tell them anything!"

"You're lying."

"You think I'm stupid? You think I'd tell them I have friends in the CIA?"

He released her. As she sat up, the silky heat of her breast brushed against his arm. So the old whore still slept naked, he thought with an automatic stirring of desire.

She rose from the bed and pulled on a robe.

"Don't turn on the lights," he said.

"There was a man outside—a police agent. What did you do with him?"

"I took care of him."

"And the body?"

"In the ditch out back."

"Oh, nice, Siang. Very nice. Now they'll blame me for that, too." She struck a match and lit a cigarette. By the flame's brief glow, he could see her face framed by a tangle of black hair. In the semidarkness she still looked tempting, young and soft and succulent.

The match went out. He asked, "What happened at the police station?"

She let out a slow breath. The smell of exhaled smoke filled the darkness. "They asked about my cousin. They say he's dead. Is that true?"

"What do they know about me?"

"Is Winn really dead?"

Siang paused. "It couldn't be helped."

Chantal laughed. Softly at first, then with wild abandon. "*She* did that, did she? The American bitch? You cannot finish off even a woman? Oh, Siang, you must be slipping!"

He felt like hitting her, but he controlled the urge. Chantal was right. He must be slipping.

She began to pace the room, her movements as sure as a cat's in the darkness. "The police are interested. Very interested. And I saw others there—Party members, I think—watching the interrogation. What have you gotten me into, Siang?"

He shrugged. "Give me a cigarette."

She whirled on him in rage. "Get your own cigarettes! You think I have money to waste on *you?*"

"You'll get the money. All you want."

"You don't know how much I want."

"I still need a gun. You promised me you'd get one. Plus twenty rounds, minimum."

She let out a harsh breath of smoke. "Ammunition is hard to come by."

"I can't wait any longer. This has to be—"

They both froze as the door creaked open. *The police,* thought Siang, automatically reaching for his knife.

"You're so right, Mr. Siang," said a voice in the darkness. Perfect English. "It has to be done. But not quite yet."

The intruder moved lazily into the room, struck a match and calmly lit a kerosene lamp on the table.

Chantal's eyes were wide with astonishment. And fear. "It's you," she whispered. "You've come back. . . ."

The intruder smiled. He laid a pistol and a box of .38-caliber ammunition on the table. Then he looked at Siang. "There's been a slight change of plans."

7

She was flying. High, high above the clouds, where the sky was so cold and clear, it felt as if her plane were floating in a crystalline sea. She could hear the wings cut the air like knives through silk. Someone said, "Higher, baby. You have to climb higher if you want to reach the stars."

She turned. It was her father sitting in the copilot's seat, quicksilver smoke dancing around him. He looked the way she'd always remembered him, his cap tilted at a jaunty angle, his eyes twinkling. Just the way he used to look when she'd loved him. When he'd been the biggest, boldest Daddy in the world.

She said, "But I don't want to climb higher."

"Yes, you do. You want to reach the stars."

"I'm afraid, Daddy. Don't make me. . . ."

But he took the joystick. He sent the plane upward, upward, into the blue bowl of sky. He kept saying, "This is what it's all about. Yessir, baby, this is what it's all about." Only his voice had changed. She saw that it was no longer her father sitting in the copilot's seat; it was Guy Barnard, pushing them into oblivion. "I'll take us to the stars!"

Then it was her father again, gleefully gripping the joystick. She tried to wrench the plane out of the climb, but the joystick broke off in her hand.

The sky turned upside down, righted. She looked at the copilot's seat. Guy was sitting there, laughing. They went higher. Her father laughed.

"Who *are* you?" she screamed.

The phantom smiled. "Don't you know me?"

She woke up, still reaching desperately for that stump of a joystick. "It's me," the voice said.

She stared up wildly. "Daddy!"

The man looking down at her smiled, a kind smile. "Not quite."

She blinked, focused on Guy's face, his rumpled hair, unshaven jaw. Sweat gleamed on his bare shoulders. Through the curtains behind him, daylight shimmered.

"Nightmare?" he asked.

Groaning, she sat up and shoved back a handful of tangled hair. "I don't usually have them. Nightmares."

"After last night, I'd be surprised if you didn't have one."

Last night. She looked down and saw she was still wearing the same blood-spattered dress, now damp and clinging to her back.

"Power's out," said Guy, giving the silent air conditioner a slap. He padded over to the window and nudged open the curtain. Sunlight blazed in, so piercing, it hurt Willy's eyes. "Gonna be a hell of a scorcher."

"Already is."

"Are you feeling okay?" He stood silhouetted against the window, his unbelted trousers slung low over his hips. Once again she saw the scar, noticed how it rippled its way down his abdomen before vanishing beneath the waistband.

"I'm hot," she said. "And filthy. And I probably don't smell so good."

"I hadn't noticed." He paused and added ruefully, "Probably because I smell even worse."

They laughed, a short, uneasy laugh that was instantly cut off when someone knocked on the door. Guy called out, "Who's there?"

"Mr. Barnard? It is eight o'clock. The car is ready."

"It's my driver," Guy said, and he unbolted the door.

A smiling Vietnamese man stood outside. "Good morning! Do you still wish to go to Cantho this morning?"

"I don't think so," said Guy, discreetly stepping outside to talk in private. Willy heard him murmur, "I want to get Ms. Maitland to the airport this afternoon. Maybe we can . . ."

Cantho, Willy sat on the bed, listening to the buzz of conversation, trying to remember why that name was so important. Oh, yes. There was a man there, someone she needed to talk to. A man who might have the answers. She closed her eyes against the window's glare, and the dream came back to her, the grinning face of her father, the sickening climb of a doomed plane. She thought of her mother, lying near death at home. Heard her mother ask, "Are you sure, Willy? Do you know for certain he's dead?" Heard herself tell another lie, all the time hating herself, hating her own cowardice, hating the fact that she could never live up to her father's name. Or his courage.

"So stick around the hotel," Guy said to the driver. "Her plane takes off at four, so we should leave around—"

"I'm going to Cantho," said Willy.

Guy glanced around at her. "What?"

"I said I'm going to Cantho. You said you'd take me."

He shook his head. "Things have changed."

"Nothing's changed."

"The stakes have."

"But not the questions. They haven't gone away. They'll never go away."

Guy turned to the driver. "Excuse me while I talk some sense into the lady. . . ."

But Willy had already risen to her feet. "Don't bother. You can't talk sense into me." She went into the bathroom and shut the door. "I'm Wild Bill Maitland's kid, remember?" she yelled.

The driver looked sympathetically at Guy. "I will get the car."

The road out of Saigon was jammed with trucks, most of them ancient and spewing clouds of black exhaust. Through the open windows of their car came the smells of smoke and sun-baked pavement and rotting fruit. Laborers trudged along the roadside, a bobbing column of conical hats against the bright green of the rice paddies.

Five hours and two ferry crossings later, Guy and Willy stood on a Cantho pier and watched a multitude of boats glide across the muddy Mekong. River women dipped and swayed as they rowed, a strange and graceful dance at the oars. And on the riverbank swirled the noise and confusion of a thriving market town. Schoolgirls, braided hair gleaming in the sunshine, whisked past on bicycles. Stevedores heaved sacks of rice and crates of melons and pineapples onto sampans.

Overwhelmed by the chaos, Willy asked bleakly, "How are we ever going to find him?"

Guy's answer didn't inspire much confidence. He simply shrugged and said, "How hard can it be?"

Very hard, it turned out. All their inquiries brought the same response. "A tall man?" people would say. "And blond?" Invariably their answer would be a shake of the head.

It was Guy's inspired hunch that finally sent them into a series of tailor shops. "Maybe Lassiter's no longer blond," he said. "He could have dyed his hair or gone bald. But there's one feature a man can't disguise—his height. And in this country, a six-foot-four man is going to need specially tailored clothes."

The first three tailors they visited turned up nothing. It was with a growing sense of futility that they entered the fourth shop, wedged in an alley of tin-roofed hootches. In the cavelike gloom within, an elderly seamstress sat hunched over a mound of imitation silk. She didn't seem to understand Guy's questions. In frustration, Guy took out a pen and jotted a few words in Vietnamese on a scrap of newspaper. Then, to illustrate his point, he sketched in the figure of a tall man.

The woman squinted down at the drawing. For a long time, she sat there, her fingers knotted tightly around the shimmering fabric. Then she looked up at Guy. No words were exchanged, just that silent, mournful gaze.

Guy gave a nod that he understood. He reached into his pocket and lay a twenty-dollar bill on the table in front of her. She stared at it in wonder. American dollars. For her, it was a fortune.

At last she took up Guy's pen and, with painful precision, began to write. The instant she'd finished, Guy swept up the scrap of paper and jammed it into his pocket. "Let's go," he whispered to Willy.

"What does it say?" Willy whispered as they headed back along the row of hootches.

Guy didn't answer; he only quickened his pace. In the silence of the alley, Willy suddenly became aware of eyes, everywhere, watching them from the windows and doorways.

Willy tugged on Guy's arm. "Guy . . ."

"It's an address. Near the marketplace."

"Lassiter's?"

"Don't talk. Just keep moving. We're being followed."

"What?"

He grabbed her arm before she could turn to look. "Come on, keep your head. Pretend he's not there."

She fought to keep her eyes focused straight ahead, but the sense of being stalked made every muscle in her body strain to run. *How does he stay so calm?* she wondered, glancing at Guy. He was actually whistling now, a tuneless song that scraped her nerves raw. They reached the end of the alley, and a maze of streets lay before them. To her surprise, Guy stopped and struck up a cheerful conversation with a boy selling cigarettes at the corner. Their chatter seemed to go on forever.

"What are you doing?" Willy ground out. "Can't we get out of here?"

"Trust me." Guy bought a pack of Winstons, for which he paid two American dollars. The boy beamed and sketched a childish salute.

Guy took Willy's hand. "Get ready."

"Ready for what?"

The words were barely out of her mouth when Guy wrenched her around the corner and up another alley. They made a sharp left, then a right, past a row of tin-roofed shacks, and ducked into an open doorway.

Inside, it was too murky to make sense of their surroundings. For an eternity they huddled together, listening for footsteps. They could hear, in the distance, children laughing and a car horn honking incessantly. But just outside, in the alley, there was silence.

"Looks like the kid did his job," whispered Guy.

"You mean that cigarette boy?"

Guy sidled over to the doorway and peered out. "Looks clear. Come on, let's get out of here."

They slipped into the alley and doubled back. Even before they saw the marketplace, they could hear it: the shouts of merchants, the frantic squeals of pigs. Hurrying along the outskirts, they scanned the street names and finally turned into what was scarcely more than an alley jammed between crumbling apartment buildings. The address numbers were barely decipherable.

At last, at a faded green building, they stopped. Guy squinted at the number over the doorway and nodded. "This is it." He knocked.

The door opened. A single eye, iris so black, the pupil was invisible, peered at them through the crack. That was all they saw, that one glimpse of a woman's face, but it was enough to tell them she was afraid. Guy spoke to her in Vietnamese. The woman shook her head and tried to close the door. He put his hand out to stop it and spoke again, this time saying the man's name, "Sam Lassiter."

Panicking, the woman turned and screamed something in Vietnamese.

Somewhere in the house, footsteps thudded away, followed by the shattering of glass.

"Lassiter!" Guy yelled. Shoving past the woman, he raced through the apartment, Willy at his heels. In a back room, they found a broken window. Outside in the alley, a man was sprinting away. Guy scrambled out, dropped down among the glass shards and took off after the fugitive.

Willy was about to follow him out the window when the Vietnamese woman, frantic, grasped her arm.

"Please! No hurt him!" she cried. "Please!"

Willy, trying to pull free, found her fingers linked for an instant with the other woman's. Their eyes met. "We won't hurt him," Willy said, gently disengaging her arm.

Then she pulled herself up onto the windowsill and dropped into the alley.

Guy was pulling closer. He could see his quarry loping toward the marketplace. It had to be Lassiter. Though his hair was a lank, dirty brown, there was no disguising his height; he towered above the crowd. He ducked beneath the marketplace canopy and vanished into shadow.

Damn, thought Guy, struggling to move through the crowd. *I'm going to lose him.*

He shoved into the central market tent. The sun's glare abruptly gave way to a close, hot gloom. He stumbled blindly, his eyes adjusting slowly to the change in light. He made out the cramped aisles, the counters overflowing with fruit and vegetables, the gay sparkle of pinwheels spinning on a toy vendor's cart. A tall silhouette suddenly bobbed off to the side. Guy spun around and saw Lassiter duck behind a gleaming stack of cookware.

Guy scrambled after him. The man leapt up and sprinted away. Pots and pans went flying, a dozen cymbals crashing together.

Guy's quarry darted into the produce section. Guy made a sharp left, leapt over a crate of mangoes and dashed up a parallel aisle. "Lassiter!" he yelled. "I want to talk! That's all, just talk!"

The man spun right, shoved over a fruit stand and stumbled away. Watermelons slammed to the ground, exploding in a brilliant rain of flesh. Guy almost slipped in the muck. "Lassiter!" he shouted.

They headed into the meat section. Lassiter, desperate, shoved a crate of ducks into Guy's path, sending up a cloud of feathers as the birds, freed from their prison, flapped loose. Guy dodged the crate, leapt over a fugitive duck and kept running. Ahead lay the butcher counters, stacked high with slabs of meat. A vendor was hosing down the concrete floor, sending a stream of bloody water into the gutter. Lassiter, moving full tilt, suddenly slid and fell to his knees in the offal. At once he tried to scramble back to his feet, but by then Guy had snagged his shirt collar.

"Just—just talk," Guy managed to gasp between breaths. "That's all—talk—"

Lassiter thrashed, struggling to pull free.

"Gimme a chance!" Guy yelled, dragging him back down.

Lassiter rammed his shoulders at Guy's knees, sending Guy sprawling. In an instant, Lassiter had leapt to his feet. But as he turned to flee, Guy grabbed his ankle, and Lassiter toppled forward and splashed, headfirst, into a vat of squirming eels.

The water seemed to boil with slippery bodies, writhing in panic. Guy dragged the man's head out of the vat. They both collapsed, gasping on the slick concrete.

"Don't!" Lassiter sobbed. "Please . . ."

"I told you, I just—just want to talk—"

"I won't say anything! I swear it. You tell 'em that for me. Tell 'em I forgot everything. . . ."

"Who?" Guy took the other man by the shoulders. "Who are *they?* Who are you afraid of?"

Lassiter took a shaky breath and looked at him, seemed to make a decision. "The Company."

"Why does the CIA want you dead?" Willy asked.

They were sitting at a wooden table on the deck of an old river barge. Neutral territory, Lassiter had said of this floating café. During the war, by some unspoken agreement, V.C. and South Vietnamese soldiers would sit together on this very deck, enjoying a small patch of peace. A few hundred yards away, the war might rage on, but here no guns were drawn, no bullets fired.

Lassiter, gaunt and nervous, took a deep swallow of beer. Behind him, beyond the railing, flowed the Mekong, alive with the sounds of river men, the putter of boats. In the last light of sunset, the water rippled with gold. Lassiter said, "They want me out of the way for the same reason they wanted Luis Valdez out of the way. I know too much."

"About what?"

"Laos. The bombings, the gun drops. The war your average soldier didn't know about." He looked at Guy. "Did you?"

Guy shook his head. "We were so busy staying alive, we didn't care what was going on across the border."

"Valdez knew. Anyone who went down in Laos was in for an education. If they survived. And that was a big *if.* Say you did manage to eject. Say you lived through the G force of shooting out of your cockpit. If the enemy didn't find you, the animals would." He stared down at his beer. "Valdez was lucky to be alive."

"You met him at Tuyen Quan?" asked Guy.

"Yeah. Summer camp." He laughed. "For three years we were stuck in the same cell." His gaze turned to the river. "I was with the 101st when I was captured. Got separated during a firefight. You know how it is in those valleys, the jungle's so thick you can't be sure which way's up. I was going in circles, and all the time I could hear those damn Hueys flying overhead, *right overhead,* picking guys up. Everyone but me. I figured I'd been left to die. Or maybe I was already dead, just some corpse walking around in the trees. . . ." He swallowed; the hand clutching the beer bottle was unsteady. "When they finally boxed me in, I just threw my rifle down and put up my hands. I got force marched north, into NVA territory. That's how I ended up at Tuyen Quan."

"Where you met Valdez," said Willy.

"He was brought in a year later, transferred in from some camp in Laos. By then I was an old-timer. Knew the ropes, worked my own vegetable patch. I was hanging in okay. Valdez, though, was holding on by the skin of his teeth. Yellow from hepatitis, a broken arm that wouldn't heal right. It took him months to get strong enough even to work in the garden. Yeah, it was just him and me in that cell. Three years. We did a lot of talking. I heard all his stories. He said a lot of things I didn't want to believe, things about Laos, about what we were doing there. . . ."

Willy leaned forward and asked softly, "Did he ever talk about my father?"

Lassiter turned to her, his eyes dark against the glow of sunset. "When Valdez last saw him, your father was still alive. Trying to fly the plane."

"And then what happened?"

"Luis bailed out right after she blew up. So he couldn't be sure—"

"Wait," cut in Guy. "What do you mean, 'blew up'?"

"That's what he said. Something went off in the hold."

"But the plane was shot down."

"It wasn't enemy fire that brought her down. Valdez was positive about that. They might have been going through flak at the time, but this was something else, something that blew the fuselage door clean off. He kept going over and over what they had in the cargo, but all he remembered listed on the manifest were aircraft parts."

"And a passenger," said Willy.

Lassiter nodded. "Valdez mentioned him. Said he was a weird little guy, quiet, almost, well, *holy.* They could tell he was a VIP, just by what he was wearing around his neck."

"You mean gold? Chains?" asked Guy.

"Some sort of medallion. Maybe a religious symbol."

"Where was this passenger supposed to be dropped off?"

"Behind lines. VC territory. It was billed as an in-and-out job, strictly under wraps."

"Valdez told *you* about it," said Willy.

"And I wish to hell he never had." Lassiter took another gulp of beer. His hand was shaking again. Sunset flecked the river with blood-red ripples. "It's funny. At the time we felt almost, well, *protected* in that camp. Maybe it was just a lot of brainwashing, but the guards kept telling Valdez he was lucky to be a prisoner. That he knew things that'd get him into trouble. That the CIA would kill him."

"Sounds like propaganda."

"That's what I figured it was—Commie lies designed to break him down. But they got Valdez scared. He kept waking up at night, screaming about the plane going down. . . ."

Lassiter stared out at the water. "Anyway, after the war, they released us. Valdez and the other guys headed home. He wrote me from Bangkok, sent the letter by way of a Red Cross nurse we'd met in Hanoi right after our release. An English gal, a little anti-American but real nice. When I read that letter, I thought, now the poor bastard's really gone over the edge. He was saying crazy things, said he wasn't allowed to go out, that all his phone calls were monitored. I figured he'd be all right once he got home. Then I got a call from Nora Walker, that Red Cross nurse. She said he was dead. That he'd shot himself in the head."

Willy asked, "Do you think it was suicide?"

"I think he was a liability. And the Company doesn't like liabilities." He turned his troubled gaze to the water. "When we were at Tuyen, all he could talk about was going home, you know? Seeing his old hangouts, his old buddies. Me, I had nothing to go home to, just a sister I never much cared for. Here, at least, I had my girl, someone I loved. That's why I stayed. I'm not the only one. There are other guys like me around, hiding in villages, jungles. Guys who've gone bamboo, gone native." He shook his head. "Too bad Valdez didn't. He'd still be alive."

"But isn't it hard living here?" asked Willy. "Always the outsider, the old enemy? Don't you ever feel threatened by the authorities?"

Lassiter responded with a laugh and cocked his head at a far table where four men were sitting. "Have you said hello to our local police? They've probably been tailing you since you hit town."

"So we noticed," said Guy.

"My guess is they're assigned to protect me, their resident lunatic American. Just the fact that I'm alive and well is proof this isn't the evil empire." He raised his bottle of beer in a toast to the four policemen. They stared back sheepishly.

"So here you are," said Guy, "cut off from the rest of the world. Why would the CIA bother to come after you?"

"It's something Nora told me."

"The nurse?"

Lassiter nodded. "After the war, she stayed on in Hanoi. Still works at the local hospital. About a year ago, some guy—an American— dropped in to see her. Asked if she knew how to get hold of me. He said he had an urgent message from my uncle. But Nora's sharp gal, thinks fast on her feet. She told him I'd left the country, that I was living in Thailand. A good thing she did."

"Why?"

"Because I don't have an uncle."

There was a silence. Softly Guy said, "You think that was a Company man."

"I keep wondering if he was. Wondering if he'll find me. I don't want to end up like Luis Valdez. With a bullet in my head."

On the river, boats glided like ghosts through the shadows. A café worker silently circled the deck, lighting a string of paper lanterns.

"I've kept a low profile," said Lassiter. "Never make noise. Never draw attention. See, I changed my hair." He grinned faintly and tugged on his lank brown ponytail. "Got this shade from the local herbalist. Extract of cuttlefish and God knows what else. Smells like hell, but I'm not blond anymore." He let the ponytail flop loose, and his smile faded. "I kept hoping the Company would lose interest in me. Then you showed up at my door, and I—I guess I freaked out."

The bartender put a record on the turntable, and the needle scratched out a Vietnamese love song, a haunting melody that drifted like mist over the river. Wind swayed the paper lanterns, and shadows danced across the deck. Lassiter stared at the five beer bottles lined up in front of him on the table. He ordered a sixth.

"It takes time, but you get used to it here," he said. "The rhythm of life. The people, the way they think. There's not a lot of whining and flailing at misfortune. They accept life as it is. I like that. And after a while, I got to feeling this was the only place I've ever belonged, the only place I ever felt safe." He looked at Willy. "It could be the only place *you're* safe."

"But I'm not like you," said Willy. "I can't stay here the rest of my life."

"I want to put her on the next plane to Bangkok," said Guy.

"Bangkok?" Lassiter snorted. "Easiest place in the world to get yourself killed. And going home'd be no safer. Look what happened to Valdez."

"But *why?*" Willy said in frustration. "Why would they kill Valdez? Or me? I don't know anything!"

"You're Bill Maitland's daughter. You're a direct link—"

"To *what?* A dead man?"

The love song ended, fading to the *scritch-scritch* of the needle.

Lassiter set his beer down. "I don't know," he said. "I don't know why you're such a threat to them. All I know is, something went wrong on that flight. And the Company's still trying to cover it up. . . ." He stared at the line of empty beer bottles gleaming in the lantern light. "If it takes a bullet to buy silence, then a bullet's what they'll use."

"Do you think he's right?" Willy whispered.

From the back seat of the car, they watched the rice paddies, silvered by moonlight, slip past their windows. For an hour they'd driven without speaking, lulled into silence by the rhythm of the road under their wheels. But now Willy couldn't help voicing the question she was afraid to ask. "Will I be any safer at home?"

Guy looked out at the night. "I wish I knew. I wish I could tell you what to do. Where to go . . ."

She thought of her mother's house in San Francisco, thought of how warm and safe it had always seemed, that blue Victorian on Third Avenue. Surely no one would touch her there.

Then she thought of Valdez, shot to death in his Houston rooming house. For him, even a POW camp had been safer.

The driver slid a tape into the car's cassette player. A Vietnamese song twanged out, sung by a woman with a sorrowful voice. Outside, the rice paddies swayed like waves on a silver ocean. Nothing about this moment seemed real, not the melody or the moonlit countryside or the danger. Only Guy was real—real enough to touch, to hold.

She let her head rest against his shoulder, and the darkness, the warmth, made sleep impossible to resist. Guy's arm came around her, cradled her against his chest. She felt his breath in her hair, the brush of his lips on her forehead. A kiss, she thought drowsily. It felt so nice to be kissed. . . .

The hum of the wheels over the road seemed to take on a new rhythm, the whisper of the ocean, the soothing hiss of waves. Now he was kissing her all over, and they were no longer in the back seat of the car; they were on a ship, swaying on a black sea. The wind moaned in the rigging, a soulful song in Vietnamese. She was lying on her back, and somehow, all her clothes had vanished. He was on top of her, his hands trapping her arms against the deck, his lips exploring her throat, her breasts, with a conqueror's triumph. How she wanted him to make love to her, wanted it so badly that her body arched up to meet his, straining for some blessed release from this ache within her. But his lips melted away, and then she heard, "Wake up. Willy, wake up. . . ."

She opened her eyes. She was lying in the back seat of the car, her head in Guy's lap. Through the window came the faint glow of city lights.

"We're back in Saigon," he whispered, stroking her face. The touch of his hand, so new yet so familiar, made her tremble in the night heat. "You must have been tired."

Still shaken by the dream, she pulled away and sat up. Outside, the streets were deserted. "What time is it?"

"After midnight. Guess we forgot about supper. Are you hungry?"

"Not really."

"Neither am I. Maybe we should just call it a—" He paused. She felt his arm stiffen against hers. "Now what?" he muttered, staring straight ahead.

Willy followed his gaze to the hotel, which had just swung into view. A surreal scene lay ahead: the midnight glare of streetlights, the army of policemen blocking the lobby doors, the gleam of AK-47s held at the ready.

Their driver muttered in Vietnamese. Willy could see his face in the rearview mirror. He was sweating.

The instant they pulled to a stop at the curb, their car was surrounded. A policeman yanked the passenger door open.

"Stay inside," Guy said. "I'll take care of this."

But as he stepped out of the car, a uniformed arm reached inside and dragged her out as well. Groggy with sleep, bewildered by the confusion, she clung to Guy's arm as voices shouted and men shoved against her.

"Barnard!" It was Dodge Hamilton, struggling down the hotel steps toward them. "What the hell's going on?"

"Don't ask me! We just got back to town!"

"Blast, where's that man Ainh?" said Hamilton, glancing around. "He was here a minute ago. . . ."

"I am here," came the answer in a shaky voice. Ainh, glasses askew and blinking nervously, stood at the top of the lobby steps. He was swiftly escorted by a policeman through the crowd. Gesturing to a limousine, he said to Guy, "Please. You and Miss Maitland will come with me."

"Why are we under arrest?" Guy demanded.

"You are not under arrest."

Guy pulled his arm free of a policeman's grasp. "Could've fooled me."

"They are here only as a precaution," said Ainh, ushering them into the car. "Please get in. Quickly."

It was the ripple of urgency in his voice that told Willy something terrible had happened. "What is it?" she asked Ainh. "What's wrong?"

Ainh nervously adjusted his glasses. "About two hours ago, we received a call from the police in Cantho."

"We were just there."

"So they told us. They also said they'd found a body. Floating in the river . . ."

Willy stared at him, afraid to ask, yet already knowing. Only when she felt Guy's hand tighten around her arm did she realize she'd sagged against him.

"Sam Lassiter?" Guy asked flatly.

Ainh nodded. "His throat was cut."

8

The old man who sat in the carved rosewood chair appeared frail enough to be toppled by a stiff wind. His arms were like two twigs crossed on his lap. His white wisp of a beard trembled in the breath of the ceiling fan. But his eyes were as bright as quicksilver. Through the open windows came the whine of the cicadas in the walled garden. Overhead, the fan spun slowly in the midnight heat.

The old man's gaze focused on Willy. "Wherever you walk, Miss Maitland," he said, "it seems you leave a trail of blood."

"We had nothing to do with Lassiter's death," said Guy. "When we left Cantho, he was alive."

"I think you misunderstand, Mr. Barnard." The man turned to Guy. "I do not accuse you of anything."

"Who *are* you accusing?"

"That detail I leave to our people in Cantho."

"You mean those police agents you had following us?"

Minister Tranh smiled. "You made it a difficult assignment. That boy on the corner—an ingenious move. No, we're aware that Mr. Lassiter was alive when you left him."

"And after we left?"

"We know that he sat in the river café for another twenty minutes. That he drank a total of eight beers. And then he left. Unfortunately, he never arrived home."

"Weren't your people keeping tabs on him?"

"Tabs?"

"Surveillance."

"Mr. Lassiter was a friend. We don't keep . . . tabs—is that the word?—on our friends."

"But you followed *us*," said Willy.

Minister Tranh's placid gaze shifted to her. "Are you our friend, Miss Maitland?"

"What do you think?"

"I think it is not easy to tell. I think even you cannot tell your friends from your enemies. It is a dangerous state of affairs. Already it has led to three murders."

Willy shook her head, puzzled. "Three? Lassiter's the only one I've heard about."

"Who else has been killed?" Guy asked.

"A Saigon policeman," said the minister. "Murdered last night on routine surveillance duty."

"I don't see the connection."

"Also last night, another man dead. Again, the throat cut."

"You can't blame us for every murder in Saigon!" said Willy. "We don't even know those other victims—"

"But yesterday you paid one of them a visit. Or have you forgotten?" Guy stared across the table. "Gerard."

In the darkness outside, the cicadas' shrill music rose to a scream. Then, in an instant, the night fell absolutely silent.

Minister Tranh gazed ahead at the far wall, as though divining some message from the mildewed wallpaper. "Are you familiar with the Vietnamese calendar, Miss Maitland?" he asked quietly.

"Your calendar?" She frowned, puzzled by the new twist of conversation. "It—it's the same as the Chinese, isn't it?"

"Last year was the year of the dragon. A lucky year, or so they say. A fine year for babies and marriages. But this year . . ." He shook his head.

"The snake," said Guy.

Minister Tranh nodded. "The snake. A dangerous symbol. An omen of disaster. Famine and death. A year of misfortune . . ." He sighed and his head drooped, as though his fragile neck was suddenly too weak to support it. For a long time he sat in silence, his white hair fluttering in the fan's breath. Then, slowly, he raised his head. "Go home, Miss Maitland," he said. "This is not a year for you, a place for you. Go home."

Willy thought about how easy it would be to climb onto that plane to Bangkok, thought longingly of the simple luxuries that were only a flight away. Perfumed soap and clean water and soft pillows. But then another image blotted out everything else: Sam Lassiter's face, tired and haunted, against the sky of sunset. And his Vietnamese woman, pleading for his life. All these years Sam Lassiter had lived safe and hidden in a peaceful river town. Now he was dead. Like Valdez. Like Gerard.

It was true, she thought. Wherever she walked, she left a trail of blood. And she didn't even know why.

"I can't go home," she said.

The minister raised an eyebrow. "Cannot? Or will not?"

"They tried to kill me in Bangkok."

"You're no safer here. Miss Maitland, we have no wish to forcibly deport you. But you must understand that you put us in a difficult position. You are a guest in our country. We Vietnamese honor our guests. It is a custom we hold sacred, If you, a guest, were to be found murdered, it would seem . . ." He paused and added with a quietly whimsical lilt, "inhospitable."

"My visa's still good. I want to stay. I *have* to stay, I was planning to go on to Hanoi."

"We cannot guarantee your safety."

"I don't expect you to." She added wearily, "No one can guarantee my safety. Anywhere."

The minister looked at Guy, saw his troubled look. "Mr. Barnard? Surely you will convince her?"

"But she's right," said Guy.

Willy looked up and saw in Guy's eyes the worry, the uncertainty. It frightened her to realize that even he didn't have the answers.

"If I thought she'd be safer at home, I'd put her on that plane myself," he said. "But I don't think she will be safe. Not until she knows what she's running from."

"Surely she has friends to turn to."

"But you yourself said it, Minister Tranh. She can't tell her friends from her enemies. It's a dangerous state to be in."

The minister looked at Willy. "What is it you seek in the North?"

"It's where my father's plane went down," she said. "He could still be alive, in some village. Maybe he's lost his memory or he's afraid to come out of the jungle or—"

"Or he is dead."

She swallowed. "Then that's where I'll find his body. In the North."

Minister Tranh shook his head. "The jungles are full of skeletons. Americans. Vietnamese. You forget, we have our MIAs too, Miss Maitland. Our widows, our orphans. Among all those bones, to find the remains of one particular man . . ." He let out a heavy breath.

"But I have to try. I have to go to Hanoi."

Minister Tranh gazed at her, his eyes glowing with a strange black fire. She stared straight back at him. Slowly, a benign smile formed on his lips and she knew that she had won.

"Does nothing frighten you, Miss Maitland?" he asked.

"Many things frighten me."

"And well they should." He was still smiling, but his eyes were unfathomable. "I only hope you have the good sense to be frightened now."

Long after the two Americans had left, Minister Tranh and Mr. Ainh sat smoking cigarettes and listening to the screech of the cicadas in the night.

"You will inform our people in Hanoi," said the minister.

"But wouldn't it be easier to cancel her visa?" said Ainh. "Force her to leave the country?"

"Easier, perhaps, but not wiser." The minister lit another cigarette and inhaled a warm and satisfying breath of smoke. A good American brand. His one weakness. He knew it would only hasten his death, that the cancer now growing in his right lung would feed ravenously on each lethal molecule of smoke. How ironic that the very enemy that had worked so hard to kill him during the war would now claim victory, and all because of his fondness for their cigarettes.

"What if she comes to harm?" Ainh asked. "We would have an international incident."

"That is why she must be protected." The minister rose from his chair. The old body, once so spry, had grown stiff with the years. To think this dried-up carcass had fought two savage jungle wars. Now it could barely shuffle around the house.

"We could scare her into going home—arrange an incident to frighten her," suggested Ainh.

"Like your Die Yankee note?" Minister Tranh laughed as he headed for the door. "No, I do not think she frightens easily, that one. Better to see where she leads us. Perhaps we, too, will learn a few secrets. Or have you lost your curiosity, Comrade?"

Ainh looked miserable. "I think curiosity is a dangerous thing."

"So we let her make the moves, take the risks." The minister glanced back, smiling, from the doorway. "After all," he said. "It is *her* destiny."

"You don't have to go to Hanoi," said Guy, watching Willy pack her suitcase. "You could stay in Saigon. Wait for me."

"While you do what?"

"While I do the legwork up north. See what I can find." He glanced out the window at the two police agents loitering in the walkway. "Ainh's got you covered from all directions. You'll be safe here."

"I'll also go nuts." She snapped the suitcase shut. "Thanks for offering to stick your neck out for me, but I don't need a hero."

"I'm not trying to be a hero."

"Then why're you playing the part?"

He shrugged, unable to produce an answer.

"It's the money, isn't it? The bounty for Friar Tuck."

"It's not the money."

"Then it's that skeleton dancing around in your closet." He didn't answer. "What are you trying to hide? What's the Ariel Group got on you, anyway?" He remained silent. She locked her suitcase. "Never mind. I don't really want to know."

He sat down on the bed. Looking utterly weary, he propped his head in his hands. "I killed a man," he said.

She stared at him. Head in his hands, he looked ragged, spent, a man who'd used up his last reserves of strength. She had the unexpected impulse to sit beside him, to take him in her arms and hold him, but she couldn't seem to move her feet. She was too stunned by his revelation.

"It happened here. In Nam. In 1972." His laugh was muffled against his hands. "The Fourth of July."

"There was a war going on. Lots of people got killed."

"This was different. This wasn't an act of war, where you shoot a few men and get a medal for your trouble." He raised his head and looked at her. "The man I killed was American."

Slowly she went over and sank down beside him on the bed. "Was it . . . a mistake?"

He shook his head. "No, not a mistake. It was something I did without thinking. Call it reflexes. It just happened."

She said nothing, waiting for him to go on. She knew he *would* go on; there was no turning back now.

"I was in Da Nang for the day, to pick up supplies," he said. "Got a little turned around and wound up on some side street. Just an alley, really, a dirt lane, few old hootches. I got out of the jeep to ask for directions, and I heard this—this screaming. . . ."

He paused, looked down at his hands. "She was just a kid. Fifteen, maybe sixteen. A small girl, not more than ninety pounds. There was no way she could've fought him off. I—I just reacted. I didn't really think about what I was doing, what I was going to do. I dragged him off her, shoved him on the ground. He got up and swung at me. I didn't have a choice but to fight back. By the time I stopped hitting him, he wasn't moving. I turned and saw what he'd done to the girl. All the blood . . ."

Guy rubbed his forehead, as though trying to erase the image. "By then there were other people there. I looked around, saw all these eyes watching me. Vietnamese. One of the women came up, whispered that I should leave, that they'd get rid of the body for me. That's when I realized the man was dead."

For a long time they sat side by side, not touching, not speaking. He'd just confessed to killing a man. Yet she couldn't condemn him; she felt only a sense of sadness about the girl, about all the silent, nameless casualties of war.

"What happened then?" she asked gently.

He shrugged. "I left. I never said a word to anyone. I guess I was scared to. A few days later I heard they'd found a soldier's body on the other side of town. His death was listed as an assault by unknown locals. And that was the end of it. I thought."

"How did the Ariel Group find out?"

"I don't know." Restless, he rose and went to the window where he looked out at the dimly lit walkway. "There were half a dozen witnesses, all of them Vietnamese. Word must've gotten around. And somehow the Ariel Group got wind of it. What I don't understand is why they waited this long."

"Maybe they only just heard about it."

"Or maybe they were waiting for the right chance to use it." He turned to look at her. "Doesn't it bother you, how we got thrown together? That we *happened* to meet in Kistner's villa? That you *happened* to need a ride into town?"

"And that the man you've been asked to find just happens to be my father."

He nodded.

"They're using us," she said. Then, with rising anger she added, "They're using *me.*"

"Welcome to the club."

She looked up. "What do we do about it?"

"In the morning I'll fly to Hanoi, start asking questions."

"What about me?"

"You stay where Ainh can watch you."

"Sounds like a lousy plan."

"Have you got a better one?"

"Yes. I come with you."

"You'll only complicate things. If your father's alive, I'll find him."

"And what happens when you do? Are you going to turn him in? Trade him for silence?"

"I've given up on silence," Guy said quietly. "I'll settle for answers now."

She hauled her packed suitcase off the bed and set it down by the door. "Why am I arguing with you? I don't need your permission. I don't need any man's permission. He's *my* father. I know his face. His voice. After twenty years, *I'm* the one who'll recognize him."

"You're also the one who could get killed. Or is that part of the fun, Junior, going for thrills? Hell." He laughed. "It's probably written in your genes. You're as loony as your old man. He loved getting shot at, didn't he? He was a thrill junkie, and you are, too. Admit it. You're having the time of your life!"

"Look who's talking."

"I'm not in this for thrills. I'm in it because I had to be. Because I didn't have a choice."

"Neither of us has a choice!" She turned away, but he grabbed her arm and pulled her around to face him. He was standing so close it made her neck ache to look up at him.

"Stay in Saigon," he said.

"You must really want me out of the way."

"I want you safe."

"Why?"

"Because I— You—" He stopped. They were staring at each other, both of them breathing so hard neither of them could speak. Without another word he hauled her into his arms.

It was just a kiss, but it hit her with such hurricane force that her legs seemed to wobble away into oblivion. He was all rough edges—stubbled jaw and callused hands and frayed shirt. Automatically, she reached up and her arms closed behind his neck, pulling him hard against her mouth. He needed no encouragement. As his body pressed into hers, those dream images reignited in her head: the swaying deck of a ship, the night sky, Guy's face hovering above hers. If she let it, it would happen here, now. Already he was nudging her toward the bed, and she knew that if they fell across that mattress, he'd take her and she'd let him, and that was that. Never mind what made sense, what was good for her. She wanted him.

Even if it's the worst mistake I'll ever make in my life?

The thump of her legs against the side of the bed jarred her back to reality. She twisted away, pushed him to arm's length.

"That wasn't supposed to happen!" she said.

"I think it was."

"We got our wires crossed and—"

"No," he said softly. "I'd say our wires connected just fine."

She crossed to the door and yanked it open. "I think you should get out."

"I'm not going."

"You're not staying."

But his stance, feet planted like tree roots, told her he most certainly *was* staying. "Have you forgotten? Someone wants you dead."

"But *you're* the one who's threatening me."

"It was just a kiss. Has it been *that* long, Willy? Does it shake you up that much, just being kissed?"

Yes it does! she wanted to scream. *It shakes me up because I've never been kissed that way before!*

"I'm staying tonight," he said quietly. "You need me. And, I admit it, I need you. You're my link to Bill Maitland. I won't touch you, if that's what you want. But I won't leave, either."

She had to concede defeat. Nothing she could do or say would make him budge. She let the door swing shut. Then she went to the bed and sat down. "God, I'm tired," she said. "Too tired to fight you. I'm even too tired to be afraid."

"And that's when things get dangerous. When all the adrenaline's used up. When you're too exhausted to think straight."

"I give up." She collapsed onto the bed, feeling as if every bone in her body had suddenly dissolved. "I don't care what happens anymore. I just want to go to sleep."

He didn't have to say anything; they both knew the debate was over and she'd lost. The truth was, she was glad he was there. It felt so good to close her eyes, to have someone watching over her. She realized how muddled her thinking had become, that she now considered a man like Guy Barnard *safe.*

But safe was what she felt.

Standing by the bed, Guy watched her fall asleep. She looked so fragile, stretched out on the bedcovers like a paper doll.

She hadn't felt like paper in his arms. She'd been real flesh and blood, warm and soft, all the woman he could ever want. He wasn't sure just what he felt toward her. Some of it was good old-fashioned lust. But there was something more, a primitive male instinct that made him want to carry her off to a place where no one could hurt her.

He turned and looked out the window. The two police agents were still loitering near the stairwell; he could see their cigarettes glowing in the darkness. He only hoped they did their job tonight, because he had already crossed his threshold of exhaustion.

He sat down in a chair and tried to sleep.

Twenty minutes later, his whole body crying out for rest, he gave up and went to the bed. Willy didn't stir. What the hell, he thought, she'll never notice. He stretched out beside her. The shifting mattress seemed to rouse her; she moaned and turned toward him, curling up like a kitten against his chest. The sweet scent of her hair made him feel like a drunken man. Dangerous, dangerous.

He'd been better off in the chair.

But he couldn't pull away now. So he lay there holding her, thinking about what came next.

They now had a name, a tentative contact, up north: Nora Walker, the British Red Cross nurse. Lassiter had said she worked in the local hospital. Guy only hoped she'd talk to them, that she wouldn't think this was just another Company trick and clam up. Having Willy along might make all the difference. After all, Bill Maitland's daughter had a right to be asking questions. Nora Walker just might decide to provide the answers.

Willy sighed and nestled closer to his chest. That brought a smile to his face. *You crazy dame,* he thought, and kissed the top of her head. *You crazy, crazy dame.* He buried his face in her hair.

So it was decided. For better or worse, he was stuck with her.

9

The flight attendant walked up the aisle of the twin-engine Ilyushin and waved halfheartedly at the flies swarming around her head. Puffs of cold mist rose from the air-conditioning vents and swirled in the cabin; the woman seemed to be floating in clouds. Through the fog, Willy could barely read the emergency sign posted over the exit: Escape Rope. Now *there* was a safety feature to write home about. She had visions of the plane soaring through blue sky, trailing passengers on a ten thousand-foot rope.

A bundle of taffy landed in her lap, courtesy of the jaded attendant. "You will fasten your seat belt," came the no-nonsense request.

"I'm already buckled in," said Willy. Then she realized the woman was speaking to Guy. Willy nudged him. "Guy, your seat belt."

"What? Oh, yeah." He buckled the belt and managed a tight smile.

That's when she noticed he was clenching the armrest. She touched his hand. "Are you all right?"

"I'm fine."

"You don't look fine."

"It's an old problem. Nothing, really . . ." He stared out the window and swallowed hard.

She couldn't help herself; she burst out laughing. "Guy Barnard, don't tell me you're afraid of *flying?*"

The plane lurched forward and began bumping along the tarmac. A stream of Vietnamese crackled over the speaker system, followed by Russian and then very fractured English.

"Look," he protested, "some guys have a thing about heights or closed spaces or snakes. I happen to have a phobia about planes. Ever since the war."

"Did something happen on your tour?"

"End of my tour." He stared at the ceiling and laughed. "There's the irony. I make it through Nam alive. Then I board that big beautiful freedom bird. That's how I met Toby Wolff. He was sitting right next to me. We were both high, cracking jokes as we taxied up the runway. Going home." He shook his head. "We were two of the lucky ones. Sitting in the last row of seats. The tail broke off on impact. . . ."

She took his hand. "You don't have to talk about it, Guy."

He looked at her in obvious admiration. "You're not in the least bit nervous, are you?"

"No. I've been in planes all my life. I've always felt at home."

"Must be something you inherited from your old man. Pilot's genes."

"Not just genes. Statistics."

The Ilyushin's engines screamed to life. The cabin shuddered as they made their take-off roll down the runway. The ground suddenly fell away, and the plane wobbled into the sky.

"I happen to know flying is a perfectly safe way to travel," she added.

"Safe?" Guy yelled over the engines' roar. "Obviously, you've never flown Air Vietnam!"

In Hanoi, they were met by a Vietnamese escort known only as Miss Hu, beautiful, unsmiling and cadre to the core. Her greeting was all business, her handshake strictly government issue. Unlike Mr. Ainh, who'd been a fountain of good-humored chatter, Miss Hu obviously believed in silence. And the Revolution. Only once on the drive into the city did the woman offer a voluntary remark. Directing their attention to the twisted remains of a bridge, she said, "You see the damage? American bombs." That was it for small talk. Willy stared at the woman's rigid shoulders and realized that, for some people on both sides, the war would never be over.

She was so annoyed by Miss Hu's comment that she didn't notice Guy's preoccupied look. Only when she saw him glance for the third time out the back window did she realize what he was focusing on: a Mercedes with darkly tinted windows was trailing right behind them. She and Guy exchanged glances.

The Mercedes followed them all the way into town. Only when they pulled up in front of the hotel did the other car pass them. It headed around the corner, its occupants obscured behind dark glass.

Willy's door was pulled open. Heat poured in, a knock-down, drag-out heat that left her stunned.

Miss Hu stood waiting outside, her face already pearled with sweat. "The hotel is air-conditioned," she said and added, with a note of disdain, "for the comfort of *foreigners.*"

As it turned out, the so-called air-conditioning was scarcely functioning. In fact, the hotel itself seemed to be sputtering along on little more than its old French colonial glory. The entry rug was ratty and faded, the lobby furniture a sad mélange of battered rosewood and threadbare cushions. While Guy checked in at the reception desk, Willy stationed herself near their suitcases and kept watch over the lobby entrance.

She wasn't surprised when, seconds later, two Vietnamese men, both wearing dark glasses, strolled through the door. They spotted her immediately and veered off toward an alcove, where they loitered behind a giant potted fern. She could see the smoke from their cigarettes curling toward the ceiling.

"We're all checked in," said Guy. "Room 308. View of the city."

Willy touched his arm. "Two men," she whispered. "Three o'clock . . ."

"I see them."

"What do we do now?"

"Ignore them."

"But—"

"Mr. Barnard?" called Miss Hu. They both turned. The woman was waving a slip of paper. "The desk clerk says there is a telegram for you."

Guy frowned. "I wasn't expecting any telegram."

"It arrived this morning in Saigon, but you had just left. The hotel called here with the message." She handed Guy the scribbled phone memo and watched with sharp eyes as he read it.

If the message was important, Guy didn't show it. He casually stuffed it into his pocket and, picking up the suitcases, nudged Willy into a waiting elevator.

"Not bad news?" called Miss Hu.

Guy smiled at her. "Just a note from a friend," he said, and punched the elevator button.

Willy caught a last glimpse of the two Vietnamese men peering at them from behind the fern, and then the door slid shut. Instantly, Guy gripped her hand. *Don't say a word,* she read in his eyes.

It was a silent ride to the third floor.

Up in their room, Willy watched in puzzlement as Guy circled around, discreetly running his fingers under lampshades and along drawers, opened the closet, searched the nightstands. Behind the headboard, he finally found what he was seeking: a wireless microphone, barely the size of a postage stamp. He left it where it was. Then he went to the window and stared down at the street.

"How flattering," he murmured. "We rate baby-sitting service."

She moved beside him and saw what he was looking at: the black Mercedes, parked on the street below. "What about that telegram?" she whispered.

In answer, he pulled out the slip of paper and handed it to her. She read it twice, but it made no sense.

Uncle Sy asking about you. Plans guided tour of Nam.
Happy Trails. Bobbo.

Guy let the curtain flap shut and began to pace furiously around the room. By the look of him, he was thinking up a blizzard, planning some scheme.

He suddenly halted. "Do you want something for your stomach?" he asked.

She blinked. "Excuse me?"

"Pepto Bismol might help. And you'd better lie down for a while. That old intestinal bug can get pretty damn miserable."

"Intestinal bug?" She gave him a helpless look.

He stalked to the desk and rummaged in a drawer for a piece of hotel stationery, talking all the while. "I'll be it's that seafood you ate last night. Are you still feeling really lousy?" He held up a sheet of paper on which he'd scribbled, "Yes!!!"

"Yes," she said. "Definitely lousy. I—I think I should lie down." She paused. "Shouldn't I?"

He was writing again. The sheet of paper now said, "You want to go to the hospital!"

She nodded and went into the bathroom, where she groaned loudly a few times and flushed the toilet. "You know, I feel really rotten. Maybe I should see a doctor. . . ." It struck her then, as she stood by the sink and watched the water hiss out of the faucet, exactly what he was up to. *The man's a genius,* she thought with sudden admiration. Turning to look at him, she said, "Do you think we'll find anyone who speaks English?"

She was rewarded with a thumbs-up sign.

"We could try the hospital," he said. "May be it won't be a doctor, but they should have someone who'll understand you."

She went to the bed and sat down, bouncing a few times to make the springs squeak. "God, I feel awful."

He sat beside her and placed his hand on her forehead. His eyes were twinkling as he said, "Lady, you're really hot."

"I know," she said gravely.

They could barely hold back their laughter.

"She did not seem ill an hour ago," Miss Hu said as she ushered them into the limousine ten minutes later.

"The cramps came on suddenly," said Guy.

"I would say *very* suddenly," Miss Hu noted aridly.

"I think it was the seafood," Willy whimpered from the back seat.

"You Americans," Miss Hu sniffed. "Such delicate stomachs."

The hospital waiting room was hot as an oven and overflowing with patients. As Willy and Guy entered, a hush instantly fell over the crowd. The only sounds were the rhythmic clack of the ceiling fan and a baby crying in its mother's lap. Every eye was watching as the two Americans moved through the room toward the reception desk.

The Vietnamese nurse behind the desk stared in mute astonishment. Only when Miss Hu barked out a question did the nurse respond with a nervous shake of the head and a hurried answer.

"We have only Vietnamese doctors here," translated Miss Hu. "No Europeans."

"You have no one trained in the West?" Guy asked.

"Why, do you feel your Western medicine is superior?"

"Look, I'm not here to argue East versus West. Just find someone who speaks English. A nurse'll do. You have English-speaking nurses, don't you?"

Scowling, Miss Hu turned and muttered to the desk nurse, who made a few phone calls. At last Willy was led down a corridor to a private examination room. It was stocked with only the basics: an examining table, a sink, an instrument cart. Cotton balls and tongue depressors were displayed in dusty glass jars. A fly buzzed lazily around the one bare lightbulb. The nurse handed Willy a tattered gown and gestured for her to undress.

Willy had no intention of stripping while Miss Hu stood watch in the corner.

"I would appreciate some privacy," Willy said.

The other woman didn't move. "Mr. Barnard is staying," she pointed out.

"No." Willy looked at Guy. "Mr. Barnard is leaving."

"In fact, I was just on my way out," said Guy, turning toward the door. He added, for Miss Hu's benefit, "You know, Comrade, in America it's considered quite rude to watch while someone undresses."

"I was only trying to confirm what I've heard about Western women's undergarments," Miss Hu insisted as she and the nurse followed Guy out the door.

"What, exactly, have you heard?" asked Guy.

"That they are designed with the sole purpose of arousing prurient interest from the male sex."

"Comrade," said Guy with a grin, "I would be delighted to share my knowledge on the topic of ladies' undergarments. . . ."

The door closed, leaving Willy alone in the room. She changed into the gown and sat on the table to wait.

Moments later, a tall, fortyish woman wearing a white lab coat walked in. The name tag on her lapel confirmed that she was Nora Walker. She gave Willy a brisk nod of greeting and paused beside the table to glance through the notes on the hospital clipboard. Strands of gray streaked her mane of brown hair; her eyes were a deep green, as unfathomable as the sea.

"I'm told you're American," the woman said, her accent British. "We don't see many Americans here. What seems to be the problem?"

"My stomach's been hurting. And I've been nauseated."

"How long now?"

"A day."

"Any fever?"

"No fever. But lots of cramping."

The woman nodded. "Not unusual for Western tourists." She looked back down at the clipboard. "It's the water. Different bacterial strains than you're used to. It'll take a few days to get over it. I'll have to examine you. If you'll just lie down, Miss—" She focused on the name written on the clipboard. Instantly she fell silent.

"Maitland," said Willy softly. "My name is Willy Maitland."

Nora cleared her throat. In a flat voice she said, "Please lie down."

Obediently, Willy settled back on the table and allowed the other woman to examine her abdomen. The hands probing her belly were cold as ice.

"Sam Lassiter said you might help us," Willy whispered.

"You've spoken to Sam?"

"In Cantho. I went to see him about my father."

Nora nodded and said, suddenly businesslike, "Does that hurt when I press?"

"No."

"How about here?"

"A little tender."

Now, once again in a whisper, Nora asked, "How is Sam doing these days?"

Willy paused. "He's dead," she murmured.

The hands resting on her belly froze. "Dear God. How—" Nora caught herself, swallowed. "I mean, how . . . much does it hurt?"

Willy traced her finger, knifelike, across her throat.

Nora took a breath. "I see." Her hands, still resting on Willy's abdomen, were trembling. For a moment she stood silent, her head bowed. Then she turned and went to a medicine cabinet. "I think you need some antibiotics." She took out a bottle of pills. "Are you allergic to sulfa?"

"I don't think so."

Nora took out a blank medication label and began to fill in the instructions. "May I see proof of identification, Miss Maitland?"

Willy produced a California driver's license and handed it to Nora. "Is that sufficient?"

"It will do." Nora pocketed the license. Then she taped the medication label on the pill bottle. "Take one four times a day. You should notice some results by tomorrow night." She handed the bottle to Willy. Inside were about two dozen white tablets. On the label was listed the drug name and a standard set of directions. No hidden messages, no secret instructions.

Willy looked up expectantly, but Nora had already turned to leave. Halfway to the door, she paused. "There's a man with you, an American. Who is he? A relative?"

"A friend."

"I see." Nora gave her a long and troubled look. "I trust you're absolutely certain about your drug allergies, Miss Maitland. Because if you're wrong, that medication could be very, very dangerous." She opened the door to find Miss Hu standing right outside.

The Vietnamese woman instantly straightened. "Miss Maitland is well?" she inquired.

"She has a mild intestinal infection. I've given her some antibiotics. She should be feeling much better by tomorrow."

"I feel a little better already," said Willy, climbing off the table. "If I could just have some fresh air . . ."

"An excellent idea," said Nora. "Fresh air. And only light meals. No milk." She headed out the door. "Have a good stay in Hanoi, Miss Maitland."

Miss Hu turned a smug smile on Willy. "You see? Even here in Vietnam, one can find the best in medical care."

Willy nodded and reached for her clothes. "I quite agree."

* * *

Fifteen minutes later, Nora Walker left the hospital, climbed onto her bicycle and pedaled to the cloth merchants' road. At a streetside noodle stand she bought a lemonade and a bowl of *pho,* for which she paid the vendor a thousand-dong note, carefully folded at opposite corners. She ate her noodles while squatted on the sidewalk, beside all the other customers. Then, after draining the last of the peppery broth, she strolled into a tailor's shop. It appeared deserted. She slipped through a beaded curtain into a dimly lit back room. There, among the dusty bolts of silks and cottons and brocade, she waited.

The rattle of the curtain beads announced the entrance of her contact. Nora turned to face him.

"I've just seen Bill Maitland's daughter," she said in Vietnamese. She handed over Willy's driver's license.

The man studied the photograph and smiled. "I see there is a family resemblance."

"There's also a problem," said Nora. "She's traveling with a man—"

"You mean Mr. Barnard?" There was another smile. "We're well aware of him."

"Is he CIA?"

"We think not. He is, to all appearances, an independent."

"So you've been tracking them."

The man shrugged. "Hardly difficult. With so many children on the streets, they'd scarcely notice a stray boy here and there."

Nora swallowed, afraid to ask the next question. "She said Sam's dead. Is this true?"

The man's smile vanished. "We are sorry. Time, it seems, has not made things any safer."

Turning away, she tried to clear her throat, but the ache remained. She pressed her forehead against a bolt of comfortless silk. "You're right. Nothing's changed. Damn them. *Damn* them."

"What do you ask of us, Nora?"

"I don't know." She took a ragged breath and turned to face him. "I suppose—I suppose we should send a message."

"I will contact Dr. Andersen."

"I need to have an answer by tomorrow."

The man shook his head. "That leaves us little time for arrangements."

"A whole day. Surely that's enough."

"But there are . . ." He paused. "Complications."

Nora studied the man's face, a perfect mask of impassivity. "What do you mean?"

"The Party is now interested. And the CIA. Perhaps there are others."

Others, thought Nora. Meaning those they knew nothing about. The most dangerous faction of all.

As Nora left the tailor shop and walked into the painful glare of afternoon, she sensed a dozen pairs of eyes watching her, marking her leisurely progress up Gia Ngu Street. The brightly embroidered blouse she'd just purchased in the shop made her feel painfully conspicuous. Not that she wasn't already conspicuous. In Hanoi, all foreigners were watched with suspicion. In every shop she visited, along every street she walked, there were always those eyes.

They would be watching Willy Maitland, as well.

"We've made the first move," Guy said. "The next move is hers."

"And if we don't hear anything?"

"Then I'm afraid we've hit a dead end." Guy thrust his hands into his pockets and turned his gaze across the waters of Returned Sword Lake. Like a dozen other couples strolling the grassy banks, they'd sought this park for its solitude, for the chance to talk without being heard. Flame red blossoms drifted down from the trees. On the footpath ahead, children chattered over a game of ball and jacks.

"You never explained that telegram," she said. "Who's Bobbo?"

He laughed. "Oh, that's a nickname for Toby Wolff. After that plane crash, we wound up side by side in a military hospital. I guess we gave the nurses a lot of grief. You know, a few too many winks, too many sly comments. They got to calling us the evil Bobbsey twins. Pretty soon he was Bobbo One and I was Bobbo Two."

"Then Toby Wolff sent the telegram."

He nodded.

"And what does it mean? Who's Uncle Sy?"

Guy paused and gave their surroundings a thoughtful perusal. She knew it was more than just a casual look; he was searching. And sure enough, there they were: two Vietnamese men, stationed in the shadow of a poinciana tree. Police agents, most likely, assigned to protect them.

Or was it to isolate them?

"Uncle Sy," Guy said, "was our private name for the CIA."

She frowned, recalling the message. *Uncle Sy asking about you. Plans guided tour of Nam. Happy trails. Bobbo.*

"It was a warning," Guy said. "The Company knows about us. And they're in the country. Maybe watching us this very minute."

She glanced apprehensively around the lake. A bicycle glided past, pedaled by a serene girl in a conical hat. On the grass, two lovers huddled together, whispering secrets. It struck Willy as too perfect, this view of silver lake and flowering trees, an artist's fantasy for a picture postcard.

All except for the two police agents watching from the trees.

"If he's right," she said, "if the CIA's after us, how are we going to recognize them?"

"That's the problem." Guy turned to her, and the uneasiness she saw in his eyes frightened her. "We won't."

So close. Yet so unreachable.

Siang squatted in the shadow of a pedicab and watched the two Americans stroll along the opposite bank of the lake. They took their time, stopping like tourists to admire the flowers, to laugh at a child toddling in the path, both of them oblivious to how easily they could be captured in a rifle's cross hairs, their lives instantly extinguished.

He turned his attention to the two men trailing a short distance behind. Police agents, he assumed, on protective surveillance. They made things more difficult, but Siang could work around them. Sooner or later, an opportunity would arise.

Assassination would be so easy, as simple as a curtain left open to a well-aimed bullet. What a pity that was no longer the plan.

The Americans returned to their car. Siang rose, stamped the blood back into his legs and climbed onto his bicycle. It was a beggarly form of transportation, but it was practical and inconspicuous. Who would notice, among the thousands crowding the streets of Hanoi, one more shabbily dressed cyclist?

Siang followed the car back to the hotel. One block farther, he dismounted and discreetly observed the two Americans enter the lobby. Seconds later, a black Mercedes pulled up. The two agents climbed out and followed the Americans into the hotel.

It was time to set up shop.

Siang took a cloth-wrapped bundle from his bicycle basket, chose a shady spot on the sidewalk and spread out a meager collection of wares: cigarettes, soap and greeting cards. Then, like all the other itinerant merchants lining the road, he squatted down on his straw mat and beckoned to passersby.

Over the next two hours he managed to sell only a single bar of soap, but it scarcely mattered. He was there simply to watch. And to wait.

Like any good hunter, Siang knew how to wait.

10

Guy and Willy slept in separate beds that night. At least, Guy slept. Willy lay awake, tossing on the sheets, thinking about her father, about the last time she had seen him alive.

He had been packing. She'd stood beside the bed, watching him toss clothes into a suitcase. She knew by the items he'd packed that he was returning to the lovely insanity of war. She saw the flak jacket, the Laotian-English dictionary, the heavy gold chains—a handy form of ransom with which a downed pilot could bargain for his life. There was also the Government-issue blood chit, printed on cloth and swiped from a U.S. Air Force pilot.

I am a citizen of the United States of America. I do not speak your language. Misfortune forces me to seek your assistance in obtaining food, shelter and protection. Please take me to someone who will provide for my safety and see that I am returned to my people.

It was written in thirteen languages.

The last item he packed was his .45, the trigger seat filed to a feather release. Willy had stood by the bed and stared at the gun, struck in that instant by its terrible significance.

"Why are you going back?" she'd asked.

"Because it's my job, baby," he'd said, slipping the pistol in among his clothes. "Because I'm good at it, and because we need the paycheck."

"We don't need the paycheck. We need you."

He closed the suitcase. "Your mom's been talking to you again, has she?"

"No, this is me talking, Daddy. *Me.*"

"Sure, baby." He laughed and mussed her hair, his old way of making her feel like his little girl. He set the suitcase down on the floor and grinned at her, the same grin he always used on her mother, the same grin that always got him what he wanted. "Tell you what. How 'bout I bring back a little surprise? Something nice from Vientiane. Maybe a ruby? Or a sapphire? Bet you'd love a sapphire."

She shrugged. "Why bother?"

"What do you mean, 'why bother?' You're my baby, aren't you?"

"Your baby?" She looked at the ceiling and laughed. "When was I ever *your* baby?"

His grin vanished. "I don't care for your tone of voice, young lady."

"You don't care about anything, do you? Except flying your stupid planes in your stupid war." Before he could answer, she'd pushed past him and left the room.

As she fled down the hall she heard him yell, "You're just a kid. One of these days you'll understand! Grow up a little! Then you'll understand. . . ."

One of these days. One of these days.

"I still don't understand," she whispered to the night.

From the street below came the whine of a passing car. She sat up in bed and, running a hand through her damp hair, gazed around the room. The curtains fluttered like gossamer in the moonlit window. In the next bed, Guy lay asleep, the covers kicked aside, his bare back gleaming in the darkness.

She rose and went to the window. On the corner below, three pedicab drivers, dressed in rags, squatted together in the dim glow of a street lamp. They didn't say a word; they simply huddled there in a midnight tableau of weariness. She wondered how many others, just as weary, just as silent, wandered in the night.

And to think they won the war.

A groan and the creak of bedsprings made her turn. Guy was lying on his back now, the covers kicked to the floor. By some strange fascination, she was drawn to his side. She stood in the shadows, studying his rumpled hair, the rise and fall of his chest. Even in his sleep he wore a half smile, as though some private joke were echoing in his dreams. She started to smooth back his hair, then thought better of it. Her hand lingered over him as she struggled against the longing to touch him, to be held by him. It had been so long since she'd felt this way about a man, and it frightened her; it was the first sign of surrender, of the offering up of her soul.

She couldn't let it happen. Not with this man.

She turned and went back to her own bed and threw herself onto the sheets. There she lay, thinking of all the ways he was wrong for her, all the ways they were wrong for each other.

The way her mother and father had been wrong for each other.

It was something Ann Maitland had never recognized, that basic incompatibility. It had been painfully obvious to her daughter. Bill Maitland was the wild card, the unpredictable joker in life's game of chance. Ann cheerfully accepted whatever surprises she was dealt because he was her husband, because she loved him.

But Willy didn't need that kind of love. She didn't need a younger version of Wild Bill Maitland.

Though, God knew, she wanted him. And he was right in the next bed.

She closed her eyes. Restless, sweating, she counted the hours until morning.

"A most curious turn of events." Minister Tranh, recently off the plane from Saigon, settled into his hard-backed chair and gazed at the tea leaves drifting in his cup. "You say they are behaving like mere tourists?"

"Typical *capitalist* tourists," said Miss Hu in disgust. She opened her notebook, in which she'd dutifully recorded every detail, and began her report. "This morning at nine-forty-five, they visited the tomb of our beloved leader but offered no comment. At 12:17, they were served lunch at the hotel, a menu which included fried fish, stewed river turtle, steamed vegetables and custard. This afternoon, they were escorted to the Museum of War, then the Museum of Revolution—"

"This is hardly the itinerary of capitalist tourists."

"And then—" she flipped the page "—they went *shopping.*" Triumphantly, she snapped the notebook closed.

"But Comrade Hu, even the most dedicated Party member must, on occasion, shop."

"For antiques?"

"Ah. They value tradition."

Miss Hu bent forward. "Here is the part that raises my suspicions, Minister Tranh. It is the leopard revealing its stripes."

"Spots," corrected the minister with a smile. The fervent Comrade Hu had been studying her American idioms again. What a shame she had absorbed so little of their humor. "What, exactly, did they do?"

"This afternoon, after the antique shop, they spent two hours at the Australian embassy—the cocktail lounge, to be precise—where they conversed in private with various suspect foreigners."

Minister Tranh found it of only passing interest that the Americans would retreat to a Western embassy. Like anyone in a strange country, they probably missed the company of their own type of people. Decades ago in Paris, Tranh had felt just such a longing. Even as he'd sipped coffee in the West Bank cafés, even as he'd reveled in the joys of Bohemian life, at times, he had ached for the sight of jet black hair, for the gentle twang of his own language. Still, how he had loved Paris. . . .

"So you see, the Americans are well monitored," said Miss Hu. "Rest assured, Minister Tranh. Nothing will go wrong."

"Assuming they continue to cooperate with us."

"Cooperate?" Miss Hu's chin came up in a gesture of injured pride. "They are not aware we're following them."

What a shame the politically correct Miss Hu was so lacking in vision and insight. Minister Tranh hadn't the energy to contradict her. Long ago, he had learned that zealots were seldom swayed by reason.

He looked down at his tea leaves and sighed. "But, of course, you are right, Comrade," he said.

"It's been a day now. Why hasn't anyone contacted us?" Willy whispered across the oilcloth-covered table.

"Maybe they can't get close enough," Guy said. "Or maybe they're still looking us over."

The way everyone else was looking them over, Willy thought as her gaze swept the noisy café. In one glance she took in the tables cluttered with coffee cups and soup bowls, the diners veiled in a vapor of cooking grease and cigarette smoke, the waiters ferrying trays of steaming food. *They're all watching us,* she thought. In a far corner, the two police agents sat flicking ashes into a saucer. And through the dirty street windows, small faces peered in, children straining for a rare glimpse of Americans.

Their waiter, gaunt and silent, set two bowls of noodle soup on their table and vanished through a pair of swinging doors. In the kitchen, pots clanged and voices chattered over a cleaver's staccato. The swinging doors kept slapping open and shut as waiters pushed through, bent under the weight of their trays.

The police agents were staring.

Willy, by now brittle with tension, reached for her chopsticks and automatically began to eat. It was modest fare, noodles and peppery broth and paper-thin slices of what looked like beef. Water buffalo, Guy told her. Tasty but tough. Head bent, ignoring the stares, she ate in silence. Only when she inadvertently bit into a chili pepper and had to make a lunge for her glass of lemonade did she finally put her chopsticks down.

"I don't know if I can take this idle-tourist act much longer." She sighed. "Just how long are we supposed to wait?"

"As long as it takes. That's one thing you learn in this country. Patience. Waiting for the right time. The right situation."

"Twenty years is a long time to wait."

"You know," he said, frowning, "that's the part that bothers me. That it's been twenty years. Why would the Company still be mucking around in what should be a dead issue?"

"Maybe they're not interested. Maybe Toby Wolff's wrong."

"Toby's never wrong." He looked around at the crowded room, his gaze troubled. "And something else still bothers me. Has from the very beginning. Our so-called accidental meeting in Bangkok. Both of us looking for the same answers, the same man." He paused. "In addition to mild paranoia, however, I get also this sense of . . ."

"Coincidence?"

"Fate."

Willy shook her head. "I don't believe in fate."

"You will." He stared up at the haze of cigarette smoke swirling about the ceiling fan. "It's this country. It changes you, strips away your sense of reality, your sense of control. You begin to think that events are meant to happen, that they *will* happen, no matter how you fight it. As if our lives are all written out for us and it's impossible to revise the book."

Their gazes met across the table. "I don't believe in fate, Guy," she said softly. "I never have."

"I'm not asking you to."

"I don't believe you and I were *meant* to be together. It just happened."

"But something—luck, fate, conspiracy, whatever you want to call it—has thrown us together." He leaned forward, his gaze never leaving her face. "Of all the crazy places in the world, here we are, at the same table, in the same dirty Vietnamese café. And . . ." He paused, his brown eyes warm, his crooked smile a fleeting glimmer in his seriousness. "I'm beginning to think it's time we gave in and followed this crazy script. Time we followed our instincts."

They stared at each other through the veil of smoke. And she thought, *I'd like nothing better than to follow my instincts, which are to go*

back to our hotel and make love with you. I know I'll regret it. But that's
what I want. Maybe that's what I've wanted since the day I met you.

He reached across the table; their hands met. And as their fingers
linked, it seemed as if some magical circuit had just been completed, as
if this had always been meant to be, that this was where fate—good,
bad or indifferent—had meant to lead them. Not apart, but together,
to the same embrace, the same bed.

"Let's go back to the room," he whispered.

She nodded. A smile slid between them, one of knowing, full of
promise. Already the images were drifting through her head: shirts
slowly unbuttoned, belts unbuckled. Sweat glistening on backs and
shoulders. Slowly she pushed her chair back from the table.

But as they rose to their feet, a voice, shockingly familiar, called to
them from across the room.

Dodge Hamilton lumbered toward them through the maze of tables.
Pale and sweating, he sank into a chair beside them.

"What the hell are *you* doing here?" Guy asked in astonishment.

"I'm bloody lucky to be here at all," said Hamilton, wiping a handkerchief across his brow. "One of our engines trailed smoke all the way
from Da Nang. I tell you, I didn't fancy myself splattered all over some
mountaintop."

"But I thought you were staying in Saigon," said Willy.

Hamilton stuffed the handkerchief back in his pocket. "Wish I had.
But yesterday I got a telex from the finance minister's office. He's
finally agreed to an interview—something I've been working at for
months. So I squeezed onto the last flight out of Saigon." He shook his
head. "Just about my last flight, period. Lord, I need a drink." He
pointed to Willy's glass. "What's that you've got there?"

"Lemonade."

Hamilton turned and called to the waiter. "Hello, there! Could I
have one of these—these lemon things?"

Willy took a sip, watching Hamilton thoughtfully over the rim of her
glass. "How did you find us?"

"What? Oh, that was no trick. The hotel clerk directed me here."

"How did *he* know?"

Guy sighed. "Obviously we can't take a step without everyone knowing about it."

Hamilton frowned dubiously as the waiter set a napkin and another
glass of lemonade on the table. "Probably carries some fatal bacteria."
He lifted the glass and sighed. "Might as well live dangerously. Well,
here's to the trusty Ilyushins of the sky! May they never crash. Not with
me aboard, anyway."

Guy raised his glass in a wholehearted toast. "Amen. From now on, I say we all stick to boats."

"Or pedicabs," said Hamilton. "Just think, Barnard, we could be pedaled across China!"

"I think you'd be safer in a plane," Willy said, and reached for her glass. As she lifted it, she noticed a dark stain bleeding from the wet napkin onto the tablecloth. It took her a few seconds to realize what it was, that tiny trickle of blue. Ink. There was something written on the other side of her napkin. . . .

"It all depends on the plane," said Hamilton. "After today, no more Russian rigs for me. Pardon the pun, but I've been thoroughly dis-Ilyushined."

It was Guy's burst of laughter that pulled Willy out of her feverish speculation. She looked up and found Hamilton frowning at her. Dodge Hamilton, she thought. He was always around. Always watching.

She crumpled the napkin in her fist. "If you don't mind, I think I'll go back to the hotel."

"Is something wrong?" Guy asked.

"I'm tired." She rose, still clutching the napkin. "And a little queasy."

Hamilton at once shoved aside his glass of lemonade. "I *knew* I should have stuck to whiskey. Can I fetch you anything? Bananas, maybe? That's the cure, you know."

"She'll be fine," said Guy, helping Willy to her feet. "I'll look after her."

Outside, the heat and chaos of the street were overwhelming. Willy clung to Guy's arm, afraid to talk, afraid to voice her suspicions. But he'd already sensed her agitation. He pulled her through the crowd toward the hotel.

Back in their room, Guy locked the door and drew the curtains. Willy unfolded the napkin. By the light of a bedside lamp, they struggled to decipher the smudgy message.

"0200. Alley behind hotel. Watch your back."

Willy looked at him. "What do you think?"

He didn't answer. She watched him pace the room, thinking, weighing the risks. Then he took the napkin, tore it to shreds and vanished into the bathroom. She heard the toilet flush and knew the evidence had been disposed of. When he came out of the bathroom, his expression was flat and unreadable.

"Why don't you lie down," he said. "There's nothing like a good night's sleep to settle an upset stomach." He turned off the lamp. By the glow of her watch, she saw it was just after seven-thirty. It would be a long wait.

They scarcely slept that night.

In the darkness of their room, they waited for the hours to pass. Outside, the noises of the street, the voices, the tinkle of pedicab bells faded to silence. They didn't undress; they lay tensed in their beds, not daring to exchange a word.

It must have been after midnight when Willy at last slipped into a dreamless sleep. It seemed only moments had passed when she felt herself being nudged awake. Guy's lips brushed her forehead, then she heard him whisper, "Time to move."

She sat up, instantly alert, her heart off and racing. Carrying her shoes, she tiptoed after him to the door.

The hall was deserted. The scuffed wood floor gleamed dully beneath a bare light bulb. They slipped out into the corridor and headed for the stairs.

From the second-floor railing, they peered down into the lobby. The hotel desk was unattended. The sound of snoring echoed like a lion's roar up the stairwell. As they moved down the steps, the hotel lounge came into view, and they spotted the lobby attendant sprawled out on a couch, mouth gaping in blissful repose.

Guy flashed Willy a grin and a thumbs-up sign. Then he led the way down the steps and through a service door. Crates lined a dark and dingy hallway; at the far end was another door. They slipped out the exit.

Outside, the darkness was so thick, Willy found herself groping for some tangible clue to her surroundings. Then Guy took her hand and his touch was steadying; it was a hand she'd learned she could trust. Together they crept through the shadows, into the narrow alley behind the hotel. There they waited.

It was 2:01.

At 2:07, they sensed, more than heard, a stirring in the darkness. It was as if a breath of wind had congealed into something alive, solid. They didn't see the woman until she was right beside them.

"Come with me," she said. Willy recognized the voice: it was Nora Walker's.

They followed her up a series of streets and alleys, weaving farther and farther into the maze that was Hanoi. Nora said nothing. Every so often they caught a glimpse of her in the glow of a street lamp, her hair concealed beneath a conical hat, her dark blouse anonymously shabby.

At last, in an alley puddled with stagnant water, they came to a halt. Through the darkness, Willy could just make out three bicycles propped against a wall. A bundle was thrust into her hands. It contained a set of pajama-like pants and blouse, a conical hat smelling of fresh straw. Guy, too, was handed a change of clothes.

In silence they dressed.

On bicycles they followed Nora through miles of back streets. In that landscape of shadows, everything took on a life of its own. Tree branches reached out to snag them. The road twisted like a serpent. Willy lost all sense of direction; as far as she knew, they could be turning in circles. She pedaled automatically, following the faint outline of Nora's hat floating ahead in the darkness.

The paved streets gave way to dirt roads, the buildings to huts and vegetable plots. At last, at the outskirts of town, they dismounted. An old truck sat at the side of the road. Through the driver's window, a cigarette could be seen glowing in the darkness. The door squealed open, and a Vietnamese man hopped out of the cab. He and Nora whispered together for a moment. Then the man tossed aside the cigarette and gestured to the back of the truck.

"Get in," said Nora. "He'll take you from here."

"Where are we going?" asked Willy.

Nora flipped aside the truck's tarp and motioned for them to climb in. "No time for questions. Hurry."

"Aren't you coming with us?"

"I can't. They'll notice I'm gone."

"*Who'll* notice?"

Nora's voice, already urgent, took on a note of panic. "Please. Get in *now.*"

Guy and Willy scrambled onto the rear bumper and dropped down lightly among a pile of rice sacks.

"Be patient," said Nora. "It's a long ride. There's food and water inside—enough to hold you."

"Who's the driver?" asked Guy.

"No names. It's safer."

"But can we trust him?"

Nora paused. "Can we trust anyone?" she said. Then she yanked on the tarp. The canvas fell, closing them off from the night.

It was a long bicycle ride back to her apartment. Nora pedaled swiftly, her body slicing through the night, her hat shuddering in the wind. She knew the way well; even in the darkness she could sense where the hazards, the unexpected potholes, lay.

Tonight she could also sense something else. A presence, something evil, floating in the night. The feeling was so unshakable she felt compelled to stop and look back at the road. For a full minute she held her breath and waited. Nothing moved, only the shadows of clouds hurtling before the moon. *It's my imagination,* she thought. No one was following her. No one *could* have followed her. She'd been too cautious, taking the Americans up and down so many turns that no one could possibly have kept up unnoticed.

Breathing easier, she pedaled all the way home.

She parked her bicycle in the community shed and climbed the rickety steps to her apartment. The door was unlocked. The significance of that fact didn't strike her until she'd already taken one step over the threshold. By then it was too late.

The door closed behind her. She spun around just as a light sprang on, shining full in her face. Blinded, she took a panicked step backward. "Who—what—"

From behind, hands wrenched her into a brutal embrace. A knife blade slid lightly across her neck.

"Not a word," whispered a voice in her ear.

The person holding the light came forward. He was a large man, so large, his shadow blotted out the wall. "We've been waiting for you, Miss Walker," he said. "Where did you take them?"

She swallowed. "Who?"

"You went to the hotel to meet them. Where did you go from there?"

"I didn't—" She gasped as the blade suddenly stung her flesh; she felt a drop of blood trickle warmly down her neck.

"Easy, Mr. Siang," said the man. "We have all night."

Nora began to cry. "Please. Please, I don't know anything. . . ."

"But, of course, you do. And you'll tell us, won't you?" The man pulled up a chair and sat down. She could see his teeth gleaming like ivory in the shadows. "It's only a question of when."

From beneath the flapping canvas, Willy caught glimpses of dawn: light filtering through the trees, dust swirling in the road, the green brilliance of rice paddies. They'd been traveling for hours now, and the sacks of rice were beginning to feel like bags of concrete against their backs. At least they'd been provided with food and drink. In an open crate they'd found a bottle of water, a loaf of French bread and four hard-boiled eggs. It seemed sufficient—at first. But as the day wore on and the heat grew suffocating, that single bottle of water became more and more precious. They rationed it, one sip every half hour; it was barely enough to keep their throats moist.

At noon the truck began to climb.

"Where are we going?" she asked.

"Heading west, I think. Into the mountains. Maybe the road to Dien Bien Phu."

"Towards Laos?"

"Where your father's plane went down." In the shadows of the truck, Guy's face, dirty and unshaven, was a tired mask of resolution. She wondered if she looked as grim.

He shrugged off his sweat-soaked shirt and threw it aside, oblivious to the mosquitoes buzzing around them. The scar on his bare abdomen seemed to ripple in the gloom. In silent fascination, Willy started to reach out to him, then thought better of it.

"It's okay," he said softly, guiding her hand to the scar. "It doesn't hurt."

"It must have hurt terribly when you got it."

"I don't remember." At her puzzled look, he added, "I mean, not on any sort of conscious level. It's funny, though, how well I remember what happened just before the plane went down. Toby, sitting next to me, telling jokes. Something about the pilot looking like an old buddy of his from Alcoholics Anonymous. He'd heard in flight school that the best military pilots were always the drunks; a sober man wouldn't dream of flying the sort of junk heap we were in. I remember laughing as we taxied down the runway. Then—" He shook his head. "They say I pulled him out of the wreckage. That I unbuckled him and dragged him out just before the whole thing blew. They even called me a hero." He uncapped the water bottle, took a sip. "What a laugh."

"Sounds like you earned the label," she said.

"Sounds more like I was knocked in the head and didn't know what the hell I was doing."

"The best heroes in the world are the reluctant ones. Courage isn't fearlessness—it's acting in the face of fear."

"Yeah?" He laughed. "Then that makes me the best of the best." He stiffened as the truck suddenly slowed, halted. A voice barked orders in the distance. They stared at each other in alarm.

"What is it?" she whispered. "What're they saying?"

"Something about a roadblock . . . soldiers are stopping everyone. Some sort of inspection. . . ."

"My God. What do we—"

He put a finger to his lips. "Sounds like a lot of traffic in front. Could take a while before they get to us."

"Can we back up? Turn around?"

He scrambled to the back of the truck and glanced through a slit in the canvas. "No chance. We're socked in tight. Trucks on both sides."

Willy frantically surveyed the gloom, searching for empty burlap bags, a crate, anything large enough in which to hide.

The soldiers' voices moved closer.

We have to make a run for it, thought Willy. Guy had already risen to a crouch. But a glance outside told them they were surrounded by shallow rice paddies. Without cover, their flight would be spotted immediately.

But they won't hurt us, she thought. *They wouldn't dare. We're Americans.*

As if, in this crazy world, an eagle on one's passport bought any sort of protection.

The soldiers were right outside—two men by the sound of the voices. The truck driver was trying to cajole his way out of the inspection, laughing, offering cigarettes. The man had to have nerves of steel; not a single note of apprehension slipped into his voice.

His attempts at bribery failed. Footsteps continued along the graveled roadside, heading for the back of the truck.

Guy instinctively shoved Willy against the rice sacks, shielding her behind him. He'd be the one they'd see first, the one they'd confront. He turned to face the inevitable.

A hand poked through, gripping the canvas flap. . . .

And paused. In the distance, a car horn was blaring. Tires screeched, followed by the thud of metal, the angry shouts of drivers.

The hand gripping the canvas pulled away. The flap slid shut. There were a few terse words exchanged between the soldiers, then footsteps moved away, crunching up the gravel road.

It took only seconds for their driver to scramble back into the front seat and hit the gas. The truck lurched forward, throwing Guy off his feet. He toppled, landing right next to Willy on the rice sacks. As their truck roared full speed around the traffic and down the road, they sprawled together, too stunned by their narrow escape to say a word. Suddenly they were both laughing, rolling around on the sacks, giddy with relief.

Guy hauled her into his arms and kissed her hard on the mouth.

"What was that for?" she demanded, pulling back in surprise.

"That," he whispered, "was pure instinct."

"Do you always follow your instincts?"

"Whenever I can get away with it."

"And you really think I'll let you get away with it?"

In answer, he gripped her hair, trapping her head against the sacks, and kissed her again, longer, deeper. Pleasure leapt through her, a desire so sudden, so fierce, it left her voiceless.

"I think," he murmured, "you want it as much as I do."

With a gasp of outrage, she shoved him onto his back and climbed on top of him, pinning him beneath her. "Guy Barnard, you miserable jerk, I'm going to give you what you deserve."

He laughed. "Are you now?"

"Yes, I am."

"And what, exactly, do I deserve?"

For a moment she stared at him through the dust and gloom. Then, slowly, she lowered her face to his. "This," she said softly.

The kiss was different this time. Warmer. Hungrier. She was a full and willing partner; he knew it and he responded. She didn't need to be warned that she was playing a dangerous game, that they were both hurtling toward the point of no return. She could already feel him swelling beneath her, could feel her own body aching to accommodate that new hardness. And the whole time she was kissing him, the whole time their bodies were pressed together, she was thinking, *I'm going to regret this. As sure as I breathe, I'm going to pay for this. But it feels so right. . . .*

She pulled away, fighting to catch her breath.

"Well!" said. Guy, grinning up at her. "Miss Willy Maitland, I *am* surprised."

She sat up, nervously shoving her hair back into place. "I never meant to do that."

"Yes, you did."

"It was a stupid thing to do."

"Then why did you?"

"It was . . ." She looked him in the eye. "Pure instinct."

He laughed. In fact, he fell backward laughing, rolling around on the sacks of rice. The truck hit a pothole, bouncing her up and down so hard, she collapsed onto the floor beside him.

And still he was laughing.

"You're a crazy man," she said.

He threw an arm around her neck and pulled her warmly against him. "Only about you."

In a black limousine with tinted windows, Siang sat gripping the steering wheel and cursing the wretched highway—or what this country called a highway. He had never understood why communism and decent roads had to be mutually exclusive. And then there was the traffic, added to the annoyance of that government vehicle inspection. It had given him a moment's apprehension, the sight of the armed soldiers standing at the roadside. But it took only a few smooth words from the man in the back seat, the wave of a Soviet diplomatic passport, and they were allowed to move on without incident.

They continued west; a road sign confirmed it was the highway to Dien Bien Phu. A strange omen, Siang thought, that they should be headed for the town where the French had met defeat, where East had triumphed over West. Centuries before, an Asian scribe had written a prophetic statement.

To the south lie the mountains,
The land of the Viets.
He who marches against them
Is surely doomed to failure.

Siang glanced in the rearview mirror, at the man in the back seat. *He* wouldn't be thinking in terms of East versus West. *He* cared nothing about nations or motherlands or patriotism. Real power, he'd once told Siang, lay in the hands of individuals, special people who knew how to use it, to keep it, and *he* was going to keep it.

Siang had no doubt he would.

He remembered the day they'd first met in Happy Valley, at an American base the GIs had whimsically dubbed "the Golf Course." It was 1967. Siang had a different name then. He was a slender boy of thirteen, barefoot, scratching out a hungry existence among all the other orphans. When he'd first seen the American, his initial impression was of hugeness. An enormous fleshy face, alarmingly red in the heat; boots made for a giant; hands that looked strong enough to snap a child's arm in two. The day was hot, and Siang was selling soft drinks. The man bought a Coca Cola, drank it down in a few gulps and handed the empty bottle back. As Siang took it, he felt the man's gaze studying him, measuring him. Then the man walked away.

The next day, and every day for a week, the American emerged from the GI compound to buy a Coca Cola. Though a dozen other children clamored for his business, each waving soft drinks, the man bought only from Siang.

At the end of the week, the man presented Siang with a brand-new shirt, three tins of corned beef and an astonishing amount of cash. He said he was leaving the valley early the next morning, and he asked the boy to hire the prettiest girl he could find and bring her to him for the night.

It was only a test, as Siang found out later. He passed it. In fact, the American seemed surprised when Siang appeared at the compound gate that evening with an extraordinarily beautiful girl. Obviously, the man had expected Siang to take the money and vanish.

To Siang's astonishment, the man sent the girl away without even touching her. Instead, he asked the boy to stay—not as a lover, as Siang at first feared, but as an assistant. "I need someone I can trust," the man said. "Someone I can train. . . ."

Even now, after all these years, Siang still felt that young boy's sense of awe whenever he looked at the American. He glanced at the rear-view mirror, at the face that had changed so little since that day they'd met in Happy Valley. The cheeks might be thicker and ruddier, but the eyes were the same, sharp and all-knowing. Just like the mind. Those eyes almost frightened him.

Siang turned his attention back to the road. The man in the back seat was humming a tune: "Yankee Doodle." A whimsical choice, considering the Soviet passport he was carrying. Siang smiled at the irony of it all.

Nothing about the man was ever quite what it seemed.

11

It was late in the day when the truck at last pulled to a halt. Willy, half-asleep among the rice sacks, rolled drowsily onto her back and struggled to clear her head. The signals her body was sending gave new meaning to the word *misery*. Every muscle ached; every bone felt shattered. The truck engine cut off. In the new silence, mosquitoes buzzed in the gloom, a gloom so thick she could scarcely breathe.

"Are you awake?" came a whisper. Guy's face, gleaming with sweat, appeared above her.

"What time is it?"

"Late afternoon. Five or so. My watch stopped."

She sat up and her head swam in the heat. "Where are we?"

"Can't be sure. Near the border, I'd guess . . ." Guy stiffened as footsteps tramped toward them. Men's voices, speaking Vietnamese, moved closer.

The canvas flap was thrown open. Against the sudden glare of daylight, the faces of the two men staring in were black and featureless.

One of the men gestured for them to climb out. "You follow," he ordered. "Say nothing."

Willy at once scrambled out and dropped onto the spongy jungle floor. Guy followed her. They swayed for a moment, blinking dazedly, gulping in their first fresh air in hours. Chips of afternoon sunlight dappled the ground at their feet. In the branches above, an invisible bird screeched out a warning.

The Vietnamese man motioned to them to move. They had just started into the woods when an engine roared to life. Willy turned in alarm to see the truck rattle away without them. She glanced at Guy and saw in his eyes the same thought that had crossed her mind, *There's no turning back now.*

"No stop. Go, go!" said the Vietnamese.

They moved on into the forest.

The man obviously knew where he was going. Without a trail to guide him, he led them through a tangle of vines and trees to an isolated hut. A tattered U.S. Army blanket hung over the doorway. Inside, straw matting covered the earthen floor and a mosquito net, filmy as lace, draped a sleeping pallet. On a low table was set a modest meal of bananas, cracked coconuts and cold tea.

"You wait here," said the man. "Long time, maybe."

"Who are we waiting for?" asked Guy.

The man didn't answer; perhaps he didn't understand the question. He turned and, like a ghost, slipped into the forest.

For a long time, Willy and Guy lingered in the doorway, waiting, listening to the whispers of the jungle. They heard only the clattering of palms in the wind, the lonely cry of a bird.

How long would they wait? Willy wondered. Hours? Days? She stared up through the dense canopy at the last sunlight sparkling on the wet leaves. It would be dark soon. "I'm hungry," she said, and she turned back into the gloom of the hut.

Together they devoured every banana, gnawed every sliver of coconut from its husk, drank down every drop of tea. In all her life, Willy had never tasted any meal quite so splendid! At last, their stomachs full, their legs trembling with exhaustion, they crawled under the mosquito netting and, side by side, they fell asleep.

At dusk, it began to rain. It was a glorious downpour, monsoonlike in its ferocity, but it brought no relief from the heat. Willy, awake in the darkness, lay with her clothes steeped in sweat. In the shadows above, the mosquito net billowed and fell like a hovering ghost.

She clawed her way free of the netting. If she didn't get some air, she was going to smother.

She left Guy asleep on the pallet and went to the doorway, where she gulped in breaths of rain-drenched air. The swirl of cool mist was irresistible; she stepped out into the downpour.

All around her, the jungle clattered like a thousand cymbals. She shivered in the thunderous darkness as the water streamed down her face.

"What the hell are you doing?" called a sleepy voice. She turned and saw Guy in the doorway.

She laughed. "I'm taking a shower!"

"With your clothes on?"

"It's lovely out here! Come on, before it stops!"

He hesitated, then plunged outside after her.

"Doesn't it feel wonderful?" she cried, throwing her arms out to welcome the raindrops. "I couldn't take the heat any longer. God, I couldn't even stand the smell of my own clothes."

"You think that's bad? Just wait till the mildew sets in." Turning his face to the sky, he let out a satisfied growl. "Now *this* is the way we were meant to take a shower. The way the kids do it. When I was here during the war, I used to get a kick out of seeing 'em run around without their clothes on. Nothing cuter than all those little brown bodies dancing in the rain. No shame, no embarrassment."

"The way it should be."

"That's right," he said. Softly he added, "The way it should be."

All at once, Willy felt him watching her. She turned and stared back. The palms clattered, and the rain beat its tattoo on the leaves. Without a word, he came toward her, stood so close to her, she could feel the heat rippling between them. Yet she didn't move, didn't speak. The rain streaming down her face was as warm as teardrops.

"So what are we doing with our clothes on?" he murmured.

She shook her head. "This isn't supposed to happen."

"Maybe it is."

"A one-night stand—that's all it'd be—"

"Better once than never."

"And then you'll be gone."

"You don't know that. I don't know that."

"I do know it. You'll be gone. . . ."

She started to turn away, but he pulled her back, twisted her around to face him. At the first meeting of their lips, she knew it was over, the battle lost.

Better once than never, she thought as her last shred of resistance fell away. *Better to have you once and lose you than to always wonder how it might have been.* Reaching up, she threw her arms around his neck and met his kiss with her own, just as hungry, just as fierce. Their bodies pressed together so tightly, their fever heat mingled through the damp clothes.

He was already fumbling for the buttons of her blouse. She trembled as the fabric slid away and rain trickled down her bare shoulders. Then the warmth of his hand closed around her breast, and she was shivering not with cold but with desire.

Together they stumbled into the darkness of the hut. They were tugging desperately at each other's clothes now, flinging the wet garments into oblivion. When at last they faced each other with no barriers, no defenses, he pulled her face up and gently pressed his lips to hers. No kiss had ever pierced so true to her soul. The darkness swam around her; the earth gave way. She let him lower her to the pallet and felt the mosquito net whisper down around them.

Making love in the clouds, she thought as the whiteness billowed above. Then she closed her eyes and lost all sense of where she was. There was only the pounding of the rain and the magical touch of Guy's hands, his mouth. It had been so long since a man had made love to her, so long since she'd bared herself to the pleasure. The pain. And there *would* be pain after it was over, after he was gone from her life. With a man like Guy, the ending was inevitable.

She ignored those whispers of warning; she had drifted beyond all reach of salvation. She pulled him down against her, and whispered, "Now. Please."

He was already struggling against his own needs, his own urgencies. Her quiet plea slashed away his last thread of control.

"I give up," he groaned. Seizing her hands, he pinned her arms above her head, trapping her, his willing captive, beneath him.

His hardness filled her so completely, it made her catch her breath in astonishment. But her surprise quickly melted into pleasure. She was moving against him now, and he against her, both of them driving that blessed ache to new heights of agony.

The world fell away; the night seemed to swirl with mist and magic. They brought each other to the very edge, and there they lingered, between pleasure and torment, unwilling to surrender to the inevitable. Then the jungle sounds of beating rain, of groaning trees were joined by their cries as they plummeted over the brink.

Even when she fell back to earth, she was still floating. In the darkness above, the netting billowed like parachute silk falling through the emptiness of space.

There was no need to speak; it was enough just to lie together, limbs entwined, and listen to the rhythms of the night.

Gently, Guy stroked a tangled lock of hair off her cheek. "Why did you say that?" he asked.

"Say what?"

"That I'd be gone. That I'd leave you."

She pulled away and rolled onto her back. "Because you will."

"Do you want me to?"

She didn't answer. What difference would it make, after all, to bare her soul? And did he really want to hear the truth: that after tonight, she would probably do anything to keep him, to make him love her?

"Willy?"

She turned away. "Why are we talking about this?"

"Because I want to talk about it."

"Well, I don't." She sat up and hugged her knees protectively against her chest. "It doesn't do anyone any good, all this babbling about what comes next, where do we go from here. I've been through it before."

"You really don't trust men, do you?"

She laughed. "Should I?"

"Is it all because your old man walked out on you? Or was it something else? A bad love affair? What?"

"You could say all of the above."

"I see." There was a long silence. She shivered at the touch of his hand stroking her naked back. "Who else has left you? Besides your father?"

"Just a man I loved. Someone who said he loved me."

"And he didn't."

"Oh, I suppose he did, in his way." She shrugged. "Not a very permanent way."

"If it's only temporary, it's not love."

"Now that sounds like the title of a song." She laughed.

"A lousy song."

At once, she fell silent. She pressed her forehead to her knees. "You're right. A lousy song."

"Other people manage to get over rotten love affairs. . . ."

"Oh, I got over it." She raised her head and stared up at the netting. "Took only a month to fall in love with him. And over a year to watch him walk away. One thing I've learned is that it doesn't fall apart in a day. Most lovers don't just get up and walk out the door. They do it by inches, step by step, and every single one hurts. First they start out with, 'Who needs to get married, it's just a piece of paper.' And then, at the end, they tell you, 'I need more space.' Then it's 'How can anyone promise forever?' Maybe it was better the way my dad did it. No excuses. He just walked out the door."

"There's no such thing as a good way to leave someone."

"You're right." She pushed aside the netting and swung her feet out. "That's why I don't let it happen to me anymore."

"How do you avoid it?"

"I don't give any man the chance to leave me."

"Meaning you walk away first?"

"Men do it all the time."

"Some men."

Including you, she thought with a distinct twinge of bitterness. "So how did you walk away from your girlfriend, Guy? Did you leave before or after you found out she was pregnant?"

"That was an unusual situation."

"It always is."

"We'd broken up months before. I didn't hear about the kid till after he was born. By then there was nothing I could do, nothing I could change. Ginny was already married to another man."

"Oh." She paused. "That made it simple."

"Simple?" For the first time she heard his anger, and she longed to take back her awful words, longed to cleanse the bitterness from his voice. "You've got some crazy notion that men are all the same," he said. "All of us trying to claw our way free of responsibility, never looking back at the people we've hurt. Let me tell you something, Willy. Having a Y chromosome doesn't make someone a lousy human being."

"I shouldn't have said that," she said, gently touching his hand. "I'm sorry."

He lay quietly in the shadows, staring up at the ceiling. "Sam's three years old now. I've seen him a grand total of twice, once on Ginny's front porch, once on the playground at his preschool. I went over there to get a look at him, to see what kind of kid he was, whether he looked happy. I guess the teachers must've reported it. Not long after, Ginny called me, screaming bloody murder. Said I was messing with her marriage. Even threatened to slap me with a restraining order. I haven't been near him since. . . ." He paused to clear his throat. "I guess I realized I wouldn't be doing him any favors anyways, trying to shove my way into his life. Sam already has a father—a good one, from what I hear. And it would've hurt everyone if I'd tried to fight it out in court. Maybe later, when he's older, I'll find a way to tell him. To let him know how much I wanted to be part of his life."

And my life? she thought with sudden sadness. *You won't be part of it, either, will you?*

She rose to her feet and groped around in the darkness for her scattered clothes. "Here's a little advice, Guy," she said over her shoulder. "Don't ever give up on your son. Take it from a kid who's been left behind. Daddies are a precious commodity."

"I know." he said softly. He paused, then said, "You'll never get over it, will you? Your father walking out."

She shook out her wet blouse. "There are some things a kid can't ever forget."

"Or forgive."

Outside, the rain had softened to a whisper. In the thatching above, insects rustled. "Do you think I should forgive him?"

"Yes."

"I suppose I could forgive him for hurting *me*. But not for hurting my mother. Not when I remember what she went through just to—" Her voice died in midsentence.

They both heard it at the same time: the footsteps slapping through the mud outside.

Guy rolled off the pallet and sprang to his feet beside her. Shoes scraped over the threshold, and the shadow of a man filled the doorway.

The intruder held up a lantern. The flood of light caught them in freeze-frame: Willy, clutching the blouse to her naked breasts; Guy, poised in a fighter's crouch. The stranger, his face hidden in the shadow of a drab green poncho, slowly lowered the lantern and set it on the table. "I am sorry for the delay," he said. "The road is very bad tonight." He tossed a cloth-wrapped bundle down beside the lantern. "At ease, Mr. Barnard. If I'd wanted to kill you, you'd be dead now." He paused and added, "Both of you."

"Who the hell are you?" Guy asked.

Water droplets splattered onto the floor as the man shoved back the hood of his poncho. His hair was blond, almost white in the lantern light. He had pale eyes set in a moonlike face. "Dr. Gunnel Andersen," he said, nodding by way of introduction. "Nora sent word you were coming." Raindrops flew as he shook out the poncho and hung it up to dry. Then he sat down at the table. "Please, feel free to put on your clothes."

"How did Nora reach you?" Guy asked, pulling on his trousers.

"We keep a shortwave radio for medical emergencies. Not all frequencies are monitored by the government."

"Are you with the Swedish mission?"

"No, I work for the U.N." Andersen's impassive gaze wandered to Willy, who was self-consciously struggling into her damp clothes. "We provide medical care in the villages. Humanitarian aid. Malaria, typhoid, it's all here. Probably always will be." He began to unwrap the bundle he'd set on the table. "I assume you have not eaten. This isn't much but it's the best I could do. It's been a bad year for crops, and protein is scarce." Inside the bundle was a bamboo box filled with cold rice, pickled vegetables and microscopic flecks of pork congealed in gravy.

Guy at once sat down. "After bananas and coconuts, this looks like a feast to me."

Dr. Andersen glanced at Willy, who was still lingering in the corner, watching suspiciously. "Are you not hungry, Miss Maitland?"

"I'm starved."

"Then why don't you eat?"

"First I want to know who you are."

"I have told you my name."

"Your name doesn't mean a thing to me. What's your connection to Nora? To my father?"

Dr. Andersen's eyes were as transparent as water. "You've waited twenty years for an answer. You can surely wait a few minutes longer."

Guy said, "Willy, you need to eat. Come, sit down."

Hunger finally pulled her to the table. Dr. Andersen had brought no utensils. Willy and Guy used their fingers to scoop up the rice. All the time she was eating, she felt the Swede's eyes watching her.

"I see you do not trust me," he said.

"I don't trust anyone anymore."

He nodded and smiled. "Then you have learned, in a few short days, what took me months to learn."

"Mistrust?"

"Doubt. Fear." He looked around the hut, at the shadows dancing on the walls. "What I call the creeping uneasiness. A sense that things are not right in this place. That, just under the surface, lies some . . . secret, something . . . terrible."

The lantern light flickered, almost died. He glanced up as the rain pounded the roof. A puff of wind swept through the doorway, dank with the smells of the jungle.

"You sense it, too," he said.

"All I know is, there've been too many coincidences," said Guy. "Too many tidy little acts of fate. As though paths have been laid out for us and we're just following the trail."

Andersen nodded. "We all have roads laid out for us. We usually choose the path of least resistance. It's when we wander off that path that things become dangerous." He smiled. "You know, at this very minute, I could be sitting in my house in Stockholm, sipping coffee, growing fat on cakes and cookies. But I chose to stay here."

"And has life become dangerous?" asked Willy.

"It's not my life I worry about now. It was a risk bringing you here. But Nora felt the time was right."

"Then it was her decision?"

He nodded. "She thought it might be your last chance for a reunion."

Willy froze, staring at him. "Did you—did you say *reunion?*"

Dr. Andersen met her gaze. Slowly, he nodded.

She tried to speak but found her voice was gone. The significance of that one word reduced her to numb silence.

Her father was alive.

It was Guy who finally spoke. "Where is he?"

"A village northwest of here."

"A prisoner?"

"No, no. A guest. A friend."

"He's not being held against his will?"

"Not since the war." Andersen looked at Willy, who had not yet found her voice. "It may be hard for you to accept, Miss Maitland, but there *are* Americans who find happiness in this country."

She looked at him in bewilderment. "I don't understand. All these years he's been alive . . . he could have come home. . . ."

"Many men didn't return."

"He had the choice!"

"He also had his reasons."

"Reasons? He had every reason to come home!"

Her anguished cry seemed to hang in the room. For a moment neither man spoke. Then Andersen rose to his feet.

"Your father must speak for himself. . . ." he said, and he started for the door.

"Then why isn't he here?"

"There are arrangements to be made. A time, a place—"

"When will I see him?"

The doctor hesitated. "That depends."

"On what?"

He looked back from the doorway. "On whether your father wants to see *you.*"

Long after Andersen had left, Willy stood in the doorway, staring out at the curtain of rain.

"Why *wouldn't* he want to see me?" she cried into the darkness.

Quietly Guy came to stand behind her. His arms came around her shoulders, pulled her into the tight circle of his embrace.

"Why wouldn't he?"

"Willy, stop."

She turned and pressed her face into his chest. "Do you think it was so terrible?" she sobbed. "Being my father?"

"Of course not."

"It must have been. I must have made him miserable."

"You were just a kid, Willy! You can't blame yourself! Sometimes men . . . change. Sometimes they need—"

"Why?" she cried.

"Hey, not all men walk out. Some of us, we hang around, for better or for worse."

Gently, he led her back to the sleeping pallet. Beneath the silvery mosquito net, she let him hold her, an embrace not of passion, but of comfort. The arms of a friend. It felt right, the way their making love earlier that evening had felt right. But she couldn't help wondering, even as she lay in his arms, when this, too, would change, when *he* would change.

It hurt beyond all measure, the thought that he, too, would someday leave her, that this was but a momentary mingling of limbs and warmth and souls. It was hurt she expected, but one she'd never, ever be ready for.

Outside, the leaves clattered in the downpour.

It rained all night.

At dawn the jeep appeared.

"I take only the woman," insisted the Vietnamese driver, planting himself in Guy's path. The man gestured toward the hut. "You stay, GI."

"She's not going without me," said Guy.

"They tell me only the woman."

"Then she's not going."

The two men faced each other, challenge mirrored in their eyes. The driver shrugged and turned for the jeep. "Then I don't take anybody."

"Guy, please," said Willy. "Just wait here for me. I'll be okay."

"I don't like it."

She glanced at the driver, who'd already climbed behind the wheel and started the engine. "I don't have a choice," she said, and she stepped into the jeep.

The driver released the brake and spun the jeep around. As they rolled away, Willy glanced back and saw Guy standing alone among the trees. She thought he called out something—her name, perhaps—but then the jungle swallowed him from view.

She turned her attention to the road—or what served as a road. In truth, it was scarcely more than a muddy track through the forest. Branches slashed the windshield; water flew from the leaves and splattered their faces.

"How far is it?" She asked. The driver didn't answer. "Where are we going?" she asked. Again, no answer. She sat back and waited to see what would happen next.

A few miles into the forest the mud track petered out, and they halted before a solid wall of jungle. The driver cut the engine. A few rays of sunlight shone dimly through the canopy of leaves. Only the cry of a single bird sliced through the silence.

The driver climbed out and walked around to the rear. Willy watched as he rooted around under a camouflage tarp covering the back seat. Then she saw the blade slide out from beneath the tarp. He was holding a machete.

He turned to face her. For a few heartbeats they stared at each other, gazes meeting over the gleam of razor-sharp steel. Then she saw amusement flash in his eyes.

"We walk now," he said.

A nod was the only reply she could manage. Wordlessly, she climbed out of the jeep and followed him into the jungle.

He moved silently through the trees, the only sound of his passage the whistle and slash of the machete. Vines hung like shrouds from the branches; clouds of mosquitoes swarmed up from stagnant puddles. He moved onward without a second's pause, melting like a phantom through the brush. Willy, stumbling in the tangle of trees, barely managed to keep the back of his tattered shirt in view.

It didn't take long for her to give up slapping mosquitoes. She decided it was a lost cause. Let them suck her dry; her blood was up for grabs. She could only concentrate on moving forward, on putting one foot in front of the other. She was sliding through some timeless vacuum where distance was measured by the gaps between trees, the span between footsteps.

By the time they finally halted, she was staggering from exhaustion. Conquered, she sagged against the nearest tree and waited for his next command.

"Here," he said.

Bewildered, she looked up at him. "But what are you—"

To her astonishment, he turned and trotted off into the jungle.

"Wait!" she cried. "You're not going to leave me here!"

The man kept moving.

"Please, you have to tell me!" she screamed. He paused and glanced back. "Where am I? What is this place?"

"The same place we find *him,*" was the reply. Then he slipped away, vanishing into the forest.

She whirled around, scanning the jungle, watching, waiting for some savior to appear. She saw no one. The man's last words echoed in her head.

What is this place?

The same place we find him.

"Who?" she cried.

In desperation, she stared up at the branches crisscrossing the sky. That's when she saw it, the monstrous silhouette rising like a shark's fin among the trees.

It was the tail of a plane.

12

She moved closer. Gradually she discerned, amid the camouflage of trees and undergrowth, the remains of what was once an aircraft. Vines snaked over jagged metal. Fuselage struts reached skyward from the jungle floor, as bare and stark as the bleached ribs of a dead animal. Willy halted, her gaze drawn back to the tail above her in the branches. Years of rust and tropical decay had obscured the markings, but she could still make out the serial number: 5410.

This was Air America flight 5078. Point of origin: Vientiane, Laos. Destination: a shattered treetop in a North Vietnamese jungle.

In the silence of the forest, she bowed her head. A thin shaft of sunlight sliced through the branches and danced at her feet. And all around her the trees soared like the walls of a cathedral. How fitting that this rusted altar to war should come to rest in a place of such untarnished peace.

There were tears in her eyes when she finally forced herself to turn and study the fuselage—what was left of it. Most of the shell had burned or rotted away, leaving only a little flooring and a few crumbling struts. The wings were missing entirely—probably sheared off on impact. She moved forward to the remnants of the cockpit.

Sunlight sparkled through the shattered windshield. The navigational equipment was gutted; charred wires hung from holes in the instrument panel. Her gaze shifted to the bulkhead, riddled with bullet holes. She ran her fingers across the ravaged metal and then pulled away.

As she took a step back, she heard a voice say, "There isn't much left of her. But I guess you could say the same of me."

Willy spun around. And froze.

He came out of the forest, a man in rags, walking toward her. It was the gait she recognized, not the body, which had been worn down to its rawest elements. Nor the face.

Certainly not the face.

He had no ears, no eyebrows. What was left of his hair grew in tortured wisps. He came to within a few yards of her and stopped, as though afraid to move any closer.

They looked at each other, not speaking, perhaps not daring to speak.

"You're all grown up," he finally said.

"Yes." She cleared her throat. "I guess I am."

"You look good, Willy. Real good. Are you married yet?"

"No."

"You should be."

"I'm not."

A pause. They both looked down, looked back up, strangers groping for common ground.

Softly he asked, "How's your mother?"

Willy blinked away a new wave of tears. "She's . . . dying." She felt a comfortless sense of retribution at her father's shocked silence. "It's cancer," she continued. "I wanted her to see a doctor months ago, but you know how she is. Never thinking about herself. Never taking the time to . . ." Her voice cracked, faded.

"I had no idea," he whispered.

"How could you? You were dead." She looked up at the sky and suddenly laughed, an ugly sound in that quiet circle of trees. "It never occurred to you to write to us? One letter from the grave?"

"It only would have made things harder."

"Harder than *what?* Than it's already been?"

"With me gone, dead, Ann was free to move on," he said, "to . . . find someone else. Someone better for her."

"But she didn't! She never even tried! All she could think about was *you.*"

"I thought she'd forget. I thought she'd get over me."

"You thought wrong."

He bowed his head. "I'm sorry, Wilone."

After a pause, she said, "I'm sorry, too."

A bird sang in the trees, its sweet notes piercing the silence between them.

She asked, "What happened to you?"

"You mean this?" He gestured vaguely at his face.

"I mean . . . everything."

"Everything," he repeated. Then, laughing, he looked up at the branches. "Where the hell do I start?" He began to walk in a circle, moving among the trees like a lost man. At last he stopped beside the fuselage. Gazing at the jagged remains, he said, "It's funny. I never lost consciousness. Even when I hit the trees, when everything around me was being ripped apart, I stayed awake all the way down. I remember thinking, 'So when do I get to see heaven?' Or hell, for that matter. Then it all went up in flames. And I thought, 'There's my answer. My eternity . . .' "

He stopped, let out a deep sigh. "They found me a short way from here, stumbling around under the trees. Most of my face was burned away. But I don't remember feeling much of anything." He looked down at his scarred hands. "The pain came later. When they tried to clean the burns. When the nerves grew back. I'd scream at them to let me die, but they wouldn't. I guess I was too valuable."

"Because you were American?"

"Because I was a pilot. Someone to pump for information, someone to trade. Maybe someone to spread the Party line back home. . . ."

"Did they . . . hurt you?"

He shook his head. "I guess they figured I'd been hurt enough. It was a quieter sort of persuasion. Endless discussions. Relentless arguments as I recovered. I swore I wasn't going to let the enemy twist my head around. But I was weak. I was far from home. And they said things—so many things—I couldn't argue with. And after a while . . . after a while it made . . . well, sense. About this country being their house, about us being the burglars in the house. And wouldn't anyone with burglars in their house fight back?"

He let out a sigh. "I don't know anymore. It sounds so feeble now, but I just got tired. Tired of arguing. Tired of trying to explain what I was doing in their country. Tired of trying to defend God only knew what. It was easier just to agree with them. And after a while, I actually started to believe it. Believe what they were telling me." He looked down. "According to some people, that makes me a traitor."

"To some people. Not to me."

He was silent.

"Why didn't you come home?" she asked.

"Look at me, Willy. Who'd want me back?"

"*We* did."

"No, you didn't. Not the man I'd become." He laughed hollowly. "Everyone would be pointing at me, whispering behind my back, talking about my face. Is that the kind of father you wanted? The kind of husband your mother wanted? Back home, people expect you to have a nose and ears and eyebrows." He shook his head. "Ann . . . Ann was so beautiful. I—I couldn't go back to that."

"But what do you have here? Look at you, at what you're wearing, at how skinny you are. You're starving, wasting away."

"I eat what the rest of the village eats. It's enough to live on." He picked at the rag that served as his shirt. "Clothes, I never much cared about."

"You gave up a family!"

"I—I found another family, Willy. Here."

She stared at him, stunned.

"I have a wife. Her name's Lan. And we have children. A baby girl and two boys . . . eight and ten. They can speak English, and a little French. . . ." he said helplessly.

"We were at home!"

"But I was here. And Lan was here. She saved my life, Willy. She was the one who kept me alive through the infections, the fevers, the endless pain."

"You said you begged to die."

"Lan was the one who made me want to live again."

Willy stared at that man with half a face, the man she'd once called her father. The lashless eyes looked back at her, unblinking. Awaiting judgment.

She still had a face, a normal life, she thought. What right did she have to condemn him?

She looked away. "So. What do I tell Mom?"

"I don't know. Maybe nothing."

"She has a right to know."

"Maybe it would be kinder if she didn't."

"Kinder to whom? You or her?"

He looked down at his feet in their dirty slippers. "I suppose I deserve that. Whatever you have to say, I deserve it. But God knows, I wanted to make it up to her. And to you. I sent money—twenty, maybe thirty thousand dollars. You got it, didn't you?"

"We never knew who sent it."

"You weren't supposed to know. Nora Walker arranged it through a bank in Bangkok. It was everything I had. All that was left of the gold."

She gave him a bewildered look and saw that his gaze had shifted toward the plane's fuselage. "You were carrying gold?"

"I didn't know it at the time. It was our little rule at Air America: Never ask about the cargo. Just fly the plane. But after she went down, after I crawled out of the wreckage, I saw it. Gold bars scattered all over the ground. It was crazy. There I was, half my damn face burned off, and I remember thinking, 'I'm rich. If I live through this, son of a bitch, I'm *rich!*' " He laughed, then, at his own lunacy, at the absurdity of a dying man rejoicing among the ashes. "I buried some of the gold, threw some in the bushes. I thought— I guess I thought it would be my ticket out. That if I was captured, I could use it to bargain for my freedom."

"What happened?"

He looked off at the trees. "They found me. NVA soldiers. And they found most of the gold." He shrugged. "They kept us both."

"But not forever. You didn't have to stay—" She stopped. "Didn't you *ever* think of us?"

"I never stopped thinking of you. After the war, after all that—that insanity was over, I came back here, dug up what gold they hadn't found. I asked Nora to get it out to you." He looked at Willy. "Don't you see? I never forgot you. I just . . ." He stopped, and his voice dropped to a whisper. "I just couldn't go back."

In the trees above, branches rattled in the wind. Leaves drifted down in a soft rain of green.

He turned away. "I suppose you'll want to go back to Hanoi. I'll see that someone drives you. . . ."

"Dad?"

He halted, not daring to look at her.

"Your little boys. You—say they understand English?"

He nodded.

She paused. "Then we ought to understand each other, the boys and I." she said. "I mean, assuming they want to meet me. . . ."

Her father quickly rubbed a hand across his eyes. But when he turned to look at her, she could still see the tears glistening there. He smiled . . . and held out his hand to her.

She'd been gone too long.

Three hours had passed, and Guy was more than worried. He was scared out of his head. Something wasn't right. It was that old instinct of his, that sense of doom closing in, and he was helpless to do anything about it. A dozen different images kept forming in his mind, each one progressively more terrible. Willy screaming. Dying. Or already dead in the jungle. When at last he heard the rumble of the jeep, he was hovering at the edge of panic.

Dr. Andersen was at the wheel. "Good morning, Mr. Barnard!" he called cheerily as Guy stalked over to him.

"Where is she?"

"She is safe."

"Prove it."

Andersen threw open the door and gestured for him to get in. "I will take you to her."

Guy climbed in and slammed the door. "Where are we going?"

"It is a long drive." Andersen threw the jeep into gear and spun them around onto a dirt track. "Be patient."

The night's rainfall had turned the path to muck, and on either side the jungle pressed in, close and strangling. They might have gone for miles or tens of miles; on a road locked in by jungle, distance was impossible to judge. When Andersen finally pulled off to the side, Guy could see no obvious reason for stopping. Only when he'd climbed out and stood among the trees did he notice the tiny footpath leading into the bush. He couldn't see what lay beyond; the forest hid everything from view.

"From here we walk," said Andersen, foraging around for a few loose branches.

"Why the camouflage?" asked Guy, watching Andersen drape the branches over the jeep.

"Protection for the village."

"What are they afraid of?"

Andersen reached under the tarp on the back seat and pulled out an AK-47. Casually, he slung it over his shoulder. "Everything," he said, and headed off into the jungle.

The footpath led into a shadowy world of hundred-foot trees and tangled vines. Watching Andersen's back, Guy was struck by the irony of a doctor lugging an automatic rifle. He wondered what enemy he planned to use it on.

The smells of rotting vegetation, of mud simmering in the heat were only too familiar. "The whole damn jungle smells of death," the GIs used to say. Guy felt his gait change to a silent glide, felt his reflexes kick into overdrive. His five senses were painfully acute; the snap of a branch under Anderson's boot was as shocking as gunfire.

He heard the sounds of the village before he saw it. Somewhere deep in the forest, children were laughing. And then he heard water rushing and the cry of a baby.

Anderson pushed ahead, and as the last curtain of branches parted, Guy saw, beneath a towering stand of trees, the circle of huts. In the central courtyard, children batted a pebble back and forth with their feet. They froze as Guy and Andersen emerged from the forest. One of the girls called out; instantly, a dozen adults emerged from the huts. In silence they all watched Guy.

Then, in the doorway of one hut, a familiar figure appeared. As Willy came toward Guy, he had the sudden desire to take her in his arms and kiss her right then and there, in view of the whole village, the whole world. But he couldn't seem to move. He could only stare down at her smiling face.

"I found him," Willy said.

He shook his head. "What?"

"My father. He's here."

Guy turned and saw that someone else had emerged from the hut. A man without ears, without eyebrows. The horrifying apparition held out its hand; a fingertip was missing.

William Maitland smiled. "Welcome to Na Co, Mr. Barnard."

Dr. Andersen's jeep was easy to spot, even through the camouflage. How fortunate the rains had been so heavy the night before; without all that mud, Siang would never have been able to track the jeep to this trail head.

He threw aside the branches and quickly surveyed the jeep's interior. On the back seat, beneath a green canvas tarp, was a jug of drinking water, a few old tools and a weathered notebook, obviously a journal, filled with scribbling. The name "Dr. Gunnel Andersen" was written inside the front cover.

Siang left the jeep, tramped a few paces into the jungle and peered through the shadows. It took only a moment to spot the footprints. Two men. Dr. Andersen and who else? Barnard? He followed the tracks a short way and saw that, just beyond the first few trees, the footprints led to a distinct trail, no doubt an old and established path. The village of Na Co must lie farther ahead.

He returned to the limousine where the man was waiting. "They have gone into the forest," Siang said. "There's a village trail."

"Is it the right one?"

Siang shrugged. "There are many villages in these mountains. But the jeep belongs to Dr. Andersen."

"Then it's the right village." The man sat back, satisfied. "I want our people here tonight."

"So soon?"

"It's the way I work. In and out. The men are ready."

In fact the mercenary team had been waiting two days for the signal. They'd been assembled in Thailand, fifteen men equipped with the most sophisticated in small arms. As soon as the order went through, they would be on their way, no questions asked.

"Tell them we need the dogs as well," said the man. "For mopping up. The whole village goes."

Siang paused. "The children?"

"One mustn't leave orphans."

This troubled Siang a little, but he said nothing. He knew better than to argue with the voice of necessity. Or power.

"Is there a radio in the jeep?" asked the man.

"Yes," said Siang.

"Rip it out."

"Andersen will see—"

"Andersen will see nothing."

Siang nodded in instant understanding.

The man drove off in the limousine, headed for a rendezvous spot a mile ahead. Siang waited until the car had disappeared, then he trotted back to the jeep, ripped out the wires connecting the radio and smashed the panel for good measure. He found a cool spot beneath a tree and sat down. Closing his eyes, he summoned forth the strength needed for his task.

Soon he would have assistance. By tonight, the well-paid team of mercenaries would stand assembled on this road. He wouldn't allow himself to think of the victims—the women, the children. It was a consequence of war. In every skirmish, there were the innocent casualties. He'd learned to accept it, to shrug it off as inevitable. The act of pulling a trigger required a clear head swept free of emotions. It was, after all, the way of battle.

It was the way of success.

"Does she understand the danger?" asked Maitland.

"I don't know." Guy stood in the doorway and gazed out at the leaf-strewn courtyard where the village kids were mobbing Willy, singing out questions. The wonderful bedlam of children, he thought wistfully. He turned and looked at the mass of scars that was Bill Maitland's face. "I'm not sure *I* understand the danger."

"She said things have been happening."

"Things? More like dead bodies falling left and right of us. We've been followed every—"

"Who's been following you?"

"The local police. Maybe others."

"The Company?"

"I don't know. They didn't come and introduce themselves."

Maitland, suddenly agitated, began to pace the hut. "If they've traced you here . . ."

"Who're you hiding from? The Company? The local police?"

"To name a few."

"Which is it?"

"Everyone."

"That narrows it down."

Maitland sat down on the sleeping pallet and rested his head in his hands. "I wanted to be left alone. That's all. Just left alone."

Guy gazed at that scarred scalp and wondered why he felt no pity. Surely the man deserved at least a little pity. But at that instant, all Guy felt was irritation that Maitland was thinking only of himself. Willy had a right to a better father, he thought.

"Your daughter's already found you," he said. "You can't change that. You can't shove her back into the past."

"I don't want to. I'm glad she found me!"

"Yet you never bothered to tell her you were alive."

"I couldn't." Maitland looked up, his eyes full of pain. "There were lives at stake, people I had to protect. Lan, the children—"

"Who's going to hurt them?" Guy moved in, confronted him. "It's been twenty years, and you're still scared. Why? What kind of business were you in?"

"I was just a pawn—I flew the planes, that's all. I never gave a damn about the cargo!"

"What *was* the cargo? Drugs? Arms?"

"Sometimes."

"Which?"

"Both."

Guy's voice hardened. "And which side took delivery?"

Maitland sat up sharply. "I never did business with the enemy! I only followed orders!"

"What *were* your orders on that last flight?"

"To deliver a passenger"

"Interesting cargo. Who was he?"

"His name didn't show up on the manifest. I figured he was some Lao VIP. As it turned out, he was marked for death." He swallowed. "It wasn't the enemy fire that brought us down. A bomb went off in our hold. Planted by *our* side. We were meant to die."

"*Why?*"

There was a long silence. At last, Maitland rose and went to the doorway. There he stared out at the circle of huts. "I think it's time we talked to the elders."

"What can they tell me?"

Maitland turned and looked at him. "Everything."

* * *

Lan's baby was crying in a corner of the hut. She put it to her breast and rocked back and forth, cooing, yet all the time listening intently to the voices whispering in the shadows.

They were all listening—the children, the families. Willy couldn't understand what was being said, but she could tell the discussion held a frightening significance.

In the center of the hut sat three village elders—two men and a woman—their ancient faces veiled in a swirl of smoke from the joss sticks. The woman puffed on a cigarette as she muttered in Vietnamese. She gestured toward the sky, then to Maitland.

Guy whispered to Willy. "She's saying it wasn't your father's time to die. But the other two men, the American and the Lao, they died because that was the death they were fated all their lives to meet. . . ." He fell silent, mesmerized by the old woman's voice. The sound seemed to drift like incense smoke, curling in the shadows.

One of the old men spoke, his voice so soft, it was almost lost in the shifting and whispers of the audience.

"He disagrees," said Guy. "He says it wasn't fate that killed the Lao."

The old woman vehemently shook her head. Now there was a general debate about why the Lao had really died. The dissenting old man at last rose and shuffled to a far corner of the hut. There he pulled aside the matting that covered the earthen floor, brushed aside a layer of dirt and withdrew a cloth-wrapped bundle. With shaking hands he pulled apart the ragged edges. Reverently, he held out the object within.

Even in the gloom of the hut, the sheen of gold was unmistakable.

"It's the medallion," whispered Willy. "The one Lassiter told us about."

"The Lao was wearing it," said her father.

The old man handed the bundle to Guy. Gingerly, Guy lifted the medallion from its bed of worn cloth. Though the surface was marred by slag from the explosion, the design was still discernable: a three-headed dragon, fangs bared, claws poised for battle.

The old man whispered words of awe and wonder.

"He saw a medallion just like it once before," said Maitland. "Years ago, in Laos. It was hanging around the neck of Prince Souvanna."

Guy took in a sharp breath. "It's the royal crest. That passenger—"

"Was the king's half brother," said Maitland. "Prince Lo Van."

An uneasy murmur rippled through the gathering.

"I don't understand," said Willy. "Why would the Company want him dead?"

"It doesn't make sense," said Guy. "Lo Van was a neutral, shifting to our side. And he was straight-arrow, a clean leader. With our backing, he could've carved us a foothold in Laos. That might have tipped the scales in our favor."

"That's what he was *meant* to do," said Maitland. "That crate of gold was his. To be dropped in Laos."

"To buy an army?" asked Willy.

"Exactly."

"Then why assassinate him? He was on our side, so—"

"But the guys who blew up the plane weren't," said Guy.

"You mean the Communists planted that bomb?"

"No, someone more dangerous. One of ours."

The elders had fallen silent. They were watching their guests, studying them the way a teacher watches a pupil struggle for answers.

Once again the old woman began to speak. Maitland translated.

"During the war, some of us lived with the Pathet Lao, the Communists in Laos. There were few places to hide, so we slept in caves. But we had gardens and chickens and pigs, everything we needed to survive. Once, when I was new to the cave, I heard a plane. I thought it was the enemy, the Americans, and I took my rifle and went out to shoot it down. But my cell commander stopped me. I could not understand why he let the plane land. It had enemy markings, the American flag. Our cell commander ordered us to unload the plane. We carried off crates of guns and ammunition. Then we loaded the plane with opium, bags and bags of it. An exchange of goods, I thought. This must be a stolen plane. But then the pilot stepped out, and I saw his face. He was neither Lao nor Vietnamese. He was like you. An American.'"

"Friar Tuck," said Guy softly.

The woman looked at them, her eyes dark and unreadable.

"I've seen him, too," said Maitland. "I was being held in a camp just west of here when he landed to make an exchange. I tell you, the whole damn country was an opium factory, money being made left and right on both sides. All under cover of war. I think that's why Lo Van was killed. To keep the place in turmoil. There's nothing like a dirty war to hide your profits."

"Who else has seen the pilot's face?" Guy asked in Vietnamese, looking around the room. "Who else remembers what he looked like?"

A man and a woman, huddled in a corner, slowly raised their hands. Perhaps there were others, too timid to reveal themselves.

"There were four other POWs in that camp with me," said

Maitland. "They saw the pilot's face. As far as I know, not a single one made it home alive."

The joss sticks had burned down to ashes, but the smoke still hung in the gloom. No one made a sound, not even the children.

That's why you're afraid, thought Willy, gazing at the circle of faces. *Even now, after all these years, the war casts its shadow over your lives. And mine.*

"Come back with us, Maitland," said Guy. "Tell your story. It's the only way to put it behind you. To be free."

Maitland stood in the doorway of his hut, staring out at the children playing in the courtyard.

"Guy's right," said Willy. "You can't spend your life in hiding. It's time to end it."

Her father turned and looked at her. "What about Lan? The children? If I leave, how do I know the Vietnamese will ever let me back into the country?"

"It's a risk you have to take," said Guy.

"Be a hero—is that what you're telling me?" Maitland shook his head. "Let me tell *you* something, Barnard. The real heroes of this world aren't the guys who go out and take stupid risks. No, they're the ones who hang in where they're needed, where they belong. Maybe life gets a little dull. Maybe the wife and kids drive 'em crazy. But they hang in." He looked meaningfully at Willy, then back at Guy. "Believe me. I've made enough mistakes to know."

Maitland looked back at his daughter. "Tonight, you both go back to Hanoi. You've got to go home, get on with your own life, Willy."

"*If* she gets home," said Guy.

Maitland was silent.

"What do you think her chances are?" Guy pressed him mercilessly. "Think about it. You suppose they'll leave her alone knowing what she knows? You think they'll let her live?"

"So call me a coward!" Maitland blurted out. "Call me any damn name you please. It won't change things. I can't leave this time." He fled the hut.

Through the doorway, they saw him cross the courtyard to where Lan now sat beneath the trees. Lan smiled and handed their baby to her husband. For a long time he sat there, rocking his daughter, holding her tightly to his chest, as though he feared someone might wrench her from his grasp.

You have the world right there in your arms, Willy thought, watching him. *You'd be crazy to let it go.*

"We have to change his mind," said Guy. "We have to get him to come back with us."

At that instant Lan looked up, and her gaze met Willy's. "He's not coming back, Guy." Willy said. "He belongs here."

"You're his family, too," Guy protested.

"But not the one who needs him now." She leaned her head in the doorway. A leaf fluttered down from the trees and tumbled across the courtyard. A bare-bottomed baby toddled after it. "For twenty years I've hated that man. . . ." She sighed. And then she smiled. "I guess it's time I finally grew up."

"Something's wrong. Andersen should've been back by now."

Maitland stood at the edge of the jungle and peered up the dirt road. From where the doctor's jeep had been parked, tire tracks led northward. The branches he'd used for camouflage lay scattered at the roadside. But there was no sign of a vehicle.

Willy and Guy wandered onto the road, where they stood puzzling over Andersen's delay.

"He knows you're waiting for him," said Maitland. "He's already an hour late."

Guy kicked a pebble and watched it skitter into the bushes. "Looks like we're not going back to Hanoi tonight. Not without a ride." He glanced up at the darkening sky. "It's almost sunset. I think it's time to head back to the village."

Maitland didn't move. He was still staring up the road.

"He might have a flat tire," said Willy. "Or he ran out of gas. Either way, Dad, it looks like you're stuck with us tonight." She reached out and threaded her arm in his. "Guy's right. It's time to go back."

"Not yet."

Willy smiled. "Are you that anxious to get rid of us?"

"What?" He glanced at his daughter. "No, no, of course not. It's just . . ." He gazed up the road again. "Something doesn't feel right."

Willy watched him, suddenly sharing his uneasiness. "You think there's trouble."

"And we're not ready for it," he said grimly.

"What do you mean?" said Guy, turning to look at him. "The village must have some sort of defenses."

"We have maybe one working pistol, a few old war relics that haven't been used in decades. Plus Andersen's rifle. He left it today."

"How many rounds?"

"Not enough to—" Maitland's chin suddenly snapped up. He spun around at the sound of an approaching car.

"Hit the deck!" Guy commanded.

Willy was already leaping for the cover of the nearest bush. At the same instant, Guy and Maitland sprang in the other direction, into the foliage across the road from her.

She barely made it to cover in time. Just as she landed in the dirt, a jeep rounded the bend. Through the tangle of underbrush, she saw that it was filled with soldiers. As it roared closer, she tunneled frantically under the branches, mindless of the thorns clawing her face, and curled up among the leaves to wait for the jeep to pass. Something scurried across her hand. Instinctively she flinched and saw a fat black beetle drop off and scuttle into the shadows. Only then, as her gaze followed the insect, did she notice the strange chattering in the branches and she saw that the earth itself seemed to shudder with movement.

Dear God, she was lying in a whole nest of them!

Choking back a scream, she jerked sideways.

And found herself staring at a human hand. It lay not six inches from her nose, the fingers chalk white and frozen into a beckoning claw.

Even if she'd wanted to scream, she couldn't have uttered a sound; her throat had clamped down beyond all hope of any cry. Slowly her gaze traveled along the arm, followed it to the torso, and then, inexorably, to the face.

Gunnel Andersen's lifeless eyes stared back at her.

13

The soldiers' jeep roared past.

Willy muffled her cry with her fist, desperately fighting the shriek of horror that threatened to explode inside her. She fought it so hard her teeth drew blood from her knuckles. The instant the jeep had passed, her control shattered. She stumbled to her feet and staggered backward.

"He's dead!" she cried.

Guy and her father appeared at her side. She felt Guy's arm slip around her waist, anchoring her against him. "What are you talking about?"

"Andersen!" She pointed wildly at the bushes.

Her father dropped to the ground and shoved aside the branches. "Dear God," he whispered, staring at the body.

The trees seemed to wobble around her. Willy slid to her knees. The whole jungle spun in a miserable kaleidoscope of green as she retched into the dirt.

She heard her father say, in a strangely flat voice, "His throat's been cut."

"Clean job. Very professional," Guy muttered. "Looks like he's been here for hours."

Willy managed to raise her head. "Why? Why did they kill him?"

Her father let the bushes slip back over the body. "To keep him from talking. To cut us off from—" He suddenly sprang to his feet. "The village! I've got to get back!"

"Dad! Wait—"

But her father had already dashed into the jungle.

Guy tugged her up by the arm. "We've gotta move Come on."

She followed him, running and stumbling behind him on the foot-path. The sun was already setting; through the branches, the sky glowed a frightening bloodred.

Just ahead, she heard her father shouting, "Lan! Lan!" As they emerged from the jungle, they saw a dozen villagers gathered, watching as Maitland pulled his wife into his arms and held her.

"These people have got to get out of here!" Guy yelled. "Maitland! Tell them, for God's sake! They've got to leave!"

Maitland released his wife and turned to Guy. "Where the hell are we supposed to go? The next village is twenty miles from here! We've got old people, babies." He pointed to a woman with a swollen belly. "Look at her! You think *she* can walk twenty miles?"

"She has to. We all have to."

Maitland turned away, but Guy pulled him around, forcing him to listen. "Think about it! They've killed Andersen. You're next. So's everyone here, everyone who knows you're alive. There's got to be some-where we can hide!"

Maitland turned to one of the village elders and rattled out a ques-tion in Vietnamese.

The old man frowned. Then he pointed northeast, toward the moun-tains.

"What did he say?" asked Willy.

"He says there's place about five kilometers from here. An old cave in the hills. They've used it before, other times, other wars. . . ." He glanced up at the sky. "Almost sunset. We have to leave now while there's still enough light to cross the river."

Already, the villagers had scattered to gather their belongings. Cen-turies of war had taught them survival meant haste.

Five minutes was all the time Maitland's family took to pack. Lan presided over the dismantling of her household, the gathering of essen-tials—blankets, food, the precious family cooking pot. She spared no time for words or tears. Only outside, when she allowed herself a last backward glance at the hut, did her eyes brim. She swiftly, matter-of-factly, wiped away the tears.

The last light of day glimmered through the branches as the ragged gathering headed into the jungle. Twenty-four adults, eleven children and three infants, Willy counted. *And all of us scared out of our wits.*

They moved noiselessly, even the children; it was unearthly how silent they were, like ghosts flitting among the trees. At the edge of a fast-flowing river, they halted. A waterwheel spun in the current, an elegant sculpture of bamboo tubes shuttling water into irrigation sluices. The river was too deep for the little ones to ford, so the children were carried to the other bank. Soaked and muddy, they all slogged up the opposite bank and moved on toward the mountains.

Night fell. By the light of a full moon, they journeyed through a spectral land of wind and shadow where the very darkness seemed to tremble with companion spirits. By now the children were exhausted and stumbling. Still, no one had to coax them forward; the fear of pursuit was enough to keep them moving.

At last, at the base of the cliff, they halted. A giant wall of rock glowed silvery in the moonlight. The village elders conferred softly, debating which way to proceed next. It was the old woman who finally led the way. Moving unerringly through the darkness, she guided them to a set of stone steps carved into the mountain and led them up, along the cliff face to what appeared to be nothing more than a thicket of bushes.

There was a general murmur of dismay. Then one of the village men shoved aside the branches and held up a lit candle. Emptiness lay beyond. He thrust his arm into the void, into a darkness so vast, it seemed to swallow up the feeble light of the flame. They were at the mouth of a giant cavern.

The man crawled inside, only to scramble out as a flurry of wings whooshed past him. Nervous laughter rippled through the gathering.

Bats, Willy thought with a shudder.

The man took a deep breath and entered the cave. A moment later, he called for the others to follow.

Guy gave Willy a nudge. "Go on. Inside."

She swallowed, balking. "Do I have a choice?"

His answer was immediate. "None whatsoever."

The village was deserted.

Siang searched the huts one by one. He overturned pallets and flung aside mats, searching for the underground tunnels that were common to every village. In times of peace, those tunnels were used for storage; in times of war, they served as hiding places or escape routes. They were all empty.

In frustration, he grabbed an earthenware pot and smashed it on the ground. Then he stalked out to the courtyard where the men stood waiting in the moonlight, their faces blackened with camouflage paint.

There were fifteen of them, all crack professionals, rough-hewn Americans who towered above him. They had been flown in straight from Thailand at only an hour's notice. As expected, Laotian air defense had been a large-meshed sieve, unable to detect, much less shoot down, a lone plane flying in low through their airspace. It had taken a mere four hours to march here from their drop point just inside the Vietnamese border. The entire operation had been flawless.

Until now.

"It seems we've arrived too late," a voice said.

Siang turned to see his client emerge from the shadows, one more among this gathering of giants.

"They have had only a few hours head start," said Siang. "Their evening meals were left uneaten."

"Then they haven't gone far. Not with women and children." The man turned to one of the soldiers. "What about the prisoner? Has he talked?"

"Not a word." The soldiers shoved a village man to the ground. They had captured the man ten miles up the road, running toward Ban Dan. Or, rather, the dogs had caught him. Useful animals those hounds, and absolutely essential in an operation where a single surviving eyewitness could prove disastrous. Against such animals, the villager hadn't stood a chance of escape. Now he knelt on the ground, his black hair silvered with moonlight.

"Make him talk."

"A waste of time," grunted Siang. "These northerners are stubborn. He will tell you nothing."

One of the soldiers gave the villager a kick. Even as the man lay writhing on the ground, he managed to gasp out a string of epithets.

"What? What did he say?" demanded the soldier.

Siang shifted uneasily. "He says that we are cursed. That we are dead men."

The soldier laughed. "Superstitious crap!"

Siang looked around at the darkness. "I'm sure they sent other messengers for help. By morning—"

"By morning we'll have the job done. We'll be out of here," said his client.

"If we can find them," Siang said.

"Find a whole village? No problem." The man turned and snapped out an order to one of the soldiers. "That's what the dogs are for."

A dozen candles flickered in the cavern. Outside, the wind was blowing hard; puffs of it shuddered the blanket hanging over the cave mouth. Through the dancing shadows floated murmuring voices, the frantic whispers of a village under siege. Children gathered stones or twisted vines into rope. Women whittled stalks of bamboo, sharpening them into punji stakes. Only the babies slept. In the darkness outside, men dug the same lethal traps that had defended their homeland through the centuries. It was an axiom of jungle warfare that battles were won not by strength or weaponry but by speed and cunning and desperation.

Most of all, desperation.

"The cylinder's frozen," muttered Guy, sighting down the barrel of an ancient pistol. "You could squeeze off a single shot, that's all."

"Only two bullets left anyway," said Maitland.

"Which makes it next to worthless." Guy handed the gun back to Maitland. "Except for suicide."

For a moment Maitland weighed the pistol in his hand, thinking. He turned to his wife and spoke to her gently in Vietnamese.

Lan stared at the gun, as though afraid to touch it. Then, reluctantly, she took it and slipped away into the shadows of the cave.

Guy reached for Andersen's assault rifle and gave it a quick inspection. "At least this baby's in working order."

"Yeah. Nothing like a good old AK-47," said Maitland. "I've seen one fished out of the mud and still go right on firing."

Guy laughed. "The other side really knew how to make 'em, didn't they?" He glanced around as Willy approached. "How're you holding up?"

She sank down wearily beside him in the dirt. "We've carved enough stakes to skewer a whole army."

"We'll need more," said her father. He glanced toward the cave entrance. "My turn to do some digging. . . ."

"I was just out there," said Guy. "Pits are all dug."

"Then they'll need help with the other traps—"

"They know what they're doing. We just get in the way."

"It's hard to believe," said Willy.

"What is?"

"That we can hold off an army with vines and bamboo."

"It's been done before," said Maitland. "Against bigger armies. And we're not out to win a war. We just have to hold out until our runners get through."

"How long will that take?"

"It's twenty miles to the next village. If they have a radio, we might get help by midmorning."

Willy gazed around at the sleeping children who, one by one, had collapsed in exhaustion. Guy touched her arm. "You need some rest, too."

"I can't sleep."

"Then just lie down. Go on."

"What about you two?"

Guy snapped an ammunition clip into place. "We'll keep watch."

She frowned at him. "You don't really think they'd find us tonight?"

"We left an easy trail all the way."

"But they'll need daylight—"

"Not if they have a local informant," said her father. "Someone who knows these caves. We found our way in the dark. So could they." He grabbed the rifle and slung it over his shoulder. "Minh and I'll take the first watch, Guy. Get some sleep."

Guy nodded. "I'll relieve you in a few hours."

After her father left, Willy's gaze shifted back to the sleeping children, to her little half brothers, now curled up in a tangle of blankets. *What will happen to them?* she wondered. *To all of us?* In a far corner, two old women whittled bamboo stalks; the scrape of their blades against the wood made Willy shiver.

"I'm scared," she whispered.

Guy nodded. The candlelight threw harsh shadows on his face, "We're all scared. Every last one of us."

"It's my fault. I can't stop thinking that if I'd just left well enough alone . . ."

He touched her face. "I'm the one who should feel responsible."

"Why?"

"Because I used you. For all my denials, I planned to use you. And if something were to happen to you now . . ."

"Or to you," she said, her hand closing over his. "Don't you ever make me weep over your body, Guy Barnard. Because I couldn't stand it. So promise me."

He pressed her hand to his mouth. "I promise, And I want you to know that, after we get out of here, I . . ." He smiled. "I plan to see a lot more of you. If you'll let me."

She returned the smile. "I'll insist on it."

What stupid lies we're telling each other, she thought. *Our way of pretending we have a future.* In the face of death, promises mean everything.

"What if they find us?" she whispered.

"We do what we can to stay alive."

"Sticks and stones against automatics? It should be a very quick fight."

"We have a defensible position. Traps waiting in the path. And we have some of the smartest fighters in the world on our side. Men who've held off armies with not much more than their wits." He gazed up at the darkness hovering above the feeble glow of candlelight. "This cave is said to be blessed. It's an ancient sanctuary, older than anyone can remember. Follow that tunnel back there, and you'll come out at the east base of the cliff. They're clever, these people. They never back themselves into a corner. They always leave an escape route." He looked at the families dozing in the shadows. "They've been fighting wars since the Stone Age. And they can do it in their bare feet, with only a handful of rice. When it comes to survival, *we're* the novices."

Outside, the wind howled; they could hear the trees groan, the bushes scrabbling against the cliff. One of the children cried out in his sleep, a sob of fear that was instantly stilled by his mother's embrace.

The little ones didn't understand, thought Willy. But they knew enough to be afraid.

Guy took her in his arms. Together, they sank to the ground, clinging to each other. There was no need for words; it was enough just to have him there, to feel their hearts beating together.

And in the shadows, the two old women went on whittling their stalks of bamboo.

Willy was asleep when Guy rose to stand his watch. It wasn't easy leaving her. In the few short hours they'd clung together on the hard ground, their bodies had somehow melted together in a way that could never be reversed. Even if he never saw her again, even if she was suddenly swept out of his life, she would always be part of him.

He covered her with a blanket and slipped out into the night.

The sky was a dazzling sea of stars. He found Maitland huddled on a ledge a short way up the cliff face. Guy settled down beside him on the rock shelf.

"Dead quiet," said Maitland. "So far."

They sat together beneath the stars, listening to the wind, to the bushes thrashing against the cliff. A rock clattered down the mountain. Guy glanced up and saw, on a higher ledge, one of the village men silhouetted against the night sky.

"Did you get some sleep?" asked Maitland.

Guy shook his head. "You know, I used to be able to sleep through anything. Chopper landings. Sniper fire. But not now. Not here. I tell you, this isn't my kind of fight."

Maitland handed the rifle to Guy. "Yeah. It's a whole different war when people you love are at stake, isn't it?" He rose to his feet and walked off into the darkness.

People you love? It filled Guy with a sense of wonder, the thought that he *was* in love. Though it shouldn't surprise him. On some level, he'd known it all along: he had fallen hard for Bill Maitland's daughter.

It was something he'd never planned on, something he'd certainly never wanted. He wasn't even sure *love* was the right word for what he felt. They'd just spent a week together in hell. *And in heaven,* he thought, remembering that night in the hut, under the mosquito net. He knew he couldn't stand the thought of her being hurt, that he'd do anything to keep her safe. Was *love* the name for that feeling?

Somewhere in the night, an animal screamed.

He tightened his grip on the rifle.

Four more hours until dawn.

At first light the attack came.

Guy had already handed the rifle to the next man on watch and was starting down the cliff face when a shot rang out. Sheer reflexes sent him diving for cover. As he scrambled behind a clump of bushes, he heard more automatic gunfire and a scream from the ledge above, and he knew his relief man had been hit. He peered up to see how badly the man was hurt. Through fingers of morning mist, he could make out the man's bloodied arm dangling lifelessly over the ledge. More gunfire erupted, spattering the cliff face. There was no return fire; the village's only rifle now lay in the hands of a dead man.

Guy glanced down and saw the other villagers scrambling for cover among the rocks. Unarmed, how long could they defend the cave? It was the booby traps they were counting on now, the trip wires and the pits and the stakes that would hold off the attackers.

Guy looked up at the ledge where the rifle lay. That precious AK-47 could make all the difference in the world between survival and slaughter.

He spotted a boulder a few yards up, with a few scraggly bushes as cover along the way. There was no other route, no other choice. He crouched, tensing for the dash to first base.

Willy was stirring a simmering pot of rice and broth when she heard the gunshots. Her first thought as she leapt to her feet was, *Guy. Dear God, has he been hurt?*

But before she could take two steps, her father grabbed her arm. "No, Willy!"

"He may need help—"

"You can't go out there!" He called for his wife. Somehow, Lan heard him through the bedlam and, taking her arm, pulled Willy toward the back of the cave. Already the other women were herding the children into the escape tunnel. Willy could only watch helplessly as the men grabbed what primitive weapons they had and scrambled outside.

More gunfire thundered in the distance, and rocks clattered down the mountainside.

Where's our return fire? she thought. *Why isn't anyone firing back?*

Outside, something skittered across the ground and popped. A finger of smoke wafted into the cave, its vapor so sickening it made Willy reel backward, gasping for air.

"Get back, get back!" her father yelled. "Into the tunnel, all of you!"

"What about Guy?"

"He can take care of himself! Go and get the kids out of here!" He gave her a brutal shove into the tunnel. *"Move!"*

There was no other choice. But as she turned to flee and heard the rattle of new gunfire, she felt she was abandoning a part of herself on the embattled cliff.

The children had already slipped into the tunnel. Just ahead, Willy could hear a baby crying. Following the sound, she plunged into pitch blackness.

A light suddenly flickered in the passage. It was a candle. By the flame's glow, she saw the leathery face of the old woman who'd guided them to the cave. She was now leading the frightened procession of women and children.

Willy, bringing up the rear, could barely keep track of the candle's glow. The old woman moved swiftly; obviously, she knew where she was going. Perhaps she'd fled this way before, in another battle, another war. It offered some small comfort to know they were following in the footsteps of a survivor.

The first step down was a surprise. For an instant, Willy's heel met nothingness, then it landed on slippery stone. How much farther? she wondered as she reached out to steady herself against the tunnel wall. Her fingers met clumps of dried wax, the drippings of ancient candles. How many others before her had felt their way down these steps, had stumbled in terror through these passages? The fear of all those countless other refugees seemed to permeate the darkness.

The tunnel took a sharp left and moved ever downward. She wondered how far they'd come; it began to seem like miles. The sound of gunfire had faded to a distant *tap-tap-tap*. She wouldn't let herself think about what was happening outside; she could only concentrate on that tiny pinpoint of light flickering far ahead.

Suddenly the light seemed to flare brighter, exploding into a dazzling luminescence. No, she realized with sudden wonder as she rounded the curve. It wasn't the candle. It was daylight!

Murmurs of joy echoed through the passageway. All at once, they were all scrambling forward, dashing toward the exit and into the blinding sunshine.

Outside, Willy stood blinking painfully at trees and sky and mountainside. They were on the other side of the cliff. Safe. For now.

Gunfire rattled in the distance.

The old woman ordered them forward, into the jungle. At first Willy didn't understand the urgency. Was there some new danger she hadn't recognized? Then she heard what was frightening the old woman: dogs.

Now the others heard the barking, too. Panic sent them all dashing into the forest. Lan alone didn't move. Willy spotted her standing perfectly still. Lan appeared to be listening to the dogs, gauging their direction, their distance. Her two boys, alarmed by their mother's refusal to run, stood watching her in confusion.

Lan shoved her sons forward, commanding them to flee. The boys shook their heads; they wouldn't leave without their mother. Lan gave the baby to her eldest son, then gave both boys another push. The younger boy was crying now, shaking his head, clinging to her sleeve. But his mother's command could not be disobeyed. Sobbing, he was led away by his older brother to join the other children in flight.

"What are you doing?" Willy cried. Had the woman gone mad?

Calmly, Lan turned to face the sound of the dogs.

Willy glanced ahead at the forest, saw the children fleeing through the trees. They were so small, so helpless. How far would they get?

She looked back at Lan, who was now purposefully shuffling through the dirt, circling back toward the dogs. Suddenly Willy understood what Lan was doing. She was leaving her scent for the dogs. Trying to make them follow her, to draw them away from the children. By this action, this choice, the woman was offering herself as a sacrifice.

The barking grew louder. Every instinct Willy possessed told her to run. But she thought of Guy and her father, of how willingly, how automatically they had assumed the role of protectors, had offered themselves to the enemy. She saw the last of the children vanish into the jungle. They needed time, time no one else could give them.

She, too, began to stamp around in the dirt.

Lan glanced back in surprise and saw what Willy was doing. They didn't exchange a word; just that look, that sad and knowing smile between women, was enough.

Willy ripped a sleeve off her blouse and trampled the torn cloth into the dirt. The dogs would surely pick up the scent. Then she turned and headed south, back along the cliff base. Away from the children. Lan, too, headed away from the villagers' escape route.

Willy didn't hurry. After all, she was no longer running for *her* life. She wondered how long it would take for the dogs to catch up. And when they did, how long she could hold them off. A weapon was what she needed. A club, a stick. She snatched up a fallen branch, tore off the twigs and swung it a few times. It was good and heavy; it would make the dogs think twice. Prey she might be, but she'd damn well fight back.

The barking grew steadily closer, a demon sound, relentless and terrifying. But now it mingled with something else, a rhythmic, monotonous thumping that, as it grew louder, seemed to make the ground itself shudder. Not gunfire . . .

A helicopter!

Wild with hope, she glanced up at the sky and saw, in the distance, a pair of black specks against the vista of morning blue. Was it the rescue party they'd been waiting for?

She scrambled up on a mound of rocks and began waving her arms. It was their only chance—Guy's only chance—for survival.

All her attention focused on those two black pinpricks hovering in the morning sky, she didn't see the dogs moving in until it was too late.

A flash of brown shot across her peripheral vision. She jerked around as a pair of jaws lunged straight for her throat. Her response was purely reflex. She twisted away and a hundred pounds of fur and teeth slammed into her shoulder. Thrown to the ground, she could only cry out as powerful jaws clamped onto her arm.

Footsteps thudded close. A voice shouted, "Back off! I said back *off!*"

The dog released her and stood back, growling.

Slowly Willy raised her head and saw two men in camouflage garb towering above her. *Americans,* she thought in confusion. What were they doing here?

Rough hands hauled her to her feet. "Where are the others?" one of the men demanded.

"You're hurting me—"

"Where are the others?"

"There are no others!" she screamed.

His savage blow knocked her back to the ground. Too dazed to move, she sprawled helplessly at their feet and fought to clear her head.

"Finish her off."

No, she thought. *Please, no* . . .

But she knew that no amount of begging would change their minds. She lay there, hugging herself, waiting for the end.

Then the other soldier said, "Not yet. She might come in handy."

She was dragged back to her feet to stand, sick and swaying, before them.

An expressionless face, blackened with camouflage grease, stared down at her. "Let's see what the good Friar thinks."

14

*M*ade *it to third base. Time to go for that home run.*

Guy, sprawled behind a boulder, scouted out the next twenty yards to the gun. His only cover would be a few bushes and, midway, a pathetic excuse for a tree. He could see the AK-47's barrel extending over the rock ledge, so close, he could practically spit at it, but still beyond reach.

Slowly, he rose to a crouch and got ready for the final dash.

Gunfire splattered the cliff. Instantly, he flopped back to the dirt. *This is a crazy-ass idea, Barnard. The dumbest idea you've ever had.*

He glanced below and saw Maitland trying to signal him. What the hell was he trying to say? Guy couldn't be sure, but Maitland seemed to be telling him to wait, to hold on. But there was so little time left. Already, Guy spotted men in camouflage fatigues moving through the brush toward the cliff base. Toward the first booby trap. *God, slow 'em down. Give us time.*

He heard, rather than saw, the first victim drop into the trap. A shriek echoed off the cliff face, the cry of a man who had just slid into a bed of stakes. Now there were other shouts, curses, the sounds of confusion as soldiers dragged their injured comrade to safety.

Just a taste, fellas, Guy thought with a grim sense of satisfaction. *Wait till you see what comes next.*

The attackers didn't delay long. A shouted order sent a half-dozen soldiers scrambling up the cliff path, closer and closer to the second trap: a trip wire poised to unleash a falling tree trunk. But now the attackers were warned; they knew that every step was a gamble, and they were searching for hazards, considering every rock, every bush with the practiced eyes of men well versed in jungle combat.

We're almost down to our last resort, thought Guy. *Prayer.*

Then he heard it. They all heard it. A familiar rumble that made them turn their gazes to the sky. Choppers.

That was the instant Guy ran, when everyone's eyes were focused on the heavens. His sudden dash took the soldiers by surprise, left them only a split second to respond. Then the maelstrom broke loose as bullets chewed the ground, throwing up a storm cloud of dust. By then he was halfway to his goal, scrambling through the last thicket. Time seemed to slow down. Each step took an eternity. He saw puffs of dirt explode near his feet, heard a far-off shriek and the thud of the poised tree trunk, the second trap, slamming onto the soldiers in the path.

He launched himself through the air and tumbled onto the ledge. Time leapt to fast forward. He yanked the AK-47 out of the dead man's grasp, took aim and began firing.

One soldier, standing exposed below, went down at once. The others beat a fast retreat into the jungle. Two lay dead on the path, victims of the latest booby trap.

Welcome to the Stone Age, Rambo.

Guy held his fire as the attackers slipped out of view and into the cover of trees. He watched, waiting for any flash of movement, any sign of a renewed attack. A standoff?

He turned his gaze to the sky and searched for the choppers. To his dismay, they were moving away; already they had faded to mere specks. In despair he watched them slip away into a field of relentless blue.

Then, from below, he heard shouts in Vietnamese and saw smoke spiral up the cliff face, the blackest, most glorious smoke he'd seen in his whole damn life. The villagers had set the mountainside on fire!

Quickly he scanned the heavens again, hoping, praying. Within seconds he spotted them, like two flies hovering just above the horizon. Was it only wishful thinking, or were they actually moving closer?

A new hint of movement at the bottom of the cliff drew his attention. He looked down to see two figures emerge from the forest and approach the cliff base. Automatically, he swung his gun barrel to the target and was about to squeeze off a round when he saw who it was standing below. His finger froze on the trigger.

A man stood clutching a human shield in front of him. Even from that distance, Guy recognized the prisoner's face, could see her blanched and helpless expression.

"Drop it, Barnard!" The command of an unseen man, hidden among the trees, echoed off the mountainside. The voice was disturbingly familiar.

Guy remained frozen in the pose of a marksman, his finger on the trigger, his cheek pressed against the rifle. Frantically he wracked his brain for a plan, for some way to pull Willy out of this alive. A trade? It was the only possibility: her life for his. Would they go for it?

"I said *drop it!*" the disembodied voice shouted.

Willy's captor raised a pistol barrel to her head.

"Or would you like to see what a bullet will do to that pretty face?"

"Wait!" Guy screamed. "We can trade—"

"No deals."

The barrel was pressed to Willy's temple.

"No!" Guy's voice, harsh with panic, reverberated off the cliff.

"Then drop the gun. *Now.*"

Guy let the AK-47 fall to the ground.

"Kick it away. Go on!"

Guy gave the gun a kick. It tumbled off the ledge and clattered to the rocks below.

"Out where I can see you. Come on, come on!"

Slowly, Guy rose to his full height, expecting an instantaneous hail of bullets.

"Now come down. Off the cliff. You, too, Maitland! I haven't got all day, so *move.*"

Guy made his way down the cliff path. By the time he reached bottom, Maitland was already waiting there, his arms hooked behind his head in surrender. Guy's first concern was Willy. He could see she'd been hurt; her shirt was torn and bloodied, her face alarmingly white. But the look she gave him was one of heartwrenching courage, a look that said, *Don't worry about me. I'm okay. And I love you.*

Her captor smiled and let the pistol barrel drop from her head. Guy instantly recognized his face: it was the same man he'd tackled on the terrace of the hotel in Bangkok. The Thai assassin—or was he Vietnamese?

"Hello, Guy," said a shockingly familiar voice.

A man strolled into the sunshine, a man whose powerful shoulders seemed to strain against the fabric of his camouflage fatigues.

Maitland took in a startled breath. "It's him," he murmured. "Friar Tuck."

"*Toby?*" said Guy.

"Both," said Tobias Wolff, smiling. He stood before them, his expression hovering somewhere between triumph and regret. "I didn't want to kill you, Guy. In fact, I've done everything I could to avoid it."

Guy let out a bitter laugh. "Why?"

"I owed you. Remember?"

Guy frowned at Toby's legs, noticing there were no braces, no crutches. "You can walk."

Toby shrugged. "You know how it is in army hospitals. The surgeons gave me the bad news, said there was nothing they could do and then they walked away. Shoved me into a corner and forgot about me. But I wasn't a lost cause, after all. First I got the feeling back in my toes. Then I could move them. Oh, I never bothered to tell Uncle Sam. It gave me the freedom to carry on with my business. That's the nice thing about being a paraplegic. No one suspects you of a damn thing." He grinned. "Plus, I get that monthly disability check."

"A real fortune."

"It's the principle of things. Uncle Sam owes me for all those years of loyal service." He glanced at Maitland. "He was the only detail that worried me. The last witness from Flight 5078. I'd heard he was alive. I just didn't know how to find him."

He squinted up at the sky as the rumble of the choppers drew closer. They were moving in, attracted by the smoke from the cliff fire. "Time's up," said Toby. Turning, he yelled to his men, "Move out!"

At once, the soldiers started into the woods in a calm but hasty retreat. Toby looked at the hit man and nodded. "Mr. Siang, you know what to do."

Siang shoved Willy forward. Guy caught her in his arms; together, they dropped to their knees. There was no time left for last words, for farewells. Guy wrapped himself around her in a futile attempt to shield her from the bullets.

"Finish it," said Toby.

Guy looked up at him. "I'll see you in hell."

Siang raised the pistol. The barrel was aimed squarely at Guy's head. Still cradling Willy, Guy waited for the explosion. The darkness.

The blast of the pistol made them both flinch.

In wonderment, Guy realized he was still kneeling, still breathing. *What the hell? Am I still alive? Are we both still alive?*

He looked up in time to see Siang, shirt bloodied, crumple to the ground.

"There! She's there!" Toby shouted, pointing at the trees.

In the shadow of the forest they saw her, clutching the ancient pistol in both hands. Lan stood very still, as though shocked by what she'd just done.

One of the soldiers took aim at her.

"No!" screamed Maitland, flinging himself at the gunman.

The shot went wild; Maitland and the soldier thudded to the ground, locked in combat.

From the cliff above came shouts; Guy and Willy hit the dirt as arrows rained down. Toby cried out and fell. What remained of his army scattered in confusion.

In the melee, Guy and Willy managed to crawl to cover. But as they rolled behind a boulder, Willy suddenly realized her father hadn't followed them.

"Dad!" she screamed.

A dozen yards away, Maitland lay bloodied. Willy turned to go to him, but Guy dragged her back down.

"Are you nuts?" he yelled.

"I can't leave him there!"

"Wait till we're clear!"

"He's hurt!"

"There's nothing you can do!"

She was sobbing now, trying to wrench free, but her protests were drowned out by the *whomp-whomp* of the helicopters moving in. An army chopper hovered just above them. The pilot lowered the craft through a slot in the trees. Gently, the skids settled to the ground.

The instant it touched down, a half-dozen Vietnamese soldiers jumped out, followed by their commanding officer. He pointed at Maitland and barked out orders. Two soldiers hurried to the wounded man.

"Let me go," Willy said and she broke free of Guy's grasp.

He watched her run to her father's side. The soldiers had already opened their medical field kit, and a stretcher was on the way. Guy's gaze shifted back to the chopper as one last passenger stepped slowly to the ground. Head bowed beneath the spinning blades, the old man made his way toward Guy.

For a long time, they stood together, both of them silent as they regarded the rising cloud of smoke. The flames seemed to engulf the mountain itself as the last of the village men scrambled down the cliff path to safety.

"A most impressive signal fire," said Minister Tranh. He looked at Guy. "You are unhurt?"

Guy nodded. "We lost some people . . . up on the mountain. And the children—I don't know if they're all right. But I guess . . . I think . . ."

He turned and watched as Willy followed her father's stretcher toward the chopper. At the doorway, she stopped and looked back at Guy.

He started toward her, his arms aching to embrace her. He wanted to tell her all the things he'd been afraid to say, the things he'd never said to any woman. He had to tell her now, while he still had the chance, while she was still there for him to touch, to hold.

A soldier suddenly blocked Guy's way and commanded, "Stay back!"

Dust stung Guy's eyes as the chopper's rotor began to spin. Through the tornadolike wash of whirling leaves and branches, Guy saw a soldier in the chopper shout at Willy to climb aboard. With one last backward glance, she obeyed. Time had run out.

Through the open doorway, Guy could still see her face gazing out at him. With a sense of desolation, he watched the helicopter rise into the sky, taking with it the woman he loved. Long after the roar of the blades had faded to silence, he was staring up at that cloudless field of blue.

Sighing, he turned back to Minister Tranh. That's when he noticed that someone else, just as desolate, had watched the chopper's departure. At the forest edge stood Lan, her gaze turned to the sky. At least she, too, had survived.

"We are glad to find you alive," Minister Tranh said.

"How *did* you find us?" Guy asked.

"One of the men from the village reached Na Khoang early this morning. We'd been concerned about you. And when you vanished . . ." Minister Tranh shook his head. "You have a talent for making things difficult, Mr. Barnard. For us, at least."

"I had to. I didn't know who to trust." Guy looked at the other man. "I still don't know who to trust."

Minister Tranh considered this statement for a moment. Then he said quietly, "Do we ever really know?"

"A toast," said Dodge Hamilton, leaning against the hotel bar. "To the good fight!"

Guy stared down moodily at his whiskey glass and said, "There's no such thing as a good fight, Hamilton. There are only fights you can't avoid."

"Well—" grinning, Hamilton raised his drink "—then let's drink to the unavoidable."

That made Guy laugh, though it was the last thing he felt like doing. He supposed he *ought* to be celebrating. The ordeal was over, and for the first time in days, he felt human again. After a good night's sleep, a shower and a shave, he could once again stand the sight of his own face in the mirror. *For all the difference it makes,* he thought bleakly. *She's not here to notice.*

He was having a hell of a time adjusting to Willy's absence. Over and over he replayed that last image of her sad backward glance as she'd climbed into the chopper. No last words, no goodbyes, just that look. He wished he could erase the image from his memory.

No, no, that wasn't what he wanted.

What he wanted was another chance.

He set the whiskey glass down and forced a smile to his lips. "Anyway, Hamilton," he said, "looks like you got your story, after all."

"Not quite the one I expected."

"Think it's front-page material?"

"Indeed! it has everything. Old war ghosts come to life. Ex-enemies joining sides. *And* a happy ending! A story that ought to be heard. But . . ." He sighed. "It'll probably get shoved to the back page to make room for some juicy royal scandal. As if the fate of the world depends on who does what to whom in Buckingham."

Guy shook his head and chuckled. Some things, it seemed, never changed.

"He'll be all right, won't he? Maitland?"

Guy looked up. "I think so. Willy called me from Bangkok a few hours ago. Maitland's stable enough to be transferred."

"They're flying him to the States?"

"Tonight."

Hamilton cocked his head. "Aren't you joining them?"

"I don't know. I've got a job to wrap up, a few last minute details. And she'll be busy with other things. . . ."

He looked down at his whiskey and thought of that last phone conversation. They'd had a lousy connection, lots of static on the line, and they'd both been forced to shout. She'd been standing at a hospital telephone; he'd been on his way out to meet Vietnamese officials. It had hardly been the time for romantic conversation. Yet he'd been ready to say anything, if only she'd given him some hint that she wanted to hear it. But there'd been only awkward how-are-yous and is-your-arm-all-right and yes-it's-fine-I'm-all-patched-up-now and then, in the end, a hasty goodbye.

When he'd hung up the receiver, he'd known she was gone. *Maybe it's for the best,* he thought. Every idiot knew wartime romances never lasted. When you were huddled together in the trenches and the bullets were whizzing overhead, it was easy to fall in love.

But now they were back in the real world. She didn't need him any longer, and he liked to think he didn't need *her* either. After all, he'd never needed anyone before.

He drained his whiskey glass. "Anyway, Hamilton," he said, "I guess I'll have a hell of a story to tell the guys back home. How I fought in Nam all over again—this time with the other side."

"No one'll believe you."

"Probably not." Guy looked off at a painting on the wall—Ho Chi Minh smiling like someone's merry uncle. "You know, I have a confession to make." He looked back at his drinking partner. "At one point, I was so paranoid that I thought *you* were the CIA."

Hamilton burst out laughing.

"Can you believe it?" Guy said, laughing as well. "You of all people!"

Hamilton, still grinning, set his glass down on the counter. "Actually," he said after a pause, "I am."

There was a long silence. "What?" said Guy.

Hamilton gazed back, his expression blandly pleasant and utterly unrevealing. "General Kistner sends his regards. He's happy to hear you're alive and well."

"Kistner sent you?"

"No, he sent *you.*"

Guy stiffened. "You got it wrong. I don't work for those people. I was on my own the whole—"

"Were you, now?" Hamilton's smile was maddening. "Quite a stroke of luck, wouldn't you say, that meeting between you and Miss Maitland at Kistner's villa? Damned odd about her driver vanishing like that, just as you were heading back to town."

Guy looked down at his glass, swirled the whiskey. "I *was* set up," he muttered. "That mysterious appointment with Kistner—"

"Was to get you and Miss Maitland together. She was in dangerous waters, already floundering. We knew she'd need help. But it had to be someone completely unconnected with the Company, someone the Vietnamese wouldn't suspect. As it turned out, *you* were it."

Guy's fists tightened on the countertop. "I did your dirty work—"

"You did Uncle Sam a favor. We knew you were slated to go to Saigon. That you knew the country. A bit of the language. We also knew you had a . . . shall we say, *vulnerable* aspect to your past." He gave Guy a significant look.

They know, Guy thought. *They've probably always known.* Slowly, he said, "That visit from the Ariel Group . . ."

"Ah, yes. Ariel. Lovely ring to it, don't you think? It happens to be the name of General Kistner's youngest granddaughter." Hamilton smiled. "You needn't worry, Guy. We can be discreet. Especially when we feel we've been well served."

"What if you'd been wrong about me? What if I was working for Toby Wolff? I could have killed her."

"You wouldn't."

"I had a 'vulnerable' aspect to my past, remember?"

"You're clean, Guy. Even with your past, you're cleaner than any flag-waving patriot in Washington."

"How would you know?"

Hamilton shrugged. "You'd be amazed at the things we know about you. About everyone."

"But you couldn't predict what I'd do! What Willy would do. What if she'd told me to go to hell?"

"It was a gamble. But she's an attractive woman. And you're a resourceful man. We took a chance on chemistry."

And it worked, thought Guy. *Damn you, Hamilton, the chemistry worked just fine.*

"At any rate," said Hamilton, sliding a few bills onto the bar, "you'll be rewarded with the silence you crave. I'm afraid the bounty's out of the question, though—budget deficit and all. But you'll have the distinct pleasure of knowing you served your country well."

That's when Guy burst into unstoppable laughter. He laughed so hard, tears came to his eyes; so loud, a dozen heads turned to look at him.

"Have I missed the joke?" Hamilton inquired politely.

"The joke," said Guy, "is on me."

He laughed all the way out the door.

15

Her father, once again, was leaving.

Early on a rainy morning, Willy stood in the bedroom doorway and watched him pack his suitcase, the way she'd watched him pack it long ago. She'd had him home such a short time, only a few days since his release from the hospital. And he'd spent every moment pining for his family—his other family. Oh, he hadn't complained or been unkind, but she'd seen the sadness in his gaze, heard his sighs as he'd wandered about the house. She'd known it was inevitable: that he'd be walking out of her life again.

He took one last look in the closet, then turned to the dresser.

She glanced down at a pair of brand-new loafers that he'd set aside in the closet. "Dad, aren't you taking your shoes?" she asked.

"At home, I don't wear shoes."

"Oh." *This used to be your home,* she thought.

She wandered into the living room, sat down by the window and stared out at the rain. It seemed as if a lifetime of sorrow had been crammed into these past two weeks she'd been home. While her father had recuperated in a military hospital, in a civilian hospital a few miles away, her mother had lain dying. It had been wrenching to drive back and forth between them, to shift from seeing her father regain his strength to seeing her mother fade. Ann's death had come more quickly than the doctors had predicted; it was almost as if she'd held on just long enough to see her husband one last time, then had allowed herself to quietly slip away.

She'd forgiven him, of course.

Just as Willy had forgiven him.

Why was it always women who had to do the forgiving? she'd wondered.

"I'm all packed," her father said, carrying his suitcase into the living room. "I've called a cab."

"Are you sure you've got everything? The kids' toys? The books?"

"It's all in here. What a delivery! They're going to think I'm Santa Claus." He set the suitcase down and sat on the couch. They didn't speak for a moment.

"You won't be coming back, will you?" she said at last.

"It may not be easy."

"May I come see you?"

"Willy, you know you can! Both you and Guy. And next time, we'll make it a decent visit." He laughed. "Nice and quiet and dull. Guy'll appreciate that."

There was a long silence. Her father asked, "Have you spoken to him lately?"

She looked away. "It's been two weeks."

"That long?"

"He hasn't called."

"Why haven't you called him?"

"I've been busy. A lot of things to take care of. But you know that."

"He doesn't."

"Well, he *ought* to know." Suddenly agitated, she rose and paced the room, finally returning to the window. "I'm not really surprised he hasn't called. After all, we had our little adventure, and now it's back to life as usual." She glanced at her father. "Men hate that, don't they? Life as usual."

"Some men do. On the other hand, some of us change."

"Oh, Dad, I've been around the block. I can tell when things are over."

"Did Guy say that?"

She turned and gazed back out the window. "He didn't have to."

Her father didn't comment. After a while, she heard him go back into the bedroom, but she didn't move. She just kept staring out at the rain, thinking about Guy. Wondering for the first time if maybe *she* had done the running away.

No, it wasn't running. It was facing reality. Together they'd had the time of their lives, a crazy week of emotions gone wild, of terror and exhilaration, when every breath, every heartbeat had seemed like a gift from God.

Of course, it hadn't lasted.

But whose fault was that?

She felt herself drawn almost against her will to the telephone. Even as she dialed his number, she wondered what she'd say to him. *Hello, Guy. I know you don't want to hear this, but I love you.* Then she'd hang up and spare him the ordeal of admitting the feeling wasn't mutual. She let it ring twelve times, knowing it was 4:00 a.m. in Honolulu, knowing he *should* be home.

There were tears in her eyes when she finally hung up. She stood staring down at the phone, wondering how that inanimate collection of wires and plastic could leave her feeling so betrayed. *Damn you,* she thought. *You never even gave me the chance to make a fool of myself.*

The sound of tires splashing across wet streets made her look out the window. Through pouring rain she saw a cab pull up at the curb.

"Dad?" she called. She went to her father's bedroom. "Your taxi's here."

"Already?" He glanced around to see if he'd forgotten anything. "Okay. I guess this is it, then."

The doorbell rang. He threw on his raincoat and strode across the living room. Willy wasn't watching as he opened the door, but she heard him say, "I don't believe it." She turned.

"Hello, Maitland," said Guy.

The two men, both wearing raincoats, both holding suitcases, grinned at each other across the threshold.

Guy shook the raindrops from his hair. "Mind if I come in?"

"Gee, I don't know. I'd better ask the boss." Maitland turned to his daughter. "What do you think? Can the man come in?"

Willy was too stunned to say a word.

"I guess that's a yes," her father said, and he motioned for Guy to enter.

Guy stepped over the threshold and set his suitcase down. Then he just stood there, looking at her. Rain had plastered his hair to his forehead, lines of exhaustion mapped his face, but no man had ever looked so wonderful. She tried to remind herself of all the reasons she didn't want to see him, all the reasons she should throw him out into the rain. But she couldn't seem to find her voice. She could only stare at him in wonder and remember how it had felt to be in his arms.

Maitland shuffled uneasily. "I . . . uh . . . I think I forgot to pack something," he muttered, and he discreetly vanished into the bedroom.

For a moment, the only sound was the water dripping from Guy's raincoat onto the wood floor.

"How's your mother?" Guy asked.

"She died, five days ago."

He shook his head. "Willy, I'm sorry."

"I'm sorry, too."

"How are you? Are you okay?"

"I'm . . . fine." She looked away. *I love you,* she thought. *And yet here we are, two strangers engaging in small talk.* "Yeah, I'm fine," she repeated, as though to convince him—to convince herself—that the anguish of these past two weeks had been a minor ache not worth mentioning.

"You look pretty good, considering."

She shrugged. "You look terrible."

"Not too surprising. Didn't get any sleep on the plane. And there was this baby screaming in the next seat, all the way from Bangkok."

"Bangkok?" She frowned. "You were in Bangkok?"

He nodded and laughed. "It's this crazy business I'm in. Got home from Nam, and a week later, they asked me to fly back . . . for Sam Lassiter." He paused. "I admit I wasn't thrilled about getting on another plane, but I figured it was something I had to do." He paused and added quietly, "No soldier should have to come home alone."

She thought about Lassiter, about that evening in the river café, the love song scratching from the record player, the paper lanterns fluttering in the wind. She thought about his body drifting in the waters of the Mekong. And she thought about the dark-eyed woman who'd loved him. "You're right," she said. "No soldier should have to come home alone."

There was another pause. She felt him watching her, waiting.

"You could have called me," she said.

"I wanted to."

"But you never got the chance, right?"

"I had plenty of chances."

"But you didn't bother?" She looked up. All the hurt, all the rage suddenly rose to the surface. "Two weeks with no word from you! And here you have the gall to show up unannounced, walk in my door and drop your damn suitcase in my living—"

The last word never made it to her lips. But he did. She was dragged into a rain-drenched embrace, and everything she'd planned to say, all the hurt and angry words, were swept away by that one kiss. The only sound she could manage was a small murmur of astonishment, and then she was whirled up in a wild maelstrom of desire. She lost all sense of where she ended and he began. She only knew, in that instant, that he had never really left her, that as long as she lived, he'd be part of her. Even as he pulled back to look at her, she was still drunk with the taste of him.

"I *did* want to call you. But I didn't know what to say. . . ."

"I kept waiting for you to call. All these days . . ."

"Maybe I was . . . I don't know. Scared."

"Of what?"

"Of hearing it was over. That you'd come to your senses and decided I wasn't worth the risk. But then, when I got to Bangkok, I stopped at the Oriental Hotel. Had a drink on the terrace for old time's sake. Saw the same sunset, the same boats on the river. But it just didn't feel the same without you." He sighed. "Hell, nothing feels the same without you."

"You never told me. You just dropped out of my life."

"It never seemed like . . . the right time."

"The right time for what?"

"You know."

"No, I don't."

He shook his head in irritation. "You never make it easy, do you?" She stepped back and gave him a long, critical look. Then she smiled. "I never intended to."

"Oh, Willy." He threw his arms around her and pulled her tightly against his chest. "I can see you and I are going to have a lot of things to settle."

"Such as?"

"Such as . . ." He lowered his mouth to hers and whispered, "Such as who gets to sleep on the right side of the bed. . . ."

"Oh," she murmured as their lips brushed. "You will."

"And who gets to name our firstborn. . . ."

She settled warmly into his arms and sighed. "I will."

"And who'll be first to say 'I love you.' "

There was a pause. "That one," she said with a smile, "is open to negotiation."

"No, it's not," he said, tugging her face up to his.

They stared at each other, both longing to hear the words but stubbornly waiting for the other to give in first.

It was a simultaneous surrender.

"I love you," Willy heard him say, just as the same three words tumbled from her lips.

Their laughter was simultaneous, too, bright and joyous and ringing with hope.

The kiss that followed was warm, seeking, but all too brief; it left her aching for more.

"It gets even better with practice," he whispered.

"Saying 'I love you'?"

"No. Kissing."

"Oh," she murmured. She added in a small voice, "Then can we try it again?"

Outside, a horn honked, dragging them both back to reality. Through the window they saw another taxi waiting at the curb.

Reluctantly Willy pulled out of Guy's arms. "Dad?" she called.

"I'm coming, I'm coming." Her father emerged from the bedroom, pulling on his raincoat again. He paused and looked at her.

"Uh, why don't you two say goodbye," said Guy, diplomatically turning for the front door. "I'll take your suitcase out to the car."

Willy and her father were left standing alone in the room. They looked at each other, both knowing that this, like every goodbye, could be the last.

"Are things okay between you and Guy?" Maitland asked.

Willy nodded.

There was another silence. Then her father asked softly, "And between you and me?"

She smiled. "Things are okay there, too." She went to him then, and they held each other. "Yes," she murmured against his chest, "between you and me, things are definitely okay."

A little reluctantly, he turned to leave. In the doorway, he and Guy shook hands.

"Have a good trip back, Maitland."

"I will. Take care of things, will you? And, Guy—thanks a lot."

"For what?"

Maitland glanced back at Willy. It was a look of regret. And redemption. "For giving me back my daughter," he said.

As Wild Bill Maitland walked out the door, Guy walked in. He didn't say a thing. He just took Willy in his arms and hugged her.

As the taxi drove away, she thought, *My father has left me. Again.*

She looked up at Guy. *And what about you?*

He answered her unspoken question by taking her face in his hands and kissing her. Then he gave the door a little kick; with a thud of finality, it swung shut.

And she knew that this time, the man would be staying.